E. V. THOMPSON OMNIBUS

Cast No Shadows

Harvest of the Sun

D1494474

E. V. THOMPSON OMNIBUS

Cast No Shadows
Harvest of the Sun

E. V. THOMPSON

timewarner
paperbacks

A *Time Warner* Paperback

This omnibus edition first published in Great Britain by
Time Warner Paperbacks in 2002
E. V. Thompson Omnibus Copyright © E. V. Thompson 2002

Previously published separately:
Cast No Shadows first published in Great Britain in 1997 by
Little, Brown and Company
Published by Warner Books in 1998
Reprinted 1999
Copyright © E. V. Thompson 1997

Harvest of the Sun first published in Great Britain in 1978 by
Macmillan London Ltd
First paperbacked in 1980 by Pan Books Ltd
This edition published by Warner Books in 1999
Copyright © E. V. Thompson 1978

The moral right of the author has been asserted.

A CIP catalogue record for this book is available from the British Library.

ISBN 0 7515 3304 1

Printed and bound in Great Britain by
Mackays of Chatham plc, Chatham, Kent

Time Warner Paperbacks
An imprint of
Time Warner Books UK
Brettenham House
Lancaster Place
London WC2E 7EN

www.TimeWarnerBooks.co.uk

Cast No Shadows

1

Menacing grey cloud lowered over Dartmoor. It rolled down the rock-strewn slopes of the Beardown tors in a silent, diaphanous avalanche of mist. As it advanced it swallowed giant towers of balancing rocks, filled hollows excavated by long-forgotten generations of grubbing tin miners and spread a cloak of damp anonymity over the moor.

Tacy Elford was acutely aware that the mist was travelling faster than she could walk.

Accompanied by her nine-year-old sister and aided by two dogs, she drove three heavily pregnant ewes ahead of her and could travel no faster. One of the ewes was lame and found it difficult to keep up with the others at their present speed.

'Look over there.' Johanna, unconcerned about the advancing mist, pointed southwestwards. 'It looks as though the prison is an island.'

Tacy looked in the direction indicated by her sister and could see what Johanna meant. The mist was spreading in an uneven pattern over the moor. From the tor behind Dartmoor prison it laid siege to the circular perimeter wall. Gaunt granite prison buildings rose from it, for all the world like grim, man-made islands, protruding from a restless grey sea of mist.

'I'm glad I'm not in there,' said Johanna. Her shiver was due in part to her thoughts, partly as a result of the mist, which had lowered the moorland temperature dramatically. 'Billy said they hang most of the people who are sent to prison. Those who aren't hung are left there to rot.'

'You should know better than to take notice of anything Billy Yates tells you,' retorted Tacy scornfully. 'You start paying attention to what he says and you'll finish up as simple as he is.'

Billy lived with his mother in a cottage on an old mine workings at Whiteworks, in a remote part of the moor. He helped the Elfords on their farm for most of the year, taking peat, farm produce and cooked foods from the farm kitchen in lieu of payment.

'His mother's told him all about prisons. She says he'll likely end up inside one of 'em if he doesn't behave himself.'

'Tillie Yates is almost as simple as Billy,' declared Tacy. 'She probably said it when she was angry with him. If she had more sense she'd realise how much something like that plays on Billy's mind. He'd have had nightmares about it. Poor Billy.'

Urging on the lame ewe, she said, 'Anyway, Dartmoor isn't *that* sort of prison. There are only French soldiers and sailors in there, not criminals. Some of them don't speak English very well, but they're no different to us, really. I should know, I meet them every time I go to the prison market.'

'That doesn't mean you know what they're *really* like,' retorted Johanna. She shivered again, but this time it was due entirely to the mist, which had now caught up with them.

'I want to pee,' she said suddenly.

'We'll be home in half an hour,' said Tacy unsympathetically. 'Wait until then.'

'I can't hold it that long,' wailed Johanna. 'I want to go now.'

Tacy was anxious to get the ewes back to Roundtor Farm before the mist became any more dense. Dartmoor was a dangerous place at such times . . . but Johanna had always been troubled with a weak bladder.

'Hurry up and go then. Over there, among those rocks if you feel shy about going here.'

She pointed to a spot where great granite rocks were scattered about the hillside, their outlines softened by the mist, 'Be quick!'

Johanna needed no urging. She hurried to the rocks and disappeared from view.

Tacy signalled to the dogs, instructing them to hold the sheep where they were. She needed to be firm with the youngest dog, Rip. It was still under training and it was Rosie who brought the sheep to a halt. Crouching low to the ground, the experienced sheepdog dared them to move.

Suddenly there was a scream from the direction of the rocks – and Tacy heard a man's voice. There was another scream and this time it continued for some seconds.

Abandoning the sheep, Tacy ran towards the rocks. As she reached them she bumped into Johanna who was shaking with fright.

Clinging to Tacy, she said, 'There's a man here. A wild man. He's . . . frightening. He spoke to me using strange words that didn't make sense!'

Tacy had a sudden glimmer of understanding. 'How is he dressed?'

'What difference does that make? I think . . . I think it might have been the Devil. Let's go, Tacy. Quickly!'

'What sort of clothes is he wearing?' repeated Tacy.

'He's dressed all in yellow. Do you think it's the Devil, Tacy?' Johanna was still trembling.

'No, I think he's an escaped French prisoner.'

Tacy occasionally took produce to the daily market held inside Dartmoor prison. She knew that prisoners-of-war unable to pay to have new uniforms made, were issued by the prison authorities with uniforms made from yellow material.

At that moment both girls heard a cry, muffled by the thickening mist.

'Which way did he go?' asked Tacy.

'I'm not sure. He ran off that way, I think,' said Johanna, pointing.

'Mudilake Marsh is over there!'

Mudilake Marsh was a large expanse of dangerous marshland. More than one moorland animal had lost its life here.

The cry came again and now it was almost as shrill as Johanna's scream had been.

'He's in the marsh. Come on, Johanna. Stay close behind me.'

'What if he's *not* an escaped prisoner, Tacy? What if it's the Devil, dressed up to look like a prisoner?'

'Don't be so stupid!' Tacy called the words back to her sister who, despite her doubts, was hurrying along behind her.

Tacy's instinct was to run, but that would be fool-hardy. That was what the unknown man had done and Tacy feared he was now trapped in the marsh. If this were so, he would be very lucky to escape with his life.

'Au secours! Au secours!'

The cry came from much closer now and slightly to one side of them.

'What's he saying, Tacy?' Johanna put the question in a fearful voice.

'I don't know . . . shh!'

Tacy stopped. The ground was spongy underfoot. They needed to be careful.

'Au secours!' The plea was accompanied by a whole spate of unintelligible words now and it sounded as though the unseen man was sobbing.

The sisters were advancing with the utmost caution when suddenly the swirling mist thinned – and they both saw the man in yellow. Despite being spattered with mud, the attire was clearly that of a prisoner-of-war.

The trapped Frenchman saw them at the same time and his relief was touching. He had sunk up to his ribcage in the mire. Now he held out his arms towards them imploringly, at the same time appealing to them in his own language.

He made an attempt to flounder towards them, but the mud held him fast. His struggles only served to cause him to sink farther into the marsh.

'Stay still!' Tacy called. 'Don't move. Keep your arms spread out on the marsh . . . No! Don't try to reach us!'

It was quite apparent the Frenchman did not understand her. He appealed to her once more, all the time struggling futilely to escape from the unrelenting grip of the marsh.

When she realised he could not understand what she was saying, Tacy turned to Johanna. Eyes wide with fright, the younger girl was still uncertain whether the man caught in the marsh was human or demon.

'Go back to where we left the ewes. Take the dogs and

follow the path down to Two Bridges. If you lose it, send the dogs on and follow where they tread. There'll be someone at the inn. Tell them to come up here as quickly as they can – and they're to bring a rope with them. Hurry now – but don't stray from the path. *Go on!*'

She shouted the last two words as Johanna hesitated, seemingly reluctant to leave her sister alone with this strange-speaking man – if indeed man he was.

The urgency in Tacy's voice got through to Johanna at last. She turned and was quickly swallowed up by the mist.

'Be careful . . . you hear?' Tacy called after her sister before returning her attention to the Frenchman. Despite her warning he was still struggling, snatching at coarse clumps of reedlike grass, only to have them come away in his hand.

The mud and water were enveloping his lower chest now. Tacy called to him yet again. 'Stop struggling, you'll only sink deeper. Spread your arms out and stay still. Like this.' She demonstrated what she wanted him to do. 'Help is coming.'

The Frenchman replied in his own language, clearly pleading with her to help him. He had not understood a word of what she had said. Indeed, he continued doing all she had told him *not* to do.

He was a young man of perhaps twenty-one, no more than three years older than herself. Somehow it made his plight all the more tragic. It seemed to Tacy he was sinking deeper in the mud of the marsh even as she looked at him.

She was not imagining it. No more than five minutes later he had sunk to his armpits – and suddenly he began sobbing.

Tacy found the sound unbearable. 'Please . . . please don't. Just stay still. Help is on the way.'

Her pleas had no more effect than her earlier ones. He realised he was sinking deeper into the Dartmoor marsh by the minute and his panic grew. Tacy stretched out a hand towards him to no avail.

His response was equally futile. The distance between their fingertips was more than two arms' length.

Tacy looked around her in desperation. If only there were a long pole, or the branch of a tree . . . but there was nothing.

Suddenly, she had an inspiration. She was wearing a cloak of brown, blanket-like material. Unfastening the clasp at her neck, she slipped the cloak from her shoulders. Swinging it through the air she aimed one end of it in the Frenchman's direction.

The first cast fell short and she tried again.

This time the long hem at the front of the cloak fell within reach of one of the Frenchman's outstretched hands. He grasped it eagerly.

As the cloak tautened between them, Tacy felt a great sense of achievement . . . but the Frenchman continued pulling. He was desperately trying to use the cloak as a lifeline to pull himself free from the marsh.

Thoroughly alarmed, Tacy cried, 'No! Just keep a grip on it. Use it to keep your head above the marsh. *Don't try to pull yourself out* . . . the cloak's not strong enough . . .'

Unable to understand her, the young Frenchman pulled even harder and Tacy was in danger of tumbling in the marsh herself.

But the cloak was old. It had been handed down to Tacy by her grandmother. Suddenly the strands of the cloth could take the strain no more. They parted. There was no sound of rending cloth. No warning of what was about to happen.

Tacy fell backwards and when she scrambled to her feet she was holding less than half of her cloak. The remainder was still grasped by the Frenchman.

He too had slipped backwards and Tacy saw to her horror that the mire was now above his shoulders.

He opened his mouth and his lips formed the shape of a scream, but only a low, despairing moan escaped. Tacy found this even harder to bear than his earlier cries of terror.

'Don't give up. Stay still. Help is on the way,' she pleaded, even though she knew he could not understand her words. Just saying them made her feel better.

The Frenchman continued moaning, all the time fixing her with a terror-stricken stare that seemed to contain an accusation.

At that moment Tacy thought she heard voices somewhere in the mist.

'Hello! Hello! I'm over here.'

There was no answering call and Tacy believed she must have been mistaken. Then she heard them again. There could be no doubt about it now, but the mist made it difficult to make out the distance or the direction of the voices. She realised it would be equally difficult for them to locate her.

'Hello . . . I'm here.'

She turned to the Frenchman who was now being forced to hold his chin up in order to keep it clear of the mud. 'Do you hear that? Someone's coming. Hold on. I'll just go a little way towards them, otherwise they won't find us.'

She could hear the voices more clearly now and they were calling her name. She ran towards the sound, shouting at the top of her voice.

The rescuers were farther away than she had realised,

but suddenly she ran into them. There were four militia-men and Johanna was with them. One of the men carried a rope.

'Where is he?' said a militiaman who wore sergeant's stripes on his arm.

'He's over here. Come quickly. There's not much time.'

Tacy hurried ahead of them. To her dismay, when she came to the marshy ground she realised it was not the right spot.

'Hello! Where are you?' She called out to the trapped Frenchman. There was no reply.

Frantically, Tacy ran first this way and that, until commonsense told her to stop and think.

After a moment she headed slightly down the slope. When she had taken no more than a dozen paces, she stopped and frowned.

'I thought it was about here . . . Perhaps I'm wrong . . .'

Suddenly, she looked down at her feet. She was almost standing on half of her torn cloak. Looking into the mist that swirled about the marsh, she saw the other half lying on top of the muddy ground.

There was no sign of the French prisoner-of-war.

2

'Prisoners . . . Halt!'

The shouted command from the Somerset Militia captain prompted a surprised and ragged response from the two hundred and fifty men marching along the narrow Devon lane.

'Prisoners . . . Fall out! All right, you can take your food and rest for a while now.'

'How the hell are we supposed to cook our rations? Breathe on it?'

The grumbled question came from a giant black man. Towering head and shoulders above his fellow prisoners, he wore trousers, a ragged, sleeveless coat and nothing else.

Barefooted, he left a group of other black men, padded to the side of the lane and sank down heavily on a rain-sodden grass bank, along the length of which were numerous pockets of pale yellow primroses.

'You don't have to worry about cooking anything,' said one of the militiamen. 'As usual, we've done the thinking for you. Cooks were sent on ahead. Your grub's ready and waiting through the gate in the field there. All you have to do is fall into line to collect it, then sit down and enjoy it, courtesy of the English Government.'

The strong, south-westerly wind had been behind the men as they marched. It dropped momentarily now and the pungent aroma of cooking fish reached the nostrils of the prisoners.

'If I wasn't so damned hungry I'd leave it where it is and let you English think how to get rid of a quarter of a ton of stinking fish stew.'

The arms of the speaker bulged with muscle and they also carried an interesting variety of scars, etched by sword and bullet.

'Eat what you can, while you can, Ephraim.'

The suggestion came from Lieutenant Pilgrim Penn. Reaching out, he picked a primrose and examined it closely. The flower reminded him of a garden in Ohio. Of his mother's flower beds. The plants had been nurtured from seeds carried with her in covered wagons on the trek westwards, as his father sought new frontiers.

'You never know, the next meal might be even worse.'

Pilgrim was probably half the age of Ephraim, but his shabby United States Marines uniform bore the insignia of a lieutenant. Ephraim's missing sleeves had carried a corporal's stripes.

'You're right there, Pilgrim. The things these English do with food would choke a hog.'

Captain Virgil Howard sat down heavily on the grass beside the muscled corporal and eased his left leg out in front of him.

'How's the leg standing up to the march?' Pilgrim asked the question anxiously. Although only seven years older than the lieutenant, Virgil was the senior commissioned officer among the American prisoners-of-war. Not only were the two men good friends but, if anything happened to Virgil, responsibility for the well-being of the men would fall upon Pilgrim's shoulders. The authority was more than a nineteen-year-old junior officer should have to assume.

The three men, Pilgrim, Virgil and Ephraim were the only members of the United States fighting forces among the prisoners. The remainder were men of the United States merchant service. All had been taken at sea by the British navy.

The three men had not been the only marines captured when the United States frigate *Delaware* was defeated in battle by two British men-of-war off the coast of Bermuda. However, during numerous changes of ship the Americans had become split up.

The three men had become separated from the last of their colleagues when, despite Virgil's barely healed wound, they escaped from a British man-of-war off one of the West Indian islands.

They were at liberty for only thirty-six hours before being recaptured by a party of British plantation owners.

The escape was the reason why the two officers had been lodged with Ephraim on board the prison hulk *Le Brave* in the Hamoaze, off Plymouth Dock.

It was usual for captured French officers to be offered parole in a small town, at a suitable distance from the coast. But American prisoners-of-war were still a novelty. The British authorities did not seem to know what to do with them.

'You stay here and rest your leg, Virgil. I'll go and fetch your food.'

Pilgrim made his way to the head of the line of men which stretched along the lane and through an open gateway into a nearby field.

Standing at intervals on either side of the lane were armed men of the Somerset Militia. They maintained a close watch on the American prisoners. One of the part-time soldiers moved to challenge Pilgrim, but a sergeant, recognising his rank, intervened and walked with him to ensure he had no more problems.

'Thank you.' Pilgrim acknowledged the militiaman's help. 'I'm fetching two meals. One for my captain. He has a leg wound that's barely healed. This march is hard on him. Do we have much farther to go?'

'About seven miles,' said the sergeant. 'But you'll notice a difference in the countryside from here on. It's moorland, and pretty bleak.'

'This prison we're going to – what's it like?' It was Pilgrim's first opportunity to talk to anyone about their destination.

'Dartmoor?' The militia sergeant shrugged. 'I'd rather be a guard than a prisoner there. They only finished building it about four years ago and I reckon the builders were glad to get away. I doubt if you'll find a bleaker place anywhere. The only time it stops raining is when it snows. Most times you won't know the difference because you can't see anything for mist.'

'It can't be as bad as that, surely?' said Pilgrim, his spirits sinking.

'No? You ask the French prisoners when you reach Dartmoor. There are about nine thousand of 'em. Some have been there since it opened.'

'Nine thousand?' Pilgrim looked at the militia sergeant in disbelief. 'How big is this place?'

'Not big enough for the number of men in there right now,' declared the sergeant. 'But you shouldn't be too badly off. You and your captain will be put in the Petty Officers' Block, I daresay. There's a bit more room there – though not too much.'

Collecting two bowls of fish stew, Pilgrim returned to where Virgil was now sitting alone. He repeated what the militia sergeant had told him.

'Whatever it's like, it can't be worse than life on that stinking hulk,' declared the American marine captain. Taking a spoonful of the soup, he pulled a wry face. 'Ephraim's right about the food. Salt haddock doesn't make a good stew.'

'It's an uppity nigger who'd dare complain about his food,' commented a merchant navy officer sitting nearby. 'Most of those we have down south are only too happy to be given anything at all to eat.'

'We're not "down south" now,' retorted Pilgrim. 'And Ephraim's not an "uppity nigger". He's a corporal of marines, who's earned his rank in battle. He's entitled to good food, same as the rest of us. I, for one, will make damn sure he gets it.'

'I don't care what he's done,' persisted the merchant seaman. 'A spoiled nigger is a dangerous nigger. You'll learn that, one day.'

With this warning, the merchant navy officer rose to his feet and walked away.

Angry by now, Pilgrim would have gone after him but Virgil put a restraining hand on his arm. He inclined his head to where the subject of their exchange was walking towards them.

Ephraim had only just sat down with his bowl of food when the militia officer began shouting for the prisoners-of-war to fall in again to resume the march.

There was much grumbling from the Americans, but the guards moved among them, threatening to use musket butts to add weight to the militia officer's orders.

'You all right?' Pilgrim's anxiety showed once more as Virgil struggled to his feet.

'I'll last another seven miles,' said the captain, gritting his teeth. 'Come on, let's fall in with the others.'

The militia sergeant had been right about the nature of the countryside through which they were soon marching. The narrow lane climbed steadily and less than an hour after their meal stop they were on Dartmoor.

For as far as could be seen there was a bleak, rolling landscape, dotted here and there with tors surmounted by bare, grey, tumbled rocks.

The rain was heavier now, preventing the prisoners from seeing for much more than a mile. However, the impression they had already gained was that the moorland went on for ever.

The moor was not entirely deserted. They were nearing their destination when a young girl of perhaps seventeen or eighteen came into view. Accompanied by two dogs, she was driving sheep inside a large paddock enclosed by freestone walls.

The sight of the lone girl brought a noisy outburst from the Americans. Few had even glimpsed a woman during many months of internment on board the prison hulk. They ignored the attempts of the militiamen to bring them to order.

The girl tried to ignore the calls of the men, as did the older and more experienced of the two dogs. The other was younger and not yet fully trained. For some moments it seemed undecided whether the sheep or the marching men were of more interest.

The men won the day. The dog ran towards them, barking noisily, ignoring the shouted command of the young shepherdess for it to return to her.

The dog's disobedience was compounded by the prisoners-of-war who whistled and shouted encouragement to the errant animal.

For some of the men it was a genuine wish to commune with the dog. After months spent in the dehumanising confines of a prison hulk, it was a link with life as they had once known it.

To others it was merely a mischievous and not-too-serious diversion.

Eventually, the captain in charge of the militiamen rode back along the line of men from the head of the column, to ascertain the reason for the noisy disorder.

Captain Henry Pollit was the only mounted member of the escort. The young dog immediately began barking at the horse. Running around it excitedly, it was urged on by the prisoners.

'Get away! Go on. Off with you!'

The officer's unsuccessful attempts to drive away the dog brought howls of glee from the American prisoners.

Henry Pollit possessed no military experience whatsoever, and was unused to commanding men. The only reason he had been granted a militia commission was because he had influential family connections in his own county.

He also possessed an exaggerated view of the importance of his command. Angered by the derision of the American prisoners-of-war and the antics of the disobedient dog, he called to one of the militiamen.

'Corporal! I'll not allow a blasted dog to threaten discipline in such a manner. Shoot it!'

The militiaman looked at the officer uncertainly. 'It's not really doing any harm, sir. It'll leave us in a few minutes.'

'Damn you, Corporal! Did you hear what I said? I gave you an order. Shoot it, or I'll take your gun and do it myself.'

Reluctantly, the corporal put the musket he carried to his shoulder and took aim.

The move brought a howl of protest from the marching men. At the same time, Pilgrim saw the girl begin to run towards the column, aware of what was about to happen to her young and disobedient dog.

He was among the men closest to the corporal. As the militiaman thumbed back the hammer on his musket, Pilgrim jumped at him without pausing to think of the consequences of his action.

He knocked the barrel of the weapon up at the very moment the militiaman pulled the trigger. A thick cloud of white smoke enveloped both men, but the musket ball sped harmlessly away, to fall to earth far away on the open moorland.

The noise of the shot succeeded where all else had failed. The dog turned and fled towards the running girl.

'Seize that man!' Furious, Captain Pollit pointed to Pilgrim. Before he could return to the column of prisoners, he was secured by two of the militiamen.

The move brought an angry response from the other American prisoners, all of whom had come to a halt. But the sound of the shot had brought other militiamen to the spot. Their muskets and bayonets were sufficient deterrent to any attempt to help Pilgrim.

'Put manacles on him. When we reach Dartmoor he'll be dealt with for assaulting a militiaman.'

One of the part-time soldiers produced a pair of heavy manacles. As they were secured to Pilgrim's wrists, Virgil limped forward and addressed the militia captain.

'I must protest, sir. Lieutenant Pilgrim Penn is an officer of the United States Marines and a prisoner-of-war. He is not a common criminal.'

'He's lucky he wasn't shot,' retorted Captain Pollit. 'He's under escort and he assaulted one of my men.'

'All he did was stop you from shooting my dog.' The girl was close enough to hear the captain's words.

Brushing long, dark hair back from her face, she spoke angrily and breathlessly. 'You should be grateful to him. The dog belongs to Sir Thomas Tyrwhitt, Lord Warden of the Stannaries. He gave it to my father for training. It's to be a present for the Prince Regent. If it had been shot you'd be in serious trouble now.'

The militia captain was startled by her disclosure. Although he had never met Sir Thomas Tyrwhitt, he certainly knew *of* him. Personal secretary and a close friend to England's future monarch, he was a man who wielded great power. There was no doubting the truth of the girl's words. But Henry Pollit was not prepared to admit he might have acted hastily.

'Your father should keep the dog at home until it's learned obedience, not send it out with a slip of a girl to stir up trouble among prisoners-of-war.'

Tacy bit back an angry retort. Instead, she looked to where Pilgrim stood between the two militiamen, his wrists manacled in front of him. 'Are you going to release him now?'

'No. He'll be taken to Dartmoor prison and punished for assaulting one of my men.'

'Then I'll have my father tell Sir Thomas you ordered one of your men to shoot his dog. You'll be hearing from him, have no doubt about that!'

Turning her back on the stubborn militia captain she spoke to Pilgrim for the first time. 'Thank you for saving the dog. I'm sorry it got you in trouble, but I'll tell Sir Thomas what happened. What's your name?'

The rowdier element among the prisoners had resumed their whistling and catcalling and Captain Pollit called to the girl. 'Stop talking to the prisoners or I'll have you arrested too.'

Pilgrim just had time to call out his name to the girl before he was pushed back among the others and the prisoners-of-war were prodded into movement once more. He would have liked to ask her name too, but they had moved away from her now. He was not even certain she had heard his words.

He thought it made little difference. He would probably never see her again – and he had other matters to worry about. In manacles now, he wondered what would happen to him when he and his fellow prisoners-of-war reached their destination.

He was certainly in trouble. What came of it would depend on how determined the militia captain was to press charges against him.

3

When the high granite walls of Dartmoor prison came into view, the American prisoners-of-war fell strangely silent. To Pilgrim, the prison resembled the drawings of grim medieval castles he had seen in books on the shelves of his grandfather's library in Washington, before Pilgrim's father took his family westwards, to Ohio.

But the pictures had lacked reality. The prison did not. The sheer size of it was awesome. It had been built on land which sloped gently away from the road. Because of this, despite its eighteen-feet-high circular perimeter wall, it was possible for a while to see something of the tall grey granite buildings rising inside the walls.

However, as the Americans drew closer, the walls themselves towered above them and nothing more could be seen of the prison buildings.

'Here we are, Pilgrim. This is likely to be our home until the war's over.'

Virgil spoke to the manacled young lieutenant, but it was Ephraim who replied. He had joined them to check whether Virgil had any orders for him when they entered the prison.

'It don't look a lot like the cabin back home on the plantation,' he said laconically.

Despite his predicament, Pilgrim smiled at the marine corporal's dry humour. He was aware that Ephraim had been born a slave. How he had escaped from his environment was something Pilgrim had never queried.

Probably the only coloured recruit in the United States Marine Corps, Ephraim had originally joined them as a blacksmith. However, he had proved himself to be a superb fighting man. Enlisted into their ranks, he had quickly earned both promotion and the respect of his fellow marines.

'With any luck the war will soon be over and we'll go home before we grow to like it here,' said Virgil.

'I'll be happy for now just to get inside and have these things taken off.' Pilgrim held his manacled wrists out in front of him. 'I swear their weight has increased tenfold since they were put on.'

'Well, if you will go around siding with some dumb dog against a puffed-up English militia officer you've got to learn to take the consequences, Lieutenant.'

The look Ephraim gave Pilgrim was more sympathetic than his words. 'Mind you, you're the first Yankee among us to have an English girl speak to him. Would you say she was pretty, Lieutenant?'

'Yes, she was.' Pilgrim thought of the girl with her black hair, and eyes that had seemed incredibly blue when she expressed her anger with the militia captain. He gave a mental shrug. After almost a year without any feminine company whatsoever, most girls were likely to appear to be attractive.

At that moment the sergeant of militia, John Straw, came back to where the three men walked together.

Addressing Virgil, he said, 'We'll be entering the prison in a few minutes, sir. There are nine thousand Frenchmen in there to watch your arrival. I thought you might want to be at the head of the men. Make some sort of impression, if you know what I mean.'

'Thank you, Sergeant. It's very thoughtful of you.'

Speaking to Pilgrim, he said, 'You ought to be up there with me.'

Pilgrim shook his head and held out his hands. 'Not with these on. You're the captain. Go on ahead. We'll march in behind you as smart as we're able.'

Virgil was stopped by one of the militiamen when he reached the head of the column of prisoners. When he insisted he be allowed to take his place at the head of the men, the militia captain was called to the scene.

Virgil told Captain Pollit the reason he wished to enter the prison at the head of his fellow Americans. He also asked for a few minutes to address the men before they reached the prison gate.

'As I see it, the French prisoners-of-war will outnumber us by about thirty-six to one. If we're to avoid trouble inside the prison, we need to establish ourselves immediately as a separate, disciplined entity and enter the prison in good order. It's equally important for my men to know what's expected of them.'

The militia captain thought about Virgil's words for a few moments, then he shrugged. 'Governor Cotgrave is quite capable of maintaining discipline, but I can't see it will do any harm. I'll call a halt for you to say your piece – but keep it brief. Governor Cotgrave will already have been informed of our approach. I don't intend keeping him waiting.'

Captain Pollit believed it would do no harm to have the senior American officer kindly disposed towards him. He was convinced his action in respect of the dog had been correct, but it might be misrepresented to the Warden of the Stannaries.

Virgil's next words dented this plan.

'There's also the matter of my second-in-command. I'd like his manacles taken off before we go in.'

'I haven't decided yet what measures will be taken against him. Until I do, the manacles remain.'

Virgil realised it would be futile to argue. He had gained one concession. He did not want to lose the opportunity to talk to the other prisoners-of-war.

The men were brought to a halt beneath the walls of the forbidding prison. Meanwhile, Captain Pollit sent a militiaman ahead to give the governor official notification of their imminent arrival. Forewarning the governor of their presence was a more acceptable reason for halting the prisoners-of-war than acceding to a request by Captain Howard.

Calling his countrymen about him, Virgil told them all he had learned about their future home. They gasped when they learned the prison was already occupied by nine thousand Frenchmen. He impressed upon them his determination that the Americans should keep their identity and remain together as a single unit.

He warned them of likely language difficulties with their fellow prisoners-of-war. It would no doubt lead to many misunderstandings between them at first. Virgil stressed that they should not try to settle their own differences. Any problems were to be brought to him, or to the committee he intended setting up to take care of the interests of American prisoners-of-war.

Looking at the faces of the men, Virgil could see he had their general agreement. Then Ephraim voiced the concern of the slaves and ex-slaves.

'Are we all going to be represented on this committee,

you're setting up, Cap'n? Will it look after *our* interests too?'

It sounded very much as though Ephraim was questioning Virgil's authority and there were angry mutterings among the southern-based merchant seamen.

Pilgrim said nothing. He, Virgil and Ephraim had already discussed what was likely to happen when they reached Dartmoor prison. Ephraim had told the officers that it was the intention of the black prisoners to break off all relations with their white countrymen if it were possible. The black prisoners had also agreed that Ephraim should assume leadership of their group.

Ephraim was by far the largest man among the American prisoners-of-war. He was a natural leader too – but he was also a marine. It was necessary to show the others he was capable of questioning white authority.

'You're all United States citizens, Ephraim. You have the same rights as everyone else.'

'They're fine words, Captain Howard – and I know you mean what you say. All the same, there are men here who've yet to meet a white man who'd take the word of a black man against one of his own kind, whether he be American, French, or English.'

He raised his voice so he could be heard by all the prisoners-of-war. 'I hope this committee is going to be fair to *everyone*. If it isn't, and any of our people have trouble, they should come to me. To Ephraim. *I'll* see they get justice. Black man's justice. You hear me?'

There were some fifty black sailors among the prisoners-of-war and Ephraim's words had the desired effect. One or two of them cheered. The others nodded their heads vigorously.

They would accept Ephraim as their leader.

'That's enough talking, Captain Howard. Get your

men fallen in. We're going inside the prison now.' The militia captain had been listening and he feared there might be trouble.

Ephraim winked at Pilgrim before he returned to the black seamen who formed a group at the rear of the column. Meanwhile, Virgil took his place at the head of the prisoners-of-war.

Virgil trusted Ephraim to maintain control over his fellow black Americans. He hoped he might have equal success with those white Americans who were not subject to military or naval discipline.

'Prisoners, quick march!'

At the order, the prisoners-of-war squared their shoulders and attempted some semblance of a disciplined, if ragged, force.

Black and white Americans marched towards the prison with at least an outward semblance of unity.

4

Led by Captain Virgil Howard and surrounded by a strong escort of Somerset Militiamen, the United States prisoners-of-war marched in through the high, arched gate of Dartmoor prison.

Over the gates was the Latin inscription, *Parcere Subjectis*.

Pilgrim had dropped back until he was marching just ahead of Ephraim. As they passed through the gates, Ephraim said, 'Look at them words. What are they supposed to mean?'

'It's Latin and means "Spare the Vanquished",' explained Pilgrim. 'The Romans used to kill their prisoners. It's what one of their poets said when he pleaded for them to change their ways and spare their captives.'

'Why have they put it up there in Latin?' asked Ephraim, clearly puzzled. 'I thought the people in this country spoke American.'

Pilgrim smiled. 'It's considered clever to inscribe Latin quotations on buildings and tombstones, things like that.'

'What's clever about carving words that nobody understands? They might as well have carved a picture.'

'You're quite right, they might as well have, Ephraim. They probably never thought of it.'

Passing beneath the archway, they marched through a small courtyard to a second rectangular yard, surrounded by a high wall. At the far end was a gate, guarded by half a dozen militiamen.

Waiting here for them was a reception committee headed by a man wearing the uniform of a Captain in the British Royal Navy. This was Captain Isaac Cotgrave, RN, the prison governor. His appointment had been made by the Transport Board, a department of the Admiralty, the body responsible for prisoners-of-war.

The Americans were brought to a halt and told to form three ranks against one of the walls.

Marching smartly up to the prison governor, the militia captain reported his arrival. Waving forward a corporal, Captain Pollit took a satchel from him and handed it to an official who stood beside the prison governor. Inside the satchel was a list of the prisoners being transferred from the hulks to Dartmoor prison.

The two officers talked for a few minutes, during which time the prison governor frequently cast glances in the direction of the latest arrivals in his prison.

Suddenly, he pointed to Pilgrim. 'Why is that man wearing manacles?'

Pilgrim was not close enough to hear the militia captain's reply – but Virgil was.

Before the men of the militia guard could prevent him, he confronted the governor and the officials about him. 'That's not true! Lieutenant Penn assaulted no one. He merely prevented your corporal from killing a young sheepdog.'

'Who are you?' the prison governor demanded angrily.

Virgil came to attention. 'Captain of Marines Virgil Howard, sir. Senior United States officer present.'

'I recognise no ranks among the inmates of my prison, *Mister* Howard. You are all prisoners. If one of your countrymen has assaulted a militiaman he can expect to be punished.'

Turning to one of the prison officials, he said, 'Have that manacled man thrown into the *cachot*, Mr Williams. We'll let him reflect upon his folly for a week or two.'

'I object most strongly, sir,' said Virgil. 'Lieutenant Penn is being punished arbitrarily, without being afforded an opportunity to defend himself.'

'Object as much as you like,' snapped the governor. 'When I've looked into the matter I'll likely have him flogged. Now, go back to the ranks, or you'll join your countryman in the *cachot*. It's not an experience I would recommend.'

Virgil would have continued to argue, but the governor turned his back on him and two of the militiamen came forward to drive Virgil back to the other prisoners-of-war.

One of the two was Sergeant Straw. As Virgil was driven back towards the others, the sergeant said quietly, 'Don't argue with Captain Cotgrave, sir. He'll do as he says. He had the reputation of being a hard captain when he was at sea. Having a shore post's done nothing to improve his temper.'

Virgil allowed himself to be pushed back to the other prisoners-of-war but instead of taking his place at their head, he found a place in their ranks beside Ephraim. With the other Americans, the marine corporal booed loudly as Pilgrim was led away.

Scowling in their direction, Captain Cotgrave told

the militia commanding officer to take the prisoners to Number Four Prison Block, where they were to be housed.

Hurrying back to his men, Captain Pollit passed the order on to Sergeant Straw. The order to fall in and turn right to march to their prison block was given, but there was no response.

Sergeant Straw repeated his order, louder this time. The result was the same. Nobody made any attempt to obey him.

The sergeant looked towards his commanding officer uncertainly. Captain Pollit stalked towards the prisoners and shouted a command for them to prepare to move off. The Americans ignored him.

His face scarlet with anger and humiliation, the officer shouted, 'What do you think you're playing at? Come to attention and prepare to move off.'

Yet again nothing happened.

The prison governor had been watching with growing anger. Now he called to the militiaman, 'What's going on, Captain Pollit?'

'The prisoners are refusing to obey orders, sir. They won't march off.'

'Won't they, indeed? We'll see about that. Order your men to fix bayonets. A jab or two should soon bring them to their senses.'

The militia sergeant looked uncertainly at his commanding officer.

'You heard what Governor Cotgrave said. Order the men to fix bayonets, Sergeant.'

When Sergeant Straw gave the order, Captain Pollit brought his men into line and gave them the order to advance upon the American prisoners.

Before the militiamen reached them, the nearest prisoners sat down. They were quickly followed by the others. Within a few minutes, all the Americans were seated upon the ground.

The militiamen halted uncertainly but Captain Pollit ordered, 'Get them on their feet. They're to go inside the gate to Block Four . . .'

One of the militiamen prodded a prisoner hesitantly. A cry went up immediately from some of the Americans that he had drawn blood.

Among the staff surrounding Governor Cotgrave was George Dykar, the prison surgeon. Now he said to the governor, 'I must protest, sir. These are unarmed men . . .'

'They are prisoners-of-war and in a state of mutiny, Mr Dykar.'

'It's a passive mutiny, sir. They pose no threat to anyone. Should serious wounds be inflicted, requiring my attention, the facts will have to be registered in my report.'

Governor Cotgrave glared at the surgeon. Neither of the men liked the other and Cotgrave was aware the surgeon would do as he said.

'Where's that captain of marines?' Seeking him out, he approached until he stood no more than seven or eight paces away from Virgil.

'You! Tell these men to stand up and march to their quarters.'

Without rising to his feet, Virgil said, 'Are you acknowledging that as senior United States officer here I have a responsibility for the well-being of the American prisoners-of-war, sir?'

'I am acknowledging nothing,' snapped Governor Cotgrave, furious at Virgil's opportunism. 'But if you are as concerned for their well-being as you claim to be, you'll persuade them to take up their quarters immediately.'

'I *am* concerned, Governor. However, I am not prepared to help you. As you told me a while ago, I am just another prisoner-of-war. Nevertheless, I can assure you that any report I forward to my Government on their behalf will be taken very seriously indeed.'

'Your country is a long way from Dartmoor,' snapped Governor Cotgrave. 'A single Dartmoor night should be sufficient to make you change your mind – and those of your countrymen.'

Turning back to Captain Pollit, the prison governor said, 'You and your men seem particularly inept at soldiering, perhaps you might prove better at guarding the prisoners. I'll have the yard lit by lanterns. You will arrange for a strong guard to be placed on the prisoners all night. They will be ready to listen to reason by morning.'

5

The confrontation between the American prisoners-of-war and the governor had been witnessed by a great many French officers, all of whom seemed to have freedom to wander about the prison at will.

There were also a number of French prisoners watching from viewpoints in the upper-storey windows of one of the nearby prison blocks.

As the governor and his entourage walked away from the seated Americans, the watching Frenchmen cheered and jeered loudly, adding to the anger of Governor Cotgrave.

When darkness fell over the prison, lamps were lit and placed upon poles around the defiant American prisoners. With the darkness, the drizzle that had been with them intermittently throughout the day, turned to sleet.

Sitting shivering with the others, Virgil called out to his countrymen, 'Move back until you're tight against the wall. Huddle together as close as you can to keep warm.'

The men were seated in the lee of a high interior wall. It afforded them some degree of protection from the bitterly cold wind. Now they edged even closer, huddling tightly together to share what scant body heat they were generating.

Ephraim was squatting on the ground close to Virgil and he said quietly, 'I know you and I can last out, Captain, but how about the others? After all, they're not marines.'

'This was their idea, remember? Besides, it doesn't matter now whether they last out or not. We've let the governor know we Americans stick together. He'll need to take that into account when dealing with us during the time we're here.'

'Do you think it might persuade him to turn Lieutenant Penn loose?'

'That would be too much of a blow to his pride, but I intend lodging an official complaint about it as soon as we can . . .'

He was interrupted by a sudden upsurge of sound from nearby. Something had been thrown over the wall behind them. It was quickly followed by many more items.

The word went around quickly and excitedly. They were being bombarded with rolled-up blankets by the Frenchmen who occupied the compound on the far side of the wall. They had been locked up for the night but, as the Americans would learn, their allies were adept at obtaining and duplicating keys. Indeed, they had the capabilities to manufacture all manner of objects.

Soon dozens of blankets had landed among the seated men. The American prisoners quickly discovered that many of the bundles also contained bottles of spirits!

Before long most of the newly arrived prisoners-of-war were huddled beneath blankets while bottles containing rum, brandy or wine were circulating among them.

The morale of the American prisoners soared enormously. Someone declared loudly that if this treatment continued they should remain seated in the prison's market square for the whole of their internment.

'What do you think we ought to do about it?' One of the militiamen guarding the American prisoners-of-war put the question to Sergeant Straw.

'Nothing.' The reply was immediate and positive. 'We were told to guard them and make sure no one escapes. That's what we're doing. Nobody said they shouldn't be allowed any scrap of comfort that comes their way. I only wish someone would throw a bottle of something warming in our direction, that's all.'

Outside the punishment cell known by the French word *cachot*, meaning 'dungeon', Pilgrim had his manacles removed by one of the prison turnkeys.

'You won't be lonely in there,' said the guard unfeelingly. 'You'll be with someone who's been locked up long enough to find his way around – not that there's much in there to be found.'

A moment later a hand was placed against Pilgrim's back and he was shoved through a low doorway and sent stumbling inside the gloomy, rough concrete *cachot*. The heavy iron door slammed shut behind him.

'Who is that?'

The question was in French, a language Pilgrim had learned as a boy from the French trappers who had passed through the hills close to his home in Ohio, heading northwestwards.

'My name's Pilgrim. What's yours?'

'You are English?' There was disbelief in the Frenchman's voice.

'No, American.'

'Ah! We heard you had entered the war against England. But so many rumours circulate in a prison. I am Henri Joffre. I will not insult you by bidding you welcome.'

The Frenchman spoke in English now, in a flat, emotionless voice. He slurred his words in the manner of a man who had grown unaccustomed to conversation. Seated on the cold, concreted floor he made no attempt to rise to his feet.

'How long have you been in here?' Pilgrim asked.

'It is difficult to measure time in the *cachot*, m'sieur, especially in winter. Some days are little lighter than night. If the gaoler forgets to bring a meal, as is frequently the case, it is impossible to tell night from day. I think perhaps it is five or six weeks?'

'Five or six weeks? In this place . . . ?'

It was dark inside the *cachot*. The only light entering the dungeon-like structure filtered through two tiny holes. No larger than a man's hand, each was set high in the wall beneath the eaves. What light there was showed the *cachot* to be perhaps six paces square, with rough concrete floor and walls. Apart from a large wooden slop bucket in one corner, it was totally devoid of furniture. There was not even straw on the floor.

Pilgrim was aghast at the Frenchman's words. He had expected to be incarcerated here for a day or two, at the most.

An uncomfortable thought suddenly occurred to him. It was possible the other man was guilty of some particularly heinous crime . . .

Hesitantly, he asked him the reason he had been cast in the *cachot*.

'I tried to escape, m'sieur. We have a market in the large square inside the gates. I became friendly with

a young girl who sets up a stall there every day. We
would talk long together. She became very fond of me
– and I of her too, of course. One day she brought some
clothes to the prison for me. Women's clothes. Night
comes early to the moor in winter. By the time the
market ended it was dark. When the traders left the
prison I went with them, dressed as a woman.'

The Frenchman was silent for a while and Pilgrim
prompted, 'What went wrong?'

In the gloom of the *cachot* the Frenchman made a
sound that might have been an attempt at a laugh.
'Nothing – at first. I walked through the gate without
being challenged. Then, on the way through Princetown
we encountered a large party of off-duty militiamen.
They had been drinking heavily. I think it was to
celebrate a victory in battle by their county regiment
over my countrymen, in the Spanish Peninsular.'

When the Frenchman fell silent yet again, Pilgrim
asked, 'Did their celebrations make you angry? Is that
how you came to be recaptured?'

'Angry? No, m'sieur. In war there are defeats and
victories in battle for both sides. Only the final battle
is of importance. I did not resent their celebrations.
Unfortunately, the drink they had consumed had also
made them amorous – and I was dressed as a woman,
you understand?'

Pilgrim thought he *did* understand, but the French
officer was talking once more.

'. . . One of the militiamen was especially persistent.
When he began taking liberties I hit him. Not as a
woman might, with the flat of my hand on his cheek,
but with my fist, on his chin. Then the other militiamen
and the traders joined in. During the mêlée I lost my
bonnet and one of the militiamen recognised me.'

Pilgrim could just make out the Frenchman's shrug as

he added, 'For escaping I expected to be punished, but when I was brought before the governor charged with assaulting a militiaman I protested most strongly. I was defending my honour, you understand. But it was to no avail. Now I have been left to rot here in the *cachot*.'

Pilgrim was dismayed, not only at the length of the Frenchman's stay in this primitive cell, but at the thought that he too was here for assaulting a militiaman! He wondered whether he would also be kept for weeks in the semi-darkness of this dungeon-like punishment cell?

6

The rain that had been falling across the high ground of the moor turned briefly to snow before ceasing altogether. However, once the snow ceased the temperature plummeted.

In the market square, the American prisoners-of-war huddled together as closely as was possible. By sharing the blankets thrown to them by the Frenchmen, a pair of men could enjoy the protection of two blankets and whatever warmth was generated by their bodies. But it could not keep the chill of the night away altogether.

In the *cachot*, Pilgrim was spending one of the most uncomfortable nights of his young life. He consoled himself with the thought that the accommodation for his companions was probably only marginally better than his own.

As yet, he was unaware they were still outside, enduring the bitter cold of the prison's market square.

Pilgrim and Henri sat on opposite sides of the bare, concrete room. Neither was talking now. Conversation had ceased when the cold, seeping in through the small apertures in the outside wall, began to numb the facial muscles of both men.

Slumped against a rough wall in the small building, Pilgrim was deep in thought when he became aware of a sound that had been increasingly impinging upon his thoughts. He suddenly realised he was listening to the chattering teeth and ragged breathing of his companion.

The sounds were alarming. 'Henri . . . ?'

'It's . . . it's all right. This . . . isn't the first . . . cold night . . . I've spent in here.'

Talking brought on a violent fit of coughing. When it ended Henri fought hard in an effort to breathe normally once more.

Pilgrim also felt desperately cold, but he knew he was in much better health than the Frenchman. Weeks spent in the comfortless *cachot* after years of imprisonment were finally taking their toll.

Climbing stiffly to his feet, Pilgrim shrugged off his coat. 'Here, take this. I can probably withstand the cold better than you . . . for one night, at least.'

When the Frenchman protested, albeit weakly, he said, 'Well, take it just for a while. Until you feel warmer. Then we'll take turns with it.'

As he wrapped the coat about the Frenchmen he could feel the man's whole, thin body shaking.

He was about to sit down on the floor once more when there was a sound at the door and the small hatch was opened. A voice which Pilgrim recognised as belonging to John Straw, the friendly militia sergeant, whispered, 'Here, take these. They'll help warm up the night.'

Something was pushed through the hatch and dropped to the floor of the *cachot*. Feeling around, Pilgrim located a bundle. It comprised two rolled-up blankets – and inside was a bottle.

Pulling the cork, Pilgrim breathed in the pungent fumes of what promised to be a cheap and fiery, but nonetheless welcome brandy.

When Henri took a first swig from the bottle he choked for so long Pilgrim thought he might expire. Then, his voice hoarse and strained, the Frenchman gasped, 'My family . . . have distilled Cognac for very many years. It is renowned throughout France . . . throughout *Europe*, but never have they produced anything that tastes better than this. I feel the heat from it exploring every part of my body.'

'There are blankets here too. They'll help keep the heat in once it's made its way around your veins.'

'My friend! Have you been sent by the gods to work miracles in this most grim of all prisons? Companionship, compassion, Cognac – and a blanket too! Will I wake in the morning to find it all gone – and you with it?'

Despite his surroundings and the predicament he was in, Pilgrim grinned. 'Well, *I'll* still be here, I don't know about the blankets – or the bottle. They're both likely to be taken away if a turnkey sees them. I suggest we do something about the contents of the bottle, at least.'

'It would be rare indeed for a gaoler to actually come inside the *cachot*, but it is not impossible. However, do not worry, there is a space above the door, between roof and wall, where we can hide them. A hole has been carefully made over the years by those who have been here before us. There are messages hidden inside, written to their families by men with no expectation of leaving Dartmoor alive. You must read them when there is sufficient light entering through the rat-hole that passes for a window. They make touching reading.'

Huddled in their blankets and with the chill of the night held at bay, albeit temporarily, the two men talked far into the early hours of the Dartmoor morning.

The brandy had put new life into the Frenchman. At times it seemed to Pilgrim he was trying to make up for all the conversation he had lacked during his lonely sojourn in the primitive punishment cell.

Yet Pilgrim was grateful for the company of Henri Joffre. From him he learned a great deal about the prison that was likely to be his home until the conclusion of the war between Great Britain and the United States of America.

Built of grey, moorland granite, the whole prison complex was contained within a mile-long, circular wall, constantly patrolled by militiamen. Within this was a second, lower wall.

The actual gaol blocks were built inside one half of the circle and the *cachot* was located within this area. There were seven prison blocks in all, arranged in a half-circle like the spokes of a gigantic wheel. One end of each block pointed to the centre of the circle.

The blocks were numbered one to seven and Pilgrim learned that Block Four contained the worst elements of the French prisoners-of-war. So desperate were they considered to be that a wall had been built about this particular block to separate them from the other prisoners.

In the remaining half of the circle was the hospital and a block known as *Le Petit Cautionnement*, or Petty Officers' Block. It contained French officers who, for one reason or another, had not taken parole, or had had it refused or taken away.

The market square was within this half of the prison area. Farmers and traders from the surrounding countryside were allowed to bring goods here for sale to those prisoners with sufficient money to purchase them.

Built into the high prison wall on either side of the main gate were the houses occupied by the governor, and the prison surgeon.

After a while, Pilgrim found his concentration wandering as the Frenchman chattered on. He began thinking of the forests and fertile plains of Ohio, so unlike the bleak moorland wastes on which the prison stood; of the home and family he had left behind in America.

His father, once a marines officer himself, was now a Congressman, representing the newly established State of Ohio, able to bring pressure to bear in the seat of government in Washington. Pilgrim wondered whether his father would use this influence in an attempt to have his only son freed.

He decided his father would probably not yet be aware that he was a prisoner-of-war. All he would know was that the ship on which Pilgrim had been serving was missing.

It had been impossible to write and have letters taken for delivery from the prison hulk on which the American prisoners-of-war had been held until now. He hoped it might be possible to send a letter from Dartmoor prison, giving his whereabouts to the family.

But first he needed to obtain his release from the *cachot*. He was younger than Henri Joffre and probably far fitter, but he hoped his fitness would not be put to the test of spending months locked away in the semi-darkness of this grim punishment cell.

7

Tacy Elford was working in the yard of Roundtor Farm. The small moorland holding was rented by her father from the Duchy of Cornwall.

The Dukedom of Cornwall was one of many titles held by George, the Prince Regent, currently ruling England on behalf of his deranged father, King George the Third.

The Duchy would remain in his possession until he took formal possession of the Crown of England. Then the title and all income from Duchy lands would pass to the next male heir to the throne. If there were not one, the income would be retained by the king and his successors, until one was born.

Included in the Duchy lands was most of Dartmoor and the surrounding countryside.

Roundtor farmhouse had been thoughtfully sited beside a narrow river, in a valley at the foot of the tor from which it took its name. The tor afforded the farmhouse protection from the prevailing westerly winds.

Dartmoor was a beautiful but unrelenting environment. Everything on and about the small isolated farm was designed to counter the effects of the harsh moorland winter weather.

The house and outbuildings formed a square, with the doors of the farm buildings opening into a central courtyard. Many of the domestic animals were brought in during the severest weather. They and the householders needed to be able to survive being cut off from the rest of the world for days – or even weeks in a particularly severe winter.

This had been no more than an average winter. Much of the snow had already come and gone, although some still lingered in pockets among the rocks of the surrounding tors.

Tacy's father, Tom, was not a well man. He had suffered for years from a chest complaint that restricted the amount of work he was able to do. At this moment he was checking on the sheep in a pen not far from the house. Pregnant ewes were gathered here, in anticipation of the lambing that would soon take place.

Tacy was throwing hay down into the courtyard from a hayloft, helped somewhat indifferently by her sister, Johanna, and Billy Yates.

Suddenly, the gate to the yard creaked open noisily on ungreased hinges, and Billy sucked in his breath.

Tacy looked up to see Sir Thomas Tyrwhitt ride his horse in through the yard gateway. The friend of the Prince Regent waved a hand before dismounting. As he tethered his horse, the young sheepdog ran across the yard to give him a warm greeting.

Tacy waved her hand in return and stopped working, but she remained in the open doorway of the hayloft.

Sir Thomas Tyrwhitt was a very important man in his own right and his close friendship with the Prince

Regent commanded additional respect. He was a local landowner and, as Lord Warden of the Stannaries, he wielded a great deal of influence in south-west England.

The appointment had lost much of the vast power it had once carried when the Stannaries – the tin-mining areas – had produced great wealth for the Crown, but it was still important enough to make him a very influential man.

He was also a generous man. Yet Tacy had always been somewhat in awe of him. She felt happier remaining on the upper floor of the hayloft.

Ignoring Billy, Sir Thomas raised his hat to Tacy and pointed to the dog. 'How is Rip coming along? Will he make as fine a sheepdog as his mother?'

'He shows great promise, Sir Thomas, but he still has a lot to learn. Mind you, we're lucky to still have him with us. He was almost shot by a militiaman yesterday.'

'It's a shame to want to shoot a dog like Rip.' Billy was indignant. 'It's not right. I wish I'd been there. I'd have showed him what I thought of him.'

Continuing to ignore the simple young man, Sir Thomas frowned. He advanced until he was standing directly beneath the open hayloft door. '*Almost* shot . . . ? Tell me about it.'

Tacy described the incident involving the American prisoners-of-war and their militia escort. By the time she ended her story, the landowner was having difficulty controlling his anger.

'That militia captain may not be aware of it but he has good reason to thank the American. Had he shot Rip I'd have had him stripped of his commission and sent back to his home in disgrace. The trouble with these part-time soldiers is that a little power goes to

their head. It's something I was discussing with the
Prince Regent only the other day . . .'

The conversation he repeated to Tacy, although undoubtedly true, was intended to impress her. Sir Thomas
never missed an opportunity to remind a pretty young
woman what an important man he was.

Nevertheless, he *was* a kindly man and Tacy genuinely liked him.

'I suppose you didn't happen to get the name of the
American? I'll send him a little something to show my
appreciation of his actions. It might make his life a little
easier if it's known I'm taking an interest in him. The
Good Lord knows, a man needs something to make
things more bearable if he's locked up inside Dartmoor
prison. But you won't have been in there, Tacy?'

'She has, Sir Thomas,' said Billy, eager to be noticed
by the landowner. 'She goes in there sometimes to sell
things from the farm. I've been in there with her. I went
along to see that none of them prisoners hurt her.'

'And I was very pleased to have your protection, Billy.
Now, will you go to the house and tell my ma that Sir
Thomas has come calling?'

When Billy had gone, beaming happily to have been
given praise from Tacy, she said, 'I go to the prison
quite often, Sir Thomas. Pa sends me there to sell peat
and sometimes eggs and chickens. Vegetables too when
we have some to spare – and I did manage to learn
something of the American who saved Rip's life. He's a
lieutenant. Lieutenant Pilgrim something-or-other. But
I don't know if they'd allow you to send anything to
him. After he'd knocked the militiaman's gun up, they
put manacles on him before marching him off with the
others. Pa says he'd have no doubt been thrown in a
punishment cell as soon as they got to the prison.'

'Your father is probably right.' Sir Thomas looked

thoughtful. 'The governor might also order him to be flogged – and that would be most unfair. This happened only yesterday, you say?'

'Yesterday afternoon. He doesn't deserve to be flogged. All he did was stop the militiaman from shooting Rip.'

'You're quite right, of course.' The Lord Warden of the Stannaries arrived at a sudden decision. 'Do you think you would recognise this American again if you saw him?'

'I'm certain of it.' Tacy hoped she had not sounded *too* positive, but the American had been young and good-looking. Quite unlike any of the young men she had met about the moor.

'Then why don't we take a ride to the prison and find out what's happening to him, Tacy?'

'You want *me* to come with *you* . . . now? To the prison?'

'That's right.'

The suggestion took Tacy by surprise.

'I'll need to ask my pa. He's up at the sheep pen, on the tor.'

'I'll come with you,' said Billy eagerly, as he returned from the house.

'That won't be necessary, Billy, but thank you all the same. You stay here and help Johanna. She'd like that.'

Behind Billy's back, and unseen by the simple young man, Johanna put out her tongue at her sister, but Sir Thomas was talking once more.

'Come on down, Tacy. We'll stop and speak to your father along the way. We shouldn't waste any time if we're to save this American from the lash.'

Tom Elford was no more enthusiastic about having his daughter go off with Sir Thomas across the moor than she was. But he knew how upset she had been the previous day, when she was telling him of the incident. Especially when she described how the American prisoner-of-war had been manacled before being marched away by the militiamen. It had brought back the memory of the help-lessness she had felt when the escaped French prisoner had died in Mudilake Marsh.

'Of course she must go, if it will help the man who saved Rip. But the governor will want to entertain you afterwards, Sir Thomas, and Tacy's not dressed for such company. You go on together now. As soon as I've fed these ewes I'll make my way to the prison and wait outside the gate for Tacy. When she's found this young man for you, she and I can return home together.'

'There's really no need . . . but that's up to you, Tom. It's your own time, to spend as you wish. Come along, Tacy. Give me your hand and climb up behind me. It's all right, girl, I won't bite you. We'll be there a sight more quickly than if you walk and I have to keep the horse moving at your pace.'

Tacy climbed up behind Sir Thomas and was forced to wrap her arms about him when he put the horse to a trot. She was relieved her father had said he would come to the prison and wait for her.

None of them saw Billy.

Naturally clumsy, he had dropped his hay fork from the hayloft, into the yard. When he went down to retrieve it, he could see through the gate to the sheep pen.

He saw Tacy climb upon the horse behind Sir Thomas, and he stood and watched them ride away.

It made him unhappy. Not because he questioned Sir Thomas's motives. Such a thought would never have occurred to Billy. Sir Thomas was a *gentleman*. As such, his motives were beyond reproach.

Billy was unhappy because *he* would never own a

horse. He would never know what it was to have Tacy riding behind him, her arms about *his* waist.

He watched the horse and its two riders until Johanna called to him crossly, 'Are you supposed to be helping me, Billy, or are you going to spend all your time down there leaning on that old fork, day-dreaming?'

'I'm coming, Johanna.'

Billy hurried to the ladder which led to the hayloft. He did not want to upset Johanna. He loved her almost as much as he did her older sister.

8

A penetrating, cold wind was blowing across the expanse of open moorland between Roundtor Farm and the prison and Sir Thomas Tyrwhitt showed little inclination to dally along the way.

The prison governor's house had been built into the high perimeter wall, to the right of the main prison gate. When they reached it Tacy slid to the ground before Sir Thomas dismounted. After he had tethered his horse, they walked together to the house.

The servant who opened the door informed them that the prison governor was inside the prison.

'He'll be in the market square,' she explained, 'only there's no market there today, on account of them troublesome Americans.'

'Troublesome?' queried Sir Thomas.

'Yes, Sir Thomas. When they arrived yesterday they refused to leave the market square and go to their prison block. They've been sitting out there in the cold ever since. They're still there. You can just see them from a window upstairs in the servants' quarters, if you've a mind.'

'And Captain Cotgrave is with them?' queried Sir Thomas.

'That's right, Sir Thomas. He's been out there for about half an hour now.'

'Then we'll go inside the prison and speak to him. You have a back door that leads inside the prison, I presume?'

'Yes, Sir Thomas, but . . .'

'Good!' Sir Thomas brusquely interrupted her. 'You can show us the way. Come along, Tacy. Let's find out what's happened to your young American.'

Sir Thomas's positive manner precluded further argument. The young servant girl had strict instructions that the door leading to the prison yard was to be kept locked at all times, but she could not refuse Sir Thomas permission to use it. She hoped her employer would understand . . .

'Cap'n, isn't that the girl whose dog got Lieutenant Penn into trouble?'

A blanket wrapped tightly about him, Ephraim nudged Virgil and inclined his head to where Tacy and Sir Thomas were walking from the direction of the governor's house.

Virgil looked up, bleary-eyed. There had been little sleep for any of the Americans during the night. The blankets donated by the French had afforded only a degree of protection against the cold night wind. The prisoners-of-war had been numbed by an insidious chill which seeped inside a man's bones and remained there.

'It certainly looks like her . . .' mused Virgil. 'But what would she be doing in here – and who's that with her? By the way everyone's jumping one of the two must be pretty important – and I don't think it's the girl.'

'What was the name of the man she said owned the dog Lieutenant Penn saved?'

'It was a Sir something-or-the-other.' Virgil took a renewed interest in the couple who were approaching the prison governor and his party.

'Look at the way everyone's scuttling his butt off to meet him.' The deference accorded to Sir Thomas was making a big impression upon Ephraim.

When Virgil struggled stiffly to his feet his muscles were cold and unresponsive, his wounded leg giving him particular trouble.

'Where you going, Cap'n?' demanded the big marine corporal.

'If it's who we think it is and he's brought the girl with him, he must be here to help Pilgrim. I want to make sure no one puts him off.'

Picking his way between the other American prisoners-of-war, Virgil limped towards Sir Thomas Tyrwhitt, Tacy and the prison officials.

The militiamen forming a half-circle around the seated prisoners were looking towards the new arrival. Virgil almost made it through their line before he was stopped. Then two of the militiamen reacted swiftly.

One seized him by the arm as the other confronted him. The bayonet attached to the second militiaman's musket puckered the material of Virgil's uniform coat, in the vicinity of his navel.

'Where do you think you're going?' The question came from the militiaman wielding the bayonet.

'I want to talk to the gentleman who has just arrived with the girl.'

'If Sir Thomas Tyrwhitt wants to talk to you he'll send for you. Get back with the others.'

Virgil held his ground. 'I'll stay here until I can attract Sir Thomas's attention.'

The militiaman increased the pressure on the bayonet pressing against Virgil's midriff and it pricked his skin through the cloth. 'The longer you stand here, the more of my bayonet you're likely to taste. Stay here long enough and you'll know how a pig on a spit feels.'

'I've faced bayonets held in the hands of *real* soldiers,' said Virgil contemptuously. 'They didn't frighten me any more than yours does. I'll stay here until I'm noticed.'

Governor Cotgrave had seen Sir Thomas the moment he left the house and entered the prison yard. He hurried to meet him, closely followed by many of the senior prison officials with whom he had been speaking.

The governor and his staff had been discussing the best course of action to take against the American prisoners-of-war.

Cotgrave favoured calling in all off-duty militiamen and forcibly removing the stubborn Americans from the yard. Most of his officials felt perhaps a day without food, followed by one more night in the open would be sufficient to break their will.

George Dykar, the prison surgeon, was opposed to both these solutions. Called from his bed, there had been no time to consume his usual morning intake of brandy. Uncharacteristically sober, he argued that moving the men forcibly would provoke violence, resulting in casualties. There might even be fatalities – on both sides.

He also pointed out that refusing food to the men and leaving them in the open for another cold night would have equally serious consequences. The Americans had spent many months in the unhealthy confines of a rat-infested convict hulk. Already weakened, they would not have the constitution to withstand another bitterly cold night.

Either way, there would certainly be more work for the surgeon and his assistants.

Dykar favoured reasoning with them. If it proved necessary, he believed they should release the young marine lieutenant.

Such a solution was strongly opposed by Governor Cotgrave. The differences between governor and surgeon had still to be resolved.

When Sir Thomas had shaken hands with the governor and the senior members of his party, he said, 'I came here to see you concerning one of your prisoners, but I seem to have arrived at a somewhat inopportune moment.'

'We are having trouble with the American prisoners-of-war who arrived yesterday,' explained Governor Cotgrave apologetically. 'The supervisor of the hulk at Plymouth warned me they were likely to prove troublesome. He was happy to be rid of them.'

At that moment, Tacy said excitedly, 'That's the American who was with the lieutenant who saved Rip.'

As Sir Thomas turned away from Governor Cotgrave, she pointed in Virgil's direction.

Aware of the governor's questioning frown, Sir Thomas explained, 'This young lady is Tacy Elford. Her father farms below Roundtor. She's training one of my dogs for me – an animal with a first-class pedigree. Going to be a champion one day. I intend presenting it to the Prince Regent. It's the reason I'm here today. A damn-fool militiaman was about to shoot the dog when one of these Americans knocked his gun up. I came here to thank him and to see if there was something I could do for him while he's here. I knew the late American ambassador to London very well. It distresses me that we should be at war with his country. After all, we share the same language and have a great deal in common. I can't for the life of me see why they've allied themselves with the French. Expediency, I suppose. Do you mind if I have a few words with the American recognised by Tacy? By his dress he would appear to be an officer.'

Even as he asked the question, Sir Thomas was walking briskly towards Virgil. Hard put to keep up with him, Governor Cotgrave was given no opportunity to interrupt his flow of words before the Prince Regent's friend reached his objective.

Frowning at the militiaman who had brought Virgil to a halt, Sir Thomas pushed the man's musket and bayonet to one side, using only a forefinger of his right hand. 'I really don't think that is necessary. This officer poses no threat to anyone.'

To Virgil, he said, 'Good morning, sir. I'm Sir Thomas Tyrwhitt. Unless I'm mistaken you're wearing a captain's insignia. I'm seeking one of your lieutenants, Pilgrim something-or-other. According to Tacy here, he prevented one of my dogs from being shot.'

'That's right, Sir Thomas.' Virgil spoke quickly, aware that the prison governor wanted to speak. 'Lieutenant Pilgrim Penn saved the life of your dog. He's been thrown in a punishment cell as a result.'

'He has been placed in a punishment cell for assaulting a militiaman.'

The prison governor was angered that the American marine captain had been allowed to put his version of the incident before he had been able to give Sir Thomas the official explanation. 'Striking a guard, or an escort, is a very serious offence. There are more than nine thousand prisoners in this prison. Discipline is of paramount importance . . .'

'Lieutenant Penn struck no one,' declared Virgil firmly. 'He knocked up the militiaman's musket so that the shot went wide of the dog. No more than that.'

'That's *exactly* what he did,' agreed Tacy heatedly. 'When the gun went off it frightened Rip and he ran back to me. Then the lieutenant stepped back among the others again. That was when the militia officer had the manacles put on him.'

'You will have spoken to everyone involved in this unfortunate incident, of course?' Sir Thomas's question was directed at the prison governor.

Captain Cotgrave was an autocratic governor, unused to either seeking or accepting the views of others. It galled him to have his actions queried by anyone. Nevertheless, he was aware of the enormous power wielded by Sir Thomas Tyrwhitt.

'The actions of the prisoner's countrymen forced me to defer my inquiries into the matter until today, Sir Thomas. They defied orders given to them upon their arrival and refused to take up their quarters.'

Sir Thomas had already been given this information by Cotgrave's servant girl, but he pretended to be shocked. 'These men have been here all night? Out in the open?'

'The night air has undoubtedly chilled them through. Hopefully, it will also have given them time to reflect upon their actions. Had I called upon the militia to move them there would have been considerable bloodshed. Deaths too, I have no doubt. I took the humane course.'

'Why would they not go to their quarters? Is there something wrong with them?'

Before the governor could reply, Virgil said, 'It was a spontaneous protest at the unfair arrest of Lieutenant Penn. The men saw what happened out there on the moor. He'd done nothing to deserve being arrested. If anyone deserves punishment it's the militia officer. The order to shoot the dog was neither necessary nor reasonable.'

'No one asked your opinion, Captain. You may rejoin the other prisoners.'

Governor Cotgrave reacted angrily to Virgil's comments, but Sir Thomas countermanded his order.

'I would like him to remain here – with your permission of course, Governor.'

The rider was added as a sop to Governor Cotgrave's pride. Nevertheless, it was a command.

'I would also like to meet the young officer who saved my dog. I have no doubt you will wish to release him in view of what we have both heard?'

Inwardly seething with anger, Governor Cotgrave carefully controlled his feelings. 'I will arrange his release immediately. Perhaps you would like to return to my house while the order is carried out?'

'I will be delighted to accept your offer, Governor Cotgrave, but shall we see this matter resolved first? I presume it won't take long once you have issued the necessary order . . . ?'

9

When the inner prison gate opened and Pilgrim appeared, flanked by two militiamen, a great cheer went up from the American prisoners-of-war. They immediately began climbing stiffly to their feet.

Pilgrim was escorted to the small group of people which included Virgil, Tacy, Sir Thomas Tyrwhitt and the prison governor.

Aware of the part Tacy must have played in his release, Pilgrim nodded his head to her in grateful acknowledgement. Sir Thomas looked from one to the other with interest. The young American could only be a year or two older than Tacy . . .

He dismissed such an idea as preposterous. They had met only briefly the day before.

Governor Cotgrave was the first to speak. 'Lieutenant Penn, Sir Thomas Tyrwhitt has come to the prison to intercede on your behalf. In view of what he, this young lady, and your senior officer have said about the incident for which you were placed in the punishment cell, I feel justice will best be served by releasing you. I will, of course, conduct an inquiry into the circumstances of your arrest.'

Inclining his head to the prison governor, Pilgrim said, 'Thank you, sir.'

Turning to Sir Thomas and Tacy, he said, 'I would like to thank both of you, too. I am very grateful.'

'It is I who should be thanking *you*,' said Sir Thomas warmly. 'According to Tacy you saved the life of the dog I intend presenting to His Royal Highness the Prince Regent.'

'It's a spirited young animal and should please His Royal Highness,' replied Pilgrim.

'As I have just said to the governor, I find it distressing that our two countries should be at war with each other. Before hostilities began I made many friends at the United States Embassy in London. As a matter of fact a namesake of yours was ambassador there. We became good friends.'

'That would be my Uncle Richard, Sir Thomas. He too is unhappy that our countries are at war.'

'Your uncle, you say! Well, I'm damned . . . begging your pardon, Tacy. Now I am doubly glad to have been able to sort out this misunderstanding, young man. I feel I have done something to repay your uncle for the many hours I spent in the embassy enjoying his warm hospitality.'

The prison governor had been following the conversation in tight-lipped silence. Now Sir Thomas turned to him. 'I would like to stand as a guarantor for this young man if parole can be arranged, Governor Cotgrave.'

The prison governor shook his head. 'I'm sorry, Sir Thomas. No decision has yet been reached by the Admiralty about parole for American officers. Much will depend upon their conduct, as you will appreciate. I regret, they have not impressed the authorities so far.'

With a gesture, he indicated the Americans who were still noisily acclaiming the release of Pilgrim. 'I doubt very much whether this demonstration will make it any easier for us to relax the conditions under which they are detained.'

'No doubt the situation will improve before too long,' declared Sir Thomas meaningfully.

Addressing Pilgrim once more, he said, 'We will talk more of parole in due course, young man. In the meantime, if there is anything you need, you have only to send word to me. I live very close to the prison and Tacy comes here occasionally to sell produce from her father's farm. She will carry any messages you might have.'

Sir Thomas smiled in Tacy's direction, but she was looking at Pilgrim.

'Thank you, Sir Thomas,' said Pilgrim. 'You're very kind. In fact, there's something you might do right now that would make me feel much happier.'

Sir Thomas frowned, but he said, 'Of course. What is it?'

'I shared a punishment cell – the "*cachot*", I believe it is called – with a French officer. He has been there for about six weeks. He could not be more precise himself, having lost all sense of time. He's a very sick man and should be seen by a doctor as a matter of some urgency.'

'Six weeks in a punishment cell? What was his offence? It must have been extremely serious.' Sir Thomas put the question to the governor who promptly turned to one of his staff for an answer.

The man in question appeared embarrassed at being singled out for attention. 'It's the Frenchman who escaped and assaulted a militiaman. It was quite a serious assault, I believe. It was feared at first the militiaman's jaw had been broken.'

'I see.' The governor looked maliciously at Pilgrim. 'You are not suggesting the Frenchman is also innocent of the offence for which he was committed to the *cachot*?'

Pilgrim smiled. 'No, he certainly hit the militiaman, but . . .' Pilgrim related the story of the Frenchman's escape, and the circumstances of his recapture.

By the time his story came to an end only the governor was unsmiling. Undeterred, Pilgrim said, 'I'm sure you'll agree, sir, he had a great deal of justification for the action he took?'

'It occurred in the course of an escape attempt,' snapped the governor. 'He was fortunate not to have been shot.'

'Perhaps,' agreed Pilgrim enigmatically. 'One thing's certain, he'll die just as surely – but more miserably – if he's left to rot in the *cachot* for very much longer.'

The governor looked from Pilgrim to the Lord Warden of the Stannaries. He could see that Sir Thomas's sympathies were with the Frenchman.

To the prison doctor, he said, 'Surgeon Dykar, will you have a look at the man in the *cachot*? If you think it advisable, have him transferred to the hospital. When he's well he may return to the petty officers' mess.'

Expressionless, he said to Pilgrim, 'I suggest you rejoin the other prisoners-of-war now.'

He next addressed Virgil. 'I presume your countrymen will now agree to take up your quarters and cause me and my staff no further problems?'

Virgil inclined his head to the governor. 'You'll have no more trouble now, sir. We'll go wherever you wish. Come on, Pilgrim. Let's get the men moving.'

As Pilgrim walked off with Virgil, heading towards their fellow American prisoners, he looked back.

Sir Thomas and the governor were talking, surrounded

by the prison officials. Only Tacy was looking in his direction. Pilgrim smiled at her and she waved a hand in return. Then she and the prison party began to move slowly towards the governor's house.

Pilgrim felt he had found an unexpected friend in Sir Thomas Tyrwhitt. He also looked forward to meeting Tacy again in the not-too-distant future.

10

'I'm not sure we weren't better off outside in the yard!'

The comment came from Ephraim as he and the others surveyed the interior of Number Four prison block. The building was likely to house the American prisoners-of-war until the war between Britain and the United States came to an end.

Although completed only a few years before, the prison accommodation left a great deal to be desired. Constructed from blocks of moorland grantie, the building had the comfortless feel of a fortress. This impression was heightened by windows which, although fitted with stout iron bars, had no glass to keep out the chill winds blowing across Dartmoor.

It had been built of Dartmoor granite. The porous qualities of the material was no doubt a contributory cause of the glistening damp which accumulated and ran down the inside of the bleak, grey walls.

Long tables and bench stools ran almost the whole length of the communal rooms, with crude lift-up lockers located at either end of each prison 'dormitory'.

Beside the lockers were stowage racks to house the hammock beds of the prisoners during the daylight hours.

'The Frenchman who shared the *cachot* with me said Number Four is the worst of all the prison blocks,' Pilgrim told Virgil and Ephraim. 'Apparently this is where the prison authorities place all the French thieves, thugs and misfits.'

'Then we'll need to establish ourselves as a separate entity right away,' declared Virgil. 'We'll begin by taking over this section of the ground floor. The Frenchmen can move elsewhere.'

The high-ceilinged room, or dormitory, that Virgil intended taking over occupied one half of the ground floor of Number Four cell block. It was divided from the other half by a wooden partition which reached from floor to ceiling. Above it was one more floor, reached by a series of concrete steps, plus a narrow 'attic' located immediately beneath the roof.

Henri Joffre had told Pilgrim the attic was occupied by prisoners considered bad even by the very worst elements among the French prisoners-of-war. They were degraded men who had lost all sense of decency. Many went about completely naked. Having gambled away even their clothes and blankets, they were ready to steal anything moveable and rob their more industrious countrymen.

The men interned here were so violent that prison guards never ventured into the 'attic' of Number Four cell block.

The announcement by the Americans that they intended to take exclusive control of half the ground floor of the building was greeted with derision by the Frenchmen already occupying the room.

At first, Virgil tried reasoning with them, suggesting that he meet with the senior Frenchmen who represented the men occupying the block.

'You're wasting your time,' declared Pilgrim. 'The other blocks have committees of prisoners to see that things run smoothly but, according to Henri Joffre, anarchy reigns here.'

'Well, it's not going to reign in this part of the building,' said Virgil firmly. 'If they won't be persuaded by reason there's nothing for it but to throw their things out and take it over for ourselves.'

Moments later the Americans were removing every article of personal belongings from the section of the building they had decided to make their own.

The move provoked howls of protest from the French and brought men hurrying from other parts of the building to see what was going on.

Pilgrim believed they would have trouble, but the uninvolved occupants of the building seemed to find the proceedings highly amusing. There *were* fights, but they were between Frenchmen from different parts of the building. No one attempted to make a physical assault on the Americans at this stage.

'That went easier than I imagined,' grinned Virgil when the last of the French belongings were heaved out through the door. 'Now we'll see if we can get hold of some soap and water and scrub this place out from end to end. The French must have been here for at least four years and I doubt if it's been properly cleaned in all of that time.'

It was two days before the prison authorities provided soap and scrubbing brushes for the Americans to clean up their quarters. By this time their scant belongings had arrived from the prison hulk.

On the second day the previous occupiers of the quarters made an attempt to return by force, but Ephraim led the resistance and the Frenchmen were quickly routed.

It was not long before the Americans settled down to a routine in their new life at Dartmoor prison. Cooks were detailed to prepare their daily rations and orderlies rostered for the various chores that needed to be undertaken.

It quickly became apparent that the greatest threat to their existence here would be boredom. Apart from a daily muster at nine o'clock every morning, there was nothing for the men to do.

The same problem had been present on the prison hulks anchored off Plymouth, but conditions there had been so cramped it had proved impossible to relieve the tedium. Here it was different.

The militia sergeant, John Straw, came to see how they were settling in. Through him, Pilgrim and Virgil were able to arrange for various writing materials to be made available to them.

With these, they began classes in as many subjects as it was possible to find tutors. Many men were unable to read or write and it was easy to find others to teach them these skills.

Virgil taught them mathematics while Pilgrim and one of the more respectable Frenchmen from another block began classes in French. If the Americans were going to share a gaol with their allies for very long it seemed to Pilgrim a sensible thing to do.

There was also a choir that became surprisingly popular. Most of the singers were black Americans. Included in their repertoire were many of the soulful songs learned during years of working on plantations in the southern states of America.

Large numbers of the Frenchmen would come along in the evenings to listen silently to the music of the black

Americans. John Straw told Pilgrim it was also popular with the guards. They made a habit of gathering on the walls close to the prison block. Here they listened to music which had its origins a long, long way from the bleak hills of Dartmoor.

But this was a prisoner-of-war establishment and tensions were never far below the surface. Soon they were to explode in a fashion that would rock the inmates and the prison authorities to the core.

11

A fortnight after the American prisoners-of-war had taken up residence in Number Four prison block, Henri Joffre paid them a visit.

Pilgrim did not immediately recognise him. In the semi-darkness of the *cachot* the Frenchman had been no more than a small, emaciated figure, his face hidden by weeks of dark beard.

Standing before him now was a trim, clean-shaven man dressed in the tight-fitting, green walking-out uniform of a captain of Napoleon's 9th Dragoons.

Shaking hands with the Frenchman, Pilgrim offered his apologies for failing to recognise his visitor before he had introduced himself.

'You need not apologise, my friend,' said Henri. 'Even had there been light in the *cachot* my face was buried in hair, and I was not dressed like this . . .'

A movement of his hand indicated his smart uniform. 'Fortunately, some of our men have become skilled tailors during the years we have spent here. You must take advantage of their talents. In fact, we have all become very industrious. No matter what is required, it can be made . . . even English money.'

'It's good to see you looking so well,' said Pilgrim. 'I was concerned about you.'

'The prison surgeon told me of your insistence that he must attend to me. I am deeply grateful. I do not think I would have survived many more nights in the *cachot*, especially after I lost the pleasure of your company. I had to spend ten days in the hospital before I was fit enough to return to the *Petit Cautionnement* – or, as the English call it, the "Petty Officers' Block". It is where they place those officers who refuse parole, or who have tried to escape.'

Henri used his hands in an expressive gesture once more, this time registering distaste for the large damp room in which they were standing. 'This is not a place for gentlemen. Those of our men who have been put in this building are not even wanted by other Frenchmen. This is why we insisted that a wall be built about them. It is not right for *any* of your countrymen to be here. For an *officer* . . . it is unthinkable!'

'It's better than the *cachot*,' Pilgrim pointed out.

'Every place is better than the *cachot*,' agreed Henri. 'But that makes no difference. This is not satisfactory accommodation for a gentleman.'

Virgil had been listening to the conversation between the two men. Now he said, 'No one's given us any choice in the matter. Even if they had, we couldn't go off and leave the others to the mercy of the riff-raff in here. To do so would be failing in our duties.'

Pilgrim had already introduced his companion to the Frenchman and Henri shrugged. 'You have been here for only two weeks. By the time the weeks have become months and the months years, you will have learned that personal survival is all that matters in Dartmoor prison. It becomes one's only duty. It is a sad lesson to have to learn. Yet, even if you feel obliged to remain here, why do you not take advantage of the market that is held in the prison square every day?'

To Pilgrim, he said, 'I told you of the woman who helped me to escape?' Without waiting for a reply, he said, 'Yes, I did. She came to the market yesterday. With her was a young girl. A very pretty young girl who asked after you. I was told it was she who arranged for you to be released from the *cachot*. I think she is perhaps unhappy you have not tried to see her.'

'It isn't that I haven't tried,' explained Pilgrim. 'We've requested the same privileges as your countrymen, but the governor refuses to discuss the matter. According to one of the turnkeys we've been branded as trouble-makers and are to be kept under close supervision.'

'Do you consider yourselves troublemakers, M'sieur Pilgrim?'

'Some of us have tried to escape once or twice in the past,' admitted Pilgrim guardedly. 'But then, so have you. Yet you and your fellow officers seem to be able to go wherever you wish inside the prison.'

'That is so,' agreed Henri. 'Of course, there are more than nine thousand Frenchmen here. The governor would find it very difficult to control so many without our co-operation. You are few. He does not feel it is necessary to make concessions to you. However, one of the turnkeys has told me another two hundred and fifty Americans are on their way. They will arrive very soon. The governor might be more inclined to listen to you when you have greater numbers. Perhaps he will allow the officers, at least, to attend the market.'

'Being given such permission will be a moral victory only,' said Virgil. 'Unfortunately, we have no money.

Representations have been made to our Government, but we've heard nothing from them yet.'

'Your lack of money need present no problem, Captain Howard. My father arranged for a considerable sum to be deposited in a London bank for my use. I will loan you all you need. Please . . . !'

He held up a hand to halt Virgil's immediate protest. 'France and America are allies, are they not? And M'sieur Pilgrim and I are friends. Had he not been able to secure my release from the *cachot* all the money in the world would not have been able to help me. You will repay me when your money arrives – as I am quite certain it will. Your Government takes good care of its own people, I know. Two of my uncles fought with your countrymen to gain your independence. One was killed. The other fell in love with your land – and with an American girl. He remained in your country.'

Returning his attention to Pilgrim once more, Henri said, 'Tomorrow I will no doubt be seeing the young lady who is so anxious about you. Would you like me to give her any message?'

Aware that others were listening and that Virgil in particular seemed highly interested in his reply, Pilgrim felt tongue-tied. 'Tell her . . . tell her I'm grateful for her concern . . . I'll come and speak to her as soon as I'm able. Perhaps you'll explain that we aren't allowed to leave the compound and visit the market.'

'I will tell her this, M'sieur Pilgrim. I will also discuss your problems with my senior officers. We have a committee to deal with French problems. Once a month they meet with Governor Cotgrave. He was at first reluctant to agree to any recommendations made by those who are his prisoners. However, experience has taught him to pay attention to what we suggest. If he does not, there is likely to occur an unexpected outbreak of trouble. This upsets him greatly. He much prefers to enjoy a quiet life. I think he will agree to allow you and Captain Howard to attend the market. When there are more of you here, we will make arrangements for the officers to come and join us in the *Petit Cautionnement*.'

'Thank you, Henri. When we feel there are enough Americans here to protect themselves against the unruly element in Block Four we'll be delighted to come and share your quarters. I'm sure they're much better than these.'

'But of course! We have servants there. At table we eat like gentlemen – not like the pigs with whom you share this building.'

As Henri made this comment there was a sudden din from the far end of the Americans' quarters. A party of brawling, ragged French prisoners spilled from the hallway beyond the doorway to the yard outside.

'We're getting used to them now,' said Virgil with a gesture of resignation. 'They're about all the entertainment we can enjoy in Block Four.'

'I will have some playing cards sent here for you,' said Henri. 'But be on guard against the men with whom you share this block. They fought for France, but I refuse to regard them as true Frenchmen. They are animals. Unfortunately, like animals, they are also dangerous. You must take care. It is rumoured they are planning to take revenge upon you for evicting them from a part of the building they regard as their own. I have heard nothing specific, you understand. At the moment it is no more than a rumour, yet it is one that should be taken seriously. If I hear more I will inform you.'

Bowing to each man in turn, Henri Joffre took his leave, his smart attire in marked contrast to the rags of his countrymen as he pushed between them on his way to the gateway that led to the remainder of the prison.

'Do you believe there's any truth in what he says about the French planning to take revenge on us?' asked Virgil.

'I think we have to take his words seriously,' warned Pilgrim. 'There's not very much happening in here that Henri doesn't know something about. Besides, he feels he owes me something. We should begin by placing guards on the doors to our part of the building – and keeping them there, day and night.'

12

When the second batch of American prisoners-of-war arrived at Dartmoor prison, Pilgrim and Virgil were reunited with many of the surviving marines and sailors from the United States frigate *Delaware*.

It was an emotional reunion – the marines had believed the two officers and Ephraim to be dead. Rumours to this effect had circulated soon after the escape of the three men from custody in the West Indies.

Also included among the new arrivals were a hundred battle-hardened soldiers from the regular United States army, with their own experienced non-commissioned officers. They had been captured at Queenston, when the Americans launched an abortive invasion into Canada.

The soldiers had been sent to England for internment because it was feared that holding them in a prisoner-of-war camp closer to their homeland would tempt them to escape.

The arrival of so many disciplined fighting men came as a great relief to Virgil. Still the senior officer present, he now felt confident that if Henri Joffre's fears were justified, the Americans would be able to hold their own against the French prisoners in Block Four.

The Americans now took over the whole of the ground floor of the building. This time, the eviction of the remaining Frenchmen was carried out by the militia guard force on duty at the prison.

Governor Cotgrave had reluctantly accepted that the French and Americans in this block did not get along with each other. Although the two nationalities were allied in their war against Great Britain, they required separate quarters if there was not to be constant friction between them.

However, the disciplinarian governor was unable to forestall violence when it eventually erupted.

The turnkey arrived early one morning to carry out his usual duty of unlocking the iron grille doors that opened from the prison block to the exercise yard.

It promised to be a fine and warm early summer day and the prisoners, both French and American, took the opportunity to get out of the overcrowded and evil-smelling dormitories as quickly as possible.

The intention of the Americans was to enjoy the fresh morning air before mustering for the nine o'clock roll call.

It was Ephraim who commented to Virgil on the uncharacteristic silence of the French prisoners as they filed out to the yard. Usually, they spilled from the building in a torrent of loud-voiced humanity.

Today they left the prison block in near silence and began forming up in an irregular line, some ten or twelve deep, facing the doors through which the Americans were leaving the building.

'They're definitely up to something,' agreed Virgil.

'I'll get our marines and the soldiers out there as quickly as I can. Meanwhile, go outside and warn the others to stay close to the building, Pilgrim. Better still, get them back inside. You go with him, Ephraim.'

Pilgrim hurried outside with the giant marine corporal close behind him – but they had left it too late to forestall a fight.

The American prisoners who had already left the building were belatedly aware that all was not as it should be. Previously warned by Pilgrim and Virgil that the French were planning revenge on them for taking over the ground floor of the prison block, they now realised the time had arrived.

They began pushing back against those still leaving the building. For a few moments there was total confusion. This was when the Frenchmen waded in to the attack.

The French prisoners-of-war had somehow managed to accumulate a wide variety of makeshift weapons. Among these were pieces of timber torn up from the attic floor, and large stones prised from the wall around Block Four.

The more vicious of the Frenchmen had armed themselves with scissors, taken apart to make crude but highly effective daggers.

Outside the prison building, Pilgrim and Ephraim battled against the tide of Americans desperately trying to regain the uncertain sanctuary of the prison block. The majority were merchant seamen, not fighting men. They were no match for soldiers who had seen active service with Napoleon's army on many successful campaigns.

The Frenchmen who occupied Dartmoor prison's Block Four were undoubtedly the very dregs of their country's army – but they were no strangers to fighting.

For many of them, brought up during the bloody years of the revolution, violence had always been part of their way of life.

As Pilgrim and Ephraim drew closer to the vengeful Frenchmen other marines and soldiers of the United States army struggled to join them. Many were more prepared for trouble than was Pilgrim.

Quite as resourceful as the Frenchmen, they too had acquired and secreted a wide variety of weapons during their internment both in Dartmoor and on the prison hulks.

They had stout sticks and stones and some had managed to acquire a variety of iron bars. When they clashed with the French attackers, their makeshift weapons were put to effective use.

Suddenly finding himself in the front line, facing the Frenchmen, Pilgrim was about to be struck with a half-scissor dagger tied to a broom-handle when a large stone struck his would-be attacker between the eyes.

Pilgrim's rescuer was Ephraim. Pushing Pilgrim to one side he picked up the makeshift pike of the fallen Frenchman and wielded it to devastating effect. He was a formidable warrior and his great size commanded respect. Within moments there was a space about him that extended for as far as his long arms and the scissor-pike could reach.

The battle was brief, but savage. Although heavily outnumbered, the Americans held their own and were soon able to check the onslaught of the Frenchmen.

Suddenly, the gate to the prison yard was flung open and armed militiamen poured inside the Block Four exercise yard. With bayonets fixed and muskets extended menacingly, they advanced upon the fighting prisoners-of-war.

The French belligerents held their line for only a few

minutes before they broke and ran. The savage battle was over, but when they fled from the compound they left a great many men lying on the ground.

Most were Americans – and among their number was Pilgrim.

The American marines and soldiers had rallied around him to form the nucleus of the American resistance. Then, at the very moment when the Frenchmen fled the field, a half-naked ruffian lunged forward with a stick that had been sharpened to a dangerous point. With this makeshift weapon he succeeded in stabbing the American lieutenant in the stomach.

Pilgrim sank slowly to the ground, both hands clutching the wound and blood oozing out between his fingers.

Even as he protested to the men bending over him that he was not seriously hurt the world began to spin about him. In mid-sentence he drifted off into a state where pain disappeared and he hovered between lethargy and unconsciousness.

Then faces and sounds drifted away and he knew no more.

13

Pilgrim recovered consciousness slowly. It was very many minutes before it registered that he was lying in a bed in the Dartmoor prison hospital.

He became aware of groaning. When he turned his head he could see other men in nearby beds, some heavily bandaged, others wearing crude splints.

As Pilgrim moved his head an English hospital orderly came along and stopped at the foot of his bed. 'Well! I'm surprised to see you back in the world of the living, dearie. The surgeon had given you up for dead – and so had I.'

'I'd like . . . a drink.' Pilgrim's tongue seemed to fill his mouth and felt as though it was made of old leather.

The orderly went to a nearby table and transferred some water from a jug to a heavy mug. As he returned, Pilgrim tried to sit up. He let out a gasp of pain. It felt as though his stomach was on fire. Then he remembered the fight . . . and the stabbing.

The orderly helped him raise his head and held the

mug to his lips. When Pilgrim lay back on the pillow once more, he was gasping, as though he had done something strenuous.

'The fight . . . ?' he spoke breathlessly. 'Were many of our men seriously hurt?'

'More Americans than Frenchmen – but only just. We've got forty of you in here. If you ask me, it's a miracle no one was killed. You came as close to it as anyone, yet here you are talking away better than some of them. Him over there, for instance.' The orderly pointed vaguely in the direction of the far side of the ward. 'He's lost half his teeth and has a broken jaw.'

The orderly straightened the blanket on Pilgrim's bed. 'Call me again if you need anything. I'll go and tell Surgeon Dykar you've come round. He'll be pleased. He doesn't like losing patients; it upsets him. Trouble is, it means he's unhappy for most of the time in this place. In the last few months we've lost more than ever before, what with gaol fever, measles and fights. Still, I'm sure it's a blessed release for some of 'em. Especially those in the block where they've put you Americans. We're supposed to be here to save lives, but there's some of them I wouldn't work very hard to keep alive.'

Having made this stark and harsh observation, the orderly went on his way, pausing here and there along the ward to speak to some of the patients.

The surgeon did not come to the hospital until the morning after Pilgrim had regained consciousness. Watching him as he made his way along the ward, inspecting the wounds of those involved in the fight between Frenchmen and Americans, Pilgrim grimaced at his rough methods. He thought he probably owed his own recovery to the fact that the surgeon had believed him to be dying and had done little to treat his wound.

The surgeon's method of removing Pilgrim's dressing could only be described as brutal, but he ignored his patient's cry of pain. Looking at the wound for a minute or two, he prodded around it none-too-gently and sniffed it. Then, breathing wine fumes over his patient, he said, 'It appears to be healing well enough by itself, so we'll leave it to take its course. You're lucky, young man. Whatever it was you were stabbed with seems to have missed your vital organs. With any luck you'll be back on your feet in a week or so.'

That afternoon Pilgrim had two unexpected visitors. One was Captain Henri Joffre. The other was Tacy. She walked self-consciously along the ward beside the Frenchman, her progress marked by appreciative catcalls and whistles from the injured and sick men.

'Good afternoon, Pilgrim.' Henri smiled down at him. 'I met a hospital orderly at the market this afternoon and asked after you. He told me you had regained consciousness. I passed the information on to Tacy and she asked if she might come and speak to you.'

'I'm very pleased to see you,' said Pilgrim, feeling ridiculously elated. 'It's good to see you both,' he added belatedly, realising he had been looking only at Tacy when he spoke. 'But I'm surprised the governor gave permission for Tacy to come in here.'

'Ah! Governor Cotgrave does not know. He is away in Plymouth and the surgeon is having his usual afternoon "rest". It was the orderly who proved obliging – and for no more than a couple of guineas.'

When Pilgrim began thanking him, Henri cut him short. 'We do not have much time. Do not waste it. I will leave you and Tacy alone for a few minutes. One of the men in my regiment was also injured in the fight. He is in the next ward. The man is a rogue, but he was a good soldier. I will visit him for a few minutes.'

When Henri had gone there was an awkward silence between Tacy and Pilgrim for a few moments. It was broken by Tacy.

'I've brought a couple of things from the stall for you. A few eggs. A piece of cheese. It's not much, but we'd almost sold out of things by the time Captain Joffre found me and said I might be able to come and see you.'

'It's very kind of you . . . Tacy. I like that name. I know a woman back home in Ohio named Tacy. She and her family are Quakers.'

'It's a Quaker name,' explained Tacy. 'It was my grandmother's name. She was a Quaker until she married my grandfather.'

'My mother was a Quaker!' Pilgrim seized on the common ground they had discovered. 'She was made to leave the Society when she married my pa.'

For a few minutes they talked about Quakers in America and in Devon, then they both fell silent once more.

'It really is nice of you to come here to see me,' said Pilgrim sincerely, 'but it's not the nicest of places for a girl to visit.'

'It's the least I could do,' said Tacy. 'Especially after what you did for Rip. I'd been hoping you would come to see me at the market. I've been here almost every day since you arrived at the prison. But Captain Joffre explained that the governor won't allow the Americans to come and buy things.'

'I thought you only came to the prison market very occasionally?' said Pilgrim.

Tacy coloured up. 'I do as a rule, but we seem to have had a few more things than usual to sell just lately.'

'I'm glad,' said Pilgrim, a little more enthusiastically than he had intended it to sound. 'Your coming here today has cheered everyone else in the hospital too.'

The fact that Pilgrim was happy to see her pleased Tacy, but she tried not to allow it to show too much.

'Do you think you'll be able to come to the market when you get out of here? Captain Joffre says he's trying to arrange for you and your Captain to be allowed to come to the market and buy things for the others.'

'If Henri says that's what he's trying to do then he'll probably succeed,' said Pilgrim. 'He's pretty good at arranging things – except perhaps his own escape.'

Tacy giggled and it was a pleasant sound. 'He very nearly succeeded. Mary – that's the girl who brought the clothes in for him – is a friend of mine. She'd do anything to get him out of here. She hopes that if she helps him to escape he'll take her to France with him. She hasn't got a very happy life here.'

Before Pilgrim could question her about her friend, she said, 'Here's Captain Joffre coming back. He seems to be in a hurry.'

When Henri reached them, he said breathlessly, 'I've just seen the orderly. Governor Cotgrave has returned sooner than was expected. Tacy and I must leave immediately.'

Tacy's expression of disappointment matched Pilgrim's own.

'I'll try to see you again – as soon as I can,' he said to her.

'I look forward to that . . . Do you think they'll let you out on parole?'

'Come. We must leave.' Captain Joffre took Tacy by the arm.

'I don't know . . . can you write?'

Tacy nodded.

'Write to me. I'll write too. Send the letters through Henri and Mary . . .'

The orderly put in an agitated appearance at the entrance to the ward and Henri began hurrying Tacy away. She turned at the end of the ward to give him a brief wave, then she was gone.

Behind her, Pilgrim lay back on his pillow and closed his eyes. He was tired after talking to her, even though it had been for a relatively short time, but he felt incredibly happy that she had come to the hospital to see him.

It seemed unbelievable that he, a prisoner-of-war in the grim, moorland prison of Dartmoor, should have been fortunate enough to meet up with someone like Tacy . . .

14

Pilgrim remained in the prison hospital for two weeks. He was the last of the American casualties involved in the fight with the Frenchmen to be released.

During this time, Virgil was able to visit him only twice. The visits were sanctioned by the governor, but for some reason he insisted that Virgil be accompanied on each occasion by two militiamen.

Despite this petty restriction, Virgil was able to report that conditions seemed to be improving for the Americans, at last. Notification had been received that the United States Government would soon deposit a large sum of money with a certain Reuben G. Beasley, an American citizen currently resident in London. He had been appointed as the United States agent in London.

Once the money had been received, the agent had been instructed to make a regular allowance to American prisoners-of-war. He had also been instructed to visit Dartmoor and listen to any grievances the American inmates might have about the conditions of their intern-ment.

There was also talk of transferring the two Marines officers and some of the more senior ship's captains to the *Petit Cautionnement*.

This news was particularly welcomed by Pilgrim. Such a move would enable him to visit the daily market and meet with Tacy there.

With nothing else to occupy his time in the hospital, he had thought a great deal about the young Devon girl. He had spoken of her to Virgil, but the Marines captain did not share Pilgrim's enthusiasm for the blossoming relationship.

'Be careful, Pilgrim,' he had warned. 'In your present condition you'd find any young girl attractive. If one is kind to you as well, you'll be in over your head before you even know you're in there swimming.'

Pilgrim realised this was a matter over which they were unlikely to agree and he changed the subject.

'The last time a move to the petty officers' block was mentioned you said you wouldn't even consider it. What's happened to make you change your mind?'

'A number of things. With the arrival of our marines and the army, we now have some good NCOs capable of taking care of things in Block Four. That reminds me, I've promoted Ephraim to sergeant. An official letter to Marines headquarters to confirm his promotion is on its way right now. I did this because some of the army NCOs from the southern states have been making things difficult for him – for the other coloured men too. We'll have trouble if we're not careful. Ephraim's now one of the most senior men in the Block. I trust him to keep things the way they ought to be, particularly among his own people. He'll no doubt welcome an opportunity to run things his way, without having us around breathing down his neck the whole of the time.'

A more frequent visitor to the prison hospital was Henri. Each time he came he carried a small gift from Tacy. Most often it was some item of farm produce or fresh bread, but once he brought a cake she had baked especially for him.

On two occasions he also brought letters from her, but Pilgrim found them disappointingly short and formal. She politely expressed the hope that his health was improving then went on to tell him domestic news of everyday happenings on the farm where she lived.

The letters gave him a glimpse of the hard-working yet apparently happy way of life she and her young sister shared on Roundtor Farm. They also indicated she had caring and loving parents, although a constant theme in the letters was the concern she felt for the health of her father.

With paper and a pencil supplied by Henri, Pilgrim was able to reply to her letters. He tried to inject something of the way he felt into the writing. Yet, despite all his efforts, he found they contained little more than a 'thank you' for her gifts and the hope that he would soon leave the hospital block and be able to attend the prison market and see her once more.

Looking through the latest letter he had written, Pilgrim realised it was every bit as formal as those he had received from her.

When Pilgrim was eventually discharged from the hospital and escorted back to Block Four, he found there had been a number of changes. Only the day before, the black Americans had moved out, *en masse*, from the ground floor of Number Four block. They had taken over part of the 'attic', where the toughest and most dangerous of the Frenchmen were housed.

The move had come about after a recently arrived American prisoner-of-war, a ship's mate from Georgia, claimed to have recognised Ephraim.

The sailor declared Ephraim was an escaped slave. Moreover, he swore that Ephraim had murdered an overseer during his flight from the plantation to which he belonged.

It was a rumour Pilgrim and Virgil had heard before, but it had never been substantiated and had not affected Ephraim's service in the United States Marine Corps.

The mate's denunciation of the runaway slave provoked anger against Ephraim among the mate's fellow American seamen, many of whom came from slave-owning southern states.

Virgil and Ephraim's fellow marines had prevented any serious trouble from erupting, but it remained a volatile situation.

A temporary solution was found by Ephraim himself. He had formed a friendship with the self-styled leader of the *Romains*, the name by which the French occupants of the Block Four attic liked to be known.

Evicting a number of his own men, the French *Romain* leader invited Ephraim and his fellow black Americans to occupy part of the 'attic' with him.

Virgil did not like the idea of splitting the American prisoners-of-war into separate racial groups. Yet he was aware the move offered at least a short-term solution to the animosity that existed between black and white Americans.

It also meant Ephraim would be able to maintain his control over his fellow black Americans even though they were separated from the other American prisoners-of-war.

Virgil was forced to accept that the problem which divided the United States of America could not be solved here on Dartmoor, amidst the added pressures that existed in a prisoner-of-war gaol.

It would take a war, and the loss of millions of lives in a divided country, to lay the foundations of a truly united nation. Meanwhile, he trusted Ephraim to maintain control over those who had gone to the Block Four attic with him.

15

'I wish we all knew a little more about this young man of yours, Tacy. It worries me, you being sweet on someone who's locked up in a prison. It doesn't seem right, somehow.'

Joan Elford voiced her concern to her daughter as they kneaded dough for bread in the kitchen of Roundtor Farm.

'I'm not sweet on him, Ma – and he's not my "young man". As for him being in prison . . . He's not there because he's done anything wrong. He's locked away because he was captured while he was fighting for his country. There's nothing wrong with that.'

'If you're not sweet on him, why wouldn't you let me read the letters he sent to you – or the ones you wrote to him?' The interruption came from Johanna.

'Because they're none of your business, that's why.' Tacy threw a glance at her younger sister that was intended to silence her. Instead, it provoked a mischievous grin.

'Billy thinks you're sweet on the American. He's unhappy about it. He told me so.'

'Billy doesn't know any better. *You* should.'

Silencing her younger daughter with a stern glance, Joan Elford returned her attention to Tacy. 'You've never written letters *or* baked a cake for any man before.'

'I've never written to a man because I've never known one who's locked away in prison, and I made the cake because Lieutenant Penn was stabbed in a fight and put in the prison hospital. There's no one else to do anything for him – and he almost died.'

'Stabbed? You never told me *that*! How did he get himself stabbed? What was the fight about?' Joan Elford was genuinely alarmed. 'If he's the sort who gets himself involved in fights, then he's *definitely* not a young man you should be getting mixed up with. I don't know what your father's doing encouraging you . . .'

'Ma!' Tacy placed flour-dusted hands on her hips and glared in exasperation, first at her highly amused young sister, then at her disapproving mother. 'Lieutenant Penn is an officer. There was a fight between American and French prisoners-of-war. Hundreds of them were involved. It was his duty to try to stop the fight. *That's* how he came to be stabbed. He wasn't *fighting* anyone. It was a French officer told me that. He'd hardly be likely to take Lieutenant Penn's side if it wasn't true, would he?'

'I don't know about that. From what I hear it's a mistake to trust these French officers. You look at young Polly Pearce, over at Sheepstor Farm – and Carol Williams, whose father is churchwarden at Ashburton. They trusted French officers. Now they're both expecting.'

Joan Elford wiped a flour-streaked hand across her nose. 'If this young man of yours is as trustworthy as you say he is, then why hasn't the prison governor given him parole, same as has been given to the French officers?'

'Nobody knows, really. The French officer that Mary Gurney's friendly with thinks it's because the Americans speak English so they could easily pass themselves off as Englishmen and escape. I expect they'll be allowed out on parole soon, though. When they do, Sir Thomas Tyrwhitt says he'll stand surety for Lieutenant Penn, so he must think he's all right.'

'What sort of a recommendation is that supposed to be? The likes of Sir Thomas don't have the same standards as ordinary people. Mind you, them as rule over all of us aren't very much better. The Prince Regent, who ought to have important things to do in London, has been spending more time on Dartmoor than he should – and it's not for the good of his estates, either. They say that between 'em, Sir Thomas Tyrwhitt and the Prince Regent have worn a path between Tor Royal and Dolly French's cottage that's easier to follow than the main road to Plymouth! It's an affront to decent folk, that's what it is.'

'Well, while Sir Thomas is spending his time with Dolly French he's leaving others alone,' said Tacy enigmatically. 'If he wants to stand surety for Lieutenant Penn I can't imagine anyone suggesting he's not a suitable person.'

'Perhaps they'll let Tacy's young man come and stay here,' said Johanna. With an air of exaggerated innocence, she added, 'Then, if Tacy has a baby I could help her look after it.'

'That's quite enough from you, young lady,' said her mother firmly. 'I should know better by now than to talk of such things in front of you. Go out and collect the eggs. While you're there – and since you're so interested in babies – go and see how the old sow is. According to my reckoning she should have had her litter a day or two ago.'

Johanna left the kitchen without argument, although she paused at the door to turn and put out her tongue at her sister. Everyone in the household of four had their own responsibilities on the farm. Johanna's was taking care of the chickens.

When the door closed behind the young girl, Tacy spoke hesitantly to her mother. 'Do you think Lieutenant Penn might possibly be given parole here?'

Seeing her mother's expression of amazement at the unexpected suggestion, she added hurriedly, 'With Pa being ill most of the time we could do with help on the farm this summer, what with the haymaking, and everything.'

'We could use extra help for perhaps two or three months of the year, girl. What would we find for him to do for the rest of the time? Besides, Billy's on hand to give us help during the busy months. Are you saying we should stop him from coming here?'

'No, of course not,' said Tacy. 'That wouldn't be fair. Billy's simple, but he's never done an unkind thing to anyone in his life. He loves coming here. It makes him feel useful. I couldn't hurt him.'

Joan Elford was aware that the young American had assumed considerable importance to her eldest daughter. She also knew the reason why. Roundtor Farm was in an isolated situation. There was not a young man of Tacy's own age living within miles. Nevertheless, it was tragic that the first young man to attract her attention should be a prisoner-of-war, incarcerated in Dartmoor prison.

When Tacy lapsed into an unhappy silence, her mother said gently, 'Don't get carried away with your dreams, Tacy. This young American is a prisoner, far from home – and he's been hurt. It's right you should show him Christian kindness, but don't get too sweet on him. I heard you telling your pa the other day his uncle had been the American ambassador in London and a friend of Sir Thomas's. With such a background he's hardly likely to want to live or work on a small farm like ours, even if we did ask him to come here. He's a gentleman. I expect he'll be paroled to somewhere like Ashburton. That's where most of the French officers go.'

'I suppose so,' conceded Tacy unhappily. 'But he doesn't behave a bit like Sir Thomas. Until he gets parole I'll still take one or two things into the prison for him.'

'Of course. It's a very kind thing to do. All I'm saying is that it would be foolish to grow too fond of him. You'll only end up being hurt if you do. If he's given parole he'll be mixing with the fine friends of Sir Thomas, not with the likes of us. Remember, too, that one day he'll be going home to America and out of your life.'

Tacy had still not replied to this observation when Johanna burst in through the kitchen door. 'Ma, Tacy! Come quick. The sow's having her babies – there's six already and more are coming. They're dropping out like maggots from a dead sheep!'

Joan Elford was not sure she approved of the simile, but she allowed it to pass.

'It's cold out there and that old sow won't let any of 'em feed until she's had them all. Start bringing them in, Johanna. You help her, Tacy, while I finish the bread. Bring them in and lay them in front of the fire.'

Piglets were a source of quick profit. Joan Elford knew from past experience that this particular sow became very agitated when giving birth. Unless the piglets were taken away from her until the last one had arrived, she was likely to roll on those already born and kill or injure some of them.

While the girls were out of the kitchen she found a piece of cloth and laid it in front of the fire. The piglets would be placed upon it to keep warm until the last of them was born. Then they would be returned to their mother.

An hour later there were thirteen tiny piglets laid in a row before the fire. The two girls were pleading that they be allowed to remain in the house for 'just a minute or two more'.

Watching the two girls crouched before the fire with the piglets, Joan Elford wished they might both remain innocent young girls for a few more years, but she realised it was not to be. Tacy was already a young woman. She would marry and leave the farm as soon as the right young man came along.

She wished Tacy could have found him before meeting the young American. Joan could see Lieutenant Pilgrim Penn bringing nothing but unhappiness into the life of her elder daughter.

16

Another two hundred Americans arrived at Dartmoor during the next few days. Among their number was a ship's captain named Steiger. He was also the owner of a small fleet of ships which sailed out of Savannah, in Georgia.

Steiger was a difficult man and furious to have been taken prisoner while he was sailing in a merchantman. He also seemed to think he should have been allocated a whole prison block to himself, but he was lodged in the other half of the block occupied by Virgil and Pilgrim.

One of the men who had been taken prisoner with him was Steiger's slave. The shipowner would not have him sharing the same section of prison building, but still expected the man to carry out all the duties of a slave.

Ephraim had other ideas.

Soon after the arrival of the newcomers, the slave abruptly ceased serving his master and disappeared from view.

It was discovered he had taken up residence in the attic with the other black Americans. It was strongly rumoured that the parting of master and slave had been engineered by Ephraim.

Steiger was furious. He and Ephraim had a fierce argument. Violence was averted only by the intervention of Virgil.

Not to be thwarted, Steiger and his crew, accompanied by a number of seamen from the southern states, laid in wait for their black countrymen, hoping to lay hands on the missing slave.

A fight ensued but this too was quickly broken up by the marines before anyone was seriously hurt. Virgil realised it was merely postponing a showdown. Trouble between the two groups of men would remain, constantly simmering beneath the surface of prison life, as would the enmity between the Americans and the Frenchmen of Block Four.

Virgil discussed the problem with Pilgrim soon after the latest incident, and spoke with irritation of the newly arrived Captain Steiger.

'Would you know whether this shipowner's name is *Conrad* Steiger?' asked Pilgrim.

'That's his name. You know him?'

'No, but I certainly know *of* him. He lived in Washington for a while after making his money as a privateer. Then he moved west and stood for Congress against my father, in Ohio. He was a bad loser. It didn't help him gain votes when it was rumoured he was involved with a slave girl. Steiger took the girl as his mistress, and after he'd had her husband sold off and shipped elsewhere, he moved back to Washington. When his wife left him he moved the girl into his house, as a so-called "servant". Apparently, it caused one of Washington's biggest scandals for years. That's the reason he moved south and went back to sea. There have been other rumours about him since. Trouble seems to follow him around. We could do without him here.'

'Well, he won't be upsetting Block Four for very much longer, but you and I aren't going to lose him. The governor's finally agreed to move you, me, and the ships' captains to the 'Petty Officers' Block'. It'll give us more freedom of movement. Once our money arrives we're to be allowed to attend the market and buy provisions for those of our men who are left here. Ephraim will be the senior American in the block, although he'll never be accepted by the southerners. However, Governor Cotgrave has agreed to give him access to us at all reasonable times and he'll be able to tell us what's going on here.'

Pilgrim was impressed. 'Things really are looking up! What persuaded the governor to change his mind? I get the distinct impression he doesn't like Americans.'

'I doubt if he's changed his mind about us, but he likes a quiet life. There are more of us now and the French officers have been agitating for some time for the transfer of our officers. I think your friend from the *cachot* had a great deal to do with it.'

Two days later nine Americans were transferred to the Petty Officers' Block. Among their number were Pilgrim, Virgil and Conrad Steiger.

Despite the prospect of greatly improved living conditions in their new block, Steiger complained bitterly because he had been refused permission to locate and bring his slave with him from Block Four.

Henri Joffre headed the party of French officers waiting to greet the Americans upon their arrival in their new quarters. Walking inside the Petty Officers' Block with the others, it seemed to Pilgrim they had been transported to a different world.

Most of the Frenchmen had been in Dartmoor prison for four years. They had used the time to make their quarters as comfortable as money and ingenuity would allow.

Each man had been allotted a carefully measured space. It was not large, but within its chalked lines were a bed and a slim wooden wardrobe. Some men had also managed to fit a stool and small table within their allotted area. In addition, many small rugs were strewn about the concrete floor.

Everything in the block had been made by craftsmen among the French prisoners-of-war and paid for from the private funds which seemed to be freely available to all the Frenchmen here.

Upon their arrival, Henri introduced Pilgrim and Virgil to fellow members of the Petty Officers' Block's 'committee'. All were either officers of high rank, or belonged to influential families in their home country.

The French officers had instigated a disciplined regime throughout the prison for prisoners of a lower rank than themselves. Only the men of Block Four contemptuously refused to acknowledge their authority, going about in their own degraded way.

Pilgrim learned that the wall around Block Four had actually been erected at the suggestion of the French officers' committee. Once completed, the dissidents inside had been largely ignored by their more law-abiding and industrious countrymen.

Henri listened patiently and politely to Conrad Steiger's complaint about the loss of his slave, before saying, 'We have a number of men in the prison who were slaves before being taken prisoner, m'sieur. However, we are all here because we were captured while serving our country. It has been decided there will be no slaves in Dartmoor prison. Only prisoners-of-war. It makes sense, if you think about it, M'sieur Steiger. Rather than acknowledge themselves as slaves, many would offer their services to the British navy – as free men. We would therefore be helping the enemy, would we not?'

Henri smiled amiably at the disgruntled American shipowner. 'If you find it essential to have a servant, you will find many excellent Frenchmen willing to oblige you – for a fair wage, of course.'

'I have no money to pay a servant,' complained Steiger bitterly. 'All the money I had with me was stolen when my ship was taken by the British.'

'I understand that arrangements are being made for you to receive an allowance from your Government,' said Henri with continuing patience. 'It should also not be too difficult to have private money transferred to an English bank, as many of us have done. In the meantime, we have established a fund to provide a temporary solution for such problems. You may repay the fund when your own money is received.'

Turning away from the complaining American, Henri returned his attention to the two Marines officers. 'Your friends will be attended to by other officers, but I have had space made for you next to me. You will be comfortable enough, I assure you. All we lack here is privacy. For the rest, I can offer you a wide choice of drinks. Would you like a Cognac . . . ? Wine . . . ? Or champagne, perhaps, to celebrate your improved status within the prison?'

17

Tacy and her father were among the vendors selling goods when Pilgrim and Virgil paid their first visit to the market the following day, accompanied by Henri Joffre.

Tacy held a basket containing cakes and eggs for sale. Her father had brought a cart loaded with blocks of peat, dried and ready for burning. It was a commodity that was always in demand within the prison.

Wealthy French officers had purchased stoves during their first winter in the cold and damp prison. Much of the moorland fuel would go to them in the Petty Officers' Block. The remainder would be burned in the kitchens, where food for the prisoners was cooked.

Tacy's face lit up with surprised delight when she saw Pilgrim. 'You're better – and they've allowed you to come to the market! I'm very happy for you. But you're far too thin. You need to put on some weight . . .'

Placing her basket on the back of the open cart, she rummaged inside and pulled out a cake. 'Here, this is full of good things. I've got some eggs here too . . .'

'Wait a minute, Tacy. I don't have any money yet.'

Tacy looked offended. 'I'm not asking you for money. They're presents.'

'I thought we'd come here to sell things, not give them away!' Tom Elford walked towards them from the front of the cart where he had been removing a nosebag from the pony. The moorland farmer looked every bit as frail as Pilgrim was himself. His smile was intended to wipe away any criticism implied in the words.

Despite the moorland farmer's smile, Pilgrim was uncertain how Tacy's father viewed her friendship with an enemy of their country.

'That's just what I was telling Tacy . . .'

Tom Elford waved Pilgrim's explanation aside. 'I was only joking.'

Extending a hand, he said, 'You'll be the young man who saved Rip – and who seems to have been the subject of more talk on Roundtor Farm than anything else I can remember for years past.'

'Pa!'

The word came out as a rebuke from Tacy, her cheeks fiery with embarrassment.

'I'm sorry . . . !' Pilgrim apologised hesitantly, still not quite certain whether or not Tacy's father was expressing disapproval.

'There's nothing to apologise for,' said Tom Elford. 'I should be thanking you. Before Tacy met up with you we'd only sent things here for sale when we had too much of something or another. Now, because we've been here so often, we have customers for all the cake and eggs we can carry, as well as all the peat we can cut. We'll be bringing crops here too, later on in the year. It will save us carrying them all the way to town.'

'Tacy's been very kind and very generous,' said Pilgrim. 'I do appreciate it. There's one thing of which you can be certain. When money starts coming through from our agents, we'll buy all the cakes you can bake to pass on to our men. It'll be a taste of home for them.'

'You don't need to wait for any money,' said Tom Elford generously. 'Have the cakes now. We'll settle up when your money arrives.'

'That won't be necessary,' said Henri. 'We have a fund in the Petty Officers' Block. It will provide money for all that Pilgrim and Virgil wish to buy.

'It makes good sense,' he added when it appeared Tom Elford would protest. 'There are many Americans here and more are coming all the time. If you are not paid immediately for what you sell to them, they will very soon run up such a debt it will not be possible for you to buy ingredients for so many cakes. Accept the money I can provide and your earnings will be limited only by the hours your family is able to spend baking.'

Tom Elford conceded that Henri's words made sense. Making and selling cakes would provide a good income. It was probable that by baking for the Americans held in the prison, the women of Roundtor Farm might make more money than he could earn from farming!

Speaking to Pilgrim once again, he said, 'I realise our countries are at war, but it won't last for ever. We none of us know what's likely to happen in the future, but if you ever have the opportunity to step outside this place you can be sure of a warm welcome at Roundtor Farm. Remember that.'

On the way home to Roundtor Farm that evening, Tacy took her father gently to task for embarrassing both Pilgrim and herself.

When he protested that he had meant no harm, she conceded it had not been a serious embarrassment and thanked him for the invitation he had issued to Pilgrim.

'It took me by surprise,' she admitted. 'The last time we spoke about it you seemed to disapprove of me even knowing him. You said I should get to meet some of the local young men and not waste my time on someone locked up in a prison.'

'I'd still like you to find a decent young man . . . All right!'

He held up a hand in a weary gesture intended to pre-empt the protest he knew she was about to make. 'I realise they're few and far between on the moor, but you'll find the right man one day. In the meantime, I meant what I said to your young American. He's very likeable. It's not his fault he's inside a prison. All he's done is fight for his country. I admire him for that. If I'd been a fit young man with no responsibilities when the war with France began, I'd have done the same.'

Tacy knew her father had always been envious of one of his younger brothers who had left the family farm on the far side of Dartmoor to enlist. Serving with Wellington's army in Spain, he had taken part in many of the battles fought there.

The occasional letters home told of a life far removed from that he had known as the younger son of a tenant farmer on a moorland farm in Devon.

'I wonder how long he'll be here?' mused Tacy, half to herself.

'As a prisoner-of-war, you mean?'

Tom Elford cast a glance at his daughter and saw she was daydreaming. It was something she had always done, since she was a small girl.

'For as long as the war lasts – and that's likely to be quite a while. Wars don't usually start and end within a few months, or even a few years. I suspect he'll be lodging in Dartmoor prison for much longer than he would care to think about.'

Smiling sympathetically at his daughter, he added, 'Time enough for you to become an old maid, if you're not careful.'

Tacy said nothing. Being able to continue to meet Pilgrim for the foreseeable future was a pleasant thought – although she hoped it might not always be inside the high walls of Dartmoor prison.

She believed that if he had to remain a prisoner-of-war for some years the authorities might relent and allow him out on parole, on similar terms to those offered to French officers. Some had been paroled for many years. A few had succeeded in bringing wives and families to England to be with them. She had also heard of one in Ashburton, who had courted and married a local girl during his years of parole.

On the other hand, if Pilgrim was not offered parole and the authorities forced him to remain inside the prison, she could always consider doing what Mary Gurney had done with Henri, Pilgrim's friend . . .

Tacy smiled at the thought of Pilgrim dressed up in some of her clothes. Nevertheless, the idea of helping him to escape from the prison and thoughts of what they might do once he was free, excited her.

Roundtor Farm was in a remote part of the moor. It might be possible for Pilgrim to remain there undetected for as long as the war between Britain and the United States lasted.

It was something that would fire her imagination for a great many hours during the weeks and months ahead.

18

The occupants of the Petty Officers' Block were awakened by the sound of an uproar. A disturbance was taking place somewhere beyond the wall that separated them from the main prison blocks.

Pilgrim and Virgil were immediately concerned that another fight might be taking place in Block Four. Suddenly, a jubilant French officer came hurrying towards them. With a delighted expression, he beckoned excitedly.

'Come. Come quickly!'

They ran close behind him up the stairs that led to the upper storey of the Petty Officers' Block. Despite their repeated questioning along the way, he either did not understand or was deliberately refusing to expand on his brief command.

The windows of the upper floor were crowded with Frenchmen. Grinning widely, those men at one of the windows moved to one side to allow room for the two marines officers.

A Frenchman pointed to where the grey bulk of Block

Four rose above its surrounding wall. Looking in that direction, Pilgrim gave voice to a cheer which was taken up by Frenchmen and Americans alike.

Flying from the roof of Block Four was not one, but *two* United States flags.

'Of course! It's Independence Day!'

Pilgrim's delight was shared by Virgil, but the senior officer sounded a note of warning. 'There's going to be hell to pay over this. We'd better get across there and try to prevent bloodshed when the militia go in to take down the flags.'

Pilgrim and Virgil hurried from the first-floor window to the ground floor, but the doors of the building were securely locked. They were unable even to leave the Petty Officers' Block.

The usual daily routine was that the doors of every block, including that which housed the officers, were locked each evening and unlocked the following morning. Today, because of the troubles in Block Four, the turnkeys had not gone the rounds to carry out their duties.

Despite loud protests from the officer inmates, the doors remained securely locked until mid-afternoon. By this time the two flags had disappeared from the roof of Block Four. Nobody knew whether they had been removed by the militia or by the prisoners themselves.

During the hours their doors were secured, the Frenchmen and Americans in the Petty Officers' Block and the other buildings continued to crowd the windows overlooking Block Four, shouting encouragement to their defiant fellow-prisoners.

When the doors were eventually opened, the noise within the prison was deafening. Hungry prisoners were banging metal plates, wooden tables and anything else capable of making a noise.

'It's about time someone let us out,' complained Virgil to the turnkey who opened the Petty Officers' Block door. 'We'll be lucky if there's time for even one meal today.'

The turnkey shrugged his indifference. 'You can blame your men in Block Four, not me.'

'Can I go over there and speak to them?'

'No,' said the turnkey. 'A couple of hundred militiamen are searching the block. They've found one flag, but are still looking for the other. I'd say there are likely to be more Americans in the *cachot* tonight than in Block Four.'

'Has anyone been hurt?' asked Pilgrim.

'One or two, but no one on either side has suffered any serious injury. The surgeon's still over there, but he hasn't taken anyone to the hospital as far as I know.'

'I'd still like to speak to the Americans who've been involved,' repeated Virgil.

'You'll need to wait 'til tomorrow,' said the turnkey. 'When the militia come out I'm to lock all the doors in the block. Governor Cotgrave's said they can all go without a meal today, as a punishment.'

'The Frenchmen are being punished too?' The question was put by Henri. 'That is not fair. The committee will complain to the governor.'

'Complain as much as you like,' said the turnkey. 'Perhaps next time your people will do something to stop the Americans getting up to their antics, instead of cheering them on.'

Henri and his fellow committee members would complain, but it was intended to be no more than an irritating thorn in the flesh of the harassed governor. Cotgrave represented the common enemy of Frenchmen and Americans, someone to be harangued whenever possible. However, he still possessed ultimate power over the prisoners. It would not do to push him too hard.

'May we go to the market now?' asked Pilgrim.

'There's no market today. The gates weren't opened because of the troubles, so your countrymen will have made no friends there, either.'

The turnkey left the Petty Officers' Block with the clamorous protests of Americans and Frenchmen ringing in his ears.

Not until the following morning was a deputation of American and French officers allowed to enter Block Four to learn what had happened during the previous day's rioting.

Ephraim came down from the attic to speak to them. In answer to Virgil's question, he admitted, 'They gave us a good going over, but there'll be a great many Englishmen this morning with a bruise or two to show for their efforts.'

'Did they eventually find both flags?' Pilgrim put the question to the sergeant of marines.

'No. They searched just about everywhere they thought it might be hidden but we managed to save the one. We'll raise it again as soon as we find something else to celebrate. Thanksgiving, perhaps.'

'Where did you hide it?' asked Pilgrim. He was aware there were few places in the prison block where a flag might be concealed.

'Where it'll stay until it's needed again,' said Ephraim. 'Wrapped around my body. Mind you, I wish I knew what the Frenchmen put into some of the dye we used to make it. When it gets really warm it stinks worse than a skunk. I'll have no friends left, come the end of summer.'

*   *   *

The events of Independence Day angered Governor Cotgrave. He called Virgil to his office to express his disapproval of the activities of the American prisoners-of-war.

'I was warned by the Superintendent of Hulks that you and your men would cause trouble,' fumed Cotgrave, glaring across his large desk at Virgil. 'I had hoped he was exaggerating. It's now quite apparent he was not.'

'I think we need to keep this matter in perspective, sir,' replied Virgil amiably. 'Yesterday was American Independence Day. The American prisoners-of-war wanted to celebrate the occasion. No doubt they would have asked your permission to fly the United States flag had they thought it would be granted.'

'Must I remind you that you are prisoners-of-war, Captain Howard? You are under British jurisdiction. Would your country have allowed *our* prisoners to fly the Union flag to celebrate a victory against America?'

'No,' conceded Virgil, 'but I look upon this as no more than a very minor disciplinary matter. You'll find my men will behave themselves every bit as well as the Frenchmen while they are here. If this is the most serious incident that occurs during your governorship you can consider yourself very lucky.'

'That remark is insolent, Captain Howard. I regret I must take it into consideration when I reply to the letter I have just received, suggesting you and your fellow officers be considered for parole. My recommendation will be that parole should be refused.'

Viewing Virgil's surprised expression with satisfaction, he said, 'Thank you, Captain Howard. You may return to the Petty Officers' Block now.'

19

'. . . But why would you *want* to consider parole? Do you think it would be so much more enjoyable to live with the English?'

Henri Joffre made a deprecating gesture with his hands. 'Their manners leave much to be desired. English food is terrible, and even their smugglers cannot obtain such Cognac as this.'

Henri held up his brandy goblet and the liquid amber of its contents reflected the light from the lamps hanging about the cell block walls. 'Even in France such Cognac is enjoyed by only a favoured few.'

'It's very fine Cognac indeed,' agreed Pilgrim, 'but there's more to life than satisfying one's stomach.'

'Ah yes!' Henri swirled the contents of the goblet he held in his hand and smiled down at it. 'I forget. You are talking, of course, of the young women who are to be found outside the prison. *English* women. Be careful, my friend. They walk in a manner deliberately intended to arouse a man's passions, but should he respond . . . !'

Again there was an expressive gesture from the

Frenchman. 'She will recoil in mock horror and protest that her honour is being threatened. Many of my countrymen in this very building have stories to tell of this. Some have lost their parole because of these women. Others have been flogged. Only last year two Frenchmen were hanged, solely on the evidence of an Englishwoman. They protested their innocence to the scaffold.'

Henri took another sip from his goblet. 'Forget all ideas of parole, M'sieur Pilgrim. Remain in the *Petit Cautionnement*. You must admit, life here is not altogether unpleasant.'

'Yet you've tried to escape,' pointed out Pilgrim.

'Of course! I am a patriot.'

Henri appeared offended that Pilgrim had thought it necessary to question his actions. 'I wished to escape not to enjoy the English way of life, but to return to France, in order to usefully serve my country once more.'

'Is Mary Gurney aware that was the reason she was loaning you her clothes?'

Pilgrim put the question casually and Henri had the grace to look at least mildly embarrassed.

'It is not something we have discussed, but she knows I am anxious to return to my country as soon as possible. My father is not a well man.'

'Perhaps Mary hopes that if she helps you to escape from here you'll take her to France with you?'

Henri shrugged. 'It is not impossible, of course, but, as I have said, it is a matter we have not discussed. Now, let us forget about English women and enjoy some more Cognac . . .'

The following day the market was allowed to take place in the prison once more. Tacy was among those offering goods for sale.

She expressed her relief at learning no harm had come to Pilgrim. 'When we arrived here yesterday I saw strange flags flying on one of the buildings. Someone said they were American flags and I knew there was trouble. When we were not allowed to come inside the prison I thought there must have been a riot and that you might have been hurt again.'

'I suppose it was a riot, of sorts – but only a very minor one. It was more high spirits, really.' He explained the significance of Independence Day to her.

'I'm glad you weren't involved,' she said, with some relief. 'But Governor Cotgrave must have been livid.'

'He wasn't pleased,' agreed Pilgrim. 'He called Virgil to his office and told him we Americans are a troublesome lot who can't expect to be granted any extra privileges while we're here. It doesn't mean very much. Our men aren't treated as leniently as the French as it is. They're not allowed to come to the market, for instance, even though money from our Government is beginning to trickle through now.'

'Perhaps all that might change very soon . . . for you, at least.'

'I don't understand . . . In what way might it change for *me*?'

Tacy had spoken without thinking. Now she seemed embarrassed. 'Perhaps I shouldn't be saying anything to you just yet, but Sir Thomas Tyrwhitt returned from London yesterday evening. His carriage happened to be coming along the road by Two Bridges when Pa was bringing sheep from over that way with Rip helping him. Sir Thomas stopped to talk about how Rip's training was coming along. Before he went on his way he said Pa was to tell me he had some good news for you. He felt it would repay you for what you did to save Rip.'

'I wonder what that could be – and when I'll hear about it?'

'Perhaps they're going to let you out of the prison on parole, like the French officers who're staying over at Ashburton.'

'It could be something like that, I suppose.' Pilgrim recalled the conversation with Henri the evening before. He also remembered the comments Governor Cotgrave had made to Virgil on the subject. 'I doubt it, though. Cotgrave has already said he's against giving parole to Americans.'

'He won't be able to do very much about it if Sir Thomas says he's to give it to you,' Tacy spoke with great confidence. 'He'll know that whatever Sir Thomas does has the approval of the Prince Regent.'

At that moment one of the French prisoners-of-war came along to buy a dozen eggs from Tacy. Before handing over his money he inspected each one carefully, insisting that she change two of them because he considered them smaller than the others.

When the Frenchman was eventually satisfied with his purchase and parted with his money, Tacy said to Pilgrim, 'Would you take parole if it was offered to you?'

He had a feeling his reply was of importance to her, but his words were guarded. 'I don't know. I would have to think about it carefully before making up my mind.'

Tacy seemed upset by his lack of enthusiasm. 'Why? Why do you say that? Surely you don't want to remain in here one minute longer than you have to? It's an *awful* place. I wouldn't wish to put my worst enemy in here!'

Pilgrim smiled, he could not imagine Tacy having a 'worst enemy'. 'Don't get the wrong idea. I'd *love* to be out of here, but not if it smacked of favouritism and all the others were left behind. I'd want Virgil to be given parole too. Anyway, even if it were offered we'd need to stay close enough to the prison to remain in touch with the soldiers and marines left behind. As officers we're responsible for them, even though we're now all prisoners-of-war.'

'Sir Thomas's house at Tor Royal is no more than a mile from here. If you were offered parole to stay there you'd take it?'

Tacy did not feel it necessary to add that Tor Royal was little more than the same distance from Roundtor Farm.

'If Virgil were offered parole at the same time and we were able to keep in touch with our men, I'd be delighted to accept parole. To be honest, Tacy, I think it's only the fact I can meet and talk with you a few times a week that's keeping me sane. It's a whole lot better than the prison hulk, certainly, but it's never possible to forget I'm a prisoner. We're shut up inside walls and the doors are locked as soon as it gets dark. Perhaps being an American makes it worse. I come from Ohio, where there are miles and miles of empty, open space. There's a sense of freedom there like you'll never have known . . .'

The way he spoke of his home was the way *she* felt about Dartmoor. If he took parole it would not be very long before he came to share her love of it.

20

Pilgrim and Virgil were summoned to Governor Cotgrave's office three days after Sir Thomas Tyrwhitt's return to Dartmoor from London.

On the desk in front of the governor was a letter bearing an impressive seal. It sat amidst a variety of other documents which he shuffled about in an apparently aimless fashion before speaking to the two prisoners-of-war.

'I have had a letter from the Transport Board, in London. It authorises me to offer parole to you and the other Americans held in the *Petit Cautionnement*.'

Pilgrim and Virgil exchanged glances in which were mingled surprise, delight and faint amusement. It was as though the conversation between Governor Cotgrave and Virgil resulting from the Independence Day troubles had never taken place.

Choosing to ignore their expressions, the governor continued, 'As you are both mentioned by name and are to be offered parole on special terms, I have decided to speak to you before I call in your countrymen.'

'Special terms?' queried Virgil. 'Are they less favour-able than those offered to the others?'

Governor Cotgrave did not reply to the question with a direct answer. 'Sir Thomas Tyrwhitt has offered you parole accommodation in his own home, at Tor Royal. It's no more than a mile from the prison. He will stand as guarantor for your behaviour – on con-dition you give your word of honour to him personally that you will not attempt to escape. As the Prince Regent is known to visit Tor Royal from time to time, Sir Thomas will no doubt require additional assur-ances from you in respect of your conduct during your parole there. In return, you will be granted a number of concessions not usually enjoyed by paroled officers. Do I take it you both agree to this rather exceptional offer?'

Pilgrim held his breath. He wanted parole and knew Virgil did too, but the captain of marines would not accept it unless he were satisfied the American prisoners-of-war remaining in the prison would not suffer as a result of their absence.

His heart sank when Virgil said, 'There are one or two matters I would like to clarify before I reply to your offer, Governor.'

'What sort of "matters"?' Cotgrave snapped the ques-tion at Virgil. He was not at all pleased for prisoners-of-war to be given any special privileges – especially American prisoners.

'I am the senior United States officer in the prison. If I accept parole I would need to know I will have regular access to my men and the other Americans. I accept that it must be at a reasonable hour, and will require your permission, of course – but I need your assurance that such permission will not be unreasonably withheld. I also insist that I be informed should any serious incident occur involving any of the United States citizens in your care . . .'

Banging the desk in front of him with his clenched fist, Cotgrave cried, 'Insist? You . . . *insist*? You are being offered parole on quite exceptional terms – far better than you deserve, yet you have the gall to try to set conditions? Not only are you ungrateful, Captain Howard, you are impertinent too!'

'Gratitude has nothing at all to do with this matter, Governor Cotgrave. I am pointing out my duty as a United States officer of marines. I have no doubt that were our roles reversed, you would act in a smiliar manner.'

Governor Cotgrave wished he could have sent both men back to the *Petit Cautionnement* and forgotten them – and any question of parole for American prisoners-of-war – but he did not dare.

The letter instructing him to arrange parole made it clear the suggestion had originated in the office of the Prime Minister. It also made it plain the order had the support of the Prince Regent himself.

Captain Cotgrave's seagoing service had not proved sufficiently illustrious to bring a peerage to the Cotgrave family. It was his hope that in his present post a combination of unbending discipline and rigid application of regulations would succeed where valour had failed. The instructions contained in the letter before him on the desk stuck in his craw, but he did not intend allowing an enemy of his country – until recently a colonial – to thwart his ambitions.

'Your devotion to duty is both understandable and admirable, Captain Howard. Under the terms of your parole you will present yourself at this prison once a fortnight. You may visit your men then.'

Pilgrim hoped Virgil might agree, but the captain now

insisted that one of the marines, possibly Ephraim, be given permission to visit him at Tor Royal. He also had a number of other points to raise with the prison governor.

Governor Cotgrave had agreed to Ephraim acting as a messenger between prison and Tor Royal only when Virgil reminded him that such a procedure had been granted to the French for much of their time in Dartmoor. He also raised the question of granting the American rank-and-file prisoners the same privileges as their French counterparts. Included in this would be the right to attend the market and be generally granted greater freedom of movement within the prison.

Aware that he was on stronger ground than he had been over the question of parole for the officers, Governor Cotgrave pointed out that the French had been in Dartmoor prison since it opened, four years before. Many had been captured some years before this. There had been ample time for the British authorities to assess their behaviour.

The Americans, on the other hand, had been in Dartmoor prison for a matter of months only. During this short time their behaviour had already left much to be desired.

This argument was countered by Virgil with details of Frenchmen who had escaped, attempted to escape, or broken their parole. The figures had been given to him by Henri Joffre and were quite staggering. The number of French officers who had tried to escape, or seriously broken the conditions of their parole ran into hundreds.

After much argument back and forth, Cotgrave had finally agreed to allow Ephraim, or a named substitute, a bi-weekly visit to Tor Royal, but he had refused to concede anything more.

While his friend was negotiating with the prison governor, Pilgrim maintained a discreet silence. Filled with admiration for the tough stand Virgil was making on the issue of the terms of their parole, he was fearful lest the captain of marines push the governor too hard and so lose the opportunity of parole for both of them.

Eventually, Governor Cotgrave brought the acrimonious interview to an end.

'Prisoners-of-war are defeated men, Captain Howard – and defeated men do not dictate terms to their victors. Should it be necessary, you will both be allowed reasonable access in addition to your fortnightly visit and, yes, your sergeant will be allowed out to report to you. Now, do you or do you not accept the terms of the parole you have been offered?'

Pilgrim held his breath until Virgil said, 'I do, Governor. But before I leave the prison I would like to visit Block Four and tell my countrymen all that has been agreed between us.'

Relieved to have finally resolved the matter, Governor Cotgrave said, 'Very well. Both of you sign the parole agreement now, then you may pay a visit to Block Four. In the meantime I will send word to Sir Thomas Tyrwhitt that you will be released tomorrow. I understand he wishes to see you settled in at Tor Royal before he returns to London.'

There were grumbles of discontent from the assembled American prisoners-of-war when Virgil broke the news of the impending parole of American officers.

Pilgrim felt sorry for them. He, Virgil and the other officers were already enjoying the comparative comfort of the Petty Officers' Block. Now they were being paroled. Meanwhile, the men here were forced to endure conditions worse than in any other block of the prison.

Furthermore, they were in constant fear of those French prisoners who had been virtually disowned by their own countrymen.

'There is no question of deserting you,' Virgil sought to reassure the Americans. 'Lieutenant Penn and I will be reporting to the prison once every two weeks and are to be allowed to visit you, to make sure you're all keeping well. In addition, Sergeant Ephraim is to be granted permission to leave the prison to report to me at Tor Royal on the weeks I don't come here. If he is unable to come to me, another named deputy will take his place.'

The news that Ephraim was to be given freedom to leave the prison did not please many of the merchant seamen. They protested noisily.

When Virgil had quietened them, he said impassively, 'I suggest you choose the substitute for my approval. The governor has also agreed I will be notified immediately if you have any serious problems.'

When Virgil's talk to the American prisoners-of-war came to an end, there were grudging good wishes from some of those who would be remaining behind, but silence from many more.

They were particularly aggrieved because many of them had been captured whilst serving on United States merchant vessels. They believed, with certain justification, that they should not be held in Dartmoor at all. They were civilians, caught up in a war in which they had taken no active part. Yet in captivity they were being treated as though they too were combatants.

However, they conceded that Virgil and Pilgrim would be able to do more to help them from Tor Royal than from the Petty Officers' Block in prison. They would elect one of their number to visit Tor Royal should Ephraim not be able to go on any particular occasion.

Despite their grumbling, there was not one man among them who did not envy Virgil and Pilgrim their imminent departure from the grim confines of Dartmoor prison.

21

Pilgrim and Virgil's release from Dartmoor prison on parole was devoid of all ceremony.

Issued with parole documents, each carried a small bundle in which was wrapped what few personal belongings he had succeeded in gathering during his imprisonment. Thus frugally equipped, they passed through the high archway and the heavy wooden prison gates slammed shut behind them.

There was no one outside to meet them and they had only sketchy directions of how they would find Tor Royal. Standing hesitantly in the lane outside the prison, beneath a watery early morning sun, they found it difficult to take in their changed circumstances. To all intents and purposes, they were now free men, albeit in the country of an enemy.

Pilgrim was surprised that Sir Thomas Tyrwhitt had sent no one to escort them to Tor Royal, but there was no one in view for as far as they could see.

To their right, the lane wound around the high tor that overlooked the prison. To the left they could see the small cluster of buildings that comprised the small prison hamlet of Princetown.

Behind the prison, hidden from view for the moment by the high, granite perimeter wall, was open moorland, stretching away for as far as the human eye could see.

The instructions Pilgrim and Virgil had been given would take them through Princetown and they set off in that direction. They expected to find the house of the Lord Warden of the Stannaries in a valley on the far side of the hamlet that had sprung up about the prison.

'Do you notice anything in particular, Pilgrim?'

The question from Virgil came when they had left the prison behind them and had an uninterrupted view of rolling moorland to their left.

'Yes. Space,' replied Pilgrim. 'I feel I can breathe freely again.'

'That's it, Pilgrim . . . the *air*. It's fresh. We've left the stench of prison behind. I've only just realised how bad it was.'

Virgil was right. Pilgrim filled his lungs once more. The air carried on it the aroma of grass and furze. It was a sweet, clean smell.

'How will you spend your time in our new surroundings?' Pilgrim put the question to his companion as they walked together.

'Sir Thomas might have some ideas on that,' replied Virgil. 'But I intend addressing a barrage of letters to our Government. I want to tell them of the conditions endured by our men on the hulks and in the prison here. I'll see if I can get them to do something about it. How about you, how do you intend occupying your time?'

'I became very unfit in the prison, especially after I came out of the hospital. I'd like to do some physical work. On a farm, perhaps.'

Virgil gave Pilgrim a knowing smile. 'Would you have any particular farm in mind? One where the farmer has a pretty young, dark-haired daughter who goes by the name of Tacy, perhaps?'

'I don't know where her farm is,' said Pilgrim truthfully, but evasively. He had already decided he would locate Roundtor Farm at the earliest opportunity.

Once Princetown was reached, they came to a large building set back on the right of the road. Beside it, a number of militiamen were being drilled under the supervision of an officer.

These were not the Somerset militiamen who had brought the Americans to Dartmoor prison from the hulks at Plymouth. The Somerset men had been replaced a few weeks before by a Welsh militia regiment.

Pilgrim and Virgil were wearing new uniforms, tailored for them by a Frenchman who worked in Cell Block Five. Made from good-quality blue cloth, the money to pay the tailor had been provided by Henri Joffre.

Both men had protested that the Frenchman should not spend his money on them. He had countered that they owed it to the United States Marine Corps to which they belonged, as well as to their country, to look their best when they left the prison and went out to live among the English.

The bright colours of the American uniform attracted the attention of an officer sitting astride his horse and watching the militiamen being drilled. Assuming the two men to be French prisoners-of-war, he sent one of his non-commissioned officers to stop them and bring them to him.

With the officer who had brought them from Plymouth in mind, Pilgrim and Virgil approached the militia officer with some apprehension.

But this was a very different man to Captain Henry Pollit of the Somerset Militia.

Mounted on a superb horse, Lieutenant Colonel Cecil Hawke was a man of aristocratic bearing. He sat upright in his saddle, watching the approaching prisoners-of-war with great interest.

As the two men drew closer, Pilgrim could see the empty right sleeve of the militiaman's coat folded neatly and pinned to the shoulder.

When they reached him, Lieutenant Colonel Hawke spoke to them in passable French to enquire what they were doing.

'We're Americans, not French,' replied Virgil. 'We've just been granted parole and are on our way to the house where we'll be staying. Here are our parole documents.'

He handed the papers to the one-armed colonel. He did not even look at them.

'Americans, eh? No wonder I didn't recognise the uniforms.'

His glance shifted to Pilgrim for only a moment before returning to Virgil. 'You were limping as you approached me. Have you been wounded?'

'I was shot in the leg during the battle in which I was made a prisoner. Fortunately I was treated by an American surgeon. He was less drastic than the man who attended you, sir.'

Virgil correctly assumed the other man to have been a regular soldier who had been retired as a result of losing his arm. He wore the insignia of a lieutenant colonel. It was a far more senior rank than was normal for an officer commanding a militia unit responsible for guarding prisoners-of-war.

Lieutenant Colonel Hawke glanced briefly down at the empty sleeve. 'The best surgeon in the world couldn't have saved my arm, Captain. I am afraid that in the wars of today mounted men are no match for the weapons of the artillery – especially when a cavalryman meets an enemy with as many guns as his squadron has horses. But I can still serve my country, albeit in a somewhat frustrating capacity.'

He nodded his head to where the militiamen were making fumbling attempts to attach bayonets to muskets.

'I despair of ever making soldiers of such material. Few have seen life outside a farmyard . . . Make them do that again!'

He bellowed the order at the sergeant who was drilling the militiamen, adding, 'This time tell them to put some life into it. An enemy's not going to stand back and wait while they fiddle around fixing bayonets!'

Shaking his head in exasperation, Lieutenant Colonel Hawke said, 'I swear that when they're given an order they check on what the weather's going to do before they decide whether or not to obey!'

Momentarily dismissing the clumsy militiamen from his thoughts, he said, 'Where will you be staying during your parole . . . Ashburton? That's where most of the French officers are.'

Virgil shook his head. 'We're to live at Tor Royal.'

The reply took the militia lieutenant colonel by surprise. 'At Sir Thomas Tyrwhitt's home? You'll be keeping illustrious company there, Captain.'

He looked at the two men speculatively. 'Is there a reason why Sir Thomas should be taking a special interest in you?'

'Yes, sir.' Virgil nodded his head in Pilgrim's direction. 'Lieutenant Pilgrim Penn was able to perform a service for Sir Thomas recently. As a result Sir Thomas learned that Pilgrim's uncle was United States ambassador in London. It seems he and Sir Thomas were good friends.'

Virgil had decided it would do them no harm to impress this colonel of militia – and he was right.

'My father fought against your people when you rebelled against us,' said Lieutenant Colonel Hawke. 'He has retained a great admiration for Americans as soldiers. He's also of the opinion we should not be at war with you now. Indeed, he firmly believes we should both be fighting Napoleon Bonaparte together.'

Waving a hand in the direction of the large building beside the makeshift parade ground, he said, 'I'm senior officer of the militia mess. You must come there as my guests before I return home. It'll make a refreshing change to talk to soldiers who know what it is to go into battle. Whose idea of "wounded in action" is more serious than tripping over their sword on parade – or dropping a bayonet and piercing their foot.'

He added the last remark as one of the militiamen pulled a bayonet free from his boot and limped from the ranks.

'All right, Sergeant, get someone to go with him to find the surgeon . . .'

Returning his attention to Virgil, he said sympathetically, 'If your leg is bothering you I would be pleased to loan you horses to carry you both to Tor Royal.'

'It's a very kind offer, sir, but we're in no hurry. It's a delight to be able to savour newfound freedom after spending months in prison.'

'Of course. I quite understand,' said Lieutenant Colonel Hawke. I am very pleased to have met up with you both. If you find you need anything – anything at all – don't hesitate to call on me.'

Unexpectedly, Pilgrim said, 'You mentioned your

father had fought against us in our war of independence. Would he be *General* Hawke?'

With an expression of delight, Lieutenant Colonel Hawke said, 'Yes . . . You've heard of him?'

'Of course. He is held up as an example of all that was fine with the British. Had there been more like him we might never have broken our ties with your country. I believe my father met him at the end of the war. He'll be thrilled to know I've made the acquaintance of the son of such a distinguished soldier, sir.'

Virgil and Pilgrim walked away from the militia parade ground in the knowledge that they had made a friend of yet another man who might possibly have an influence upon their future.

22

Pilgrim and Virgil were still discussing the militia lieutenant colonel when they reached the lane which led
to Tor Royal. Here, much to Pilgrim's delight, they
found Tacy and her young sister Johanna waiting for
them.

'I was beginning to think you weren't coming,' said
Tacy brightly.

'You knew we were being released today?' Pilgrim
found it difficult to hide his pleasure at seeing her.

'Yes, Sir Thomas told father last night you'd be coming
to Tor Royal this morning.'

'And you decided to come and meet us?'

'Well . . . there wasn't much happening at the farm.
It was something to do . . .'

'That isn't true!' exclaimed Johanna indignantly.
'There's a whole lot to do at the farm. You told Pa
you'd work late tonight to get it done if he'd let you
come here and meet him.'

She jabbed a finger in Pilgrim's direction.

Tacy tried hard not to look discomfited by her young

sister's impish revelation. 'I thought you might have trouble finding Tor Royal. Lots of people miss the turn-off from the road. They think this is just some old track because you can't see the house until you're almost up to it.'

'Then it's a good thing you've come to show us the way,' lied Pilgrim. 'We'd have probably walked right past without even noticing it.'

'You can hardly miss it,' snorted Johanna derisively. 'Tor Royal is bigger than our farmhouse and all the buildings put together.'

'Have you been to Tor Royal often?' Virgil put the question to Johanna as they began to draw ahead of Tacy and Pilgrim.

'Lots of times,' replied the young girl positively.

'She *hasn't*,' said Tacy to Pilgrim. She spoke quietly, lowering her voice so it would not carry to her sister. 'She's got a vivid imagination.'

'Is that why she said you *did* have work to do on the farm, when you'd said you hadn't?'

Tacy's glance went to his face quickly, before dropping away. 'I *do* have work to do, but it's nothing that won't keep. I thought it would be nice for you to have someone to meet you when you left the prison. A familiar face. Had Sir Thomas been with you, Johanna and I would have gone home again and you'd never have known we'd been waiting.'

Pilgrim was taken aback. 'You mean . . . you wouldn't even have come to say "Hello"? Why not? You know Virgil and me – and you know Sir Thomas.'

'I know him, but I wouldn't dare speak to him unless he spoke to me first. He's a rich and important man. I'm only the daughter of a moorland farmer – a *tenant* farmer.'

'Such things don't matter very much in my country,'

said Pilgrim. 'A man with nothing can head westwards, find a place he likes and settle there on as much land as he can manage. It doesn't matter who he is, or where he's from. He's accepted for what he is, and what he can achieve.'

'But you're from an important family. I heard you and Sir Thomas talking.'

'My pa's respected because he fought for the independence of our country and proved himself a good leader. My uncle became an ambassador because he's a clever man and was an adviser to General Washington in the early days. But that's because it's what they *wanted* to be. I've another uncle who's a trapper somewhere up Canada way, one who's working down in Mexico, and another who, the last we heard of him, had taken a Cherokee wife and was living with her and her tribe up in the Blue Mountains. He went there after almost getting himself hung for shooting someone.'

Tacy did not know who, or what, a 'Cherokee' was, but it sounded exciting.

'Tell me about America.' Tacy was happy just to be with Pilgrim, but she wanted to learn as much as possible about him and the country from which he came. She also liked listening to his voice.

'It's a great big country, Tacy. A huge country, with land for the taking. Nobody even knows quite how much there is.'

'Doesn't anyone live there at all?'

'Only the Indians and they don't do anything with the land. They just hunt over it and fight each other whenever they meet up.'

'But . . . what do the Indians do when you take their land from them?'

Pilgrim frowned. 'They just move on westwards.

There's so much land in America there's plenty for everyone.'

'What will happen when there's no more land for them to move on to?'

'That'll never happen, Tacy. There's more than enough land for everyone to do just what they want and still leave some for everyone else.'

'How much land does your family own?'

'If you stood on one of these hills and looked around, it would be just about as much as you could see in every direction.'

It was a bald statement of fact, not made in an attempt to impress her. Yet it was altogether too much for Tacy to take in. At that moment they came to a gap in the high-banked hedge and Pilgrim stopped.

The view from here was across a wide valley. Beyond it the moor stretched for as far as could be seen, dotted here and there with tors of varying heights.

Many of the tors were dominated by tumbled heaps of rock. A light sprinkling of ponies and sheep grazed in scattered groups across the landscape. There was not a dwelling, or any sign of human habitation to be seen anywhere.

Pilgrim drew in his breath sharply. 'This could almost be Ohio,' he said. 'When we were making our way westward we passed through country just like this.'

'Then you'll feel at home here.'

'I think I might,' agreed Pilgrim. 'I think I could feel very much at home.'

When he spoke he was looking not at the countryside but at Tacy.

They looked at each other for a few seconds and felt themselves drawing closer. The moment was broken by Johanna. She and Virgil had stopped and the young girl called back, 'You can see Tor Royal from here.'

When Tacy and Pilgrim caught up with the others, Johanna pointed to the rooftops of a substantial house, just visible through a line of trees.

'That's Tor Royal.'

'Yes,' said Tacy. 'We'll leave you here.'

Her statement took Pilgrim by surprise. 'Won't you at least come to the house with us?'

'No.'

'Why not?' Pilgrim was puzzled. 'You've met us and showed us the way here. I'm sure Sir Thomas will be delighted to see you both.'

For a moment Tacy thought he was teasing her. When she realised he was not, she said, 'As I said just now, Sir Thomas is a titled man who mixes with royalty. My pa is only a tenant farmer. He needs to work as hard as he's able, in order to pay the rent for his farm and make a living.'

Tacy felt very unhappy in a way she could not entirely explain. 'We live in a very different world to that of Sir Thomas.'

She thought of what Pilgrim had just told her about his life in America and the land owned by his family there. Even allowing for a degree of boastfulness it seemed his family owned more land than Sir Thomas Tyrwhitt.

Unconsciously or otherwise, Pilgrim had told her that his family were on a par with the Lord Warden of the Stannaries. Perhaps he had not intended that his words should be interpreted in such a way, but she now realised, beyond all possible doubt, that Pilgrim belonged in the world of the Dartmoor knight.

'Come on, Johanna, we've a lot of work to do back at the farm. We've showed Lieutenant Penn the way. We must go home now.'

23

'Well, did you meet up with your young American?'

Joan Elford put the question to Tacy as both her daughters entered the kitchen. Behind them, Billy staggered in through the open doorway, his arms laden with more peat than could comfortably be carried.

Her attention momentarily diverted, Joan said crossly, 'Billy! I've told you before, don't try to bring it all in at once. You'll strain something. Make two journeys, as any sensible young man would.'

'It's all right, Mrs Elford, it's not too heavy for me. I'm really strong, you know I am.'

Billy looked at Tacy before lowering his heavy load with some difficulty to the stone floor beside the kitchen fireplace.

He had hoped to impress Tacy with his strength. Much to his disappointment, she did not appear to have even noticed him enter the room bearing his heavy load.

Joan returned her attention to her daughter. 'You haven't answered me, Tacy. Was your young lieutenant released from the prison?'

'Yes, he was.' Johanna answered on behalf of her sister. 'We met him at Princetown. Tacy walked all the way to Tor Royal with him, but it doesn't seem to have made her very happy. She's hardly said a single word to me all the way home.'

'Why don't you just mind your own business, Johanna? Nobody was speaking to you. Anyway, I've said before, he's not *my* young lieutenant and there's nothing to talk about. I'm going upstairs to change my clothes. Then I'll clean out the cow's shed before I milk her.'

Tacy hurried from the kitchen leaving everyone there looking at each other in surprise. It was rare for her to give way to such a bad-tempered outburst. After a few moments, Joan wiped her hands on her apron and set off after her daughter.

'Who's made Tacy unhappy?' asked Billy, unable to comprehend what was happening. 'I'll go and speak to him if it'll make her happy again.'

'I don't think it'd do any good, Billy,' said Johanna. 'It's that American who saved Rip when the militiaman was going to shoot him. Our Tacy's sweet on him. Perhaps he doesn't feel the same way about her. I don't really know. Anyway, I'm going outside to clean out the henhouse. You can come and help me, if you like.'

Billy knew that if he went to help Johanna he would end up doing all the work, but he did not really mind. It would help to take his mind off Tacy for a while. He did not like to think of her being unhappy, whatever the reason.

'Do you want to tell me about it, Tacy?'

Joan stood in the doorway of the room shared by both her daughters. Tacy had not begun to change into her working clothes yet. She was sitting in a chair looking out of the window, her back to her mother.

'Not really.'

'You can do better than that, my girl. When you left here this morning you could hardly stand still for more than two moments at a time, you were so excited about the release of this young American of yours. What happened to change your mood like this? What did he say to upset you? Was he nasty to you?'

'Like I told Johanna, he's not *my* American – and no, he wasn't nasty. In fact he was as nice as I could have wished him to be. Perhaps that's the trouble, he was *too* nice.'

Joan frowned. 'I'm sorry, I don't understand . . .'

Tacy shrugged miserably. 'It's what you've been telling me all along, really. About Pilgrim and Sir Thomas being two of a kind.'

Suddenly alarmed, Joan tried to remember the conversations between Tacy and herself in which she had compared the unknown American with the Lord Warden of the Stannaries.

She could remember nothing of what she had said about the American – but she *had* warned her daughter on many occasions about Sir Thomas.

'What is it you're trying to say, Tacy? Did this American try to do something to you?'

'Of course not!' Tacy was indignant. 'I don't mean that he's like Sir Thomas in *that* way. No, it's what you told me about him being rich. We spoke about his family today. From what he said to me, it seems they're even richer than Sir Thomas.'

She shrugged in a dejected manner. 'When we were looking out across the moor, up by Tor Royal, he said it reminded him of where he lived in America. I asked him how much land his family owned. He said if you stood on a high hill and looked around, all the land for as far as could be seen belonged to them.'

Owning so much land was a difficult concept for Joan to accept. 'Perhaps that wasn't exactly what he meant. It could be that, like us with the moor, they have grazing rights over that much land.'

Tacy shook her head miserably, 'No, Ma. He said they own it – and that's exactly what he meant. His family must be rich, Ma. Very rich.'

Joan looked in silence at her daughter for some minutes. Then she said, 'You really have been smitten by this young man, haven't you?'

Tacy nodded her head unhappily. 'I like him an awful lot, Ma.'

Joan held out her arms and Tacy rose from the chair and came to her, much as she had done as a child whenever things were going wrong in her young life.

Stroking her daughter's hair gently, Joan said, 'I *am* sorry, Tacy. Had I known the way you felt about him I would never have let you go up to that old prison so often.'

Pulling away from her, Tacy managed a weak smile. 'It's not your fault, Ma. You did warn me.'

She managed a shaky laugh. 'It's funny, isn't it? So many girls are made miserable because their men pretend to be far richer than they really are. Yet here's me unhappy because Pilgrim's probably told me the truth!'

'You mustn't feel too bad about it, Tacy. He's not the only man in the world. There'll be another nice young man come along for you before too long, you just wait and see.'

'Thanks, Ma,' Tacy grimaced, 'but I think perhaps I'll forget about men for a while. Right now I'll go out to the yard and sort out that old cow of ours.'

24

Pilgrim found it strange to be inside a house once more, with the routine of everyday life going on about him.

There were many servants employed at Tor Royal. Each of them behaved politely enough, but he had the impression they believed he or Virgil were likely to explode at any moment! However, Pilgrim and Virgil were received warmly by Sir Thomas Tyrwhitt.

Also staying at Tor Royal were Sir Thomas's sister, Winifrith Cudmore, and her daughter, Sophie. Making the introductions, Sir Thomas explained that because he remained unmarried, various members of his family were in the habit of paying him extended visits.

They came, he said, to enjoy the tranquillity of Tor Royal and the moor on which it was built. Then they spent much of their time suggesting the names of suitable women who might enjoy sharing such an idyllic lifestyle with him.

Sophie seemed somewhat subdued, although she was polite enough when she was introduced to the two Americans.

By way of contrast, Winifrith Cudmore acknowledged them with undisguised disapproval. After an almost discourteously brief period of time, she ushered her daughter from the presence of the two men.

The newly paroled officers could not fail to notice her attitude, but it was left to Virgil to put it into words.

'Mrs Cudmore would appear not to approve of our presence in your house, Sir Thomas. I sincerely hope we won't prove an embarrassment to you.'

'Embarrassment? Dear me, no, Captain. The trouble is, Winifrith *will* try to run my life for me. No, that's not strictly true. She tries to run the lives of *everyone* she meets. She has tried to find a wife for me on more than one occasion. She's peeved because I never consulted her about bringing you to Tor Royal on parole, that is all. Take no notice. I will not have her, or any other woman, running my life for me.'

He looked meaningfully at Virgil before adding, 'She's also had problems with young Sophie, I understand. The situation came very close to a scandal. She became involved with some young army officer working in the War Office. He's being packed off to his regiment in the Spanish Peninsular and Winifrith's brought Sophie here. They'll stay until the scandal has died down. No doubt Winifrith is still a little wary of young men who wear a uniform.'

Sir Thomas smiled disarmingly. 'But you must not allow my family and their problems to spoil your day. I've arranged a small dinner party this evening. We'll celebrate your release from that dreadful prison. I was responsible for having it built on Dartmoor, you know? But I never intended that *gentlemen* should be locked up there.'

The dinner party was a small affair. Only nine people

sat around the dining table, including those who were
staying at Tor Royal.

One of the dinner guests was the militia officer, Lieutenant Colonel Hawke. He had been invited because
Virgil had told Sir Thomas of the conversation the
soldier had held with the two paroled prisoners-of-war
earlier in the day.

Cecil Hawke was delighted to be at Tor Royal and he
was a bluff and lively guest.

The remaining three around the dinner table were the
Reverend Alfred Cotterell, vicar of the moorland parish
of Sheepstor, his wife Agatha and their daughter.

Jemima Cotterell was a very pleasant young girl,
about two or three years older than Sophie.

Sophie and the vicar's daughter seemed to know each
other, but Pilgrim observed a look cast in Jemima's
direction by Winifrith during a conversation between
the girls. He drew the conclusion that Sir Thomas's
sister considered the vicar's daughter hardly more suitable as a companion for Sophie than were the two
Americans.

However, it became increasingly apparent during the
course of the evening that Winifrith Cudmore's love for
alcohol was as much of an embarrassment as Sophie's
love for the army officer who was being despatched to
the war in the Peninsula.

By the end of the meal she had consumed twice as
much champagne as anyone else at the table and her
voice had grown in volume.

The company was not large enough for the men
and women to go their separate ways after dinner.
Instead, they all adjourned to the drawing room – losing
Winifrith somewhere along the way.

No one commented upon her absence, but after she
had been missing for a while, Sophie left the party,

murmuring something to Sir Thomas on her way fror
the room.

When she returned, Sophie sat down on the settee
alongside Virgil. She seemed more relaxed now he
mother was not with her and engaged Virgil in polit
conversation. She asked the circumstances of his captur
and questioned him about the conditions for capture
soldiers and sailors inside the Dartmoor prison.

She shuddered at his description of life there and the
turned the conversation towards more personal detail
about his family and their home in the United States c
America.

Pilgrim was being equally assiduously questione
by the wife and daughter of the clergyman, but h
did not seem to be enjoying the experience as muc
as the captain of marines.

The party did not break up until almost midnigh
when the clergyman reluctantly placed his empty glas
upon the small table beside his comfortable armchai
and said it was time he took his family home. He ha
a funeral to conduct in the morning.

The militia colonel reluctantly decided he too shoul
return to his barracks in Princetown. The remainin
members of the party went out into the night to se
them off.

The clergyman's carriage rumbled away from th
house with a hand waving a white handkerchief fror
one of the windows. Pilgrim commented to Sophie tha
it was an almost forgotten luxury to be free to walk i
the night air.

Sophie glanced towards Virgil before replying, '
don't suppose you saw many horses inside the priso
either?'

'No . . . except those which drew carts to and fror
the prison.'

'Uncle, may I take Pilgrim and go and check on your favourite hunting mare? Virgil might like to come too.'

Sophie put the question to Sir Thomas, adding, 'She looked as though she was close to foaling earlier this evening.'

'If you don't mind, I think I'll go on to bed,' said Virgil. 'It's been an exciting day.' In truth, his wounded leg was bothering him. He needed to rest it.

Sir Thomas hesitated. 'I'm not certain your mother would approve, Sophie . . .'

'She wouldn't, but you don't have to tell her – and it's not as though we'll be alone. One of the grooms is staying in the stable, just in case the mare foals during the night.'

'Well . . . all right,' agreed Sir Thomas reluctantly, 'but don't be long. There's quite a bite to the wind. I don't want you coming down with a chill, or your mother *will* take me to task.'

Afraid he might change his mind, Sophie startled Pilgrim by reaching out and taking his hand, whispering, 'Come along, before Uncle has second thoughts about it.'

Once out of Sir Thomas's hearing, she said, 'Uncle Thomas has very old-fashioned ideas of how I should behave. I suppose that's because he's never married and had children of his own.'

'His caution is quite understandable,' said Pilgrim. 'After all, I've only arrived in his house today. He doesn't really know very much about me.'

'Nonsense!' declared Sophie. 'He was friends with *your* uncle for years. Besides, I *can* trust you, can I not? I feel I shall go quite mad if I'm not able to talk to someone my own age for a while. You can tell me about yourself – and about Captain Howard.'

'You *can* trust me, but you don't really know any more about me than does Sir Thomas.'

'You're beginning to sound just like him!' retorted Sophie. 'Anyway, we're at the stable now. Look! There's a light on in the mare's stall.'

There was not *one* groom, but two in the stall and the mare was in the throes of labour.

She was not having an easy time. Although the night was growing cold, one of the grooms was stripped to the waist and perspiring profusely. He was also bloody from fingertips to shoulder.

He looked up as they entered the loosebox and glanced from Pilgrim to Sir Thomas's niece.

'This is no place for you right now, Miss Sophie. The mare's in trouble.'

'Don't be ridiculous,' snapped Sophie haughtily. 'What's wrong with her?'

'The foal is the wrong way round and won't come out. I've tried to turn it, but the mare's too far on. She needs help bad, but she's so highly strung we can't do things for her the way we should. She needs someone to hold her head still while we get on with things at this end.'

'Can I hold her?' Pilgrim volunteered his help.

'It might be better if I were to do that,' said the other groom. 'She feels safe with me. Do you know anything about horses?'

'We've got quite a few at home,' replied Pilgrim. 'I've helped with more than one difficult birth – and I've never lost a foal yet.'

'Then see if you can help Alfie. I'll hold her head and try to keep her still – but you'd better take that fancy coat off if you don't want to get it bloodied.'

Pilgrim stripped off his French-made Marines coat and rolled up his sleeves.

The birth of the foal was difficult. Very difficult. It

was eventually pulled from the body of its mother by sheer brute force. By this time Sophie too was helping.

While this was going on Sir Thomas had come from the house, concerned about Sophie's continuing absence. He was accompanied by Virgil. Despite his troublesome leg, Virgil was anxious that his countryman should not find trouble on his first night of freedom.

'Is it alive?' Sir Thomas asked the question as the foal slithered to the ground.

The foal supplied an answer by spasmodic movements of its legs that grew in strength.

'It's a fine young stallion foal,' said Pilgrim proudly. 'It needed to be strong to survive all it's been through. He'll prove a good stayer.'

'He wouldn't have survived at all had Pilgrim not been on hand to help,' declared Sophie. 'He's worked hard.'

'Everyone's worked hard,' said Pilgrim, 'including you, Sophie. But the little fellow's going to be worth all our efforts.'

'We've a great many fine horses at Tor Royal,' said Sir Thomas. 'You're welcome to ride any of them whenever you wish. They'll enjoy the exercise.'

'So would I,' declared Pilgrim, 'but I'm not certain the terms of my parole allow me to ride horses . . .'

'Nonsense, dear boy! But if you're in any doubt, take out the big grey from the stable across the yard. It belongs to the Prince Regent. Say you're exercising it on his behalf and it'll be a brave man who takes you to task for it.'

'Yes, take Henry out,' said Sophie eagerly. 'I'll come with you. Captain Howard can come too. There are some wonderful rides on the moor around Tor Royal. I'll show them to you.'

'We'll discuss it another time,' said Sir Thomas hu
riedly. He took a large watch from his pocket. '
nigh on two o'clock. It has been a very exciting d
for everyone, now I think it is time we all went
our beds. If we remain here very much longer we
see the sun rise and I have much to do tomorrow,
more properly, I should say *today.*'

'It's been a wonderful day, Sir Thomas,' declared P
grim. 'One I shall remember for the rest of my days.

'There will be many more,' promised Sophie eager
Glancing at Virgil, she added, 'We'll all work very ha
to make your stay in that prison seem no more thar
bad dream.'

'I do hope so,' declared Sir Thomas fervently. 'I thir
this war between our two countries is the height
foolishness. I have said as much to the Prince Rege
on many occasions . . .'

Shortly afterwards, Virgil and Pilgrim wished ea
other goodnight as they entered their adjacent rooms

'It's wonderful to be leading civilised lives agair
declared Pilgrim. 'I think I'm going to enjoy my sta
here.'

'I trust so,' said Virgil cautiously. 'It's certainly bett
than life inside the walls of the prison. I like Sir Thomas
niece, too . . . She's a good-looking girl – yet she
desperately unhappy and lonely. As for her moth
. . . well, she's trouble if ever I saw it!'

25

Although it had been very late when he retired to bed, Pilgrim woke soon after the household came to life. When he remembered where he was, he lay in bed for a while, just listening to the sounds in and about the house.

He tried to identify the various activities that had been absent from his life for such a long time.

There were the muted voices of servants; the sound of a hard brush sweeping on stone and the squeaking of a pump as water was drawn for use in the house. Somewhere farther away in the yard it sounded as though a carpet was being vigorously beaten.

In addition to all the household noises, birdsong in the gardens provided a constant background to all the other sounds. He was able to identify the soft, pleasant murmuring of a dove but the songs of most other birds were unfamiliar to him.

There had been no birdsong within the bleak confines of the Dartmoor prison.

Pilgrim lay listening for perhaps twenty minutes

before deciding he wanted to be a part of the world he could hear. Rising from his bed he first of all washed in a bowl, using water from a jug placed on a marble-topped table in a corner of his room.

When he went downstairs he was surprised to find Sir Thomas already seated at the dining table, taking breakfast alone.

The landowner invited Pilgrim to join him, explaining he was riding to Cornwall to attend a Stannary meeting. It was possible, he added, he would not be returning that night.

During breakfast, Sir Thomas tried to explain to Pilgrim what his duties as Lord Warden of the Stannaries entailed.

As he talked, it became apparent to Pilgrim that the title had meant a great deal in years gone by. When mining operations dwindled, so too did the authority wielded by the Lord Warden.

When he finished eating, Sir Thomas dabbed his mouth with a napkin. 'It's a grand morning. Why don't you take one of the horses and go for a ride?'

'It's a very kind offer,' replied Pilgrim, 'but today I think I would rather go for a walk. I want to savour the feeling of being part of the world once more.'

'Of course.' Pulling out his watch, Sir Thomas peered at it and said, 'I must leave now. I need to be at my destination by lunchtime. Enjoy your freedom, Pilgrim, and please treat Tor Royal as though it were your home.'

For almost an hour after he had finished his breakfast, Pilgrim wandered about the grounds, watching gardeners, estate workers and the house servants going about their various duties. Then he went to the stables and for a while watched the foal he had helped bring into the world.

When he returned to the house and asked after the others, Pilgrim was told by the butler that he was still the only guest up and about.

Pilgrim decided he would not wait about the house until the others woke.

'When Captain Howard rises, will you please tell him I've gone for a walk on the moor?'

'Yes, sir . . .' The butler hesitated before asking, 'Do you mind if I ask which direction you intend taking, sir?'

Mindful of the terms of his parole, Pilgrim replied resentfully, 'Why? Are you concerned the prison authorities will inquire after me?'

'I don't think they are likely to do that, sir, but you are new to the moor. Mists often come down here without any warning. It's very easy to get lost. If you're caught in mist your best plan is to stay exactly where you are and wait for someone to come out and find you. That's why I would like to know the direction you intend taking.'

Sheepishly, Pilgrim said, 'Of course. Even in the prison we were aware of how suddenly the weather here could change. Thank you for thinking of it.'

He hesitated a moment before saying, 'I shall head northeastwards. I believe the farm of the Elford family is that way?'

'That's right, sir. Drop down into the valley and you'll find it a comparatively easy walk. I know the farm – and the Elfords too. They're one of the nicest families on the moor. Enjoy your day. I hope the weather stays as fine for you as it is now.'

Pilgrim set off with the rising sun in his eyes. As he walked, he thought wryly that the weather seemed to crop up in conversation with every Englishman he had met on the moor. He decided it was because it dominated every activity that went on here and so was vitally important in their daily lives.

However, the weather could hardly have been better than it was right now. He walked along relishing his freedom.

Following the curve of the tor, he became aware from the position of the sun that he was gradually heading farther northwards. Then, as he dropped down towards the valley floor, he could hear the sound of tumbling water.

A clear, fast-flowing stream ran along the valley. Picturesque and shallow, the tumbling water divided around numerous polished granite rocks.

For a few minutes Pilgrim stopped to watch a small, black and white bird as it darted about the stream, spending as much time beneath the surface of the water as it did above. It seemed to be searching for food as it darted here and there with incredibly fast movements.

He had been walking for perhaps half an hour when he came upon a young man cutting oblong slabs of peat and stacking them with exaggerated precision nearby.

At the same time, Pilgrim could see the roofs of a house and outbuildings farther along the valley.

Billy had seen Pilgrim approaching in the distance, but he did not cease working until Pilgrim was no more than a few paces away. Leaning on his long-handled peat cutter, he looked at the American uncertainly.

'Hello.' Pilgrim was the first to speak. Indicating the partly visible farm with a nod of his head, he said, 'Is that the Elfords' farm?'

'That's right.' Billy's face wore a puzzled expression when he spoke again. 'Why do you talk so funny?'

Pilgrim realised he was talking to a simple young man and he smiled. 'I expect I sound funny to you because I'm an American. You've probably not met one before.'

Billy's puzzlement became a frown. Looking at Pilgrim reproachfully, he asked, 'Are you the American who upset Tacy? The one they let out of the prison yesterday?'

Pilgrim was taken aback by the accusation. 'I didn't even know Tacy *was* upset! What am I supposed to have done?'

Billy shrugged. 'How should I know? All I can tell you is that she was in a funny mood when she came back from seeing you. She went straight up to her room and didn't speak a word to me for the rest of the day.'

'I'm sorry to hear that. I don't think it can have had anything to do with me, but I'll try to find out.'

'You won't upset her again? I don't like to see her upset.'

Pilgrim smiled sympathetically at the earnest young man. 'I promise to try very hard not to upset her. What's your name?'

'Billy. I live over there . . .' He nodded his head vaguely in a southerly direction '. . . but I like coming to help on the farm. Mr Elford lets me take all the peat we need and Mrs Elford gives me eggs and milk. Bread and cakes too when she bakes 'em.'

'Then you're a fortunate man, Billy. I've tasted some of Mrs Elford's cakes. You'll not find better anywhere. My name's Pilgrim. I'll be on my way now, but I've no doubt we'll meet up with each other again.'

Pilgrim extended his hand and, after a moment's surprised hesitation, Billy took it and the two shook hands.

When Pilgrim had gone on his way, Billy looked from the departing American to his hand. He beamed happily. No one had ever shaken his hand before. It made him feel very important.

26

Coming from the dairy, Joan Elford saw the tall, rather thin, uniformed young man as he turned to secure the gate after entering the farmyard. She realised immediately who he was, but was uncertain what her attitude would, or should, be.

She stood in the kitchen doorway, undecided, as he approached.

Crossing the yard, Pilgrim removed his hat and tucked it beneath his arm as he neared the waiting woman. He slowed down when she remained silent.

'Mrs Elford . . . ?' Pilgrim spoke hesitantly, remembering the conversation he had just had with Billy. He felt sure this woman must be Tacy's mother. It was possible she too believed he had said or done something to upset Tacy.

'You'll be one of the American officers who's staying up at Tor Royal.'

'That's right, ma'am. Lieutenant Penn. Pilgrim Penn.'

There was an awkward lull in the conversation. It was broken, hesitantly, by Pilgrim. 'I came to thank Tacy and

Johanna for showing me and Captain Howard the way to Tor Royal yesterday.'

'I'm the only one at home at the moment. My husband and Johanna have gone to the prison market. Tacy's out with the two dogs. She's rounding up sheep to have them ready for Tavistock market later this week.'

Although Pilgrim believed he was hiding his disappointment well, it was evident to the farmer's wife.

'May I go and look for her?'

'You'd be wasting your time. I couldn't even tell you in which direction to begin looking,' said Joan, untruthfully. 'But she'll be bringing the sheep into the home pen soon. We'll be able to see her from the house. Won't you come in and have a cup of tea while you wait?'

Pilgrim would much rather have gone off on his own, seeking Tacy, but he said, 'That's very kind of you. It's been a long time since I tasted tea.'

Pilgrim needed to duck his head in order to enter through the kitchen doorway. As he did so the smell of baking hit him. For a moment he could almost have been in the kitchen of his own home, far away in Ohio.

When he expressed his thoughts to Joan, she said, 'Were you in the habit of visiting the kitchen in your house . . . in America?'

'Of course. Aren't all children?' Pilgrim was puzzled by her question.

'They certainly are in *this* house, but the kitchen's where we all eat, as well as being where the cooking's done.'

'It must be very cosy during the cold winter months.' Pilgrim continued the polite small talk.

Joan shrugged. 'It's as cosy as anywhere else. Mind you, like just about every moorland house, you can't get rid of all the draughts – nor the damp. You can see where the wet's coming in over by that window.' She pointed to the offending spot of dampness. 'It comes straight through the wall.'

Pilgrim smiled. 'You'll never know what damp and draught are until you've lived in a log cabin. When the mud between the logs is new a heavy rainstorm will wash it out quicker than you can fill it in. When it gets old and dry the mud shrinks and lets in the wind.'

Joan looked at the visitor quizzically. 'You've lived in a place like that?'

'Pilgrim nodded. 'That's right, ma'am, but it was sheer luxury after living for months in the back of a wagon.'

Joan looked confused. 'But . . . Tacy said your family owns a great deal of land.'

Delighted that Tacy should have spoken of him to her mother, Pilgrim explained, 'We do, but so do a great many folk in Ohio. Land is there for the taking.'

The concept of simply taking over vast tracts of land without paying rent to anyone was beyond the comprehension of the Dartmoor farmer's wife. She was certain that *ordinary* people did not have such vast landholdings – and it did not seem compatible with the type of home he had just described to her.

'Are you telling me your family owns all this land and yet you live in a wooden cabin?'

Pilgrim smiled. 'No, ma'am. Not any more. We lived in it for more than a year, though, while a proper house was being built for us. Now we've got one of the finest houses in Ohio.'

Listening to Pilgrim talk, Joan was undecided whether or not Tacy was right about this very likeable young American. She had believed he was probably exaggerating the wealth of his family in order to impress

Tacy. Now she realised her daughter had probably been right. Pilgrim's family had a substantial landholding.

'Does your father farm the land himself?'

'When he's home, but that's not so often these days. We were the first settlers in our part of Ohio so folk got used to asking him about things. When it was decided to send someone to Congress it seemed natural for them to elect my father.'

Observing Joan's frown, Pilgrim explained, 'Congress is very much like your Parliament, I guess.'

'Oh, I see.'

If confirmation was needed about his place in society, this was it.

Sir Thomas Tyrwhitt had also been a Member of Parliament until only a few years ago and she told Pilgrim so.

'Sir Thomas seems to have a finger in a great many pies around here.'

'He's a very important man. So, too, I suspect, is your father.'

Pilgrim smiled once more. 'I'm not sure Pa would agree with you about that. He says he's just a natural-born fighter. He's had to fight for everything he's ever wanted. Now *he's* got it he's fighting so that other folk can have what *they* want . . .'

Pilgrim's voice trailed away. While he was speaking he had glanced through the window. He could see one of the dogs and some sheep.

'Would that be Tacy arrived back?'

Joan also looked through the window. 'Yes. At least, I can see Rip, so she won't be far away.'

'Would you mind if I went out to meet her?'

After what Pilgrim had just told her about his family background, Joan was not pleased that he should be taking such an interest in her elder daughter. Wealthy men

– and the sons of wealthy men – did not interest themselves in working girls with a view to *marrying* them. However, if he went out to meet Tacy now the two of them would hardly be out of sight from the farmhouse.

'Tell Tacy not to be too long. With Johanna away she'll need to clean out the pigs, as well as tending to the cow.'

Rip saw the approach of Pilgrim before Tacy did. It was not until the dog began barking that she looked in Pilgrim's direction, shielding her eyes with her hand against the sun.

Pilgrim waved to her. Tacy's return greeting was a decidedly perfunctory gesture and he remembered Billy's words.

'Hello! It's such a fine morning I thought I'd take a walk over here to see you and your farm.'

'You've chosen a bad day,' replied Tacy. There was little enthusiasm in her voice. 'Pa and Johanna are at the prison market and I have a lot to do.'

'Then I've probably chosen a *good* day. I can make myself useful and help you.'

Pilgrim was puzzled by Tacy's attitude towards him. She had always seemed to be prepared to go out of her way in order to see him. Only yesterday she had waited for him upon his release from the prison.

Yet today she was behaving in a decidedly off-hand manner. He suddenly remembered her mother's message and passed it on.

'In that case, if you're serious about helping me you could make a start on cleaning out the pigs.'

It was not what Pilgrim had in mind when making his offer of help. He had expected they would be working together, but he said, 'All right. Where will I find all the things I need?'

Now it was Tacy's turn to be taken by surprise.

After she had explained where everything was kept, she watched him walking back to the farm and felt increasingly guilty. She had thought he would object to carrying out such a menial task, yet he had raised no objections whatsoever.

As she had done so many times during the past twenty-four hours, she wished he was an ordinary man and not a gentleman . . .

27

Pilgrim hardly had the appearance of a gentleman when Tacy returned to the farm, half an hour later. His smart uniform coat was now hanging behind the kitchen door in the farmhouse. In its place he was wearing an old smock, over a pair of well-patched corduroy breeches. Both items of clothing belonged to her father.

He was also perspiring heavily, but the pigsty was cleaner than Tacy had ever seen it.

'You've got some fine hogs here,' Pilgrim said, gesturing towards the old sow and her piglets. 'They're as strong and healthy as any I've seen at home.'

'I didn't mean for you to clean out the sty on your own,' said Tacy guiltily. 'I was on my way to give you a hand when the sheep broke out of the pen. I had to gather them up again.'

'It's all right, I enjoyed the work,' said Pilgrim truthfully. 'Once the old sow realised I wasn't going to hurt her family, we got along fine. Mind you, it took a while to convince your mother I was serious about cleaning them out.'

Tacy knew her mother would have something to say to her about it later, but Pilgrim was talking again.

'I've just about finished here. What needs doing next?'

'There's a whole lot of junk to be cleaned out of the old cowshed,' said Tacy. 'Your people up at the prison have asked if we can supply them with more milk, so we've two more cows and a calf being brought over here this afternoon . . . But it's something I can do any old time. You've done enough work for one day. More than enough.'

'We can do it together,' declared Pilgrim. 'And we can talk while we work. That's really why I've come over here today. So I can talk to you.'

The idea appealed to Tacy and they walked across the farmyard together, watched by Joan Elford through the kitchen window.

The farmer's wife had taken an instant liking to Pilgrim. He had a ready smile and possessed none of the 'airs and graces' she associated with gentlemen. He had been perfectly ready to wear old clothes that even her husband objected to wearing. Nevertheless, she still had deep reservations about his friendship with Tacy. The girl was more fond of him than was good for her. Joan was firmly convinced it was a friendship that would bring nothing but heartache for her daughter.

If Tacy still nurtured any doubts about Pilgrim's ability to sustain hard, physical work because he was a 'gentleman', they were quickly dispelled when they began clearing out the old cowshed together.

She was used to working hard on the moorland farm, but she found it difficult to maintain the pace he set.

As they worked, Pilgrim chattered away happily and Tacy discovered she was enjoying his company even more than she had imagined.

Yet again she found herself wishing his family circumstances were more similar to her own.

Such thoughts made her quieter and more withdrawn than she would otherwise have been. After they had been working together for some time, Pilgrim suddenly stopped work.

'Have I done something to upset you, Tacy?'

Startled, Tacy replied, 'You're helping me with my work. Why should that upset me?'

'I don't necessarily mean today – although you haven't said very much to me . . . not that we've spent enough time together for me to know how you usually behave! But on my way to the farm today I met someone named Billy. He wasn't pleased when he learned I was coming here. He seemed to think I'd made you unhappy yesterday. He warned me not to do the same again.'

Tacy managed a self-conscious laugh. 'You don't want to take any notice of anything Billy says, but he's quite harmless. He wouldn't hurt a fly, really.'

'He thinks the world of you.'

'Billy's grateful to anyone who's kind to him,' said Tacy.

'So nothing I said or did yesterday made you unhappy,' Pilgrim persisted.

'Of course not!' Tacy lied. 'We weren't together for very long, were we?'

'I couldn't think of anything, but it had me worried for a while. As you say, Billy's a little simple. He probably imagined it.'

Setting to work again he said, 'Right, let's get this finished off then we'll see what else needs to be done.'

Pilgrim continued chatting quite freely to Tacy and they worked together happily until soon after noon. At this time Joan came to the cowshed to fetch them both back to the farmhouse.

As they entered the kitchen together, Billy came into the farmyard. Tacy's mother called to him, 'You're just in time, Billy. We're going in for something to eat.'

For a moment it seemed Billy had not heard her; he was staring at Pilgrim in disbelief. 'You . . . you're the American! You been working?'

'That's right, Billy,' Pilgrim smiled at him. 'I've been cleaning out the hogs and helping Tacy get the cowshed ready for the new cows the Elfords are buying.'

When Billy looked from Pilgrim to Tacy and her mother there was a bewildered and hurt expression on his face. 'But . . . *I* was going to help you clear the cowshed, Tacy. You said I could.'

'Did I? I'm sorry, Billy. I forgot.'

'You *promised*, Tacy. You know I like helping you do things.'

'There'll be lots of other things for you to do, Billy,' said Joan, in an attempt to soothe Billy's hurt feelings. 'More than you can manage, no doubt. Come inside and have something to eat now.'

'No! She promised . . .'

Suddenly and unexpectedly, Billy turned about and ran from the farmyard, ignoring the calls of Joan and Tacy to come back.

'Oh dear! Poor Billy. I've never seen him so upset,' said Joan, deeply concerned. 'It isn't like him to behave this way.'

'I'll go and bring him back,' said Tacy.

'You'll never catch him,' said Pilgrim, looking after the running figure of Billy.

'Yes I will.'

Tacy pointed to the top of the rock-strewn tor behind the sheep pen. 'He'll be up there. Ever since he was a young boy he's gone there when something's happened to make him unhappy.'

'Then let me go and find him,' said Pilgrim. 'I'll bring him back.'

'He won't come for you,' declared Tacy.

'I think he will,' said Pilgrim confidently. 'Anyway, I'd like to try.'

As he hurried towards the farmyard gate, Tacy went to follow him, but her mother reached out and gripped her shoulder. 'Let him go, Tacy. I think he understands what's upsetting Billy. It's right for him to go.'

28

Pilgrim soon discovered that the smock he wore was more suited to working in a farmyard than climbing a Dartmoor tor. However, he persevered and was soon approaching the summit of the hill.

The granite boulders here were much larger than they had appeared to be from the farmyard.

He thought he might have difficulty locating the unhappy young man. Then he rounded a piece of broken granite more than twice his own height and here he found Billy. He was seated with his back to another giant rock and was desperately unhappy, as was evident by the tears running down his cheeks.

He made a feeble attempt to cuff them away as Pilgrim approached. Billy was aware of Pilgrim's presence but, without looking up, he drew up his knees, rested his forehead upon them and wrapped his arms about his head.

Pilgrim sat down beside him and felt the coarse granite rock warm against his back.

'I seem to be making a habit of upsetting people just

lately, Billy. Tacy yesterday and now you today. I'm sorry, I truly am.'

'Go away.'

Billy did not raise his head from his knees and the words were muffled.

'I'll go away in a few minutes, Billy, but there are a couple of things I want to say first in a man-to-man talk, with just the two of us here.'

Billy made no reply, but Pilgrim knew he was listening.

'First of all, why do you work for the Elfords? Do they pay you well?'

The question was so unexpected, Billy raised his head and gave Pilgrim a puffy-eyed glare.

'I wouldn't take money from them,' he declared indignantly. 'They feed me and let me take as much peat home as we need. I work for them because they're kind to me, and I like them. I like Tacy, especially.'

'I can't think of any better reason for working for anyone, Billy. They appreciate your help too, they've told me so. With Mr Elford not being so well they've come to rely on you. You're very important to them. I couldn't take your place – and I certainly don't want to.'

'Then why did you help Tacy clear out the cowshed today, when she said I could do it?'

Billy's question was still resentful, but the belligerence had gone.

'For the same reasons you help them, Billy. Because Tacy's been kind to me. She brought Sir Thomas to the prison and had me released from the punishment cell. She brought cakes to the prison when I had no money to pay for them, and she came to see me in the prison hospital when I'd been hurt.'

Pilgrim had Billy's full attention now. 'I want to repay Tacy for her kindness – just as you do. Like you, the only way I can think of to do that is to help her and the Elford family on the farm.'

Pilgrim eased his back off the hard rock. 'There'll never be any question of me taking your place, Billy. You'll be here long after this war is over and I've gone back to America. Tacy and her family *need* you. I don't want to do anything to upset them, or you either, but I'd like to do as much as I can to help during the time I'm here. Far from taking over what you do about the farm, I believe that together we can do a whole lot more to help them. You'll know of some of the things they might have always wanted to do, but couldn't because there was neither the time nor enough hands to do it. Is there anything particular you can think of right now?'

Billy had been concentrating very hard on what Pilgrim was saying. He frowned now as he tried to think.

Suddenly his expression lightened. 'They could do with having the wall built up properly around the big sheep pen. They can't put sheep in there any more because they keep getting out. Then there's that old tumbledown barn in the corner of the yard. Tacy's always said if it was rebuilt they could keep more calves – or perhaps a lot more chickens.'

'There you are, Billy. If you and me work hard during the time I'm here we could do all those things and make Tacy and her family *really* happy. It'd make me happy too. When the time comes for me to go home to America I'd leave with the knowledge that I'd been able to do something lasting to repay their kindness. Not only that, whenever you looked at what we'd done together you could feel proud because it was your idea and resulted from us working together.'

Pilgrim could see by Billy's expression that he had won, but he added, 'What do you say, Billy? Shall we work together and do all we can to make this the best farm on the moor for the Elfords? We can do it, you and I.'

Fired with Pilgrim's enthusiasm, Billy climbed to his feet and nodded his head vigorously, his earlier unhappiness dispelled. 'Yes . . . and we could dam up that old stream and make a pond for them . . . and repair the roof on the long barn. I'd have time to cut more turf too. They could sell it all at the prison and make a lot more money.'

'There you are, Billy. With all the ideas you have, there's no end to the things we can do together for the Elfords. That's if you don't mind having me around to work with you, of course.'

'I'd like it. I expect I can think of a lot more things too.'

'I don't doubt it, Billy.' Pilgrim smiled at his companion and there was a genuine warmth in the expression. 'Shall we go back to the farm together now?'

Billy hesitated and Pilgrim realised he probably felt embarrassed because of the manner in which he had left the farm.

'I . . . I don't know if I'll have time to have anything to eat today. I promised I'd go and fetch the two cows and a calf from Mr Pearce's farm. It's quite a way from here.'

'I'll tell you what then, Billy. You go and fetch the cows while I go back to the farm and ask Mrs Elford to keep something for when you get back. But won't you need one of the dogs to help you?'

Billy grinned happily. 'You don't need to worry about that. I just have to give my special whistle and old Rosie'll come running to me. Rip'll come too, I expect.'

'Then I'll get on back to the farm and tell them what you're doing. They'll be worrying about you. I'm glad we've had our talk, Billy. I look forward to working with you and doing as much as can be done for Tacy and her family. They're good folk.'

'I'm glad too, Mr Pilgrim. Nobody's ever spoken to me about things the way you have – except Tacy, sometimes. We'll make it the best farm anywhere. Tacy'll be happy then.'

The two young men shook hands for the second time that day.

As Pilgrim walked back to the house, he heard a shrill whistle, repeated three or four times. Then he saw the two farm dogs running along the valley, making for the now unseen, but very happy, Billy.

29

Tacy and her mother were concerned when they saw Pilgrim returning from the tor alone and he had difficulty assuring them that Billy was no longer unhappy.

'He was very upset when he ran off,' said Joan.

'Well, he's perfectly happy now,' said Pilgrim. 'He's taken the dogs with him and gone to fetch the cows and the calf you've bought.'

Joan was still dubious. 'Billy usually takes days – weeks even – to recover from the sort of upset he's had today.'

'Not this time,' said Pilgrim confidently. 'He's gone off thinking of all the things he's always wanted to do for you and will be able to do now he's got some help.'

'That's all very well for now,' said the farmer's wife. 'But what happens when he realises there's going to be no miracle – that Roundtor Farm won't change overnight to being a gentleman's farm? We need to work hard here to survive. There isn't the time, or money, to do all the things that need doing, and you won't be around for ever. The war between our countries could end any day. When it does you'll go home and that'll be the end of all these plans you have for Roundtor.'

Joan was being deliberately blunt and pessimistic. She had seen Tacy's barely concealed delight when Pilgrim was talking of spending time working with Billy at Roundtor Farm. It was not only Billy who seemed to think this young American was the saviour for whom the farm had been waiting.

'Billy realises I might not be around to see all our plans made good. But he and I agreed that together we'd do all we could in the time I have here. Somehow I think that's likely to be a year or two, at the very least.'

'That's as maybe,' retorted Joan, unreasonably disturbed by his words. 'All the same, you'll not be working every day of the week, month in and month out at Roundtor. Sir Thomas will expect you to spend some time with him and his friends, at Tor Royal.'

'I certainly owe it to Sir Thomas to fall in with his wishes,' agreed Pilgrim patiently. 'But I understand he spends much of his time in London. Working here will help keep me out of mischief while he's away. I might even be able to persuade Captain Howard to come and give a hand occasionally.'

Pilgrim was a little puzzled by Joan Elford's lack of enthusiasm for the suggestion that he and Billy should work to improve Roundtor Farm. 'Perhaps I'm being a little presumptuous. You might not want me to come here quite so often?'

Joan realised she had been less than gracious in her response to Pilgrim's offer of help. She felt suddenly guilty. 'It isn't that . . . You can come to Roundtor as often as you like.' The words were accompanied by an apologetic smile. 'But you mustn't think you have to work whenever you come calling. We get by, especially now we have a market for our cakes up at the prison.'

Whatever happens on the farm, we'll still have money coming in. All the same, we're glad of any help we can get. If you actually *enjoy* farm work we'll be grateful to you for helping out.'

Tacy was relieved at her mother's conciliatory words. She had listened with increasing alarm to her apparent determination to put Pilgrim off coming to Roundtor and helping on the farm.

Further discussion was brought to an unexpected halt by a woman's voice. It came from somewhere beyond the farmyard gate and was calling Pilgrim's name.

Peering through the kitchen window, Pilgrim said, 'That's Sir Thomas's niece, Sophie. What can she want? I'd better go and find out.'

He hurried from the kitchen, leaving Tacy and her mother standing in the doorway, looking after him. The two Roundtor women were witness to Sophie's peal of laughter when she saw him.

'Pilgrim! What on earth are you doing in that ridiculous garb?'

Sophie spoke loudly, apparently unaware that the two women were standing in the farmhouse doorway and able to hear all she was saying.

'Are you taking part in a masquerade?'

'I'm wearing clothes that are eminently practical for farm work,' retorted Pilgrim. 'But I don't imagine you've ridden all the way here from Tor Royal to discuss how I'm dressed.'

'No – although those clothes are certainly worthy of comment. A message arrived at Tor Royal from the prison. An agent has arrived there to talk about aid from the American Government for your countrymen. Virgil thought you should both be there to hear what he has to say. He's already gone on ahead.'

'I'll go straight there,' said Pilgrim.

'Will you please wear your smock back to Tor Royal afterwards – and those breeches, of course. It would cause great merriment.'

Ignoring her taunts, Pilgrim said, 'I'll go to the farmhouse to change, before going to the prison.'

'We'll go there together. Then I'll ride back to Tor Royal and tell them you won't be back for lunch. But I still think you should remain in those clothes. They must be in need of some amusement at the prison.'

When Pilgrim returned to the farm kitchen, he told Tacy and her mother that he had to leave.

'Oh?' said Tacy icily. 'Has Sir Thomas's niece come to tell you that you shouldn't be spending the day on a farm and must return home now like an obedient boy?'

Pilgrim looked at Tacy sharply. Her earlier iciness had thawed while they were working together in the cowshed. It seemed to have returned with increased intensity.

'Sophie's called to say Virgil and I are needed at the prison. The United States agent has arrived to tell the men of our Government's plans to help us while we're here.'

'Then you'd better go, and not keep her waiting, hadn't you? No doubt *she'll* go with you, to keep you company.'

'Possibly, but I doubt if she'll be allowed inside the prison, as you are.'

Puzzled by Tacy's sudden swings of temperament, Pilgrim asked, 'Will it still be all right for me to come here again, when I can?'

Tacy shrugged her shoulders. 'That's up to you, I'm sure. No doubt you have lots of other things to occupy your time.'

'Of course it will be all right,' said Joan Elford unexpectedly, her sympathy suddenly going out to the perplexed young man standing before her. 'Come as often as you wish.'

As Pilgrim set off for Tor Royal, walking beside Sophie's horse, Tacy's unhappiness was so apparent that her mother put an arm about her shoulders and squeezed affectionately.

'I think this has brought the situation home to you far more clearly than any words of mine might. He's a nice young man, Tacy. A rather special young man who's very far from home. But don't allow yourself to care too much for him. He belongs with the likes of Sir Thomas Tyrwhitt and those who visit Tor Royal, not here, at Roundtor.'

When Tacy made no reply, she added, 'I don't doubt he means well, but helping on a farm is no more than an amusing pastime for him. He's no need to work anywhere. One day he'll tire of it and we'll see no more of him.'

30

On the way to Dartmoor prison, Sophie questioned Pilgrim closely about the family at Roundtor Farm. She was particularly interested in Tacy and the manner in which they had first met. He added that had it not been for her he would probably never have met with Sir Thomas and been paroled to Tor Royal.

'It's a very good reason to be grateful, certainly,' agreed Sophie. 'But her family has gained from it too. It would seem they now have a very lucrative business selling their wares at the prison market. There's no reason at all for you to spend time on their farm, dressed as a peasant and performing menial tasks for them. It's demeaning, Pilgrim. What would your family think?'

'I don't think the Elford family see farm work as demeaning. Neither do I. There's nothing wrong with physical work. My father is a congressman now, but when we first settled in Ohio he cleared the land and built our first cabin with just me to help him.'

'That was different. He wasn't just building a cabin,

he was helping to build a whole new country. Now he's a leader of that country.'

Pilgrim realised he would be wasting his time if he tried to explain the American way of life to Sophie. She would not understand. She had been brought up to accept without question that birth and not ability dictated the place of a man in society.

He led the conversation away from Roundtor Farm and they spoke of less controversial subjects for the remainder of the journey to Dartmoor prison.

Virgil was waiting for Pilgrim in the governor's office. Together they were escorted to Block Four, where they met up with the United States agent.

Both men found Reuben G. Beasley a disappointment. He was already talking to the American prisoners-of-war, including those from the Petty Officers' Block, when they arrived there – and he was being given a difficult time.

As they entered the building an angry howl had just escaped from the throats of the assembled men. The noise increased when the Americans saw the two marines officers.

'What's going on?' Virgil shouted the question to Ephraim above the din. The marines sergeant had come across the room to meet them.

'Beasley's come to Dartmoor with nothing more than talk to offer the men right now – and very little more in the future, if you ask me.'

'Then why *is* he here?' Pilgrim asked.

Ephraim shrugged. 'Probably to justify the fat fee our Government's paying him to take care of our interests. Whatever the reason, it seems there's nothing coming our way just yet.'

'Well, we're not going to get anywhere in here with

this din going on. I'll see if the governor will let Lieutenant Penn and me use his office to have a chat with Beasley. We might be able to get some sense out of him there.'

Calming the men with difficulty, Virgil told them what he intended doing. He promised he would let them know the result of his talks. Then, much to the perspiring agent's relief, the three men were escorted from the block, followed by a number of the frustrated prisoners-of-war and the jeers of the remainder.

Before they left the yard, Ephraim caught up with them and spoke to the frightened agent. 'This money that's supposed to be coming to American prisoners-of-war . . . is it just for the army and navy men?'

'No,' replied Beasley, 'it's to be granted to every United States citizen who's been taken prisoner by the British.'

'Whether they're black or white?'

As the agent hesitated, Virgil said firmly, 'It will go to everyone who is being kept in here because he's an American citizen, Ephraim. I'll make out a list of names and have it sent to Mr Beasley. No one will be left out.'

'That wasn't what was being argued before you arrived, Cap'n. Steiger was in there saying none of the Government money should go to anyone who's believed to be a slave. He said it would make them "uppity". Them's his words, Cap'n Howard, not mine.'

'And I stand by them . . .'

Virgil had not realised that Conrad Steiger had walked from the Block Four building behind him. '. . . Give a nigger money to make him independent and he'll think he's as good as us. It's a bad precedent. It might mean nothing to you men from the north, but those of us who are from the south will one day have to deal with the trouble you stir up.'

'I'll make a note of that, Mr Steiger,' said Agent Beasley.

'No you won't,' said Virgil firmly. '*I'll* make out the list of who is to receive our Government's money. Every American in this prison will receive an equal share, whether he's black or white.'

Ephraim acknowledged Virgil's words, but said, 'The men trust you, Cap'n Howard, but Mr Steiger won't take this lying down. If we're to stay clear of trouble in here you're going to have to do something about him. If you don't, some of us surely will.'

'You heard that, Howard! That was an out-and-out threat. The governor should be told about this . . .'

'It's quite likely he will, Steiger. Unfortunately, if he does you're likely to be the loser. I hear you're applying for parole? You won't get it if word reaches the governor's ears that you're a troublemaker. I suggest you make your way back to the Petty Officers' Block right now and leave me to deal with what needs doing here.'

Surrounded by some of his southern friends, Conrad Steiger made his way to the gate leading from the Block Four compound. He was not a happy man, but he *had* applied for parole. He did not want anything to spoil his chances of leaving the prison. He would say nothing more – for now.

'Steiger's the worst of the southern men here, but there's a great many men who feel the same way as he does, Cap'n. They're beginning to push us just a little too hard.'

'Keep things under control, Ephraim. Trouble will help no one, least of all you and your people.'

Ephraim shrugged. 'We were born to trouble, Cap'n. If we don't find it, as sure as there's a heaven and a hell it'll find us.'

'You can handle it, Ephraim. Just don't go looking for it, that's all I ask.'

'I hear you, Cap'n. For all our sakes I hope you'll say the same thing to Steiger.'

In the governor's office, Reuben G. Beasley showed Virgil and Pilgrim the correspondence he had received from the United States Government. They had promised to make an allowance to the prisoners-of-war of one and a half pence a day.

'So far, promises are all I have,' complained the unhappy agent. 'I tried to explain this to your men, but they wouldn't listen. They blame me for not coming up with money for them.'

'I can understand their point of view,' said Virgil. 'They're desperate for money. They have no comforts whatsoever. Can't you use these letters to borrow money for them?'

Reuben Beasley spread his hands wide in a gesture of helplessness. 'No one's likely to loan money without charging interest.'

'How much interest do you think they would want?' asked Virgil.

'I haven't asked anyone,' admitted the agent. 'After all, who would want to loan money to the men of an enemy country?'

'This war won't last for ever,' retorted Virgil. 'The written authority of the United States Government should be enough for any bank, or wherever else you go to borrow the money.'

Reuben Beasley looked unhappy, 'I'm sorry but I can't commit the United States Government to repaying a loan.'

'Of course you can. You can. You've been appointed our agent here – and you're in possession of letters showing our Government's intent to pay money to the prisoners.'

'Yes . . . but not to pay interest on a loan.'

'Dammit, man! The men you're supposed to be taking care of don't have a cent between them. To pay every American in here a month's allowance wouldn't take much more than a hundred English pounds. If you feel you can't stand security for such an amount then let me do it. Our Government's not going to quibble over a few pounds of interest.'

'If they do then *I'll* pay it,' said Pilgrim. 'As Captain Howard says, stop making excuses and get some money for the men.'

Turning to the prison governor who had been seated at his desk listening to the discussion without saying anything, Pilgrim said, 'You'll witness my agreement to this, Governor Cotgrave?'

Governor Cotgrave nodded his head, still without speaking. This was something he wanted no part of. Possession of money by prisoners was a two-edged sword. Some would use it to buy a few small luxuries and be more content with their lot. Others would become involved in the type of gambling which had reduced some of the French prisoners to the level of animals.

The men confined to the upper levels of Block Four were reduced to scavenging for their very existence. Those who proved less successful than their fellows at such means of survival quickly became so emaciated they succumbed to the first minor ailment that came their way.

'Well . . . as long as you're prepared to accept full responsibility for any interest charged . . .' Beasley was still reluctant to support the idea.

'Governor Cotgrave, do you have pen and paper, please?'

When the governor pushed the items across his desk, Pilgrim picked up the pen and acknowledged in writing his responsibility for whatever interest would be charged on a loan up to the amount of two hundred pounds.

When it was written, he passed the paper to the American agent, saying, 'There! Now you have no excuse whatsoever for not providing at least a single month's allowance to the prisoners here. I expect you to produce the payment within days, Mr Beasley, you understand?'

Looking pained, Reuben G. Beasley said, 'I'll do my best, Lieutenant Penn, but our Government has been extremely tardy, to say the least. I have even been forced to pay my own fare from London.'

31

That night it began to rain. It rained with a ferocity unimaginable to anyone who did not live on Dartmoor. All across the moor an intricate skein of streams carried the water to a hundred small rivers and the rivers became raging torrents.

To Pilgrim, looking out from a sitting room window at Tor Royal, it seemed as though God must have decided to send another unheralded deluge to cover the face of the earth.

'Have you ever experienced rain like this in America?'

Sophie had entered the room silently and she came to stand beside Pilgrim at the window.

He shook his head. 'I once saw rain like it during a hurricane in Florida, but it didn't last all that long. Is it often like this here?'

'I've never known rain quite like this before, but Dartmoor weather is often more extreme than it is anywhere else, whether it's rain, wind or snow.'

She gave him a sidelong glance. 'You won't be able to visit your farmer's daughter in this.'

'No . . . and it looks as though it will continue for a month!'

'I sincerely hope not,' Sophie spoke with considerable feeling. 'I want it to be fine by this weekend.'

Something in her voice caused Pilgrim to turn and look at her. 'Is something special happening then?'

'No! No, nothing's happening. Nothing at all. It's just . . . well, weekends are special somehow, aren't they?' Sophie seemed inexplicably flustered, but she was saved from further embarrassment by Virgil.

Putting in an appearance at the doorway, he called, 'Sir Thomas has suggested we have a game or two of cards as the weather precludes anything else.'

'You go,' Sophie said to Pilgrim. 'I'm not fond of cards. I shall take one of Uncle's books to my room and read for a while.'

When Pilgrim explained Sophie's absence to her mother and Sir Thomas, it brought a comment from the landowner that he thought she had looked somewhat pale and drawn that morning. He hoped the sudden change in the weather had not brought on a chill.

'It's more likely to be the letter she received yesterday evening from one of her London friends,' replied his sister. 'I expect it told her all that is going on in the capital and she is wishing herself back there.'

'That's a fairly healthy state of mind,' said Sir Thomas. 'She's a high-spirited girl and there's not a great deal of social life here.'

'Sophie is twenty-one years of age. It's high time she found herself a suitable husband and settled down,' retorted Winifrith. 'But where marriage is concerned she is not set a very good example by *some* members of her own family.' She glared pointedly at Sir Thomas.

'Quite! Shall we cut the cards for who is going to deal? I think you and I should be partners, Winifrith, against

Virgil and Pilgrim. We will make it an international contest . . .'

By the end of the second day of rain, everyone in the house was beginning to get on each other's nerves. Sophie, especially, appeared to find being confined to the house particularly irksome. She was irritable with everyone.

On the third morning the household awoke to discover the rain had ceased. However, it had been replaced by a dense mist. On the moor it was impossible to see anyone at a distance of more than three paces.

Despite this, Pilgrim found it a welcome relief to be able to get out of the house, even though a visit to Roundtor Farm was out of the question until the mist thinned considerably.

While Virgil wrote letters and Sir Thomas was out with the Tor Royal head gardener, assessing the extent of the damage caused by the rain, Pilgrim made his way to the stables. He thought he might check on the progress of the foal.

To his surprise, he found Sophie there, grooming her own horse.

'It's something to do,' she explained. 'Another day in the house with my mother would drive me mad.'

Pilgrim smiled sympathetically. 'I must admit, the house seems somewhat smaller after being inside for a couple of days.'

Sophie was silent for a few moments. Thinking she probably wanted to be on her own for a while, Pilgrim begain to walk towards the stall where the foal was kept.

'Don't go, Pilgrim. Stay here and talk to me for a while.'

When Pilgrim returned, Sophie was silent for a few

more moments, then she said, 'Do parents in America control the lives of their children to the same extent as they do in England?'

'I'm not sure I know just how much control they have here. In America it depends pretty much on the family, I guess – and whether you're a son or a daughter. Were you thinking of anything specific?'

'Oh, you know,' said Sophie vaguely. 'Deciding who you can, or cannot marry. That sort of thing.'

'In some American families it still matters, I suppose,' replied Pilgrim thoughtfully, 'but that's among the more wealthy families in the east. Virgil will know more about that than I do. Further west folk tend to grow up more quickly and make up their own minds about most things, including marriage.'

Pilgrim thought he knew why she was asking the question and he sympathised with her. 'But I guess things are different here?'

'I don't see why they should be!' said Sophie angrily. 'I don't see why anyone should decide about something that's going to affect the whole of someone else's life.'

When Pilgrim made no reply, she said with slightly less passion, 'Would your parents try to stop you if you wanted to marry someone they thought was not suitable? That young girl at Roundtor Farm, for instance?'

Her question took Pilgrim by surprise. 'Tacy? I hardly know her well enough to have thoughts about anything as serious as marriage!'

'Well, suppose you had, would they object?'

Pilgrim thought seriously about the possible implications of his reply. He decided to give her a truthful answer – but only as it applied to him.

'I think my pa would say I'm as much of a man as I'm ever likely to be and can make up my own mind. Ma would probably say I'm too young to marry anyway. But if she felt it was to the girl I really wanted she wouldn't stand in my way.'

He looked at her apologetically. 'That doesn't help you a lot, does it?'

Sophie seemed about to say something, but changed her mind. She shrugged. 'I suppose it confirms what I've known all along, really. The only person who can make up my mind about it all – is me.'

'You're not thinking of doing something silly, are you, Sophie?'

'Silly? Silly for whom, Pilgrim? For me? My mother – or for everyone else?'

At that moment there was the sound of the door being opened and Winifrith entered the stables. She looked from Pilgrim to her daughter suspiciously.

'One of the servants told me I would find you here, Sophie. Had I realised Lieutenant Penn was with you I would have come here earlier.'

Addressing Pilgrim, she said icily, 'Such things probably don't matter in your country, Lieutenant Penn, but in England a young woman is at grave risk of being compromised if she is taken off by a man, away from the company of others. It's something no *gentleman* would think of doing.'

'Mother! You really have surpassed yourself this time. Pilgrim took me nowhere. I was here grooming my horse when he came to check on the foal.'

Unabashed, Winifrith said, 'It doesn't matter how you both arrived here. You are in the stables together. An *English* gentleman would have apologised and left immediately.'

'Had he been an *observant* English gentleman, Mrs Cudmore, he would no doubt have noticed the stable-hand just two stalls along from here, as I did.'

The stablehand had been mucking out a nearby stall

and had heard every word of the exchange. He stood up now and grinned in Pilgrim's direction.

'I think you owe Pilgrim an apology,' said Sophie to her mother.

Carefully avoiding looking at Pilgrim, Winifrith said, 'No mother need apologise for trying to protect the good name of her daughter – and I'm sure I don't know why it is necessary for you to groom your own horse. Sir Thomas employs stablehands to do that – and not to skulk around eavesdropping.'

The stablehand hastily ducked from view and Winifrith said, 'I shall expect to see you back in the house within fifteen minutes, Sophie. If you have not returned by then I shall come looking for you once more.'

With this, she turned about and made her way to the stable door. Opening it, she stepped outside into the mist which swirled in around her.

'Since my mother refuses to apologise then I must do it for her,' said Sophie unhappily. 'It's the second time it has happened. She did the same thing when I took a walk with Virgil. I am truly sorry, Pilgrim.'

'You can't take the blame for your mother's behaviour,' said Pilgrim. 'Anyway, as she said, no mother can be blamed for trying to protect her daughter.'

'Protect? No, Pilgrim, *humiliate* is a more accurate word. She *enjoys* humiliating me.'

Sophie began vigorously brushing the startled horse. 'God! I shall be glad to be rid of her!'

They were words Pilgrim would remember.

32

Not until Sunday morning did the heavy mist disappear from Dartmoor. But Pilgrim was unable to visit Roundtor Farm. He, Virgil, Sir Thomas, Winifrith and Sophie were to attend a service at Sheepstor church. They would then spend the remainder of the day at the vicarage with the Reverend Cotterell and his family.

At the very last moment, Sophie complained of a headache. She announced she would remain at Tor Royal and not go with the others to Sheepstor.

'This is very tiresome of you, Sophie,' complained her mother. 'Could you not have mentioned it earlier?'

'Mother, I do not choose when to have a headache. It just happens. I think I shall go to my room and remain there for a while.'

'Then I'll stay home with you,' declared her mother.

'That's the very *last* thing I want!' said Sophie heatedly. 'You would be coming up to my room every five minutes, demanding to know how I was. I would have no rest at all. If you go to Sheepstor with the others I have no doubt I will recover in half the time.'

'Well! That's all the thanks I'm given for caring about my daughter,' said Winifrith, to everyone in general. 'But I realised long ago that the young people of today do not recognise the values we were taught as being important. So be it. Come, Thomas, we must not keep Reverend Cotterell waiting.'

As Winifrith led the way from the room, Pilgrim spoke quietly to Sophie. 'Are you really going to be all right?'

She nodded. 'Yes – but thank you for caring, Pilgrim. You and Virgil. Thank you for everything.'

Her words disturbed Pilgrim. They sounded somehow as though they were a farewell. He thought about it for a long time. However, by the time the party reached Sheepstor, he had convinced himself he was worrying unnecessarily. Everyone had been closeted in Tor Royal for far too long during the period of rain and mist.

Sophie and her mother, in particular, had found it difficult. Both were basically city dwellers. They found the limitations of country life irksome. A day spent apart from each other would be good for both of them.

The visit to Sheepstor lasted much longer than anyone could have anticipated.

After the morning service and a very pleasant day at the vicarage, the party attended Evensong. When this service was over they intended returning to Tor Royal.

However, when they left the church, the mist had descended once again. It was extremely dense and they discussed whether or not it would be safe to undertake the journey across the moor.

Even as they talked, the mist was becoming thicker. It was hardly possible to see one's hand when held at arm's length.

Eventually, it was decided the Tor Royal party would have to spend the night at the vicarage.

Winifrith expressed her concern for Sophie, but Sir Thomas assured her she would be all right at Tor Royal with the servants to take care of her.

Winifrith looked squarely at Pilgrim when she said, 'Yes, of course she will. There is no one there to take advantage of her.'

Pilgrim thought it would be a relief for Sophie to be free of her mother for a few more hours.

The mist had not entirely dispersed when the party left the Sheepstor vicarage the next morning, but it had thinned to such an extent it no longer posed a danger to moorland travellers.

It was a happy party that travelled home. Only Winifreth was particularly quiet. Pilgrim believed, somewhat ungenerously, that her lack of conversation was due in part to the large quantity of port she had consumed during the previous evening.

When the carriage came to a halt before the main entrance to Tor Royal, the party was helped to the ground by a footman and greeted at the door by the butler.

'Good morning, Sir Thomas, Mrs Cudmore; gentlemen. We are all happy to see you safely back at Tor Royal. The staff were concerned last night that you might have tried to journey back though the mist. I assured them you would decide to remain at Sheepstor.'

The butler looked past them before adding, 'Will Miss Sophie be returning later, Sir Thomas?'

Winifrith looked at him sharply. 'What do you mean, "returning later"? Isn't she in the house?'

The butler seemed confused by the question. 'No, madam. She left the house soon after you, yesterday.

She said her headache was better and she had decided to go to Sheepstor after all. She went on her horse – and took two saddlebags of clothes with her. She said they were for Miss Jemima to distribute to the poor women of Sheepstor village.'

'Took clothes . . . ? Let me through!'

Winifrith pushed past the others and hurried through the hallway to the stairs.

'What do you think can have happened to Sophie?' Virgil put the question to Pilgrim, as Sir Thomas hurried after his sister.

'I believe she's probably had as much of her mother as she can take. It's my opinion she's gone off to make a life for herself.'

Pilgrim told Virgil of the conversations he had held with Sir Thomas's niece.

'She's spoken to me in a similar vein,' admitted Virgil. 'Do you think we ought to tell her mother?'

'No,' said Pilgrim firmly. 'Whatever she's doing, Sophie has thought it all out and made her plans accordingly. We'd be wrong to interfere in any way.'

A few minutes later, Sir Thomas came down the stairs. He was mopping his brow and appeared harassed.

'The girl's gone,' he said. 'Packed her personal belongings and a few clothes, and taken off bound for God-knows-where. Her mother's having a fit of hysterics in her room.'

Tucking the handkerchief inside his sleeve, a fleeting smile crossed his face. 'Who'd have thought young Sophie had the nerve to do such a thing? Mind you, I don't really blame the girl. I can't imagine anything worse than the thought of spending the foreseeable future in the company of Winifrith.'

'What will Mrs Cudmore do now?'

'She seems to think Sophie has run off to London to

stay with one of her friends there. We'll be taking the carriage and setting off after her this afternoon. It will mean leaving you both on your own, of course, but no doubt you'll be able to find plenty to keep you occupied.'

Sir Thomas gave them a benevolent smile. 'You both seemed to get along well with the Cotterells and their charming daughter. You're welcome to take one of the horses whenever you feel like paying a call on them.'

Sir Thomas waved Virgil's protest aside before it was even uttered. 'Yes, I know all about the terms of your parole. I'll write a letter stating you are travelling beyond the limits of your parole area with my express permission. That should be sufficient to keep you out of trouble, I think.'

The handkerchief came into play once more. 'Now, if you will excuse me, I must arrange to have the carriage made ready and my clothes packed.'

He shook his head. 'The more I see of other people's children, the happier I am that I never married. I hope you two young gentlemen will take note!'

When Sir Thomas had gone from the room, Virgil said, 'I wish Sophie well. Now, do you have anything planned for the remainder of the day, Pilgrim?'

'I thought I might take a walk to Roundtor this afternoon. Why don't you come with me?'

'I don't think you need my company. I'll keep myself amused here. Go off and meet your young country girl – but remember Sir Thomas's warning. Don't get too serious about her.'

33

As he approached Roundtor, Pilgrim saw Tacy working in the hillside sheep pen with Johanna. The sisters were building up one of the walls.

Tacy saw him approaching. For a moment she seemed pleased to see him, then the expression became one that was less easily read.

'I thought I'd come across to see how you made out during the bad weather,' he said when he was within calling distance.

'We had a flood come down the slope behind the pen,' said Johanna before her sister could reply. 'It washed part of the wall away. We're building it up again now.'

'You're making a very good job of it,' said Pilgrim. 'I'm surprised Billy isn't here to help you.'

'So am I,' said Tacy, 'but perhaps the streams between here and his cottage have risen too high for him to get here. If he doesn't come tomorrow I'll go and find out whether anything is wrong.'

Looking about him across the still sodden moor, Pilgrim asked, 'What happened to your sheep?'

'All the ewes escaped,' said Tacy. 'Ma and Pa are out looking for them. They've found a few and shut them up in the yard, but Pa's not very well, so they can't cover as much ground as they ought to.'

'We've got a leak in the roof of the house too,' said Johanna. 'Water poured into the room where Tacy and me sleep. We've had to move in with Ma and Pa.'

'That's right.' When Tacy spoke, Pilgrim thought she looked tired.

She brushed a long lock of hair back from in front of her face and said, 'The roof's going to have to wait until we've caught all the ewes and can get someone in to work on it. Pa's not fit enough to go clambering around up there.'

Picking up another stone and adding it to those on the freestone wall, Tacy said, 'No doubt you, Sir Thomas's niece and the others have been comfortable enough up at Tor Royal.'

'Well, life hasn't been without incident,' replied Pilgrim, 'but I'll tell you about that some other time. More to the point right now is that I've done a little bit of work on roofs in my time. Do you have anything I can use for new thatch?'

'Loads of it,' replied Tacy. 'But . . . are you sure?' Although she expressed doubt, Tacy was secretly delighted. 'You fix the roof and you'll be Ma's friend for life. She wept when it happened and water poured in.'

'Tell me where I can find the thatch, then you carry on here. I'll borrow the ladder from the barn and make a start. Who knows, I might even have it finished by the time your ma and pa return home.'

The repairs to the thatch were not completely finished

by the time Tom and Joan Elford returned home, but they were well on the way.

In fact, Pilgrim did not fully complete his work until it was almost too dark to see what he was doing.

Climbing down to the ground, he expressed the opinion that the roof was now as good as new. He explained that, in addition to repairing the storm-damaged section of the roof, he had checked out the remainder. He was confident it would withstand any future severe weather.

'God bless you, Pilgrim!' said Joan fervently, calling him by his Christian name for the first time. 'I've been dreading the thought of it raining again and ruining more of the precious things Tom and I have managed to get together over the years. Now, let me cook something for you. It's a meal well-earned, I'd say!'

'Thanks all the same, but I have to be getting back to Tor Royal. The terms of my parole are that I should be indoors an hour before sunset. Not all the servants at the house are happy about us being there. If one decided to report me to Governor Cotgrave at the prison, I would be in trouble.'

'It's very nearly dark now. By the time you reach Tor Royal it's going to be too dark to see your way – and you don't know the moor.' Joan expressed her concern.

'I'll walk back with him.'

Tacy saw the fleeting expression of disapproval on her mother's face and she added, 'I know the moor better than anyone. I'll have Pilgrim at Tor Royal more quickly than anyone else could.'

'It's all right, I'm sure I can find my way,' Pilgrim protested.

'And I'm equally certain you can't,' said Tacy firmly.

'Take Johanna with you,' suggested her mother.

'Oh, Ma! I'm tired. I've been heaving stones all day up in the sheep pen.'

'Come on, Pilgrim, we're wasting time and you're right. A couple of the servants up at Tor Royal have brothers in the navy who might be fighting Americans right now. They wouldn't think twice about reporting you for being out late.'

Tacy's manner brooked no further argument. A few minutes later she and Pilgrim were striding out together across the moor.

There were many stars out, but no moon. They had not gone far before Pilgrim admitted to Tacy that, had she not insisted she come with him, he would probably have become hopelessly lost.

'I know that, and so does Ma. That's why she didn't make any real fuss about me coming with you.'

They walked on in silence for a few moments, then Tacy said, 'Is anyone likely to come out looking for you from Tor Royal?'

'No, but Virgil will be worried.'

'How about Sir Thomas's niece?'

It seemed a casual question, but Pilgrim remembered Tacy's reaction to Sophie when she had come to Roundtor Farm.

'She's not at Tor Royal.'

Pilgrim told Tacy the manner of Sophie's leaving and her mother's belief that she had run off to London.

'Do you believe she's gone to London?' Tacy had detected doubt in Pilgrim's voice when he talked of Sophie's disappearance.

'I'm not at all sure. There was a man in her life before she came to Devon. Someone she really cared about. I think she might be with him – but that's a wild guess. I could be hopelessly wrong.'

'Are you sweet on her?'

The question took Pilgrim by surprise. After a moment's thought, he said, 'I hadn't known her long enough to think how I felt about her. I liked her, yes, although sometimes I felt that she and I came from different worlds. I guess I sometimes find your social distinctions difficult to understand.'

'Do they *really* not matter so much in America?'

'If they do, then I've certainly never noticed them in the same way I have here.'

Pilgrim's words gave Tacy much to think about. The main barrier between Pilgrim and herself was their vastly differing backgrounds. His family was rich. Hers, although not poor by Dartmoor standards, needed to work very hard to make a living.

If such things *really* did not matter in America it might change everything between them.

They were close enough to see the lights of Tor Royal now and Tacy came to a halt. 'There's the house. I'll leave you here.'

'Thanks very much for walking me home, Tacy.' They both stood close in the darkness, seemingly trying to find words to say.

'I'd better go now – and you shouldn't leave it any later going inside.'

'No, you're right.'

'Goodnight then.'

As she started off, he called, 'Tacy!'

'Yes.' She stopped only a couple of paces away.

'Wait for me in the morning. I'd like to walk to Billy's house with you.'

Tacy disappeared into the darkness and Pilgrim wished he could have found some excuse to persuade her to stay with him for a while longer.

Then her voice came back to him.

'Pilgrim?'

'I'm here.'

'Goodnight. See you in the morning.'

34

The next morning Pigrim was on his way to Roundtor Farm when, in the distance, he saw someone hurrying towards Sir Thomas Tyrwhitt's house. The figure was coming from the direction of Princetown.

Pilgrim's attention was drawn to the figure by the bright yellow of his clothes. It was the colour of the uniform issued to many of the Dartmoor prisoners-of-war.

Turning back, Pilgrim reached Tor Royal only a minute before Ephraim.

'What's wrong? Has there been more trouble at the prison?'

Out of breath from hurrying, Ephraim nodded his head vigorously.

'Come inside. I'll call Captain Howard.'

As Pilgrim led the way to the sitting room, the breathless Ephraim eyed the luxuriously furnished interior of Sir Thomas Tyrwhitt's house.

'Come in here and sit down.'

Pilgrim waved Ephraim to an armchair but the giant marines sergeant perched himself gingerly on the edge of a wooden chair which seemed hardly stout enough to take his large bulk.

Pouring a brandy despite the early hour, Pilgrim handed it to Ephraim. 'This might help you get your breath back while I go and find the captain.'

Ephraim took the drink gratefully and Pilgrim hurried away.

When Pilgrim returned with Virgil, the glass was empty and Ephraim was standing at the window looking out at the neatly trimmed lawns and the colourful flower beds.

Turning to greet them, Ephraim said, 'This is a better view than the one from Block Four, Cap'n.'

'There's no disputing that, Ephraim, but what's brought you here this morning? Lieutenant Penn says there's trouble at the prison.'

'That's right, Cap'n, and it's likely to get worse. Little Mo's been given a bad flogging. At least fifty lashes, I'd say. It's taken all the skin and most of the flesh off his back.'

'Little Mo? Should I know him?' The name meant nothing to Virgil.

'He was Steiger's slave. They were captured together.'

Pilgrim and Virgil both remembered the man now. Much lighter-skinned than most of his fellow Negroes, he was a small, rather frail man. Pilgrim winced at the thought of him taking a flogging.

'Who had him flogged? Cotgrave?'

'No, it wasn't the governor, Cap'n. It wasn't even an official flogging. It was Steiger.' Ephraim spoke angrily. 'He's not admitting it, but it was him who ordered it.'

'How do you know?' Pilgrim put the question to Ephraim.

'We were mustered in the Block Four yard yesterday

morning. The captains and shipowners from the Petty
Officers' Block were there too. Some money had finally
arrived from the agent. Each man was given three
shillings and nine pence, English money. A month's
allowance. Steiger objected to money being given to
Little Mo. He said it should come to him. That he's
the one who should decide if and when any money
was going to be handed out to Little Mo. When it was
given over anyway, Little Mo was told by Steiger that he
was still a slave and should remember what happened
to slaves when they didn't obey their masters.'

Ephraim's fists clenching and unclenching rapidly
were the only outward sign of his anger.

'Sometime during the night, or this morning, Steiger's
men got him. It wouldn't have been difficult. Little Mo
has problems with his breathing so he slept out on the
attic landing, close to the window. He was found this
morning lying at the bottom of the steps on the ground
floor. He'd been tied to a railing and gagged. Then he'd
been flogged until he passed out – and after that too,
I suspect. He's in the prison hospital now, more dead
than alive.'

Virgil's expression was grim when he asked, 'What's
the mood among your people?'

'They're angry, Cap'n. For a while it's not going to be
safe for a white man – any white man – to be caught by
them on his own anywhere in the block.'

'You can't be absolutely sure this is Steiger's doing.'

Virgil was clutching at straws. Pilgrim was aware of
it, and so was Ephraim.

'We don't have a signed confession, Cap'n, but we
don't need one. Anyway, nothing is a secret for ever
inside Dartmoor. Sooner or later we'll know the names
of the men who carried out the flogging. When we do,
they'll be killed. I couldn't stop it, even if I wanted to.'

Virgil nodded acknowledgement of Ephraim's statement before speaking to Pilgrim. 'I think we'd better pay the prison a visit right away. Governor Cotgrave is going to have to make a few decisions before the day's out.'

'I've got something else for you to think about along the way, Cap'n – and this concerns Steiger too.'

Pilgrim pulled a wry face. 'I told you Conrad Steiger was trouble, Virgil. What else has he done, Ephraim?'

'You've both heard the story of Steiger taking a slave girl as his mistress, I suppose, and of having her husband sold off and shipped away?'

'We've heard it,' agreed Virgil. 'But it's only an unsubstantiated rumour, as far as I'm concerned.' Virgil did not want to provide more fuel for the hatred against Steiger that had already taken hold in the attic floor of Dartmoor Prison's Block Four.

'It's more than a rumour, Cap'n, that's for sure now. The woman's husband was among the latest batch of prisoners-of-war to be brought to Dartmoor. He's vowed to get Steiger before this war's over. I, for one, believe him.'

Listening to Ephraim's revelations, Pilgrim resigned himself to the fact that he would not be visiting Roundtor Farm today. Tacy would need to go in search of Billy without him.

35

Tacy waited for Pilgrim until mid-morning. When he had not arrived she told her mother she would go to Billy's home without him.

'Well, you just be careful,' said Joan. 'I'd send Johanna with you, but with your pa the way he is at the moment you can't both be away from the farm. If it wasn't that I was so worried about Billy I wouldn't let you go there, either.'

'I'll be all right. If . . . if Pilgrim *does* arrive, don't let him come after me. The moor isn't very safe at the moment. He'd probably get lost anyway.'

'He'll be all right here until you return.' Joan looked at her daughter quizzically. 'You two didn't have an argument last night on your way to Tor Royal?'

Tacy shook her head. 'We were the best of friends when I left him. I expect he's had to go to the prison or something. He'll get here if he can.'

On the way from the farmhouse, Tacy thought of the walk in the darkness with Pilgrim. She felt it had somehow brought them closer. So close, she had expected him to try to kiss her when they parted. She had been disappointed when he did not. Tacy was aware she was deeply in love with Pilgrim. To try to convince herself otherwise would be self-deceit. She shrugged off the uncomfortable thought that Pilgrim's failure to come to the farm might be because he realised how she felt about him and did not reciprocate her feelings.

It was easy to believe that all was well with the world when walking the moor on a day like this. There was very little wind and only a few small white clouds in the blue sky. The ground was spongy underfoot, but Tacy knew the moor well and kept clear of the dangerous places.

The streams contained more water than usual, as a result of the recent heavy rains. When she came to the first, the water was flowing so fast and high over the stepping-stones it would have been dangerous to attempt a crossing. There was a stout clapper bridge upstream where she was able to cross in safety, but it meant an extra half-mile on her journey.

The second stream she met with was much shallower and she was able to wade across safely, the water coming no higher than her knees.

Soon she came within sight of the ruined mine buildings that surrounded the home of Billy and his mother.

Billy came to the door in response to her persistent knocking. He seemed surprised and strangely ill-at-ease to find her there.

'Everyone at Roundtor Farm's been worried about you, Billy. We didn't expect you during the rain, or the mist, of course, but we thought you might have come to us when the weather improved.'

Billy spoke without looking directly at her. 'I tried to get there on the first day, but the streams were too high. The water was pouring over that old clapper bridge, upstream from the crossing. I . . . I haven't tried these last couple of days because Ma's not very well. I didn't like leaving her.'

'What's wrong with her, Billy? Can I come in and see?' At any other time she would not have needed to pose such a question. It was unusual for Billy not to have invited her inside the cottage.

'She's upstairs in her bedroom. She hasn't moved from there for two days. I'm worried about her, Tacy.'

'Let me have a look at her. You should have come to the farm and told us.'

'I was going to . . . There hasn't been time, that's all.'

There was something in Billy's manner that puzzled Tacy. Something she could not fathom. He was pleased to see her, she did not doubt that, but there was an evasiveness in his manner that was out of character.

'Is your ma's illness the only reason why you've stayed away, Billy? There's no other reason you haven't been to Roundtor? None of us have offended you in any way?'

'No, Tacy. There's nothing like that. It's just . . . well, I just haven't been able to come there, that's all.'

They had reached the upstairs bedroom where Billy's mother was lying. Tacy entered the room and wrinkled her nose. The room smelled foul.

'Open the window, Billy. It could do with some fresh air in here.'

'Ma don't like having the air in her room.'

'Your ma's probably too ill to know what's good for her. Open it.'

While Billy struggled with the stiff window, Tacy went over to the bed. She pulled back the bedclothes, the better to look at Tillie Yates, and two dark, bright eyes looked back at her fiercely.

'What you doing here, Tacy Elford? Can't a woman have some peace when she's not feeling very well?'

'It's because you're not feeling well that I'm here. What's wrong with you?'

'I told you. I'm ill – but I'm better than I was. For days I couldn't eat a thing without bringing it up again. Now I reckon I could – that's if we had any food in the house.'

'I'll bring some across to you in the morning – unless Billy comes back with me to collect it now.'

'Why haven't you brought any with you before this? When you was here yesterday – and the day before?'

Tacy was puzzled. 'I haven't been here before. Today's the first time I've tried to get here, what with the storm and the mist.'

'Don't you lie to me, Tacy Elford. I've heard you downstairs talking to my Billy. Laughing too. At me being up here and not able to get up and about to see what you was up to, no doubt.'

Tacy would have argued with the woman, but she changed her mind. Tillie Yates had never been altogether sensible. The illness seemed to have made her more unbalanced than usual.

'Well, it doesn't matter. I'll see you have some food. Will you come back to Roundtor Farm with me to collect it, Billy?'

'I . . . I don't know.' Billy was definitely not happy about something. 'I don't really like to leave her when she's like this.'

'Liar!' Tillie spat out the word. 'You haven't bothered about leaving me before, when you've wanted to go downstairs to speak to *her*.'

'It's all right, Billy.' Tacy put out a hand to stop the protest Billy was about to make. 'We'll go now and talk about it downstairs.'

'Don't you keep him talking half the night again, either. I'm a sick woman, I need my rest . . .'

Tillie could still be heard complaining when Billy and Tacy reached the bottom of the stairs.

'I'm sorry, Tacy . . .'

'It's all right, Billy. Do you have anything to eat for tonight?'

'I caught a rabbit yesterday. It's cooking in a pot now.'

'Good! I think your ma needs something to build her strength up. Give her some of the rabbit stew and I'll see what I can bring from home. I doubt if it'll be today, though. There's a lot to be done at Roundtor and only me and Johanna to do it. My pa isn't too well either.'

'What about Lieutenant Pilgrim? Hasn't he been helping?'

'He should have been there today, but I think something must have happened at the prison. Anyway, never you mind about it. You just do what you can to help your ma get better and I'll get some food across to you as soon as I can.'

'Thanks, Tacy. You're very good to us.'

Billy seemed far more upset than the situation warranted and Tacy said, 'Are you sure there's nothing else worrying you, Billy? We're friends, remember?'

Once again Billy seemed desperately unhappy, but he shook his head. 'No, I'm all right.'

'Then just take care of things here and we'll get some food to you as soon as possible. If you need anything in the meantime, just call on us. You can cross the stream at the clapper bridge now, and the water level's still dropping. Goodbye, Billy.'

On the way home to Roundtor Farm, Tacy tried to put behind her the thought that Billy was keeping something back. Yet she could not help thinking he was worried about something more than his mother's illness. She determined that on her next visit she would question him more closely. She would discover what it was that was troubling him.

36

Pilgrim reached Roundtor Farm the following morning as Tacy was preparing a heavily laden basket of food to take to Billy and his sick mother.

After briefly explaining the reason why he had not come to the farm the previous day, Pilgrim said he would accompany her to the Yates's home today.

Tacy desperately wanted Pilgrim to come with her, but there were many things to be done about the farm. Due to the recent bad weather and the state of her father's health, they were falling behind with the work.

Reluctantly, she suggested it would help her more if he remained at Roundtor and helped with some of the chores.

Her mother's relief at Tacy's suggestion was short-lived. Tom Elford, looking decidedly frail, was seated in the kitchen. He said, 'There's no need for Pilgrim to spend every day he's here working at something or the other. I'm feeling a lot better today. The pair of you go off to Billy's. What doesn't get done here will wait for another day.'

'Now, Tom. I don't want you working outside yet. You're not well enough . . .'

'I'm well enough to use my tongue and tell Johanna what needs doing. Go on, Pilgrim. Get on your way to Billy's with Tacy, before her ma changes my mind for me.'

'Are you quite sure? I don't mind working here to help out.'

'Of course I'm sure. If you can come again tomorrow and help out I'll be very grateful to you – but don't get thinking you *have* to work every time you come to Roundtor. You and our Tacy are still young. Life will force work upon you both soon enough. Learn to take the opportunity for a day off when it comes your way now. Off you go.'

Tacy gave her father a hug, then she and Pilgrim went out of the house together.

'I wish I was as happy as you are about sending the two of them out together for a day on the moor.' Joan voiced the concern she felt to her husband. 'That young man has no reason at all to show a sense of responsibility while he's in this country.'

'But he will,' said her husband. 'He's that sort of man – and I believe he's genuinely fond of our Tacy.'

'She feels far more strongly than that about *him*,' declared Joan unhappily. 'I would have thought that reason enough not to send them off alone.'

'Does that mean Tacy *might* have a baby soon?' asked Johanna brightly. 'Can I look after it instead of working out on the farm?'

'I've told you before about talking such nonsense,' said her mother sharply. 'I've no doubt I'll have far more trouble with you than I've ever had with Tacy when you're of an age. Now, if any of us are to get any work done today you can both get out of my kitchen for an hour. I can't work with you cluttering up the place.'

It was a glorious day for walking on the moor, even though Pilgrim was burdened with the heavy basket of provisions destined for Billy and his mother.

When they reached the stream which had been dangerously swollen the previous day, they discovered the water level had dropped considerably. Even so, the fast-running water was lapping the top of most of the unevenly spaced stepping-stones.

Despite Tacy's protest that she could cross perfectly well by herself, Pilgrim went first. After depositing the basket on the far bank, he came back to help her.

She had crossed this stream many times before, but she allowed him to help her and to retain a hold on her hand when they were both on the same side as the basket.

As they set off together once more, Pilgrim looked about him and said, 'This really is beautiful country, Tacy.'

'I think so,' she agreed.

'You'd like Ohio too. Sometimes you wake up there in the mornings and feel that if you reach up far enough you could touch the sky. You'd love it.'

'Perhaps I'll go there some day and see it for myself.'

'I'd like to think you will, Tacy.'

She looked at him uncertainly, hoping there might be a hidden meaning in his words, but he was not looking at her.

Tacy wondered whether he was aware his statement might have been misconstrued and was wishing he had not made it.

She shrugged off the thought. 'Pa often says that when he was young he used to dream of one day going off to see the world. Poor Pa. With all his dreams, he's never gone farther than a mile or two off the moor. I don't think he ever will now.'

'You never know,' replied Pilgrim sympathetically.

After a moment's hesitation, he asked, 'What will happen if he ever becomes too ill to run the farm? Will you, Johanna and your ma carry on, or will you move somewhere else?'

'Where could we go?' asked Tacy. 'We'd still need to keep ourselves. But if anything happens to Pa I suppose we'll have to find somewhere else to live. It's always been Pa's hope that Johanna and I would be married before anything happened to him and that one of his sons-in-law would want to carry on farming at Roundtor.'

When Pilgrim made no immediate reply, they walked on in silence.

Deciding it was time they spoke of something else, Tacy told Pilgrim about her visit to Billy's home the day before, and of his peculiar manner towards her.

'It might just be that he's particularly worried about his mother being ill,' suggested Pilgrim. 'Or perhaps he's feeling guilty because he hasn't been to Roundtor to do any work, even though your pa is ill too.'

Tacy shook her head. 'That's what I told myself, first of all. But the more I thought about it the more convinced I became that Billy was lying to me and didn't feel comfortable about doing it.'

'Why should he lie? You saw his mother. If she really is sick there was no need for him to be embarrassed about it. You don't think you were imagining it?'

'No, I've known Billy too long. He was hiding something from me, and that's not like him.'

'Well, perhaps we'll find out today what it is that's bothering him.'

Walking along beside Tacy, their arms and hands touching frequently, Pilgrim was determined not to allow anything to spoil the happy mood he was in today.

37

For the remainder of the walk from Roundtor, Tacy and Pilgrim spoke of generalities, enjoying the warmth of the day and each other's company.

Eventually they came within view of a small jumble of derelict buildings and spoil heaps. Tacy stopped and pointed. 'That's where Billy lives. In the cottage on the left.'

The cottage was almost as derelict as the other mine buildings but, unlike the others, the roof of the cottage was intact.

As they walked along together, Pilgrim had occasionally shifted the basket from one arm to the other. Now he stopped and placed it on the ground, flexing both his arms.

'Go on ahead and knock at the door. Tell Billy I'm here with you and give him time to get used to it. He still doesn't know me all that well. It might not be a good idea to spring surprises on him, especially if he has something on his mind.'

'That's a good idea.' She smiled and inclined her head in the direction of the basket. 'Has it grown heavier since we left Roundtor?'

'I'm probably not as fit as I should be. Go on, I'll catch up with you.'

Pilgrim's gaze followed Tacy as she walked away from him, towards the house. She wore a thin summer frock which showed off her slim figure. She really was a very lovely young woman. His affection for her was growing stronger with every day that passed. He had never felt this way about anyone before.

Had he met her in the United States he would have been able to tell her how he felt and their relationship would have progressed rapidly. He had much to offer her there. But here in England . . . ? He was a paroled prisoner-of-war, liable to be recalled to prison at the whim of the British Government. It was a wonder her parents allowed her to spend so much time in his company.

Pilgrim watched as Tacy walked up to the front door. She paused for a moment before knocking. Then she walked inside the cottage without waiting for a reply.

Suddenly someone ran from behind the house. He was able to catch only a glimpse before the running figure disappeared behind a spoil heap. It was sufficient for him to see that it was a young girl.

Pilgrim was puzzled. No one had ever mentioned that a young girl lived in Billy's house – and why had she run away in such a manner?

He was intrigued. Billy must know of the girl's presence. She must be the reason there had been such a puzzling change in his attitude towards Tacy.

Picking up the basket, Pilgrim carried it the remaining distance to the cottage.

Entering through the front door he was met by Tacy. He followed her to the kitchen which was situated at the back of the house. Here he noticed there was an outside door that might have been used by someone fleeing from the house.

Billy was here, but he seemed ill-at-ease and there was no warmth in his greeting. Pilgrim understood immediately why Tacy was concerned about him. Something was making the simple young man decidedly unhappy.

'Hello, Billy. It seems a long time since we last met. How's your mother?'

'She's getting better,' replied Billy. His words were devoid of the enthusiasm he had shown when he and Pilgrim had last spoken.

'Billy says she should be up and about again in a couple of days.' Tacy spoke to fill the uncomfortable gap that widened after Billy's words. 'That's good news, isn't it?'

'Very good,' agreed Pilgrim. 'It must be very lonely out here when you don't have your mother to talk to. Is it only the two of you living here?'

'Yes.'

If there had been any doubt in Pilgrim's mind that Billy was hiding something, it was dispelled now. Billy did not enjoy telling lies. Pilgrim wondered why he felt it necessary to do so.

'I was just telling Billy that I'm really impressed by his housekeeping,' said Tacy. 'I've never seen the house so neat and tidy.'

Looking about him, Pilgrim was in full agreement with her comments. There was not a dirty plate or dish in sight and everything was stowed away neatly. The hard dirt floor too had been brushed clean.

'Will you take me up to see your ma, Billy? I'd like

to ask her if there's anything she needs. There might be things she wouldn't tell you about.'

Billy nodded, but once again, he seemed less than enthusiastic and Pilgrim determined he would get to the bottom of this particular mystery.

'You go on upstairs with Billy, Tacy. I'll stay down here. Mrs Yates won't want a stranger paying her a visit when she's not feeling well.'

When the others had left the kitchen, Pilgrim opened the door quietly and slipped outside. He made his way to where he had seen the young girl disappear.

There was no one behind the spoil heap, but a roofless and doorless building stood nearby. It had probably once been a small storehouse.

Treading lightly, Pilgrim made his way towards it. He reached the doorway and was about to pass inside when a young girl fled from the building and tried to slip past him.

Pilgrim caught her by the arm and the girl immediately bit him. Instead of releasing his grip, he wrapped both his arms about her in such a way that she could neither bite, nor strike him. She could still kick, but as she wore no shoes it proved quite ineffectual.

'Let me go.' She had a shrill, young voice, but as she struggled violently he realised she was not quite as young as he had first thought. She was probably fifteen years old, or thereabouts.

'Stop your struggling. No one intends hurting you, but you're not going to get away.'

Eventually, when Pilgrim's words got through to her, the struggling grew weaker, then stopped altogether.

'Let me go, then.'

'Sure – but remember I can probably run faster than you. Just tell me what this is all about. Who are you and what are you doing here?'

'Who are *you*?' she countered. 'And what's that uniform you're wearing?'

Pilgrim released his hold on her and for a few moments they stood warily facing each other.

'My name's Pilgrim Penn. What's yours?'

'That's only answered one of my questions. Why are you wearing that uniform?'

'I suggest we go to the house. There are quite a lot of things that need clearing up – but I still don't know your name.'

It was Billy who provided the answer. He had heard the commotion from the house and he came running, with Tacy close behind him.

'Are you all right, Emma?' His concern for the girl was such that Tacy and Pilgrim exchanged surprised glances.

'I think you ought to tell us what this is all about, Billy.' Pilgrim made the suggestion.

'It doesn't matter what they say, Billy. I'm not going back to Charlie and Bella. I'll top myself first. I swear I will.'

'As far as I know there's no one with the slightest interest in taking you anywhere, but who are Charlie and Bella?'

Pilgrim's question was directed at Emma, but it was Tacy who broke in with the answer.

'I know! It's that pair of tinkers who were passing through the moor a week or two ago. They came to the door with a grindstone, offering to sharpen scissors, or anything else needing a good sharp edge. When they'd gone I found two of our chickens were missing. There weren't as many eggs as there should have been, either. I thought then they must have had someone else working with them. Was that you?' Tacy put the accusation to Emma.

Scared but defiant, the young girl said, 'You can't prove nuffing – and if he tries to take me in for it I'll bite him a sight harder than I did just now.'

'Why do you keep suggesting I'm going to take you somewhere or the other, Emma?'

Pilgrim's question was asked quietly. He had been looking more closely at the girl and his sympathy went out to her. Her clothes were old, frayed and ill-fitting. She was pinched-faced, barefooted and under-nourished, but she and her clothes were clean. He was of the opinion she had not always been a tinker's girl.

'Why do you think Pilgrim might take you back to the tinkers?' Tacy prompted her.

'Well, he's wearing a uniform, ain't he? And I belong to Charlie and Bella. At least, they've always said I do. Charlie said he paid for me all kosher-like.'

Pilgrim frowned. 'People aren't animals, Emma. They can't be bought and sold.'

Even as he was speaking, Pilgrim thought uncomfortably of the men who occupied the attic floor of Block Four, inside Dartmoor prison.

Brushing such thoughts aside, he said, 'Anyway, what do you think this uniform means?'

'I dunno! Militiaman, soldier or constable, I suppose. Whichever it is, it means you're not going to be taking my side.'

'It's a Marines uniform, Emma. An American Marine – and America is at war with England. I'm a prisoner from Dartmoor prison. They've let me live outside the prison only for as long as I behave myself. I'm hardly likely to want to get anyone else in trouble, am I?'

'You've been locked up inside Dartmoor gaol?' Emma looked at Pilgrim with an expression of awesome respect for a few moments. Then her expression hardened. 'That don't make no difference. Charlie's been put away more'n once but it hasn't made him any better. It hasn't stopped him trying to get me in trouble, neither. He tries it on every time Bella's back's turned.'

The look exchanged between Pilgrim and Tacy was a mixture of pity, anger and disgust, but it was Billy who spoke now.

'I won't let him get you into trouble any more, Emma, and neither will Pilgrim. You can trust him.'

'I don't trust no one,' she replied fiercely. When she saw the hurt expression that came to Billy's face, she added hurriedly, 'Except you, Billy. You're the first one I've ever trusted.'

When she was satisfied she had placated his hurt feelings, she returned her attention to Pilgrim. 'Well, now you've found me here, what you going to do about it?'

'Pilgrim's already told you he doesn't intend doing anything,' said Tacy. 'But we'll need to decide what's going to happen to you now.'

'Why? I'm all right here. If ever Billy gets fed up with having me around, I'll just move on to somewhere else.'

'I won't get fed up with you, Emma. You can stay here for as long as you like.'

As though suddenly afraid he was being disloyal to Tacy, Billy explained, 'Emma's helped me a lot while Ma's been ill. She's made food and cleaned up the place. She's even done some washing.'

'I thought the place was looking especially clean,' said Tacy approvingly. 'But it's not me you need to convince. You know what your ma is like about having strangers around.'

Billy did know. When his mother had been ill a few years before, Tacy had brought some food for her. She had stayed to carry out some much-needed tidying, only to be chased from the cottage by a nightdress-clad Mrs Yates.

Standing in the doorway wielding the broom hastily dropped by Tacy, Tillie Yates had triumphantly declared that if ever Tacy returned she would teach her such a lesson she would never dare come snooping around the house again.

She had come to accept Tacy as a visitor since then, but would tolerate no one else.

Billy looked unhappily from Tacy to Emma and back again. 'Where can she go? She doesn't know anyone except me.'

It was apparent to both Tacy and Pilgrim that Billy was seriously smitten with the young tinker girl.

'Let's not worry too much about it just yet, Billy. It's no problem while your ma's upstairs ill. In the meantime I'll talk to my ma. Perhaps she'll let Emma come to stay with us. Then you can see her whenever you come to work at Roundtor.'

Tacy's suggested solution seemed to cheer up Billy somewhat, but he was still not entirely reassured. Realising this, Tacy added, 'She could come over to see you whenever she wished. Then perhaps one day your ma will let her come back here to live.'

'Don't I have no say in what's going to happen to me?' The question was put to Tacy by a scowling Emma.

'I'm just making suggestions,' said Tacy, taking offence. 'I don't even know whether my ma will let you stay at Roundtor Farm – but I'm quite certain Billy's ma won't have you here once she's up and about.'

Tacy looked at Emma. 'Where will you go if she sends you away?'

Reality took the place of belligerence and Emma said, 'I don't have any place to go. All right, if your ma says I can come to your place I'll come there – but you don't own me. None of you own me. If I don't like it, I'll leave. I mean it.'

'You're quite free to do exactly as you want, Emma,' said Tacy gently. 'But I think you'll be happy at Roundtor, and I believe Billy will be relieved to know you're somewhere safe, too.'

38

'I'm sorry for not telling you about Emma before you found her at the house, Tacy. But she was so frightened about being caught and taken back to the tinkers, she made me promise to tell *no* one. No one at all – and it was you who told me a promise must never be broken . . .'

'Billy! You don't have to keep apologising to me about it. I *do* understand.'

Tacy and Billy were cleaning out the cowshed together and it was at least the sixth time that day Billy had apologised to Tacy for not telling her about Emma. She was trying very hard not to become exasperated with him.

When Joan Elford had heard the story of Emma, and Tacy had suggested she come to stay at Roundtor Farm, she had been dubious about having a self-confessed thief living in the house.

However, when Emma arrived, scrubbed and as tidy as was possible in view of the threadbare frock she wore, the farmer's wife had weakened.

She quickly realised the young girl was trying desperately hard not to show that what the Elford family thought of her really mattered. Joan had relented and given Emma a warm and impulsive hug. The tinkers' girl had a new home.

Emma had settled in well, proving to be as hardworking as she was clean. She was also very, very kind to Billy.

He, in his turn, was so besotted with her that Johanna would have been quite jealous had Emma not made a fuss of her too.

While Tacy and Billy cleaned out the cowshed together, Pilgrim was helping Tom Elford fit a new axle to the small farm wagon. In the house, Emma, Johanna and Joan were baking cakes in the farm kitchen.

'I was a bit upset at first because you hadn't told me about Emma right away,' admitted Tacy to Billy, 'but once I knew the full story I was proud of you. I don't think I would have been able to keep such a secret to myself.'

Billy's cheeks glowed with pleasure at her words. He had been desperately concerned that his secretiveness would cost him his friendship with Tacy. His relationship with her still meant a great deal to him.

'I *wanted* to tell you about her. I would have too, soon.' He gave her a look that revealed the affection he had for her. 'Had it happened a while ago I would have been even more unhappy about finding someone else I like so much, but it's easier now you have Pilgrim. Do you love him, Tacy?'

Billy's unexpected and direct question took Tacy by surprise. 'What . . . ? I . . . That's not the sort of question you ask someone, Billy.'

'Why not?'

'I . . . Well, it just isn't, that's all.'

Billy was puzzled by her evasiveness. 'I think he loves you.'

'What makes you think that? Has he said anything to you?' Tacy asked eagerly.

'He doesn't have to, does he? He wouldn't come here and work like he does if he didn't. I mean, he doesn't need to work. I like Pilgrim. He's been kind to me, and to Emma.'

'It's time I started on the milking,' said Tacy abruptly. 'Hurry up and finish off in here, Billy. Then you can go and turn some of the peat on the stack down by the big rock.'

A few minutes later Tacy sat on the low stool milking the cow, her cheek resting against its warm body, thinking of Billy's words.

She tried not to dwell upon her feelings for Pilgrim, nor his for her. They spent a great deal of time together, but more and more often recently it seemed they were always accompanied by someone else – usually by Johanna.

When they *were* alone Tacy often felt Pilgrim was on the verge of saying something of importance to her, but it never came to anything.

She wondered whether it was because he did not care as passionately for her as she did for him?

'Have you fallen asleep against that old cow? You'll certainly get no milk unless you work at it.' The voice of Joan broke in on her daughter's thoughts. 'I've just come out here to get some fresh milk because I want to do some baking. What were you up to, girl?'

'Oh, just thinking, that's all.'

'What about?'

'Nothing in particular,' Tacy lied as she set to work to draw milk from the cow. 'We seem to have had a lot of new people come to the farm this year. First Pilgrim, sometimes Virgil and Ephraim, and now Emma. What do you make of her, Ma?'

'It'll take more than a day or two to get to know that one,' her mother replied, 'but if first impressions are anything to go by, I quite like her.'

'Billy's absolutely head-over-heels in love with her,' said Tacy.

'Of course he is. Billy doesn't expect much from life. If someone shows him anything approaching affection he'll do anything for them. You should know that. Now, I'll take the milk you've got and put it in this jug. Then I'll go back to see what's happening in the kitchen.'

When she had gone, Tacy carried on with the milking and thought of what her mother had said about Billy. She wondered whether he and she were very different. Tacy decided not to dwell on how she might react if Pilgrim ever displayed more than a gentle affection for her. It was an exciting thought.

She only just succeeded in saving the wooden bucket as the cow kicked out at it. She decided it was not a good thing to have exciting thoughts when she was milking a cow.

'How long do you think this foolish war between our countries is likely to last, Pilgrim?'

Tom Elford put the question to Pilgrim as they began bolting the new axle into place on the cart, prior to attaching the wheels.

'Not too long, I hope.'

Pilgrim was perspiring heavily. Tacy's father was as well as he would ever be, but he was not a strong man. Most of the hard work involved in replacing the axle had been performed by Pilgrim.

'. . . From all accounts the French are being driven back into France by your General Wellington. Once that war comes to an end there should be no quarrel between our two countries. There'd be none now if British ships hadn't taken to stopping ours on the high seas and impressing seamen with British backgrounds for your navy.'

Not wanting to enter a discussion about the rights, or wrongs of the British actions, Tom Elford said, 'I suppose you'll be off home as soon as the war's over.'

'It'll no doubt take a while before they get around to returning prisoners.'

'Our Tacy will miss you.'

'Do you really think so?'

There had been a time when Pilgrim would not have felt it necessary to question such a statement. In the days when he had still been in prison he had imagined how things would be between himself and Tacy if only he was outside the prison walls. When he had been granted parole he thought his dreams were about to come true.

There were still times when he thought so, but somehow there always seemed to be an invisible barrier raised between them. He had never been able to decide whether it was placed there by Tacy or by himself. Perhaps it was there because he was reluctant to do anything that might upset her and so destroy the very easy relationship they enjoyed at the moment.

He had come close to it on more than one occasion when they were alone, but always backed off. He was constantly aware of being a prisoner-of-war. There was little of any substance he could offer her until this war was over.

'I know so, lad. One of her mother's biggest worries has always been that one of these days you'll go off back to America, leaving our Tacy behind with a broken heart.'

Tom Elford smiled wryly. 'I shouldn't be talking to you like this, should I? A father's duty is supposed to be to warn off young men, not encourage 'em.'

'I wouldn't do anything to hurt Tacy, Mr Elford. I think far too much of her for that.'

Tom Elford lifted a wheel clear of the ground with difficulty and eased it on to the greased end of the new axle. 'That's what I keep telling her mother – and it's what I believe, or I wouldn't be talking to you like this right now. Tacy's a good girl, Pilgrim. All the same, I'd like her to have more from life than I've been able to give her mother. There's more drudgery to a woman's life on a moorland farm than most.'

'I'm not sure Mrs Elford would agree with you. She's one of the most contented women I've ever met.'

'It's nice of you to say so, boy, but it's not because of what I've been able to give her. I've just been lucky to find her, I suppose. I don't know why, but she loves me enough to take up a tinker's life if that's all I had to offer.'

Seeming to concentrate on what he was doing, Tom Elford said, 'Our Tacy takes after her mother in that way. She'll make a man a good wife some day. I only hope I live long enough to see her settled with him.'

Straightening up, Tom Elford stood back from the wheel with satisfaction. 'There, that's one of them done. If the other one goes on as easily I'll say it's the best job I've ever seen done.'

He suddenly grinned. 'If only we could sort folk's lives out as easily as mending a farm wagon. Come on, let's get that other wheel on then we'll go inside the house and have a drop of something. I was given some cider the other day in exchange for a few chickens. I've been waiting for the right opportunity to sample some of it . . .'

39

Sir Thomas Tyrwhitt returned to Tor Royal, accompanied by his sister Winifrith, in the autumn of the year. They had discovered no trace of Sophie in London. It seemed her whereabouts was as much of a mystery to her friends as it remained to her mother.

Winifrith suspected the two Americans of knowing more about Sophie's disappearance than they had disclosed. She made no secret of her suspicions, especially after she had been drinking heavily.

Pilgrim, in particular, became a target for her sharp tongue. He began to dread the evenings when Winifrith dined in at Tor Royal.

A couple of weeks after his return, Sir Thomas Tyrwhitt held a farewell party for Lieutenant Colonel Hawke. The duties of the one-armed army officer and his militiamen had been taken over by a contingent of Irish militiamen.

Lieutenant Colonel Hawke and his men were due to march away from Dartmoor the following day.

'I won't be sorry to see the last of Dartmoor,' Cecil

Hawke confided to Virgil and Pilgrim as they stood in a corner of the crowded Tor Royal room. 'All the same, I wish I were leaving you in better company. On my brief acquaintance with them, I find the discipline of these Irishmen leaves much to be desired. I had intended holding this party at the mess, but I think Sir Thomas was wise in persuading me it might be better to hold it here.'

He did not add that he had suggested to the land-owner that the presence of the two American paroled prisoners-of-war might prove too provocative to the indisciplined Irish militiamen.

Pilgrim believed the militiaman's assessment of the men who were assuming responsibility for the secur-ity of the prisoners-of-war in Dartmoor was probably accurate. The party had been in progress for little more than an hour, yet already some of the younger officers were becoming rowdy.

At that moment the Reverend Cotterell entered the room, accompanied by his wife and their daughter.

The glance of Jemima went around the room quickly. When she saw the two Americans her face lit up with an expression of pleasure.

Pilgrim was taken by surprise. Then he realised the smile must have been for Virgil. He had visited the Sheepstor vicarage almost as often as Pilgrim had been to Roundtor. Virgil and Jemima must know each other quite well.

For a moment, he felt a twinge of jealousy that they were able to meet each other on occasions such as this and he and Tacy could not.

The feeling soon passed. He remembered the look Winifrith had given to Jemima on the first occasion they had visited Tor Royal. She did not consider the vicar and his family socially acceptable at Tor Royal.

She would be outraged by the presence of the daughter of a tenant farmer at such a function. Pilgrim would not want Tacy to be the subject of her acid tongue.

Reverend Cotterell waved in the direction of the two Americans and the vicar and his family made their way towards them.

'I was not expecting there to be quite such a crowd here,' said the Sheepstor vicar as he accepted a drink from a servant. 'But you have been a popular commanding officer, Colonel Hawke.'

Cecil Hawke snorted loudly as a loud shout went up from the far end of the room. 'I fear some of the young men here this evening would accept an invitation from the Devil himself if free drinks were on offer.'

It rapidly became a very noisy evening. At the height of the party, Pilgrim glanced across the room to see Jemima looking uncomfortable as she stood talking to an Irish militia officer. He was swaying ever closer to her as he talked, the drink in his glass coming perilously close to spilling over her as he leaned forward.

'Excuse me a moment.' Pilgrim broke off his conversation with one of Cecil Hawke's officers and hurried across the room. Seeing where he was headed, Virgil put down his drink and followed him quickly.

'Hello, Jemima. Is everything all right? Perhaps you would like another drink?'

Jemima's relief at his intervention was evident, but the Irish militiaman was less pleased. He was not prepared to relinquish her so easily.

Focusing upon Pilgrim with some difficulty, he said haughtily, 'I don't know how you behave in the colonies, sir, but it's not done here to interrupt a gentleman when he's talking to a lady.'

'I'm not aware how the men in your colonies behave,

either, sir, but I certainly wouldn't dream of interrupting a *gentleman* anywhere in the world.'

Controlling his anger, he offered his arm to Jemima, and said, 'Shall we find that drink for you?'

It was a moment or two before the implication of Pilgrim's words sunk in to the befuddled mind of the militiaman. When it did, he flushed angrily.

'I think you intended that remark to be insulting, sir.'

'I really don't give a damn *what* you think,' said Pilgrim quietly. 'But I *do* care when a man who has had more drink than he can hold makes a nuisance of himself in the presence of a lady.'

'I agree wholeheartedly,' said Virgil, moving quickly to place himself between Pilgrim and the Irish officer. 'Indeed, were I not on parole in this country I would call you out, sir. Regrettably, were I to do so you would die and I would no doubt be charged with your murder.'

Some of the militiaman's fellow officers had become aware that their drunken colleague was in danger of provoking a major incident. Three of them crossed the room hastily. While one paused to murmur apologies to Jemima, the other two hurried the protesting militia officer away.

When they had passed beyond hearing, Pilgrim turned to apologise to Jemima.

'I'm sorry, Jemima, but his attitude was quite unacceptable . . .'

He broke off when he saw the expression on her face.

'You were wonderful, Pilgrim. I am truly grateful to you.'

Suddenly aware that her praise was a little too gushing, she turned to Virgil. 'You too, Virgil. It was most gallant of you. Indeed, I feel you gave the militia-man a much-needed lesson in manners, but . . . would you really have fought a duel on my behalf?'

'Probably not.'

Virgil had the impression Jemima was disappointed by his reply and he added, 'A militiaman is *not* an army officer. He was also very drunk. Killing him would have been closer to murder than I care to come.'

Mrs Cotterell was beckoning across the room to her daughter, but before she moved off, Jemima said, 'It's very difficult to talk here tonight, but please come to the vicarage some time soon, Pilgrim. I really am *most* grateful to you for coming to my assistance.'

40

The Irish militia officer was not the only person at Sir Thomas Tyrwhitt's party to have drunk too much. Shortly after the incident involving Jemima, Pilgrim was leaving the room when he came face-to-face with Winifrith.

Giving him a malicious look, she said, 'I saw you making up to that vicar's daughter, just as you did to poor Sophie. Were you encouraging her to run off and leave her parents too? It was a sad day when my brother allowed you to come to Tor Royal.'

'That is most unfair, Mrs Cudmore. I have no more knowledge of Sophie's whereabouts than you.'

'I don't believe you – and I never will.'

Winifrith turned to go back the way she had come, but her words had been heard by a number of guests standing nearby.

Among them was Lieutenant Colonel Hawke.

'Pardon me, ma'am, but am I to understand you are not aware of your daughter's whereabouts?'

'And what business is it of yours, pray?' replied Winifrith belligerently.

'None at all, ma'am,' said the militiaman coldly. 'I was merely trying to be helpful by telling you where your daughter is likely to be.'

'You know where Sophie is?' The shock of his words momentarily sobered Winifrith.

'I do.'

Lieutenant Colonel Hawke was being deliberately reticent. He did not like Winifrith and was beginning to wish he had said nothing.

'Then tell me, for God's sake! Don't you know that Sir Thomas and I spent weeks searching London for her?'

'You won't find her in London, ma'am. When I saw her she was on her way to the war in the Spanish Peninsular. She was in the company of a captain wearing the uniform of the Rifle Corps. I thought she was probably married to him, but it seems I could have been mistaken.'

'A captain in the Rifle Corps! Did you hear that, Thomas? It's that *dreadful* young man she met before I brought her down here.'

Returning her attention to Lieutenant Colonel Hawke, she demanded, 'When did you see her? How long ago?'

'A long time,' said the militiaman, frowning in concentration. 'It was immediately after those few days of heavy rain and fog, as I remember. I was in Plymouth seeing off a friend who was on his way to join Wellington's staff. I tried to speak to your daughter . . . Sophie, is it? But she turned away and I thought she had not recognised me. There was no time to pursue the matter, a port is a busy place when soldiers are embarking.'

Winifrith tried to gather her wits, then with a stifled howl she fled from the room.

'Oh dear! I seem to have distressed the lady,' said Lieutenant Colonel Hawke, but with little contriteness in his expression.

Turning to Pilgrim, he said in a low voice, 'I only hope I have given the poor girl ample time to carry out her intentions, whatever they are, before her mother catches up with her.'

As Lieutenant Colonel Hawke walked away, Pilgrim was left wondering why he was not really surprised by the news that Sophie had run away from her mother to be with the man she loved.

Once again Winifrith Cudmore threw the household at Tor Royal into turmoil when she made another hurried departure in search of her missing daughter.

She set off for London the day after the party. As before, she was accompanied by her patient, titled brother.

Their destination was once more London, but on this occasion Winifrith knew exactly where she was going. She intended taking the War Office by storm. She would demand that they send an immediate despatch to Lord Wellington, ordering him to have Sophie Cudmore returned to England immediately.

In the unlikely event of the War Office officials refusing to make her demand one of their top priorities, she intended setting off for the Spanish Peninsular herself. Woe betide either Wellington or Napoleon if they did anything that might thwart her plans.

Sir Thomas told all this to Pilgrim and Virgil while he was waiting for his carriage to be loaded with his sister's luggage.

'I do hope the officers at the War Office will accommodate her,' he said, displaying a rare, nervous concern. 'I believe the war on the Continent has turned in our favour. It would be most distressing if Winifrith did anything to upset Wellington at such a critical stage in his campaign.'

He saw the expressions of barely concealed amusement on the faces of the two American marines and said, 'Yes, it sounds quite ridiculous, gentlemen, but I *know* my sister. I fear the War Office and my Lord Wellington do not.'

At that moment Winifrith descended the staris. She stalked past Pilgrim and Virgil without deigning to look at either of them as she made her way to the waiting carriage.

'Goodbye, gentlemen,' said Sir Thomas. 'I have no doubt there will be many occasions during the coming days when I will envy you the peace and tranquillity of Dartmoor.'

41

Pilgrim was on his way downstairs to breakfast the morning after the departure of Sir Thomas and Winifrith, when he met with a servant on the stairs.

'I was just coming up to your room to find you, sir,' she said. 'There's a girl at the back door asking to speak to you. I told her it was too early to bother you, but she said I was to tell you it was urgent.'

Pilgrim thought immediately it must be Tacy. Something must have happened at Roundtor Farm. Possibly it had to do with her father . . .

He hurried downstairs and through the kitchen to the back door, only to discover it was not Tacy who was waiting there but Mary Gurney, the girl who had befriended Henri.

She would not say anything to Pilgrim immediately, but drew him away from the house, out of hearing of the servants. When she was certain they could not be overheard, she blurted out, 'Henri is in desperate need of your help, Pilgrim. He's escaped from the prison.'

'Again?' Pilgrim was alarmed. 'Does he have a plan this time?'

'Yes . . . Well, he *did* . . . but you must come to speak to him. It's very important.'

Mary was so agitated she was unable to stand still. 'Please come with me.'

'Of course.' Pilgrim hurried after Mary as she set off. 'Where is he now?'

'Not far away. I left him hiding behind a wall along the lane to Tor Royal. I'll show you.'

Only a very short distance from the house Pilgrim saw Henri. He was not hiding behind a wall, as Mary had stated, but was sitting upon it. He was not dressed as a French soldier, but was wearing clothes that befitted an English gentleman.

Henri greeted Pilgrim effusively, but with little outward sign of agitation. 'My friend! You are looking very well. Freedom is good for you.'

'It's *your* freedom we're concerned about right now, Henri. What are you doing here? More to the point, what do you *intend* doing?'

'Ah yes! I escaped with a very carefully laid plan in mind but, as with many plans, things have gone wrong. I should have escaped over the wall of the prison soon after dark. It was arranged with one of the prison turnkeys. A man would be waiting for me with a horse to guide me to a boat on the river – the Tamar, I believe. The boat is leaving at noon today to rendezvous with a party of French smugglers. I should have been on board by now.'

'Why aren't you? What went wrong?'

Henri spread his hands wide. 'It is the new militiamen. They have not yet settled in and keep changing their routine. I was crouching beneath the wall on the inside of the prison for much of the night. Not until it was almost light was I able to climb over the wall. Unfortunately, by this time my guide had become frightened, fearing all was not well. He had gone, taking the horse I was to ride with him. Only Mary remained – but there are no riding horses on her father's farm.'

Henri smiled at Pilgrim apologetically. 'I suggested we should come to speak to you. I felt certain you would be able to obtain the loan of a horse on my behalf.'

'You'd have it returned by tonight,' promised Mary. 'My brother's waiting for Henri at Morwelham Quay. He'll bring it back.'

Pilgrim frowned. 'How is Henri going to find his way to this Morwelham Quay without a guide?'

'I've told him how to get there. It's not hard to find – but he must be there by noon. The boat has to set off by then.'

'That is not the only reason why I must leave very soon,' said Henri. 'As you well know, there is a nine o'clock roll call in the prison. It will be discovered I am missing and they will begin searching for me. I do not wish to be caught and sent to the *cachot* once again. I doubt if I would find another friend such as you there.'

Pilgrim was thinking fast as Henri was talking. 'I think I might be able to get a horse for you, Henri, but if it isn't returned by this evening I'll be forced to give an explanation for its loss – and then it will be *me* for the *cachot*.'

'My brother will bring the horse back by this evening, I promise!' declared a very agitated Mary. She was close to tears. 'He's got to come back to tell me that Henri is safely on board the boat. If . . . if anything goes wrong I'll come to Tor Royal and say I stole the horse and gave it to Henri to help his escape. But it won't go wrong. It *won't!*'

'You would do this for me?' Henri was fully aware that by taking such a course of action, she would be inviting a sentence of death for horse stealing. He looked at her with an expression that contained both incredulity and affection.

'Of course.'

Suddenly and unexpectedly, Henri cupped Mary's face in his hands and kissed her.

When he released her, Mary's cheeks had turned scarlet, but she gazed at him happily.

'Have you ever known such devotion?' Henri said to Pilgrim.

'I'll go and get you a horse. Mary will take you to an old sheep pen, halfway between here and Roundtor Farm. Wait for me there. I'll bring the horse as quickly as I can. We must hurry if you're not to miss the boat. Go now and I'll be as quick as I can.'

When Pilgrim returned to the house his breakfast was ready, but he told the servants he had promised to make an early start at Roundtor Farm and would forego the meal.

The same reason was given by him for wanting to take a horse from the Tor Royal stables, but here he encountered an unexpected problem. He was informed by one of the grooms that a party of dignitaries would be arriving at Tor Royal by carriage later that morning. Sir Thomas Tyrwhitt had arranged for them to be provided with horses from his stable and taken out on the moor. It was intended to give them an idea of the sport they might expect when the hunting season began. It was an arrangement that had been made some weeks before.

'So you see, sir, there's not a spare horse to be had today.'

This was disastrous news. If Henri was not sent on his

way within the hour, mounted on a good horse, capture would be inevitable for him.

Then Pilgrim had a sudden brainwave. 'What about the Prince Regent's horse? Is it going out with today's party?'

'No, sir.' The groom looked doubtful. 'But he's in peak condition. He won't be satisfied with just a brief trot from here to Roundtor.'

The groom, in common with all the other Tor Royal servants, was aware that Pilgrim spent most days at the Elfords' farm.

'Then I'll make certain he has a good run. Will you saddle him up for me, please. I'll go as soon as he's ready.'

The Prince Regent's horse was saddled quickly and Pilgrim rode off. He found Henri and Mary waiting for him at the appointed place.

Henri was a cavalry officer and knew horses. He was filled with admiration for the big stallion. Walking about the animal, he said, 'My friend, you have done me proud. This is a horse fit for a king.'

Pilgrim smiled broadly, but he did not enlighten the Frenchman. One day he would tell him, but not now.

'It is indeed,' he agreed. 'Go now. Catch your boat and see that the horse is returned on time. Good luck, Henri – and find some way of letting us know you have reached France safely.'

'Of course! I will send you a keg of the finest brandy. But now I must say farewell to my Mary. Would that she were coming with me.'

Minutes later, Henri was galloping away, heading for Morwelham Quay and freedom.

Standing beside Pilgrim, tears running down her cheeks, Mary waved until Henri passed out of sight.

'You're a brave girl, Mary. It's something Henri is very aware of. You haven't seen the last of him.'

'I hope not,' sobbed Mary. 'I love him very much. But his father is ill. He had to get home quickly. Now I must get home too. Thank you for getting the horse. I'll see it's returned to you. Will you be at Roundtor?'

Pilgrim nodded.

'It'll be brought there to you.'

Pilgrim was walking away in the direction of Roundtor when Mary called to him.

When he turned, she said, 'Give my love to Tacy. You can tell her about Henri, if you like. She'll say nothing to anyone. Besides, I've done nothing she wouldn't do for you if the need arose.'

Her words gave Pilgrim much food for thought as he walked to the Elfords' farm.

42

For two hours after arriving at Roundtor Farm, Pilgrim had to keep the news of Henri's escape a secret. Tom Elford and Johanna had gone to the prison with cakes and produce from the farm, leaving Pilgrim, Tacy and Billy at work repairing the roof of the cowshed.

There had been a strong wind blowing across the moor during the night. It had caused one of the roof timbers, riddled with woodworm, to finally collapse.

Not until the roof had been shored up and three pieces of timber replaced did Billy leave the others and go off across the moor to cut peat. Winter was approaching and sales of the moorland fuel to Dartmoor prison had been so good it had left the farm short.

When the young man had gone, Pilgrim told Tacy of the morning's happenings.

She was very excited at the news of Henri's escape and Mary's part in it, but was also fearful of what would happen if the prison authorities learned of Pilgrim's involvement – as they surely would if the Prince Regent's horse was not returned to Pilgrim that day.

This was a possibility that had been niggling at Pilgrim all morning and he shared Tacy's concern. 'Is Mary's brother as reliable as she says he is?'

'He's all right – when he's not been drinking.'

Pilgrim was hammering a final nail into a wooden beam. He missed and struck his thumb. Shaking his hand in a vain bid to get rid of the pain, he asked, 'What do you mean by that? Is he a drunkard?'

'Michael could never settle down to farming and he hated the moor. He was always arguing with his father about something. Eventually he left the farm and moved to Tavistock.'

Pilgrim knew Tavistock to be a fair-sized market town on the western fringe of Dartmoor, but Tacy was still talking.

'His going away didn't make much difference to the family. There were plenty more brothers and sisters to do the work on the farm. In fact, the main problem has always been to feed them all. They were probably pleased to get rid of one. Though I believe Michael's been in trouble with the town constable in Tavistock once or twice, for being drunk.'

Pilgrim looked at Tacy aghast. 'This is the man who's been entrusted to return the Prince Regent's horse to me?'

Pilgrim began to wonder what he had done!

'It'll be all right.' Tacy hoped she sounded more confident than she felt about the outcome of Pilgrim's actions in support of his French friend. 'Mary and Michael have always been pretty close. He's not the most reliable of men, but I don't think he'd do anything to let her down. Mary can certainly he relied on. If she's said she'll take the blame if anything goes wrong, that's exactly what she'll do. She'd sacrifice anything for Henri – even her life. Anyway, I've heard that Michael hopes to marry soon. He's probably settled down a lot more than when I knew him.'

Pilgrim sincerely hoped Tacy was right. If Henri escaped safely and the horse was returned, it would be a very satisfying incident. He did not like deceiving Sir Thomas Tyrwhitt. The owner of Tor Royal had been very generous to Virgil and himself. Nevertheless, the United States and France were both at war with Britain. Helping a French prisoner to escape by using a horse belonging to the man who ruled England would make a good story once the war was over.

Henri's escape pleased Tacy for quite another reason. Pilgrim had been shown that love was capable of overcoming the vicissitudes of war and prison walls. She hoped the lesson might not be lost on him.

They were still tidying up after repairing the roof, when a fearful Emma came running across the yard to the cowshed from the house.

'Pilgrim! Tacy's ma told me to come and tell you. Some militiamen are coming towards the farm. One of 'em's riding a horse.'

Pilgrim's immediate thought was that Henri must have been captured and the militiamen were coming to arrest him, bringing the Prince Regent's captured horse as evidence of his complicity in the escape.

He ran to the door and looked out. Beyond the farm he could see half a dozen uniformed men accompanied by an officer, riding a horse. The mount had none of the breeding of the stallion from Tor Royal and Pilgrim breathed a sigh of relief. This was probably one of many search parties out scouring the moor for the escaped prisoner-of-war.

When he returned to the cowshed, he saw Emma clambering up among the rafters.

'What are you doing up there?' he demanded.

'The militiamen might be looking for me. I'll hide away up here until they're gone.'

'They'll not be interested in you, Emma. I believe a French officer has escaped from the prison. They'll be looking for him.'

Emma was not convinced. 'I'm not taking any chances. If they don't find the Frenchman they might take me instead.'

Pilgrim smiled. 'If they search the farm, as well they might, they'd find you up there and want to know the reason why you're hiding from them. The best thing you can do is come down here with us. They'll probably think you're Tacy's sister and won't even ask any questions of you.'

Emma thought carefully about his words. She was a bright girl and realised there was much sense in what he said, but she was still doubtful. 'Are you sure they're not looking for me?'

'Of course he is,' said Tacy. 'Anyway, Pilgrim knows most of the militiamen, don't you?'

Pilgrim shook his head. 'Not any more, the ones I knew have been replaced by Irish militiamen.'

Looking through the open door of the cowshed he watched the men approach the gate. He felt a sudden unease when he recognised the man on the horse. It was the officer who had been involved in the argument with him and Virgil at the Tor Royal party.

'Irish militiamen?' Emma dropped to the ground from her refuge among the beams. 'I thought all Irishmen were tinkers. All those I've met have been.'

Pilgrim smiled despite his misgivings at seeing the Irish officer. 'I wouldn't repeat that in front of the militiamen, Emma. I don't think the officer, in particular, would take it very kindly.'

Before the militiamen entered the farmyard, Pilgrim dusted himself down and put on his uniform coat. Then he walked from the cowshed accompanied by Tacy and Emma.

His sudden appearance caused considerable excitement among the militiamen and he realised it was the sight of his uniform. These men were newly arrived at Dartmoor. They could probably not distinguish between a French and an American uniform. All they would know was it was not an English one.

His suspicions were confirmed when two of the men ran towards him, muskets extended menacingly.

They stopped when they reached him and one of the militiamen waved the muzzle of his musket dangerously close to Pilgrim's face.

'You. Are you the escaped prisoner?'

Pilgrim pushed the muzzle away from his face. 'I'm not an escaped anything. I'm a United States prisoner-of-war on parole from Dartmoor prison.'

The militiaman seemed to hear only what he wished to hear. Calling to the officer, he said, 'It's a prisoner all right, sir. But he says he's not a Frenchman.'

'Bring him here,' called the officer.

'You heard the lieutenant. He wants to speak to you.' The second militiaman prodded Pilgrim.

Trying hard to control his anger, Pilgrim made his way with as much dignity as he could muster to where the militia officer sat upon his horse.

'What's your name?' The Irish lieutenant looked down at Pilgrim unsmilingly.

'Lieutenant Pilgrim Penn.' The last time Pilgrim had seen this haughty young man, he was drunk and being helped from the room.

'Are you paroled to this farm?' It was evident that Pilgrim's recognition of the other man was not mutual.

'No.' Pilgrim spoke with considerably more patience than he felt towards this arrogant young man.

'Your parole licence, if you please.'

Pilgrim reached inside a pocket and a wave of despair hit him. He had removed the licence the previous day when the coat was given to one of the Tor Royal servants to brush and clean.

He began to explain to the militia lieutenant what had happened, but his explanation was cut short.

'You are aware that you are required to carry your parole licence with you at all times?'

'Yes, but as I was explaining . . .'

'You can explain it to the governor at Dartmoor prison. Two of you take him there. If he tries to escape – shoot him! He might be telling the truth, or he might not. It doesn't matter. He's in breach of his parole regulations. No doubt the governor will take him back where he belongs. Inside the prison.'

43

The militiamen made a search of the farmhouse and outbuildings, despite the objections of Joan and Tacy Elford, before Pilgrim was led off across the farmyard by the two militiamen.

He offered no resistance. His two guards were so excited at having a prisoner, their reaction to any form of protest would have been both unpredictable and dangerous. Besides, their officer had given them *carte blanche* by telling them to shoot him if he made an attempt to escape.

Should he be shot when they were out of sight of Roundtor Farm there would be no one to dispute the militiamen's version of events.

Pilgrim believed the officer's instruction had been given in a moment of inexperienced bravado, rather than an instruction to the two men that they should dispose of their prisoner. However, he did not intend antagonising them in any way and putting it to the test.

As Tacy passed by the officer sitting importantly upon his horse, she ceased her haranguing of the militiamen to call to Pilgrim, 'Shall I go and tell Sir Thomas Tyrwhitt what's happened here?'

'Yes. Tell him I've been arrested and sent to the prison by the militia officer who insulted Jemima Cotterell at Colonel Hawke's farewell party.'

Pilgrim knew Sir Thomas was in London and not at the house, but he hoped the use of Sir Thomas's name might help his cause.

The immediate effect of his words was to prompt one of the two militiamen accompanying him into giving him a painful prod in the back with his musket.

The action was seen by Joan who was standing in the doorway of the farmhouse kitchen, wiping flour-coated hands on her apron.

She too recognised the danger Pilgrim was in from their over-enthusiasm. 'Emma, follow Pilgrim and the militiamen all the way to Dartmoor prison, while Tacy runs to Tor Royal. Keep your distance, but don't let them out of your sight. If they do anything they shouldn't, you'll bear witness against them.'

'Wait!'

The officer's shout brought Pilgrim and his escort to a halt. Peering intently at Pilgrim, he said, 'How do you know what happened at Tor Royal?'

Pilgrim looked at the Irish lieutenant impassively. 'I was at the party too. I am paroled to Sir Thomas Tyrwhitt at Tor Royal. As I recall we were introduced, Lieutenant Kennedy.'

'You're one of the Americans who is friendly with the vicar's daughter?'

The Irish lieutenant seemed suddenly to be uncertain of the action he was taking and Tacy chose this moment to say, 'Sir Thomas Tyrwhitt is a personal friend of Lieutenant Penn's family. Pilgrim knew Colonel Hawke too. He'd never have dreamed of arresting him.'

In the course of their many conversations together, Pilgrim had told Tacy of the regard in which his father had held Lieutenant Colonel Hawke's father when they had fought on opposite sides in his country's war to gain its independence.

Pilgrim was grateful for Tacy's intervention. He was caught up in a dangerous situation. There was the added complication of the Prince Regent's horse. His arrest might precipitate the discovery that the animal was not in his possession.

All these things had gone through his mind before he replied to Lieutenant Kennedy's question.

'I am – and the man who offered to call you out is my commanding officer.'

Lieutenant Kennedy was silent for some moments as he mulled the situation over in his mind. Arriving at a decision, he said to the two militiamen guarding Pilgrim, 'You can rejoin the others for now.'

'But what about the prisoner?' one of them protested.

'He's not the man we're looking for. He poses no threat to anyone. Rejoin the others.'

Grumbling because their brief prospect of glory had been brought to a premature end, the two men reluctantly rejoined their companions who were now drinking water from a bucket provided for them by Joan Elford.

Dismounting from his horse in order that he might speak more confidentially to Pilgrim, Lieutenant Kennedy had lost his bombastic manner. He was almost apologetic when he asked, 'Did I make an absolute ass of myself the other evening?'

Surprised and greatly relieved at the welcome change of attitude from the militiaman, Pilgrim replied sarcastically, 'You didn't exactly cover yourself in glory. But be thankful you're alive. Had Captain Howard not been aware how drunk you were, he might well have called you out – and he's the best shot in the United States Marine Corps.'

'I'd had a great deal to drink,' admitted the unexpectedly contrite lieutenant. 'Far more than I am used to. I had been celebrating my birthday.'

When Pilgrim offered no comment, the young Irish lieutenant asked, 'Do you think Captain Howard would accept a written apology? I would send one to the young lady too, of course.'

After a moment more's hesitation, he added, 'Perhaps I should apologise to Sir Thomas Tyrwhitt as well.'

'I think your fellow officers were able to spirit you away before Sir Thomas became aware anything was amiss,' said Pilgrim. 'It might be as well if he remained in ignorance of what went on.'

He looked to where Tacy waited uncertainly beside the farmyard gate, ready if need be, to fire a final verbal volley at Lieutenant Kennedy before hurrying off to enlist the aid of Sir Thomas Tyrwhitt.

'Am I still under arrest, or may I rejoin my friends? There's a lot to do about the farm and work has come to a halt on my account.'

Lieutenant Kennedy looked at Tacy admiringly before replying to Pilgrim. 'You seem to have found a most attractive and spirited champion, Lieutenant Penn. You must explain to me some time how you Americans manage to allure such young women. Yes, you may return to her. I am searching for an escaped French prisoner. I have no wish to disrupt the lives of local residents.'

Looking pointedly at Tacy, he added, 'Besides, I shall certainly be passing this way again.'

Mounting his horse once more, Lieutenant Alan

Kennedy inclined his head in Tacy's direction. Calling on his men to resume their search for the escaped French prisoner-of-war, he turned his mount towards the farmyard gate.

The two militiamen who had expected to convey Pilgrim to Dartmoor prison scowled as they passed him by. The others smiled sheepishly in his direction.

As they passed through the gate, the Elford family and Emma gathered around Pilgrim and he thanked them profusely for their support.

'Had it not been for you – all of you – I would be on my way to the *cachot* – the punishment cell – inside the prison right now.'

He grimaced and explained to Joan Elford, 'I've been there before, fortunately only briefly. I didn't enjoy the experience. That's where I met Henri, Mary Gurney's friend.'

'Talking of Henri, didn't I hear one of the militiamen say they were searching for a Frenchman named Henri something-or-other?'

'That's right, Ma,' replied Tacy. 'It's the same man. He's escaped again.'

The glance exchanged between Tacy and Pilgrim was not lost on the farmer's astute wife.

'I hope Mary isn't involved in his escape this time – or anyone at Roundtor, either. The militiamen we've had at Dartmoor until now have been willing to turn a blind eye to a lot of what's gone on. I don't think these Irishmen are going to be as understanding.'

44

Mary's brother, Michael, reached Roundtor, riding the Prince Regent's horse, in the early evening. Mary was walking beside him, smiling happily.

Michael was full of praise for the stamina and speed of the horse. At the same time he expressed concern at the level of militia activity on and about the moor.

'There are patrols on roads all over the place,' he said. 'It's a good thing Henri went when he did. He'd never have got off the moor now.'

'They're all over our part of the moor too,' declared Mary. 'That's why I set off to meet Michael. I was anxious about him.'

'Did any of the militiamen stop and question you?' asked Pilgrim.

'No. When Mary met me we left the roads and came across the moor. She knows it better than anyone you'll meet – with the possible exception of Billy Yates.'

Pilgrim was relieved. The Prince Regent's horse was distinctive in size and colouring. He did not want any militiaman remembering it at a later date.

'Did Henri get away safely?'

Michael grinned. 'He did. He even found time to call at an inn between Tavistock and Morwhelham on his way there.'

Pilgrim was aghast. 'What did he think he was doing? His accent could have given him away. Had he been brought back to Dartmoor we'd all have been in trouble.'

'He said he was thirsty. As a matter of fact his accent was commented on at the inn. He told them he was an Irishman, over here to buy bloodstock. Those at the inn didn't know any different. Henri said he could have wined and dined for a week at the expense of the country's horse breeders, if he'd had the time.'

In spite of his concern for what *might* have happened, Pilgrim admired Henri's effrontery.

'The boat left on time,' said Michael. 'They'll have cleared Plymouth by now. If the weather holds they'll make good time. By nightfall tomorrow Henri should be back in his own country.'

'Thanks to Mary,' said Pilgrim.

She was a short distance away, talking to Tacy. Dismounting from the Prince Regent's horse, Michael patted the animal affectionately, then, lowering his voice, he said to Pilgrim, 'I think Mary was hoping he would take her with him. As it is, I doubt if she'll ever see him again.'

Mary's hearing was more acute than her brother had realised. Rounding on him, she cried, 'I *will* see him. He told me so. Pilgrim was there.'

'That's so,' agreed Pilgrim. 'I also know that Henri is very fond of you, Mary – and so he should be after the risks you've taken for him.'

'I've done nothing that Tacy wouldn't do for you. The only difference is that she's got you here. Henri and I are going to be hundreds of miles apart until this war is over. I won't even know what he's doing.'

'He'll find some way to get word to you, don't you worry. Henri's one of the most resourceful men I've ever met.'

Pilgrim hoped he was right. Mary would be desperately unhappy if she never heard from him again – and Henri was still an officer in Napoleon's army. He was liable to be sent anywhere he was needed.

Pilgrim was also thinking about the remainder of Mary's opening statement. He thought of how Tacy had sprung to his defence when the Irish militiamen were going to take him away.

He looked to where she was taking Mary inside the farmhouse, an arm about her friend's shoulders. He wondered what *her* thoughts were at this moment.

Mary and Henri would soon be hundreds of miles apart, yet Mary seemed to have very few doubts about the way Henri felt about her.

Despite the fact he and Tacy spent almost every day in each other's company, she would be far less certain of how Pilgrim felt about her.

He told himself yet again there was a very good reason for this, but he wondered whether Tacy would agree with such reasonableness.

Pilgrim decided that when the time was right he would have a talk with Tacy. Explain honestly how he felt about her and the situation in which they found themselves.

He had very little experience with women, but Pilgrim believed she would prove understanding.

Later that evening, Pilgrim breathed a huge sigh of relief when he handed the Prince Regent's horse over to a groom. He even managed a grin when the groom commented that the animal looked as though it had been ridden harder than at any time in its life.

Virgil came to the stables to meet him and, as they walked back to the house, Pilgrim told Virgil what had occurred.

The captain of marines saw the humour in the situation. At the same time he pointed out what might have happened had things not gone according to plan.

'Sir Thomas would have been very upset. He would quite rightly have regarded it as a breach of his trust. No doubt we'd both have had our paroles revoked.'

'I'm sorry, Virgil. I never even considered you might become involved.'

Virgil was struggling with his conscience. Suddenly he put a hand across Pilgrim's shoulders. 'Ignore what I've just said, Pilgrim. Life is so comfortable here I'm forgetting who and what I am. What we both are. We're first and foremost officers of the United States Marine Corps. Our country is at war with Britain, and France is an ally. We're on parole and have given our word we'll not take advantage of our position to attempt to escape, but we've given no promises about not helping others. You were right to do what you did and you've managed it without apparently affecting anyone adversely. Well done.'

Virgil gave Pilgrim a wry smile. 'I'm sure you'll understand if I don't submit a report commending your actions until after we return to the States. Now, you're not the only one to have had an interesting and exciting day. Come inside the house and meet someone. On the way I'll try to fill in as much of the story as I can . . .'

45

Had Winifrith Cudmore delayed her departure from Tor Royal by little more than twenty-four hours, her journey would not have proved necessary. She would also have changed the destinies of a number of people, including that of her daughter.

When Pilgrim entered the house with Virgil he was flabbergasted to see Sophie seated on a settee in the drawing room. She was suntanned, but appeared very tired and looked desperately unhappy.

'But . . . your mother's gone to London looking for you! She thinks you're in Spain,' said Pilgrim, inanely.

'She's unlikely to learn very much from the War Office in London,' explained Virgil. 'Sophie has come direct from the battle front, landing at Plymouth only this morning. News of the war in Spain is unlikely to reach London for another day or two. Even then there will be nothing to indicate that Sophie's returned to England.'

Pilgrim looked from Virgil to the unhappy woman

and back again. 'I'm sorry . . . I really don't understand what's happening.'

'Sophie was married in Spain. To the army officer Winifrith was trying to keep her from.' Virgil seemed to find it difficult to carry the explanation any farther and Sophie herself completed the explanation for him.

'Harry, my husband, was in the Rifle Corps. He . . . he was killed in the fighting near San Sebastian. He and his men were surprised by a French cavalry force.'

Tears welled up in Sophie's eyes and began to roll down her cheeks, but she continued. 'I was in camp when I heard about the action. I set off to try to find him but there were only a few survivors. One was a badly wounded sergeant. He brought me Harry's signet ring. Harry had given it to him for me, before he died . . .'

As she spoke, she wound the signet ring in question around and around in a distressed manner on a finger of her right hand.

'The sergeant died before he could pass on a report to anyone else. As a result Harry has been listed only as "missing". Although I know the truth, he won't be listed among the casualties for some time . . .'

Sophie closed her eyes as though in pain, but it did not stop the tears.

'You don't need to tell me any more, Sophie. You've had a very, very unhappy time. Here, Virgil's poured a brandy for you.'

Sophie took the drink with some difficulty because her hand was shaking alarmingly. She took a couple of gulps of the fiery drink and then stood up.

'I . . . I'm sorry, but I think I'll go to my room now.'

'Of course.'

Pilgrim and Virgil stood up and watched in silent sympathy as she headed for the door.

With her hand on the door knob, she turned to look

back at them. 'Thank you both for your kindness. I am glad I found you here and not my mother.' Although she addressed her words to both of them, she looked only at Virgil. Then she opened the door and was gone.

Without speaking, Virgil poured some of Sir Thomas Tyrwhitt's brandy into two glasses and handed one of them to Pilgrim before he sat down heavily upon one of the padded leather chairs.

'She's a courageous girl. A *very* courageous girl,' he said, eventually. 'She gave up everything for the man she loved, only to have him killed within a few weeks of their wedding.'

He took a deep draught of the brandy in his glass, then sat looking down at the remainder before speaking again.

'When she first arrived back here, she told me a little more about what happened. It was almost as though she was desperate to tell someone. She cried a lot too, but it's hardly surprising.'

Finishing off the still quite considerable amount of drink left in his glass, he stood up and refilled it once more, holding out the bottle to Pilgrim, who shook his head.

'She went off looking for her husband's body, you know, but the French were advancing. She would have been taken prisoner by them had some of her husband's regiment not taken her back forcibly.'

'She certainly deserves more happiness than she's found,' agreed Pilgrim, 'especially after throwing convention to the wind in order to go off with him.'

Pilgrim looked up at Virgil. 'Will you write and let Winifrith know she's here?'

'I have no intention of writing to Winifrith,' declared Virgil firmly, 'but I do feel we owe it to Sir Thomas to let him know. However, Sophie needs a little time to put herself back together before she meets up with either of them. I'll write to Sir Thomas, perhaps tomorrow, or the day after – and send the letter off a day or two after that. I somehow feel Sir Thomas will understand.'

Virgil sat down heavily and gave Pilgrim a sad smile. 'With any luck the news might take another day or two getting from Sir Thomas to his sister. Given another week or more, Sophie might be more capable of coping with her mother.'

46

Pilgrim told Sophie's story to Tacy as he turned the handle of a butter churn for her at Roundtor Farm three days later.

He had been unable to visit the farm during the intervening period. Trouble had flared up once more between the French and American prisoners-of-war in Dartmoor prison. On this occasion the fault lay with the Americans. Pilgrim had been at the prison instigating an inquiry on behalf of Virgil.

Listening to Pilgrim now, Tacy was torn between very real sympathy for Sophie and a feeling of uneasiness because the Tor Royal owner's niece was once more living beneath the same roof as Pilgrim.

Sophie was a very attractive woman. She now had the added appeal of having travelled to Spain in romantic circumstances, becoming involved in the war there and being dealt a tragic blow by fate.

Tacy felt she had little with which to challenge the appeal of such a woman.

Sensing something of what she was thinking, Pilgrim

added, 'Sophie's been through a very unhappy and difficult time, but Virgil seems to have found a new role as her comforter. I believe it's one he's finding much to his liking.'

'Don't you mind about that?'

'Mind? Why should I?'

'Well . . . you and Sophie seemed to be very friendly before she went away. You might have expected her to turn to you for comfort.'

'She couldn't have a better man than Virgil to help her right now. He's seen far more of life than me. She'll get better advice from him than I'm capable of giving her.'

Turning the handle of the churn vigorously, Pilgrim added, 'I've had experience with my pa of opening up new lands, making a new home and of fighting both Indians and the British. I just haven't met enough girls, or women, to be of any help with their problems.'

He paused in his work and looked at Tacy. 'I know you better than any other girl I've ever met, Tacy. Yet I can't even find words to tell you some of the things I want to say.'

For a moment Tacy thought he was at last about to declare his feelings for her, but as the moments passed and he said nothing further, her optimism seeped away.

She remembered the other times she had felt the same way. As the occasions multiplied without anything being said about Pilgrim's feelings for her, she had begun to believe any idea of a romance between them was in her mind alone.

Suddenly the thought entered her head that Pilgrim might be trying to tell her something very different. That he did not want to come to Roundtor Farm any more. After all, he had no need to work. Perhaps he would be happier just enjoying life at Tor Royal with the friends of Sir Thomas Tyrwhitt. With Sophie too, despite his denial.

'Are you trying to say you'd rather not come to work at Roundtor any more?'

Her question took Pilgrim by surprise. 'Why should I say that? I *like* coming here.'

'Well, if it's not that, what is it you find so difficult to say?' Tacy decided to take the initiative and discover just what it was he found so difficult to say to her.

The tone of her voice was somewhat less belligerent, but her attitude caught Pilgrim off balance. He *had* been on the verge of saying some of the things she had been wanting to hear for so long. To open his heart and tell her how he really felt about her. At the same time he intended explaining why he had not attempted to do anything about it.

Instead, he floundered embarrassingly. 'Nothing. At least . . . nothing important. No, that isn't right, either . . .'

At that moment, Emma came to the kitchen door, across the farmyard, and called out, 'Pilgrim! Mrs Elford said to tell you a man in uniform is coming towards the farm, riding a horse. She says it looks a bit like that officer who almost arrested you.'

'What can he want?' Pilgrim had met the Irish militiaman once or twice during the past few days, but he did not feel entirely at ease in his presence.

'I expect he's come to see Tacy,' declared Johanna, mischievously. She had brought a bucket of milk from the cowshed as Emma called her message from the farmhouse. 'That's what he came here for the day before yesterday.'

'That's not true, Johanna, as well you know!'

Glaring angrily at her grinning sister, Tacy explained, 'Lieutenant Kennedy came looking for you. He said there'd been some trouble among the Americans up at the prison. He thought you ought to know.'

Pilgrim remembered meeting up with Alan Kennedy on that day as he passed through Princetown on his way to the prison. It meant the militiaman's excuse for visiting Roundtor was a deliberate lie. He must have taken advantage of Pilgrim's absence to visit Tacy.

The knowledge did nothing to endear the Irishman to Pilgrim. He found some consolation in the fact that Tacy thought it necessary to explain away Lieutenant Kennedy's visit.

But Johanna had not yet done with her mischief making. 'If he only came to speak to Pilgrim, why didn't he go away again when he found he wasn't here, instead of staying talking to you for *ages*?'

'You're just trying to cause trouble,' said Emma, who had come from the house. 'I was with Tacy the whole of the time the militiaman was here. He probably said as much to me as he did to her – not that I wanted him to. I don't much care for him.'

While they had been talking, the subject of their conversation had reached the farmyard gate. He waved to them in a friendly manner before dismounting.

Leading his horse inside the farmyard, he called cheerily to Pilgrim, 'I thought I would find you here. I called in to tell you I've just escorted twenty of your fellow Americans from the prison to Tavistock. They've been granted parole there.'

His words were for Pilgrim, but his glance rested upon Tacy for far longer than it did upon the United States marine.

'I expect Virgil or I will be given a list of their names when one of us next goes to the prison.'

Pilgrim knew it was more likely to be him than Virgil. The marines captain had been troubled by his wounded leg of late. As a result, most of the prison visits had been left to Pilgrim.

Not that Virgil was particularly upset about being restricted to the house at the moment. Sophie's concern for his comfort and well-being had been heightened by her experiences on the battlefields of Spain. She seemed to find an escape from her own deep sadness by helping Virgil in every way she could.

'There were some extremely interesting men among them,' said Kennedy. 'I was talking to one of them who owns a whole fleet of merchantmen. He was complaining bitterly about being held as a prisoner-of-war. I'm inclined to agree with him. He should never have been taken in the first place.'

'That sounds like Conrad Steiger,' commented Pilgrim. 'He'll always find something to grumble about to anyone who's prepared to listen.'

Lieutenant Kennedy frowned at Pilgrim's apparent lack of concern for his countryman. 'At least he'll be staying with a family who should appreciate his background. He's gone to live in the home of a man who owns a store as well as a small freight company. He has recently bought a share in a trading vessel, so they'll find plenty to talk about. There are also three pretty young daughters in the house.'

Pilgrim thought that Steiger was the last man who should have been billeted in a house where there were three young women, but he kept his thoughts to himself.

Lieutenant Kennedy switched his attention to Tacy. 'Would it be your sheep held in a pen about half a mile along the valley from here?'

Tacy nodded. 'Yes, some ewes and a young ram are going to market tomorrow. It'll save having to feed them through the winter. Why do you ask?'

'As I came by I noticed that some of the stones have been knocked to the ground. One sheep was actually standing on the wall. I drove it back inside, but unless the damage is repaired it won't keep them there for long.'

Tacy was alarmed. 'If they get out we'll never find them in time to take them to market. I'll need to fix the wall right away – and find any of the sheep too, if they've got out.'

'I'll come and help you,' offered Alan Kennedy immediately.

Pilgrim had been watching the militiaman. He believed he had only mentioned the broken wall in the hope that Tacy would want to deal with it immediately, thus affording him an opportunity to accompany her.

'It's all right, Tacy,' said Emma promptly. 'You and Pilgrim carry on with the butter-making. I'll go.'

Tacy hesitated. Whether it was because she did or did not want Kennedy's company, Pilgrim could not tell, but Emma was talking once more.

'You can send Billy to help when he comes back. He'll have the wall fixed in no time.'

Billy was away from the farm with the pony and cart. He was conveying peat to the house in preparation for the winter months that would soon be upon them.

Lieutenant Kennedy tried unsuccessfully to hide his disappointment. With far less enthusiasm than before, he said, 'My offer still stands. I'll come and help with the wall and the sheep.'

As Kennedy led his horse out of the farmyard behind Emma, Tacy said, 'I think Lieutenant Kennedy's rather nice, don't you?'

Pilgrim's grunted reply was decidedly non-committal and Tacy persisted, 'Don't you like him, Pilgrim?'

'Not much. He's not an officer I would want in my command.'

'Why not?' Tacy asked the question in apparent innocence.

'He's got a bit of growing up to do. He's never been in action and still believes war is fun. It isn't. Officers who think it is are a danger to the men they command.'

Tacy had hoped Pilgrim's dislike of Alan Kennedy might stem from jealousy because the young Irishman was paying her too much attention. She felt disappointed.

Tacy would have been far happier had she been able to read Pilgrim's mind. His first two meetings with the militiaman had not been propitious. Since then Lieutenant Kennedy had gone out of his way to be pleasant to him, yet he still neither liked, nor trusted the man.

Pilgrim too was wondering whether his continued dislike had its roots in Kennedy's current interest in Tacy.

47

Virgil allowed three days to pass before sending a letter to Sir Thomas Tyrwhitt, informing him of Sophie's return to Tor Royal and the true circumstances of her disappearance.

A week later a brief note was received from Sir Thomas's secretary. It said no more than that Sir Thomas had asked him to acknowledge the letter, send his love and condolences to his niece and explain that he was accompanying the Prince Regent on a visit to the north of England.

The secretary declared Sir Thomas would reply at length as soon as he returned.

Virgil revealed the contents of both letters to the Tor Royal butler, with the result that the whole household awoke to each new day wondering whether it would see the return of Sir Thomas and the formidable Winifrith Cudmore.

As the days passed and she had still not descended upon them, the household became even more apprehensive about the intentions of Sir Thomas's uncertain-tempered sister.

It was inconceivable that she would do nothing at all. The household staff sympathised wholeheartedly with Sophie, aware of all that had happened to her after she ran off from Tor Royal. They watched with undisguised approval as she slowly put the pieces of her shattered life back into place with the patient help of Virgil.

Despite the initial reservations held by some of the servants, the two Americans had settled into the household well and had gained the respect of most of those who worked there. There was particular sympathy for Virgil. His wounded leg was presenting increasing problems for him, but he bore his pain and discomfort without complaint.

Not until four weeks had elapsed did Sir Thomas return to Tor Royal. He was alone and he was able to lift, at least temporarily, the threat of the imminent arrival of Winifrith.

Genuinely fond of his niece, he greeted her warmly. Holding her to him, he murmured, 'Poor Sophie, you must have been through some absolutely dreadful experiences. Thank heavens that you, at least, have returned home to us safely. I sincerely trust your mother will do the same.'

Sophie pulled away from him. 'Mother . . . ? I am sorry, Uncle, I don't understand . . .'

Sir Thomas looked at her in astonishment, 'Do you mean you don't know? But of course not, how could you? My child, your mother left for the front, in Spain, some weeks ago. She was determined to fetch you back to England. At this very moment she is probably causing Lord Wellington more problems than Napoleon, and all because he is unable to produce you on demand.'

Sophie gazed at him in disbelief. 'You mean . . . she's gone to Spain looking for me?'

'That's exactly what I mean. When she could obtain no satisfaction at the War Office, she declared they were all totally incompetent and set off to find you for herself.'

Sophie's mouth opened twice without any words escaping, then she gave way to sudden, uncontrollable laughter.

Virgil thought it a wonderful sound. After weeks of desperate unhappiness, Sophie had begun to smile occasionally once more, but it was the first time he had heard her laugh out loud since her return from Spain.

Once she had brought her merriment under control, Sophie wiped tears from her eyes and said, 'Oh dear! I really should not find it amusing to have caused everyone so much trouble. Poor mother will absolutely *hate* the conditions she will encounter on the campaign. Lord Wellington has the scent of victory in his nostrils and is pushing the French army hard. Poor Harry always said the war would be won or lost in the course of the next few months. It's doubtful whether the British army will retire to quarters for the winter, as is usual. Mother will suffer dreadful hardships, only to eventually learn that I am already safely back in England!'

The sadness had returned when Sophie spoke of her late husband, but it disappeared once more when she said, 'I know I should be feeling terribly guilty, but if only mother didn't constantly interfere so in my life, matters would never have come to this.'

Screwing up her face in a moment of sudden anguish, she added, 'And Harry might still be alive today if she had not interfered and had him transferred to active service. She deserves to suffer a little, at least.'

'I am quite certain your mother means well, my dear,' said Sir Thomas, his arm about Sophie's shoulders. 'Although we none of us agree with the way she goes about things, she *does* have your best interests at heart.'

He cleared his throat noisily. 'However, I do agree that she has an unfortunate tendency to want to organise other people's lives for them. But you must try not to worry too much about her. I will have a letter to Lord Wellington sent off with the official despatches from the War Office. He will be informed you are safe and well, back here at Tor Royal.'

Showing little enthusiasm, Sir Thomas added, 'When the news reaches Winifrith I am quite sure she will return to Tor Royal immediately. Indeed, she may know already. If that is so, she will no doubt already be on her way home to us.'

48

'Them two are sweet on each other, ain't they?'

Emma added the question to her statement as Virgil and Sophie rode away along a curving valley, not far from Roundtor.

Sophie turned to give a final wave to Pilgrim before horses and riders passed from view behind the slopes of the tor.

Pilgrim and Emma were busily securing the roof of a low, dry-stone lean-to shelter they had built inside one of the many sheep pens scattered about this part of the moor.

Their task was being carried out at the suggestion of Tom Elford. The farmer was suffering another of his bouts of ill health. However, in common with all moorland dwellers, he could still read nature's signs. All the indications were that it was going to be an early and probably severe winter.

There was not room in the buildings about the small Roundtor farmyard for all the sheep he owned. This year he intended bringing as many sheep as possible close to the farm, in a bid to minimise his losses.

While Pilgrim and Emma worked, Tacy and Johanna were at the prison market selling bread and cakes to the prisoners-of-war. The Americans had just received some of their overdue allowance. They had money to spend on such small luxuries.

Virgil and Sophie had been out riding and decided to call at Roundtor Farm to speak to Pilgrim.

'I think they're very happy in each other's company,' agreed Pilgrim. 'It's pleasing to see. Virgil's been in a lot of pain with his leg just lately, and Sophie has been through a pretty horrific experience.'

'It's very special to find someone nice when you've been through bad times,' said Emma with feeling. 'I'm glad I've found Billy.'

'He's very happy to have you too,' said Pilgrim.

He was on the roof of the lean-to, laying squares of turf across a framework of sticks and weighing them down with stones picked up from the moor.

'If your captain and Sir Thomas Tyrwhitt's niece can go around and show they think a lot of each other, why can't you and Tacy do the same?'

'I've thought about that,' said Pilgrim. 'It's rather complicated, but I want to speak to Tacy as soon as I can, to tell her how I feel about her . . . What I think about everything.'

'I suggest you get round to it pretty quickly,' said Emma. 'And you want to keep her away from that Lieutenant Kennedy. He's no good for her. He's no good for any girl.'

'Why do you think that, Emma?'

'I don't *think* nothing,' said Emma vehemently. 'I haven't told anyone else – and I won't, either – but he tried it on with me that day when we went out to repair the sheep pen.'

Pilgrim was taken aback by her revelation, but was inclined to be sceptical.

'Was it a serious attempt to do something, or was he just making suggestions?'

'It was serious enough to give me a bruise here.' Emma touched her right breast, briefly. 'I needed to bite him good and hard before he let me go. Then he told me I was an "uppity little bitch". I won't tell you what I called him, but I'd keep an eye on him and Tacy, if I was you. I've met his sort before. They think there are two sorts of girls in the world – and Tacy and I belong to the sort that are suppposed to be here for them to do what they want with.'

She looked up at him as he squatted on the roof of the crude shelter thinking of what she had said. 'I don't want you telling any of this to Billy. He'd feel he had to say something to Lieutenant Kennedy. That would land him in serious trouble. Billy's no match for a militia officer, even though he's worth ten of that one. Yes, and most other men too.'

'You think a lot of Billy, don't you, Emma?'

'Of course I do. He may not be as clever as some, but I know a good man when I find one. I ought to, I met enough of the other sort while I was a tinkers' girl.'

'But you haven't always been a tinkers' girl, Emma. Sometimes you say or do things that no tinkers' girl would know anything about. How did you come to get mixed up with them in the first place?'

'I dunno. I can't really remember a time when I wasn't with 'em. Though sometimes, when Mrs Elford says something nice to me, I seem to remember someone just like her. Someone I feel belonged to *me*, but that's all.' Emma shrugged. 'I expect I just dreamed about it, that's all.'

With a struggle, she lifted a granite boulder above her

head and Pilgrim took it from her. She looked at him in silence for a few moments. Then, in her characteristically blunt manner, she asked, 'Do you love Tacy?'

The question took Pilgrim completely by surprise. He only just succeeded in preventing the rock he was holding falling from his arms and crashing through the turf roof.

'What sort of a question is that?' he demanded.

'A very simple one, I'd have thought. Do you love her?'

'I'm . . . I've never met anyone like her before.' He felt embarrassed and gave her an evasive reply, but it was not one that Emma was prepared to accept.

'That's not what I'm asking you.'

'I would think the way I feel about Tacy is something between me and her and no one else.'

Pilgrim felt the snub was wholly justified, but gradually curiosity got the better of him. He had known Emma for long enough to realise she must have a very good reason for asking such a question.

'Why do you want to know, Emma?' The question was asked almost reluctantly.

Emma paused in the act of handing up another boulder. She lowered it to the ground again before replying. 'I know how Tacy feels about you, but I don't know your feelings for her. I don't think she does, either. If the two of you *do* love each other, then that's all right. You won't need anyone else, will you?'

Emma sat down on the stone she had just placed on the ground and looked up at him. 'On the other hand, if Tacy's just wasting her time loving you, there's no reason why she shouldn't have a bit of fun with this Lieutenant Kennedy, I suppose.'

Resting elbows upon knees, she cupped her face in her hands and said, 'She'll know it won't mean anything, not to him, anyway, but that won't matter. I mean, look at the life she leads at Roundtor Farm. It's nothing but work from the time the sun rises, until it sets again – and beyond that too, more often than not. I ask you, what sort of life is that for *anyone*? It's all right if you're doing it because you're with someone you love, and who loves you. That makes it all worthwhile. If you're not . . . ? Well, then you've got to take what you can from life, when you can, haven't you?'

Squatting on the uncompleted turf roof, Pilgrim said, 'You're full of surprises, Emma. I'd never have thought of you as a philosopher, but that's what you are, right enough.'

'What's that mean?' asked Emma aggressively. 'Why am I a philo . . . a . . . what you said I was?'

'It's a compliment. Philosophers are clever people. They think a lot about things, Emma. They make others think about things too.'

'Well, that's all right then. I don't mind being one of them if it makes you think about Tacy. She's one of the nicest people I've ever met. I'd like her to be really happy.'

'If you mean that, then you should warn her off Lieutenant Kennedy. She'll find no happiness keeping company with him.'

'I didn't say she would,' retorted Emma. 'I said she could have some *fun* with him, if that's what she wants. But I'll make sure she goes into it with her eyes wide open, don't you worry about that.'

'I'd rather she had nothing to do with him at all, Emma.'

Giving him one of her direct looks, Emma said, 'If that's what you *really* want then I think you'd better do something about it. If I was you I wouldn't leave it too long, Pilgrim.'

Her attention suddenly shifted away from him and her expression softened.

Following the direction of her gaze, Pilgrim saw Billy had just come into view around a curve of the hill. Two dogs were driving perhaps a dozen sheep ahead of him.

Standing up and handing him the rock on which she had been seated, she said, 'Here, take this old stone. I'm going to meet Billy. Like I said, life shouldn't be all work and nothing else, should it?'

As Emma hurried off to meet Billy, she gave an occasional carefree skip. Billy was still some distance away, but Pilgrim could see his wide and happy grin as he waved to Emma.

They were an unlikely couple. The worldly-wise tinkers' girl and the simple young man who knew nothing of the world beyond Dartmoor. Yet they were ridiculously happy in each other's company.

Pilgrim smiled to himself, thinking of what Emma had said to him. She had deliberately provoked him into thinking about his relationship with Tacy.

He alone knew how much he thought of her. He had believed she was aware of his feelings. He also thought she clearly understood why he was unable to express his feelings at this time. Now he realised she had probably misinterpreted his reticence as a lack of any deep and real feeling for her.

He would need to do something about it – and do it soon if he was to nip in the bud any relationship between Tacy and Lieutenant Kennedy.

49

The hopes Pilgrim entertained of telling Tacy how he felt about her suffered a setback the following morning.

The day began early for the Tor Royal household. As a result of the pain and discomfort caused to Virgil by his leg wound, Sophie had expressed her concern to Sir Thomas Tyrwhitt.

The Dartmoor landowner had called in an eminent surgeon from Plymouth. His opinion had been that part of the musket ball which had caused the wound was still lodged in Virgil's leg. The surgeon suggested the piece of lead had possibly moved recently, causing the extra pain Virgil was suffering.

The surgeon expressed his willingness to operate in a bid to locate and remove the offending body, but he warned Virgil there was a very real danger of infection following upon such an operation. Should this occur, he declared it would prove necessary to amputate the limb.

Virgil had always held the opinion that British surgeons resorted to amputation far too readily. It was a view strongly held by his father, who had been in charge of medical services for the army of the United States during the War of Independence.

He thanked the surgeon and Sir Thomas, but declined to be operated on in England. He would wait until the operation could be performed by a United States surgeon.

Offended by Virgil's lack of faith in his ability and that of his British colleagues, the surgeon pointed out that the war might continue for many years to come. He suggested that although the presence of the musket ball was not life-threatening at present, another year might find Virgil permanently crippled by his wound.

Sir Thomas was now able to use his considerable influence once more. After a long discussion with Virgil, he arranged for him to be interviewed by the senior naval surgeon at the Plymouth naval hospital.

If the naval surgeon agreed with the prognosis of his civilian colleague, Virgil would be recommended for repatriation to the United States.

Today was the day Virgil was to travel to Plymouth for his examination. He would be riding there in Sir Thomas's own carriage, accompanied on the journey by Sophie and by Sir Thomas himself. The Dartmoor landowner had business in the busy sea port.

Two militiamen would be accompanying Virgil as an armed escort, but they would be travelling on the outside of the carriage.

The party set off early, leaving Pilgrim to prepare himself for another day at Roundtor Farm – but today was likely to be more important to him than any other.

He had lain awake for much of the night thinking about Tacy and the possibility that there might be a future for them together.

He had decided to tell her of his feelings and his hopes

and fears for the future. Once it had been said, much would depend upon her own thoughts and feelings for him.

The outcome of Virgil's medical examination was also likely to have an impact on Pilgrim's present way of life. There were a number of naval men in the prison now of equal rank to Pilgrim, but Virgil particularly wanted him to rank as the senior officer. He intended to promote him to the rank of brevet captain in the event of his own repatriation.

It was a responsibility Pilgrim did not particularly want, but he would not sidestep his duty.

All these thoughts were in his mind that morning as he finally set off for Roundtor Farm.

The house was well behind him when he glanced back and caught a glimpse of bright yellow in the lane that led from the direction of Princetown.

It was the colour of a prisoner-of-war's uniform. For a brief moment Pilgrim thought of ignoring its implications and carrying on to Roundtor.

Instead, he retraced his steps and met with Ephraim at the entrance gate to Tor Royal.

'Morning, Lieutenant. I'm on my way to the house to see Cap'n Howard. It's a matter I think you should hear about too.'

'Captain Howard isn't at the house, Ephraim. He's gone into Plymouth with Sir Thomas Tyrwhitt.'

Pilgrim told the marines sergeant the reason for Virgil's journey, and asked, 'Will your news wait until tomorrow? I'm sure the captain won't mind coming to the prison to see you.'

'For all I care about the man involved, it could wait for ever, but I reckon it's something both you and Cap'n Howard should know about right now. Things might already have gone too far.'

'What sort of "things", Ephraim?'

Pilgrim asked the question although he was already convinced he would not want to know. He could see the day at Roundtor and his planned talk with Tacy slipping farther and farther away.

'You'd better tell me all about it. Who is it who's got himself in trouble?'

'Steiger.'

Pilgrim was startled. 'But . . . he's out on parole. How is it you've heard about it and Captain Howard and I haven't?'

'He *was* on parole, Lieutenant, but he's not any more. It seems he went a bit farther than he should have with a young girl – and I'm not talking about distance from the place to which he was paroled. He and the youngest daughter of the man he was staying with were left alone in the house. Steiger plied her with drink then got her into his bed. She screamed when she realised what was happening and folk came running. Steiger was given a beating, then handed over to the town constable and returned to the prison.'

'Damn the man! His actions could undo all the goodwill that's been built up with the local people by us *and* the French. I hope the governor will keep him inside the prison now. It's the best place for him.'

'I wouldn't say that, Lieutenant.'

There was something in the way the opinion was expressed that caused Pilgrim to say sharply, 'I think you'd better explain that remark, Ephraim.'

'When he was brought back to the prison he was thrown in the *cachot*.'

'So? I can't think of a better place for him. A couple of days in there might help teach him he's not such a great man as he'd like everyone to believe.'

'It might teach him a whole lot more than that, Lieutenant. You remember me telling you that the husband of the slave girl there was so much trouble about was now a prisoner-of-war in Block Four?'

When Pilgrim nodded, Ephraim continued, 'When it was learned Steiger had been brought back to the prison and thrown in the *cachot*, the girl's husband, Steiger's whipped slave and two of the biggest ex-slaves in Block Four staged a fight. It took a whole lot of militiamen to break it up and some of them got hurt. As a result, all four were thrown in the *cachot* too.'

'With Steiger?' The very thought of it made Pilgrim's blood run cold. He had an intense dislike of Conrad Steiger, but . . .

'When did all this happen?'

Ephraim shrugged nonchalantly, 'A couple of days ago. Maybe three.'

'Good God, Ephraim! You know as well as I do what might have happened in the *cachot*. Why didn't you come to tell Captain Howard or me about this before today?'

'I don't owe Steiger any favours, Lieutenant. He's had a day of reckoning coming to him for a very long time. All the same, if the others have done to Steiger what they boasted they would do, it's probably time he was brought out now.'

'Damn you, Ephraim,' said Pilgrim angrily, 'you should have got word to us long before things reached this stage!'

Even as he reprimanded the black sergeant, Pilgrim was aware that had *he* been in his place, he would probably have behaved no differently. There was no doubt at all that Steiger deserved whatever punishment was meted out to him. Nevertheless, it could

not be allowed to continue now it had been brought
to Pilgrim's attention.

'We'd better go to the prison right away and speak to
the governor. If Steiger's still alive he's got to be brought
out of the *cachot* right away.'

50

The governor of Dartmoor prison listened with growing irritation as Pilgrim suggested that Steiger should be released from the *cachot* immediately if a violent confrontation between black and white Americans were to be averted.

'Steiger has been returned to my prison because serious allegations have been made against him by a well-respected citizen of Tavistock. Very serious allegations indeed.'

'I realise all that,' said Pilgrim patiently. 'He will no doubt go on trial to answer the allegations, in due course. If he is found guilty I expect him to be punished according to the laws of your country. That will be acceptable to the other Americans too. Unfortunately, if he remains in the *cachot* with the men who are in there with him right now I doubt if he will survive to stand trial.'

Pilgrim knew he had not yet fully convinced the governor but he felt it was very important to have Conrad Steiger released from the *cachot*.

'I'll be perfectly honest with you, Governor Cotgrave. I have no liking for Steiger. But if he dies while he's in the *cachot* the men in there with him are going to be held responsible for his death. It will provoke a bloodier riot than anything you've experienced in Dartmoor so far. It will be black American against white American and will involve some of the most violent men in your prison. It will also be on record that I warned you it was about to happen.'

'Don't threaten me, Lieutenant Penn. I will consider reasoned arguments, but not threats. Besides, what happens in the future will not concern me. I am leaving my post here at the end of next month. I would like to say I am sorry to be leaving, but that would not be honest. The authorities in London seem to believe the end of the war with France is in sight. When that happy day comes French prisoners-of-war will be repatriated. It has been suggested that *all* American prisoners will then be brought to Dartmoor prison.'

Leaning back in his chair, Captain Cotgrave said, 'I will be happy to forego the pleasure of welcoming your countrymen to Dartmoor, Lieutenant Penn. However, I have no wish to add to the problems of my successor. I will have your Mr Steiger released from the *cachot*, examined by the surgeon, and placed under house arrest in the Petty Officers' Block.'

'Thank you, Governor. You will be doing your successor a great service.'

Governor Cotgrave detailed one of the two gaolers who had been present in the room throughout the discussion to go and release Steiger. When he had gone, the governor said to Pilgrim, 'Before you leave I would like you to go through the occurrence book with me. There have been a couple of deaths. Captain Howard always took details and wrote to their relatives.

There have also been a number of new admissions. You might like to check their names and status . . .'

Pilgrim looked through the occurrence book and was copying out the names of the recent admissions to the prison when there came an urgent knocking at the door. It was repeated before the governor had time to answer and, somewhat irritably, he instructed whoever was outside to 'Come in!'

It was a medical orderly, the one who had been particularly friendly to Pilgrim during his period in the prison hospital.

Extremely agitated, the orderly addressed himself to the governor. 'Begging your pardon, sir, but Mr Dykar says would you come to the hospital right away. It's the man who's just been released from the *cachot*.'

'What is it? Is he ill? Surely Mr Dykar can deal with him. Why does he want me there?'

'It's not that he's ill, sir. It's more . . . well, it's what's been done to him while he's been in the *cachot*.'

'What's happened? Has he been attacked? Is that it?'

'Not exactly . . .' The medical orderly licked his lips, ill-at-ease. 'It's worse than that, sir . . . I think you should come to the hospital.'

'Oh . . . very well! You had better come with me, Lieutenant Penn. Why the medical orderly can't tell me what's happened, I really don't know.'

At the hospital, they found the surgeon in his office. There was a strong aroma of brandy in the air. After suggesting they should be seated, he offered his visitors a drink.

'We are not here on a social visit,' snapped a tight-lipped governor. 'Your orderly told me there was some sort of emergency. Is there, or is there not?'

'I wouldn't call it an emergency, Captain Cotgrave.

At least, it is not a medical emergency. However, it might provoke serious incidents affecting discipline in Block Four.'

'For goodness' sake, Dykar! Have all my medical staff taken to talking in riddles? If you have something to tell me then say so – and tell it to me in plain English.'

When Surgeon Dykar glanced pointedly at Pilgrim, the governor said impatiently, 'Lieutenant Penn is here on Captain Howard's behalf. He should be made aware of anything likely to affect discipline in Block Four.'

'It's Mr Steiger. The prisoner who has just been released from the *cachot*.'

'I have gathered that much, Mr Dykar. What exactly is wrong with him? Has he been attacked by the other men in the *cachot*? If so I will have them severely flogged in addition to any other punishment I might award them for the disturbance they recently caused.'

'He refuses to make any complaint against them, Governor. He also refuses to allow me to carry out a full medical examination on him.'

Governor Cotgrave expelled his breath noisily in an expression of impatience.

'I am still no wiser, Mr Dykar. Will you please come to the point and tell me why I was asked to come here. What – if anything – is wrong with Mr Steiger?'

'He has been effectively castrated, Governor. It would appear that a ligature of some description was tied around the base of his testicles so tightly it prevented the flow of blood to them. As a result they have become gangrenous and died.'

'Good God!' His impatience gone, Governor Cotgrave was genuinely shocked by the surgeon's revelation. 'Who did this to him? The other prisoners in the *cachot*?'

'He refuses to say anything.' The surgeon hesitated before saying, 'I suspect he has been abused in other ways too but, as I say, he allowed me to examine the gangrenous area but refuses to allow me to carry out a full medical examination.'

Rounding on Pilgrim angrily, Governor Cotgrave said, 'Is this the type of behaviour that goes on in your own country, Lieutenant Penn?'

'I am as shocked as you are, Governor, but not entirely surprised.' He told both men something of Conrad Steiger's background history and what he knew of two of the men who had shared the *cachot* with him.

Ending his explanation, he said, 'It by no means excuses what has been done to Steiger, but I think you now know *why* it happened.'

'Why was I not told this before?' asked the angry governor. 'Had I known, this appalling incident might have been prevented.'

'I suspect it was for the same reason I was not informed Steiger was sharing the *cachot* with the others until today. Those who might have prevented it thought he was still on parole. Those who knew had been waiting for an opportunity to take their revenge on the man. Some of them have been nursing their hatred for years.'

'Nevertheless, Steiger had a number of friends among your white countrymen, Lieutenant Penn. They will not accept what has happened without taking some form of reprisal.'

'I agree wholeheartedly, Governor. What will you do?'

'I will have the white and black Americans segregated immediately. It means there will be a degree of overcrowding for a while, but they will have to put up with that.'

He glared at Lieutenant Penn. 'In future, Lieutenant, I want to be made aware of anyone, or anything like this that is likely to create trouble in my prison, do you understand?'

'Perfectly, Governor Cotgrave. Perhaps you will reciprocate by informing me immediately a United States prisoner-of-war is accused of committing an offence and thrown in the *cachot*. I believe we both have lessons to learn from this unfortunate occurrence.'

As the men exchanged angry and defiant looks, there came an urgent knocking at the door. It was thrown open before the surgeon had time to invite the visitor inside.

It was a medical orderly and he spoke breathlessly to the surgeon. 'I think you'd better come to the ward quickly, sir. It's the man who was released from the *cachot* a short time ago.'

'Steiger? What's he done now? Has he changed his mind and agreed to a medical examination?'

'No, sir, and he'll not agree to anything now. He's just been found hanging from a beam in the blanket store. He's dead, sir.'

51

News of the suicide swept through Block Four, carried on the mysterious yet remarkably efficient information network that extended to every corner of Dartmoor prison.

At first it was generally believed he had killed himself as a consequence of the charges made against him while he was on parole in Tavistock.

Not for two days did rumours begin to circulate that his death might have been precipitated by other considerations.

By this time Block Four had been cleared of those white Americans who could be given a place in the Petty Officers' Block without upsetting the Frenchmen already there.

Pilgrim had been asked by the governor to make out the list. Working swiftly, he was satisfied he had isolated the white southerners who might otherwise have stirred up serious trouble in Block Four. By so doing, he hoped to be able to maintain peace between the two American factions.

The ploy succeeded. A number of minor incidents did take place between black and white prisoners-of-war in the Block Four compound, but hardly more than was usual in a restrictive environment, where the slightest difference was likely to be magnified tenfold.

Meanwhile, the Royal Navy doctor in Plymouth had confirmed the prognosis of the surgeon called in on Virgil's behalf by Sir Thomas Tyrwhitt.

Virgil's wound required urgent treatment. Whether it was to be by a British or American surgeon was a matter for him to choose. He chose a United States surgeon and was immediately placed at the top of the list of American prisoners-of-war due for repatriation.

As a result of all that was happening, Pilgrim spent the daylight hours of three days inside Dartmoor prison. During this time he was unable to send word to Roundtor Farm of the reasons for his prolonged absence.

On the evening of the third day, Pilgrim had gone to bed early, leaving Virgil and Sophie alone in the downstairs sitting room. Sir Thomas Tyrwhitt was attending a dinner for the tenants of the Duchy of Cornwall at the inn at Two Bridges.

Pilgrim was half-asleep when there came a soft knock at his bedroom door.

'Come in!'

Pilgrim thought it must be one of the servants with a query about his proposed movements on the following day.

To his surprise, the door opened and Virgil limped into the room. 'Hello, Pilgrim. I hoped you might still be awake. I wanted you to be the first to know.'

'Know what?'

Pilgrim sat up in bed, unable to see Virgil's face because the light from the lamp in the hall was behind him.

Virgil sat on a chair close to Pilgrim's bed. 'I've just asked Sophie to marry me. I want her to come to America with me when I'm repatriated. She's said "Yes".'

The announcement took Pilgrim by surprise. He was aware that Virgil and Sophie had become very close in recent weeks, but marriage . . . !

Leaping from his bed, Pilgrim shook his friend's hand vigorously. 'Virgil . . . I don't know what to say. I'm delighted for you. Delighted for both of you. Give me a couple of minutes to get dressed and I'll come down and congratulate Sophie too. This calls for a celebration – or should we wait for Sir Thomas to come home?'

'I've already sent a servant to the inn at Two Bridges to tell him,' said Virgil, his happy smile apparent even in the dim light within the room. 'Hurry and get dressed. I'm so glad you're pleased. I was concerned you might think I was behaving foolishly. Doing all I have told you *not* to do, in fact. Not that it would have made any difference,' he added.

Ten minutes later Pilgrim was in the sitting room, raising a glass to the health of the couple. Less than an hour later Sir Thomas returned to the house and joined in the celebration.

'I find it most difficult to decide which of you is getting the better of the bargain,' he declared. He was decidedly maudlin, a result of the drink he had consumed at the Two Bridges party. 'I hope you realise what a special and resourceful young woman you are getting for your wife, Virgil? I have no intention of finding a wife for myself but, were I to do so, I would be looking for someone just like Sophie. So, if you are willing to accept the recommendation of a confirmed bachelor, you have it.'

'Thank you, Uncle. I could not have wished for a more generous blessing.'

'I mean every word of it, Sophie – and you are getting a fine man. I have no doubt he will take care of you in a manner of which I and your mother would approve.'

'Talking of mother . . . Am I required to seek her approval before marrying?'

Sir Thomas shook his head. 'You are a widow, Sophie. Your own woman. It would have been nice to be able to inform her but, as I understand it, time is crucial to your plans. Virgil will be repatriated as soon as a ship is made available. Unless the ceremony is conducted before then, there are liable to be all sorts of complications which might well prevent you travelling to America. I presume you will wish the service to be conducted by the Reverend Cotterell, at Sheepstor?'

'Yes. We both know him and we would like to be married here, on Dartmoor.'

'Splendid. I will speak to him tomorrow morning. We must have the first banns published this Sunday and the marriage can be arranged for three weeks on Monday. Would that be satisfactory for both of you?'

'That will be wonderful, Sir Thomas. Thank you very much.'

Virgil looked towards Pilgrim. 'I seem to remember telling Pilgrim he should not contemplate marriage while he was a prisoner here, in your country, Sir Thomas. I feel I ought to eat my words now. I'm also rather surprised he has not been the one to set the precedent. I was quite sure he would announce his intended marriage long before this.'

Sir Thomas looked from Virgil to Pilgrim with a puzzled expression. 'Marriage? To whom?'

'Really, Uncle, you must be the only one at Tor Royal who isn't aware of Pilgrim's feelings for that young girl who lives over at Roundtor Farm. He's been there practically every day since he was paroled to Tor Royal. Why, he even dresses like a farmhand when he's there, in a bid to impress her.' She smiled mischievously in Pilgrim's direction as she was speaking.

'Well I'm damned! – begging your pardon, Sophie. I didn't realise you were keen on young Tacy, Pilgrim. Well, you could do far worse. She's a nice young thing.'

Sir Thomas frowned. 'But on my way to Two Bridges earlier this evening I saw her in the company of one of those young Irish militia officers. They were walking across the moor driving a couple of sheep in front of them. I thought they seemed a whole lot closer than I would like a daughter of mine to be with a young man who isn't going to be around for very much longer. It was hardly the thing for a young single woman to be doing unless she had some understanding with the young man concerned. It seems you are not the only one with designs on young Tacy, Pilgrim. You might well have left things too late.'

52

Disturbed by what Sir Thomas Tyrwhitt had told him about seeing Tacy walking on the moor with a militia officer – and Pilgrim had no doubt it was Lieutenant Kennedy – he had hoped to go to the farm the following day. But it was not to be. There was still trouble inside the prison.

The potential troublemakers had been removed from Block Four, but the men moved to the Petty Officers' Block were not finding it easy to settle in. There was no one like Henri Joffre to help them and relations between the French and Americans had sunk to a low ebb within the prison.

Things were going badly for the French on the battle-fields of Europe. The French prisoners-of-war felt the United States of America should be doing much more to relieve the pressure on their troops in the Peninsula.

In truth, there was little the United States could achieve on their behalf. Their navy was tiny in comparison to the mighty fleets of the British. It consisted of no more than a few frigates, backed up by the ships manned by privateers.

The crews of these vessels fought well when the odds of battle would allow, but single ship victories would not gain them access to the high seas and permit the movement of large numbers of troops from America to Europe, even if they were available.

For the Americans in Dartmoor prison, a cause for continuing resentment was still the meagre and irregular sums of money arriving from their Government.

As a result of long internment and close proximity to their native land, it had been possible for the French to organise an increasing flow of funds for their needs. Indeed, many of the men in the Petty Officers' Block were living almost as comfortably as they would have been in their own land.

They employed servants to wait upon them and the latest fad was to bribe the guards to allow younger American prisoners out of Block Four to become personal servants to senior French officers.

Some of the captured American merchant seamen were as young as thirteen. They were eager to escape the confines of their prison block and earn more money than their Government was paying them.

The tardiness of the United States Government was bringing other problems too. Many of the Americans were of English stock. Indeed, some were first-generation Americans.

Taking advantage of both these factors, the British authorities were offering attractive incentives to any prisoners-of-war who chose to defect and serve in the British navy.

This had increased tension within the prison. Those suspected of considering changing sides were brought before a 'court' of their fellow prisoners. If found guilty, they were severely flogged.

As a result of prison grudges, many innocent men were denounced and 'tried' by their peers. Not all were acquitted by colleagues who were themselves by no means always impartial.

Pilgrim had many meetings with black and white Americans and with the governor too, in a bid to resolve the difficulties of all involved.

Walking back to Tor Royal after a particularly tense day spent trying to sort out the problems of his countrymen, Pilgrim felt that what he wanted more than anything else was to relax in the kitchen of Roundtor Farm with Tacy and forget his responsibilities for a while.

He was sorely tempted to ignore the terms of his parole and walk on to Roundtor, even if it did mean being out after dark.

Commonsense won the day. It would be too risky. One of the kitchen servants at the house had recently lost a brother off the coast of America. He had been killed in a fierce battle between HMS *Shannon*, one of the most efficient frigates in the British Navy, and the United States frigate *Chesapeake*, manned by a virtually untrained crew.

The battle had been won by *Shannon* but at a cost of eighty-three of her crew. The Tor Royal servant's brother had been one of them.

Pilgrim had expressed his sympathy to the servant, but the words of condolence had been ignored. The other servants had also known the dead sailor. There was a tense atmosphere in the Dartmoor house right now. He felt the servants would not hesitate to report him if he broke the terms of his parole.

Thinking his own thoughts, Pilgrim had reached the lane leading from Princetown to Tor Royal when a girl rose up from the long grass of the bank just ahead of him.

For a brief illogical moment, Pilgrim thought it might be Tacy.

Instead, it was Mary Gurney.

'Mary! Have you heard from Henri?' He realised this must be the reason she was here, apparently waiting for him.

'He reached home safely! A letter came during the night and he's sent presents for you and for me.'

Mary's happiness shone from her like a light. Reaching down into the long grass, she lifted a keg by one of its two rope handles. It seemed to be very heavy.

'He sent this for you.'

Pilgrim knew without removing the bung that the keg would contain a superb Cognac. He did not doubt Henri's claim that his father produced the finest Cognac in France would be proven to be quite true.

He grinned. 'I'm surprised Henri didn't bring it himself. He certainly has the nerve.'

'I wish he had,' said Mary fervently. 'But he did the next best thing. Look.'

She wore a long gold chain about her neck. Attached to it was a locket. Snapping it open with her fingers, she held it out towards Pilgrim. Inside was a miniature portrait of Henri.

'That's exquisite, Mary. Valuable, too. It's gold and pretty old. I'd say Henri has probably sent you a family heirloom. It's a very generous gift.'

Mary beamed happily. 'I thought it might be, but I'm more pleased that he put a likeness inside for me. Now, when I'm having a bad day I can always open it up and see him looking at me.'

'I'm very pleased for you, Mary, but it's no more than you deserve. Had it not been for you Henri would still be inside the prison. What does he say in his letter?'

Mary looked mildly embarrassed. 'I'm not exactly sure. It says the brandy is for you and the locket for me, but . . . I don't read very well. One of my sisters read it for me and there were lots of words she didn't understand. I have it here. Would you read it to me, please?'

She reached inside the neck of her dress and pulled out a letter, handing it to him.

Pilgrim scanned through the letter before reading it aloud to Mary. There was nothing he felt obliged to leave out. It was a warm and affectionate letter, in which Henri praised Mary for her part in his escape. The letter explained that the locket he was sending had belonged to his mother, and her mother before her.

There was much too about Henri's feelings for Mary. He ended the letter by promising to come to England to see her when the war between their countries came to an end.

By the time Pilgrim reached the end of the letter, Mary was pink with pleasure.

'There's a lot more in it than my sister read,' she said. 'Thank you, Pilgrim.' Then, hesitantly, she asked, 'Do you think he means what he says? About coming back here after the war, I mean?'

'Henri is a man of his word, Mary. If he says he'll be back, you can be assured he will. I can see you living on a French vineyard yet.'

'I'd like that,' she said, colouring up even more. 'But how about you and Tacy? I went to Roundtor Farm looking for you earlier. It was lucky I'd hidden the keg before I went up to the house. There was a militia officer there with her. I don't know what he was doing, but I didn't like him very much. I asked Tacy about you and she said she hadn't seen you for almost a week. She said she'd heard you were spending a lot of time over at Sheepstor with Reverend Cotterell's daughter.'

Pilgrim was startled. 'That's not true, Mary! Virgil's spent some time there lately – but only because he's marrying Sir Thomas's niece at Sheepstor church in a little over two weeks' time. They're planning their wedding. Whoever told her that is just mischief making.'

'I didn't think it would be true,' declared Mary. 'I told Tacy so. But I think you should get across there as quickly as you can and tell her yourself. Perhaps she'll decide to get rid of that militiaman then. I don't like any of 'em and never have, but I could dislike this one more than most if I set my mind to it.'

53

That night Pilgrim had a serious conversation with Virgil. He explained the problems he was having at the moment finding an opportunity to tell Tacy how he felt about her, and discussing the future he envisaged for them both.

Virgil listened in silence before asking, 'Just how *do* you feel about her, Pilgrim?'

'I feel about her as you do about Sophie, Virgil – but it's been with me for a whole lot longer.'

Virgil was puzzled. 'In that case, why haven't you said anything to her before this?'

'Would you have disclosed to Sophie how you felt about her if you hadn't been told you were being returned to America on the next boat?' Pilgrim countered.

Virgil frowned. 'I don't know. Probably not.'

'You know you wouldn't, and for the same reason I've said nothing to Tacy. You can see an end to your captivity now, Virgil. I can't. What would I have to offer Tacy if I told her now that I loved her and wanted to marry her? Could we set up home and live on a penny-halfpenny a day? And *where* would we live? You and I are paroled to Tor Royal, but I couldn't ask Sir Thomas to allow me to have a wife here too.'

Pilgrim began pacing the room in his frustration. 'It might be old-fashioned, but I was brought up to believe the most important thing in life was to behave honourably – especially in dealings with women. I've had little to do with them before meeting Tacy, so I can't measure my feelings for her against anyone else I've known. I only know that I want to be with her more than I've ever wanted anything. If things were different I would ask her to marry me and I'd be the happiest man in the world if she said "yes". But I can give her nothing at all right now. Rightly or wrongly, I've thought it would be better for her if I said nothing about my feelings.'

'You're an honourable man, Pilgrim. No one can find fault with that – but being honourable is one thing. Not letting Tacy know how you feel is something very different. She *needs* to know. Keep your feelings to yourself and she'll end up thinking you don't care at all. The only person likely to gain from such a situation is this militiaman, Kennedy. I don't think he deserves to be given any advantage as far as Tacy is concerned, do you?'

Pilgrim shook his head. 'That's why I wondered whether you would go to the prison tomorrow in my place. It's not going to be an easy day. Governor Cotgrave's men have "lost" three of our men. They're in the prison somewhere, I'm certain of it, but no one knows where. If you take that problem on I can go to Roundtor Farm and try to explain to Tacy how I feel about her – and why I haven't said anything before this.'

'You go and sort out your problems, Pilgrim. Leave me to deal with things at the prison. I'll take one of Sir Thomas's horses, that will be easier on my leg. But whatever you do, don't lose Tacy to this militiaman. He's no good for her and she's a very special girl. By the way, Sophie and I have already discussed the guests we are going to invite to our wedding and we'd both like Tacy to come. Before you leave in the morning I'll write out an invitation. You can take it with you. I'll leave for the prison early and then ride on to Sheepstor. There are still a great many things to be sorted out before the wedding.'

'Will you tell Sir Thomas what we're doing?'

'He's in Cornwall for a couple of days, attending a tenants' meeting. So all you have to do is go to Roundtor Farm tomorrow, sort out things with Tacy and come back here as happy a man as I am.'

By the time Pilgrim was dressed the next morning, Virgil had already left for the prison. Pilgrim had lain awake for much of the night, going over the things he intended saying to Tacy. He now felt he would be able to find the right words to tell her how he felt and explain the reasons why he had said nothing before today.

He was leaving the house when a party of men rode in through the entrance gates. They were dressed in uniforms similar to those worn by naval officers – but these were not naval men. Pilgrim felt immediately uneasy.

Riding up to the house, a man who seemed to be in charge of the party said to Pilgrim, 'From your uniform I take it you are one of the American prisoners-of-war paroled to Tor Royal? Which one are you?'

Still apprehensive, Pilgrim replied, 'Lieutenant Penn. Pilgrim Penn. And you, sir?'

'Chief Officer Cunningham of His Majesty's Revenue Service. I have reason to believe you are in possession of a keg of brandy on which no Excise duty has been paid. Will you produce the keg for us, Lieutenant Penn, or shall I order my men to search the house for it?'

'That won't be necessary. I *was* given a keg of brandy a couple of days ago. Whether duty was paid on it or not, I don't know. I'll fetch it for you.'

Pilgrim did not want Sir Thomas Tyrwhitt to suffer the embarrassment of having his home searched by Revenue men. At the same time, he realised that someone in the house, one of the servants, must have informed the Revenue men about the brandy. It was probably someone who was particularly bitter about the death of the kitchen servant's brother.

'You won't mind if two of my men accompany you, Lieutenant Penn? We don't want the contents of the keg mysteriously disappearing along the way, do we?'

The keg of brandy was in Pilgrim's room. When he showed it to them it was carried triumphantly from the house by one of the two Revenue men.

The keg was examined by the Chief Officer. His examination completed, he looked triumphantly at Pilgrim. 'There are no Excise marks on this. It's almost certainly smuggled. Would you like to tell me where it came from?'

'I told you, it was a present – from a man who was once a prisoner-of-war in Dartmoor prison.'

'A Frenchman?'

Pilgrim nodded.

'Who is the man who delivered it to you?'

'He gave no name,' lied Pilgrim. He was relieved that the Revenue officer was not aware it had been given to him by a woman. 'And I had never seen him before.

I would like to add that Sir Thomas Tyrwhitt knows nothing at all of this.'

'Sir Thomas Tyrwhitt?' It seemed the Chief Revenue Officer did not recognise the name. 'Who is he?'

'He's secretary to the Prince Regent,' said Pilgrim. 'This is his house. Weren't you aware of that when you came here?'

'I'm new to these parts,' snapped the Chief Officer. 'Where is Sir Thomas Tyrwhitt now?'

'He's visiting some of the Prince Regent's tenants in Cornwall.'

'He's a very important man in these parts,' volunteered one of the Revenue men. 'He's also the Lord Warden of the Stannaries, and was once Member of Parliament for Plymouth.'

'Then he'll no doubt be pleased to learn we've rid his house of a lawbreaker,' declared the Chief Officer. 'We've got what we came here for. Let's take him off to Plymouth.'

'Wait!' Pilgrim was dismayed by the news that he was being arrested and taken away. 'Can I write a note to my commanding officer? He's in Dartmoor prison on a duty visit. I'd like to tell him what's happening.'

'Does he know anything about the brandy?'

'Nothing at all,' replied Pilgrim hurriedly. He did not want Virgil caught up in this sorry business.

'Hm! Well, yours was the only name given to me, so we'll leave him out of this, but I don't think there's any need for you to be writing notes to anyone. I'll leave word with the house servants of your whereabouts. They can tell him. Now, let's get back to Plymouth and find out whether you know more about this brandy than you've told us.'

54

Before leaving Tor Royal, Pilgrim's wrists were shackled and he was told to walk behind the lead horse and before the remainder of the mounted Revenue men.

They had almost reached the gate when there was a shrill shout behind them. It was Sophie. The Chief Revenue Officer pulled his horse to a halt and waited uncertainly as she lifted the hem of her dress clear of the ground and ran to them.

'What on earth do you think you're doing with Pilgrim?' She directed her question at the Chief Officer. 'Where are you taking him?'

'Who are you, ma'am?' The Chief Officer asked the question, aware from the manner of her dress that she was not a house servant.

'I am Sir Thomas Tyrwhitt's niece. Lieutenant Penn is a guest in my uncle's house, paroled on the express orders of the Prince Regent. Now, reply to my questions, if you please.'

Just for a moment, Pilgrim glimpsed a touch of

Winifrith in Sophie and he hoped it might have the desired effect.

'I'm sorry, ma'am.' The Chief Revenue Officer was decidedly uncomfortable, but he had no intention of backing down. 'I received information that an American prisoner-of-war staying here was in possession of brandy smuggled in from France and on which no duty had been paid. A keg of such brandy has been recovered from Lieutenant Penn's room.'

Sophie frowned. 'Is this true, Pilgrim?'

'I was sent a keg of brandy by a French friend whom I met whilst in Dartmoor prison. I had no way of knowing whether or not duty had been paid on it.'

This at least was the truth, even though he had very strong suspicions that it had not.

'There you are then,' said Sophie ambiguously. 'Why don't you go away and sort it out, leaving Pilgrim here.'

'I'm sorry, ma'am. My duty is to take him in custody to the Customs House in Plymouth.'

'That is absolutely ridiculous,' declared Sophie. 'Sir Thomas Tyrwhitt is going to be infuriated by your inflexible attitude. It may well cost you your position in the Revenue service.'

'I'm sorry, ma'am,' said the Revenue Officer unhappily, 'but I must carry out my duties as I see them.'

'I have never heard of anything quite so preposterous,' said Sophie in a Winifrith-like manner once more. 'Well, if you must persist in this idiotic stance, then at least allow Pilgrim to *ride* to Plymouth. I'll have one of the grooms saddle up a horse.'

'I'm sorry, ma'am, I can't guarantee the return of a horse from Plymouth . . .'

'You don't have to,' snapped Sophie. 'The groom will accompany you to Plymouth. Another will be sent to find Sir Thomas in Cornwall. He'll have something to say about this, I can assure you.'

Sophie turned and hurried away in the direction of the stables, leaving the Chief Revenue Officer, surrounded by his silent men, wondering just what manner of hornet's nest he had stirred up.

'May I ask whether the information about the keg of Cognac was given to you by one of the house servants?' asked Pilgrim. 'One of them recently lost a brother in the war. She's particularly aggrieved at having Captain Howard and myself in the house.'

'The information was received from an officer in the militia,' replied the Revenue officer. 'Where he got it from, I don't know. But it was true enough, you can't deny that. I may be new in this part of the country, but the law is the same in any part of England.'

'I'm not denying anything,' said Pilgrim amiably. 'I was given a present. I wasn't told I needed to consult a whole lot of English law books before accepting it.'

He hoped he sounded more confident than he felt about the whole business. It was possible Henri's present would put him back inside Dartmoor prison once more – or even result in him being returned to the hulks. It was a punishment that had been meted out to more than one prisoner-of-war who had been dubbed a troublemaker.

A Tor Royal horse was supplied and the journey to Plymouth was made in comparative silence, but it was far more comfortable than if Pilgrim had been made to walk. Before leaving Tor Royal Sophie had insisted that the shackles be removed from Pilgrim's wrists. The Revenue Officer agreed, but only after Pilgrim gave his word that he would not try to escape.

The headquarters of the Revenue Service was on the waterfront at Plymouth. From his high, barred window,

Pilgrim could look across the water and see the squat, ugly shapes of the prison hulks. It was a stark reminder of what might happen to him should Sir Thomas not be able to secure his release.

Pilgrim remained in the Revenue cell for two days. During this time he was frequently questioned by the Chief Revenue Officer and others, in a bid to draw from him the name of the 'man' from whom he had received the keg of Cognac.

Pilgrim's reply never varied. He declared the keg had been brought to him by a man whom he assumed to be no more than a common carrier. He repeated what he had told the Revenue Officer earlier. He was unfamiliar with British law and had no idea he was doing wrong by accepting such a gift.

He remained unmoved at threats that the militia officer involved had been asked to ascertain whether Pilgrim was known to have had other dealings with smugglers.

By the end of the second day, Pilgrim realised that his unchanging story was beginning to worry the Chief Revenue Officer. The knowledge gave him fresh hope.

At dusk that day, when Pilgrim was eating an indifferent meal, he heard voices in the corridor outside his cell. One of them was that of a woman. With a thrill of renewed hope, he recognised it as belonging to Sophie.

A key grated in the lock, the door swung open and the next moment it seemed the small cell was filled with people.

After hugging him and murmuring words of sympathy, Sophie grimaced at the plate of food he had placed on the wooden platform, the only piece of furniture in the room.

'How utterly dreadful! Poor Pilgrim. I wouldn't feed such food to a dog!'

Behind Sophie was Sir Thomas Tyrwhitt and other men who were variously introduced to Pilgrim as the Mayor of Plymouth, the Chief Collector of Customs, a deputy lieutenant of the county and Plymouth's chief magistrate.

Minutes later, Pilgrim was being led from the building. On the way he caught a brief glimpse of the man who had arrested him. The expression on his face indicated to Pilgrim that the threats made by Sophie before he was escorted from Tor Royal had not been idle ones. For a moment he allowed himself to feel sorry for the unfortunate Chief Revenue Officer.

Then he was inside Sir Thomas Tyrwhitt's carriage. He sank back against the seat, thankful that Sophie and his host had been able to rescue him from the Revenue cell.

Before the coach moved off a Revenue officer emerged from the building carrying the keg of brandy that had been the cause of all the trouble. He handed it up to the coachman to be returned to Tor Royal and to Pilgrim.

On the way back to Dartmoor, Sir Thomas questioned him about conditions in the Revenue cells and Sophie happily informed him that she and Virgil could look forward to their wedding now there was no longer a cloud over Pilgrim's future.

55

It did not take Sir Thomas Tyrwhitt very long to learn that one of his servants had reported Pilgrim for being in possession of the keg of smuggled brandy.

It was the kitchen maid whose brother had been killed on board HMS *Shannon*.

The owner of Tor Royal dismissed the girl on the spot, but when he heard of the action taken against her, Pilgrim pleaded with Sir Thomas to keep the girl on.

'She had only recently heard of the death of her brother. Knowing he had been killed by Americans it must have been very difficult for her to have to work for two of them here in your house.'

'Her brother was a sailor on board a warship. He was aware of the dangers he faced. In fact, he died winning a notable victory. I have read the newspaper reports of the battle. Her brother was one of eighty-three British casualties. Your country's ship had a hundred and forty-six before her colours were struck.'

Pilgrim was silent for some moments while he digested

this news. He had served for a while on the USS *Chesapeake* and knew many of the crew members.

'Then we have both suffered a loss,' he said. 'Nevertheless, I understand it was her only brother. You would be granting me yet another favour were you to allow her to continue working in your house.'

After giving it some thought, Sir Thomas said, 'Very well, Pilgrim, but I will give her to understand she owes her post here to you. She will also be told she cannot expect to progress beyond the kitchen while she is here. The girl will also make a personal apology to you for all the trouble she has caused.'

The arrangement suited Pilgrim. He intended asking the girl to whom she had passed on the information concerning the brandy.

It was an embarrassing and emotional meeting. The girl came to offer her apology when Pilgrim was in the drawing room with Virgil and Sophie.

Pilgrim once again commiserated with her over the loss of her brother, keenly aware she was only a young girl. When he told her the English sailor had died in the company of some very brave men, many of them Pilgrim's own friends, she burst into tears and fled from the room. He caught up with her in the passageway outside the drawing room.

'I'm sorry to have upset you, but I'd like to ask you just one question,' he said. 'Who was it you told about the keg of brandy?'

For a moment it seemed the kitchenmaid would refuse to reply, but Pilgrim said gently, 'The answer is important to me, Katie.'

Sniffling loudly, the girl said, 'I told a man I sometimes meet in Princetown. A militiaman. I didn't really tell him to get you into trouble, sir. I was upset about my brother and was telling the militiaman that while he was getting himself killed by Americans, you was here drinking brandy brought in for you by smugglers. That's all it was. He said he would tell one of his officers, to see what could be done about it. I don't know which one it was though and I don't think I can find out. We . . . we're not friends any more.'

'Thank you, Katie.' Pilgrim thought he could guess the name of the officer. 'I'm glad we've got things sorted out between us and that you still have your work here. You can go now.'

Dropping him an awkward curtsy, the young servant girl fled in the direction of the kitchen.

'So you think it was a militia officer who reported you to the Revenue men?'

The drawing room door had been left open and Sophie put the question to Pilgrim when he returned to the room.

'I'm certain of it. The Chief Revenue Officer said so when he was questioning me.'

'Oh dear! Had I known I would never have invited the militia officers from Princetown to the wedding celebrations. It would be difficult to withdraw the invitations now.'

'Don't worry about it,' said Pilgrim casually. 'I'll probably have it sorted out before then.'

That afternoon, Pilgrim made his way to Roundtor Farm. It seemed a very long time since he was last there. Others thought the same.

Entering the kitchen, he found Joan Elford hard at work, baking. A delicious smell of pastry and cooked apples permeated the air in the spacious room.

Close to the fire, Tom Elford sat in a high-backed wooden rocking chair, eyes half closed. He looked both tired and ill.

'Well! Look who's paying us a call,' said the farmer's wife. 'We're honoured, young man. We didn't expect to see you at Roundtor again. We all thought you were moving among the county's high society now.'

'Not unless the county's society divide their time between Dartmoor prison and the Revenue gaol in Plymouth. That's where I've been.'

Brushing back a lock of hair that kept breaking free and dangling in front of her face, Joan looked at him in disbelief. 'Are you saying you've been locked up in a Plymouth cell?'

'Only for the last two days. Before then I was kept busy at the prison. There was some serious trouble involving our prisoners-of-war. Virgil is being sent back to America for treatment to his leg wound and he wants me to take over from him. It means I'm going to have to spend more time there, I'm afraid.'

'You can tell us all about that later, but what's this about you being locked up in the Revenue cells?'

Pilgrim told her of the happenings of the past couple of days and Tom Elford kept his eyes open for long enough to say, 'Well, I'll be blowed! What goings on!' at the end of the story.

'I feel sorry for young Katie up at Tor Royal,' said Joan. 'She and her brother were very close, but there was no need for her to do what she did. That was downright spiteful.'

'I'm surprised that young militia officer who's been seeing so much of Tacy never said anything about it,' said Tom Elford, pushing back on his chair and setting it rocking gently.

'I'm not,' said his wife with considerable feeling. 'Even if he knew about it he wouldn't have said anything that might make our Tacy feel any sympathy for Pilgrim. In fact, I wouldn't be at all surprised to learn he

had something to do with reporting the whole business
to the Revenue men.'

'Neither would I,' agreed Pilgrim. 'There was certainly a militia officer involved.'

'Then it was probably him,' declared Joan firmly.
'I wouldn't trust him an inch farther than I could
throw him.'

Briskly dusting the flour from her arms, she said,
'You keep an eye on those cakes for me, Tom. Don't
let 'em burn. I'm going across to the dairy to fetch in
some more milk.'

'I'll go,' volunteered Pilgrim.

'I doubt if you'd find anything,' she said. 'We've
shifted things around a bit since you were last here.
Mind you, if you've come to help there are one or two
things you could be doing. Come along, I'll show you.'

As they stepped outside the door into the farmyard,
Pilgrim asked, 'Where's Tacy right now?'

'She's up at the prison market, selling cakes. Tom's
having another of his bad times. We need to get some
money put by for the winter in case he doesn't get any
better.'

After murmuring a few words of sympathy, Pilgrim
said, 'I hoped I might see Tacy at the market when I was
spending so much time at the prison. I really couldn't
get away, you know. It might have been different if the
terms of my parole didn't mean I had to be in Tor Royal
after dark. But, as was proved by the incident with the
Revenue men, I need to abide by the rules. Not all
the servants there are happy about having Americans
staying in the house. It only needs a word in the right
place to have my parole revoked. I can't expect Sir
Thomas to keep getting me out of trouble.'

'When we were in the kitchen I had the impression
you knew it was Lieutenant Alan Kennedy?'

'I haven't been able to prove it,' admitted Pilgrim, 'but he's the one I strongly suspect.'

'You're probably right,' agreed the farmer's wife. 'He's spending far too much time with our Tacy these days. I don't like it. I don't like it one little bit.'

They had reached the dairy now. When they entered its cool interior, Pilgrim looked about him. Everything seemed to be in the same place as when he was last here. He looked at his companion questioningly.

She did not seem in the least bit embarrassed. 'I wanted to get you away from the house to have a talk to you, out of Tom's hearing. To tell you the truth, I'm worried about this Lieutenant Kennedy and the way he's running after Tacy. He doesn't always come to the farm first, as you do. I suspect he watches the farm to see when she goes off on her own. Then he'll meet up with her, pretending it's by accident. I don't believe it is. I've taken to sending Johanna or Emma out with her whenever she leaves the house, to try to make certain she's not on her own when she meets up with him. The trouble is I can't watch her all hours of the day and night. Besides, having two people doing the work of one all the time and with Tom so ill, it means things aren't getting done about the house. To make things worse, Billy's ma is ill again. He and Emma are staying over there for a while.'

Taking a jug of milk from a wooden bucket, Joan Elford reached up on a shelf and took down a large pat of butter. 'I'll be perfectly honest with you, Pilgrim. When you first started coming to Roundtor I had my doubts about you and Tacy. I could see no future for her, but give you your due, you've always behaved like a gentleman and I've come to trust you. That's more than I can say for Kennedy. I can't bring myself to like him. I really don't know what Tacy sees in him, unless it's because she believes you're cooling off and don't *want* to come here quite as often as you once did. I probably shouldn't be telling you this, but I'm doing it because I'm worried about Kennedy, and because I trust you. Our Tacy cares very much for you. I think she's hurt because you don't seem to feel the same about her.'

'But I *do*, Mrs Elford,' said Pilgrim unhappily. 'I always have.'

Arriving at a sudden decision, he took a deep breath and said, 'You've trusted me with your thoughts, so I'll do the same with you. You tell me I've behaved like a "gentleman" and that's what I've tried to do. Now I think I've probably behaved *too* honourably. I did so because I didn't want to take Tacy into a relationship that could go nowhere. I'm a prisoner-of-war. I can't ask Tacy to marry me because I can't afford to keep her on the money my Government is allowing me and if I do anything wrong, no matter how minor, I'm liable to be thrown back into prison.'

Pilgrim shrugged. 'At least, that's the way I've *been* feeling, until lately. When I was last here Emma told me that if I wasn't careful I'd lose Tacy to Lieutenant Kennedy. That got me to thinking about things. When Virgil announced that he was going to marry Sophie, Sir Thomas's niece, and take her back to America with him I made up my mind to say something to Tacy. I don't want her to think I don't really care for her. I do. I've decided to explain to her why I haven't done anything about it before. Then she'd at least know the way I feel and we can talk about things.'

Pilgrim shrugged despairingly. 'That's what I was planning to do the morning the Revenue men arrested me. I felt that if only we could talk about it we'd be able to work out a solution. I intended speaking to her first, to see how she felt, then to you and Mr Elford. Well, now I've done things the wrong way round, but at least *you* know the way *I* feel. If you're unhappy about it I'll need to think of something else. But I *do* want to marry Tacy one day and take her back to America with me. She'd have a good life there, I promise you.'

Joan looked at Pilgrim with a strange mixture of expressions fighting for control of her face. Suddenly, she stepped forward and wrapped her arms about him to give him a fierce hug.

'You're a good man, Pilgrim. You're all I've ever hoped for as a husband for our Tacy.'

Stepping back from him, she beamed at him in tearful happiness. 'You know, when Tacy first told me about you, I thought my world was about to collapse about my ears. Yet, right now, I can't think of anyone I would rather put my trust in. You and Tacy had something very special when you first met. I realised it and it frightened me. What she felt then is still there, of that I'm certain. We just need to do something to remind *her* of it.'

56

Pilgrim saw the Elford pony and cart before he was halfway between Roundtor Farm and Dartmoor prison. Lieutenant Kennedy, leading his horse, was walking beside Tacy. Johanna was on her other side.

When she saw him, the youngest member of the Elford family waved gaily and ran towards him, throwing herself at him when they met.

'Pilgrim! Where have you been? We were beginning to think we weren't going to see you again. I've missed you.'

Swinging her off the ground, Pilgrim said, 'I've missed you too, Johanna – and I swear you've grown since I last saw you.'

As he set the young girl on the ground once more, Pilgrim was looking at Tacy and Lieutenant Kennedy as they came closer. He was unable to read Tacy's expression, but Lieutenant Kennedy's feelings were plain enough. They showed in his scowl.

With Johanna holding his hand, he advanced to meet them. Pointedly ignoring the militiaman, he said, 'Hello,

Tacy. It seems a long time since we met. I've missed you.'

'Really? I thought you would have been so busy over at the Sheepstor vicarage that you wouldn't have any time to think about us at Roundtor.'

Tacy's manner was stiff and cool. Frowning, Pilgrim asked, 'What makes you think I've spent any time at Sheepstor?'

'Are you saying you *haven't* been there?' Tacy countered.

'That's exactly what I'm saying.'

Pilgrim glanced briefly at Lieutenant Kennedy before saying, 'I don't know where your information has come from, but it seems I've been confused with Virgil. He's spent some time there, making arrangements for his marriage to Sophie.'

'Oh!' It was apparent the news came as a surprise to her.

She too glanced at Lieutenant Kennedy before asking, 'If you haven't been to Sheepstor, where *have* you been? Not that there's any reason why you should spend all your time at Roundtor,' she added hastily. 'You can please yourself what you do.'

'Unfortunately, I *can't*,' said Pilgrim. 'I'm a prisoner-of-war. When Virgil leaves I'll be the senior American officer on Dartmoor. It means I now have a lot more to do in the prison. That's where I've been for much of the time I would like to have spent at Roundtor, as Lieutenant Kennedy would no doubt have told you, had you asked him. He knows all about the trouble they've had inside the prison.'

Once again Tacy glanced at the militia officer, but he was looking at Pilgrim impassively.

'I also have a great many rules I must obey while I'm on parole,' continued Pilgrim. 'I must never forget

I'm an enemy in your country. If I do, there's always someone ready to remind me. That's why I've spent the last couple of days locked up in a cell in the Revenue building in Plymouth. Someone reported that I'd been given a keg of Cognac on which no duty had been paid. I'm quite sure Lieutenant Kennedy could have told you about that too.'

'What are you insinuating, Penn? That I had something to do with your arrest?'

'Are you telling me you didn't?'

Lieutenant Kennedy glared at Pilgrim for some moments, before his glance slipped away. When he spoke again, it was to Tacy.

'I think that for some reason Lieutenant Penn is determined to be offensive and provocative, Tacy. Rather than remain here and cause you embarrassment I will return to Princetown. No doubt he and I will meet elsewhere to discuss whatever is troubling him. In the meantime, I trust you will allow me to see you again?'

'Of course. I look forward to it.'

As the militiaman rode away, Tacy swung around to confront Pilgrim. There was nothing in her expression to suggest Joan Elford's assumption that her daughter was in love with him.

'Do you have any proof that Alan had you arrested by the Revenue men?'

'I know it was a militia officer. Had it been anyone else I feel sure Lieutenant Kennedy would have told you about it. He was quick enough to have you believe I was visiting the Sheepstor vicarage.'

'I'm not so certain he did. He might just have said that one of you from Tor Royal was spending a lot of time at Sheepstor. I probably assumed it was you.'

'Why should you do that?'

Tacy shrugged. 'Well, you haven't been here for some

time and we've heard nothing from you. I thought you must be going there instead. Anyway, you had no right to be rude to Alan the way you were. I want you to apologise to him the next time you meet him.'

'Apologise?' Pilgrim looked at her in angry disbelief. 'He had me arrested and has tried to poison your mind against me and you want *me* to apologise to *him*?'

'You don't know any of those things for certain. You just said so yourself. You have no right to be so rude to one of my friends.'

'Oh! So he's a friend now, is he?'

Pilgrim was confused and not a little hurt that she was taking Lieutenant Kennedy's side against him.

'He's not *my* friend. I like Pilgrim much better.' The support came from Johanna who had taken Pilgrim's hand once more.

'No one's asking your opinion,' said Tacy.

She was almost as confused as was Pilgrim. She did not really know why she was so angry with him. She had been delighted when she saw him coming across the moor to meet her just now. But it had all gone terribly wrong.

She was not even very fond of Lieutenant Kennedy herself. Yet somehow she had managed to back herself into a corner on his behalf and she could see no way out. Instead, she lashed out verbally at Pilgrim once more.

'Are you going to apologise to him?' she demanded to know.

Pilgrim was hurt by her attitude, but he could not back down now. 'No. I know I'm right about him. But, please . . . can't we forget all about him for a while. I came to meet you because I want to talk to you.'

Jerking the reins of the pony she was leading, she startled the animal into faster movement, the small cart jolting over the rough ground behind him.

'When you're ready to apologise to Alan for being rude to him you can come and tell me what it is you have to say. Until then we don't have anything to say to each other.'

Tacy began running and the pony ran with her. She left Pilgrim standing with Johanna, staring after her in dismay.

Yet, had she looked back, it was doubtful whether Tacy would have seen him clearly. She had missed Pilgrim very much indeed for more than a week and had been terribly hurt when she believed he was going to the Sheepstor vicarage to see Jemima Cotterell. Now, when he had returned with a very good reason for not coming to Roundtor she had driven him away. *Deliberately* driven him away.

Tacy stumbled on a tuft of coarse grass and angrily cuffed away the tears that had prevented her from seeing the obstacle.

At that moment she felt that the bottom had dropped out of her whole world.

From a window, Joan saw Tacy leading the pony and cart towards the farmhouse. Johanna was some distance behind, hurrying across the moor after her.

She reached the gate to the farmyard at the same time as her elder daughter and opened it for her. 'Haven't you seen Pilgrim? He was here earlier but left to go and meet you.'

'Yes, we saw him.'

'Then . . . why isn't he with you now? There was something he wanted to talk about with you. I've been looking out for you to return so you and he could talk without having Johanna listening to everything that was being said.'

Johanna reached them in time to hear the last part of

what her mother said. As Tacy backed the pony and cart inside the cart shed, the younger girl said, 'You're too late. Pilgrim spoke to Tacy, but she sent him packing.'

'It wasn't me he was talking to,' retorted Tacy. 'It was Alan. Pilgrim accused him of all sorts of things but didn't have any proof for any of them.'

'You mean the business of him being arrested by the Revenue men? I don't think there can be any doubt about Alan Kennedy's involvement in that.'

'He told Lieutenant Kennedy off for telling Tacy he'd been seeing that girl over at the Sheepstor vicarage, when he hadn't,' said Johanna.

'He was very rude to Alan,' persisted Tacy. 'And he wouldn't apologise. I said I didn't want to talk to him until he did. Anyway, I don't want to talk about it.'

'I like Pilgrim better than that militia officer,' said Johanna positively. 'He gives me the creeps.'

'You should at least have listened to what Pilgrim had to say,' said her mother. 'You and he have been good friends for a long time.'

'I've said I don't want to talk about him, haven't I?' said Tacy. 'If you two want to, then you can do it while you're putting the pony away. I'm going into the house.'

With this, she turned about and hurried away.

'Aren't you going to make her come back and finish what she's supposed to be doing?' asked Johanna spitefully.

'No, you can do it,' said her mother. 'I think it'll be best if we leave her alone to think her own thoughts for a while.'

'That's not fair,' complained Johanna as her mother walked thoughtfully towards the farmhouse. 'I suppose if she starts crying again she'll be let off doing any more work today.'

'Crying *again*?' Joan turned back towards Johanna.

'That's why she was hurrying home in front of me after Lieutenant Kennedy had gone off and she'd had words with Pilgrim. She thought I wouldn't see, but I did. I don't know which of 'em she was crying for, though.'

Walking slowly back to the house, Joan hoped Tacy had been shedding tears for Pilgrim. If so, there was hope for her. If the tears were for Lieutenant Kennedy . . . ?

It was a possibility she did not want to consider.

57

'What do you think we ought to do about Tacy's invitation?'

Sophie put the question to Virgil as they sat in Sir Thomas's study, writing out wedding invitations.

'We've sent it off to her, we'll just have to hope she'll come.'

'But Pilgrim hasn't been to see her for almost two weeks now. It seems that whatever there might have been between them is over.'

'I don't believe that,' said Virgil, as he carefully placed the page he had just written on the desk in front of him, to allow the ink to dry. 'They've had some sort of a falling-out, that's all. I believe Lieutenant Kennedy had something to do with it. It will blow over. Pilgrim is already more of a man than Kennedy will ever be. Tacy will see it for herself, if she hasn't already. She's a sensible girl. Anyway, the invitation is from us to one of our guests. She was the first person I knew here and she was very kind to Pilgrim and myself in those early days.'

'Do you think it will be all right, having Tacy, Pilgrim and Lieutenant Kennedy there together?'

'It's an excellent opportunity for Tacy to compare her suitors. I know who'll come out best from the comparison.'

'I hope you're right, Virgil. I don't want anything to happen that might mar the day for us.'

Rising from his seat at the desk, Virgil crossed the room and embraced his bride-to-be. 'Nothing's going to spoil the day. It will be the first of many happy and memorable days for both of us. You just wait and see.'

The threat to the wedding plans of Virgil and Sophie came not from the triangle of Pilgrim, Tacy and Lieutenant Kennedy – but from Winifrith, Sophie's mother.

The two Americans, Sophie and Sir Thomas were in the Tor Royal dining room, enjoying a pleasant dinner, when they heard the sound of a loud voice in the hall.

'I *thought* I heard a carriage a few moments ago,' said Sir Thomas. 'It would seem we have unexpected visitors.'

He dabbed the corners of his mouth with his napkin and had half-risen to his feet when the door was flung open and Winifrith swept into the room, the Tor Royal butler hesitating uncertainly in the doorway.

'Good God!' Sir Thomas sat down again, heavily. 'It's you!'

'That's right, it's *me*!' confirmed the knight's sister. 'And while I've been risking my life gallivanting half-way around the world, *you* . . .' She jabbed a forefinger in a sword-thrust at Sophie. '. . . You are sitting here as though butter wouldn't melt in your mouth. What sort of a daughter is it who makes her mother chase all over Europe looking for her?'

'I don't think I ever suggested you should chase

around Europe looking for me.' After a distressed glance at Virgil, Sophie regained much of her composure. She replied to her mother in a deceptively mild manner.

'You know exactly what I am talking about, young lady, so don't adopt that innocent attitude with me. I have suffered far too much already because of you. I'll take no more of your nonsense.'

Looking about the table, she glared at each of the Americans in turn before saying, 'I've no doubt you were encouraged in your wilfulness by those no one would expect to know any better. I've had a great deal of time to think about things on my way home in an absolutely disgusting ship. We'll return to London and not visit Tor Royal again until this war is over and those who have fought against us have gone home, where they belong.'

'*We* are going nowhere, Mother. At least, not together . . .'

'That's quite enough from you, Sophie! Your defiance comes as no surprise to me. No surprise at all, but we'll pursue it in the morning. I have had a dreadful time. All I want now is a drink, some food, then a good night's sleep.'

'Really, Winifrith, I find your whole attitude wholly incomprehensible.'

The usually mild-mannered owner of Tor Royal was as angry as the others had ever seen him as he rose to his feet and confronted his sister.

'After suffering the tragedy of having her husband killed on the battlefield, Sophie had to find her own way home to us. Yet all you are apparently concerned about is the slight to your authority. No words of affection for your daughter. No joy that she is safe. Dammit, Winifrith, you have always been selfish and overbearing, but I find your behaviour at this moment quite unbelievable!'

'You haven't had to suffer the indignities and discomforts I've known these past weeks . . . but we'll discuss this in the morning . . .'

'We'll discuss it now, Mrs Cudmore. There are a few things you should perhaps think about in the privacy of your room.'

Virgil's words were spoken quietly and politely, but for a moment Pilgrim thought Winifrith was about to suffer an attack of apoplexy.

'How *dare* you speak to me in such a manner! This is a family matter. Nothing at all to do with you . . .'

'It has a great deal to do with me,' said Virgil firmly. 'Sophie and I are to be married next Monday and we will be leaving for America at the end of the week.'

For a few moments, Winifrith stood with her mouth opening and closing soundlessly, reminding Pilgrim of a landed fish. Then she reached out, pulled a chair away from the table and sat upon it – but only for a few moments.

Leaping to her feet once again, she said, 'This is absolute nonsense. There will be no wedding. You do not have my permission.'

'That did not stop me before. It will certainly not stop me this time,' said Sophie. 'Besides, your permission is neither needed nor asked for. I am not an underage daughter, but a widow who has passed the age when parental consent is needed. You are welcome to attend the wedding, but it *will* go ahead, whether you are there or not.'

Winifrith sat down once more and this time she remained seated. 'I never thought I would live to see the day when my daughter would show such ingratitude to her mother – and after all I have suffered on your behalf! You have not heard the last of this, my girl. As for coming to America with you . . . !'

'No one has asked you to come to America, Mother – and no one will. In fact, were you to come to America I would persuade Virgil to take me to Africa, or Europe, or any place where you *weren't*.'

Sophie rose to her feet abruptly and inclined her head to her fellow diners. 'I'm sorry, Uncle, Virgil, Pilgrim, but I am no longer hungry. As Mother said, we should have saved this conversation for the morning. I am retiring now. Good night.'

Sophie left the room, followed immediately by Virgil.

Pouring a very large brandy from a decanter standing on a nearby sideboard, Sir Thomas carried it to his sister.

'You will be in need of this, Winifrith. You have just lost a very important battle. I fear that unless you have a radical change of attitude you may also lose your daughter. Think of what I have said, Winifrith. No! It is far more important that you think of what *Sophie* has said. Come, Pilgrim. We will go and arrange for Winifrith's luggage to be taken to her room.'

58

'Are you quite sure this frock looks all right, Ma? It's not cut too low at the front?'

'It looks absolutely beautiful, Tacy, and so do you, girl.'

Tom Elford answered his daughter's question in a voice that was as tired as the man, but he managed a wan smile for her.

It was the day of the wedding of Virgil and Sophie. The whole of the Elford family was assembled in the kitchen. Tacy was dressed in a brand-new gingham dress. It had been made especially for the occasion by one of the moorland's itinerant tailors. But now she seemed suddenly reluctant to leave the house.

In truth, she had not been enthusiastic about accepting the invitation to the ceremony and the reception which was to take place at Tor Royal afterwards. It was an afternoon wedding and meant she would be walking back across the moor in the dark. At least this was one excuse she put forward for suggesting she should decline the invitation.

Her mother used all her persuasive powers in order to make Tacy change her mind. She pointed out that it was a rare honour to be invited to a reception at Tor Royal; one that had never before come the way of anyone in the Elford family.

'I'm still not certain I want to go . . .'

'You must, Tacy. It's an experience that'll likely come only once in a lifetime.'

'All right, then I suppose I need to be on my way. I only hope it doesn't rain again, that's all.'

Tacy was to walk to Tor Royal. It had been arranged she would travel in a carriage from there to the church at Sheepstor. When the service was over she would return in the same carriage for the wedding reception which was being held at Sir Thomas Tyrwhitt's house.

As Tacy adjusted a shawl about her shoulders, Joan Elford said, 'Have a wonderful time, Tacy. You'll be the loveliest girl there, I'm certain of it.'

With a doubtful smile, Tacy left the farmhouse and struck out across the moor.

She looked back once and waved to the family who were standing in the doorway of the kitchen. Her father was with them, supported by the arm of her mother. His condition was a growing worry to the whole family.

But this was not a day for thinking of such things. She walked briskly, holding the hem of her dress clear of the wet ground. She had not gone very far before becoming aware that the wet from the grass was soaking through the satin shoes her mother had produced from a trunk in her bedroom.

They were beautiful shoes, but totally impractical for walking across the moor. After confirming she was out of sight of those in the farmhouse kitchen, Tacy paused and removed the shoes. She would go barefooted until she reached Tor Royal.

Tacy was proud of her new dress. It was the only item of clothing she had ever possessed that had been especially tailored for her. The pale blue of the patterned material suited her colouring and she thought it the most beautiful dress she had ever seen.

Until she reached Tor Royal.

Her wet shoes now back on her feet, Tacy was shown into a room occupied by men and women from Sir Thomas Tyrwhitt's circle of friends. These women were dressed in expensive gowns of satin, cut in the latest fashion. They also wore fur-trimmed coats and every one of them had on a hat.

Tacy had anguished over the only three hats owned by the Elford family, deciding eventually to go bare-headed. It was a mistake among this company.

She realised people were staring at her. The polite ones looked once and quickly looked away again. Others stared at her for longer.

Suddenly, she was confronted by Winifrith, who was as overdressed for the occasion as Tacy was under-dressed.

'Who are you, girl? What are you doing here?'

Before Tacy could reply, she was rescued by Sir Thomas Tyrwhitt.

'Tacy, how delightful to see you – and how wonderful you look. Winifrith, this is Tacy, the daughter of Tom Elford who farms Roundtor. She has been a very good friend to Virgil and Pilgrim.'

Leading Tacy skilfully away from his vitriolic sister, he said, 'Come and meet Doctor Dykar and his wife. You may have already met them at the prison. I'm sorry neither Virgil nor Pilgrim is here to greet you, but they have already left for the church. Pilgrim is acting as Virgil's groomsman. My duty is to give Sophie away – and I'm as nervous as a young boy! Here we are.

Mr Dykar, Mrs Dykar . . . this is young Tacy Elford, a member of one of the oldest moorland families. I'm quite certain she will be able to answer any question you might have about Dartmoor. Do enjoy yourself, my dear.'

For some twenty minutes Tacy remained in conversation with the Dykars. She found it somewhat hard going. It was a relief when a servant entered the room and announced that the carriages were ready to take them all to Sheepstor.

Tacy entered a carriage with the Dykars and a number of other guests but she was not expected to make conversation with them. The state of the moorland roads precluded normal conversation.

At the church, in the crowded pews, Tacy was more aware than ever that the dress she had thought to be so wonderful when she left Roundtor Farm did not stand comparison with those worn by the other women guests. Soon she came to believe that everyone who so much as glanced in her direction was thinking the same.

One of the congregation standing not very far from her was Lieutenant Alan Kennedy. She felt certain he must have seen her but he made no acknowledgement of the fact.

Once the bride entered the church on the arm of her uncle, Tacy forgot all else. Sophie wore an embroidered wedding dress of cream batiste and carried a posy of pink and cream roses.

Stepping out to join her from the front pew, Virgil wore the full dress uniform of a captain of the United States Marine Corps, as did Pilgrim, who stood beside him. Both uniforms had been made at Tor Royal by a tailor brought in from the garrison at Plymouth.

It was a brief but moving ceremony and as Tacy

watched Sophie walking along the aisle to the church
door, on the arm of her new husband, she thought she
had seldom seen a woman looking so happy.

When the guests left the church, the carriages were
waiting. Rather than push herself forward, Tacy waited
for everyone else to board first. As Winifrith seemed
to be involved in a self-imposed task of seeing people
safely on board, she too was one of the last left standing
outside the church.

When it seemed too late to do anything else, Tacy
realised she would be obliged to share a coach with
Sophie's mother. The thought of it terrified her!

Suddenly a coach that was already moving off was
brought to a halt. The door swung open and Pilgrim
said, 'Here, Tacy. There's room for one more in here.'

Pilgrim had not been to Roundtor since he and Tacy
had argued about the apology she felt was due to Alan
Kennedy. For just a moment she hesitated. Then, behind
her Winifrith shouted to the driver of the stationary
coach to move off and allow the vehicles behind to get
on their way.

She hesitated no longer. Putting one foot on the step,
she allowed herself to be hauled by Pilgrim inside the
carriage.

59

The return journey to Tor Royal in the carriage was no more comfortable than the outward one had been. Conversation was almost impossible and Pilgrim had not been telling the truth when he said there was room for her inside the carriage.

The passengers on the seat where she sat next to him were crammed uncomfortably close together and she was aware of his closeness to her.

Soon after the carriage got underway Pilgrim leaned towards her and she thought he was telling her that he liked her dress. She could not be certain because at that moment the coachman whipped up the horses until the coach was jolting along the uneven road at what felt like a breakneck speed.

Eventually they arrived at Sir Thomas's home and Tacy enjoyed a few moments' malicious pleasure when she looked at the two other girls who had been in the carriage with her. They were by no means as elegant as when they set out. Their ornate hats were askew, the feathers of one decidedly ruffled. Their hair, which had begun the journey pinned up in elaborate hairstyles, needed urgent attention.

Tacy's long hair, on the other hand, had been brushed back and tied behind her neck. It still looked almost as neat as when she had boarded the carriage.

Pilgrim handed Tacy down and as they walked together towards the house, he said, 'Tacy? Can we be friends again?'

The delight she felt should have provided him with the answer he wanted, but before she could speak, Sir Thomas hurried from the house. 'Ah, there you are, Pilgrim! You should have been on the first carriage. Pardon me for taking him off like this, Tacy, but, as Virgil's groomsman, there are one or two duties Pilgrim needs to perform.'

As he hurried Pilgrim away, he was saying, 'I trust you have a speech ready and that things go to plan now, Pilgrim. It seems Winifrith has taken a hand and suddenly order has become chaos . . . !'

From the moment Pilgrim left her side, things went from bad to worse for Tacy. Sophie greeted her warmly enough, but Winifrith displayed great rudeness by hurrying Tacy on in order to introduce some of the more influential guests.

When the guests sat down for a formal meal, Tacy's embarrassment became a nightmare. There were so many knives, forks, spoons and glasses she had no idea where to begin.

She tried following what others were doing, but even here she made mistakes. She managed to drop a knife on the floor and bump heads with one of the servants when she tried to retrieve it. Then she was shaking with nervousness to such an extent, she dropped a spoonful of soup on her dress.

'Oh, you poor dear!' said a lady seated on Tacy's left,

extremely loudly. 'But, of course, that's why we have table napkins.'

Removing the item in question from a silver ring beside Tacy's plate, she shook it out and dropped it on her lap. On the far side of the table a young girl wearing an expensive dress of dark green silk tittered, only to be elbowed into silence by a stern-faced woman beside her.

Tacy spent most of the meal with her eyes cast down upon her plate, only the high colour of her cheeks revealing her acute embarrassment.

The meal seemed to go on for ever, but finally port began to circulate around the table and the speeches began. It seemed everyone had something to say about either bride or groom. Pilgrim, Virgil and Sir Thomas all spoke.

Then Winifrith wanted to say something. She had been drinking heavily and her cheeks were as flushed as Tacy's. She was eventually persuaded by Sir Thomas to make her speech to the newly married couple in private, later in the evening.

The speeches over, everyone left the dining room and made their way to the candle-lit terrace. A canvas canopy had been set up here. With the adjacent drawing room, it would provide an area for socialising and dancing.

Twice on the way from the dining room Tacy had passed within touching distance of Alan Kennedy. On each occasion he had carefully averted his glance, pretending to be in deep conversation with his companion of the moment.

Pilgrim had smiled in her direction once, but Sir Thomas was holding a deep conversation with him. Tacy thought that now would be a good opportunity for her to slip away unnoticed and return to Roundtor Farm.

She succeeded in finding a servant and asked her to locate her shawl. In order that she might leave quietly, she told the girl to bring it to her outside the main door of the house.

When she had it, Tacy slipped quietly away into the darkness. She looked back only once, when the small orchestra struck up a tune for the dancers.

The house was bathed in light, and lanterns shone out from every window. In any other circumstances it was a sight she would have viewed with delight. But she had just spent a miserable couple of hours during which she had become increasingly aware she did not belong among those who frequented houses like Tor Royal.

The knowledge carried much wider implications too. Pilgrim was at home in such company. That had been perfectly obvious to her. Perhaps it was this which hurt most of all. The confirmation that they belonged in different worlds.

As she left the grounds of Tor Royal behind, Tacy thought she heard sounds close behind her. At first she believed it must be her imagination. When she heard it again, she decided it must be a sheep, or perhaps one of the moorland ponies.

Walking steadily down the hill from Sir Thomas's house she reached a stream in the valley bottom. Here she paused for a moment and listened again. There was a sound as though someone or something had stumbled – then she heard a muffled curse.

'Who's that? Who's there?'

'It's all right, Tacy. It's me. Alan.'

The slurring of his words might have been because he was out of breath. Tacy thought it was more likely a result of the amount of drink she had seen him consuming at the dining table and afterwards.

'It's not all right. Why are you following me?'

Lieutenant Kennedy took shadowy form in front of her, breathing heavily. 'I saw you leave and as I hadn't had an opportunity to talk to you during the wedding reception, I came after you.'

'You had plenty of opportunity to talk to me, had you wanted to, but you didn't. Why, Alan? Was it because you didn't want your grand friends to see you talking to a farm girl? Is that why you wouldn't talk to me at Tor Royal?'

'It wasn't like that at all, Tacy. You and I are friends. I'll walk home with you.'

'No you won't. You've had so much to drink you'd end up hopelessly lost on the moor.'

'Then let's stay here for a while. This is the first time you and I have been able to meet without having someone else spying on us. Let's make the most of it.'

He moved closer to her and she could smell the brandy on his breath.

'Go back to Tor Royal, Alan. I'm going home.'

As she turned away, he reached out and grabbed her arm. 'Don't play hard to get with me, Tacy. You've enjoyed yourself these past few weeks haven't you, leading me on the way you have? Now it's my turn to enjoy myself – and it's no good playing the outraged little virgin with me. I know what you've been up to with that American – with many others too, I've no doubt. Come on, it's time to stop playing games with me.'

He had a painful grip on her arm and now he pulled her towards him, clumsily attempting to lift the skirt of her dress with his free hand.

'Let me go! You're hurting me.'

Tacy struggled to break free. She had been holding her soft shoes, now she dropped them and began pummelling the Irish militiaman. As she did so they both stumbled momentarily and one of her feet slipped into the brook.

'Stop struggling! Stop it, I tell you!'

Suddenly, he ceased fumbling with her skirt and swung his arm. The flat of his hand exploded against the side of her face and she was momentarily dazed. Her foot turned on a smooth stone and she slipped, to lie half in and half out of the stream.

Kennedy went with her. Kneeling in the water, he dragged her to the grass of the bank. His hand went inside the top of her dress and, struggling furiously once more, she screamed.

Suddenly, he was pulled bodily from her.

'What the . . . ?' The remainder of the question was lost as the militiaman's head was thrust into the water of the stream.

'Perhaps this will cool your ardour.'

It was Pilgrim! As Tacy sat on the bank, pulling her dress up about her shoulders, there was a desperate thrashing of limbs in the water and a spluttered, 'Help!' before the sound ended in a frightening gurgle.

As the sounds of the struggling grew feebler, Tacy cried out in alarm, 'Don't drown him.'

'Why? Do you still care for him, after what he tried to do?'

'I don't care what happens to *him*. I'm thinking of what they'll do to you if he dies.'

'In that case we'll let him up.'

Pilgrim released his hold on Kennedy's hair and rose to his feet. The militiaman's head rose above the surface of the water. Choking and retching, he dragged himself to the far bank of the stream. He lay here alternately choking and noisily sucking in great gulps of air.

'Are you all right?' Filled with concern, Pilgrim dropped down beside Tacy, who was on her hands and knees.

'I've lost my shoes. They belong to Ma.'

'She'll understand. You're more important than shoes. I'll come down here and find them in the morning. Right now I'll see you safely home.'

He lifted her to her feet and she said, 'You're soaking wet. You should go home and change or you'll catch a chill.'

'Not tonight, I won't. There are things I want to say to you, Tacy. Things that should have been said a long while ago.'

As they walked away, Lieutenant Alan Kennedy began coughing painfully. Turning her head, Tacy said, 'What about him?'

'He'll be all right. If he's got any sense he'll go straight back to Princetown. Then he won't have to explain his condition to any of the wedding guests. After that he'll spend the rest of his service on Dartmoor trying to avoid both of us. Now, forget him. We have some catching up to do. Give me your hand. I don't want you disappearing before I've said what needs saying.'

60

Holding Tacy's hand, Pilgrim waited to speak again until they could no longer hear Lieutenant Kennedy fighting for breath.

'Are you upset by what happened back there tonight, Tacy? Had you grown very fond of Lieutenant Kennedy?'

'The answer to both your questions is "No". I was too angry with him. Frightened, too, for a while. But I was never particularly fond of him. I was flattered by his attentions and . . . I suppose that was all, really.'

She had been about to say she thought that by allowing the militiaman to pay her attention it might provoke an appropriate response from Pilgrim. She decided it would be better left unsaid.

Suddenly, she shivered involuntarily and Pilgrim expressed immediate concern. 'You're cold. Here, borrow my coat.'

He began unbuttoning his uniform coat, but she stopped him. 'No, it's all right. My shawl never went in the stream. It's warm and dry – anyway, your coat's every bit as wet as my dress. It'll be muddy too.

It's such a pity, you looked so smart at the wedding.'

Finding her hand once more, Pilgrim said, 'At least the wedding went well. I was very pleased for Virgil and Sophie's sakes. She, in particular, has had her share of tragedy. Virgil's got a painful time ahead too, with that wounded leg of his, but I'm convinced they'll come through it together. The greatest thing in their favour is that Sophie's mother will remain in England when they set off for America. She's a very difficult woman.'

'She'd have turned me away from the wedding if she'd had her way. She wanted to know what I was doing there when I arrived at Tor Royal.'

'I can well believe it. I'd have been excluded too had she been able to think of some way of doing it. She was bitterly opposed to Sophie marrying Virgil. In fact, she's opposed to her doing anything unless she's approved of it first. I believe she's aggrieved most of all because the wedding had been organised before she returned to England. She's that sort of a woman.'

'So I've heard. But she was right you know – about me, I mean. She knew right away I didn't belong among all those people who were at Tor Royal. It didn't take *me* very long to realise *that*.'

'What are you talking about, Tacy? You looked wonderful.'

'No I didn't. I *thought* I did, before I got there. When I put on my new dress at home, I believed it must be the most beautiful dress in the whole world. It's the best one I've ever owned, but it was home-made, with gingham bought from a moorland pedlar. The dresses worn by all the women at the wedding showed it up for what it was – cheap and home-made. Everyone else knew it, too.'

'I think you're wrong, Tacy. If anyone looked at you it

was because they realised you were the most beautiful woman at Tor Royal.'

Tacy put momentary pressure on his hand and said, 'If you'd said something like that weeks ago there would have been none of the trouble we've had tonight with Alan.'

'I would have said it *months* ago had I known of an honourable way to do it. It's what I've always thought about you.'

'Then why *haven't* you told me so before now?'

'I was trying to do the right thing. I felt I couldn't say anything until I could see a way forward for us. I knew that once the way I felt was out in the open there would be no way that things between us could stand still.'

'There *is* no way forward for us, Pilgrim. Anything we do can only be enjoyed for today. You and I have no tomorrow together. If there ever was any doubt in my mind, it ended when I went to Tor Royal. As I said, when I arrived there, the most wonderful thing in my life was my new gingham dress. It didn't take me many minutes to realise that had it been given to any one of the women or girls at the wedding they would have passed it on to their servants to be torn up and used as dusters.'

'That's not true, Tacy – but even if it were, what has that to do with you and me?'

'Don't you see, Pilgrim? The people at Tor Royal today are those you're used to mixing with every day. It's a different world to the one I live in.'

Bringing Tacy to a sudden halt, Pilgrim pulled her around to face him. 'Now just you listen to me for a moment. Are you suggesting that men like Lieutenant Kennedy or women like Winifrith Cudmore are *better* than you?'

'No, but they're *rich*. They know how to dress and

how to eat, and what to do when they meet other people.'

'Anyone can learn about such things, if they want to. It doesn't make them better than someone else. I've already told you about the early days of my own family. We headed west carrying all we owned in a couple of wagons. Our first home was a log cabin that we built ourselves. The folk we travelled with were farmers, carpenters, blacksmiths – and all the other occupations that go to making up a community. Some of them worked hard and made it. Others worked equally hard, and didn't – but we all of us worked, men, women and children. What's more, most of us remained friends. Those who succeeded and those who didn't. Those who've become rich and those who haven't. I'm not saying America doesn't have social barriers, Tacy, I know it does. But that's mainly along the east coast, where the British influence was always strongest. They cling on to what's familiar to them.'

There was passion in Pilgrim's voice now as he continued, 'The country's expanding westwards now, Tacy. Out on the frontier men and women are judged by what they *are* and by what they can do, *not* by what their parents or grandparents did in the past. *They're* the sort of people I'm used to. Folk who are working hard and taking chances in order to carve out a good life for themselves and their children . . .'

Tacy shivered and Pilgrim was immediately solicitous. 'I'm sorry, there's me getting carried away with my "speechifying", as Ma calls it when Pa does it, while you're wet and cold. Let's get you home. We can talk about all this some other time.'

'Shouldn't you be getting back to Tor Royal? We don't want you getting into trouble.'

'Nobody's going to look for trouble tonight – not if

Lieutenant Kennedy goes straight back to his quarters, as I feel sure he will.'

Tacy shivered again, but this time it had nothing to do with the cold. She had thought of what would have happened to her had Pilgrim not come to her rescue.

'Come on, let's hurry.'

'All right, but there's no need to run. You were explaining to me about things in America. I'm impressed, but what difference does it make? We're in England.'

'We are now, but I won't always be a prisoner-of-war. One day I'll be returning to the United States. When I do I want you to be with me.'

'What do you mean, you want me with you? I can't just leave everything and go gadding off to a country I'd hardly heard of before I met you.'

'I'd like you to go to America with me the same way Sophie is with Virgil. Marrying me here first and travelling there as my wife.'

Tacy stopped suddenly, pulling him to a halt. 'Do you realise what you are saying? You've never given me so much as a hint of the way you feel about me, whether as a friend, or anything else. Yet here you are suddenly talking of marriage and of me going to America with you! How much have you had to drink today?'

'Quite a lot. I think that's what's given me the courage to tell you all the things I have tonight. I've tried *not* to say them before because I thought it wouldn't be fair until an end to this war was in sight. But when I thought I might lose you to Lieutenant Kennedy, I knew I had to say something. You didn't make it easy, Tacy. Telling me to apologise to him was more than I could stomach.'

'I'm sorry.' Tacy was silent for some moments, then she said, 'Do you realise that he's been the one who's brought us together like this?'

'Yes.'

'I'm glad he has, Pilgrim.'

'So am I.'

In the darkness he drew her to him to kiss her for the first time, but she suddenly pulled back.

'What is it?' For a moment he thought she might have had second thoughts about him.

'It's your coat. It's wet and *freezing*!'

He was at a loss about what to do for a moment, then Tacy was moving closer to him again. 'Here, I've pulled my shawl about me. Shall we try again . . . ?'

61

When Tacy and Pilgrim arrived at Roundtor Farm a lamp was alight in the kitchen and they could see the shadow of someone moving.

'Ma's still up,' said Tacy. 'I'd hoped I might be able to creep in without her seeing me. I'd have not told her what happened until the morning.'

'It would have been easier for you,' agreed Pilgrim, 'but I'll come in with you.'

When they reached the door, Tacy stopped for a moment and said quietly, 'I'm very glad we're friends again, Pilgrim.'

'Oh! Are we only friends now?'

'You know what I mean.' She kissed him quickly and then lifted the latch on the kitchen door.

Tacy was relieved to see that her father's high-backed chair was empty. It meant he was in bed. She did not want him becoming over-excited by her explanation of what had happened to her. Johanna would be in bed too.

Joan was making up the fire but she turned around

when she heard the door opening. Her expression became one of horrified disbelief as she saw Tacy in the light from the kitchen lamp.

Pilgrim grimaced; Tacy was in a worse state than he had realised.

'My dear soul! Look at the state of your nice new dress . . . and of you too!' She included Pilgrim in her critical assessment. 'What on earth has happened to you both?'

A hint of suspicion crept into her mind and she said, 'What have you both been up to?'

'Can we get some clothes for Pilgrim, Ma – and put his uniform round the fire to dry? He must get back to Tor Royal before too long.'

'You know where the working clothes are kept, Pilgrim. In the outhouse. Change there while I breathe some life back into this fire. The trouble is, I've only just made it up for the night. While you're changing, Tacy can make a start on telling me what you've both been up to. She left the house looking like a princess and now she's come back for all the world like one of those tinkers Emma used to travel with – and who were back here this afternoon . . .'

Pilgrim changed in the outhouse by the light of a candle, carried with him from the kitchen. It took him only a matter of minutes, but by the time he returned carrying a bundle of wet clothing with him, Tacy had given her mother an outline of what had happened to her when she left Tor Royal.

Her mother greeted Pilgrim with, 'It seems we were both right about that militia officer.'

'I'm afraid so,' said Pilgrim. 'He certainly showed his true colours tonight.'

'That isn't all he would have done had you not been

on hand to help her,' said Joan grimly. Her voice broke as she added shakily, 'He might well have murdered her. A dress can be replaced, but not a daughter. Thank you, Pilgrim.'

'I'm not at all sure you'll be wanting to thank me when you hear what I have to say, Mrs Elford. The chances are you'll be losing her anyway.'

'What do you mean?' She looked from Pilgrim to Tacy, not understanding. 'What else has happened?'

'I've asked Tacy to marry me once the end of this war is in sight. It means we'd be setting up home in Ohio, in America.'

Reaching behind her, Joan found her husband's chair and sat down heavily. Shaking her head as though dazed, she said, 'I know I shouldn't be surprised but everything's happened so quickly, and coming on top of everything else . . .' She looked thoroughly bemused.

'You don't disapprove, Ma? You and Pa aren't going to say I can't marry Pilgrim?'

'After what he's done tonight? Anyway, would it make any difference if we said "no"? You'd only do what Sir Thomas's niece did. Run off and marry him just the same. But we won't try to stop you, child. Just as long as you wait and try to behave yourselves until we can see an end to this foolish war between our countries. Your pa feels the same, I know. We've talked about it more than once.'

'Does that mean Tacy *will* be having a baby soon? Can I hold it?'

No one had noticed Johanna come down the boxed-in staircase that led from the bedrooms to a corner of the kitchen.

'Your ears are far too big for a young girl,' said her mother, rising from the chair. 'One of these days you'll take off in a high wind and we'll never see you again.

Tacy and Pilgrim are only talking of getting married. It won't happen for a long time yet.'

'Can I go up and tell Pa? He heard me come from the bedroom and said I was to ask how Tacy got on.' She frowned. 'How did she get so muddy – and why is Pilgrim wearing them old working clothes?'

'Tacy slipped as they were crossing a stream on the way home. Pilgrim pulled her out – and, no! Tacy will go up and tell Pa herself, once she's taken her muddy dress off. I'll soak it overnight and hope the mud comes out. But first I want to give them both a kiss and say that I'm very happy for them . . .'

Tom Elford shared his wife's pleasure at the news that Tacy and Pilgrim intended marrying as soon as there was an end in sight to the war.

After hugging his daughter and shaking Pilgrim by the hand, he lay back on his pillows and gave his future son-in-law a wan smile.

'You don't need me to tell you I'm not a well man, Pilgrim. It's good to have been able to see the man that at least one of my daughters is to marry. I'd thought that her future husband might one day take over Roundtor Farm, but Tacy will have a far better life in America with you. All there is here for a man and his wife is a constant battle to eke out a living. A tenant farmer on Dartmoor will never grow rich, or be able to give his wife and family the things he'd dearly love them to have.'

'Now, Tom, don't start talking of such things. Not tonight. Anyway, it's not true. Not as far as you're concerned. You've given me all I've ever asked from life. A loving husband and two of the finest daughters a woman could wish for. If Pilgrim and Tacy are blessed with as much in their life together they'll never want for happiness, at least.'

Tom Elford reached out and grasped his wife's hand, not trusting himself to speak.

'But if Tacy and Pilgrim go to live in America I'm not going to be able to take care of their babies, am I?'

'I shouldn't worry yourself about that, young lady. The time will come all too soon when you have babies of your own to look after.'

'That's not going to be for years and years,' Johanna pouted. 'I don't want to have to wait *that* long.' Suddenly she brightened. 'Oh well, if Tacy isn't going to have a baby for me to look after, then I'm just going to have to help Emma look after her baby, aren't I?'

'What are you talking about, child? Emma's not going to have a baby. She isn't married – and has no thoughts of getting married, as far as I know.'

Johanna remained silent and would not meet her mother's eyes and Joan Elford looked at her speculatively. 'Is there something you know that I don't, Johanna? I think you'd better tell me.'

'I promised Emma I'd keep it a secret,' said Johanna, unhappily.

'So there *is* something? Come on, girl, what is it? Is Emma expecting a baby?'

Johanna nodded, her eyes downcast.

'Well, who'd have thought it! There's her dangling poor young Billy along on a piece of string and all the time she's carrying someone's baby. I wonder who the father is? I hope it's not that tinker man who was around here today. It'll break Billy's heart if he finds her and they go off together.'

'It's no tinker's baby,' declared Johanna. 'It's Billy's.'

Seeing the scornful expression on her mother's face, Johanna said heatedly, 'It *is* Billy's. Emma told me. Besides . . .' Johanna dropped her eyes from her mother's face once more.

'Go on, girl, what is it you were going to say?'

'I *know* it's Billy's. I caught them together up in our hayloft a few weeks ago. Emma said I shouldn't say anything because it might get Billy into trouble. She said it would be all right, because she and Billy were going to be married very soon, anyway.'

62

Emma was working hard in the garden of the Yates cottage. All around were the man-made hills of waste, extracted from an underground skein of tunnels, dug when this had been a working mine.

The vegetable garden had produced nothing for many years. Indeed, there was now only the faintest of outlines to show where it had once been. Emma was making a start on digging it over, determined it would one day provide all the vegetable needs of those in the cottage.

It also got her out of the way of Mrs Yates. Billy's mother was up and about once more, but still not well enough to be left alone.

Neither had she accepted Emma's presence in *her* cottage, although it was cleaner than it had ever been and Emma had proved herself an impressive cook. She had the knack of producing a palatable meal from the skimpiest of ingredients.

It was of Mrs Yates Emma was thinking as she worked. She would like to have been accepted by her, for Billy's sake. He was torn between loyalty to his mother and his love for Emma, and he found it difficult to cope with his feelings.

Because of Mrs Yates's improved health, Emma had sent Billy to Roundtor Farm, promising she would remain at home and take care of the convalescing woman. They were out of provisions and the work Billy did for the Elfords was the only way of obtaining more.

So busy was Emma with her thoughts and the task she had set herself, she did not see the ragged man making his way stealthily towards her from the cover of one of the spoil heaps. He was dirty from the top of his greasy and battered high-crowned hat to the filthy ankles exposed between sockless feet and trousers that did not reach to within a handsbreadth of his decrepit shoes. The clothes in between were threadbare and full of holes.

Not until he was almost within touching distance of her did the man speak. 'Hello, Emma, my dear. I hope you didn't think you'd seen the last of old Charlie?'

Emma swung around at the sound of the man's voice, an expression of stark fear on her face. Swinging up the spade she was holding so it was between them, she said, 'You keep away from me, Charlie. If you don't I'll slice your head off with this, I swear I will.'

'Now what sort of talk is that, Emma? You *belong* to me, you know that. Didn't I pay good money for you when you would have been turned out by your own mother? You was *indentured* to me, girl, that's the word them smart lawyers use, but it means the same. You came to me when you was too small to pay your way. I taught you how to earn a living and how did you thank me? By running away, that's how.'

'You taught me to lie and cheat and thieve for you,

Charlie. As for the rest, I only have your word for how you came by me – and that's never counted for very much, has it?'

'It'll count enough for a magistrate to order you back to me, you see if it don't.'

'You wouldn't dare take me before a magistrate. What I could tell him about you would have you dangling on the end of a hangman's rope – you *and* Bella, if I'd a mind to tell about her too.'

Casting a quick glance in the direction of the spoil heap from whence Charlie had appeared, Emma said, 'Where *is* Bella?'

'She's standing right behind you.'

Without thinking, Emma turned her head to look behind her. Before she had time to take it in that she had been tricked, Charlie hit her on the side of the head, knocking her to her knees.

Before she could recover, the tinker had snatched the spade from her hand and flung it from him before taking a cruel grip on her arm.

'That fooled you, didn't it? Bella's been dead these past three weeks. That's why I've come looking for you. You can take her place.'

'No! Let go! Let go of me,' Emma shrieked at him.

'Oh no. You've run away from me once. By the time I've finished with you you'll never try it again.'

By twisting her arm, Charlie forced her to her knees once more, then, one-handed, he loosened a piece of thin rope coiled about his waist beneath his shirt, and passed one end about her neck.

His intention was to secure the rope about her neck and lead her away, but before he could accomplish his purpose he was interrupted by Tillie Yates.

She emerged from the cottage like an avenging angel. No one who saw her would have suspected she was a sick woman. In her hands she wielded a heavy, long-handled brush.

She ran at Charlie. Before he could recover from his surprise she swung the broom and struck him on the side of the head.

Releasing Emma and the rope, he wrapped both arms about his battered head and staggered away, pursued by Billy's mother.

Unwinding the rope from about her neck, Emma darted to where the spade lay. Snatching it up, she too went after Charlie.

A swing from the spade struck him in almost the same place as had the broom, but the sharp-edged blade of the spade was a far more vicious weapon. It almost severed one of his ears.

Spurting blood and screaming in pain, the brutal tinker fled across the moor, pursued part of the way by a vengeful Emma.

When it was apparent the tinker would not stop running until he had put a considerable distance between himself and the two women, Emma turned and looked back towards the house.

Tillie Yates was crouching on the ground, close to where she had attacked Charlie. Mouth open, she seemed to be having great difficulty in breathing.

Emma ran back to her. Dropping the spade, she knelt beside the woman, thoroughly alarmed by her pallor. 'You shouldn't have done that, Mrs Yates. You still aren't well.'

Putting an arm about her she tried to raise her to her feet, but received no assistance from the older woman.

'No . . . no good. Has . . . Has the tinker gone?'

'Yes. You were marvellous. But let's get you into the house.'

'It'll be . . . no good, girl. Take care . . . take care . . . Billy. He needs . . . someone . . .'

Suddenly, Tillie Yates sagged in Emma's arms and the breath escaped from her in a soft, lingering sigh.

'Mrs Yates! Mrs Yates . . .'

In her panic, Emma shook Billy's mother. The only effect it had was to cause her to fall sideways.

'Oh my God!'

Emma let the other woman slip to the ground and rose to her feet. She ran a few paces and then turned and ran back.

Kneeling down once more, she put her ear to Tillie's mouth, but could neither hear nor feel anything.

'What am I going to do? What _can_ I do?'

Tillie Yates lay crumpled on the ground and suddenly Emma began running. She ran away from the house, running as she never had before.

63

Billy had spent the morning gathering sheep from the hills and valleys about Roundtor with the aid of the two dogs.

He was well pleased with his work. Rip was at last fulfilling his earlier promise. He was now a first-class sheepdog. Billy thought Sir Thomas would be proud of him one day.

It was good to be working for the Elfords once more. Billy had told Mrs Elford that his mother was much improved and that Emma had insisted he come back to work again. In his simple, honest manner, he had explained there was no food left in the pantry of the Yates cottage.

'I'll give you a basket of food to take back with you,' said Joan. 'Now, off you go and find Tacy. She'll tell you what needs to be done.'

She would have liked to tackle Billy about Johanna's revelation that Emma was carrying his baby, but she decided that could wait for an hour or two, at least.

Pilgrim was working at the farm today. He had gone

out with the pony and wagon to fetch in some of the peat that had been stacked on the moor by Billy. Winter was very close. The peat needed to be brought to the farmyard and stacked beside the kitchen door. Here it would be easily accessible in even the worst weather.

Tacy would be working in the dairy for most of the day and a somewhat rebellious Johanna had been detailed to clean out the buildings occupied by cows, pigs and chickens.

At noon, Billy made his way back to the farm. He and the dogs had rounded up more than fifty Elford sheep. He considered it to have been a good morning's work.

He was feeling pleased with himself. When Joan walked from the farm to meet him he was eager to tell her what he had done.

'Rip did really well,' he said. 'Mr Elford was right when he said he'd turn out to be a good dog. Sir Thomas is going to be pleased with him.'

'I haven't come out here to talk about Rip, Billy. I'd like to have a word with you about Emma – and the baby.'

Billy looked completely baffled. 'Baby? What baby are you talking about, Mrs Elford? I don't know no baby.'

Joan was about to tell him what she had heard, but she changed her mind. She realised that to say any more right now would be gross interference.

'I must be getting you confused with someone else, Billy. Don't take any notice of me. Come inside the house and have something to eat. You'll have worked up an appetite this morning.'

She decided she would speak to Emma when next she came to Roundtor.

Joan Elford met with Emma far earlier than she had

anticipated, but there was no opportunity to discuss the young woman's condition with her.

She and Billy had almost reached the farmyard gate when they heard a shout from some distance behind them. When they turned, they saw a figure running towards them.

'It's Emma,' said Billy, in alarm. 'What's she doing running like that?'

'She's likely to do herself a mischief if she's not careful,' replied Joan, half to herself.

Emma was running at breakneck speed when she suddenly stumbled and fell to the ground. She picked herself up immediately, but Billy was already running to meet her. Joan hurried after him.

In the farmyard, Tacy came from the dairy in time to see what was happening. She called to Pilgrim and they both hurried after her mother.

When Billy reached Emma, she burst into tears. Clinging to him, she cried, 'I'm sorry, Billy. It's all my fault. I'm so sorry.'

Billy was thoroughly bemused. It was left to Joan to ask her what it was she had done.

Gasping for breath, Emma directed her reply to Billy. 'It's your ma, Billy. I . . . I think she's dead – and it's all my fault.'

'How . . . ?' Billy looked at her in stunned disbelief.

'You'd better come back to the house and tell us what's happened,' said the farmer's wife, but Emma shook her head vigorously.

'We must go back to the cottage . . . Billy and me.'

'All right, but calm down for a few moments first.' Joan took charge once more, as Pilgrim and Tacy reached them. 'Sit down here and tell us exactly what's happened.'

Sitting down heavily on the grass, Emma tearfully

told them of the arrival of Charlie and of the events that ensued. When she spoke of Tillie Yates's last moments, she broke down once more and kept repeating, 'It was all my fault. If I hadn't been there it wouldn't have happened.'

'You can't blame yourself for what some bullying tinker does, Emma. Besides, poor Tillie's been ill with that heart of hers these last three or four years. She could have gone at any time. Billy knows that. I've often said that she's only been hanging on because if she went there'd be no one to take care of Billy.'

'Her last words were about him,' said a tearful Emma. 'She said I was to take care of him.'

'I've no doubt at all she knew full well you would,' said Joan, adding meaningfully, 'Mind, you're going to need to have someone looking after you before too long.'

When Emma gave her a startled look, she added, 'But we'll talk about that some other time.'

Turning to a confused and bereft Billy, she said, 'I'm very sorry about your ma, Billy. She might have kept herself a bit too much to herself for most folk's liking, but she brought you up knowing right from wrong. That couldn't always have been easy with no man about the place.'

Giving him a motherly hug, she said, 'Now, you get over to her cottage – all of you – and carry her inside. I'll go back and tell Tom and Johanna what's going on, then I'll come over there and do what needs to be done.'

She hurried away, murmuring about 'Not knowing what the moor is coming to with all these goings on. First a militiaman and Tacy, and now a tinker and poor Tillie Yates . . .'

64

The funeral of Tillie Yates took place on the day Virgil and Sophie departed from Tor Royal, leaving Pilgrim as the senior United States officer in charge of the American prisoners-of-war.

The two events were emotional for everyone concerned. For Pilgrim the day began soon after dawn, when the newly married couple departed for Portsmouth. The parting came as a great wrench for him. He and Virgil had served together for a number of years, sharing war, escape and captivity.

Before leaving, Virgil promised that he would use the influence of his family and friends to bring the plight of the United States prisoners-of-war in Dartmoor prison to the attention of their Government.

The parting was equally emotional for Sophie and her mother. Theirs had always been something of a love/hate relationship. Fully aware they might never see each other again they had reached a tacit agreement not to quarrel during their final days.

However, Winifrith had felt unable to extend the

armistice to include Virgil. She continued to ignore him. Even on this, the day of his departure with her daughter. She did no more than give him a perfunctory shake of the hand, with a grudgingly expressed hope that American surgeons would be able to cure his wounded leg.

Sir Thomas, Winifrith and Pilgrim, together with all the house servants, stood outside the main entrance to Tor Royal. They continued to wave to the departing couple until the carriage taking them to Portsmouth passed from view, with Virgil and Sophie still fluttering handkerchiefs from the open windows.

Hurrying back inside the house ahead of the others, Winifrith retired to her room. She would not be seen for the remainder of the day.

'I'm going to miss that girl,' said Sir Thomas, in apparent surprise. He and Pilgrim were entering the house together. 'I've grown used to having her about the place. Still, she could not be in better hands. Virgil is a good man. He has sound commonsense and I understand he comes from a good family too.'

'Among the best in America,' agreed Pilgrim. 'Sophie will find herself at the very centre of east coast society.'

'Good!' Sir Thomas nodded his satisfaction. 'She'll fit in well, I have no doubt at all.'

Glancing at his companion, he said, 'You are going to miss Virgil.'

'Very much, and not only as a friend. I've taken over many of his duties in recent weeks, but he's always been here for me to discuss any problems with. I'm on my own now.'

'Well, if you ever feel the need to talk things over with anyone, you have my ear – although I fear I must return to London very soon now.' Giving Pilgrim a mischievous smile, he added, 'I'll see if I can persuade

Winifrith to come with me. It should make life easier for you here.'

Pilgrim felt it would be best if he made no reply.

'What are you doing for the remainder of the day, Pilgrim?'

'I have Governor Cotgrave's permission to attend a funeral at Sheepstor.'

'Of course! The mother of that young lad who works for the Elfords is being buried. He's rather simple, is he not? He and his mother have been living in one of the old mine cottages down at the old Whiteworks mine. What will happen to the boy now? Will he move in with the Elfords, d'you think? If he does I'll have the old cottage pulled down. I don't want it attracting vagrants. There seem to have been a great many of them around the moor lately.'

'I think Billy would like to remain in his mother's cottage,' said Pilgrim. 'He *is* rather simple, but he's honest and hardworking. Tom Elford also says he's better than most of the shepherds on the moor. He's certainly bringing that dog of yours on. Billy's also been fortunate enough to find a girl with enough sound commonsense for both of them.'

Pilgrim paused to allow Sir Thomas to pass through the front door of the house ahead of him before continuing. 'She's been living in the cottage while Billy's mother's been ill and has put the place in good order. She's even made an impressive start on the garden.'

Sir Thomas frowned. 'Are you suggesting I should condone having them both living there although they're not married? I would come in for a great deal of justifiable criticism were I to allow that.'

'My understanding is that they intend marrying quite soon, Sir Thomas.'

After a few moments' thought, Sir Thomas said, 'Very well. Have a word with Billy and this girl. Tell them that if they marry before Christmas they can take a tenancy of the old mine cottage. What amount of rent do you think they'll be able to afford?'

The question took Pilgrim by surprise and he said hesitantly, 'Neither of them is earning money. Billy works for the Elfords in exchange for food and fuel. Until Mrs Yates became ill, Emma was working at Roundtor Farm for her board only.'

Sir Thomas gave Pilgrim a shrewd look. 'What you're telling me is that they are unable to pay any rent for the cottage?' He shrugged. 'Very well. Tell them if they continue to make improvements to the cottage I'll see to it they have the tenancy on a peppercorn rent. Now, I feel chilled through after standing outside seeing off the newlyweds. Let's go to my study and have something to warm us up. You'll certainly need something. A moorland funeral is a cold and solemn service at the best of times.'

65

The funeral of Tillie Yates was a brief, perfunctory affair. In a box in the bedroom of his late mother Billy had found money to pay for only the simplest of burials.

The coffin containing her body was carried across the four miles of moorland between the old mine cottage and Sheepstor in the Elfords' cart, pulled by their pony, led by Pilgrim.

Following behind for the long walk were Billy, Emma and Joan and Tacy Elford. Tom Elford was not fit enough to attend the funeral and Johanna had been told to remain behind with him.

At Sheepstor church the small party of mourners was joined by two members of a moorland family who had known Tillie when she was a young girl.

The weather was as depressing as the occasion. Menacing dark clouds had built up above the moor and a chill northerly wind was a sharp reminder that winter was in the offing.

After the coffin had been laid in the ground and the gravedigger had begun the sombre task of filling in the grave, the party climbed inside the cart and made its way back to Roundtor Farm.

In the kitchen, Joan Elford bustled about, preparing a hot meal for all of them. It was now that Pilgrim repeated what Sir Thomas had said to him about the tenancy of the Yates's lonely old mining cottage.

Tom Elford had come down to his usual seat to share the warmth of the kitchen with the others. Taking a faintly smoking pipe from between his teeth, he said, 'That, at least, is a bright spot for you in a very unhappy day, Billy.'

Instead of being pleased, Billy appeared thoroughly bemused, 'But ... Emma hasn't said she wants to marry me!'

There was a wave of laughter in the kitchen that helped to release some of the unhappy tension that had built up in everyone.

'I think she'd better say "Yes" before too long,' said Joan. Her words prompted Emma to give Johanna an accusing glance.

'Have you asked her to marry you, Billy?' The question came from Tacy.

'No, he hasn't,' said Emma. 'But perhaps he doesn't want to marry me.'

'I *do*,' declared Billy unhappily. 'But ... what do I have to do to get us married?'

There was not one person in the kitchen who did not feel overwhelming sympathy for Billy. He had never known a father. Brought up in a remote part of the moor, he had met very few people. The Elfords were the only *family* he knew. Marriage was as much of a mystery to him as mathematics.

'If you really want to marry me and for us to be with each other for always, I'll be happy to wed you, Billy. We'd make a good couple, I know it.'

Joan Elford clearly approved of her decision and it was to her that Emma turned now.

'I don't know any more about arranging a wedding than Billy does. Will you help us, Mrs Elford?'

'Of course I will – and I'm very happy for both of you. We really shouldn't even be thinking of weddings on a day when Billy's ma's been laid to rest, but Tillie herself was never one for doing what was expected of her. She'd not have minded.'

'Well, if you're going to arrange Billy's wedding for him, perhaps I'll be allowed to act as his groomsman, same as I did for Virgil,' said Pilgrim. 'I'd like that.'

'Well! Such talk has brightened up a sad day, and no mistake,' declared Joan. 'Tom, where did you hide that cider we keep for special occasions? I think this is as good a time as any for it to be brought out.'

Tacy accompanied Pilgrim for part of his walk back to Tor Royal later that evening. There was a light drizzle in the air but, although it was cold, neither of them noticed.

'What an eventful day it's been,' said Tacy. 'First we bury Billy's ma, then it's decided that he and Emma will get married!'

'It's also the day when Virgil and Sophie set off for America to begin their new life together,' Pilgrim reminded her.

'Of course! Theirs was yet another unexpected marriage.'

Giving Pilgrim a sidelong glance, Tacy added, 'They do say that things always happen in threes. I wonder who'll be the third couple to be married?'

'Perhaps it'll be Mary and Henri,' said Pilgrim, in apparent innocence. He had seen her glance and was aware of the reply she wanted him to make.

Smiling sadly at her expression of disappointment, he said, 'I'd like to be able to say it might be us, Tacy, but that isn't possible just yet. You know that as well as I do.'

'No one could possibly be starting married life with less than Billy and Emma,' she pointed out. 'Yet they're going to marry.'

'They don't have a lot,' Pilgrim admitted, 'but they do have a place to live and Billy doesn't live on parole with the threat of a recall to prison hanging over his head. If the British Government suddenly decided it was a good idea, I and all the other prisoners-of-war could be sent to Botany Bay, or anywhere else. No couple can be expected to begin married life with a threat like that hanging over their heads.'

'I sometimes wonder if you really *want* to marry me, Pilgrim Penn,' Tacy pouted.

Pilgrim stopped and turned Tacy to face him. 'You already know the answer to that. If you didn't, you wouldn't dare to even suggest it.'

The drizzle had become light rain now. There was every indication that the cloud over the moor would lower and the rain become heavier, but the young couple did not seem to care at all about the weather.

66

A few days later, Pilgrim was working at Roundtor Farm when Ephraim came to find him.

Johanna saw the marines sergeant entering the farmyard and called out to tell Pilgrim of his presence before eagerly running to meet him.

'You haven't been to see us for *ages*,' she complained, when she reached him. 'Why not?'

'It's not you I've come to see this time, either, young lady, beautiful though you are. I'm here to see Captain Penn.'

Ephraim grinned at her before picking her up easily and swinging her up to a seat on one of his broad shoulders.

'Here I am, Ephraim.' Pilgrim came from the dairy, wiping his hands on the smock he wore over his uniform shirt and trousers. He had been helping Tacy with some cheesemaking. 'Is there trouble at the prison?'

'Not exactly, Cap'n. I've come to tell you that Captain Cotgrave's gone. He left with no fuss or farewell speeches, as far as I can make out. The new governor arrived yesterday. He's another naval man, a Captain Thomas Shortland. He sent for me this morning to say he's calling a meeting this afternoon of all senior prisoner-of-war officers. He wants you there and says I'm welcome to attend too. I'd like to do that, if it's all right with you?'

'Of course it is. What time this afternoon is the meeting?'

Ephraim shrugged. 'He didn't say, but Governor Cotgrave always finished his midday meal at about two o'clock. I reckon that'll be the time Shortland will be expecting you to be there.'

'Fine! We'll walk to the prison together. In the meantime, I'm sure Mrs Elford will be able to put together some home cooking to make your walk here worthwhile.'

Pilgrim was not wrong. When Ephraim walked inside the kitchen with Johanna still on his shoulder, bending extravagantly low to go through the door, and setting the young girl giggling uncontrollably, Joan Elford told him he had arrived just in time to eat.

A meal was laid on the table that Ephraim declared was better than anything he could remember tasting.

'That's not much of a compliment,' retorted the farmer's wife. 'Pilgrim is always telling us how awful the food is inside the prison.'

'I can't argue with that, ma'am,' agreed Ephraim. 'But I seem to have spent a whole lifetime being given awful food. Eating like this is rare indeed. It's food a man would happily kill for. I thank you, ma'am.'

Whether or not it had been his intention, Ephraim's complimentary remarks meant that he would return to the prison with his pockets stuffed with samples of Joan Elford's cooking.

*　　*　　*

On the way to the prison with Ephraim, Pilgrim questioned him about the new governor.

'It's too soon to know him just yet,' said Ephraim cautiously. 'He smiles a whole lot more than Cotgrave, but my momma told me never to put too much trust in a master who seems happy to know you the first time you meet. She said you can usually make a solemn master smile, but with the one who's already smiled at you there's no way to go but down.'

'I'll remember that,' said Pilgrim. 'Did she give you any other words of wisdom?'

'Every day,' replied Ephraim. 'But it didn't stop her being passed on to a team of raftmen when the last "master" lost more money than he had on him during a card game in Baton Rouge. True, when he sobered up he rode hell-for-leather down to New Orleans to buy her back.'

Ephraim said no more and Pilgrim prompted, 'Did he? Buy her back, I mean?'

Ephraim shook his head, looking straight ahead. 'She wasn't with the raftmen when they arrived, and no one was saying what happened to her. Not that it would have mattered, she was only a slave.'

'Were you her only child, Ephraim?'

The big marines sergeant shook his head. 'No. I had an older brother, but he was what they called a "bad nigger". He was forever running away, making for the northern states. Trouble is he kept getting caught. After a couple of times they gelded him. Then, when that didn't stop him they whipped him so hard he died.'

Still looking ahead, Ephraim said, 'There was a sister too. She was about the same age as Johanna when she was sold on. I never did see her again, though I heard she had a couple of children by the overseer on the plantation where she went.'

'We've known each other a long time, Ephraim, yet that's the first time you've ever told me anything about your family.'

Ephraim gave Pilgrim a faint smile. 'What family, Cap'n? A plantation nigger ain't allowed to have any family. That's another thing momma told me. We don't have no say in making the rules, but it sure as hell don't pay to break any of 'em . . .'

Ephraim broke off his conversation abruptly. 'Talking of family . . . if that man ever knew his father I'd be very surprised.'

Pilgrim looked up to see a militia officer on a horse riding towards them. It was Lieutenant Alan Kennedy. He was accompanied by about a dozen militiamen.

'Let's step out and get within shouting distance of the prison, at least, before we meet up with him.'

'I don't think he'll cause us any trouble,' said Pilgrim, with more confidence than he felt. 'But why don't you like him?'

'He's caught three escapees in the last week. Two French and one American. He's claimed that every one of them assaulted his men. As a result they've been flogged before being locked up in the *cachot*. If we're not careful he'll find some reason for having *us* arrested. He dislikes prisoners-of-war – especially if they happen to be American.'

'I think I know the reason for that, Ephraim.' Pilgrim told the marines sergeant of his various meetings with the Irish militia officer.

'Is that so?' said Ephraim. 'If you don't mind, Cap'n, I'll pass on the word about Lieutenant Kennedy. I don't think he's going to enjoy a very easy time for the short time he's got left on Dartmoor.'

'Short time? Where's he going?'

'Word is the Irish militia are due to be relieved by

some Scots militiamen. No one knows when, but it could be any day.'

'That will be a great relief,' said Pilgrim. 'I worry on the days I don't go to Roundtor, in case Lieutenant Kennedy goes around there looking for Tacy again.'

As they talked, Lieutenant Kennedy and his militiamen turned off the road and headed across the moor. 'Well, it seems you sure scare him, Cap'n. Let's hope it stays that way.'

67

'Come in, Captain Penn. Come in with your sergeant and join the others.' The apparent bonhomie of Captain Thomas Shortland, the new governor of Dartmoor prison, was exactly as Ephraim had described it to Pilgrim. It bordered on the effusive.

'You probably know most of the others here?' Governor Shortland waved a hand and his smile now included the assembled officers in its warmth.

Pilgrim nodded to the French officers seated around the walls of the governor's office.

'Well, gentlemen, now we are all gathered here, I will introduce myself. I am Thomas Shortland, a captain in the Royal Navy. Having spent the whole of my career on fighting ships I can understand many of the frustrations you are suffering as the result of being taken prisoner and unable to serve your country further. I have also learned to respect you as gallant adversaries in battle.'

His glance moved to Pilgrim and he said, 'I am addressing the French officers, Captain Penn. I have not fought your countrymen, but I have no doubt they too serve your country well.'

Pilgrim was irritated by the condescending manner of Dartmoor's new governor. He merely nodded his head in acknowledgement of Shortland's words, saying nothing.

For the remainder of the meeting, Captain Shortland spoke of his impressions of the French prisoners-of-war and of the pleasure it gave him to observe the manner in which they had settled down to life in Dartmoor, their orderliness and cleanliness and realistic adaptation to prison life.

Ominously, he said nothing at all about the Americans in this part of his introductory speech. After expressing his opinion that the war would soon be over, thus enabling them all to return to their homes and loved ones, Shortland brought the meeting to an end. It came as no surprise to Pilgrim when the new governor asked him to remain behind as the others were leaving. It seemed there was a number of matters the governor wished to discuss with him.

When the Frenchmen and Ephraim had left, Governor Shortland invited Pilgrim to bring his chair to the opposite side of his desk.

When Pilgrim had moved to face him, Governor Shortland leaned back in his chair and brought his smile into play once more. 'You heard what I had to say to the Frenchmen, Captain Penn. They are model prisoners. Were all the inmates of Dartmoor prison equally well-behaved, my term of office here would be a very pleasant one.'

The smile faded and he said, 'Unfortunately, the behaviour of those of your countrymen interned here falls far short of the standards attained by the French.'

Governor Shortland then read out a long list of misdemeanours committed by the Americans, adding, 'There have also been no fewer than three escapes in the last week alone. Such conduct is totally unacceptable, Captain Penn. Why can your men not accept their lot, as the French do?'

'There are a great many reasons, Governor. First of all, many of the American prisoners-of-war are resentful because they feel they should not be imprisoned at all. They have nothing to do with the forces of our country. They are sailors, merchants and traders who were going about their lawful business when war was declared between our two countries. Some have lost everything they ever had, including their freedom. In return, the United States Government has given them little. It took a very long while before an allowance of a penny-halfpenny a day was made to them. It does not go far.'

Thomas Shortland nodded in apparent agreement and made a note on a piece of paper on the desk in front of him.

Encouraged by the new governor's apparent sympathy, Pilgrim continued, 'They are also comparatively new to captivity. The French have had years to become organised. They have sufficient funds, not only to provide for their needs but also to bring a little luxury into their lives.'

Warming to his subject, Pilgrim said, 'There are a great many petty restrictions applied to the United States prisoners-of-war – but not to the French. The majority of Americans are kept in a prison block walled off from the remainder of the prison and are not allowed to attend the market. In addition, they suffer from having to parade outside in the yard of their block every morning, whatever the weather.'

'The morning parade is not restricted to the American prisoners, Captain Penn. The French are paraded too.'

'Yes, but the majority of them have reasonable clothing to protect them against the cold. Most of my men have little warm clothing, and no money with which to purchase any.'

Captain Shortland made another note on the paper in front of him, but this time gave no indication of whether or not he agreed with what Pilgrim had said.

For the next fifteen minutes the discussion continued, with Pilgrim airing many of the grievances held by the American prisoners-of-war.

When he ended, Captain Shortland put down his pen, leaned back in his chair and the smile returned, although now Pilgrim thought it was a trifle more forced than it had been before.

'Thank you for your help, Captain Penn. I feel our meeting has been most fruitful. Such frankness can only be in the best interest of everyone. I have a difficult duty to perform here, but I intend to carry it out as I did the command of one of His Majesty's ships: with firm but fair discipline. I will look into the grievances you have aired here today and put right those I consider to be justified. In return I shall expect the attitude of your men to change accordingly. I will not tolerate indiscipline from them.'

'If their conditions improve you'll have no trouble from them, Governor. They are civilised men.'

'I doubt if Governor Cotgrave would agree with you, Captain – and they have yet to prove it to me. I am quite willing to give them a chance, but one only.'

'Thank you, sir.'

Pilgrim turned to leave the office, but he had hardly reached the door when Governor Shortland called to him.

'By the way, I do not consider it possible for the senior United States officer to carry out his duties efficiently from a distance. I would like you to forego your parole and move back to the prison. You will be billeted in the Petty Officers' Block, of course.'

Pilgrim swung back to face the new governor once more. 'But . . . Sir Thomas is away. I promised him I would exercise supervision over the servants in his absence. I have made other commitments too.'

'You are a prisoner-of-war, Captain Penn. You realise that. Making commitments in such a situation is irresponsible – and who is this "Sir Thomas" of whom you speak?'

'He is the man to whom I am paroled. Among other duties, he is secretary to the Prince Regent and Warden of the Stannaries.'

If Thomas Shortland was impressed by Sir Thomas's duties, he did not show it. 'Obviously a man who serves his country well. He will understand the need for a man to be where his duty lies. And these other "commitments" of which you speak?'

'I am helping at a moorland farm while the farmer is ill – and have promised to do duty as groomsman at the wedding of a young Dartmoor man.'

'No doubt the farmer has family to carry on his work until he is well again. As for the wedding . . . when is it due to take place?'

'In about three weeks' time.'

'As I have already said, I am a reasonable man, Captain. You may take leave from the prison on the day of the wedding. Is there anything else?'

Pilgrim realised it would be useless to argue further with Governor Shortland. He shook his head unhappily.

'Very well. You may have forty-eight hours to settle affairs outside the prison. On your return we will have another meeting. Goodbye, Captain Penn.'

68

'But *why*, Pilgrim? Why does this have to happen, just when we had things sorted out between us? It's . . . it's not *fair*.'

Pilgrim had reached Roundtor Farm a few minutes before. Making his way to the dairy, he had found Tacy working and broken the news of his impending return to Dartmoor prison.

'I'm a prisoner-of-war, Tacy. It's something that's always easy to forget when I'm with you and we're so happy together. It brings home what I was telling you the other day. The reason I hadn't declared the way I feel about you before then. I'm not my own man, Tacy. I won't be until this war is over.'

Turning a stricken face in his direction, Tacy suddenly flung herself at him. Clinging to him, she said, 'I'm so sorry, Pilgrim. I'm only thinking of how unhappy *I'm* going to be without you. It's *you* who has to go back to live in that horrible prison. I wish Captain Cotgrave had never left.'

'I felt the same way when I left his office. But on

the way here I started thinking. Most of the Americans locked up in the prison will never be given an opportunity to take parole. They're living in appalling conditions and have nothing to look forward to, from one day to another.'

Reaching up a hand to stroke her hair, he said, 'They certainly don't have anyone like you. At least Shortland was prepared to listen to what I had to say about them. If he does something to improve the unhappy life they're leading, my loss of freedom will have been worthwhile – for them, at least. Besides, I'm going to the Petty Officers' Block, so I'll be able to see you when you bring goods to the prison market.'

'It won't be the same. We'll need to behave almost as though we're strangers.'

Looking up at him, she said, 'If things become too awful for you in there, I'll help you to escape, the same as Mary helped Henri. You could hide here, at the farm, and no one would ever find you.'

'Aren't you forgetting Lieutenant Kennedy?'

'He wouldn't dare come to Roundtor after what he tried to do to me.'

'He'd dare a whole lot more than that to have me thrown in the *cachot* and you arrested as an accomplice.'

'If he did we'd tell what he did to me.'

'We couldn't. It would be said that we'd made it all up just because he'd arrested us. No, Tacy, we'll need to go along with what the governor wants – for now, at least. He may change his mind at some time in the future.'

Tacy's face expressed the anguish she was feeling. Dropping her gaze, she said hesitantly, 'Would . . . would the governor let you stay out if . . . if I was having a baby?'

When he had recovered from his initial shock, Pilgrim

was aware that the suggestion had stirred feelings in him that were out of place in his present situation.

'I doubt it very much, Tacy. He might even take added delight in keeping me in prison.'

'If you thought it would help . . . you could.'

'No, Tacy, I wouldn't do that even if it *would* help. It isn't how I want things to be for us.'

Tacy clung to him once more and now she began to cry. 'I don't want you back in that prison, Pilgrim. I don't want you to go.'

'It will be all right, Tacy, I promise you. Things will work out for us in the end.'

He was still holding her close when her mother entered the dairy. She had seen Pilgrim's arrival at the farm and was disturbed when he had gone straight to the dairy without coming to the house first.

When he had not come out again after what she thought was a reasonable period of time, she had left the kitchen to find out what was happening.

She was startled when Tacy turned a tear-stained face towards her.

'What's going on here?'

Suddenly, with considerable alarm, she remembered Emma's condition. 'Is there something I should know about?'

'The new governor of Dartmoor had ordered Pilgrim to move back inside the prison,' Tacy wailed.

'Why? Have you done something wrong, Pilgrim?'

'No. It seems Governor Shortland has differing ideas to Captain Cotgrave on how the prison should be run. One of them is that senior officers responsible for their men should be living in the prison with them. He's given me forty-eight hours to settle my outside affairs, then I have to return.'

'What does Sir Thomas think about it?'

Pilgrim had released Tacy when Joan entered the dairy and now he gave a helpless gesture. 'He's not at Tor Royal. I don't think he's in London, either. He told me he was going to Scotland on the Prince Regent's business.'

'You must write to him. He'll have you out of there in no time.'

'Perhaps, but Sir Thomas has far more important matters to concern himself with than what's happening to an American prisoner-of-war.'

'Nonsense! You write to him. There's no reason at all why you should be locked up inside the prison. Things went along well enough with you on parole before this new governor came. There's no reason at all why you shouldn't enjoy parole, the same as all those French officers.'

Another thought came to her. 'What about young Billy's wedding? You promised him you'd be his groomsman.'

'I told the governor about that. He said I can leave the prison for the day to carry out my groomsman's duties.'

'Well, that's something, I suppose, but I still don't agree with the high-handed way he's behaving. It's the same with all these people who are put into important posts. They feel they've got to change things, to show they can do it better than the ones who were there before them.'

Looking at her distraught daughter, Joan showed her understanding. 'We're all going to miss you, Pilgrim. Tacy especially. You stay out here with her for a while. I'll go in and tell Tom what's happening. He'll feel as angry as I do about it, I've no doubt.'

Having enjoyed life outside the prison walls for so many months Pilgrim found difficulty adjusting to being locked up once more.

Although the regime in the Petty Officers' Block was much more relaxed than in the other blocks, he was unable to forget that the life of which he wanted to be a part was going on only a mile or two away.

Every few days he was able to meet with Tacy at the prison market but, as Tacy had pointed out, nothing was the same.

On the days when Tacy came to the prison, she was always accompanied. It was usually by Johanna, although on two occasions Emma came with her.

It was Emma who informed Pilgrim that Lieutenant Kennedy had been seen riding in the vicinity of Roundtor during recent days. She gave him the information while Tacy was busy serving a French officer at the back of the cart.

'Does Mrs Elford know about Kennedy?' Pilgrim asked anxiously.

Emma nodded.

'Good. Make sure Tacy doesn't go anywhere on her own – you need to be on your guard too. Fortunately, it won't be for too long. The Irish militia are overdue for relief from prison duty. Kennedy will be gone then and we can all breathe more easily.'

'What are you two whispering about?' Tacy finished serving the Frenchman and came to join them. 'If Emma wasn't marrying Billy next week I could easily be jealous.'

'Emma was telling me Lieutenant Kennedy has been seen about Roundtor lately. I don't like it. He knows I'm not there and might try to take advantage of the fact there's no man about the place.'

'There's Billy!' Emma sounded offended. 'He wouldn't let anything happen to Tacy.'

'I realise that,' said Pilgrim hastily. 'But you know yourself that he's not at Roundtor the whole time. There must be a whole lot of work to be done at the cottage.'

'Don't worry,' said Emma, only slightly placated. 'I won't let Tacy go out on the moor on her own.'

'Perhaps Mr Elford will be well soon?' said Pilgrim hopefully. 'That would make things a whole lot easier for everyone.'

Tacy shook her head sadly. 'Ma and I were talking about Pa only last night. I'm afraid we've all got to accept that he's never going to get any better. He seems to be a little bit weaker every day, but he's determined to go to Sheepstor for Billy and Emma's wedding.'

'Is that wise this weather?' Pilgrim glanced up at the dark sky.

'He'll be all right if it doesn't get any worse. Besides, it might be the last chance he'll ever have to leave the farm.'

Pilgrim murmured his sympathy, but at that moment

Ephraim was seen approaching with another inmate of Number Four Block. They were buying supplies for all their companions who were still not allowed direct access to the market.

The purchasing of the Americans was brought to a premature halt today. They had hardly begun when militiamen began moving among the market vendors, telling them to pack up their goods and move out of the prison.

Captain Shortland had tightened prison security in a number of ways. He now insisted that all market traders must be clear of the prison before dark.

Today, the traders were moved off earlier than usual. Dark clouds were building up ominously in the west and a bitterly cold wind had sprung up. Tacy had said it was likely winter would come early to Dartmoor this year.

Pilgrim watched with a heavy heart as Tacy and Emma drove the pony and cart from the prison yard. He and Tacy had been able to spend little time together after settling the misunderstanding between them. He felt there was still far too much that remained unsaid.

He had sent a letter to Sir Thomas, addressed to his London office, explaining all that had happened. He had not asked directly for his help and knew he had no reason to expect it. Yet there remained a hope at the back of his mind that the owner of Tor Royal might take it upon himself to seek to have Pilgrim's parole renewed.

'You thinking you ought to be going out with them, Cap'n?'

'That's about it, Ephraim,' said Pilgrim wistfully. 'It's a selfish thought, I suppose. I have at least spent some months enjoying life outside these prison walls. That's more than most have done.'

'True,' agreed Ephraim. 'But I don't suppose a man stops wishing for something or other until the day he dies.' He pointed up to the sky. 'Even then he's probably sitting up there somewhere, wishing he wasn't dead.'

Pilgrim smiled. 'How about you? What sort of things do you wish for?'

'Well now, that's not easy to answer, Cap'n. I've wished for many different things in my life. When I was small I wished I'd been born a white man. I wished very hard for that. When my ma was taken away from me, I wished she'd come back. Then one day I realised that wishing wasn't going to get me anywhere at all. I decided I'd have to do things for myself. The first was to get myself off the plantation. When that was done, I set out to make something of myself. Now I'm a sergeant of marines. All right, so I'm stuck in this prison, but so are a great many more Americans. I'll just take one day at a time now, Cap'n – how about you?'

'Perhaps I should do the same, Ephraim, but, unlike you, I'm still wishing. I'm wishing I was out of here and able to spend most of my days at Roundtor Farm.'

'Then you just wish away, Cap'n. That Tacy Elford is a girl worth wishing after. Take her back to America with you. If you need someone you can trust to work for you there, just call on Ephraim. Whatever needs doing I'm your man.'

'Thanks, Ephraim, I'll remember that. In the meantime, we're both stuck here, in Dartmoor prison. Keep me posted on what's happening in Block Four and we'll try to hold things down until this war is over. According to Governor Shortland we don't have very long to go.'

'I hope you're right, Cap'n. Of course, when you get back to the United States you know exactly what you're going to do. When we get shipped back we need to make sure the ship carrying us puts in to a northern port. If it takes us anywhere down south we're likely to find ourselves lined up on the jetty, being auctioned off to the highest bidder. That ain't going to go down very well with those of us who've served time in prison on behalf of America.'

Ephraim shrugged apologetically. 'You've got enough to worry you right now, Cap'n, but if you're really concerned about those of us in Block Four, I hope you'll give some consideration to what I've just said, when the time comes for our release.'

70

There had been a sprinkling of snow during the night preceding the wedding of Billy and Emma. The reluctant arrival of morning gave a promise of more. A heavy blanket of sombre grey cloud hung low over Dartmoor.

As Pilgrim walked to Princetown to meet with the others, large, soft snowflakes drifted down to earth and settled upon his uniform coat.

He waited for some twenty minutes for them to arrive. The time was spent stamping up and down and slapping his arms in a vain attempt to keep warm.

When the others eventually arrived they were travelling in the Roundtor Farm cart, pulled by their patient moorland pony.

Tom Elford was not with them.

'I didn't want him to run the risk of catching a chill,' explained his anxious wife, taking Pilgrim to one side. 'To tell you the truth, I was in two minds about leaving him at all. If it wasn't for the fact that we're all the family Billy and Emma have, I would have stayed home with him. I've still half a mind to go back. I can't run the risk of us all getting snowed in at Sheepstor, with Tom at home on his own.'

Billy and Emma stood nearby uncertainly, aware of what Joan was talking about, but not able to hear her words. Both looked ill-at-ease and unnaturally formal in the new clothes which had been yet another present from the Elford family.

'You of all people *must* be at the wedding,' declared Pilgrim. 'Look, you all go on ahead. I'll walk to Tor Royal and borrow one of Sir Thomas's horses. I have to be back at the prison tonight or I'll be in serious trouble. If the snow becomes too bad I can always bring Tacy back on the horse behind me, even if the rest of you are forced to remain behind.'

Joan's expression showed the doubt she felt about the idea. 'Will Sir Thomas loan you a horse at a moment's notice?'

'He's not at home, but the groom will let me have one. Go on to Sheepstor, I'll catch up with you before you get there.'

Joan agreed reluctantly, but when the small farm cart passed from view she was still looking back at him uncertainly.

Sir Thomas's groom was reluctant to saddle a horse for Pilgrim, until he was reminded that Sir Thomas had left instructions that Pilgrim could take out a horse whenever he wished. It had been before Pilgrim's return to the prison, but he did not remind the man of this.

When the groom finally agreed to saddle a horse for him, Pilgrim told him that if the snow became particularly bad he would have the animal housed in the prison governor's stable and see that it was returned to Tor Royal when the weather improved.

Once the decision had been made, the groom became

more helpful. He even found a waterproof riding coat for Pilgrim to wear.

As he rode the horse out of the Tor Royal drive, Pilgrim thought he was likely to be glad of the coat. Snow was beginning to fall quite heavily now. It was settling too. It felt somehow ghostly riding a horse whose hooves were making no sound on the snow-covered ground.

There were no other travellers on the road and he saw no sign of the party from Roundtor Farm. He had not travelled far before it became difficult making out the road beneath the crisp white blanket of snow. He was greatly relieved when suddenly he saw the outline of houses ahead of him. He had reached Sheepstor.

The Elfords with Billy and Emma were already at the church but there was still an hour to wait before the service was due to begin.

Fortunately, Reverend Cotterell came to the church soon after Pilgrim arrived and invited the whole party to the vicarage for a hot drink.

'I am most relieved you were able to reach Sheepstor safely,' he said, as they walked from the church. 'I feared you might not be able to make your way through the snow. It has arrived early this year. All the portents point to a harsh winter ahead of us.'

'I'm beginning to doubt the wisdom of coming,' said a worried Joan Elford. 'I've left a sick husband at home alone. No one will call in to see to him if we can't get home after the wedding.'

'Then we'll bring the service forward,' said the Sheepstor vicar immediately. 'While you are enjoying your drink I'll be getting ready.'

Snow was still falling as the party made its way to the church from the vicarage but, despite the bad weather, there were far more villagers attending the wedding than had been at the funeral of Tillie Yates.

It was a moving ceremony even though Billy was more nervous than anyone had ever seen him. The usually supremely confident Emma was equally nervous. It was a whispered and tremulous 'I do' that sealed the union of the young couple.

The ceremony over, Sheepstor villagers crowded around the newlyweds to offer their congratulations. Somehow, word of the marriage of the young moorland man to the tinkers' girl had spread around the area and moved the hearts of the Dartmoor villagers.

A number of small gifts had been collected and brought to the church for them: pots and dishes, a home-made leather-seated stool and a number of other small items.

A gift that particularly delighted Emma was a quantity of vegetable seeds that included onion, cabbage, carrots and turnips.

It was a happy party that filed from the church, but joy turned quickly to dismay. There must have been close to a foot of snow on the ground in front of the church – and it was still falling heavily!

As if this was not sufficient disaster in itself, Joan turned to say something to Pilgrim and slipped. He tried to grab her, but she fell heavily to the ground, twisting her ankle.

A couple of village men hurried to help Pilgrim lift her to her feet, but when she tried to put her right foot to the ground, she cried out in pain.

Helped back inside the church porch, Joan was close to tears. It was partly as a result of the pain of her injury, but mainly the culmination of a day spent worrying about her husband.

'Tacy, bring the pony and cart to the lychgate. Pilgrim can help me to get in it and we'll set off for Roundtor right away.'

'My dear woman!' Reverend Cotterell voiced his alarm. 'You must not even *consider* travelling home with such an injury. What if the cart went off the road – as is highly likely? You couldn't possibly walk. Oh no! You'll stay at the vicarage until the weather has improved sufficiently for you to leave.'

'I've only turned my ankle – and I *must* get home,' declared the distraught woman. 'Poor Tom . . . !'

'Don't you worry about Mr Elford,' said Pilgrim. 'I'll take Tacy back to Roundtor with me on Sir Thomas's horse.'

'Emma, Johanna and me'll take the pony and cart,' declared Billy importantly. 'You just stay here and get that ankle better, Mrs Elford. Leave everything to me. I'm a married man now, remember?'

Billy's statement forced a smile from Joan, in spite of her predicament. 'Bless you, Billy, but . . .'

'No buts, Mrs Elford,' said Reverend Cotterell positively. 'You'll stay at the vicarage until I think you are fit to travel. Off you go, Pilgrim. You and the others too, Billy. You'll be slower than Captain Penn, so let him go on ahead and explain things to Mr Elford. Now, where's Sadie Herrick? I saw her in the church just now. She'll put something on that ankle that'll have it mended more quickly than any doctor.'

'Here I am, Reverend.'

A small, toothless woman pushed her way through the crowd around Joan Elford. 'You just get her up to the vicarage. I've some opodeldoc, turpentine and some of me secrets already mixed up at home. I'll put it on that there ankle today and she'll be fit for dancing round a maypole in no time.'

The woman went on her way, cackling happily, and Pilgrim said to Tacy, 'We'd better make a move. I won't be happy until I've delivered you safely to Roundtor Farm, but I fear it's going to be a very unpleasant ride.'

71

Pilgrim's forecast that the ride from Sheepstor to Roundtor Farm would be 'unpleasant' was a gross understatement. It was a nightmare.

It snowed for the whole of the journey. For much of the time Pilgrim was hunched forward in the saddle, shielding his face from the driving snow. More than once the horse strayed from the now indefinable road. It was only Tacy's almost uncanny knowledge of the moor that brought them back again.

Arms gripped tightly about Pilgrim's waist, she would frequently peer around him, directing him to 'Go to the left of that tree', or advising him, 'You'll see rising ground on your left, soon. The road curves around the bottom of it.' Again, 'You should see a fast-running stream on your right in a minute. Tell me when you catch sight of it and I'll give you new directions.'

Almost unbelievably, it seemed to Pilgrim, just when he felt he would be unable to travel much farther, he recognised the snow-draped houses of Princetown. Now he too knew where they were.

When they finally reached Roundtor, he declared, 'That was little short of a miracle. Tacy, you're the cleverest, as well as the most beautiful navigator I've ever come across!'

Helping Tacy to slide to the ground he swung off the tired horse to stand on the ground beside her.

He looked up at the sky and was forced to close his eyes against the falling snow. 'I'd feel happier if the others had remained behind at Sheepstor with your ma.'

Tacy nodded her agreement. 'So would I, but Billy could find his way here blindfold. He knows the moor better than anyone I know. Let's go in and tell Pa what's happening. I've no doubt he's been watching the snow fall and worrying about us. You'll have something hot to drink too? You needn't set off for the prison for a couple of hours.'

'I'll put the horse in the stable and rub it down first. I mustn't leave it too late getting back. Once darkness falls I'll never find my way back – and it will come early tonight.'

When Pilgrim entered the kitchen after stamping snow off his boots on the doorstep, he was shocked to see how frail Tom Elford was looking. His condition had deteriorated in the few weeks since Pilgrim had left Tor Royal and returned to Dartmoor prison.

After shaking hands with him, the sick farmer echoed the words Pilgrim had spoken earlier to Tacy. 'I'd have felt a whole lot easier in my mind had you and the others arrived here together. Still, at least Joan will be in the warm, even though she's turned her ankle. Is it a bad injury?'

'It's painful, but Reverend Cotterell is confident a Sheepstor woman can fix it for her. As for the others,

Billy should be here with Emma and Johanna by the time I leave.'

Tom Elford nodded. 'But what am I thinking of? Pull a chair up to the fire while Tacy pours you some tea. I've kept the kettle boiling for more than an hour. Now, while we wait for the others tell me all that's been happening up at the prison. There'll be little comfort for any of you up there, I don't doubt . . .'

Two hours later, when Pilgrim declared reluctantly that he would have to make his way back to the prison, Billy had still not arrived with Emma and Johanna.

'They should have been back by now,' said Tacy when she and Pilgrim left the farmhouse and were out of the hearing of her father. 'I'm worried, Pilgrim. We should all have travelled back together.'

The snow had eased off a little but the wind had increased. Pilgrim knew there would be drifting on the higher ground over which Billy and the others would have to travel.

'Perhaps they'll be here by the time I saddle up the horse,' said Pilgrim optimistically. 'You said yourself that Billy knows the moor better than anyone.'

They had not arrived by the time Pilgrim had left the farmhouse. He hated leaving them with such uncertainty hanging over their heads about the others, but if he did not he would never make it back to the prison before it was too dark to see his way.

He was on the outskirts of Princetown when he heard a sound on the road ahead of him. He was about to call out, to enquire whether it was the party bound for Roundtor, when it came into view.

It was not a pony and cart, but two figures, leading a pony. In the near-darkness he would have passed them by, had not a voice he recognised called, 'Pilgrim?

It *is* you?'

'Emma . . . and Billy! Where's the cart . . . and where's Johanna?'

In a voice choked with emotion, Emma said, 'She's gone, Pilgrim.'

'Gone? What do you mean, she's gone? Gone where?' Pilgrim stared at them through the gloom, not under-standing, not *wanting* to understand what he believed Emma to be saying.

'We've lost her . . . in the snow.' Suddenly the words came pouring from her. 'The cart went off the road. We couldn't get it back on, so Billy took the pony out of the shafts. Johanna was riding it because she found walking hard going in the deep snow on the high ground. Then the pony fell – twice. So Johanna said she'd walk behind it. I walked with her for a while, then I went up front with Billy, telling Johanna to hold on to the pony's tail and not let go. I looked back a couple of times, to make sure she was all right. Then, when we reached some high ground, we ran into a blizzard. It was hard going for a while. When it eased off a bit I looked back – and Johanna wasn't there any more.'

'Where was this?'

Emma looked at Billy who had said nothing until now.

'Below Black Tor,' he said in a barely audible voice. 'About a mile back.'

'Didn't you go back to look for her?'

'Of course we did,' said Emma. 'We went back to where we'd last seen her and searched all around from there to where we found she'd gone. Billy floundered around in the snow like a mad thing and we both shouted for all we was worth, but . . . there wasn't a thing.'

Suddenly, Billy broke down and began to cry. 'It's all

my fault,' he said. 'They shouldn't have let her come with me. They shouldn't have trusted me to bring her home. I'm too simple to take care of myself, let alone anyone else. That's what my ma always used to say. They shouldn't have let Johanna come with me.'

Still holding the reins attached to the pony, Billy crouched down in the snow, rocking backwards and forwards in abject misery.

'Such talk will help no one,' said Pilgrim sharply. 'Emma, it's not far to Roundtor now, do you think you can find your way there alone?'

She nodded. 'What you going to do? It's too dark for you and Billy to go back there now. Even he couldn't find his way in the dark on a night like this.'

'I need him to give us an idea of where Johanna was last seen. We'll go to the barracks and get some militiamen with lanterns. Off you go now. Another thing . . . no matter how desperately upset they are, you're not to let Tom Elford or Tacy come out to try to help us. We don't want to have to start searching for anyone else. Take the pony with you. If you *do* lose your way, let the pony guide you. He knows his way to Roundtor.'

Taking the pony's reins from Billy, he passed them to her, then reached down and rested a hand on Billy's shoulder. 'Come on, Billy, there's no time to lose. Tacy has said many times that no one knows the moor as you do. Now's your chance to prove it. Johanna's life is in your hands.'

72

'But . . . this is a matter of life or death for a young girl. If we don't find her very soon she has no chance of survival in this weather.'

'I'm sorry, I can't risk the lives of my men. Besides, I have only a few men left in the barracks.'

Arriving at the militia barracks in Princetown, Pilgrim had learned with dismay that the duty officer was the one man he had hoped he would never again have dealings with.

Lieutenant Alan Kennedy was as unhelpful as Pilgrim had anticipated he would be.

'We're talking of the life of Johanna, for God's sake. You *know* her. Speak to your men. Call for volunteers.'

'I've told you, Captain Penn, I cannot allow my men to risk their lives on a night like this.'

Trying hard to control his rising anger, Pilgrim said, 'Then let me speak to your commanding officer. He'll probably lead the men himself – as any man worth his salt would.'

'The commanding officer is in Plymouth with the bulk

of our men. As it happens, they are there to escort another batch of Americans to Dartmoor.' Smugly, he said, 'Were your countrymen not so notoriously unruly, it would not have been necessary to send so many men on a simple escort duty. Then we might have had men to spare here.'

Pilgrim had an overwhelming urge to hit the militia officer but it would achieve nothing.

'Thank you, Lieutenant Kennedy. I hope your conscience allows you a good night's sleep tonight. Come, Billy, I know where we'll find some real men.'

As they walked away, Billy said, 'Where we going, Pilgrim? Where will we find the men you spoke of?'

'At the prison, Billy . . . God and Governor Shortland willing.'

Governor Shortland listened with growing concern as Pilgrim told him of the missing girl. During the brief period he had been in charge of the prison he had proved himself to be a more humane man than his predecessor. He also had a daughter who was about the same age as Johanna.

Pilgrim had gone directly to the governor's house with his request and also to ask him to take care of Sir Thomas's horse until the weather improved.

'What do you expect me to do, Captain Penn? The militia lieutenant was telling you the truth. Most of the militiamen are at Plymouth waiting for the weather to break in order to bring more prisoners-of-war here. I cannot spare more than a few of the militiamen who are on duty at the moment.'

'I'm not asking for militiamen, Governor. I'm asking you to allow prisoners-of-war to search for Johanna. American prisoners-of-war.'

Before Shortland could voice a refusal, Pilgrim added,

'I'll stand as guarantor for their conduct and return to the prison, Governor. I'll take only marines and soldiers. Disciplined men. *Please*, Governor. A young girl's life depends upon your decision.'

Pilgrim thought the prison governor was about to refuse the request, despite his pleas. But just then Shortland's daughter came to the front door. She slipped her hand inside her father's and smiled up at Pilgrim.

'Very well, Captain Penn. Go to the main gate. Tell the duty officer I will be joining you there in a few minutes.'

No more than ten minutes later, Pilgrim was standing in the ground floor of Block Four, occupied by the United States prisoners-of-war.

He outlined the problem, warned of the atrocious conditions they would be facing on the moor, then called for volunteers. Every man in the room stepped forward.

'Thank you, but I'll take only soldiers and marines. That should give us rather more than a hundred men.'

'Some of the prison guards and militiamen on duty have expressed a wish to help,' said Governor Shortland. 'I can let you have a dozen of them. The men may also draw lanterns from the store. You will no doubt have need of them.'

'Thank you, Governor. Right, shall we go . . . ?'

It was virtually impossible to distinguish the road that linked Princetown with Sheepstor. Even Billy was forced to stop on a number of occasions and retrace his steps.

Eventually, he stopped and said, 'This is where I last saw Johanna. I looked back and she was still there, clinging to the pony's tail.'

'Right, we'll go back along the road for a quarter of a mile, or so, just in case she headed back that way. Spread out in a line on either side of the road and we'll work our way back towards Princetown. Every man has a lantern, but we'll have only every other one lit. We'll keep the others in reserve. All right, Billy, lead us back along the road a way.'

It had begun to snow once more and when the men fanned out to begin their search, problems were encountered immediately. There were many hollows and gullies on the moor itself. More than once men disappeared and needed to be hauled out of deep snow by their companions.

It was a desperate feat of endurance to make any progress at all. During the course of a couple of hours they only managed to cover about half a mile. By this time the snow had closed in on them in a ferocious blizzard. Billy warned Pilgrim that there was a dangerous bog to one side of the road, even though it was now hidden beneath a two feet deep covering of snow.

Still nothing had been found of Johanna. Pilgrim wanted desperately to continue with the search, but prison life and rations had not enabled the men to maintain the standard of fitness soldiers and marines had once enjoyed. A number were close to exhaustion.

It was with a heavy heart that Pilgrim passed the order along the line of men on either side of him to call off the search and muster on the road.

Billy too was in a state of near-collapse. Even so, he pleaded with Pilgrim to allow the men to continue the search for 'just a while longer'.

'We can't, Billy,' replied Pilgrim through lips that were numb with cold. 'The men are exhausted; you're exhausted – and so am I. The weather's worse than it was when we began the search. If we go on as we are we'll begin to lose men. I'm sorry, we must call it off.'

'Then I'll stay out here on my own,' said Billy, in desperation. 'Leave me a lamp. I'll carry on searching.'

'You're closer to collapse than anyone. I've watched you staggering for the past half an hour or more. You'll come back to Princetown with us, then make your way to Roundtor Farm to be with Emma.'

Billy sank down in the snow at Pilgrim's feet and began to sob. 'Poor Johanna. She's out there somewhere, Pilgrim. Lying in the snow, probably dead already! I can't go back to Roundtor, Pilgrim. I can't face Tacy and Mr Elford and tell them I let Johanna get lost in the snow. After all they've done for me, I've let this happen. It's all my fault.'

'It's nobody's fault, Billy. Nobody could have cared more for Johanna than you. It's just a terrible, tragic accident, that's all.'

Pilgrim hoped he sounded convincing. In truth, he believed the Elfords would feel as he did, that Billy had behaved irresponsibly by allowing Johanna to walk behind the pony by herself. But perhaps he too was to blame, for not insisting that Billy, Emma and Johanna remained at Sheepstor with Mrs Elford.

'Come on, Billy, let's get back to Princetown. You make your way to Roundtor while I get the men back to Dartmoor. I wish I could come to the farm with you, but that won't be possible.'

It took more than an hour to reach Princetown, so thick had the snow become and so fierce the blizzard.

They entered the town in single file, each man holding the coat of the man in front of him and the lead changing every few minutes.

The militiamen among them organised some hot soup for the searchers before they floundered their way back to the prison.

It was here too that a muster was carried out and it was discovered one of the marines was missing.

The missing man was Ephraim.

73

For Johanna, the journey in the snow from Sheepstor had become excruciating long before the pony fell over for the first time.

Chilled to the bone, she was so cold that her fingers throbbed painfully if she breathed on them for too long. Her legs and feet too felt frozen. As a final humiliating misery, she had failed to realise the uncomplaining pony's back had been soaked by the snow while it was pulling the cart. Soon after she settled astride the patient animal she realised her drawers were soaked through, adding to the freezing cold of her legs and bottom.

When the pony slipped and fell for the first time, Johanna was caught off guard. Falling with it, she was fortunate not to become trapped beneath its body as it struggled to rise.

When it happened again she was more alert and jumped clear in time. The animal was helped up and stood shivering from a combination of fear and cold.

Billy suggested she walk at the pony's head with him and Emma, but the snow was too deep for her short, thin legs. It was now she hit upon the idea of walking behind the pony. Clinging to its tail she could tread in the footsteps of the others. Emma walked with her for a while, but then went up ahead, to join Billy.

This worked for much of the time. However, if Johanna did not concentrate on where she was walking, she found herself struggling through the deeper snow on either side of the tracks made by the others.

Occasionally the party strayed from the road when they reached higher ground and the blizzard increased in ferocity.

She was tiring too. Twice in quick succession she lost her footing and fell in the snow. On the first occasion she maintained her hold on the pony's tail, struggling to regain her footing as her light body was dragged along behind the pony.

When it happened again her cold fingers lost their grip on the pony's tail. Picking herself up she floundered frantically through the deep snow until she was able to reach out and grasp the tail once more.

It was at this point that Billy looked around to check that she was still with them. He tried to smile, but the concerned expression on his face seemed to have been frozen there.

Only moments later, it seemed to Johanna, they walked into a blinding swirl of driving snow. She ducked her head quickly, but it was too late. She had snow up her nose, in her eyes and in her half-open mouth.

Unable to see, she made the mistake of releasing her grip on the pony's tail in order to brush the snow from her face.

It was a foolhardy thing to do, but the hand holding the tail was the one she always used for such things.

Unfortunately, they had strayed off the road yet

again. Her foot caught in something and she fell into the snow.

When she picked herself up she could not see the others.

Johanna panicked momentarily. Floundering after the pony, she fell again. Struggling to her feet once more she put up an arm in an attempt to ward off the driving snow. At the same time, she found herself in snow almost to her waist.

She fought her way forward for some minutes before making a terrifying discovery. There were no tracks of man or beast in front of her!

Turning ninety degrees to her left, she struggled forward once more, but found nothing. She turned back and tried another direction, stumbling blindly ahead.

Belatedly, she began shouting, but realised almost immediately it was a futile waste of her energy. It was as though she had put several blankets over her head before calling out. Her voice went nowhere.

She tried to control her panic and think logically. Surprisingly, she did not resort to tears. She remembered that when she had been following the pony the snow had been blowing in her face.

That was it! The snow had been driving at her from dead ahead. Turning her head slowly, she discovered that the snow was now blowing in from her left. Moving in that direction, she set off once more.

She continued on this course until she encountered a drift of snow so deep she was forced to make a cautious detour around it until she once again had the wind in her face.

But she was going downhill now. She knew this was not right. She turned to retrace her footsteps once more, but quickly lost her way again.

Suddenly, she felt thoroughly frightened. Her bottom lip was pushed out and it began to tremble.

Yet again, Johanna paused to take a grip of herself. She had to get back to the road somehow. When Billy and Emma realised she was no longer with them they would surely come back and search for her.

She forced her way through the snow, travelling tortuously in the direction in which she believed she should be moving, until she began to walk downhill yet again.

She turned. As she did so, she lost her footing – suddenly it seemed the whole ground was collapsing beneath her and she was falling through space.

She landed with a jolt, but the snow that had fallen with her helped to break her fall.

Above her was the hole she had made in the snow, with dark sky showing through it and flakes drifting down to where she lay.

There was a noise behind her and Johanna looked around in alarm. It was a startled sound, as though her sudden arrival had frightened something – or someone!

At this moment Johanna was more fearful than when she had been lost in the snow. Then she heard another sound. To her great relief she recognised the bleating of a sheep. Now she realised what had happened to her.

She had fallen into a gully occupied by a number of sheep. Snow must have drifted over them, but their movement and the heat of their bodies had created a cavern in the snow.

Johanna was greatly relieved. She was not afraid of sheep – but they were of her. They began milling about and the movement brought a fall of snow from the artificial roof of the cave.

She moved back from them and before long their panic subsided. Squatting down some distance away, she was forced to move after a few minutes because a flurry of snow blew down through the hole she had made in the snow roof of the gully.

Now she began to feel really cold and could not control her shivering. Not wanting to dwell on the hopelessness of her situation, she wished the sheep would allow her to creep among them and share their warmth . . .

74

Johanna started up in a sudden fright and realised she must have slept. An exhausted sleep.

Her unexpected movement caused another momentary panic among the sheep which had gradually moved closer while she was asleep.

Now they fled from her again. For a few minutes they milled around in the darkness, bleating and jostling. Johanna feared that at any minute their movements would bring the snow roof down upon them.

'It's all right . . . I won't hurt you.'

Johanna spoke soothingly, but with some difficulty because her teeth were chattering so wildly.

Desperately cold, she looked upwards, but could see nothing. For a moment she feared the hole had become covered over.

The thought struck terror into her. If snow had blocked the hole, she was trapped underground with the sheep and they would never be found.

Then she felt snowflakes drifting down upon her upturned face and she realised darkness had fallen.

Far from feeling relief at the discovery, she became thoroughly frightened. In the darkness, no one would come looking for her. They would not know *where* to look!

Now, for the first time, tears came, unwanted. There were not many but she felt them in her eyes.

She sank down to the ground and covered her face with her hands. It was while she squatted like this that she thought she heard a sound. At first she thought it must be the sheep again. Then she heard it once more.

It sounded like someone shouting, far away.

Johanna stood up and realised how cold and stiff she was. She began shouting as loud as she could in a thin, shrill voice. The sound startled the sheep and they began milling about again, bleating their alarm.

She shouted until her throat hurt and she started to cough. When she stopped, the sheep were still making a noise and she could hear nothing.

Then she thought she saw the outline of the hole above her and realised someone must be nearby, with a lamp.

She began shouting again, even more loudly this time.

Just when she was beginning to feel she had been mistaken, the snow roof suddenly collapsed, about halfway between herself and the sheep. At the same time she heard someone cry out in pain.

'Billy . . . ? Is that you?'

'Johanna? It's me . . . Ephraim! Are you all right?'

'Oh, Ephraim, I'm so glad you've found me. I was getting awful frightened . . .'

Johanna scrambled over the heap of newly fallen snow and found Ephraim. He was sitting up on the floor and made no attempt to rise, but he did pull her to him and give her a huge hug.

'You're *freezing*, child – and soaking wet too. Here, help me off with my greatcoat – and shout while you're doing it. There are men up top. They're quite a way away, but we've got to make them hear us.'

As he struggled to remove his coat in the darkness, they both shouted as loudly as they could, driving the sheep to distraction.

When they paused, they could hear nothing above the bleating of the sheep. Ephraim said, 'Try again. The sheep are helping. It was them I heard just before I found you.'

Three times they called, but could hear nothing outside of the snow-roofed gully. During all this time, Ephraim had remained seated and now Johanna asked, 'Are you all right, Ephraim?'

'No. I landed awkwardly when I fell. I seem to have done something to my knee. I can't move my leg.'

'I'm sorry! Can I do anything?'

'Yes, you can wrap that coat around you and try to put some warmth back in your body. It's got pockets. Put your hands in them. Then get to shouting again.'

They both shouted for another ten or twelve minutes before Ephraim said, 'I don't think they heard us, Johanna. I was afraid they wouldn't. I seemed to have strayed from the others in the line when I heard the sheep bleating. Then, when I got close enough to see the hole in the snow, I heard you. Before I could call out to the others I'd fallen down here.'

'That's what happened to me,' said Johanna. 'After I lost Billy and Emma I just wandered around in the snow until I fell down here.'

'Billy was up there with us. He and Captain Pilgrim. We've all been very worried about you, Johanna.'

'Poor Billy. I expect he's blaming himself for losing

me. He always lays the blame on himself when anything happens, even if he's had nothing to do with it at all.'

'Tell me about Billy, Johanna. Tell me all you know about him.'

Ephraim wanted to keep Johanna talking, to take her mind off the cold. It also gave him something other than his injured knee to think about. He wanted to put off thinking about the cold and the situation they were both in.

It had been all right while he was wearing the greatcoat. Without it his limbs were beginning to go numb. The temperature was dropping rapidly on the moor. The men had commented upon it as the search progressed.

He would like to have been able to stand up and beat his body with his hands to keep the circulation moving, but standing was out of the question. His leg injury was worse than he had admitted to Johanna, but he did not want her worrying about him.

'Your teeth are chattering!' Johanna said suddenly, while she was telling him about the days when Billy had first come to Roundtor Farm seeking work.

'Are they? Your story about Billy was so interesting I didn't even notice.'

'Your coat's *much* too big for me. We can share it. You can have one of your arms in a sleeve and put your hand in a pocket. I can put *both* my arms in the other sleeve. That way we'll both stay a bit warmer.'

'That's a very good idea, Johanna. Why didn't I think of that? I've got something else here we can share.'

He unwrapped a large piece of cloth from around his body and put it around both of them. As he moved, he had to bite his lip to prevent himself crying out with pain as he moved the injured leg. He hoped help would reach them by early the next morning. He did not believe he would be able to last any longer.

But ensuring that Johanna survived was more important at the moment.

'Here! I've just found a couple of prison biscuits in my pocket. I bet you've never had anything like these before?'

'No . . .' said Johanna doubtfully, taking them from him.

'Well, save them until the morning. Then you can see what you're eating. Now, you were telling me about Billy coming to your farm . . .'

'I'd like permission to take my men out on the moor again, Governor.' Pilgrim stood in front of Governor Shortland's desk and made his request.

It was the morning after the abortive search for Johanna. Despite his exhaustion, he had lain awake for much of the night, thinking about the missing young girl and Ephraim. Wondering what might have happened to them.

'One of your men escaped when you took them out last night, Captain Penn. How many might I expect to lose today?'

'Ephraim didn't make an escape, Governor. I'm convinced of that. He's out there somewhere. Perhaps he found Johanna and for some reason couldn't leave her. She might be hurt . . .'

'I am not prepared to take the risk of having more prisoners escape, Captain. Your request is not granted.'

'Governor, I know Sergeant Ephraim as well as though he were my own brother. I *know* he wouldn't have run off, certainly not while we were searching for Johanna.

He knows the girl and is very fond of her. He'd move heaven and earth to find her.'

'I am sorry, the answer is still "no".'

'Then let me go alone. I'll return Sir Thomas's horse and call at Roundtor Farm, just in case Johanna or Ephraim have turned up there. If not, I'll take Billy Yates out with me and have another look around the area where both Johanna and Ephraim were lost.'

Pilgrim pleaded with the prison governor. 'I know the snow is still deep out there, but it isn't snowing right now. I might find something we missed last night.'

Captain Shortland's inclination was to refuse this request too. However, during the couple of weeks he had been in charge of the prison he had heard a great deal about Sir Thomas Tyrwhitt and the power he wielded. It had become apparent that his influence extended far beyond Dartmoor. He was a power in London too and had brought about Captain Penn's parole against the wishes of Captain Cotgrave.

If called upon to justify his own decision to withdraw Pilgrim's parole, Governor Shortland felt he could satisfy the Admiralty, at least. But he did not want to be accused of being particularly biased against the American prisoners-of-war.

'Very well, *you* may go. I am told there is likely to be a partial thaw today. That might make your task easier. I wish you luck in your search, Captain Penn, but I fear that after a night on the moor in such weather, any chance of finding the girl alive must be remote.'

As Pilgrim rode away from the prison, he thought of the governor's words. He did not want to dwell upon the likelihood that the governor would be proven right, yet commonsense told him there must be little chance that Johanna had survived the night.

There was constant traffic between the militia barracks and the prison and an early morning attempt had been made to clear the road through Princetown. However, once outside the small settlement, the snow was still deep.

Fortunately, Pilgrim was familiar with the track to Roundtor Farm. He was able to choose a route that included sheltered spots where the snow was thinnest, avoiding places where there was likely to be drifting.

Paths had been cleared criss-crossing the Roundtor farmyard and as Pilgrim entered the yard both Emma and Tacy ran from the house to greet him.

Both girls spoke at the same time.

'Have you found Johanna?'

'Where's Billy?'

Startled, Pilgrim said, 'We found nothing last night, but I'm going out to look once more. I intended to take Billy with me. He left us at Princetown last night to come on here. Has he gone out again already?'

The colour drained from Emma's face and she replied, 'Billy hasn't been seen since he went off with you yesterday afternoon.'

'Then where can he be now? It was dark when we parted, but he'd been loaned a lantern and it had stopped snowing. I can't believe he'd lose himself on the way here from Princetown.'

'I don't think he intended coming to Roundtor,' said Emma shakily. 'He blamed himself for losing Johanna. He wouldn't have been able to cope with the thought of facing Tacy.'

'Then where do you think he would have gone?'

'Back to the cottage at Whiteworks, perhaps?'

'What's going on? Has Johanna been found . . . ?'

Tom Elford called from the kitchen doorway. Looking frail and ill, he leaned against the doorframe for support.

'Pa! You shouldn't be out of bed, let alone standing out here in the cold.'

Tacy hurried across the farmyard to him.

'We've found nothing yet, Mr Elford, but I'm going out searching again now.'

'On your own? You don't know the moor . . .' Breathing in the cold, winter air as he talked he began coughing uncontrollably.

'I'm on my way to find Billy. He'll come with me.'

'You can tell him I want words with him. If it wasn't for his stupidity . . .'

Another bout of coughing cut off whatever he intended saying. Moments later, still chiding him for coming out into the cold air, Tacy took him inside.

'I'll make my way to the cottage and see if Billy's there,' said Pilgrim. 'Mr Elford's right. Without Billy I'll be no good out there on the moor alone. We've already lost Ephraim. He went missing during the search last night.'

Pilgrim was not certain that Emma even heard him. Her thoughts were still with Billy.

'I'll come with you to the cottage,' she said suddenly. 'I . . . I don't know what I'll do if he's not there.'

'Come on then. The sooner we get started, the better.'

With Emma riding behind him on the horse, Pilgrim was passing out through the farmyard gateway when Tacy came running after them from the house.

'Wait! Where are you going?'

'To the cottage first of all, to look for Billy. Then back out on the moor to find Johanna. I hope we might find Ephraim with her.' He repeated the circumstances of Ephraim's disappearance. 'I don't think he got himself lost,' he added. 'Ephraim's far too sensible to do a thing like that.'

'I hope you're right,' said Tacy fervently. 'Just thinking that Ephraim might possibly be with her gives me new hope.'

She turned to Emma. 'Don't be too upset by what Pa just said. He's frantic with worry about Johanna – we both are, but at heart he knows that Billy would never knowingly have done anything to put her in danger. The only good thing about all this is that Ma isn't here to upset herself about what's going on.'

'I'm worried for Billy too now,' said Emma unhappily. 'He *does* feel he's to blame. I'm frightened of what he might do if he believes something's happened to her.'

'We won't talk about that,' said Pilgrim firmly. 'We're going out to find Billy, Johanna and Ephraim – and we're going to succeed.'

As they were talking, there was the sound from one of the farm's outbuildings of a dog barking, no doubt excited by the sound of voices. It gave Pilgrim an idea.

'I'd like to take one of the dogs along with us. Could I have Rip?'

Tacy looked doubtful. 'He doesn't know you very well – and the snow's awfully deep out there. We'd be in trouble from Sir Thomas if anything happened to him.'

'I'll tell Sir Thomas that I insisted,' said Pilgrim. 'He'd be a great help. He's got sharper hearing than we have. If he heard Johanna, he'd lead us to her.'

After only a moment more of hesitation, Tacy nodded. 'Take him. I'll pray that you find her safely. Pray that you'll find everyone.'

76

Rip thought snow was great fun. He gambolled excitedly in the wake of the horse ridden by Pilgrim and Emma as they retraced the path made by the horse on Pilgrim's way to Roundtor earlier that morning.

However, when Pilgrim turned off and headed for Whiteworks cottage through deep snow, the dog found the going more difficult. He leaped through the snow for a while before sitting down and barking until Pilgrim turned the horse around and rode back to him.

Dismounting, he passed Rip up to Emma before mounting the horse once more. They rode on with the dog between them, the animal apparently thoroughly enjoying the new experience.

It took much longer than was usual, but eventually they reached the cottage and Emma slipped from the horse's back.

With Rip leaping after her, frog-like, through the snow, she made her way to the back door of the cottage.

As Pilgrim tied the reins of the horse to the gate, Emma opened the kitchen door and let out a horrified scream.

When Pilgrim reached the doorway she was kneeling on the floor beside a sluggishly moving Billy. Hanging from a hook in a beam, once used for curing bacon, was a piece of rope with a broken end.

On the floor, beside Billy, was a noose which also had a broken end. A chair lay on its side, nearby.

Leaning over her husband of less than twenty-four hours, Emma lifted him to a sitting position and kneeled beside him, hugging him to her.

'Billy . . . ! Billy . . . ! What did you think you were doing? Why . . . ?'

Billy looked up at her, bleary-eyed, his face screwed up in anguish. 'I'm sorry, Emma. I couldn't face Tacy and Mr Elford. It was all my fault, letting Johanna get herself lost.'

He glanced up at the piece of rope dangling from the hook and looked away again quickly. 'I . . . I just didn't want to live any more, Emma . . . but the rope broke.'

When Billy raised his head, Pilgrim saw a rope burn encircling his neck.

'There was no cause to do anything like that, Billy. We're going out now, you and I, to find Johanna. Tacy said I was to tell you she knows it wasn't your fault that Johanna got herself lost. She doesn't blame you. No one does. Anyway, we're going to find her, you'll see.'

Emma hugged Billy close, her face screwed up in an expression of anguish. 'You mustn't ever do anything like this again, Billy. We're married now, you and I. We're man and wife and will share everything – both the good and the bad things. Being married means we help each other. You must never run off and do things by yourself when something's wrong. You have me now. Before very long there'll be a baby too. We need you – and I want to keep you.'

It became impossible to say more because Rip thought

it was time he joined in. Pushing between the couple he attempted to lick Billy's face.

Suddenly, Billy gave Emma a grateful and unexpected hug. Standing up, he said, 'I'm ready now, Pilgrim. I . . . I'm sorry I've caused everyone so much trouble.'

'Friends don't look upon the things they do for each other as trouble, Billy. I'm thankful we've found you safe and sound. Now, let's go and find the others.'

Unexpectedly, Emma turned and hugged Pilgrim too. 'I'm glad Billy and I have you for a friend, Pilgrim. I only hope things work out for you and Tacy. Now, off you go, both of you, and find Johanna and Ephraim.'

There had been a surprising amount of traffic on the road between Sheepstor and Princetown that morning. As they rode along, Pilgrim and Billy passed a couple of heavy wagons, more than one horse and rider, and a number of men on foot.

Travelling proved to be much easier today. There still seemed to be as much snow covering the moor as there had been the night before, but Billy assured Pilgrim it was beginning to thaw.

'There's lots of it, so it will take some time,' he explained. 'But in a couple of days' time there'll only be snow left in the gullies on the higher ground. Mind you, it still won't be easy to travel around the moor because the rivers and streams will be running very high.'

When they eventually reached the area where Billy believed Tacy had disappeared, they found a gnarled moorland farmer here with a cart laden with hay.

When Pilgrim explained the reason he and Billy were here, the farmer shook his head pessimistically. 'You're not going to find anyone alive on the moor after such a night. I'm out looking for my sheep, but I expect to find more than half of 'em dead, for all they're wearing a coat made for 'em by the Good Lord Himself.'

'I'm surprised you expect to find *any* of them alive in snow such as this,' said Pilgrim.

'That's because you don't know much about the moor, or about sheep,' said the farmer with blunt honesty. 'They'll find themselves a hollow in the ground, or a space between some big rocks and stay there. When the snow drifts and covers 'em, they'll move around to make themselves some breathing space. Leastways, those with a farthing's worth of sense will. Others will just stand out in the snow and die. Sheep aren't the brightest of animals.'

Pilgrim had been listening to the philosophical farmer with increasing excitement. 'These "hollows". Are there any around here?'

The farmer nodded. 'A few. Some of the old tinners dug out one or two tunnels that have collapsed over the years too. That's where I'm going to look now.'

'Can we come with you?'

The farmer shrugged. 'You can please yourself, but if you're coming along with me one of you can carry some hay. The other one can bring along this shovel. Might as well be useful as not.'

The first spot the farmer led them to with impressive accuracy was little more than a faint dip in the ground. Here they found three sheep. Two were dead. The third was hauled out of the hollow unceremoniously and left with a bundle of hay in the tracks they had made.

The farmer explained he would pick up the ewe on the way back and take her to his farm in the wagon. 'There's a much deeper place over here a ways,' he said, leading them through snow that came above their knees.

Rip was making his way through the snow with them, walking between the farmer, who was leading the way, and the others. Suddenly, he pricked up his ears and made a strange sound in his throat.

'Rip's heard something,' said Billy.

'Likely it's more of my sheep,' said the farmer. 'We're getting close now. But if the dog can hear them it means there's something alive in there.'

A few paces farther on, Rip raised his head and began barking excitedly.

The farmer immediately rounded on the others. 'I don't want him barking. If he frightens the sheep he'll bring down the snow on them and it'll be hard work to get them out . . .'

'Shh! Listen!'

Pilgrim had been only half concentrating on what the farmer was saying. Rip had stopped barking without being told and Pilgrim had heard something else.

The farmer stopped talking, his lips narrowing indignantly.

Immediately, they heard the bleating of sheep – and then they heard something else. It was a shrill, young voice calling for help.

'*It's Johanna!*' Billy was suddenly beside himself with excitement and now Rip began barking furiously.

The young dog became quiet when Billy gave him an order, but the farmer had an expression of disbelief on his face. 'Well I never did!' he exclaimed. 'It is a young girl and it sounds as though she's in with my sheep.'

A few minutes later, Pilgrim spied a hole in the snow and said, 'There! It looks as though someone's fallen through . . .'

'Don't go too close!' warned the farmer. That's one of the diggings I was telling you about. It's pretty deep. You'll hurt yourself if you fall through the snow.'

'Then how are we going to get in?'

'From down there.' The farmer pointed down the

slope. 'We'll dig into it gradually and make a tunnel, same as the sheep have.'

'You and Billy go and make a start. I'll be with you in a moment. I want to call down to Johanna. To let her know what we're doing.'

As the others made their way through the snow to the point where they would begin digging, Pilgrim cautiously edged his way closer to the hole in the snow.

Both the sheep and Johanna were silent now. When he felt he was as close as he could safely advance, he called, 'Johanna, are you there? Can you hear me?'

'Yes . . . Yes, I can hear you,' said Johanna excitedly. 'Who is it?'

'It's Pilgrim. Billy and a farmer are with me. We're going to start digging through the snow towards you. Are you all right?'

'I'm very cold. Ephraim's here with me, but he hurt himself when he fell and he's not moving. I think he's hurt bad.'

'So he *did* find you! We won't be long getting through to you. Stand beneath the hole, in case the snow collapses while we're digging – and don't worry. We'll have you out of there very soon.'

Retracing his steps, Pilgrim hurried after Billy and the farmer. He joined them in their task, digging through the snow with his bare hands.

Their activity excited Rip. He alternated between barking and digging, his tail wagging furiously.

It was half an hour before the spade wielded by Billy suddenly broke through into the snow tunnel, causing the sheep to bolt to the far end of their sanctuary.

Billy was the first to reach Johanna. Still wrapped in Ephraim's overcoat, she hugged him fiercely, before treating Pilgrim in the same manner.

When he had extricated himself from her embrace,

Pilgrim made his way farther inside the tunnel, causing consternation among the sheep.

They eventually fled past him and broke out of the newly made opening.

On the dirty snow of the cave floor, curled up as though asleep, lay Ephraim.

Johanna had followed Pilgrim and now she said, 'I was shivering during the night and I couldn't stop. Ephraim wrapped something around me, then he gave me his overcoat and cuddled me until I went to sleep. When I woke up this morning, Ephraim wouldn't answer when I spoke to him and he hasn't moved. He's awfully cold.' Looking up at him, wide-eyed, she asked, 'Is he dead?'

Pilgrim crouched down beside his sergeant and felt for a pulse, but it was unnecessary. As soon as he touched the ice-cold body, he knew the answer to Johanna's question.

Standing up, he found his vision too blurred to see anything about him.

'Yes, Johanna, I'm afraid he is. But he saved you. Had he known that, he would have died a happy man. Come along, Billy will take you home to Roundtor. The farmer can help me carry Ephraim out to his wagon. It's a poor enough carriage for a brave man, but Ephraim wouldn't have minded.'

'All right.' Johanna looked at the dead man, tearfully. 'I'm sorry Ephraim died. Would you like to wrap this around him?'

From beneath the overcoat she unwrapped the 'piece of cloth' Ephraim had wrapped about her during the long, bitterly cold night.

It was the United States flag that had once fluttered defiantly over Dartmoor prison's Block Four.

With the home-made United States flag wrapped around him as a shroud, Ephraim was the first man to be buried in the, as yet, unconsecrated burial ground of the unfinished Princetown church.

The church had been built by French prisoners-of-war. Although most of the exterior was completed, there was still much to be done inside.

All the United States marines from Dartmoor prison attended the funeral, as did the soldiers, many of the merchant seamen and Governor Shortland, with members of his staff. Among the Americans, only a hard-core of men from the southern states were not present.

The service was conducted by Reverend Cotterell from Sheepstor. Not unnaturally, he chose to base his eulogy on 'Greater love hath no man than this, that a man lay down his life for his friends'.

It was a very moving service. Pilgrim thought it was one of which Ephraim would have approved.

Pilgrim would have liked to spend some time with Tacy afterwards, but on such an occasion as this, he felt it important that he march his men back inside the prison as a single unit.

He had time only for a brief conversation with her, but was relieved to hear that Billy had been forgiven by the Elford family. They agreed it should never be mentioned again.

After marching his countrymen into the prison and dismissing them, Pilgrim was told Captain Shortland wished to speak to him.

When Pilgrim entered the governor's office, Captain Shortland seemed somewhat uncomfortable. Pilgrim wondered what might have gone wrong.

There was a letter on the desk. Picking it up, Shortland said, 'I have just received this from the Admiralty. It seems they have heard from Sir Thomas Tyrwhitt. He points out that your parole was the direct result of the Prince Regent's intervention. Sir Thomas has also said His Royal Highness is not used to having his wishes countermanded. I am ordered to release you on parole immediately. I regard this whole business as being highly irregular, but it is an order I dare not disregard.'

Standing up from his desk, the prison governor turned his back on Pilgrim and stared out of the window.

'I find myself in a difficult situation, Captain Penn. As I have just said, I cannot refuse to grant your parole. Indeed, I have no wish to do so. However, in the short time we have known each other, I have come to rely upon you. Having someone I know and can trust in my dealings with your countrymen is of great importance to me right now. There are more American prisoners-of-war on the road to Dartmoor at this very moment. It will bring the total to nine hundred.'

The figure came as a surprise to Pilgrim. It would

almost double the number of Americans in Dartmoor prison. However, it should make no difference to his parole and he said so.

'That is quite true, Captain, but among these men are a few known troublemakers. One in particular. Like the sergeant you have just lost, this man is an ex-slave, as are many of his companions. The number also includes the entire crew of a ship from one of your southern ports. There has already been a serious fight on their way here in which two men have died.'

Captain Shortland turned to face Pilgrim once more. 'If you take parole there will be no American officer left who possesses your experience of prison problems. You are respected by both sides, Captain, and trusted by the black Americans. I fear the chief troublemaker among the newcomers is likely to bring new problems with him. He has been in shackles for much of his time as a prisoner-of-war. He will arrive here in chains and is unlikely to have them removed unless he undergoes a dramatic change in his attitude towards his imprisonment.'

Remembering his own introduction to Dartmoor prison, Pilgrim said, 'I must protest, Governor! No man should be kept in chains for so long, whatever he's done.'

'I agree with you. However, unless he can be persuaded to accept prison discipline, he cannot be allowed to disrupt the routine here. I have more than nine thousand men in my charge, Captain Penn. It is difficult enough keeping order without the added tensions caused by the differences among Americans.'

'My understanding is that the American authorities have similar difficulties to cope with in our prisoner-of-war camps, when English, Irish and Scots prisoners are thrown together,' Pilgrim retorted. 'I doubt whether any prison governor expects his task to be an easy one. You've said nothing to persuade me I should forego parole and remain here surrounded by problems that are not of my making, and about which I can do nothing. I have no intention of providing you with a scapegoat, should something go seriously wrong. It's hardly an attractive proposition – except for you, perhaps.'

For a few moments Pilgrim thought Governor Shortland was about to make an angry reply to such outspoken remarks. Much to his surprise, the governor agreed with him.

'You are quite right, of course, Captain Penn. The presence of a responsible prisoner-of-war officer does ease my burden here considerably. What would make prison life more palatable for *you*?'

Pilgrim thought of Tacy and the pleasant life he had led for a while, shared between Tor Royal and Roundtor Farm. Nothing could compensate for the rupture of his relationship with Tacy.

But he stood before the governor now as the senior officer representing the interests of the United States prisoners-of-war.

'I could make a number of recommendations that might help to relieve some of the tensions and grievances that exist at the moment.'

'That's what I thought. Sit down and tell me about them, Captain Penn. We'll see whether anything can be done to put them right.'

Pilgrim left Governor Shortland's office despondent because he had agreed to forego parole, at least for the foreseeable future, although he had succeeded in gaining a number of concessions for the American prisoners-of-war – and for himself too.

The most important one was perhaps the one involving the accommodation of his countrymen.

The living quarters of black and white prisoners had been partitioned off to keep them apart, the exercise yard too being divided, but this solution had not been a total success. Their close proximity provided a constant reminder of the deep differences between many of those in the two groups of men.

The black Americans still gathered in the evenings to sing some of their plaintive and moving music from the plantations of America's southern states. But now some of the more extreme of the white southerners had formed their own choir to perform at the same time as their black countrymen. Their repertoire included a number of crude songs deriding those with whom they shared Block Four.

Missiles had begun to fly in both directions over the dividing wall, causing injuries among the two opposing groups of music makers. Feelings were beginning to run high once more. If ever men from the opposing groups were allowed to meet, fights were inevitable.

The influx of another four hundred and fifty men would greatly exacerbate the situation.

At Pilgrim's suggestion, the governor agreed that when the newcomers arrived all the white Americans would be moved to accomodation in another building.

Pilgrim had also tried to have the market thrown open to all United States prisoners-of-war, but Shortland insisted this must be put off until the tension between black and white Americans had eased. All he would agree to was that twice the present number of men from each racial group would be allowed to attend the market to buy goods for the others.

Pilgrim gained other concessions. One of the most important was that the French troublemakers were to be forcibly removed from the attic floor they shared with the Americans in Block Four. They would be transferred to the prison hulks in Plymouth harbour. The black Americans would have the whole attic floor to themselves.

Another concession was that the morning parade outside the prison blocks in all weathers was to cease. The men would also have a daily surgery.

Governor Shortland then informed Pilgrim he had been advised by American Agent Beasley that the United States Government intended raising the daily allowance of the prisoners-of-war by a penny.

It seemed little enough, but Pilgrim knew it would work wonders for the morale of the men.

On a personal level, Captain Shortland gave Pilgrim permission to leave the prison one day a week to pay a visit to either Tor Royal or Roundtor.

It was not the same as enjoying his former freedom, but it would suffice for now. The governor had promised Pilgrim he would be granted full parole once more should a more senior American officer be sent to the prison.

The governor also passed on a piece of news that came as a great relief to Pilgrim. Lieutenant Kennedy and the Irish militiamen were being relieved that very day. Their place was being taken by Scots militiamen.

Pilgrim would no longer need to worry about Tacy meeting up with Kennedy on the moor when she went about her daily work.

78

Pilgrim and Tacy were able to enjoy only one day of his weekly freedom before snow enveloped the moor once again.

This fall of snow was even more severe than the one which caused Ephraim's death. Those who lived on the moor declared it was the worst weather in living memory.

So deep was the snow that supplies were unable to reach the prison from Plymouth. It was necessary to fall back on the prison's emergency stocks of food. Even these were not readily available. Working parties needed to dig paths through waist-high snow to reach the storehouse from the various cell blocks.

In places the snow had drifted against the prison walls to a height of ten foot. The weather was so cold that the militiamen were withdrawn from their stations on the walls.

This was sufficient to tempt eight American seamen from the last batch to arrive at the prison to make an ill-planned break for freedom over the prison wall.

For most, their freedom was short-lived. The escape was made at night and dawn found six of them clamouring at the prison gate to be taken back inside.

A seventh ploughed through the snow until he reached a hut within sight of the prison. He was found here two days later by a hardy moorland farmer. Hungry and cold, the escapee was only too pleased to give himself up.

The last of the escapers suffered the fate of Ephraim, but his body was not found until the snow disappeared from the moor, three weeks later.

With the thaw, the inmates of the prison looked for something else about which to grumble. The black and white Americans were now far enough apart for the heat to have been taken out of their mutual antipathy and each side sought another target.

A natural and mutual choice was Reuben G. Beasley, the United States Government Agent – until the extra penny a day promised to each man was received at the prison. Suddenly, the agent found an unfamiliar popularity among his imprisoned countrymen.

At the same time, Governor Shortland announced that he was throwing open the prison market to the Americans.

There was method in this unexpected relaxation of the rules concerning the Americans. Shortland had received a letter from the Admiralty. In it, their Lordships pointed out that when peace came, the French prisoners would be returned to their homes. Dartmoor prison would be virtually empty unless new occupants could be found.

The letter confirmed that all the United States prisoners-of-war held throughout the country would be transferred to the Dartmoor prison. At present there were more than seven thousand of them, occupying prisons and hulks scattered about Britain.

* * *

The news of the entry of the Allied armies into Paris and the abdication of Napoleon Bonaparte reached the prison blocks before it was given to those who occupied the Petty Officers' Block.

Pilgrim heard the cheering as he stood with Tacy and Mary Gurney in the prison market square. It was cheering such as had never before been heard inside the prison walls. He guessed the reason even before an excited French inmate ran into the market square, shouting the news in his own language.

'What is it?' asked Tacy who had been startled by the outburst of sound.

'The war with France is over,' explained Pilgrim. 'The Frenchmen are cheering because they know they will be home in a matter of weeks. Some will be leaving within days probably.'

'Does that mean the war with America will end now too?' asked Tacy, suddenly concerned. 'Will you be going home just as quickly?'

Pilgrim shook his head. 'I doubt it very much. A separate peace will have to be negotiated with our Government. That could take many months.'

Mary had been listening with growing excitement. Now she said, 'Does this mean that Henri will be allowed to come back to England to see me?'

Pilgrim could see from Mary's uncertain expression that she was both excited and fearful at such a prospect.

'It does, Mary, although it might take some time for travel between the two countries to get back to normality.'

'It didn't stop Henri while we were at war, I doubt if it will now.' Grinning suddenly, she said, 'I doubt whether he'll be riding such a fine horse as when I last saw him.'

'The best thing you can do is forget all about that,' said Pilgrim hurriedly. 'If a whisper of what happened ever reached the ear of Sir Thomas I could say goodbye to any hope I have of getting parole again.'

'I'd never tell him,' said Mary, 'nor anyone else neither.' Fingering the locket she wore about her neck, she added wistfully, 'But it would be lovely to see Henri again.'

When Pilgrim said farewell to Tacy and Mary and returned to the Petty Officers' Block, he was surprised to find an air of silent gloom about the place. He had expected the French officers to be overjoyed at the prospect of returning to their homes.

He said as much to one of the officers who had been a friend of Henri.

'To go home will be a great joy, Captain, but think about it. Would you want to return to America as an officer in a defeated army? Would you not imagine that when your friends and your loved ones looked at you they were thinking that perhaps if you had fought a little more boldly your country might have been victors and not the vanquished?'

'I doubt very much whether anyone in France will think that,' said Pilgrim, at the same time fully understanding the feelings of the French officer.

'Probably not,' agreed the Frenchman, 'but we are proud men, Captain. There will be many times when we *think* that is what is in their minds.'

Another French officer had been listening to the conversation. Now he joined in.

'There is yet another reason why we are not celebrating, Captain Penn. Many of us who fought for France did so under the personal command of Emperor Bonaparte. We believe he is the finest general there has ever been. A masterly leader. Should we be happy that such a man has been defeated and stripped of office? No, Captain Penn, today is not a day for celebration for officers who fought for France. It is a day of sadness. I would willingly have spent the remainder of my life locked up in Block Four had it helped France to win the war.'

Looking as despondent as he sounded, the officer turned away, only to swing about suddenly to face Pilgrim once more.

'There is another matter you should ponder, Captain. It took vast armies to defeat France. Those armies have not yet been disbanded. What will happen if they are turned against America? It is my fervent hope that it will never happen, Captain, but one day you may come to know how we are feeling today.'

79

French prisoners-of-war began leaving Dartmoor prison only a few days after the war between France and Britain came to an end.

With such great numbers to deal with, the process took a great deal of time. It was two months before the final batch of prisoners was ready for repatriation. Their departure resulted in an unforeseen tragedy.

Before passing out through the gate, each prisoner had to present his bedding, no matter how tattered and dirty. The rule was 'no bedding, no discharge'.

One French prisoner discovered his bedding had been stolen and handed in by one of his fellow prisoners. Frantically he sought to explain this to the guard at the gate, but the militiaman was adamant. Unless he produced his bedding, the prisoner would not be allowed to pass through to freedom and repatriation.

Desperately, the man fled back to the prison block. Unable to locate his bedding, he tried to find something that would be acceptable in place of the missing items, but to no avail.

One final agitated plea to the guard went unheeded. The Frenchman was told he would have to remain behind. In a final act of near-insane desperation the unfortunate Frenchman, proclaiming to all and sundry that he had been a prisoner-of-war for eleven years and could endure no more, pulled a knife from his clothing. In front of the man who had so cruelly denied him his freedom, he slit his own throat, dying in minutes.

The last to leave the prison were some of the most senior French officers who had been on parole in neighbouring villages and houses.

One was a high-ranking general who had been housed in the home of a titled landowner. He returned to Dartmoor prison briefly while the final arrangements for his departure were made.

Here he was paid farewell visits by many of the gentry who had entertained him in their homes. In return they had been entertained by the Frenchman, who received a very generous allowance from his family, in the home of his host.

Among the visitors was Sir Thomas Tyrwhitt, newly returned from an extended overseas journey, made on behalf of the Prince Regent.

After paying his respects to the departing French general, Sir Thomas asked to speak to Pilgrim.

The two men met in the presence of the governor in that official's office and Sir Thomas greeted Pilgrim with all the warmth of an old friend.

'I had hoped we would never have to meet inside these walls again, Pilgrim. I wrote a letter demanding your release as soon as I heard your parole had been terminated. Then I heard you had agreed to Captain Shortland's request that you reside in the prison once more.'

Captain Shortland had been in charge of the prison

for some months now. Long enough to acknowledge the importance of the man seated before him.

'That is correct, Sir Thomas. When I first came here as a very inexperienced prison governor, Captain Penn very kindly agreed to set aside his parole and return, in order that I might better understand the problems of his countrymen. The arrangement has proved extremely satisfactory for myself and for the Americans. The problems I had were very quickly resolved. I am happy to say that Captain Penn will soon be able to take his parole once more. We agreed he would only remain in prison while he is the senior United States officer in my jurisdiction. As soon as the last French prisoner-of-war has gone, all American prisoners-of-war held in England will be brought here. There are at least two colonels among them. When they arrive, Captain Penn may return to Tor Royal, if you so wish.'

'Of course I wish it,' said Sir Thomas. Giving Pilgrim a mischievous look, he added, 'That is of course if you will wish to return to Tor Royal when you learn that Winifrith accompanied me from London. She tells me it is her intention to stay for a while.'

The last Frenchmen left Dartmoor prison in June 1814. Only then was it discovered that more than two hundred Americans had left with them.

They had used a simple enough ruse.

During their years of internment, some twelve hundred French prisoners-of-war had died, most through the various outbreaks of disease that frequently ravaged the inmates of the moorland prison.

Their deaths were recorded in a haphazard fashion, the bodies buried in unmarked graves on the moor beyond the prison perimeter wall.

As a result, it was a comparatively simple matter

for an American with a rudimentary knowledge of the French language to assume the identity of one of the deceased men and so be repatriated to France with his French allies.

Governor Shortland was furious about such a lapse of security. Angry accusations of complicity were thrown at Pilgrim in the privacy of his office, but the governor took no measures to punish the remaining Americans.

With the departure of the French prisoners-of-war, prison life improved beyond measure for the Americans. The governor was anxious to keep them happy.

They were allowed to move into the recently vacated blocks at will. In addition, they took on many of the tasks for which the Frenchmen had been paid. Carpenters, builders and artisans of all types came into their own, receiving an extra sixpence a day for their work.

Among many other tasks, they were employed fitting out the inside of the church, built but not completed by the French. In order to ensure they never took advantage of their new status, the prisoners were employed in teams. If any man escaped, the pay of his companions was confiscated – and it was paid some three months in arrears.

The result was that the prisoners now had a very good reason for preventing their fellow countrymen from escaping.

This was the situation in the prison when United States prisoners from all over the country began to arrive at Dartmoor.

Included among the first arrivals were the two colonels of whom Governor Shortland had spoken earlier. Both were regular army men – and neither had any time for a brevet captain of marines who had been used to commanding his fellow Americans inside the prison.

The two officers were of similar seniority. Each was

determined to become the man responsible to Governor Shortland for his fellow prisoners-of-war.

There was, and would continue to be, bitter rivalry between them, but one thing they were both agreed upon. Captain Pilgrim Penn of the United States Marine Corps had no place in their intended chain of command.

Within a fortnight of their arrival, Pilgrim found himself outside the prison gate, setting off to resume his parole at Tor Royal once more.

80

Pilgrim had told Tacy the time of his release on parole from Dartmoor prison. He had expected her to be waiting for him, either on the road to Princetown or, as on the occasion of his release with Virgil, at the entrance lane to Tor Royal.

To his disappointment, she was in neither place.

However, he could find nothing to complain about in his welcome at Tor Royal. The servants made him feel as though he was a member of the family returning home.

Sir Thomas, too, greeted him with equal warmth.

'I am very relieved you are out of that place once more, dear boy,' he said, shaking Pilgrim's hand vigorously. 'I had hoped the sad differences between our two countries would end with victory over the French. Unfortunately, there has been some bitter fighting on both sides of the Canadian border this year. I fear our generals are not ready for peace just yet . . .'

Breaking off, he led Pilgrim from the hallway. 'But we can discuss this foolish war later. You will want to clean up and remove the stench of that place from your nostrils. The servants have been told to heat lots of water and prepare a bath for you. I have also taken the liberty of having a new uniform made for you.'

When Pilgrim exhibited surprise, Sir Thomas said, 'A travelling tailor visited Tor Royal last week. His skill is well above the average. I have employed him on many occasions. I had nothing for him to do this time, then I remembered there was an old uniform of yours hanging in the wardrobe of your room. I had him copy it. I am quite certain you are going to be well pleased with the result.'

After thanking his generous and thoughtful host, Pilgrim was about to make his way upstairs when Sir Thomas called to him.

'By the way, a package arrived for you from London. It's from that agent employed by your Government to look after their prisoners-of-war.'

Believing the package contained documents about official business, Pilgrim did not bother to open it immediately. He would need to have it sent to the two colonels at the prison. They were responsible for official business now.

Not until he had enjoyed the unaccustomed luxury of a hot bath and put on the splendid new uniform did he open Beasley's package.

As he had thought, it contained a number of letters about prisoners, their numbers and the amount to be paid to them. But, to Pilgrim's delight, the package also contained two letters from America for him. One was from Virgil, the other from his mother.

He read Virgil's letter first. It told him how things were in the United States at the time of writing and informed him that the operation on his leg had been a complete success. He would always walk with a slight limp, but at no stage had the American surgeon contemplated amputation.

He went on to give Pilgrim the exciting news that he and Sophie would be parents by the end of the year. Sophie had written a conciliatory letter to her mother, giving her the news that she was to be a grandparent. The letter had been sent to her London address, so if she was not there it might take a while to reach her.

The letter went on to say that Virgil and Sophie were currently living in a very nice house in Washington, given to them by Virgil's parents who had taken to Sophie immediately.

Virgil further reported that in spite of the surgeon's skill, the United States Marine Corps had decided he would be unable to carry out the full duties of a marines officer. He had been promoted to major and pensioned off on half pay.

However, Virgil informed Pilgrim that he had no intention of leading the life of a retired man. He had been asked by Pilgrim's uncle to join the United States Diplomatic Service. This was the man who had been ambassador to London and a friend of Sir Thomas. It seemed he was now head of the Diplomatic Service!

It was the letter of a very happy man. Virgil managed to convey the fact that Sophie too was thoroughly delighted with her new life in America.

Such tidings did not prepare Pilgrim for the news given to him in his mother's letter. It concerned his father who had always prided himself on being an active man; a man of action. It seemed he had not been content merely to take care of Ohio's interests in Congress in Washington.

A strong band of Shawnee Indians had been carrying out some horrific attacks on settlements in the west of the state and the settlers had called for help from their Government. It was not immediately forthcoming and Pilgrim's father had organised a small army of volunteers and set off in pursuit of the Indians.

They located the Indians quickly. In a fierce battle the Shawnees had been comprehensively defeated. However, during the fight Pilgrim's father had been wounded in the head. As a result, he had lost his sight. Surgeons were unable to say with any certainty whether the loss was temporary or permanent.

Pilgrim's mother had contacted the same uncle mentioned by Virgil in his letter and asked him to bring his influence to bear in order to have Pilgrim returned to America.

It was disturbing news and threw Pilgrim's immediate plans into disarray. He was convinced his uncle would succeed in having him returned. There was a number of senior British officers in American custody. Their Government would be quite happy to have one of them returned in exchange for a junior American officer.

Before such an exchange was put into operation there was much that Pilgrim was determined to do.

When Pilgrim went downstairs, resplendent in his new uniform, he met Winifrith in the hall. After a quick, malevolent glance in his direction, she would have passed him by without a word had he not spoken to her.

'Mrs Cudmore, would I be right in thinking you've not yet received Sophie's letter?'

'What letter?' she asked sharply.

'I've just received one from Virgil. He says Sophie's written to you. As it hasn't reached you yet I think you should read the letter he's sent to me.'

'I don't care to read other people's letters, young man,' said Winifrith haughtily.

Pilgrim grinned. 'I think you might change your mind on this occasion. I certainly won't be able to keep the news to myself. I feel you ought to know about it before I tell Sir Thomas.'

Pilgrim watched as curiosity fought a duel with Winifrith's determination to remain aloof from him.

Eventually, as he had thought, curiosity won the day.

'Thank you, it's most kind. Perhaps you will be good enough to tell me which portions I may read and those I may not.'

Pilgrim pulled the letter from his pocket and handed it to her. 'You can read it all. It's a letter from a very happy man who has an equally happy wife. I'll leave you to tell Sir Thomas of the news it contains.'

81

Pilgrim set off to visit Roundtor Farm late that same afternoon. He left behind him a household buzzing with excitement. Everyone in the house was aware that 'Miss Sophie' was expecting a baby in far-off America.

All agreed it was a wonderful happening and were delighted that she appeared to have found happiness after the tragic loss of her first husband and the misery of life with her domineering mother.

Yet, for today at least, there was little of the domineering woman evident in Winifrith.

Sir Thomas told Pilgrim that after reading Virgil's letter she had hurried off to find him and tell him the news.

'I have never known her to be so excited about anything,' he said. 'She even *kissed* me! I cannot remember the last time she kissed *anyone*! Then she told every servant she met up with, before rushing off, declaring she was so overcome with emotion she needed to go to her room and lie down.'

Beaming at Pilgrim, he had added, 'You have made

Winifrith a very happy woman by allowing her to read your letter, Pilgrim, and when she is content life is easier for all of us!'

Sir Thomas had announced his intention of opening some vintage champagne before dinner that evening, to celebrate the news.

Pilgrim promised to be back to share in the celebration, but informed Sir Thomas he wanted to go to Roundtor first. He was concerned that all might not be well there.

Sir Thomas had suggested he should take a horse, but Pilgrim had preferred to walk. It meant he would have more thinking time, and he felt it was needed.

He had said nothing to Sir Thomas about the other letter he had received. Today was not an appropriate time to pass on such news. Nevertheless, the implications of it were immense. The Ohio lands owned by his father were extensive, to say the least. It would be impossible for a blind man to maintain control over them.

Pilgrim winced at the thought of such an active man as his father being blinded. He had a few minutes of very deep pity for the man he both loved and admired. The man to whom nothing had ever been accepted as impossible. It was a cruel blow.

As he walked across Dartmoor in the warm sunshine, Pilgrim's thoughts returned to the decisions that had to be taken – and with some urgency now. He had told Tacy often enough that he could not offer her marriage until the end of his internment was in sight.

That moment had seemed so far away even a few hours ago. But now it had arrived. Pilgrim knew that his uncle was not a man who put off things that needed urgent attention – and Pilgrim's father was his only brother.

Pilgrim had no doubt at all that arrangements for

a cartel with himself at the centre of it were already underway. He needed to set his plans and convince Tacy of the need to carry them into effect as quickly as was possible.

Roundtor Farm had always given Pilgrim an impression of being permanently busy. He could not remember an occasion when there was not someone working in the yard, or when they had not seen him approaching and hurried out to meet him: Tom or Joan Elford, Tacy or Johanna, or perhaps Billy or Emma. They were usually working and chatting, or calling across the yard to one another.

Today there seemed to be no one at the farm. Pilgrim felt uneasy. Then, as he went in through the gate to the farmyard, he heard a sound from the cowshed and headed in that direction.

Tacy was here, milking one of the cows, her cheek resting against the warm body of the animal as she worked.

She turned her face towards him as he stood in the doorway blocking out much of the light, and he saw the tears on her cheeks.

'Pilgrim . . . I'm sorry . . . I forgot all about coming to meet you this morning . . .' Suddenly she abandoned her task. Rising to her feet she threw herself at him and as he held her close she clung to him and began sobbing.

'What is it, Tacy? What's happened? Is it . . . your father?'

She nodded, but it was a few minutes before she felt able to talk. 'He collapsed in the kitchen early yesterday afternoon. I had to go to Tavistock for a doctor. He arrived late last evening. He said it's Pa's heart. There's . . . there's nothing he can do for him. He's dying.'

Pilgrim held her more tightly. 'I'm very, very sorry, Tacy. Is he conscious?'

Tacy nodded vigorously against his chest. 'Yes, but he can only talk with difficulty and can't move more than half his body.'

'Can I see him?'

'Of course. Ma's been with him for most of the day. We've decided that one of us should stay with him all the time. The doctor said . . . he said he doesn't know when it will be but . . . Pa can't last very long.'

Pilgrim knew this was not the right time to talk of any of the plans he had been making on his walk to the farmhouse. They must wait for another day – even though there might not be many days left.

He came downstairs after seeing Tom Elford feeling even more depressed about what the future held for Tacy and himself. The poor man was quite obviously deteriorating fast. He had been unable to say anything to Pilgrim that made any sense.

While Tacy went upstairs to keep her father company for a few minutes, Pilgrim sat in the kitchen while Joan made him some tea.

'It's a very sad business,' said the farmer's wife. 'It's something I should have seen coming a long time ago, but you tend to shut such things out of your mind in the hope it will never happen. There could never be a good time for such a thing to happen, but this is a particularly bad one. Young Emma will be having her baby any day now and I'll be needed over there. In the meantime, Billy can't leave the poor girl on her own, so we don't have him to help us out and one of us needs to be with Tom all the time. Johanna's over at Billy's too at the moment. I sent her there with a pie and some cakes I made.'

'I'll be able to help out now I'm out on parole once

more,' said Pilgrim. Aware of what was likely to happen, he added, 'At least, for a while. But it probably won't be very long before the Americans have left Dartmoor too.'

'When the end comes for poor Tom we'll need to leave Dartmoor as well,' said Joan unhappily.

'You leave . . . ? Why?'

'Because the tenancy of the farm is in Tom's name. The Duchy won't allow me to take over the tenancy. We'll have to go.'

'But . . . *where* will you go – and what will happen to the farm?'

'The Duchy steward will find a new tenant, but he won't find it easy. There aren't many these days prepared to take over such a farm. There's not enough profit in it. But it's a happy enough life for those prepared to work at it. Now, I'll leave you with your tea and go back up to Tom. You and Tacy haven't had much opportunity to sit and chat in recent months. She's had to take a lot on her young shoulders just lately. It'll be nice for her just to sit and be with you. She might not say too much about it to you, but she's missed you, Pilgrim.'

'I've missed her too, Mrs Elford. I don't think I realised quite how much until today.'

82

'You are very quiet this morning, Pilgrim. Did you drink too much champagne last night?'

Sir Thomas put the question to him the following morning, at breakfast. The previous evening had been one of celebration at Tor Royal. All the servants had been invited to drink a glass of champagne with their employer and his sister, to toast the news of Sophie's impending motherhood.

Later, a few of Sir Thomas's close friends had dropped by too.

'I seem to recall he was not saying very much last night either,' remarked Winifrith.

Her manner towards Pilgrim had undergone a remarkable change since reading Virgil's letter. It was not only because of the news that she was to become a grandmother – although this seemed to delight her. It was as much the manner in which Virgil had written about Sophie, and the life she was leading in America.

The letter had never been intended for her eyes, yet it made it very clear that Virgil was deeply in love with

Sophie, and that she was happy and had been made welcome by her husband's family.

The letter had also mentioned that Sophie had written to her. It meant that despite all the differences they may have had in the past – and Winifrith conceded to herself there had been many – Sophie had not broken all ties with her. This knowledge had delighted Winifrith more than she would ever confess to anyone.

'Do you not share everyone else's pleasure that Sophie and Virgil are having a child?'

'I'm *very* happy for them both,' said Pilgrim. 'It's not that. It's . . . I had another letter at the same time. From my mother . . .'

After some hesitation, Pilgrim told them the contents of the second letter.

Sir Thomas was immediately sympathetic, and asked why he had said nothing about it the previous day.

'Yesterday was not a day for such news, Sir Thomas,' said Pilgrim. 'There was far too much happiness at Tor Royal. I would never have forgiven myself had I allowed it to be marred in any way.'

'I have no doubt you were given all the sympathy you needed from that young girl at the farm you visited yesterday evening,' said Winifrith shrewdly. 'The one you invited to Sophie's wedding.'

'I couldn't tell her either,' Pilgrim said unhappily. He explained about Tacy's father.

'That is very sad,' said Sir Thomas. 'Very sad indeed. I knew Tom was ill, but I never realised it was quite so serious. He is a comparatively young man too. The family must be absolutely devastated.'

'They are,' agreed Pilgrim. 'And it isn't just the state of Tom's health they have to worry about now. His wife was telling me that if anything happens to him they will have to leave the farm.'

Sir Thomas nodded. 'That is so. The tenancy dies with Tom Elford. The Duchy land steward will need to find another tenant.'

'It seems very hard on the Elford family,' protested Pilgrim.

'Perhaps,' agreed Sir Thomas. 'But I doubt very much whether the tenancy laws are very different in your country, Pilgrim.'

'I don't think you need concern yourself too much with their troubles,' said Winifrith. 'You'll probably be on your way home before anything happens to this farmer.'

'It already concerns me very much,' said Pilgrim. 'You see, I went to Roundtor yesterday to ask Tacy to marry me and return with me to America when I go.'

'Good Lord!' Sir Thomas looked at Pilgrim in utter astonishment. 'I knew you had become very friendly with the Elford family – and Tacy is a splendid girl, of course,' he added hastily, 'but I never realised you were contemplating marriage.'

'The girl accepted you, of course?' The way Winifrith put it was as much a statement as a question.

'I never asked her,' admitted Pilgrim. 'She was far too upset about her father to discuss marriage and the possibility of leaving her family.'

'Yes, of course. If you go there today please offer Mrs Elford my deepest sympathy and say I will call on them at the earliest opportunity,' said Sir Thomas.

'You had all this on your mind last night, while we were celebrating Sophie and Virgil's good fortune?' The question came from Winifrith.

'As I said before, it would have been quite inappropriate to say anything about it yesterday.'

'There's rather more to you than is immediately apparent,' said Winifrith bluntly. 'If I am not very careful I will have to reassess my opinion of Americans. But . . . this girl? She is the daughter of a Dartmoor farmer. A tenant farmer. From all I have heard of your family, you should be looking for a girl of a much better class. One of the girls you met at Sophie's wedding, for instance . . .'

When Sir Thomas tried to protest at her outspoken criticism of Tacy, she impatiently waved him to silence and carried on talking to Pilgrim.

'I know you are not British,' she said, arrogantly, 'but your family is obviously wealthy, and considerable landowners, I believe. You need to be careful this girl is not marrying you for your money. You must also think of your own family in America. They will no doubt expect you to marry someone of whom they will approve?'

Managing with some difficulty to control the anger he felt at her words, Pilgrim said, 'Tacy has not yet said she'll marry me.'

Winifrith snorted. 'That is because you have not yet asked her. Of course she'll marry you. No girl in her position would refuse such an offer.'

'I sincerely hope you're right,' said Pilgrim. 'Because it's my intention to ask her to marry me before I'm sent back home. As for my family . . . my mother is from good farming stock – Quaker farming stock – and no one has ever said she wasn't good enough for my father – least of all my father himself. If I take Tacy home as my wife – and that's what I intend doing – she will be welcomed in my home as the daughter my parents always hoped they might have one day. She'll fit in very well with their ways because she shares the same standards they've always lived by: hard work, honesty and loyalty. Such qualities are things that are not restricted to any particular social class, Mrs Cudmore – any more than are prejudice and rudeness.'

Still fighting hard to control his anger, Pilgrim rose from the table. Turning to his host, he said, 'I will leave now, Sir Thomas, before I say something to abuse your hospitality. I will pass on your sympathy to the Elford family – and thank you.'

When Pilgrim had left the room, carrying his anger stiffly, Sir Thomas rounded on his sister. 'You deserved all he said to you, Winifrith – and a great deal more. Your behaviour was quite inexcusable.'

'I agree with you, Thomas,' said Winifrith enigmatically. 'I thought he behaved rather splendidly. Now we need to find out whether this farmer's daughter is worthy of him, do we not?'

Winifrith swept from the room with her brother's protests ringing unheeded in her ears.

83

As Pilgrim walked from Tor Royal to Roundtor Farm he was still angry with Winifrith, but the exchange with her had served to sharpen his perception of the situation as it affected Tacy and himself.

He wanted her to marry him. The sooner a wedding could be arranged, the better it would be for all of them, or so he reasoned.

The thought of marrying Tacy occupied his mind during the mile-long walk and he determined that today he would broach the subject with her.

His first question when he entered the Roundtor Farm kitchen was about Tom Elford. He was told the farmer's condition was unchanged. He was conscious, but finding great difficulty in communicating with his family.

Tacy was with her father and Pilgrim went upstairs to see them both. After greeting Tacy, he said 'Hello' to her father. There was a more positive response from the sick man today, but it was quite unintelligible.

Pilgrim remained in the room for some ten minutes,

before leaving father and daughter together and returning downstairs, to the kitchen.

Johanna sat in a corner of the kitchen, pale-faced and close to tears. Speaking to her, Pilgrim said, 'It must be time to start work. What's been done this morning so far?'

Johanna shook her head. 'Nothing.'

'Nothing at all? Then I suppose you and I will need to get out there and make a start, Johanna. We'll work together this morning. First of all we ought to clean out the cowshed, then give food to the cows and pigs. After that you and I will collect the eggs. Come on, it's a long time since I did any farmwork. Let's see how much I've forgotten.'

Johanna was a reluctant starter, but once they began she was able to put some of her unhappiness behind her.

They had been working together for more than an hour before Tacy came from the house to join them. By then they were at work cleaning out the pigs.

When Tacy said she intended milking the cows, Pilgrim said he would come and help her in the cowshed. To Johanna he said, 'You carry on and finish here, then you and I will find something else to do together.'

Tacy protested that it would not take two of them to milk the cows, but Pilgrim bundled her outside and propelled her very firmly towards the cowshed.

'What are you doing?' Tacy protested, finally pulling away from him. 'There's only work for one here . . .'

'I know all about that,' replied Pilgrim, 'but I need to talk to you. I can't do it in front of your sister.'

'What's so important that can't be said in front of Johanna?'

They were in the cowshed now, but instead of releasing her arm, Pilgrim turned her to face him. 'Tacy, I have

something very important to say to you, but first I want
to ask you something. Do you love me?'

The blunt question took Tacy completely by surprise.
'What? What did you say . . . ?'

'I asked if you loved me.'

Tacy opened and closed her mouth a number of times
before she finally said, 'I think you know the answer to
that question, Pilgrim.'

'Tacy, this is too important for me to guess your
answer. Do you love me? *Truly* love me?'

Tacy searched his face, seeking a reason for his question, but his expression told her nothing.

'Yes . . . Yes, I love you very much, Pilgrim. But . . .'

'There can be no "buts", Tacy. I love you very much
too – and I want you to marry me. As quickly as
possible.'

Tacy was in a virtual state of shock now and she
stuttered, 'I . . . but . . . what are you saying? Why
now? You have always said you could say nothing to
me about the future until you were a free man! Why
are you saying this now?'

'Because I'm likely to be a free man very soon . . .'

There, in the cowshed, with only the cow as a witness, Pilgrim told her of his mother's letter and of Sir
Thomas's promise that he would have Pilgrim's return
to the United States expedited as quickly as possible,
once the request for his release was received.

Her thoughts in turmoil, Tacy said, 'But . . . I couldn't
consider leaving the family right now.'

'I realise that, Tacy. But I want you to marry me as
quickly as possible. Then, whatever else happened, you
and I would be man and wife. Nothing that happened
in the future would be able to change that.'

Suddenly, tears welled up in Tacy's eyes. 'Pilgrim,
you'll never know how much I've wanted to have you

ask me to marry you, but . . . but to ask me now . . . !
It's cruel! I can't leave the family the way things are
right now – and if I were married to you then I would
have to . . .'

At that moment, Joan shouted from the house, 'Tacy
. . . Johanna . . . come here. Quickly!'

There was an urgency in her voice that caused both
girls to run for the house. Pilgrim hurried after them.

When he reached the house, mother and daughters
were upstairs in the bedroom where Tom Elford lay.
By the time he reached the top of the stairs the farmer
had taken his last breath and Pilgrim was greeted with
a wail of despair from Tom Elford's family.

At the very moment that Tom Elford died at Roundtor
Farm, Emma Yates gave birth to a lusty son at the
Whiteworks cottage.

When she went into labour, Billy had wanted to run to
fetch Joan Elford right away, but Emma realised the baby
was in a hurry to arrive. Even as she was giving birth, she
directed Billy to do all that needed to be done to bring their
son into the world before he set off for Roundtor.

By the time Billy reached Roundtor Farm there was
nothing more that could be done to help Tom Elford.
His grieving wife set off across the moor to see what
she could do to help the child that had been born into
the harshness of Dartmoor life.

Behind her, Tacy told Pilgrim that although she
wanted to marry him more than anything else she
would ever want, she could not consider leaving her
mother and Johanna now.

It was useless for Pilgrim to try to reason with her.
Much as she wanted to marry Pilgrim, she believed it
was her duty to remain to face the uncertain future with
her family.

84

Tom Elford was laid to rest in the little churchyard at Sheepstor, on a day that Pilgrim believed God had surely intended for happier pursuits.

As the sombre party gathered about the graveside, the Reverend Cotterell's oratory was disturbed by the raucous sounds from a nearby rookery.

High above the tiny graveyard, the liquid notes of a high fluttering skylark rose and fell in a melodic requiem. Farther away, soaring over the tor that had given its name to the village, a young buzzard practised a broken-voiced imitation of the plaintive call of its wheeling parents.

In the churchyard itself, the cries of Emma and Billy's baby son reminded the mourners that, like the moor itself, there was a constant resurgence of new life, waiting to replace the old.

In addition to those members of Tom Elford's family who lived on and about the moor, there were many other mourners present. Among them were Sir Thomas Tyrwhitt and a number of moorland farmers.

Many had met Tom Elford on perhaps no more than a half-dozen occasions during his lifetime, but he was a respected man, a moorland farmer like themselves. One day they would hope for just such a gathering as this for their own funeral rites.

On the return journey to Roundtor, Emma and the baby rode on the farm cart with Joan, Tacy and Johanna. All the members of Tom's family had needed to leave immediately after the ceremony in order to reach their homes before dark.

Billy walked at the pony's head and Pilgrim rode one of the Tor Royal horses. The two dogs, left dutifully on the cart during the funeral service, now gambolled around them, enjoying the day, but there was very little cheer among the small Roundtor party as they reached the farmhouse.

Here, Joan had prepared a meal for everyone. While they were eating, Pilgrim posed the question that nobody seemed to want to ask.

The question of what the future held for them all.

'I'm sure I don't know,' said Joan unhappily. 'Tom's brother John said we can go to stay with them, but it's on the far side of the moor. I have a sister who lives over that way too. I haven't seen her for some years, but if her own family hasn't grown too much she might put us up for a while. Until we can find somewhere of our own, at least. Wherever we go, I don't want to leave the moor.'

'How long do you have before you need to move out?' asked Pilgrim.

'A month is usual. It depends whether they have anyone else waiting to move in.'

'I don't want to go,' said Johanna tearfully, her bottom lip trembling.

'There's no need for you to go until you're good and

ready.' Emma spoke so quietly that it almost passed unnoticed.

But Joan heard. 'What do you mean by that, Emma? How can we stay?'

Emma, breast-feeding the baby, looked up at Pilgrim uncertainly and he answered for her.

'First of all, let me say that this is *my* idea. It somehow didn't seem right that strangers should move into Roundtor Farm, after all the years of work you've put into it. Last night I had a talk with Sir Thomas. This morning, immediately before the service, I put my idea to Emma. I don't think she's even had a chance to discuss it with Billy yet . . . but the idea is this. Sir Thomas says that if Billy is agreeable, he'll speak to the Land Steward and see to it that Billy is offered the tenancy of Roundtor Farm.'

'Billy . . . ? At Roundtor?' Joan stared at Billy for long moments before shifting her gaze to Emma. Incredulity was gradually replaced by acceptance. After a while she said, almost as softly as Emma had spoken, 'Yes . . . Yes, you could do it, Billy. You and Emma. I'd like that. Tom would have been happy with it too.'

'You can stay here with us until you have something sorted out,' said Emma eagerly. 'You can stay for as long as you like, can't they, Billy?'

Billy had been listening in disbelief and still seemed unable to accept what he had heard. He could only look from one to the other, speechless.

'We couldn't do that,' said Joan. 'But what will happen about the stock? We'll need to sell it to get some money together for our new start.'

'Can I make another suggestion here?' asked Pilgrim. 'Once again, I've not discussed it with anyone because there hasn't been time. Tacy already knows that arrangements are being made to return me to the United

States as soon as possible. I've also asked her to marry me – but that was before her father died. She wouldn't agree to marry me then because she felt she couldn't leave the family while he was so ill. I could understand that, but I have no intention of losing Tacy. What I'm suggesting now is that you leave all the livestock and furniture – everything – for Billy and Emma. If Tacy and I can be married, you and Johanna can come to America with us. Once there you can decide what you want to do. If, as I'm hoping, you'll come to Ohio with us, I'll have a house built for you there. If that doesn't suit then *you* can choose where you want to live. I'll give you the value of all your stock and everything you've left behind here. You could open a store – or an eating-house, whatever you wanted. The standard of your cooking is a guarantee that you'll succeed. But you can do anything you want and I'll back you. What do you say?'

Pilgrim put the question eagerly, but Joan seemed to be finding it difficult to comprehend what he was offering her.

'But . . . why should you do all this for us?'

'Because I love Tacy. When I marry her, I'll be your son-in-law. I'll consider it my duty to make you happy in your new land and it will repay you in a small way for all you've done for me here.'

Joan tried to take it all in, but she failed. 'I couldn't do it, Pilgrim. It's frightening enough to think of moving to a new house on the moor. But to travel to America . . . ! No, I couldn't.'

'Yes you could, Ma.' This time the plea came from Tacy. 'It will be a wonderful new start for you – and for Johanna especially. You'll be able to put all the unhappiness you've known here behind you. Please . . . *please* say you will.'

'It hasn't been all unhappiness, Tacy. Your pa and I – you girls too – have had some very happy times here, on the moor. In fact, most years have been happy ones. It's only recently, when your father's been so ill, that things haven't gone well. That doesn't mean you can't marry Pilgrim and go to America. You'll have my blessing. You would have your father's too. We spoke about it often before he died.'

'I couldn't do that, Ma. I couldn't go off and leave you both with things the way they are right now.'

'And I couldn't leave your pa, newly laid in his grave. It wouldn't be right . . .'

The discussion waged back and forth for more than an hour, but Joan Elford remained adamant. She did not feel able to leave England now, or in the foreseeable future.

Tacy, although tearful, was equally convinced she could not leave her mother and Johanna while their future was so uncertain.

Eventually, bitterly disappointed, Pilgrim announced he would need to leave in order to be back at Tor Royal at the time decreed in his parole.

Tacy put on her coat to walk with him, not looking at her mother as she followed him out through the door.

85

'I'm sorry, Pilgrim. Truly I am.' Looking as grief-stricken as she sounded, Tacy reached out and took Pilgrim's hand. They were walking from Roundtor Farm, Pilgrim leading the Tor Royal horse. 'But you must see that I can't leave Ma and Johanna, the way things are right now. I just can't.'

'There's no need for anyone to be left here. Your ma and Johanna would have a wonderful life in America, Tacy. You all would.'

'I know, Pilgrim. I want to marry you and live with you in America more than I've ever wanted anything. But I can't leave Ma and Johanna right now. Pa has been her whole life for so long. Now she's lost him. She's feeling afraid and alone. She also believes she'd be deserting him if she went away from Dartmoor. She won't always feel like this, I'm certain of it.'

'I know that, Tacy, but I have a duty to my father too. I can't wait for this war to end before I return to America. I must go when a cartel is arranged for me.'

He pulled her to a sudden halt. 'Of course, we *could* get married right away. Then you could come to join me in America as soon as you felt able to leave your ma.'

'That wouldn't work – for very many reasons,' she said
unhappily. 'I'll certainly come to you in America, if you still
want me to, when things are settled here, but that might
take a year, or even more. I don't want to tie you to a wife
who's going to be thousands of miles away for as long as
we can look ahead. If you still want me when things are
different, I'll come to you. We can be married there.'

'I'll still want you, Tacy, but it will be so difficult with
us being so far apart – and our countries are still at war.
That's going to make it doubly difficult for letters to go
backwards and forwards between us.'

'I know.' Tacy felt every bit as unhappy as did Pilgrim.
'And I do love you – but there's nothing else I can do.
Please, say you understand . . .'

Suddenly, the events of the day caught up with her
and she began to cry. When Pilgrim held her to him she
sobbed as though her heart was breaking – and to Tacy
it felt as though it was.

Winifrith watched from her bedroom window as Pilgrim
trudged to the stables to hand over the horse before walking up to the house. He looked thoroughly dejected.

She was in the hallway when he entered Tor Royal
and she greeted him with, 'Well . . . when is the wedding to be?'

Pilgrim would have liked to ignore her, but it was not
easy to disregard the presence of Winifrith Cudmore.

'There isn't going to be a wedding.'

'The girl turned you down?' Winifrith's surprise was
not feigned.

'Not exactly . . .' In spite of the antipathy he felt
towards this woman, Pilgrim found himself repeating
the conversation he had held with Joan Elford and Tacy.

'It's refreshing to find a daughter who puts her duty

to her mother before her own happiness. Nevertheless, both she and her mother are wrong. But you look as though you have need of a drink, young man. Come along to the study . . .'

'No, thank you. I couldn't stomach either food or drink right now. If you'll excuse me, I'll go to my room.'

The Tor Royal grooms were locking the stables when Winifrith arrived in riding kit demanding that a horse be prepared for her to ride. 'Side-saddle, if you please!'

When the head groom protested it was not safe for Winifrith to be out riding alone after dark, she retorted, 'I have no intention of riding alone. You will come with me. I need someone to guide me to Roundtor Farm . . . and take me the easy way. My days of jumping horses over obstacles ended many years ago. As for it being dark . . . there is a wonderful moon tonight. Only a fool could lose his way. Come along now, I have no intention of spending the whole night wandering about the moor.'

Joan Elford was making up the kitchen fire when she heard sounds in the farmyard. She would have been in bed long before this had she not spent the last couple of hours affirming to Tacy that she would not change her mind and go to America. Tacy had just gone to bed in tears.

Feeling the loss of her husband more than at any time since his death, Joan was about to go up to the empty bedroom she had shared with him for so many years.

Wondering who would be about at this time of the night, Joan went to the kitchen door. When she opened it, she was brushed to one side as a large woman, dressed in stout riding clothes, swept into the kitchen.

'You'll be Joan Elford,' said Winifrith, turning to face the newly widowed woman.

'Yes. I . . . I don't think I know you . . . ?'

'Winifrith Cudmore, Sir Thomas Tyrwhitt's sister. Please accept my condolences on the loss of your husband. I lost mine many years ago, so I am aware of how you will be feeling at this moment. However, it isn't the dead I have come to talk about, but the living. I am here to prevent you making the same mistakes I have made during my years as a widow.'

'I'm sorry . . . I don't understand . . .'

At that moment, Tacy appeared on the stairs. Her eyes puffy as the result of too much crying, she looked at Winifrith in amazement. 'Mrs Cudmore! What are you doing here? Has something gone wrong at Tor Royal? Is it Pilgrim . . . ?'

'Nothing has gone wrong that can't be put right,' said Winifrith brusquely. 'I admire your principles, young lady. Putting duty before personal happiness is admirable in a young girl. However, I hope your sacrifice will not be necessary. Now, go upstairs again, if you please. I have come to speak to your mother. I would appreciate a little privacy.'

One did not argue with Winifrith. Tacy retreated upstairs once more, but she could be heard whispering an explanation of the voices to Johanna.

'Do you have another room, Mrs Elford? I would rather our conversation was not overheard.'

'Of course . . . We use it so seldom I'd almost forgotten it.'

Joan was flustered by this woman and her positive attitude to everything and everyone. Hurriedly she led the way to the only other ground-floor room in the farmhouse. It smelled somewhat musty but, asking Winifrith to be seated, she opened the window to let in some of the night air.

'Now,' said Winifrith, when the other woman had also

taken a seat on the edge of a wooden chair. 'You know why I am here?'

'I . . . I think so. But if you have come on behalf of Pilgrim, I must tell you I have no intention of changing my mind.'

'Only a fool would take such a stand before hearing what needs to be said, and I doubt very much whether you are one, Mrs Elford. Captain Penn told me of the proposition he put to you – and which you have apparently turned down. It is both generous and practical.'

'I realise that . . .'

Winifrith held up her hand and silenced the other woman before she could complete a sentence.

'Let me finish, please. When I lost my husband, I felt much as you do now, I suspect. I determined to take on the duties of both father and mother to my daughter. I believed it was what my husband would have wished. I was wrong.'

'I'm not trying to keep control of Tacy. I've told her she can marry Pilgrim and go to America, if that's what she wants.'

'So Captain Penn told me. I have no doubt you knew what her answer would be before you suggested it to her. She is a dutiful daughter, Mrs Elford, a girl who would not leave you at such a tragic time. Yet, knowing this, you have deprived your daughter of an opportunity to make a good – no, an *excellent* marriage. It would be a happy one too, I have no doubt. Take my very sincere advice, Mrs Elford, and change your mind. Unless you do, she will come to hate you for what you will have done, as my daughter learned to hate me. I can assure you, it will cause you more grief than you have for your husband at this very moment.'

Winifrith reached out and touched the other woman's hand for just a moment. 'If you put your own wishes before those of your daughter, you will have lost more than a husband, Mrs Elford.'

'But . . . I couldn't go away and leave him . . .'

'Your husband is in his grave. He is dead,' said Winifrith, being deliberately callous. 'He can feel nothing. You must think now of the future of your daughter – of both your daughters. Where would they be better off? What would your husband tell you? I suspect he would not hesitate to advise you to look to the future. It does not mean you need forget the past. But it must be kept where it belongs. In the past.'

Joan was in tears as she said, 'But . . . who will tend his grave? There will be no one who cares.'

'The vicar of Sheepstor is a caring man. He will care for your husband's grave and pray for his soul too. You do the best you can for his children, Mrs Elford. I don't think you need me to repeat what is best for both of them. In your heart you already know.'

Winifrith stood up. 'I must return to Tor Royal now. Captain Penn is in his room, prevented from sleep by his unhappiness. Do you have anything I can tell him to ease his pain?'

The two women walked back to the kitchen before anything more was said. Here, Joan Elford looked down at the floor by her feet for a long time. When she looked up, the tears had gone.

'Tell him he and Tacy can marry as soon as it can be arranged. Tell him . . . Johanna and I will come to America. Tell him . . .'

She had heard the stifled squeal of delight from the landing at the top of the stairs and she said, 'No, Mrs Cudmore. Perhaps you will allow Tacy to accompany you home to Tor Royal. I think she might like to tell him herself . . .'

Epilogue

Pilgrim and Tacy were married within the month. Three weeks later they, with Joan Elford and Johanna, were on their way to America. They settled in Ohio, where Pilgrim took over the running of the Penn estates and also followed his father into Congress. He was assisted in all he did by his English wife, who became one of the best-known and best-loved women in the young State of Ohio.

Meanwhile, in Europe, Napoleon Bonaparte escaped from his island exile and returned to France to raise an army and challenge the Allied armies once more. His return to power was short-lived, but it meant that Dartmoor prison once more rang to the sound of French voices.

The Americans in Dartmoor prison, numbering some six thousand men, had to wait for almost a full year before the prison was thrown open and they marched to freedom. Before this, they would experience great frustration and tragedy.

An attempt at a mass escape was foiled when the

tunnels they had intended should pass beneath the prison walls were discovered and blocked up by Captain Shortland.

Then, in December 1814, a peace document was drawn up between America and Britain. Due to the distance between the two countries, its ratification was not received in London until March 14th, 1815.

In April, the American prisoners-of-war were still locked up in Dartmoor prison – and their frustration boiled over into a riot.

It was in reality a very minor disorder, but it had disastrous consequences. The rioters confronted soldiers of the Somerset and Derbyshire militia and in an atmosphere of confusion and panic, the militiamen opened fire on the unarmed prisoners.

When the one-sided battle ended, seven Americans were killed and sixty wounded, two of these dying later.

This orgy of violence galvanised the authorities into action. Later that same month, many weeks after a ceasefire between the two nations had been agreed, the Americans began to leave for their native land.

For thirty-four years the brooding, granite prison lay empty on the great moorland of Dartmoor. Then it once again heard the clank of chains as it was brought into use as a convict prison.

It still serves the same purpose today. Men passing beneath the same archway as did Pilgrim, Virgil and Ephraim in 1813, still look up and see carved in the stonework, the words, *Parcere Subjectis* – 'Spare the Vanquished'.

Once inside, they tread the paths of long-forgotten men, many of whom would never again cast a shadow in the world outside the walls of Dartmoor prison.

Harvest of the Sun

BOOK ONE

CHAPTER ONE

Pride of Liverpool, Australia-bound from England, struck a reef off the coast of south-west Africa at 11 p.m. on the twenty-third day of February in the year eighteen hundred and forty-six. The tragedy occurred during the death throes of one of the most violent storms ever experienced in the region.

For three days the captain and his crew had tried to keep the ship bows-on to the hurricane wind that blew from the south and the waves that fought each other and threw themselves angrily upon the creaking ship. The captain had seen three of his ship's five masts snapped off close to the leaking deck by a combination of water and wind. He had watched, helpless, as five of his crew were washed overboard whilst attempting to repair a smashed hatch-cover. The battle to save his ship had been lost long before the sharp teeth of unseen rocks sank into her belly.

Below decks Josh Retallick was squatting on the floor of a cabin when the violent pitching of the ship came to a shuddering, timber-splintering stop. He had one arm about an iron stanchion, the other holding Miriam, who lay on a bunk, their three-year-old son Daniel clutched tightly in her arms.

'My God! What's happened?'

Miriam struggled to a sitting position as a thousand-ton wave fell upon the stricken ship and ground it farther on to the jagged rocks of the reef. The screams of the steerage passengers trapped in a holed compartment rose above the thunder of the sea and the shrieking of the wind, and it did not need the cries of a seaman in the passageway outside the cabin to tell Josh the ship was going to sink.

'Quick! We've got to get up top.'

Josh pulled Miriam to her feet and snatched the complaining Daniel from her. He reached for the door and pulled it open. Over his shoulder he called, 'Take hold of my belt – and don't let go. Our lives depend on staying together.'

'Josh, there are some things we need—'

'There's no time. We're going to be hard put to save ourselves.'

Pride of Liverpool added emphasis to his words by writhing on the rocks as they stumbled out into the passageway. The ship was doomed. Even as they cleared the cabin water burst through the bulkhead at the far end of the passageway and swirled knee-deep about them. There was no light to guide Josh to the companionway, and beyond the hatchway to the deck there was only an unknown wild darkness.

A wave attacked the ship and sent Josh and Miriam staggering drunkenly about the passageway, but the rocks did not relinquish their hold. They had the stern of the vessel fast in their teeth and held on with the tenacity of a bull-baiting terrier, pulling the ship down.

The passageway was a scene of panic and confusion. The occupants of the other cabins all had the same instinctive aim — to get up to the deck. To achieve it they clawed and screamed as they fell over fellow-passengers.

Josh could afford to behave no better when he reached the foot of the ladder only to find it jammed with men and women fighting for a place on the steps. Unceremoniously he forced a way through them, flinging aside those who were incapable of climbing up to the deck but would not move forward or back. Once Miriam slipped and Josh had to reach back to grasp her wrist, hauling her up behind him, saved from falling by the others jamming the ladder.

They made the deck and were nearly swept over the side as a wave struck the bow and washed the length of the ship. The water took with it all those passengers and crew who had reached the deck before them.

Now he was here, Josh was uncertain which way to go. All was blackness and confusion, the howling of the wind and the crashing of the sea loud enough to numb the mind.

Another wave poured over the bows of the ship, but this one smashed in a hatch-cover and the water tumbled into a forward hold. It acted as ballast, and the ship righted herself temporarily. Moving out on to the level platform of the deck Josh could hear indistinct voices shouting near the stern. It was here he had seen two of *Pride of Liverpool*'s boats and he cautiously made his way in their direction.

He reached the shattered stump of the mainmast and clung to it while another wave rushed past them, its cold waters swirling waist-high. There were screams in the angry night, and Miriam gasped as the water tore at her, but she never loosened her grip on Josh's belt. Daniel's cries had by now died away to a frightened whimper and his arms gripped tight about his father's neck. Josh could do no more than give him a quick reassuring hug as he listened for sounds in the stormy night.

He heard the voices again – and heard something more. The creaking of a pulley. A boat was being swung out on its davits over the ship's side. Straining his eyes into the night Josh thought he could make out its shape no more than twelve feet away.

He would have to make his move now, before the next wave swept the ship's deck.

'Now, Miriam! With me!'

He lunged towards the outline of the boat, dragging Miriam with him. As *Pride of Liverpool* gave another dying shudder he reached it, his hand gripping its clinkered side.

'Inside. Quickly!'

Handing Daniel to Miriam he heaved them both into the boat.

There was a curse of surprise from inside; but the boat was already slipping outwards away from the ship's side, and Josh barely had time to scramble in himself before it was dangling clear of *Pride of Liverpool*.

'Who's that?' The startled call came from the other end of the boat. 'Are you crewmen or passengers?'

'Passengers.'

'This is a crew boat. We can't take passengers.'

The boat swung inwards, crashing against the side of the ship, and the ropes that held it creaked in protest.

'If you don't keep it away from the side, you'll *have* no boat.' Josh called back.

The wind carried most of his words away, and Josh sensed rather than saw the seaman edging towards him. Then another wave pounded the passenger ship and ground her farther on to the rocks of the reef.

'*Isaiah!* Help me free this rope. If it jams, the boat's lost.'

A voice shouted from the darkness as the bow of the boat swung into the ship's side with considerable force.

The sailor who had been moving towards Josh went back to help his companion.

Pride of Liverpool was breaking up fast now, the rocks tearing great holes below the waterline. The small boat had its troubles too. It was buffeted repeatedly against the side of its mother ship with ever increasing force. While the two seamen struggled with the fall-rope Josh made Miriam and Daniel crouch in the bottom of the boat, then he moved forward to try to keep the bow from smashing to pieces.

A spar and sail from one of the remaining masts were part of the tangled wreckage caught against the davit, and Josh was able to free some of the heavy sodden canvas and stuff it between the boat and the ship.

As he worked he could hear shouts and screams from farther away along the deck of the ship. It was too dark to see, but he gained the impression of activity around another boat on the far side of the deck.

Another wave was thrown up over *Pride of Liverpool*, and a wall of water raced from stem to stern at the very moment that some of the crew were leading a large party of steerage passengers along the deck. More than twenty people were swept off their feet by the sea and carried away into the night, their screams lost in the wind.

Helpless, Josh heard them passing only feet away from him. The same wave lifted the boat up and away from the ship, and as Josh leaned out to hold the canvas in position there was a bump against the clinkered planking not a yard from him.

Josh plunged his hand over the side into the water and as something brushed past he grabbed at it. His fingers took a hold on a thin dress. He held his grip against the pull of the water as two tiny hands clawed their way over his clenched fist and gripped his wrist.

Slowly, his muscles cracking against the relentless pull of the greedy sea, he began to bring the unseen little girl in towards the side of the boat.

Suddenly the whole world went topsy-turvy. The boat tilted dangerously, its stern dropping four feet in a breathtaking fall. Miriam screamed as she and Daniel began sliding uncontrollably down the boat. Then the bow slipped too. For a split second the boat hung level before falling twelve feet to the sea. It landed with a crash that would have burst the seams of a lesser-built vessel.

Josh still had his fist closed, but the girl had gone in the first moment of the fall. As the boat bounced and pitched he crawled to where he had left Miriam and Daniel.

'Miriam . . . ?'

'We're here, Josh. We're here. . . .' Her voice broke. She had thought him lost in the sudden awful plunge to the sea and now she reached out for him.

'Thank God!'

He bruised his shoulder on a thwart as he crawled beneath it to take Miriam and Daniel into his arms. Then they all three crouched huddled together in the bottom of the boat, drenched by the sea and spray but sheltered from the howling wind.

Not until then did Josh open his right hand and release the fragment of calico cloth torn from a small girl's dress. It dropped to the floor of the boat and was washed away by the water that lay inches deep there. Outside in the vastness of the great ocean a ship perished and a little girl went to meet her creator wearing a torn dress.

CHAPTER TWO

All through that weary night Josh, Miriam and Daniel clung together in the bottom of the boat as cold water slopped about them and the storm raged above. Daniel was sick. He was sick until the spasms completely exhausted him and then he lay motionless in his mother's arms. He was so still that Miriam frequently pressed her head to his chest to satisfy herself his heart was still beating.

More than once during that long darkness the feet of the two crewmen stumbled over the trio, and once one of them tried none too gently to kick them aside in the restricted space. Josh knew they were unwanted and resented, but he felt too ill to do more than accept the crewmen's curses and try to keep out of their way.

When dawn finally arrived wrapped in a cold grey shawl it found the small family group huddled together in the bow of the boat. The two seamen were bent over heavy creaking oars, pulling at them in ragged unison. Looking at the sea that heaved about them Josh thought their efforts were totally futile. Nevertheless, they were still afloat.

One of the seamen, as tall and thin as his companion was short and stocky, had been watching the small family group since it was light enough to see. When he spoke Josh recognised the voice of the man who had tried to make them leave the boat the night before.

'Can you pull an oar?'

Josh shook his head wearily and licked salt-caked lips before replying.

'I've never had to – but I'll try if it will be any help.'

'Trying won't help none in this sea. It'd most likely turn us over. You can either row or you can't.'

'You'd best do some bailing and get rid of the water in the boat,' said the other seaman. 'There's a bucket in the locker just by you.'

The locker was built into the bow of the boat, and Josh had

been leaning against the door. Unfastening it with difficulty against the movement of the sea he saw a metal-bodied bucket amongst a jumble of other things. Pulling it clear he began bailing. A great deal of water had been shipped during the night, and Josh scooped up bucketful after bucketful and flung it over the side.

The waves still heaved themselves high above the boat but they no longer fought with each other. They were now long swollen rollers, each following its precedessor, undefeated and hugely powerful, vast muscles of the sea. It was almost as though the sinking of *Pride of Liverpool* had been the sole objective of the fierce storm. Now it had been accomplished nature was relaxing. Only occasionally did the wind ruffle the creamy crests of the waves, and already the sky was lighter than it had been for days.

When Miriam raised her head to him Josh was shocked by her appearance. There was a great weariness in her eyes, and fatigue had etched deep lines on her face, but easing the sleeping Daniel to a more comfortable position in her arms she mustered a wan smile.

'We're safe now, Miriam. The storm is nearly over.'

'And the ship? Has it gone?'

It was the sailor who had suggested Josh begin bailing who answered her.

'The ship wouldn't have lasted more'n five minutes after we got away, missus.'

'What about all the others . . . ?'

Miriam did not complete her wide-eyed question.

The seaman shook his head. 'It's a miracle any of us is here. There were times during the night when I didn't expect to see the light of day again. Aye, it's a miracle right enough.'

He leaned on an oar that was thicker around than his own brawny arm.

'Seeing as how we're likely to be in each other's company for a while, we'd best introduce ourselves. Sam Speke from Kent, missus. A sailor all me life.'

He inclined his head towards the man on the seat behind him. 'And that's Isaiah Dacket.'

'I'm Josh Retallick. This is Miriam and my son Daniel.'

Sam Speke nodded acknowledgement, and the other man whose eyes had not left Miriam since she woke now shifted his gaze to Josh.

'You're the one who came aboard as a convict at Falmouth.'

For a moment Josh was genuinely startled by the words. The events of the night had cast away thoughts of everything else. Now he remembered and his spirits sank.

'Yes.'

'You was leading a riot in which some soldiers got killed, so I heard.'

'Then you heard wrong. I was trying to stop a riot, not lead one.'

Josh did not expect the seaman to believe him. Why should he? The jury at the Assize Court in Bodmin Town had not believed him. They had found him guilty. But it was no longer of any real significance. The fury of the storm, its power and destructive capability had shown the decisions of man to be trivial by comparison.

Yet Josh wished his past life might have sunk with *Pride of Liverpool* and allowed him to emerge from it a free man.

The son of a Cornish copper miner, Josh had received an exceptional education from the local Wesleyan preacher, William Thackeray. As a result he had been able to serve an apprenticeship and become an engineer in the mine where his father worked.

The same preacher had also schooled Miriam, who had been Josh's girl-friend since she was a barefooted girl running wild on the Cornish moor. When her father had been tragically killed at the hands of a group of vengeful miners led by Josh's father, Thackeray had married Miriam — even though she was carrying Josh's child.

But William Thackeray taught more than reading and writing, and it was a mutual interest in a union of miners that brought the three of them together again — for a brief while. It was not long before the preacher caused a violent confrontation between soldiers and miners — after ensuring that Josh would arrive on the scene in time to take the blame for the disturbance.

Josh's only share in the riot was an eighteen-inch sabre-slash across his back and a musket-ball through his arm. It was enough to earn him a sentence of transportation for life.

Only the determination and influence of Josh's former employer had secured for Josh the status of 'privileged prisoner' travelling on a passenger ship with a cargo of mine-engines to be installed in an Australian copper mine. It was this same man who had also arranged for Miriam and Daniel to travel on the same ship after she had left her husband. It was to be their chance to begin a new life together. Miriam had joined *Pride of Liverpool* as Miriam Retallick, and Josh had the satisfaction of knowing that this part of their secret at least would be safe.

'It doesn't matter, Josh. It doesn't matter.'

His mind came back to the present to find Miriam grasping his hand and whispering urgently to him.

'Whatever crime he was supposed to have committed couldn't have been so bad, I reckon,' put in Sam Speke. 'Otherwise they'd never have let him roam free on the ship.'

'Not unless he's got some friends in high places,' retorted the scowling Isaiah Dacket.

Josh had been looking at Miriam. Now he turned his head and raised his eyes to Isaiah Dacket's face. The sailor held his gaze defiantly for a few moments before his resolution wavered and he looked away. Angrily, he pushed the heavy oar an arm's length away from him as though it was to blame for his sudden discomfort.

Isaiah Dacket was deeply resentful of Josh's privileged treatment for a reason unknown to the others. The tall seaman had himself suffered the rigours of imprisonment – but with no one ready or able to help him. Isaiah Dacket had been taken prisoner when he was involved in the sale of other human beings, a willing crewman on a French slave-ship.

An orphan, Isaiah Dacket had been placed in the Royal Navy by the Parish when he was eleven years of age. Eight years later he was a deserter. It was then he discovered the money to be made by a seaman with no principles. He had no qualms about being part of such a trade. Indeed, he enjoyed it. For the first time in his life Isaiah discovered men whose lot in life was more wretched than his own – and they had with them women who were there for the taking.

But such a way of life could not last. More and more countries were outlawing slavery and making determined attempts to stamp it out. One morning, a day out from west Africa, the slave-ship was surprised by a French man-of-war. Isaiah spent two years in a stinking French prison where his suffering owed as much to his attitude towards the authorities as to his slaving activities.

Released under the terms of an obscure amnesty, Isaiah immediately returned to the sea on an English merchantman. He carried with him a hatred of Frenchmen and enough dark memories to bring him awake in a cold sweat in the middle of the night.

Isaiah Dacket could never forgive Josh for not having suffered as he had – or for having a woman of his own. One who had not been bought for a specified time, cash in advance. There had been no love in Isaiah's life, and, though he would have poured scorn on anyone who put it into words, he was fiercely envious of any man who had the love of a woman.

'If we stay out here talking and glaring at one another, we won't reach land until nightfall,' said Sam Speke.

'Land? Where?' Their tiredness suddenly forgotten, both Josh and Miriam scrambled to their knees in the bottom of the boat and peered out over the bow. The sudden movement woke Daniel. He sat upright in Miriam's arms, clinging tightly to her as his eyes sought something familiar in these extraordinary surroundings.

Josh and Miriam were eager for a first sight of land, but as each wave carried them upwards they looked into the sunrise in vain.

It was some minutes before Josh realised that what they could see on the horizon was not the gold of a tropical sunrise but a high bank of sand rising from the water's edge and extending for as far as could be seen.

Excitedly he pointed it out to Miriam and their son. Daniel was unimpressed.

'I'm hungry!' he exclaimed, with all the indignation of a three-year-old.

'If we got rid of some of this water in the bottom of the boat, we'd reach shore a lot sooner and find something to eat,' grumbled Isaiah Dacket.

Josh had already decided he did not like the surly Dacket. He would never be able to forget his attempt to prevent them from embarking in the boat during those last terrifying minutes on board *Pride of Liverpool*. He wondered how many others had been turned away from sanctuary in the boat.

Miriam could have been reading his thoughts.

'Do you think any other boats got away?'

Josh shrugged. 'Perhaps – but I doubt whether many passengers were in them.'

They might never know. In this sea a boat could be a mere hundred yards away and remain hidden.

Josh's glance went back to the tall swarthy sailor, and Miriam saw it.

'Don't let him rile you, Josh. We're alive. What was said last night is past. If it hadn't been for the sailors, we should have drowned.'

Josh remembered the tiny fingers slipping from his wrist. He fell silent and resumed bailing with excessive vigour.

It was early afternoon before they reached the shore. The fickle wind seemed reluctant to release them and veered round to westward, blowing from the shore. It was infuriating because the land was so tantalisingly close that grit blown from the sand dunes stung their faces and ground between their teeth.

Not until the ebbing tide turned did the boat begin to move in towards the beach again. By now the two seamen were near to exhaustion, their shirts soaked with the perspiration caused by pulling at the heavy oars in the heat of the fierce midday sun.

But the long delay in landing gave Josh ample opportunity to examine the strange and forbidding coastline in some detail. What he saw was not reassuring. The beach was a wide strip of sand heavily studded with rocks and long dark reefs. Behind it the sand dunes they had first sighted rose to great heights, their rounded slopes chiselled into concentric patterns by the wind.

The boat was only yards from the beach when Josh looked out over the side and suddenly saw a low barrier of glistening black rock protruding from the sea immediately ahead of them.

'Look out! Rocks!'

Sam Speke instantly dug his oar into the water in an attempt to slow the boat. His companion was less quick to react. Isaiah Dacket gave one more powerful stroke, causing the boat to slew sideways on to the beach. It was picked up by the next breaker, and seconds later the small party suffered their second shipwreck in the space of twenty-four hours.

The boat was dashed sideways against the reef, and with the sound of splintering wood ringing in their ears the occupants were flung into the water.

Held by the rocks the boat lay on its side for a moment or two until the next wave turned it upside down and carried it in towards the shore.

Josh floundered towards Daniel, who was choking and screaming a few feet from him. As he caught the boy and lifted his head clear of the water Josh's feet touched solid sand. He reached out a hand for Miriam and they waded ashore coughing and choking from the salt water they had swallowed.

Behind them the two seamen fought to drag the boat in through the surf that pounded heavily against the shore. Handing the badly frightened Daniel to Miriam, Josh went to their aid.

The three men righted the boat and, helped by the breakers, dragged it on to the beach. Waiting for the water to drain out through a foot-wide hole punched in the bottom, they heaved the boat up beyond the highest line of sun-dried seaweed.

As well as the hole, half a dozen of the planks had sprung apart. The longboat would never put to sea again.

'You should have seen those rocks,' exclaimed Isaiah Dacket angrily. 'Look at the bloody boat now – smashed.'

'It got us ashore safely,' retorted Josh. 'That's the main thing.'

'Is it? You don't know where we are. This is the place called the Skeleton Coast – and you'll soon see why. There's been many a fine ship wrecked here, and you'll find the bones of hundreds of good seamen picked clean by the crabs and bleached by the sun. Ashore we may be. Safe? I doubt it.'

Spitting scornfully on to the sand, Isaiah Dacket strode away to wade into the sea and recover an oar that was floating close inshore.

'Don't take no notice of Isaiah, Mr Retallick,' said the more affable Sam Speke. 'He's not the happiest of men but he's as fine a seaman as you'll find anywhere.'

'He's going to have to learn to be a good landsman,' commented Josh. 'Otherwise he'll be even more miserable.'

Turning away, he walked over to where Miriam was stripping the clothes from Daniel. After wringing the water from them she laid them out on the sand to dry. The sun beating down on them was so hot that steam began rising immediately.

'He's not worried, anyway.' Miriam smiled, nodding in Daniel's direction. His recent ducking and protested hunger already forgotten, the small boy sat enjoying his nakedness. Picking up handfuls of dry sand, he allowed it to escape between his fingers. All the drama of the shipwreck and the storm were already fading in his memory.

'You'd best put some clothes about the boy's shoulders, missus. This sun's fierce enough to peel the skin off an orange.'

As Miriam hurriedly put Daniel's wet shirt about his shoulders, Josh helped Sam Speke to pull the wet canvas sail from the holed boat's locker. It was stiff and heavy, but with it they could rig a shelter that would keep the sun off and allow the breeze to pass beneath it and help cool them.

When it was done Miriam put Daniel in its shade.

'What now, Josh?' she asked quietly.

Standing beside him, her hair hung damp and lank about her shoulders and her eyes appeared abnormally large in her tired face, but she was still able to stir feelings inside Josh that had no place here at this time.

'I want to go up to the top of those dunes and see what's on the other side.' Josh looked along the empty shoreline. 'We might even see some more survivors – or perhaps a boat.'

Miriam knew as well as Josh that no others had escaped from the ship with their lives, but it was not a thought to put into words just yet. The memory of their own skirmish with death was too cose.

'I'll come up there with you,' Sam Speke said to Josh. 'It'll be better if there are two of us; there's no telling what might be about. It looks empty enough from here, but this is a strange land.'

'I'd rather you stayed with Miriam and the boy,' Josh said pointedly.

'Isaiah'll do that,' replied the seaman. Then he caught Josh's expression.

'Oh, don't you worry about him. He'll have plenty to do.' Securing a loose rope on the canvas, he called to the tall seaman.

'Me and Mr Retallick's climbing up to the top of the dunes to see if there's anything about. While we're gone you can get a fire going and catch some fish for our supper. There's a good hook and line in the boat's locker.'

'You giving the orders now, Sam Speke? Fancy yourself as the bos'n of this party, perhaps?'

'All I fancy is fish for supper.'

'How can Isaiah get a fire going?' asked Josh as he paused to look back on the first gentle slope of the dunes.

'The same way as any sailor lights his pipe on a wet and stormy night,' replied the burly sailor, pulling a pigskin pouch from inside his shirt. 'A seaman learns on his first trip how to keep his baccy dry and the way to light it whatever the weather. By the time we get back there'll be a good fire going and fish to eat.'

After the first slope the going became harder. The soft coarse sand slid away beneath their feet and they sank ankle-deep with every step.

They struggled upwards but arrived at the ridge only to find a higher one beyond it. It was the same picture when they conquered that one. There was always one more that was higher. By now Josh's legs felt as though they had weights attached to them. Two months on board ship had done nothing to tone up his leg muscles. The two men climbed for an hour, yet when Josh turned around he was still close enough to the beach for Miriam and Daniel to return his wave.

The two men rested for a while on the next ridge. Sand dunes stretched on either side like a vast crumpled blanket, and they could see the narrowing ribbon of beach curve away until it was lost in the shimmering haze of distance. Beyond it was the sea. Calm now, it was coloured a deep dark blue with here and there a patch of light-green shallows, or a white-fringed black reef. In other circumstances Josh would have looked at it and thought it incredibly beautiful.

In the whole of the vast panorama the three people on the beach below them provided the only sign of life. In the burning heat of the tropical afternoon not even a bird stirred.

'Do you think anyone else got off the ship?' Josh asked the question, seeking confirmation of his own belief.

The seaman shook his head slowly. 'No. There wasn't a chance for any of 'em. We had but four boats on the whole ship, and I saw two of them smashed myself. I reckon the other one went the same way. Even if it had been lowered it would have gone straight down on to the rocks. No, Mr Retallick, there's only us left alive from the old *Pride of Liverpool*.'

'Then why didn't we try to get more people off with us in our boat? It would have held twenty or thirty others.'

Sam Speke looked everywhere but at Josh's face. 'It was the only way, Mr Retallick, believe me it was. In a shipwreck you've got to act quick. Them as is there gets away with their lives. Them as isn't don't. I've seen it all before and so has Isaiah. I was wrecked once on the Scillies and once on the coast of Jamaica. It was off the Scillies where I saw a brave captain make the crew of his boat stay close to the ship until they'd picked up so many survivors the boat became top heavy and capsized. All of 'em was drowned.'

He looked at Josh now. 'I don't expect you to understand, Mr Retallick, but you and your family are on land and alive. You remember that whenever you get to thinking we should have done something else.'

There was a note of aggressiveness in Sam Speke's voice that told Josh far more than the seaman's words. For all his reasoning the burly seaman knew he had behaved in a cowardly manner on *Pride of Liverpool* at the height of the storm. He had thought only of saving his own life. He would deny it and defend his motives vehemently, but the truth of it would stay with him for ever.

However, Josh found it easier to accept his explanation knowing Miriam and Daniel had been brought ashore safe and well.

Sam Speke sent dry sand trickling from one hand to the other. 'There's been more ships than enough wrecked along this coast. I can't recall hearing of anyone being taken off afterwards. It isn't called the Skeleton Coast for nothing. A wise captain keeps his ship well offshore from it. It's a place to know about from over the horizon. We can't hope that any vessel will pass close enough to see us.'

He dropped the sand to the ground and stood up. Dusting his hands against his trousers, he gave Josh a faint smile. 'Come to think of it, I've never heard tell of anyone going inland and living to boast about it, either. But I don't suppose that's going to stop us from climbing up that next ridge to look and see what's there.'

Miriam searched along the beach for small pieces of wood while Isaiah tore two of the thwarts from the boat and split them into long splinters with the aid of his seaman's knife. Miriam was surprised at the amount of wood to be found half-embedded in the sand, some of it well above the high-tide mark She thought it had doubtless been carried there by some great storm even worse than the one they had survived. One old plank was drilled with worm holes large enough to put her fingers inside, but it was dry and helped the fire get away to a good start.

As the first flames burst into life Isaiah fed it with wood shavings while Miriam knelt beside it and fanned it into life.

When the flames were biting into the larger pieces of wood Miriam brushed a long tress of hair back over her shoulder and looked up with eyes smarting from the smoke. Isaiah was standing close, looking down at her, and there was something in his eyes that made her body go suddenly tense. Slowly she rose from the sand to face him.

'You're a handsome woman to be married to a convict,' said the seaman.

Miriam did not correct him.

'What I am is of no concern to you.'

'I like spirit in a woman—just so long as her man has some control over it.'

'What you like is your own business. But I advise you to choose your words carefully in front of Josh.'

'You don't have to worry about me. Isaiah Dacket knows when to hold his tongue. I know a few other things too. You remember *that* when we get to where there's people. Your husband's a convict, sentenced to transportation. Any influential friends he might have are a long way from these parts.'

The seaman gave Miriam what might have been an attempt at a smile.

'You'll need someone to look after you when he's gone.'

'Taking good care of my son as well, of course?'

The sarcasm was lost on Isaiah Dacket.

'I'd treat him right. You wouldn't have to worry about that.'

Maintaining her self-control cost Miriam a great effort.

'Isaiah Dacket, I think you'd better save all that breath you're wasting for catching fish – and I hope you'll have a lot more success or we'll all starve to death.'

Isaiah Dacket turned away without a change of expression. Taking the line from the boat he made his way down to the water's edge.

Josh and Sam Speke returned just before the sun sank over the glittering horizon. A number of large fish were cooking on makeshift spits over the fire, and the two men sank to the ground within reaching distance of the sizzling food.

As they ate, Daniel leaned against Josh, worn out from the heat of the tropical day and the bewildering turn his young life had taken. He tried to stay awake to eat all the hot fish Miriam fed to him, but once the edge of his hunger had been dulled he found it hard going.

'Well? Is neither of you going to say more than "This fish tastes good"? What did you see from up there?'

Miriam put the question even though their very silence told her the climb to the top of the dunes had been a waste of time.

'There was nothing to see,' replied Josh.

'Only plenty of sand,' corrected Sam Speke.

'How far could you see?'

Miriam tried to glean some hope from their terseness.

'Twenty miles. Twenty-five, perhaps.'

'And there is nothing but sand for that distance inland?'

Josh nodded glumly.

'Well, we did think there could have been a mountain or something well to the south,' said Sam. 'At least, Josh saw it. I wasn't so sure. Not that it would make any difference,' he finished lamely. 'It would just be rock instead of sand, that's all.'

The news was depressing but it came as no surprise to anyone.

Night descended very rapidly in this part of the world, and as Isaiah Dacket lifted another spit of fish from the fire and threw on a piece of wood firefly sparks rose from it and chased each other into a star-sprinkled darkness.

'We'll have to move off first thing in the morning and find water,' said the tall seaman. 'The keg in the boat's dry. Without water we'll be lucky to last through the day.'

'That's true enough, Josh' – the burly Sam Speke had dropped the formal 'Mr Retallick' at Josh's insistence – 'it gets terrible hot in these parts. We've got to have water.'

'That needn't bother us. Not while we're by the sea,' Josh replied. 'We've got all the water we need.'

Isaiah snorted in disgust. 'You drink that and we'll have to tie you down. Sea water puts madness into a man's blood. But I doubt if a landsman would know about such things.'

'No,' agreed Josh quietly, 'but any man who's had anything to do with making engines knows how to purify water. Was the bucket saved when the boat capsized?'

'Yes,' Miriam answered. 'We've got two buckets from the boat's locker under the canvas – one metal, the other leather.'

'Good. What else is in there?' Isaiah Dacket was curious.

'There's some rope; a piece or two of canvas; a boat-hook; anchor; couple of tin mugs. . . .'

'Then we've got all the things we need to purify sea water and take plenty with us.'

Sam Speke looked at Josh as though he had pronounced he would turn the sand into gold.

'It's easy enough, Sam.' Josh smiled at the seaman's disbelief. 'It simply involves boiling the sea water and cooling the steam quickly. Then all we have to do is collect the water that forms.'

The seaman looked no less awed.

'Don't worry about it. You'll see for yourself tomorrow. However, it's going to take time to fill that fresh-water keg. We'll be here for a couple of days. The best thing we can do is get plenty of rest and eat as much fish as we can catch. We can salt some, too, with the salt we collect from the sea water. Then we'll be leaving here better prepared to face a journey.'

'So now everyone gets to be captain,' said Isaiah Dacket. 'No doubt it'll be the woman and the boy's turn tomorrow – while I'm left to catch all the fish.'

'If you do as well as you did today, you'll have done enough,' said Josh. 'Now I suggest we make up that fire and get some sleep. I feel as though I haven't closed my eyes for a week.'

Josh, Miriam and Daniel were to sleep beneath the canvas awning while the two sailors took the inside of the boat. Although they had been wrecked on a tropical shore, the night was surprisingly cool. After wrapping some of the loose canvas about Daniel, Josh and Miriam lay down together on the unyielding sand and held each other close.

Since the night when Daniel had been conceived, high on Cornwall's Bodmin Moor, much had happened to keep the two of them apart. It was not until Josh had taken passage as a privileged prisoner on the ill-fated *Pride of Liverpool* bound for Australia that they had come together as man and wife. They were still learning to know each other again. Even having their bodies touch was a wonderful renewed experience for them both.

'Josh?' Miriam's whisper was very close to Josh's ear. 'What will we find when we leave this place? What are we looking for?' It was the tremulous query of a young girl, suddenly uncertain of what the future held.

'Who knows what we'll find? Maybe a village. A farm. People like ourselves. Sam says the Cape Colony is somewhere to the south of us. There are lots of people there. English and Dutch mostly.'

'How far away is that?'

'Sam didn't know. He's not exactly sure just where we are. But if we head south and get clear of this desert I'm sure we'll find them. I believe there are probably people inland too, but we can't risk trying to cross that sand.'

'And what happens when we do find them, Josh? What happens to us?'

He pulled her even closer and kissed her forehead.

'Don't worry about that now. There'll be a place for us. I'll turn my hand to anything to give us a living.'

'But you are still a convict as far as the rest of the world is concerned. What will happen when people find out?'

'Why should they find out? I was convicted in England. We're thousands of miles away from all that now.'

'No, Josh. Isaiah knows all about it. He'll talk to whoever will listen. He doesn't like you.'

Josh fell silent. The grim memories of prison and the horrors of the prison hulk flooded back to him. This time it would be worse. He would be tortured by the thought of what was happening to Miriam and Daniel, unprotected in a strange land. He determined that whatever happened he would not become a convict again and no man would send him back to prison.

Miriam was aware of the tight knot of unhappiness inside her man. She began to wish she had said nothing. Then she remembered Isaiah's words and knew she had been right to speak.

'Josh?'

'H'm?'

'Don't ever trust Isaiah, Josh. Whatever happens never put any trust in Isaiah Dacket.'

Again there was silence.

'Josh?'

'Yes?'

'I love you—and Daniel needs you. I'll kill anyone who tried to part us now. Don't let it happen, Josh.'

Josh felt her tears warm against his cheek and he held her to him until the soft whispering of the surf lulled them both to sleep.

CHAPTER THREE

As Josh had predicted, the distilling of the sea water was a slow process. The water had to be boiled in the metal bucket, the steam cooled in one upturned tin mug and allowed to drip into the other. It meant someone had to stay by the fire the whole time to transfer fresh water to the keg and ensure that none of the delicately balanced apparatus fell into the fire.

But there were compensations. The wind had dropped to a breeze coming off the sea and, although the weather was hot, it was not unbearably so, making the three days they spent at the spot where they had landed a pleasant interlude after the horrors of the storm.

It was an opportunity for Josh and Miriam to get to know their two companions.

There was nothing complicated about Sam Speke. He was a slow-moving, slow-thinking reliable man of infinite patience. He had taken it upon himself to look after Daniel, and nothing the small boy wanted was too much trouble for him. The burly seaman spent the whole of one afternoon making a wide-brimmed canvas hat and matching sleeveless jacket for the boy, stitching both items with a sailmaker's needle, using fishing-line for thread.

'There, that'll keep the sun from burning you,' he said, putting the home-made garments on the boy. Daniel paraded in them proudly and from that moment refused to take them off.

Isaiah Dacket was a very different character. Even when he was in a good mood he was taciturn to the point of rudeness. Much of the time he spent immersed in his own thoughts, excluding those about him. In worse mood he muttered to himself and glared angrily at anyone who spoke to him. His uncertain temperament provided additional fuel for Miriam's uneasiness about him.

Miriam had much time to think as she worked hard in a largely unsuccessful attempt to preserve the fish that Isaiah Dacket caught in plenty. She tried to pack into two days a method of curing that required nine, using the salt produced from the distilling. It was not long enough. Although she rubbed salt well in, and finished off the process by smoking the partially cured fish, the end result was an evil-smelling product that she was glad to pack away into the pouches that Sam Speke made from the invaluable canvas.

On their third day ashore the castaways received a grim reminder of the fate they had so narrowly escaped.

The outgoing tide left two bodies behind on the beach only a hundred yards from their fire. One was identified by the two seamen as a fellow-crewman from *Pride of Liverpool*. The other body was that of an unknown boy aged about sixteen. He was committed, nameless, to a shallow sand grave alongside the man whose rough-hewn cross declared him to be the late 'Brendan O'Keefe. Seaman. *Pride of Liverpool*. Died 23rd February 1846'.

The following morning the shipwrecked party moved off along a coastline shrouded in early-morning mist with the keg and the leather bucket full of fresh water. Each of the travellers wore a canvas hat made by Sam Speke and carried a canvas pouch of fish which was already registering a strong protest against the hasty method used for curing.

The men took it in turn to carry the eight-gallon keg between them, and Josh also had Daniel riding on his back in a make-shift canvas sling. They had with them the tin bucket, mugs, and a boat-hook which closely resembled a pike-staff. This, together with the two knives carried by the seamen, comprised their total armoury.

Their plan was boldly simple. They would head southwards, following the coast, until they encountered people.

It was hotter now they were moving, fully laden. The dawn mist was soon burned away and the sun blazed down upon them from a clear blue sky. Even the beach underfoot was hot, and they walked as close to the sea as possible to take advantage of the firm damp water-cooled sand.

Miriam had an additional problem that she tried to keep from the others. She steadied the pouch she carried with fingers that were stiff and painful, the skin cracked and raw from two days of plunging them in brine water and working rough-grained salt into the fish.

All that day they trudged along the water's edge on weary legs unused to such exercise. They covered fifteen miles and sighted two wrecks. The first was a few hundred yards out from the shore, only the stern protruding from the teeth of the reef that had torn it to pieces not many years before.

The second wreck was much older, and they reached it at the end of the day. It was twenty yards inland, protruding from the sand dunes as though it had been carried ashore and half-buried by a giant hand. The castaways had yet to learn that the sands of the Skeleton Coast were never still. They advanced and retreated as the mood and the wind took them.

They had been speculating on the strange shape of the wreck for the last two miles, its plump dumpy lines provoking a keen professional interest from the two seamen.

When they finally reached it they examined it in great detail, pointed out the unusual method used to fit together the now crumbling timbers.

'I've never seen the likes of this,' muttered Isaiah Dacket, walking around the wide rounded bow, the timbers of which had been scoured to a fine smoothness by the sand.

'I have, many years ago,' said Sam Speke thoughtfully. 'But she wasn't still sailing. She was laid up in Lisbon, as unseaworthy a ship as you'd find anywhere, fit only for the breakers — but the Portuguese wouldn't hear of it. Belonged to one of their great admirals years and years ago, so I was told. That ship had the same pot-bellied look about it as this one.'

'I expect it'll burn as well as English wood,' said Isaiah Dacket practically, tugging at a piece of the timber. It broke away with a sound like a musket-shot.

He was right. It burned well and threw out a good heat.

As no one seemed anxious to sample the fish Miriam had preserved they set about catching fresh fish.

There were some low rocky outcrops just off the shore, and the ebbing tide had left one or two small pools. It was Sam Speke who found the first huge crab. Nearly a foot across its shell, it scuttled sideways from the rocks into a pool as Sam approached.

The sailor stalked it cautiously until he was able to pounce upon it and grasp it without endangering his fingers in the hard bony claws. Holding it in the air, he called triumphantly to the others, 'This will make a fine meal. Quick, now, look around for more while I put this one into the bucket.'

The crab struggled valiantly, its powerful claws grabbing helplessly as it attacked the air, but there was no escape.

Between them they found an incredible nine large crabs, and as darkness fell they all sat around a blazing fire enjoying a meal of delicious crab meat.

'All it needs to round this off is some bread and soft butter and a pint of good strong ale,' said Sam Speke wistfully as he threw away the last piece of broken shell.

'I'd settle for a warm woman to share my bed,' said Isaiah Dacket softly to Sam Speke. 'It was just our luck to get one who brought her own man along.'

'What's ale?' asked Daniel.

'Ale?' Sam Speke reached out and picked up the boy, swinging him kicking into the air above his head, hoping the others had not heard Isaiah's comments. 'Well, now, ale is something that makes good men feel better, bad men feel worse and young fellows like you feel ill.'

Daniel's chuckles brought a smile to Miriam's face. She had not heard Isaiah's remark – but Josh had. He frowned, remembering what Miriam had said to him about the sailor on their first night ashore. He guessed the surly seaman must have said something to her while he and Sam Speke were away. He determined Miriam would not be left alone with Isaiah Dacket again.

That night their sleep was disturbed by thunder rumbling in the north-east. Once when Josh woke he could see lightning flickering in the sky beyond the lofty sand dunes. But it was far away, and when Miriam murmured in his arms and pulled him to her he quickly forgot the distant weather.

The next morning the sky was dark and glowering above them and lightning tracked an angry course downwards to the sand of the dunes. Thunder grumbled all about them, but it was the wind that was to prove most troublesome. The wind direction had changed during the night and now it blew from the hot sand inland in ever-increasing fury. It culminated in a furious sandstorm that they heard minutes before it arrived bringing a choking cloud of sand in its wake.

They barely had time to gather their handful of possessions and scramble to shelter on the lee side of the wrecked ship before the battering wind was upon them. Josh held his hands over Daniel's ears so he would not be frightened as the wind buffeted the shell of the old ship and it creaked and groaned at the ferocity of the onslaught. Fortunately, the ancient wreck had weathered many such winds and would not yield to this one.

For an hour the five people huddled together while wind and sand howled about them. The sand trickled into their ears, stung their eyes and collected about their lips. At the height of the storm the sand became so dense that they began to breathe it in and choke upon the cloying particles. Any available piece of cloth was held up to nose and mouth as they coughed up the lung-clogging sand. Kerchiefs, the end of Miriam's dress and men's shirts all found a new use.

Then, as suddenly as it had arrived, the wind passed on. Opening red-rimmed eyes, the five castaways saw the dense cloud of sand racing away in a funnel-like spiral across the grey Atlantic waters.

But this strange land had not yet exhausted its supply of surprises. While they still crouched in the shelter of the wreck, so covered in sand as to appear part of the dunes, there was a sudden eruption of the sea a mere twenty yards along the beach. As they watched in astonishment a glistening sleek head broke the surface of the water and a fat bull seal rode the next breaker up on to the beach. Wheezing and groaning, he heaved himself clumsily across the sand until he was at least twelve feet from the sea.

Not until then did he remember he had broken the natural laws of caution. Pausing, he raised his nose in the air and looked about him. His big soft brown eyes passed over the castaways, moved on – then swung back.

With a startled snort the big seal began to make a clumsy and desperate turn in the sand.

It was too late. The bull seal would pay the full price for his error. The two seamen jumped to their feet and sprinted the short distance that separated them from the seal, pulling knives from their belts as they ran. Josh was on his feet scrambling after them a split second later.

Isaiah was the first to reach the panic-stricken creature, throwing himself at it as it humped down the beach to the sea. It was a close race, but even as the creature's front flippers raised a splash from the edge of the ocean Isaiah buried his knife-blade in its throat. The bull seal tried to throw itself forward into the safety of deeper water, but Isaiah's knife flashed again, the blade a dull red in the poor light before it struck again. Then Sam Speke was there, and his knife pierced the blubber protecting the creature's ribs. Josh plunged into the water to help, and between them the three men rolled the dying seal back up the beach. Miriam pulled Daniel's head in towards her and turned her own face away so she would not have to see the look in the creature's too-human brown eyes.

It was all over in a matter of minutes. In the distance the thunder still grumbled and lightning illuminated a black-shrouded sky, but bright sunshine was pursuing the shadows along the beach. By the time it reached the ancient wreck Isaiah had slit the seal from throat to rear flippers and the men were congratulating themselves on their good fortune, the discomfort of the sandstorm forgotten. Even Isaiah Dacket looked happy as his fellow-seaman praised the speed with which he had moved.

'I never knew you could move so fast, Isaiah,' chortled Sam Speke. 'And look at the size of the creature! It must weigh five hundred pounds. We shan't go hungry for a while now.'

Isaiah, his arms coated to the elbows with a grisly mixture of blood and sand, resumed his natural dolefulness before replying. 'There's meat enough,' he agreed, 'but how long will it keep in this heat?'

'Don't worry about that.' Miriam overcame her revulsion now the soft-eyed creature was dead, though she still avoided looking at it. 'I'll get a fire going. Josh, you fetch a bucket of sea water. We'll need as much salt as we can possibly get – and you must dig a hole down where the sand is wet. We'll bury the meat as it's cut up. That way it will be out of the sun and will absorb salt water until I'm ready to rub more salt into it.

We'll try smoking some of it too. I think both methods will work better on this meat than they did on the fish. We can't possibly take it all with us, but I'll make sure we waste as little as possible.'

'How long will it take?' asked Josh.

Miriam shrugged, trying not to think of the pain in her fingers. 'Far longer than we've got if I were to do the job properly. But I'll do what I can in three days.'

While the two seamen continued their messy task Miriam got a fire started and, with Daniel 'helping', set to work tearing pieces of wood from the old wreck. Josh was down at the water's edge digging a pit in the wet sand, using his hands and a plank from the old ship's decking.

Isaiah paused to wipe the back of a bloody hand across his forehead and slap angrily at the flies that the wind had brought from inland and that gathered in buzzing black clouds about the seal meat. Seeing that the others were out of hearing, he spoke to his companion in a low voice.

'Do you think we'll ever see England again, Sam?'

The burly seaman grunted. 'There's a chance.'

'But not much of one with the convict and his family to slow us down.'

'I can't say as I've noticed them lagging behind.'

Sam Speke paused in his work to give the other man a long searching glance.

'Sam! Be honest, now. I know you're soft on the boy – and I fancy the woman – but we're shipwrecked. We've got to look after ourselves. Just as we did on board ship before this lot jumped into the boat with us.'

Sam Speke winced. 'I'm not proud of what we did then, Isaiah.'

'But we're *alive*, Sam. That's better than being dead. *You* know that.'

Isaiah brushed a trickle of perspiration from his nose, attacked the flies again and did another rapid check on the whereabouts of Josh and Miriam. They were both fully occupied.

'Listen to me, Sam. There's food enough for everyone now. We can leave on our own during the night. We'll take the water and as much meat as we can carry. They'll still have enough meat left to last them for a couple of weeks.'

'Only if they stay here. They won't be able to carry much off with them. And what are they supposed to do for water if we take it with us? They've got no means of lighting a fire once it's gone out.'

Isaiah Dacket hesitated a shade too long to convince Sam Speke that he really believed what he said next.

'They'll manage. He'll think of something. He's an engineer and much cleverer than the likes of you and me. Are you with me, Sam? Tonight?'

'And if we get to safety – to where there's civilised folk? I suppose you'll send 'em back here to find Josh and Miriam and Daniel?'

Isaiah Dacket thought his argument had won his shipmate over. 'Of course we will. Why, we'll be helping them, won't we? Getting them rescued quicker than if we carry on the way we're going with them in tow. You'll come, then, Sam?' His voice was a hoarse excited whisper.

'I wouldn't come with you, Isaiah Dacket – not if you promised to make me Admiral of the Queen's navy, I wouldn't.'

The tall seaman's mouth dropped open, but Sam Speke had not finished.

'I'm not used to having to sleep with one eye open Bristol fashion. That's what it would come to if I travelled with you. If we ran short of water or food, I wouldn't dare to let you behind me for fear I'd feel your knife in my back.' Sam Speke shook his head sadly. 'We were good shipmates in *Pride of Liverpool*, Isaiah, but I don't like the man you are shoresides.'

Isaiah Dacket's mouth clamped shut and he hacked savagely at the fat carcase of the seal.

'You're a fool, Sam Speke. You'll regret not taking this chance. They'll hold us back until we die in this God-forsaken country. You'll see. All the way to hell you'll regret you didn't heed my words.'

At that moment a very hot Josh came up the beach for the first of the meat for the water's-edge cache and the two seamen fell silent.

For the remainder of that day and far into the night they worked on the seal meat, cutting and storing, salting and smok-

34

ing. They also gorged themselves on the fatty meat. It smelled and tasted of fish, but Josh thought he had never tasted a finer steak.

They stayed at that camp for three more days. A Cornish country housewife would have thrown up her hands in horror at the methods used in an attempt to cure the seal meat as quickly as possible, but Miriam did her best with the resources she had. Her hands were much worse now, and there was no hiding their state from the others. Josh insisted that she keep them bound up with strips of her under-skirt while he and Sam Speke continued with the salting, but they did not appear to be healing.

They intended to carry with them as much smoked and salted meat as they could manage and, when they had sufficient, Miriam boiled down the inches-thick blubber and provided a bucket of seal oil to take with them.

The heat was great when they set off in the dawn of the fourth day. There was no cooling wind now. What wind there was still blew from the hot sand dunes inland. To make matters worse their fishy diet had brought Josh and Isaiah Dacket out in a crop of boils that did nothing to help either man's temper.

During the morning storm clouds blew up again and they could hear thunder grumbling away inland. They saw more of the dust spirals too. First one and then another snaked down the side of the dunes a mile ahead and spun out to sea, the spiralling plume of sand bending and changing shape with each unpredictable change of direction that was made.

'This is a terrible land.' Miriam eased her aching legs and tried to straighten her torn fingers as they made a midday halt. 'It's savage all through.'

'I don't think we've seen the half of it yet,' said Sam Speke. 'I've heard tales about this part of the world as would set your ears burning.'

'What sort of tales?' asked Josh.

'I'd rather not say, Josh.' Sam Speke threw a quick glance at Miriam. 'But sooner or later we'll meet up with the natives whose land this is and you'll likely see for yourself.'

'What he means is that if they say they fancy your woman it won't be for her looks. It'll be because they think she'll cook well.' Isaiah grinned maliciously.

Miriam looked to Sam Speke for confirmation and he shrugged uncomfortably. 'Take no notice of either of us, Missus Retallick. We're just repeating the old sailors' tales you hear on board ship. Neither of us has ever met anyone who's set foot here.'

'I'm quite sure Isaiah enjoyed telling us about it,' said Josh curtly. 'Now we've got something to look forward to. Let's get moving. Up you come, Daniel.'

The next day they were all in even worse shape. The sun shining on their faces had cracked their lips, and their legs and arms were chafed from the dried-in salt water in their clothes and the perspiration that ran from their bodies in the gruelling heat. Only Daniel was free from chafes and sores. But now there was a slight change in the featureless landscape. At first Josh thought he was mistaken, that perhaps the beach was wider here. But by midday they were all sure. The sand dunes were flattening out with clumps of thick coarse grass dotted here and there. Then, most exciting of all, they saw the peaks of a small range of mountains standing mauve against the blue sky far inland from them.

Another mile and the grass had become thicker and there was even an occasional bush. Finally, ahead of them the sand dunes disappeared altogether and they could see trees.

It gave the party a new lease of life. They stumbled forward excitedly, expecting at any moment to catch their first glimpse of people, convinced that their ordeal in the scorching sun was almost over.

But they did not know this part of south-west Africa, were unaware that for every promise made the land demanded a dozen disappointments in payment.

Their first was not long in coming.

What had appeared from a distance to be an expanse of flat featureless country turned out to be the estuary of a mile-wide sluggish river, oozing muddy brown water that stained the sea as far as the horizon.

Unslinging the heavy bundle from her shoulder, Miriam sank wearily to the ground, disappointment adding to the pain in her fingers and sore limbs. Josh eased Daniel from his back and, freed from restraint, perspiration ran down past the waistband of his trousers.

True to character, it was Isaiah who voiced the despair they all felt at encountering what was an unsurmountable barrier at the very place where they had been hoping their troubles would be at an end.

"We'll never cross that! We're finished. We might just as well give up and die now.'

'If you die here, you'll die alone,' said Josh firmly. 'As soon as we're rested we'll head up-river towards those mountains.'

'Walk inland? You're mad! How far away do you think those mountains are? They must be fifty or even sixty miles from here. It'll get hotter with every step you take away from the sea and, if the heat doesn't kill you, you'll die of starvation. Besides, what will you do when you get there? One place is much the same as another in this land, be it mountain or sand.'

'What's the alternative? To sit here chin in hands wishing we had a boat? No, we'll follow the river inland. At least we'll have water. If we can see nothing from the mountains, we'll discuss our next move then. You with us, Sam?'

'Of course I am – and so is Isaiah. He knows it's the only way for us to go. Isn't that so, Isaiah?'

The tall seaman glared at each of the two men in turn, then without a word took a tin mug from his bag and went to the water-keg.

'It's all right, Josh. He'll be with us, you'll see,' Sam Speke said in a low voice.

Josh shrugged. He was becoming impatient of Sam Speke continually making excuses for his companion. 'He can please himself. The hell with him. I've got my own family to look after.'

'If either of you has anything to say about me, then out with it. Don't whisper behind my back.' Isaiah threw the tin mug to the ground petulantly. 'I expect such goings-on from a convict, but not from you Sam. All right, I'll tell you what I think about going inland to those mountains. Look at us. We're covered in sores and boils. The woman can scarce pick anything up because of her torn fingers. If it was just Sam and me, I'd give it a try. Without the woman and the, boy we'd stand a chance. With them we might just as well stay here and wait for death. They've been a drag on us ever since we got off the ship.'

'Oh! Stop this stupid quarrelling.'

Miriam got to her feet as quickly as she could, willing her legs not to buckle beneath her.

'I'm as ready to move on as anyone else. So is Daniel.' She saw Josh's sudden grimace of pain as he moved. The boils on his legs and arms were worse than the others'. 'It's all right, Josh. Daniel can walk for a while. If anyone slows us down, it won't be a Retallick.'

'You don't have to force yourself to go on because of anything Isaiah says.' Josh was angry. 'We'll rest a while longer.'

'No, Josh. It's all right; really it is.' Miriam put a hand on his arm and squeezed it reassuringly. 'And it's time we moved on. We've got a couple of hours of daylight left. Let's make the most of it.'

They followed the course of the river until dusk, making perhaps four more miles. The mountains seemed no closer, but the nature of the country had changed yet again. The tall sand dunes were still dominant to the north, but down here by the river there was green grass backing off from the mud at the water's edge. Farther away from the water coarse spiky grass thrust upwards from the sandy soil, and there were many bushes and a few stunted trees.

There were also birds. They first saw them close to the estuary – tall long-legged birds standing higher than a heron in the water, curved dark beaks disturbing the water as they sifted it noisily, heads questing from side to side.

The birds took little notice of the small party of humans walking close by until Daniel ran towards them clapping his hands in excitement; then they took to the air with a clatter of noise, exposing the pink underside of their wide wings. They moved in a fluctuating pink cloud to the far side of the muddy river, leaving the newcomers to this land of surprises marvelling at their collective beauty.

That night the party camped on the river-bank alongside a dead tree whose trunk and branches were ravaged by the tunnelling of ants. Here they had their first encounter with mosquitoes. The insects descended in dense clouds, zooming and stinging and making life very uncomfortable. Not until the castaways had a good fire going with smoke billowing about them did the mosquitoes look elsewhere for a bloody meal.

But later that night the camp received a call from a much more dangerous visitor.

Everyone was asleep and the fire had burned low when Josh suddenly came awake. He was a light sleeper and knew an unusual sound had brought him awake. He lay listening for some minutes, the night seeming deep and still. Then he heard the sound again. It was a soft nerve-tingling cough — but it came from no human throat.

His heart pounding, Josh rose slowly and silently, standing clear of Daniel and Miriam. Across the dying fire someone else was awake and on his feet.

'Is that you, Josh?' Sam's hoarse whisper reached across to him.

'Yes. What's out there?'

'I don't know — but I saw its eyes. They were big and yellow like a cat's. Put some more wood on the fire. Maybe if we build it up whatever it is will go away.'

Josh picked up a length of the dead tree and, stirring up the ashes, provoked a flicker of life. Putting the piece of wood on the dull red ashes, he followed it with another.

From the darkness there was a sharp rattling cough. This time it came from a different place.

A piece of dry bark on the fire flared briefly and the light was reflected in two yellow eyes. At that moment the cough became a growl and the creature of the night bounded in to the attack.

At first Josh could see only the eyes, but then the heart of the fire shifted and he glimpsed the sand-coloured body of a leopard.

A sound, half-fear, half-bravado, left Josh's throat. At the same time there was a bellowed 'Haaa!' from Sam Speke as he lunged across the clearing with the outstretched boat-hook to intercept the leopard's charge, scattering the fire in a shower of sparks.

The makeshift naval spear took the animal in the ribs and it rounded on Sam with snarling spitting anger, but the noise of human voices accomplished more than the boat-hook. A concerted shout from Josh and Sam Speke caused the animal to lope off into the night.

In the last hectic few moments Josh had tripped over the water-keg and now he rose to his feet shakily, aware that a tawny death had passed very close to him.

'What's all the noise?'

'What's going on?'

Isaiah made his enquiry from one side of the fire as Miriam held Daniel to her and called from the other side.

'It's all right. It was only some animal come to see what we were doing here. That's all,' said Sam Speke.

'Thanks to your quick thinking "seeing" was all it did. I'm in your debt, Sam.'

'I'm sure we'll owe each other more than that before we're out of this, Josh. I didn't do nothing.'

Sam Speke was embarrassed by Josh's thanks.

'What was it, Josh. *What* nearly happened?'

'Everything's all right, Missus Retallick. You get the boy to sleep again. You'll be all right now. We scared the creature off. It won't come back again.'

'Then why's the water-keg turned over on its side spilling water everywhere?' asked Isaiah.

Josh seized hold of the keg and turned it right side up, but most of the contents had already spilled out on to the dusty ground. Anxiously shaking it, Josh estimated it now held no more than a gallon. This was a disaster.

Josh showed his dismay.

Sam said: 'We can get more water in the same way as we got this. We couldn't have fixed you up so easy. Don't you worry about it. Get back to sleep if you can. I'll sit here and keep watch for a while just to make sure that creature's gone.'

'We ought to take it in turns,' declared Josh.

'You two do what you like,' grumbled Isaiah. 'I've seen nothing. All that's woken me is you two shouting about something you imagine you saw. I'm going to sleep.'

'You too, Josh,' said Sam Speke. 'If it makes you feel any better, I'll give it a couple of hours then wake you. You can take the watch until dawn.'

Josh agreed and lay down beside Daniel and Miriam. But before he slept he had to tell Miriam what had happened to waken the camp.

Miriam reached across Daniel and her torn hands gripped Josh's very tightly when he had finished his story.

'I knew from the very beginning that I liked Sam Speke,' she said in a choked voice. 'Now I know why. He's a good man, Josh.'

In spite of his frightening experience Josh was soon asleep again and Sam Speke never woke him. He remained awake until the sky glowed red in the pre-dawn; then he, too, fell asleep.

Josh woke and saw him crouched against the tree-trunk, his arms hugging the boat-hook to him, and he managed a smile. He was making up the fire when Isaiah threw off his canvas blanket and climbed to his feet to make off in the direction of the river. He returned in such a hurry Josh thought he must have seen the leopard.

'What is it?'

'It's the river. . . . It's gone!'

'Gone? Don't be so—'

'Then have a look for yourself!'

Isaiah's shouting woke the others, and as Josh ran up the brief slope that separated them from the river Sam Speke lumbered after him.

Incredible though it was, Isaiah had been telling the truth. The water had gone. There was now nothing between them and the far bank but a wide trough of flat mud that was already hardening in the early-morning sun.

'I've never seen the likes of this before.' Sam Speke rubbed the sleep from his eyes as though he was still dreaming. 'One day there's a mile-wide river, the next morning it's gone! What do you make of it, Josh?'

'It must have something to do with those storms we've been seeing in the direction of the mountains. There's been a lot of rain up there and it must have run off down this river-bed. From the look of it now I'd say it stayed dry for most of the year.'

'And so will we if we don't get some water pretty quickly,' volunteered Isaiah. 'There's not much left in this keg. Now the river's gone we'd best get across and head back for the coast again.'

'I'd still like to get to those mountains and have a good look at this country from the top,' declared Josh.

'That's madness!' exclaimed Isaiah. 'Even you must see that, Sam. If we follow the coast, we've got a source of water and food – and we'll be heading towards the Cape settlements. Going inland doesn't make sense.'

Sam could not make up his mind. There was logic in his shipmate's argument, but he felt he owed Josh some loyalty.

Miriam provided him with a respite.

'Can I say something?' Without waiting for a reply she went on, 'I'm a bit worried about Daniel this morning. He's not very well. He's miserable and has a bit of fever. He's very sleepy, too. It isn't like him. I'd be much happier if we could stay here for today.'

'I thought the Retallicks wouldn't hold us up,' gloated Isaiah, throwing Miriam's words of the previous day back at her.

'Of course we'll rest up today. We could all do with it. We've been pushing ourselves pretty hard and the little chap's done very well,' said Sam Speke. 'It'll give us a chance to look for water in the river-bed and make up our minds what we're going to do. Personally I can't see why we shouldn't do as Josh suggests.'

Isaiah showed his displeasure by wandering off on his own.

Daniel slept for most of the morning and seemed a little brighter at midday when Sam Speke brought him a roughly carved boat he had made from a piece of wood found along the bank of the dried-up river.

Daniel was pleased with the small gift and immediately began pushing it through a sand sea at his feet.

'That was very thoughtful of you, Sam,' said Miriam. 'There's not much in this country for a small boy.'

'It was nothing. I enjoyed making it. I've whittled many of them on board ship. When I have the time I'll make a really good one for him.'

This was the first opportunity Miriam had found to have a private talk with the seaman. With the other two men out seeking water in the river-bed she determined to make the most of it.

'Do you have any sons of your own, Sam?'

'No, Missus Retallick. I've been at sea since I was eight and never found the time to take a wife, let alone settle down and raise a family.'

'Since you were eight? That was a very young age to be going to sea.'

'Well, it wasn't really being at sea at first—not on a merchant-man, that is. My father was a fisherman. I used to go out with him. Then his boat was wrecked and my father lost, so I took on as a seaman in a deep-sea boat. I was twelve by then.'

Miriam looked at him sympathetically. 'You've had a hard life, Sam.'

The seaman looked surprised. 'Hard? No, it's been a good life mostly. Better than Isaiah's. You mustn't think too badly of him, Missus Retallick. He never knew either of his parents and was brought up by the Parish. They sent him off to sea as soon as he was big enough to hold a rope. He's had to fight for every-thing he wanted for as long as he can remember. It's not easy for him to understand that others aren't the same.'

'You're probably right, Sam. All the same I wish we had two like you here instead of Isaiah Dacket.'

Sam Speke coloured up and, mumbling that they would have no real trouble with Isaiah, he excused himself, saying that he wanted to look for the leopard's tracks.

It was another hour before everyone returned to the camp for a meal of near-rancid seal meat. While they were eating they discussed the events of the night and their future movements. To Josh's surprise he found that the others had accepted they would go on to the mountains. Even Isaiah raised no further objections and agreed they should move to a new camp before dark. Sam had found a site he was sure would afford them greater pro-tection should the prowling leopard return to trouble them.

Daniel was now noticeably better, and the move of a mere half-mile was quickly accomplished. The new camp was in the shelter of a tall pile of huge balancing boulders. They were the first large stones Josh had seen since coming ashore. With dense thorn-bushes on two sides they had only to build a fire in the gap that was left and they had a stockade to protect them against any animal of the night.

There was shade here, too, most important in the airless heat of the afternoon. During the last two days the heat had become almost unbearable. It bounced back from the sandy soil and left a haze dancing above the ground like smoke from a skillet of boiling fat.

Josh had managed to locate a reluctant source of water in the middle of the river-bed by digging a hole two feet deep with his hands. The water seeped into it slowly and never rose to more than a depth of two inches, but with patience it could be scooped up and poured into the keg using a tin mug.

The men took turns at this tedious task and in the heat of the afternoon Sam Speke was lying beside the hole with the sun beating down upon his back when he was surprised to have Isaiah join him.

The tall seaman's words quickly told Sam that he had not accepted the trek to the mountains as readily as Josh had believed.

'We'll be here for days at the rate that water's coming through.'

'That's all right. We haven't got a ship to catch.'

'We'll be lucky if we ever see a ship again, Sam,' Isaiah prophesied gloomily. When Sam Speke made no reply he went on, 'We could still go back to the coast – just you and me.'

'I thought we'd already decided that.'

'You mean *he's* decided it.' Isaiah jerked a derisory thumb in the direction of the camp. 'I didn't notice him paying much heed to what anyone else wanted.'

Sam Speke had asked both Josh and Miriam to make allowances for the tall seaman. Now he tried to do the same. The sea had been father and mother to Isaiah Dacket, and Sam Speke knew he was uneasy away from it.

'We'd make out, Sam. You and me. It'd be like it always was. If we go on with the convict, we'll never see other folks again. He doesn't want to find people.'

'Now, what sort of foolish talk is that? He wants to find them just as much as we do.'

'He doesn't, Sam,' Isaiah persisted. 'You're not thinking

about it. He's a convict. As soon as he gets to where there's decent folk he'll be sent off to Australia to serve out his sentence. It stands to reason that the longer he stays away from others the longer he remains a free man.'

Isaiah saw that Sam Speke remained unmoved and he changed his approach. 'I'm not blaming him, Sam. A man has to look after his own. But there's no reason why *we* should suffer for it.'

His thoughts not on what he was doing, Sam Speke stirred up the dirt in the bottom of the hole and it muddied the water. He left the mug there to wait for it to settle and turned to his companion.

'Isaiah, I told you once before what my feelings are about leaving the others and going on with you. I think I've got more chance of coming through alive if I stay with Josh. You had your chance to put a point of view and chose to say nothing. Now you come to me and talk of sneaking off in the night and leaving the others in the lurch. I wonder how tough things would have to be before you did the same to me?'

Isaiah began to protest that he would never do such a thing, but Sam Speke cut him short.

'Go away, Isaiah, before I forget we were shipmates and treat you as I would anyone else who suggested we left three people to face certain death.'

'You weren't so particular when we were helping each other to get off *Pride of Liverpool*,' retorted the tall seaman.

'No. But I think of it with shame, not as something to be proud of. You'd be a better man if you felt the same.'

'I'm still thinking as a man who intends coming out of this alive, Sam. That woman and boy have addled your brain. When you've got your senses back we'll talk about it again.'

Sam Speke watched the angry seaman walk away from him and wondered whether he ought to speak to Josh about him. He decided against saying anything. Relations were already strained between the two men. He would only make it worse. He turned back to the water in the hole. The dirt had settled now. He hoped that the same might happen with Isaiah – that if he were left alone his resentment of Josh might go away.

Because of their stockade they were able to sleep in safety that night, but they maintained a guard. Armed with only a seaman's knife and the boat-hook, his main task was to keep the fire built as high as was possible.

Josh took the first shift. The temperature fell quickly when the sun went down, and it was pleasant to sit close to the fire and look out across a land shaded to a soft silver by the ripe moon. It became even more pleasant when Miriam slipped from the shadow of the rocks and nestled against him in the circle of his arm.

'Do you think everyone on Sharptor is looking at the same moon tonight, Josh?'

Sharptor was the small mining community on Bodmin Moor from which they both came.

'It's nice to think they might be,' Josh replied softly. 'They seem so far away now.' He took one of her hands. The skin was healing slowly, but Miriam would always carry the scars to remind her of these weeks in her life. 'These last few years haven't been easy for you and they don't seem to be getting any better.'

'Oh, they are, Josh.' She squirmed in his arms and her shadowy dark eyes looked up at him. 'We're together, and that's all I've ever wanted. Here, Sharptor or Australia. The place isn't important. I just want to be able to look up and see you near. Then I can forget everything else.'

'But there's Daniel to think of. What of his future?'

Miriam gathered her thoughts before answering.

'He'll be all right, Josh. He'll grow up to accept all manner of things we've never dreamed of. He'll see more, learn more and achieve far more than he would had he stayed in a Cornish mining village. All he could have looked forward to there would be having to support me when he became old enough to work.'

'I wish I could be as certain as you. I must admit I've had second thoughts about coming inland. Am I being selfish, Miriam? Am I more eager to find a place where I can keep my freedom than in trying to locate other people? Or did I just dig my heels in because Isaiah was against coming inland?'

Miriam smiled. 'You wouldn't be a Cornishman if you didn't resent someone else telling you what you ought to do. But I believe you made the right decision. It was far too hot on the beach with no shade at all. We wouldn't have survived another week there. It will be cooler in the mountains.'

'I hope we'll find water too. I'm worried—'

'Sh! We've found enough water in the river-bed to last for a day or two. There will be water in the mountains and we'll find it. Have faith, Josh. We weren't brought together after such a long time to have everything end here in this strange land.'

Josh held her close and said nothing more.

CHAPTER FOUR

The next morning something so extraordinary happened that it might have been conjured up by Miriam's confident faith in their future.

Sam Speke had the dawn watch. He afterwards swore he had not slept – and the well-made-up fire supported his statement. Yet someone managed to come to within six feet of the camp and leave two ostrich-egg shells filled with water in full view.

It was not until Daniel woke that they were even noticed. His loud 'What's that?' and pointing finger began the mystery. None of the castaways had ever seen such huge eggs before, and they approached them very cautiously.

Josh was the first to remove the dried grass stuffed into a hole at the top of each egg and discover they held water. Isaiah tried to dissuade him from tasting it, saying it might have been poisoned, but Josh tilted one of the great eggs and poured some water into his hand. Transferring it to his mouth he declared that, though brackish, the water was every bit as good as their own.

Who their benefactors were nobody would hazard a guess. Sam Speke insisted they must be invisible spirits, and Isaiah Dacket shook his head unhappily.

'They can't mean any good by it. Why else would they sneak in without showing themselves?'

Miriam accepted the water as a welcoming gesture from the unknown people whose land they now found themselves in.

'If they meant us harm, they could have killed us all during the night,' she declared. 'As for not showing themselves – we are strangers. For all they know, we might kill *them*.'

She emptied the water from the eggs into the keg, and when they broke camp she left the empty shells lying on the sand.

That day they travelled only until noon. By then the heat had become unbearable. As soon as a suitable camp site was found they all collapsed into its shade. It was so hot that breathing became an effort. Not until the shadows grew long and the heat became less oppressive did they stir again.

The mountains looked no nearer than they had the day before. This, together with the knowledge that there were unseen humans about — friendly though they might be — helped to make it a subdued and unhappy camp that night.

Isaiah Dacket had the morning watch and he was determined not to be taken by surprise by the visitors of the previous night. As the dawn light grew brighter he stood up alert for anything that might occur.

For a long time there was nothing to be heard but the morning insect noises and the song of a solitary bird in a tree by the dried-up river-bed. Then Isaiah heard a faint sound in the bushes to one side of the camp. It sounded to him as though someone was creeping stealthily towards them. Seizing the boat-hook, Isaiah went out of the camp and made straight for the place where he thought he had heard the noise.

'All right, you come out of there. I know where you are.'

There was not a sound.

Isaiah began prodding the boat-hook into the bushes. There were too many large and sharp thorns on the branches for him to go searching for the natives he felt sure were hiding there. It did not occur to him that the same consideration would have kept others out.

'D'you hear me? Come on out, now.'

Again there was complete silence, and Isaiah began prodding angrily into the bushes and cursing noisily.

The sound woke the others, and Josh called to ask what was happening.

'There's someone in here,' growled the angry seaman. 'I'll have 'em out in a minute.'

'How do you know they are there?' asked Miriam. 'Did you see them when they left the water?'

'What water?'

Isaiah swung around to look at her.

Miriam pointed. There, standing upright on the sandy soil not two yards beyond the perimeter of the camp, were two ostrich eggs. One of them was actually standing in one of the footprints Isaiah had made when he had gone out in pursuit of their elusive benefactors.

Isaiah took it as a personal affront. Charging across to the bushes on the opposite side of the camp, he thrashed about with the boat-hook in a vain attempt to flush out those who he imagined had humiliated him.

It was ten minutes before he returned scratched and hot and scarcely able to contain his rage.

'If I had a musket, they wouldn't be so keen to make a monkey out of me. A musket-ball would find them soon enough, that's for sure.'

'You'd shoot someone – for giving you water?' Miriam was aghast.

Isaiah stood looking at her for a long time, his mind groping for a reply. Finally he said, 'Damn you, woman! I wouldn't expect you to understand.'

Aware of the grinning faces of Josh and Sam Speke he stomped to the fire and lit his pipe with his back to them.

'I wonder who these people are?' mused Josh as he picked up one of the eggs and gazed about the parched scrubby country.

'They'll show themselves in good time,' said Miriam. 'For now let's just be grateful to them.'

When Isaiah had recovered sufficiently from his rage to talk again he was less philosophical about the unseen strangers.

'We should have left the water where they put it and not touched it. One day they'll show themselves and come to us expecting gifts. They'll want more than a drink of water, you can be sure of that.'

'If we have more than water, they'll be welcome to it,' replied Josh. 'I should think water is the most valuable gift it's possible to offer anyone in this place. I only wish they'd leave some food, too. My stomach heaves each time I look at seal meat.'

Isaiah spat into the sand at his feet. 'You're too soft – all of you. I know these people. I've met them farther up the coast. You can't make friends with them and you daren't trust them. If you do, they'll likely as not turn on you and cut your throat.'

'How many throats did you see cut?' Josh enquired.

'I don't have to jump off a yardarm to know it'll kill me,' the seaman retorted, his anger flaring anew. 'I can take the word of them as knows.'

Sam said: 'Don't take too much notice of him, Josh.'

Josh said nothing. It was apparent that he and the tall surly seaman could not agree on anything.

It was fortunate for everyone that Josh was keeping watch at dawn the next morning. The sun had shown only a thin orange rind in the eastern sky when he saw a movement about a hundred yards distant. He sprang to his feet, but it was a moment or two before he realised he was looking at three humans. There were two women, and a boy the size of Daniel.

From all the accounts he had heard Josh had expected the people of this land to be big, black and warlike. The three approaching the camp were all well below five feet in height with skins of soft golden brown reflecting the colour of the early-morning sunshine. The women were naked from the waist up, while the boy wore no clothing at all. They came this morning openly and with no attempt at concealment.

It was a very exciting moment and one to be shared. Josh went quietly to Miriam and shook her gently awake. Startled, she sat up and opened her mouth to speak, but Josh silenced her. He felt it would be better not to wake Isaiah for a while.

The three visitors were so small that, had it not been for the breasts of the two women, Josh would have said they were all children. The youngest was, in truth, newly matured, but what she lacked in years she made up for in natural dignity.

The two women each bore an ostrich egg. Without a glance at Josh and Miriam they stopped outside the camp and carefully placed their gifts on the ground. They knew they were being watched but chose to ignore the fact. This was a gesture of trust. They knew nothing about the strangers who watched them from only a few yards away and must have felt very vulnerable, but they did not allow it to show.

When the women had placed the eggs safely on the ground they turned and walked away. Josh became aware that Miriam had a tight hold on his arm, her fingernails digging painfully into his flesh in her excitement.

The visitors had almost reached a tumbled pile of rocks which would hide them from view when the younger of the women found it impossible to maintain her dignity for a moment longer. Perhaps her action was prompted by the relief she felt that the tall white strangers had not harmed her. Whatever the reason she suddenly stopped and turned to stare at Josh and Miriam for about ten seconds. Then, with a quick smile that lit up her whole face, she raised a hand to them before turning and running after her companions.

Miriam and Josh had just seen a tragic fragment of a once numerous and gifted race. Their visitors were of the Bushman people.

'Oh Josh! They were just too lovely for words. And to think we've been worried about them! Did you see that beautiful smile?'

Her delighted cries woke the others, and with great excitement Miriam described their visitors to them. Sam Speke was relieved they had proved to be nothing more sinister than two women and a boy. Predictably, Isaiah did not agree.

'You should have woken us,' he muttered. 'It might well have been some sort of trick.'

'Isaiah! Don't you ever see anything nice in anything or anyone? It was a gesture of friendship on their part and nothing more. I'm quite certain of that.'

'All right, if that's what you want to believe, I'll keep my advice to myself in future.'

Isaiah shrugged his shoulders and turned to walk away, but Miriam moved quickly and blocked his path.

'Now, you listen to me, Isaiah Dacket. There are only four of us plus a child here. The rest of the passengers and crew of *Pride of Liverpool* were drowned — remember? We know there are people in this land and they might well have resented our presence. Instead they've chosen to bring us gifts of water. Isn't that something to be thankful for? A reason to be grateful and glad to be alive? It would make life so much easier if you sometimes agreed with the rest of us and didn't spoil the few good things that happen.'

Isaiah opened his mouth twice as though he was about to say something in reply, but then he clamped his mouth tight shut and walked stiffly past her.

'You might as well not have spoken,' said Josh.

'I had to try.' Miriam's dejection was showing. 'His resentment is such a destructive thing I'm afraid it will spill over and engulf us all.'

Before they moved on from that camp Miriam made up her own small gift to the Bushman women. She guessed they would collect the eggshells once the castaways moved on and she left behind three strips of smoked seal. As an afterthought she also poured some yellow seal oil into one of the eggshells. The oil was no great loss; already it was going rancid. In other circumstances Miriam would have discarded it, but she had grasped one of the elementary rules for staying alive in this hostile world of near-desert. Never throw away anything that might prove edible, however unpalatable it might seem.

This exchange of simple gifts might have been the sign for which the Bushmen had been waiting. An indication of mutual friendship.

The Bushmen were a shy and sensitive people, used to going their own way, with customs that had changed little since the Stone Age. Because of this they had become a misunderstood and tragically persecuted race, hunted and killed like animals by tribesman and white man alike wherever they were found. It was fortunate for Josh and his party that the Boers, pushed out of the Cape Colony farther south, had not yet trekked this far north. The Bushman family group who had found them had never before seen a European; had not yet been given good reason to fear them or to tip their arrows with the special poison so rarely used amongst themselves – the poison for which only one man among each group held the formula and who would offer up a special prayer to accompany its use. The poison for hunting man.

They showed themselves to the shipwrecked party when they had called a halt with the sun beating down upon them from directly overhead. When they actually arrived nobody knew. Had it not been for Daniel they might not even have shown themselves then.

The castaways were resting in the shade of the inevitable balancing rocks. Miriam closed her eyes for a few minutes and when she opened them again she could not see Daniel.

Hurriedly Miriam jumped to her feet, a shout on her lips. She as quickly bit it back.

Her movement had brought Josh to wakefulness and he climbed to his feet at Miriam's urgent whisper.

'Over there, Josh. Look!'

Twenty-five yards from the camp Daniel and the Bushman boy were squatting together examining the boat Sam Speke had carved.

Daniel's explanation of his toy was lost on his new companion, but when Daniel pointed out a feature of particular interest the Bushman boy nodded obligingly. He smiled happily, fascinated by the flow of strange words from the tongue of the white boy. When he himself broke in with a comment of his own, the language was a strange mixture of words and incredible rapid clicks which came from the throat of the Bushman boy yet seemed independent of the words he spoke. Daniel was fascinated by the sounds and tried to imitate them, much to the other boy's amusement.

Then three Bushmen stepped from the cover of some bushes only a few yards beyond the two children. They were the two women Josh and Miriam had seen previously and an old wrinkled man. He carried no weapons of any description, signifying that he came in peace and trust with no ill-intentions. Crossing to where Daniel and the Bushman boy held their mutually unintelligible conversation, they, too, examined the carved boat.

Josh had started forward anxiously as the newcomers approached his son, but Miriam stopped him with a quick gesture.

'No! Stay here. See that Isaiah does nothing foolish. I'll take care of Daniel.'

She walked slowly but deliberately from the camp towards Daniel and the Bushmen. The young girl who had smiled at her on the previous visit saw her coming. Her eyes widened fearfully like a nervous doe hearing a strange new sound. For a moment Miriam thought the girl would turn and flee but she maintained her slow walk towards them. She smiled, and to her relief the young girl relaxed and her mouth opened in a beautiful tooth-displaying grin that had not yet caught up with the maturity of her body.

'Hello!' Miriam said to the visitors. 'I would like to say you are very welcome but I'm quite sure you wouldn't understand a word of it.'

The two women and the old Bushman all clapped their hands together briefly and said something to Miriam in their inimitable language. A sharp burst of words from the older woman brought the Bushman boy to his feet to perform the same brief ritual.

For a few moments there was a hesitant silence. It was not an uncomfortable or embarrassed void; rather, a pause while all of them tried to think of a mutual means of communication, each side eager to express its evident goodwill to the other.

Then Miriam had an idea.

'Come!'

She beckoned for them to follow her, but the women hesitated. Miriam called to Daniel and, taking him by the hand, began to walk towards the camp, hoping the Bushmen would follow. Daniel held out his free hand to his new-found friend, and with none of the reticence of his elders the Bushman boy took Daniel's hand and walked into the camp with him.

The two children had bridged the gap, and with the old man taking the lead the women followed.

Josh had wakened the others, and for once Isaiah was not scowling. He was looking at the younger of the two Bushman women, his gaze on her golden breasts that stood out proud and firm from the young body.

Miriam's stomach knotted as she recognised the hunger in the seaman's expression, and she moved between him and the girl. Fortunately, the girl was totally inexperienced in the ways of white men and was unaware of his look; there was so much to be seen in this small camp.

Miriam took the Bushman group to their store of seal meat and gave each of them a fair-sized strip of the oily meat. They accepted the gift casually, with no sign of gratitude. To have shown gratitude would have been the height of bad manners. It would imply that they had thought the givers to be mean.

But the manners of the younger girl did not inhibit her excitement at the sight of some strips of hard-furred seal skin, rough-cured by Isaiah, that they had brought with them. Her delight was so great that Miriam turned to the seaman.

'Can I give them a couple of pieces of this seal fur? I'm sure it will help us in the future.'

'It's all right with me,' agreed Sam Speke. 'They're welcome to as much as they like.'

'No!' Isaiah Dacket jumped to his feet and advanced to the canvas pack. 'Don't give everything away on our first meeting. Save some to trade later. We'll cut one piece longways into two. Here, give it to me. I'll do it.'

He took the piece of seal hide from Miriam and laid it carefully on the ground. Drawing out his knife, he first cut a shallow mark down the centre of the strip and then cut it expertly into two. Standing up, he handed one piece to the older of the two women and then stepped to her young companion.

'Now, me young beauty. This'll make you a fine belt. There's enough here to go twice around that little waist. Here, I'll show you.'

Putting his arms about her near-naked body he wound the strip of skin about her tiny waist.

The young girl was wide-eyed with fear until she realised what Isaiah was doing, then she relaxed and took the ends of the strip from him. Crossing them over she tucked them between the new belt and her body. She was so engrossed in admiring her present that she was oblivious of Isaiah's hands lingering on her body, resting heavily on her hip bones.

'Yes, that's right, my beauty,' he murmured. 'You look at it often. It'll help you remember who has first call on you when the time comes.'

Miriam went white with anger, and Josh took a step towards the tall seaman. Sam Speke put a hand on his arm and restrained him long enough for common sense to prevail. If there was a scene now, the Bushman group might guess the reason and go away never to return. The friendly relations that had been forged already were too important to jeopardise. Nothing Isaiah said would have been understood by their visitors.

But the elder Bushman woman was not so naïve as her companion. She said something quietly to the young girl, who instantly slipped from the sailor's grasp and moved away from him.

The male Bushman looked at each of the men in turn and

then without hesitation walked to Josh. Standing in front of him, he made a brief speech in his own language. Josh could only shake his head apologetically.

The Bushman realised Josh was not understanding him and began using a simple but readily understood sign-language.

First he told Josh his name was Hwexa. The name contained one of the incredible 'click' sounds that were strange to the castaways' ears. Then he asked Josh if their journey were to the distant mountains. Josh nodded that it was. The Bushman then indicated that he wished Josh and his companions to accompany him and pointed in a direction a few degrees off their course to the mountains.

'Do you think it could be a trap, Josh?' asked Sam Speke when Josh put the Bushman's suggestion to the others.

'I don't see why he should come into our camp and risk his own neck for that,' Josh replied. 'If he'd wanted to kill us, he could have crept up on us during the night. No, I don't believe he means us harm.'

For once Isaiah was in full agreement.

Josh indicated to the Bushman that they were ready to follow him.

All the members of the Bushman group smiled their delight at the decision and with the two women still admiring their seal-skin belts they moved some distance away while the Europeans broke camp as quickly as they could.

Waiting only until the little Bushmen were out of immediate hearing, Josh rounded on Isaiah Dacket.

'You can put this down as one of your lucky days,' he said angrily. 'If it hadn't meant showing you up for the lecher you are, you'd have felt the weight of my fist just now.'

'I don't know what you're talking about.'

Isaiah began to turn away but Josh's hand shot out and, gripping the sailor's shirt-front, he swung him round to face him again.

'I'm talking of you molesting that young girl. You keep well away from her. She's just a child.'

'She's no child. You know nothing about these people. Their women aren't coddled and pampered like English women. They're taught that their purpose in life is to please a man.

What's more, they only accept a gift from a man if they're ready and willing to give him what he wants in return. That's their way.'

'I don't accept your word for that, and you'd better forget what you've heard from others. These women and children will be left alone. Is that clearly understood?'

'Since when have you been leading this party?'

'Since I decided you'd leave that young girl alone.'

Isaiah Dacket was not ready to accept Josh's assumed authority but neither would he go farther without some support.

'Sam! You're not going to stand by while a convict gives the orders, are you?'

'I'll do more than stand by, Isaiah. I stand with him – and not only over the girl, either. If I hear you speaking foul-mouthed in front of Missus Retallick one more time, I'll put you on your back. Remember it, Isaiah Dacket. I'll not waste words on you again.'

The tall seaman's face showed his frustrated fury.

'From a Cornish Wesleyan I expect no more than pious clap-trap, but I never thought to hear it from you, Sam Speke.'

Swinging his canvas pack on to his shoulder, the angry seaman marched away to where Hwexa was watching the argument with great interest. Josh and the others wasted no time in following him.

Later Josh found the opportunity to talk to Sam Speke.

'I'm obliged to you for your support, Sam; but there's no need for you to fall out with Isaiah on my account.'

'I'm used to speaking my own mind,' replied the seaman. 'I doubt I'll change now.'

'We both appreciate that, Sam,' said Miriam, who was walking just behind Josh. 'But I'm a miner's daughter, brought up among miners. Isaiah isn't likely to say anything I haven't heard before. My only concern is that he might offend one of the little women. I believe we'll need their help to get clear of this desert.'

'We'll have to do our best to make sure that he doesn't,' commented Josh and he determined to keep a very close watch on the tall seaman.

They walked for about a mile before they reached the Bush-man village. It was such a well-hidden inconspicuous group of temporary huts that they were in the midst of them before they realised it. Even the cooking-fires produced hardly any smoke.

Hwexa led them to a hut that appeared to have been made especially for them. It was certainly larger than any of the others, although it was constructed in exactly the same way: a half-circle of sticks stuck into the ground, bent over and tied with strips of soft bark. The whole was covered with coarse dry grass and branches of bushes to blend with its surroundings.

The fire in front of this hut was much larger than any of the others, giving additional proof that the shipwrecked party had been expected even though Josh could not imagine how the Bushmen had been able to anticipate their arrival.

There were twelve huts altogether in the little 'village'. Unaware of the nomadic ways of the Bushmen, Josh had been expecting a village on a grander scale than this one.

No sooner had they put down their belongings than a crowd of silent but intensely curious Bushmen gathered about them. They were mostly women and, although they were all light-skinned, the young girl to whom Isaiah had given the seal-skin belt stood out among them for her golden skin and shy beauty.

One thing immediately apparent to Miriam was the absence of children. Apart from the boy they had already met there was only one other child, a babe-in-arms, in the village. This, too, was a direct result of the harsh environment and the fragile barrier that divided life and death in this primitive country. If there was a particularly hard and prolonged drought or a shift of animal migration, nature stepped in and the Bushman women did not conceive. If this natural method of birth control failed during such a time of hardship, then the traditional and basic rules of survival were invoked. The old women of the village took the baby from its mother at birth and it was never seen again. There could be no exception to this rule. The desert provided just enough, and no more. If the baby were not killed, then the chances were that neither mother nor child would survive to see better years.

Once again it was the young Bushman boy who broke down the barrier of shyness between the newcomers and the villagers. He saw the bucket containing the rancid seal oil and, dipping a finger into it, immediately transferred it to his mouth. He had already tasted the gift Miriam had left for his mother and found it very much to his liking.

In an instant his mother was at his side, scolding him in a sharp rebuke liberally laced with angry 'clicks'.

Miriam laughed. This seemed a good opportunity to rid herself of the evil-smelling seal oil. She offered the bucket to the boy's mother.

The Bushman woman was reluctant to take it at first, but Miriam insisted and eventually the woman accepted it with obvious delight.

But such a present was one to be shared, as were most things in this tiny close family community. The woman put the bucket down and called for Hwexa to come forward and issue a fair share to a representative of each 'hut'.

The distribution drove away all shyness from the Bushmen. Within minutes the village was noisy with chatter, and more than one smile was flashed in the direction of their guests.

A generous supply of water had been left for the use of the newcomers, the eggshell containers being buried in the sand on the shady side of the hut. Now the Bushmen came and brought strange root-vegetables for the bewildered Miriam to cook, and a woman produced an evil-smelling paste, indicating it should be put on their boils.

Once the Bushmen had all had a good look at the strange newcomers the crowd quickly drifted away to their allotted tasks. Although life in this temporary village appeared disorganised and casual, this was a totally false impression. The castaways had joined a very efficient little community. The Bushman was master of his environment – but it was a mastery that had to be worked at and constantly asserted. Death was the only gift the desert handed out freely.

Shortly before dusk there was another break in the routine of the village. For a full hour there had been an air of excitement building up although no one had left and nobody had arrived. Josh felt it, and so did Miriam. They found themselves waiting expectantly for something to happen.

Then, as though there had been some silent signal, more wood was thrown on to fires, the women gathered at the edge of the village and the reason for their suppressed excitement came into view. It was the remainder of their menfolk, who had been out on a hunting expedition. Armed only with tiny bows and stone-tipped arrows they had been hunting for two days.

The reward for their perseverance was a large bushbuck. Cut into rough pieces, the hunters carried it into their village and deposited it upon the ground in the centre of the circle of huts.

The hunters received a vociferous welcome and, like the seal oil, the deer was distributed to each family group, Josh and his party receiving an over-generous share. A large hindquarter was carried to their fireside by the leader of this small band of Bushmen who had returned with the hunters. He was beaming with the sheer pleasure of bringing them such a gift, and there was something about his smile that made Miriam think of the young girl, Bele, who had visited their camp. In fact, Xhube, the chief, was Bele's father.

His brief speech of welcome, like his own name, was liberally sprinkled with the clicks that defied that Europeans' tongues and was totally unintelligible. But his smile needed no interpretation. They were welcome guests in his village.

He did not stay talking for long. He could tell by the way their glances wandered to the portion of deer meat that they were hungry for fresh food. It was a hunger he had known many times. He would not prolong their waiting.

Josh and the others had not tasted fresh meat since leaving England two months before. They did not count the seal meat which had been so fishy it was difficult to accept it as anything else but fish. So much had happened to them during those two months that England might have been a lifetime away. Already, in an uneasy way, they felt part of this strange and harsh new country.

Josh in particular, with only captivity awaiting him elsewhere, was looking at it with the eye of a prospective settler.

Every fire in the small village was cooking meat, and the smell hung tantalisingly on the still evening air. When their own meat was almost ready for eating one of the Bushman women came to their fire carrying a quantity of hot cooked root-vegetables wrapped in a broad fibrous leaf. They were of the same type as those previously brought to Miriam and which remained uncooked because she had been reluctant to try them.

Having already witnessed the Bushmen's idea of a delicacy in their enjoyment of the rancid seal oil, Miriam was apprehensive about tasting the vegetable; but the Bushman woman was waiting, and she had no choice. To Miriam's relief it was quite palatable – enjoyable even.

She served up a filling and tasty meal to the four male members of the party and they ate it squatting around a pleasant-smelling fire. Even the dour Isaiah looked almost mellow.

That night the camp fires of the Bushman village burned late as a dance was held to celebrate the end of a successful hunt and the presence of the tall white strangers.

The rhythm and dancing were like nothing Josh or Miriam had ever witnessed before. The musician sat in the shadows playing a primitive form of stringed instrument while all the other members of the tribe formed a small tight circle and shuffled around and around keeping time by clapping and chanting to the strange exciting rhythm. Only a couple of very old and incredibly wrinkled women did not join in.

Gradually the dancers worked themselves up into an ecstatic state that communicated itself to the European watchers.

The Bushman men and women were half-shuffling, half-hopping around the narrow circular depression they had worn into the soft ground. They kept this movement up for longer than an hour without any sign of weariness. Even the hunters who had that day trotted miles with the fruits of their hunt on their shoulders were enthusiastic participants.

At this point the small Bushman boy broke from the circle and extended a hand for Daniel to join him. Daniel went unhesitatingly, and the teeth of the Bushman dancers gleamed white in the firelight as they made room for him. Within minutes the small boy from the mining village on Bodmin Moor had become a part of the dance. He shuffled and hopped and swayed to a dance that was being performed when a Pharaoh sat on the throne of Egypt and denied the right of the people of Israel to leave his land and his service, and when the tribes of the British Isles were themselves as primitive as these little men of the African wastelands.

It was Isaiah Dacket who brought the celebrations to an early and embarrassing close.

Unnoticed by the others he had begun to edge towards the dancers when Daniel was taken into their circle. Miriam saw him when he was no more than a yard from them, half-hidden in the shadows farthest from the firelight. Clapping his hands in time to the music, he was leering at Bele, who wore her seal-skin belt as she danced.

Guessing his intention, Miriam spoke urgently to Josh.

'Look! Isaiah's over there beyond the dancers. He's watching Bele. Stop him before he does something, Josh.'

But she was too late. Even as she was speaking Isaiah Dacket lurched forward and clumsily forced his way into the circle behind the young slim Bushman girl. Immediately the rhythm faltered and the dancers stopped in some confusion.

An older woman spoke quickly to the young Bele, and the girl ran from the circle. The others followed in an embarrassed silence, and Isaiah Dacket was left standing alone in the disturbed circle of sand.

One of the women brought Daniel back to Miriam and with a broad smile on her face said something that Miriam knew was a compliment about his dancing ability. Miriam could only smile in return, wishing once again that there was some way she could communicate with these happy and generous people, to say 'thank you' – and to apologise for the actions of the tall seaman.

When she looked back at the circle Isaiah Dacket had gone.

Josh and Sam went out into the darkness looking for him.

'If you find him first, stay with him,' Josh said. 'And whatever you do don't let him start anything stupid.'

'He's a fool,' growled Sam Speke. They were well out of the hearing of Miriam now. 'But it's a foolishness that affects many sailors. He sees a girl he fancies and his brain moves down into his trousers!'

Isaiah was not successful in his amorous search for the young Bushman girl, and when Sam Speke found him he was already on his way back to their own fire. Curling up close to it, he shared his hard bed with nothing but his own angry thoughts.

*

Later that night when the moon stood high over the mountains, touching its peaks with a silver brush, the fires of the Bushman village burned low. But the men of the little tribe were gathered around the low fire of Xhube's hut.

'It is agreed, then,' he said. 'We will take the white men to the mountains of Gaua.'

'It is your will,' said Hwexa, uncle of Xhube. 'We will do as you say. It matters not that some do not agree.'

Xhube looked at the expressions on the faces of his men shadowed in the dull light of the fire and saw doubt among them. This was a family group. Every one of the men was related to him by birth or marriage. He had long ago learned to read their faces and know what they were thinking.

'It matters,' he said. 'Give me your thoughts and I will give you mine.'

Hwexa had expressed his opinion openly and it was to him Xhube looked.

'The holy painted cave of Gaua is in the mountains,' said Hwexa. 'It would give the God great offence if a white man were to enter. It would bring great troubles to our people.'

'Then we must lead them away from the painted cave,' countered Xhube. 'If we do not go with them they are more likely to find it. The path to the cave is not hard to see.'

'The white men are not children to be taken by the hand and led by us. They will go wherever they wish.'

'We will find a way, Hwexa – but not if we remain here.'

'Then use Bele to turn their steps from the painted cave. The tall white man would see no path if she walked before him.'

Xhube's face tightened momentarily. The girl was his first-born and the only one of five children to have survived the harsh years since.

'It would not please Gaua if such an important task was undertaken by a woman,' he said quietly. 'Bele will stay far from the eyes of the tall white man.'

'What of the other thing, Xhube? The bones of the white men who came in the time of our fathers' fathers?'

'I have thought about that. It is not right a man's body should stay in the sight of the sun. They must be buried by their own people. I will take these white men to them.'

'Is that wise? What if they think we killed them?'

'They will not think that. The bones have been lying on the mountain since before the time of my father and your father, Hwexa. The white men will see that. Is there anything else?'

Hwexa shook his head. 'No, it will be as you say.'

Xhube looked at the face of each of his men for confirmation of his decision. It was freely given. 'It will be as you say,' said each man.

'Good. When the sun warms us we leave for the mountains of the sacred cave of Gaua.'

'Xhube?' The young man who spoke was his half-brother. 'Why do the white men go to the mountains?'

The Bushman leader smiled. 'I, too, asked myself that question. Look about you, my brother. If you came to this land for the first time, knowing nothing of it, where would you first look?'

The young Bushman turned his head instinctively towards the silver peaks of the mountains.

'It is so. You did not need your tongue to give me an answer. Your eyes turned to the mountain of Gaua's cave. So, too, did the eyes of the white men. That is why they have to go there.'

'And when they have been there? What then, Xhube, son of my brother?' asked Hwexa softly.

'I think they will not return to the place of hot sand. They will go on beyond the mountains. To the land of the Herero.'

Xhube smiled sadly, his thoughts those of a leader whose people were not welcome in the lands of other tribes, whose very survival depended upon occupying land no others wanted, where others could not live.

'When they go perhaps our people will have a friend on the far side of the mountains for the first time.'

Xhube said it with hope, yet as a Bushman he was conditioned to expect nothing from anyone outside his own tribe.

CHAPTER FIVE

The Bushmen removed all traces of their village quickly and efficiently. By the time a thin wedge of sky separated sun from mountains there might never have been a Bushman encampment among the tall grass and bushes. This was the way the little tribe always left their stopping-places. It was not because of any love of tidiness; it was self-preservation. The places where a village could be sited to allow them to view the surrounding countryside without themselves being seen were few and had to be protected. By exercising care they would feel safe returning to this site time and time again.

The Bushmen did not follow the course of the river as Josh expected them to do but struck across country, and by the third day the ground was beginning to slope steadily upwards. Soon they were picking their way between weathered granite rocks and toiling up steep paths as the mountains rose dramatically from the parched plain.

Looking ahead, Josh estimated that the highest peak must be at least eight thousand feet high. It would not be necessary actually to scale the summit. He only needed a good vantage-point from which to see all sides of the mountain 'island'.

When they paused for a brief rest he pointed out a saddle-shaped pass some three thousand feet below the summit to the Bushman leader.

Xhube nodded that he understood, yet when Josh took what would appear to be the obvious route to it the Bushman leader touched his arm and shook his head, indicating another route — one that would take them diagonally away from the pass.

When Josh showed signs of uncertainty Xhube squatted into a crouching position by a flat expanse of sand and motioned for Josh to sit beside him. Miriam and the two sailors joined the group, and Xhube began to tell them a vivid tale in the now familiar and remarkable Bushman sign-language.

Using a stick to create line drawings in the sand and quick movements of his sensitive hands to mould shapes in the air, he told them a story as detailed as any Josh had heard related by one of his own countrymen.

Xhube described how two white men had come to this area from the sea. It had been many years before – two grandfathers ago. Xhube's forefathers had seen them soon after they landed and followed their progress. Once they had drawn close, intending to speak to them, but one of the white men had pointed a stick at them and caused it to make the sound of small thunder. Immediately, one of the Bushmen was stung in the side by a snake that could not be seen. It had drawn much blood, and the Bushman died in great pain. After this the Bushmen had kept a respectful distance between themselves and the white men.

Even when it became obvious the white men were weak from lack of food and water the Bushmen had been reluctant to draw near.

Xhube described how the two men weaved an erratic course towards these mountains, staggering along the way and occasionally falling to the ground. Still the ancestors of Xhube only looked on from a safe distance, but never allowing the white men to leave their sight.

They followed them up this very slope – and now the two men were falling down more frequently, sometimes crawling on their hands and knees. Then somewhere farther up the mountain they found a narrow sandy gully where there was shade but no water. Here the men lay down, too weak to go farther.

During that night one of the white men died, but his companion clung desperately to life during the next long scorching day.

Then – and here Xhube's magic fingers faltered for the first time – then, as the arms of the sun slipped from around the mountains, the second man died. Not silently as had his companion, but by putting his stick into his mouth and calling from it a thunderclap that had burst forth from the gully and flown from cliff-face to mountain sending the antelope that lived on the mountains leaping all ways in terror.

The Bushmen, too, had been frightened, but they had stayed long enough to climb part of the mountain and see from a distance that both the white men were now still. Then they had left the mountain.

Since that time no Bushman had entered the gully. The bodies were still there, and with macabre accuracy Xhube's fingers traced ribs, teeth and the hollow eye-sockets of a skeleton. His uncle Hwexa had looked down on the bodies from the height of a cliff-path many years before. Rain had never been known to fall on this slope of the mountains and it was dry and hot. Bones would be preserved for many, many years. Until one day a wind would blow between the rocks and gullies and touch the bones of the long-dead men. Then they would crumble to dust. But Xhube said that would not happen for many years. For now the skeletons remained.

When the sign-language story ended the little Bushman was surrounded by his own people as well as the survivors from *Pride of Liverpool*, and every one of his listeners was spellbound by his graphic tale.

'That was magic!' breathed Miriam, breaking the silence. 'I would never have believed one man could tell us so much without uttering a single word.'

'It was a sight more than that!' exclaimed Isaiah. 'Sam, you know what I'm talking about? What one of those men carried with him!'

'Yes, I'd say it was a musket,' said Sam Speke slowly.

'There can be no doubt of it!' Isaiah was more excited than Josh had ever seen him. 'And if it's as dry up here as Xhube says, then the musket and any powder that's left might be usable!'

'For what?' queried Josh.

'For what?' echoed the seaman. 'Why, for hunting – that's what. And for protecting us when we move on from here. There's not a native or any wild animal as would threaten us twice if we had a musket with us.'

Xhube saw the excitement of the white men and was well pleased. He would take them to the place where the skeletons lay. By so doing he would lead them away from the cave of Gaua and the risk of incurring the wrath of the Bushman God.

'Well, come on! What are we waiting for?' Isaiah was impatient to locate the skeletons and check on the musket he was sure was there.

Moving ahead of them along the path, Xhube beckoned them on.

The party toiled upwards for another thousand feet before the Bushman stopped and began unslinging his belongings. The other Bushmen followed his example. It became apparent that this was not merely another stop for rest. The Bushmen were making a camp.

Isaiah immediately protested that they should go on and reach the skeletons now. Xhube listened politely until the seaman stopped talking, then he raised his hand silently and pointed with a finger.

What had appeared to be just another shadow between the rocks above them could now be seen to be the entrance to a gully. They had reached the place Xhube had described.

'I'll keep Daniel here and stay with Xhube and his people,' declared Miriam. 'I don't want to see any skeletons.'

Josh hesitated. He had grown to like the little people they had fallen in with. He trusted them too. And yet. . . . He decided he would not leave Miriam and Daniel alone with them.

'I'll stay, too. I've seen enough bodies in my time.'

'You please yourselves. I don't care if no one else comes. I'm going in there.'

As Isaiah strode off Josh said, 'Go with him, Sam. Give whoever is in there a decent burial if you can. I doubt if Isaiah will think of it. He's interested only in that musket.'

Sam Speke hurried after his fellow-mariner, and Josh helped Miriam to set up camp in a sandy hollow between some towering rocks.

The entrance to the gully was in shadow but only twenty paces on it took a sharp turn to the left and widened out into a narrow sand-floored valley with a sheer cliff-face on one side and high tumbled rock on the other.

The seamen found the skeletons at the far end of the tiny valley at a place where it ended abruptly in a sheer rock-face.

They lay side by side, the bony fingers of one reaching out as though he had tried to touch the other in death. Except for sand-dust that lay thick upon them they might have been there for no more than a few months.

Yet the clothes that held the bleached bones together were of another age. In the Portuguese style, they had been tailored when America was still a British colony – almost eighty years before!

The two seamen could not immediately see a gun, but when Isaiah bent low over the skeletons he saw not one but two weapons.

One was a pistol dangling loosely from the slack belt of the skeleton with the outstretched hand, his disconnected skull resting wearily upon a dusty sleeve.

The other weapon confirmed Xhube's graphic story. A long-barrelled musket, it lay beneath the other man's skeleton, the end of the barrel gripped between loose-toothed jaws and a gaping hole in the top of the skull to mark the passing of a musket-ball. A finger-bone protruding from the trigger-guard of the musket provided a mute addendum to the story.

Isaiah unceremoniously pulled the musket from beneath the brittle skeleton, and at his touch the human form disappeared and became no more than a bundle of bones wrapped in old rags.

'Look, Sam! There's powder and shot here, too.' Impatiently Isaiah tugged a horn of powder and a pouch of musket-balls from the skeleton's belt.

Sam was more gentle as he removed the pistol and powder from the belt of the second skeleton. The pouch of lead shot was on the other side of the belt – and there was something else. The drawstring of a once fine large leather bag was looped about the belt.

Pulling it free with difficulty, Sam heard a dull jingling inside it. He loosened the drawstring, and the slanting rays of the sun found themselves in sudden competition with the contents of the bag.

It held a sizeable fortune in gold coins.

Sam Speke's gasp of incredulous surprise made Isaiah Dacket look up sharply. He had placed the flintlock musket on the ground and was busily searching the clothing of its late owner. He had chosen the wrong body. The only secret there was the secret of death.

Before Sam Speke could stop him Isaiah Dacket dipped his hand into the bag and pulled out a coin. He put it to his mouth and bit into it. His teeth left a faint mark in its surface.

'It's gold, Sam. Pure gold! There must be at least seven pounds' weight. We've found ourselves a fortune.'

Sam Speke could only nod his head, utterly bemused. In other circumstances, in more civilised surroundings, having so much money in his grasp would have terrified him. Here, on the side of a mountain with nothing but scrub and desert on all sides, the find lacked the same impact.

Not so for Isaiah Dacket. He could hardly control his eagerness to have his share of the valuable coins.

'We're rich, Sam. We're rich! When we get out of here we'll be able to pay our passage back to England. Travel in style. No need to go aloft in all weathers or clean out stinking bilges. We won't be working all the hours God gave us. We'll be passengers, waited on by poor sailors. And when we get home we won't have to work again! Just think of it, Sam.'

'I am thinking of it.' Sam Speke tugged the drawstring of the bag closed deliberately, and the tall seaman looked at him quickly.

'Is that what you'd have said if you'd found the gold instead of me, Isaiah?'

'Why, of course I would, Sam.' Isaiah's voice oozed friendship. 'I'd share anything I found with you. Two ways, straight down the middle. I swear it.'

'This will be shared more than two ways. There's four of us — five, if we include the boy. And what about Xhube and his people? They brought us here.'

Isaiah's face showed utter disbelief.

'You can't share it with all of them. What would they do with it?'

'If I thought he'd use it, then Xhube would have his share. But I don't suppose he'd even know what gold was.' Sam Speke slipped the bag inside his shirt. 'I'll keep it until it can be shared out between the rest of us.'

'You're mad, Sam! We don't have to share it with anyone else. The Retallicks don't even know we've found it. Getting a musket and pistol will be enough to keep them happy. Let the gold be just between you and me. Anyway, Josh Retallick won't be able to do much with his share. He'll be back in prison when he gets to where he could spend it.'

'All the more reason for Missus Retallick and the boy to have money. They'll likely have need of it.'

'Sam. . . .' Isaiah pleaded with his companion to reconsider, but Sam Speke cut his protests short.

'There's no more to be said about the matter. Now, give me a hand to dig a couple of graves in this sand. They won't be deep, but it will show we cared enough to bury them.'

'What difference is that going to make now? There's little enough left of 'em as it is. They'll rot as well above ground as beneath it.'

'Happen you're right, but I'm not walking away from an un-buried man with his gold in my shirt. It's little enough to do. Come on, down on your knees and dig.'

Isaiah had no alternative but to help Sam bury the remains of the two unknown men who had perished so tragically many years before.

When their task was finished the twin mounds were scarcely discernible. Sam felt they should be marked in some way and he found enough stones to pile upon each other to make a small monument at the head of each grave. He knew even the promise of their gold would not persuade Isaiah to raise a prayer for the souls of the long-dead men, so he stood in silence by himself for a few moments, thinking a small prayer, too self-conscious to utter the words aloud.

While he was doing this Isaiah was examining the musket, peering down the long barrel, blowing sand from it and gingerly cocking the weapon. Then he twisted the top from the elaborately engraved powder-horn and, shaking some of its contents into palm of his hand, examined the black powder carefully. He sniffed it, rubbed it gently between his hands and blew on it gently. The examination over he said, 'I can't see anything wrong with either the gun or the powder. It's dry – drier than some I've used in cannons. I don't see any reason why it shouldn't fire, although some of the musket parts are just as dry. If I can cadge a spoonful of that seal oil back, we'll have ourselves a musket every bit as good as a modern one. Now, show me that pistol.'

Isaiah took the pistol and after a keen inspection handed it back to Sam Speke, declaring it to be in an even better condition than the musket.

By the time the two seamen emerged from the gully Josh had begun to worry about them. He was relieved to see them and pleased they had found the weapons. He examined the guns with great interest; it was the first time he had held one in his hands.

He was excited about the gold, too, but he had some gold coins sewn into the belt he wore beneath his shirt and so he had less need of it than the others. His money had been brought on to *Pride of Liverpool* by Miriam, royalties earned from the man-engines invented when he was a mine engineer.

But he was delighted for Sam Speke's sake. Although the seaman showed few outward signs of excitement, Josh knew the gold could provide him with a future far more comfortable than the crew's quarters on some merchantman. He also thought Sam should keep the gold for himself. 'You found it. There can be no other claim upon it, so it's yours by right.'

'It's for all of us,' said Sam Speke doggedly. 'When the time is right it'll be shared five ways.'

'If it's all the same to you, I'll take my share now,' declared Isaiah Dacket.

'No, you won't.' The stocky seaman gave his shipmate a long hard look. 'I'm keeping the gold until we are out of this mess and all go our separate ways. Then I'll share it out – but I'll hold on to yours until Josh has left with Missus Retallick and the boy.'

'He'll be going to prison on his own,' asserted Isaiah Dacket.

Sam Speke shook his head. 'No. Not unless *he* says something to put himself there – and I doubt he's fool enough for that.'

Isaiah Dacket's face grew redder and redder as he struggled to control his temper. 'There's only one fool here,' he blurted out. 'That's you, Sam Speke.' With that he threw the musket into the crook of his arm and walked towards the Bushman fires to obtain some seal oil.

'Poor Isaiah!' said Sam Speke, looking after his fellow-seaman. 'He's never seen so much gold before. He can't wait to hold his share of it in his hands.'

'And what about you, Sam?' Miriam asked gently. 'Doesn't

it mean just as much to you?'

Sam Speke frowned as he thought about it.

'No,' he said finally, 'I don't think it does. I mean, when I found it up there in the gully all I could think about was the man I'd taken it from. I wondered what he meant to do with it. I felt sorry for him because he'd died without being able to use it. I felt he'd been cheated.' The burly seaman gave Miriam a sheepish smile. 'You'll think that's foolish talk.'

'Oh no!' Miriam rested her hand on his arm for a moment. 'I think you're a good man, Sam Speke, and I've said so before.'

The seaman's neck and face darkened to the colour of a roach's fin, and Josh rescued him by changing the subject.

'Do you think these guns will work, Sam?'

'Isaiah says they will. He knows about such things. He was a gunner's mate in King William's navy and looked after the two cannon we had on board *Pride of Liverpool*.'

The tall seaman certainly appeared to be knowledgeable about firearms. He used the seal oil to grease all the moving parts on his musket, then wiped them clean again. He ran a ramrod with a lightly greased strip of cloth down inside the barrel of the musket and as carefully dried that, too. Finally he had the musket ready for firing. Pouring a small measure of powder into the long barrel, he followed it with a small wad from the pouch. Then he took a musket-ball and wrapped it in a tiny strip of cloth torn from his own shirt. Thumbing the wrapped musket-ball into the barrel of the musket, he rammed it home carefully with the ramrod. Then he shook a little of the black powder into the firing-pan and, selecting a flint from the pouch, screwed it into the cock.

'Now comes the real test,' said Sam Speke in a low whisper. 'Xhube reckons it never rains on this slope of the mountains. We'll know for sure in a moment. If there's ever been any damp hereabouts, the powder will have picked it up and there'll be nothing more than a fizzle when Isaiah pulls the trigger.'

Just then a remarkable freak of timing occurred that would have placed Isaiah Dacket securely in Bushmen legend had the outcome been different.

A large antelope not expecting to encounter anything representing danger on this usually deserted mountain slope leaped into sight against the skyline a mere seventy yards away. For several seconds it froze in astonishment at the unprecedented scene before it.

Isaiah Dacket threw the musket up to his shoulder and squeezed the trigger. The 'little thunder' reverberated from cliff-face to rock-pile. Isaiah had not fired a musket for some years. He had no knowledge of whether this one threw a musket-ball true, and the measure of gunpowder used had been a guess. But the musket-ball sang only inches wide of its target, and the startled antelope threw up its head and bounded from view.

'Hard luck, Isaiah!'

'But the gun works, shipmate.' Isaiah accepted the commiserations of his companions with surprisingly good grace, but the effect of the shot upon the Bushmen bordered on complete panic. As the sound of the shot reverberated around the mountainside they scattered in terror, some of the women screaming as they ran to get away from the 'stick-that-made-thunder'. Only Xhube, who had recounted the story of the musket, was not totally unnerved. It was his voice calling to his people that brought them all back, although some of the younger women were actually trembling with fear.

They kept their eyes averted from Isaiah and the musket and, although Xhube tried to explain what had happened, they were totally unable to grasp the principles involved and Xhube himself had only the very vaguest idea.

They spent a hot night on the mountainside with the stars so clear overhead they hardly needed any other light; but the flickering yellow flames of a fire provided a comfortable glow, and as they sat around it Isaiah checked Sam Speke's pistol. Satisfied that it was in perfect working order he handed it back to his shipmate.

'That's a fine pistol, Sam. It's French and the inlay is silver. I wonder what a man with a silver-inlaid pistol and a bag of gold was doing in this place?'

Sam shrugged. 'Whatever it was never got done.' He balanced the pistol thoughtfully in his hand and then held it out to Josh.

'Here, you take this. You'll likely find some use for it. There's plenty of powder and shot to go with it.'

'But I've never touched one of these in my life!' protested

Josh. 'I wouldn't know how to use it.'

'Then it's time you learned,' replied Sam. 'I'll show you how, and maybe you'll have a chance to practise later on. You'd best not try while we're here or Xhube's people won't stop running until dawn.'

Sam Speke showed Josh how to load and prime the pistol. It had two barrels and two triggers. Sam made Josh load and unload it, then practise priming and aiming, and also showed him how to squeeze the trigger without jerking it off aim. All the while this was going on Isaiah sat nursing his musket and scowling at his own thoughts. Josh thought it unlikely the seaman would have checked the pistol so thoroughly had he known that he and not Sam Speke would use it.

Although they were not desperately short of food, their stocks were running low, and when a keen-eyed Bushman sighted an eland near the bottom of the slope the next morning there was great excitement among the little men. The largest of the deer family, this was a particularly fine animal. Almost six feet high at the shoulder, it must have weighed more than all the men of the small tribe put together.

Eland were not often found on this side of the mountains, and Xhube made an immediate decision. The top of the mountain would be there tomorrow. Such a vast supply of meat as this large creature promised was all too seldom encountered. It could not be passed up, and such an important hunt needed to have the tribal head leading it. Only Hwexa and three of the older men of the tribe were left behind with the women and the white castaways.

It was no hardship to remain upon the mountain slope in the shade of the rocks for a day. A couple of hours after dawn the sun was already heating the rocks and it promised to be even hotter than on the previous days.

With the aid of Sam's knife, a piece of canvas and a length of fishing-line, Miriam was making a shapeless wide-brimmed hat for Daniel. The boy himself and his little Bushman friend were playing a game with a number of small stones. Josh had found an interesting quartz fault in a border and was explaining it to Sam Speke while Isaiah Dacket wandered off with his musket, hoping to make amends for his wasted shot of the previous day.

The Bushman women had their own work to do. While their men hunted the spiral-horned eland they combed the mountain slopes for whatever food might be found. Mostly they sought the tuberous-rooted plants that sometimes grew in this shallow sandy soil, watered by springs that occasionally flowed from the mountain fed by the storms high on the far side. But the Bushman women scorned nothing that might provide food. There were many insects that were considered to be particular delicacies.

Bele followed the slope for some distance, working her way along the ridge above the camp. She searched a shallow depression that had once held water, knowing that the incredible plants of this country could lie dormant for years waiting for the next trickle of water to come and promote near-miraculous growth. Bele was not disappointed. In a sandy bed between two rocks and sheltered from the full blast of the sun she found some veldt tubers, roots resembling mild onions.

Digging one up, she laid it to one side, and had begun to uproot another when a long silent shadow reached out and stopped a foot from her hand. Bele started up to see Isaiah standing watching her, his musket resting easily in the crook of his arm. She was startled more than frightened. Among the Bushman people it was unknown for a man to hurt a woman. Isaiah did his best to put her at ease. He smiled, an unaccustomed expression for his face.

'Don't mind me,' he said. 'Go on digging your roots.'

Bele understood his actions, if not his words, and she crouched down and began digging with the short sharp stick all the women carried for the purpose. She was uneasy at having Isaiah watch her, but it was merely a feeling born of her shyness.

The seaman moved closer to stand by her shoulder and look down at what she was doing. The gun was supported solely by his left hand now, leaving his right hand free. As he leaned over to watch, his fingers brushed against her bare shoulder as though by accident. Bele had just unearthed a large juicy tuber and she held it up to show him, smiling happily at her success.

Isaiah leaned lower to look at her find and let his hand rest fully on her shoulder for a moment before it moved on, his fingers tracing the line of her collar-bone.

The smile left Bele's face as Isaiah's hand dropped suddenly lower and he grasped one of her breasts. She tried to stand; but the seaman pushed his knee into her back, knocking her off balance. Bele screamed as he dropped the musket and pushed her flat to the ground. She screamed again as Isaiah tugged at the cord holding the narrow strip of animal skin she wore as an apron below the seal-skin belt the seaman had given to her.

The thongs of the apron dug into the skin of her hips before they broke and Isaiah cast the apron away to one side. By now Bele was struggling violently, and as the seaman tried to stifle her cries with his hand she bit deep into the flesh at the base of his thumb.

Cursing, Isaiah pulled his hand back and struck her heavily across the mouth. Her generous lower lip caught on her teeth, and she tasted blood. He struck her again but with clenched fist this time, and Bele felt as though her head had exploded into a thousand shooting stars. The sensation lasted only seconds, but it was long enough for her to have his weight upon her and his legs kneeing hers apart.

Bele screamed yet again and redoubled her struggles, but there was no stopping the thoroughly aroused seaman now. Still raining punches upon her face, he took her while she moaned and writhed in semi-conscious pain and blood bubbled from her battered lips.

But Bele's screams had been heard, and one of the Bushman women reached her just as Isaiah pushed himself up from her with chest heaving as he gasped in warm air.

Hardly pausing in her rush forward the Bushman woman picked up a piece of stone and swung it against Isaiah's head.

The seaman heard her coming and was moving away from the blow as it struck. It did no more than glance from his forehead, grazing the skin.

Another woman came up the slope and leaped at Isaiah with her hands extended before her like claws. He brushed her aside as easily as a doorway curtain; but now other women were converging on the spot and, snatching up his musket, Isaiah backed away from them.

78

Bele began to regain consciousness, and two of the women picked her up and, half-carrying and half-dragging the semi-conscious girl, took her down the slope. The remainder of the women began picking up stones and hurling them at the sea-man. Some of the stones were as large as a man's fist, and one of them took Isaiah in the mouth and he felt a tooth go.

Throwing the musket to his shoulder, he aimed at the woman who had thrown it and pulled the trigger.

The sound in the confines of the rocks was deafening, but the shot went wide of its intended target. However, unlike Isaiah's previous shot at the antelope, the musket-ball did not disappear harmlessly into the wastes of the mountainside. It snicked a bloody furrow across the skin on the upper arm of one of the older women before tearing into the back of young Bele.

The two women supporting her felt her body jerk in their hands as the thunder of the shot assaulted their ears. Fear and thoughts of self-preservation took the place of concern for their young relative and, dropping her to the ground, they fled from the scene in terror.

Isaiah Dacket was also in a hurry to get away but he had to reload his musket first. He knew there were still the men of the tribe to face and was thankful that the hunters had gone after the eland. He worked his way down the slope, loading the musket along the way, his eyes only on powder and shot. That was how he almost stumbled over Bele at the moment he was ramming the musket-ball down the long barrel with the ram-rod.

The little Bushman girl was dying. Blood stained the seal-skin belt that was still twisted about her waist, and it spilled on to the ground from her open mouth. But her eyes held his. There was no fear in them now she had crossed the threshold of pain. Her expression was one of sorrow. Deep unfathomable sorrow.

It unnerved Isaiah Dacket. He stepped to one side of her and sidled past her body but he could not avert his gaze from her face. The beautiful doe-like eyes followed him until he backed out of sight behind the next pile of rocks.

Josh and the others heard the shot and were still wondering

what had happened when the first of the women stumbled half-hysterical into the camp. She tumbled out breathless words to Hwexa, and he and one of the old men snatched up all the weapons to hand and ran away up the mountain slope carrying little Bushman bows and bone-bladed spears.

Josh was even more concerned when Miriam hurried to the distressed Bushman woman only to have her run away from her in terror, pausing just to snatch the hand of the small Bushman boy and take him with her.

Before this happened Josh had thought perhaps the tall seaman had shot a deer and the Bushmen had gone to help him with it. Now he knew something far more serious had occurred.

'Get Daniel and hide in those rocks over there,' he said to Miriam. 'Sam, you stay with them. I'm going to find out what's happening.'

Miriam did not argue. She picked up Daniel, who was still protesting at being parted from his young companion, and had started for the rocks when there was another shot. Seconds later Isaiah Dacket ran into the clearing.

'Quick! Get out!' he shouted. 'The Bushmen are after us.'

'What for . . . ?' Josh asked as the seaman reloaded the musket with frantic haste.

'There's no time for talking. We've got to move. They'll be after us all now.'

Josh was about to argue that they had done nothing to cause the little Bushmen to attack them when an angry arrow fired from the extreme range of one of the small bows looped through the air and landed with a soft hiss in the ground at his feet.

Then Hwexa showed himself and, reaching back with his arm, hurled a bone-bladed spear with all the strength of an angry and determined man. Josh jumped out of its way just in time, and the bone blade shattered into splinters on the rock behind him.

Isaiah brought the musket up to his shoulder to fire, but as he had Hwexa lined up with the long barrel and squeezed the trigger Josh knocked the gun up and the musket-ball sped harmlessly through the air.

'What did you do that for? I'd have got him. He wouldn't have thrown no more spears!' cried the angry seaman.

'You'll "get" no one until you've told me what happened out there to turn them against us like this.'

'There was an accident. One of them got shot—but I'm not staying here to talk about it, and neither will you if you value your life.'

Isaiah was lying. Josh was certain of it, but now was not the best time to try to extract the truth from him. The little Bushmen were closing in quickly, moving forward from rock to rock.

Josh fell back to where Sam Speke was keeping Miriam and Daniel sheltered behind him. On the way Josh managed to snatch up one of their canvas bags with preserved seal meat in it. To attempt to collect the water-keg was out of the question.

They retreated from the camp along the way they had come, but had not gone more than a few hundred yards when they saw the hunting party returning far below them and Hwexa making his way down to intercept them.

There was a fairly level strip of ground running northwards at the foot of a tall cliff, and to Josh it seemed there might have been a faint path along it.

'We'll go that way,' he pointed northwards. 'If Xhube and his men decide to come after us, they'll try to circle around us. We need to stay fairly high if we are to see them coming.'

The wisdom of his words was soon apparent. Hwexa reached the returning hunters, and minutes later the group of Bushmen split into two parties—half the men coming straight up the mountain towards them, the remainder doubling back on a curving course that would put them ahead of Josh and the others.

Isaiah Dacket was leading the way and he set a gruelling pace. As the only one aware of what had happened he knew how determined the Bushmen would be to catch them. Whatever might be the fate of the others he would certainly die—and it would not be a pleasant death.

But no matter how fast they travelled the Bushmen who were trying to cut them off went faster. By the time Josh and the others had covered a mile the Bushmen were well ahead. But then the little men turned towards them and had to scramble up the steep and rocky slope, and this slowed them down.

There was no doubt in Josh's mind now that he and the

others were following a path. It was as wide here as a wagon track and smoothed by centuries of Bushman feet.

'We've got to go faster to beat those Bushmen.' Josh took a firm grip of Daniel and broke into a trot. The boy protested breathlessly, but the little men were scrambling towards them in a last desperate attempt to cut them off. However, the Bushmen had lost their race.

The path swung around a tall single boulder and then suddenly ended at the mouth of a tall cavern set in the cliff-face.

Nobody needed Josh's urgent call to seek refuge in its shadows. They flung themselves through the entrance gratefully. Josh handed Daniel to Miriam then, turning back to the mouth of the cave, loaded his pistol and prepared to meet the expected rush of the Bushmen.

Xhube kneeled by the body of his daughter. His eyes burned and the muscles of his throat knotted as though they would choke him. Yet none of his people must be allowed to see his grief lest it be interpreted as weakness.

His hands longed to reach out and touch her young face in a vain attempt to give her back the gift of life he had first passed to her through the body of his wife. His heart cried out to tell of the twofold love he had borne for his daughter since the death of her mother.

But Bele, too, was now dead, and his eyes told him of many things he would rather not have known. Her young body had been abused by the man who had killed her. One of the lost white men he himself had ordered his people to help. It was now his duty as her father and the leader of his people to avenge her death. The white men must die.

His grief was disturbed by news from the hunters he had sent to intercept the murderers.

'The white strangers have gone into the sacred cave of Gaua. We were too late to stop them.'

The Bushman messenger had been part of the hunt, had raced to cut off the retreat of Josh and the others, then run back to his chief, yet his breathing was no heavier than that of the others standing about him.

But his news could not have been worse.

Xhube stood up and looked at the faces of his people. Now it was not only the murder of Bele that had to be avenged. The strangers had offended the god Gaua by entering his great painted cave. This was undoubtedly the worst day in the history of Xhube's people.

He looked down again at the body of his daughter. Ripping off the seal-skin belt she wore, he threw it far from him. Speaking to Hwexa, he said, 'Bring my daughter. She shall sit before the cave of Gaua and her spirit will witness the death of the strangers so it may rest when she is laid in the ground. Gaua can look from his cave and see that we, too, have been wronged.'

CHAPTER SIX

'I think you're lying!'

Josh's words were the answer to Isaiah's explanation that his musket had gone off accidentally and the ball had struck and killed one of the Bushman women.

'You think what you like. I don't expect you to believe anything I tell you – but that's what happened.'

At that moment a remarkable natural phenomenon occurred inside the great cave. The midday sunlight slanted through a cleft in the top of the cave and touched a previously unseen lake of deep-blue water. The reflected light illuminated the whole cave as though a million candles had been lit. It was this incredible and beautiful daily happening that had first made the cave a holy place for the Bushmen and their deity Gaua. This, and the truly remarkable graffiti that covered the walls of the cave to a height of more than twelve feet.

Josh had been having his heated argument with Isaiah Dacket at the entrance of the cave with the eyes of Miriam and Sam Speke upon him, and it was Daniel who first saw the sun's magic transformation of the inside of the cave. His delighted cry of 'Pretty!' brought all heads around.

It was much more than pretty. The scene was awe-inspiring in its beauty. The height of the great cave and the colours conjured up by the reflected light reminded Josh of the sun shining through the stained-glass windows of the village church at St Cleer in faraway Cornwall. But the parish church had possessed nothing to compare with the painted walls of this cave. Here, in reds, blacks, browns and whites, were a hundred stories and centuries of history. There were vivid action-packed hunting scenes, battles, births and deaths, and celebrations.

There were many animals depicted, too, most of them unlike any that Josh and Miriam had ever seen. But it was the figures of the men that really lived in the pictures. Painted with a minimum of brush-strokes the history of the Bushman came alive. Here was the little man of the wastelands at the moment of painful birth, his mother far removed from the village lest death come to her or her child and force the superstitious Bushmen to abandon that place. Farther along the wall the pictures traced the Bushman's life through the dangers and privations of a nomadic existence culminating in his death and his reunion with long-gone ancestors in a Bushman's heaven on the moon.

One could study these pictures and obtain a deep understanding of the little man they depicted – his ways, his thoughts and his religion. Here was the soul of the man.

But this was not the time for such a study. Of far more importance at the moment was the presence of water. Now Josh knew they had some chance of survival – if the Bushmen did not manage to kill them.

He was the first to recover from the wonder of the painted cave and see the little men moving in to the attack. They advanced from rock to rock, wriggling on their bellies like lizards.

Josh shouted to the others and, taking out his loaded pistol, aimed it at a low rock which was sheltering a Bushman. The report of the pistol was deafening in the confines of the cave but it achieved the desired effect. The lead ball glanced off the rock with a sound like a finger plucking a high note on a harp-string. The Bushman promptly bolted from his hiding-place, two others leaving theirs to flee with him.

It was the first time Josh had ever fired a gun, and he had not been prepared for the way it had bucked in his hand, or the choking cloud of gunpowder smoke that drifted back into his face from it, but he had hit the target he had aimed for and he was well pleased. He reloaded the barrel he had fired, content in the knowledge that this was a tool he could master if ever he put his mind to it.

The watchers in the cave had to wait for an hour before the Bushmen made their next move. It was a macabre and unexpected one.

The Bushmen arrived in a tight group, fifty yards from the cave, and Isaiah Dacket put up his musket to fire at them. Once again Josh stopped him.

'Wait! They aren't attacking this time. Let's see what they intend doing.'

But Isaiah Dacket had seen they were carrying something

between them and he had a shrewd idea what it was. Side-stepping Josh, he aimed the musket and fired. It was a snap shot, made in desperation without a proper sighting, and the musket-ball went harmlessly above the heads of the clustered Bushmen.

The sound of the shot caused great consternation among the little men, but Xhube's stern voice prevented them from dropping the body of Bele on the spot and running away.

Hwexa backed his nephew's words. 'Only a fool runs from thunder,' he declared. 'To hear it is to know that the lightning has already struck.'

Although the Bushmen heeded the words, they made great haste to the spot Xhube pointed out to them and, laying down their tragic burden, quickly scurried away to seek shelter amongst the scattered rocks.

This thing was against all their customs. When a Bushman died the body was buried in a shallow grave as quickly as possible and the whole tribe immediately moved far away so that the spirit would not follow and seek to remain with them. It was only out of respect for Xhube's leadership that they broke with tradition on this occasion. Even so, it was left to Xhube to prop the slight figure of his daughter's body up against a rock, seated so that the sightless eyes would gaze unblinkingly towards the holy cave of Gaua and witness the vengeance of her father.

Inside the cave Isaiah's desperate shot went without comment as the beleaguered party watched what was happening outside. Not until Xhube turned to face them and raised his arms in a promise to Gaua that he would avenge the death of his daughter and the desecration of the holy cave were they able to recognise the victim.

'Oh no!' The cry of deep anguish was forced from Miriam.

Josh was momentarily stunned. Then fierce anger welled up inside him. He turned on Isaiah Dacket at the moment the tall seaman aimed his musket with the intention of downing the little Bushman chief by the side of his dead daughter.

This time Josh did not try to persuade the sailor not to shoot. His clubbed fist struck Isaiah on the temple and knocked him sideways. Staggering across the cave on rubber legs, the sailor tripped and measured his length on the hard stone floor of the cave.

The long barrel of the musket began to swing towards Josh, but stopped suddenly when Isaiah looked into the two barrels of the shaking pistol, Josh's knuckles gleaming white as he gripped the weapon fiercely.

'Do it, Isaiah! Point that musket at me and give me an excuse to kill you.'

Isaiah Dacket dropped the musket to the ground quickly.

'Pick it up, Sam, and watch what's going on outside.'

Without looking at his shipmate Sam Speke did as he was told, careful not to step between the two men. He could see the anger in Josh and was afraid the pistol would go off accidentally.

When Sam Speke moved out of the way Josh gained control of himself, although he found it difficult to speak to Isaiah in his normal voice.

'So your gun went off "accidentally" and just happened to kill the girl you've been after since she first came to our camp? I think I could tell you a story that would come much closer to the truth!'

Some of Josh's anger returned again at the thought of what Bele had probably suffered at the seaman's hands.

'I ought to throw you out of this cave and let Xhube and his men have you.'

'You can't do that, Josh.' Sam Speke was thoroughly alarmed. 'You haven't seen what these people do to a man. Whatever Isaiah's done you can't let that happen to another human being.'

'And why not? He's put all our lives at risk as well as killing a young girl who did nothing but give us her friendship.'

'Josh, Sam's right. I feel just as upset as you about this, but you can't give Isaiah to them.' It was an emotionally choked Miriam who spoke.

Josh looked at Miriam and knew what she was thinking. Her father, crazed with drink, had also raped a girl, years before in Cornwall. He had been hounded to his death at the bottom of a deep mineshaft because of it. She would not allow any man to be handed over to certain death.

'No, you're right. But he'll answer for it when we reach civilisation.'

Isaiah Dacket showed no sign of the relief he felt. The first people they were likely to encounter would be Boers. If Josh made a complaint to them about the murder of a Bushman, he would make himself a laughing-stock. No Boer would penalise a white man for killing any native — but especially a Bushman. To a Boer, or indeed any native, a Bushman was something to be exterminated. A Bushman neither planted crops nor kept herds. He would not accept the rights of others to do so. It was beyond his comprehension that the land over which his people had roamed at will for thousands of years could be owned or taken possession of by others. As for cattle, they were merely slow-moving game — an easy meal.

There was another, economic, reason for hunting Bushmen. Taken young enough a Bushman woman would make a passable unpaid servant. Not so the men. A love of freedom was too deep-rooted in a Bushman to be beaten out of him, whatever his age. Killing him was the only solution.

All this was known to Isaiah Dacket, but he had no intention of being around to witness Josh's discomfort when he learned of the Boer way of thinking. He had plans.

On the way to the mountains with the Bushmen, Isaiah had observed that whenever they left camp the little men always buried a few ostrich eggshells full of water beneath the sand in a shady spot. Isaiah was satisfied he could find the camps again — and he would not be sharing the water with anyone. Josh's reaction to the death of Bele had made escape a little more difficult but he had little doubt that the dawn would find him many miles from Josh and the Bushmen.

Xhube's men made two forays before nightfall. They were not determined attacks, and a single shot on each occasion had been sufficient to drive the little men back to the shelter of the rocks. Josh's guess was that the attacks had been Xhube's way of holding the interest of his men. This would be a long siege. Time was entirely on the side of the little Bushman. He knew how much food they had in the cave.

Now that Isaiah had been deprived of his musket and his knife it meant that the watches would have to be shared between Josh and Sam, although in the grey dark of the pre-dawn they would both need to be on guard at the cave entrance.

The cave was wide enough for Josh to feel safe having Isaiah sleeping on the side farthest away from all the others while he or Sam kept watch.

Sam Speke kept the first look-out while Josh and Miriam, with Daniel, lay on the hard floor of the cave, well back in the deep black shadows. While Daniel slept Miriam wept for the young Bele, and Josh did his best to comfort her. Then the events of the day caught up with him and he dozed off.

He was brought awake by the sound of a shot, but it had come from so far away that Josh could not immediately identify it. Then from much closer he herd a groan of pain. Josh pulled the pistol from his belt before waking Miriam.

'There's something wrong. Take this pistol and stay with Daniel. Be ready to move quickly if I call.'

On hands and knees Josh crawled towards the cave entrance. There was something lying across it, and as he moved closer the shape moved and groaned. It was Sam Speke.

Josh rose to his feet and half a dozen paces took him to Sam's side. He took a quick look out from the cave. The moon was directly overhead, lighting the whole clear space before the cave. There was not a single shadow in which a Bushman could have been hiding, and the space was empty.

Sam Speke groaned again and stirred painfully.

In the moonlight Josh saw a dark patch staining the side of the seaman's forehead, and when he put his hand down to it his fingers came away sticky with blood. Then Josh knew this had not been the work of a Bushman. He made a rapid search of the area around the unconscious seaman, and when he could not find the musket he knew for certain this was Isaiah Dacket's doing.

'Miriam. Sam's been hit on the head and he's bleeding. Get some water and something to use as a cloth. Hurry! I want to bring him round and talk to him.'

By the time Miriam arrived with her underskirt soaked in water Sam was already regaining consciousness. A few minutes later he was sitting up, holding his head between his hands and cursing himself for a stupid fool.

'I never even heard him, Josh. And now he's taken the gold with him – and he's got the musket.'

'We've still got the pistol – and your life. It's my fault. I should have known he would try something like this. We should have bound him. But—'

A terrifying sound cleaved the night air and took his words away. It was a man's scream. Rising to a horrifying crescendo, it jerked along on the highest note for a full half-minute before dying away in bubbling breathlessness. It was another half-minute before Miriam's fingernails freed themselves from Josh's arm. Nobody said a word as they waited for the agonised sound to repeat itself.

There was nothing but the moonlight and a million silent stars.

'It is done,' said Hwexa.

'It is done,' agreed a weary-hearted Xhube.

The other Bushmen murmured their approval.

'This one has the stick that makes thunder,' said Hwexa. 'Now we can go to Gaua's cave for the others without losing more of our people.'

There was a moment's hesitation before Xhube declared, 'No! It is over. This is the white man who killed Bele. Now he is dead. There will be no more killing on the mountain.'

'You are forgetting the anger of Gaua. The white men and the woman and child are in his sacerd cave. They must die for that.'

'That is not Gaua's will.'

Xhube spoke as though from a great distance, and the others recognised the signs. Xhube was hearing the voices that sometimes came to him at moments like this.

'Gaua himself took the white men into his sacred cave and gave them his protection. This one was not a good man. Gaua turned him out and led him to us to pay for Bele's life. Now it is done and we will go.'

'We will go,' echoed Hwexa, and the three words were repeated by every one of the little golden-skinned warriors.

CHAPTER SEVEN

For the remainder of that night Daniel was the only occupant of the great painted cave of Gaua who slept. Sam's head throbbed painfully, but he sat keeping watch in the shadows of the cave entrance as the night gave way to the dark-grey dawn.

Still the expected attack did not come. Then, as it became lighter, Miriam said, 'Bele's body, Josh – it's gone!'

It was a few more minutes before they could be sure, and then Josh knew that Xhube and his small family tribe had gone away. He was sure of it even before the sun reached over the mountain and shone on the sandy plain below them, revealing the tiny Bushmen moving away from the mountain, travelling in single file.

Josh felt no animosity towards them, only a great sorrow. The little people had helped strangers to their land, asking nothing in return. Their reward had been murder and anguish. Josh doubted whether future travellers would find them as ready to make friends.

He lost some of his compassion when he and Sam Speke found Isaiah Dacket. The tall seaman was lying spread-eagled on the ground and the Bushmen had meted out a crude justice before spearing the life from him. Had he lived, Isaiah Dacket would have raped no other young girl.

Josh felt sick and was glad Miriam and Daniel had been left in the cave, but Sam Speke suffered no such queasiness. He searched the mutilated seaman and was jubilant to find the bag of gold slung on its cord about Isaiah's neck. His happiness was complete when he found the musket where Isaiah had dropped it after firing the shot that had wakened Josh. Only then did Sam Speke think of burying his late shipmate.

It was a very shallow grave and neither man bothered to pile stones upon it.

'Josh,' the seaman spoke as they scraped the last of the earth over the body, 'I'd like you to know that with Isaiah gone no one need ever know you've seen the inside of a prison hulk.'

The full impact of Sam Speke's statement took a few moments to sink in. He was right. Josh trusted the burly seaman and, with Isaiah Dacket dead, he realised he could hope for a future once more.

'I'm obliged to you, Sam. Not only for my sake, but for Miriam and Daniel, too.'

'Daniel's a fine boy, Josh. He'll grow up a boy to be proud of, and with this gold you'll be able to give him a good start in life.'

With their thoughts on the future the two men walked to the cave without a backward glance at the shallow grave that marked the violent passing of an English seaman.

There was no longer any choice about the direction they should take. They could not return to the coast for fear of meeting up with Xhube and his small tribe. It would be stretching his forgiveness too far.

The only way lay inland, across the mountains. But, as always in this parched land, they had to be sure of a supply of water. Isaiah had not been the only one to observe the Bushman habit of leaving a supply of water at camp sites, and so Josh and his party trekked to the site of their last unhappy camp to see if they could find some of the ostrich-egg containers.

They found something far more useful – the water-keg. It was probably too heavy and clumsy for the Bushmen to carry with them and of so stout a construction that to destroy it would have required unwonted effort. Josh chose to think that the leader of the little people had left it as a final generous gesture of friendship towards them.

They took the keg back to the great cave to fill with water for their journey and had a last look at the remarkable paintings. Then they set their faces to the east and headed for the low ridge Xhube had turned them from on their way up the mountain.

The ridge must have been four thousand feet above the surrounding country, but the view they had hoped to see was not there. Instead there was a wide broken valley with another ridge two miles in front of them.

It was the story of the sand dunes over again. For four days they slithered and scrambled down crumbling banks and toiled up steep slopes. Always there was another mountain ahead of them.

On the third day they found a valley where it was apparent that a river occasionally flowed. Here there was lush vegetation and plenty of animal life. Sam shot and killed a bustard, a bird as big and fat as a large turkey. It required no special skill. The big bird showed no inclination to move away and allowed Sam to approach to within easy shooting range.

They ate well that night, and it proved to be a turning-point in their gruelling trek across the mountains.

The next morning they topped a rise and instead of gazing out across more peaks and valleys they found themselves five thousand feet above a transformed land. Before them were miles of rolling bush veldt. It was not brown and parched like the land on the far side of the mountains, but green and fertile. The recent rains had brought plenty of water here – and it was still running. Water gushed from a spring below them, sparkling in the sunlight as it tumbled into a sheer hundred-foot drop from a smooth rock-shelf.

'We've done it, Josh. I told you we were right to come this way.'

Miriam hugged Josh in delight, and he squeezed her to him happily.

'There's life out there, too,' said Sam Speke more soberly.

'You mean all those animals?'

There was a great herd of zebra far in the distance, though from up here it was impossible to identify the species.

'No. I mean the fire over there.'

Sam pointed farther out towards the horizon, to one side of the grazing animals. A barely discernible wisp of smoke threaded the still, hot air.

'There's our civilisation. I hope it turns out to be all we are hoping for.'

Josh looked thoughtfully towards the distant fire. It *had* to be all right. They needed to make contact with people again and were totally committed to travelling in this direction. There could be no return across the mountains.

'We'll head towards the fire tomorrow. But we'll be cautious. I'd like to know what sort of people they are before we call on them.'

The ground was much steeper on this side of the mountains, and they descended slowly and cautiously, reaching the plains below by mid-afternoon. After filling the keg at the stream they followed the foot of the mountains for a while, keeping an almost vertical cliff-face on their right.

They had only travelled half a mile when they discovered a fissure in the cliff-face. It was no more than a six-foot-wide notch and would be ideal for a camp. A fire built at the entrance would provide an efficient barrier against any prowling creatures of the night, but as a double protection they cut down some of the thorn-bushes that seemed to grow everywhere in these lands and built a low barrier across the entrance beyond the fire.

Trees were more numerous here, and with the fire piled high with slower-burning wood they felt secure enough to bed down without a guard when darkness fell with typical tropical abruptness.

Sam Speke was the first to wake the following morning and seconds later he shook Josh with vigorous urgency. Josh sat up, and his hand went immediately to the loaded pistol.

Sitting cross-legged on the ground beyond the thorn-hedge were a dozen natives. Each was naked except for a short animal-skin 'apron' secured about his waist.

Sam also picked up his gun, and there was a nervous movement among the men beyond the fire. One of them stood up slowly and deliberately, leaving his spear lying on the ground beside him.

Unlike the golden-skinned Bushmen, this man was very dark-skinned and tall – taller than either Josh or Sam Speke – and his body was well formed and muscled. The castaways had met up with a hunting party of the Herero tribe.

'We come in peace. We have no guns.'

The Herero warrior spoke English slowly, his voice deep and melodic. Josh and Sam looked at each other in delight. Being able to communicate with these people meant there was far less chance of a misunderstanding occurring between them. It also meant they must be close to English-speaking people. Things were looking brighter already.

'We, too, come in peace,' replied Josh. As proof of his words he tucked the pistol back into his belt.

Behind him Miriam had awakened, and sight of her caused much interest among the Herero beyond the thorn-barrier which this morning looked frail and ineffectual.

'You have journeyed far?'

The Herero's manner was polite, his command of English good, but Josh found it necessary to concentrate on what was being said as the other man's pronunciation was unusual.

'We come from beyond the mountains. From the sea. Our ship was wrecked.'

A frown crossed the Herero's face, and he said something in his own language to those sitting beside him. One of them replied at some length.

'Do you think they mean us any harm?' Miriam whispered to Josh.

'I don't think so.' Josh's reply was as low as Miriam's query had been as he included Sam Speke, 'But keep your musket primed, Sam. Just in case.'

The Herero turned back to them.

'It is far from the other side of the mountains. Did you meet with any of the gatherers on the way?'

The question was casual – too casual. Josh sensed a sudden dangerous air of expectancy among the tall black men beyond the flimsy hedge. He knew that for some reason his answer would be important – but he did not know what he was expected to say.

'I don't know who "the gatherers" are. We met some small people on the other side of the mountains.'

Immediately the tension mounted.

'The small people are the gatherers. They helped you? They are your friends?'

Josh looked from the face of the man who had spoken to his companions and he knew what his answer had to be, though he choked on the words.

'We fought with them. One of my people was killed.'

'Ah!' The sound went up from many throats, indicating that a number of the Herero understood what had been said. Suddenly the tension was gone.

'It is always so with the gatherers,' said the Herero spokesman. 'They are not to be trusted. How many days since did this happen? We have killed three of the gatherers but know there must be more.'

He seemed disappointed when Josh told him the Bushmen were more than four days away.

'It does not matter. You are with friends now. The Little Father will be pleased to see you.'

'The Little Father?'

The Herero smiled and made the sign of the cross with his forefingers. 'The one who comes to us from the Great Father.'

'A missionary!' Josh and Miriam spoke as one, and Sam grinned at them.

'I knew I was right to follow you, Josh. You was born lucky. Shipwrecked a thousand miles from anywhere, a hundred different ways we can go – and you guide us right to some missionary's doorstep!'

They were not exactly on the missionary's doorstep. The Herero – his name was Mutjise – was leading a hunting party a hundred miles from the village where the mission station was situated and it took them another four days of hard travelling to reach it.

Along the way Josh learned to like and respect the tall muscular Hereros. They were cheerful and good-tempered and carried Daniel for much of the way on their shoulders. The only thing Josh found difficult to understand was their unreasonable hatred of the Bushmen. It was an attitude he was to find among men far more sophisticated than the Herero – and with the same apparent lack of cause.

On the way to the Herero village they met up with a great deal of game, including many animals Josh had never seen before. Elephant, giraffe and the tall ungainly bird, the ostrich, among them. Sam Speke shot two zebra and a giraffe, and the hunters were overjoyed. They would return with more meat than they had expected.

Unlike the Bushmen, the Herero were quite familiar with firearms, although none of them possessed one. Instead, they hunted with long-handled, broad-bladed assegais which they could hurl incredible distances; but they were quite content to allow the sailor to hunt for them.

They arrived at the Herero village an hour before dusk. At this time the bare-breasted women surrounded by wide-eyed naked children, were busy preparing a meal of maize porridge washed down with slightly curdled milk for their men. The men themselves were returning from the grazing-lands about the village, driving their numerous cattle into dusty wooden pens on the edge of the village.

There had been no attempt to conceal this place. It had all the bustle and dust of a small town. Round mud huts with thatched roofs were bunched together in orderly family groups while cattle, goats, children and dogs cluttered the packed earth 'streets'.

The arrival of the hunting party was greeted with acclamation, but this meat would not be distributed amongst all the people as a matter of course. It would go only to the families of the hunters. As had been the case with the Bushmen, the white strangers came in for much attention, Miriam most of all. She was the first white woman most of the villagers had ever seen. Certainly there had not been one here before.

Mutjise led them straight to the centre of the village, to where the mission church stood, its symbolic wooden cross standing high above the surrounding huts. When they arrived at a small hut standing in the shadow of the cross, Mutjise signalled them to wait. Pushing aside the blanket that served as a door, he went inside.

While they waited Josh and the others took in the details of their surroundings. The beehive-shaped huts were deceptive. At first sight they appeared tiny, but there was room in each of them for a whole family. As Josh estimated there were at least five hundred huts in the village it added up to a sizeable population.

There were many shady trees left standing, too, and the hard-packed earth beneath them was evidence that full use was made of their shade during the hot days. There seemed no shortage of water. On the far edge of the village Josh could see orderly green patches of vegetation. These people were cultivators as well as herdsmen. They were altogether a more prosperous and settled people than the little Bushmen of the desert, who lived out their precarious lives on a day-to-day basis.

'Good evening. I have been awaiting your arrival with great excitement. You are the first visitors from the outside world I have received here in Otjimkandje.'

Josh had been looking towards the pens where hundreds of cattle were raising great palls of dust as they milled about restlessly prior to settling down for the night. At the sound of the voice he swung around, startled. He had heard the accent before. It brought back memories of a German mine-captain who had once terrified the small mine where Josh's father had worked — the man who by his callous disregard for Cornish miners had caused much hardship among them. His contempt for human life had been such that he had once tried to leave injured miners entombed in a tunnel after a roof-fall.

Miriam, too, had known the German mine-captain and like Josh her initial reaction to the voice was one of dismay.

But missionary Hugo Walder was as strong a man as any to have come out of Germany and he had none of the faults of his mining fellow-countryman. Hugo Walder's capacity for loving his fellow-men was as large as the frame that held his great heart. In his early fifties, the missionary stood well over six feet tall with a large-boned frame and huge hands that would tackle any task, no matter how menial. With an eagle nose dominating a full-bearded face he was a formidable figure.

He took in the state of the ragged travel-weary party as he grasped first Sam Speke's hand and then Josh's hand, learning their names before turning to Miriam.

'My child! What a terrible time you must have had. This is no country for a woman to travel through on foot. But who is this little gentleman?'

Hugo Walder swung Daniel easily off his feet and held him out at arm's length to look at him.

'You are so young to have travelled so far!' Daniel grinned at him. 'And so brave and cheerful.' With a gentle friendly shake he lowered Daniel to the ground. 'Come, you must be hungry. I have food ready. Please come into my little house.

Holding the blanket aside, Hugo Walder ushered them inside

the hut. It was as though they had stepped over the threshold into another world. A civilised world of tables and trestle stools; of shelves with books and piles of newspapers; crockery and cutlery; oil-lamps and grass mats. In a corner of the room was a discreetly curtained-off bed, in another a small writing-desk with brass-handled drawers. Around the walls portraits of severe-faced men and women looked down. There was another picture, larger than the others, of a blood-stained Christ hanging on the cross of Calvary with tearful men and women kneeling about him.

'Welcome to my home,' said the missionary. 'While we are eating, your own huts will be made ready. I knew how many of you there were but very little else.'

'How did you know we were coming?' Josh put the question that was in all their minds.

Hugo Walder smiled. 'A runner was on his way here with the news of your presence before you knew you had been seen. Since Jonker and his tribe of Afrikaners moved into this country it is as well to know everything that happens. You were brought to Otjimkandje by Mutjise, son of Tjamuene who is the chief of this tribe of Herero. Tomorrow you will meet Tjamuene, but while you are in the village you will be my guests. That is less likely to offend Jonker.'

It was apparent that Jonker the Afrikaner had considerable authority here, but Josh's questions about him would have to wait. The big German missionary was ushering them to places at the rough-planked table which, together with the two long wooden stools, had been brought from the church for the occasion.

The missionary offered a prayer before the meal and they all sat with bowed heads as he said, 'Lord, bless all who eat at this table. And for deliverance from the trials I am sure they have suffered we thank you. Amen.'

'Amen,' they repeated.

The meal was of hot meat and gravy poured liberally on top of a generous base of thick cornmeal porridge and was served by two Herero women. It did little to cool them, but it was a happy gathering and there could be no doubt of the missionary's very real pleasure at having guests.

'It came as a great surprise to me when I heard you were found in the north, in the mountains. Where had you come from—and where are you going?'

Josh told Hugo Walder of the storm and the shipwreck as the missionary's expression changed from one of concern to incredulity.

'You were shipwrecked on the coast and crossed the desert to the mountains? You crossed that desert on your own and are here to tell of it? It's a miracle! There is not a Herero who would even attempt it, and I fear you will meet many people who will not believe you. Before today I would not have believed it possible.'

'We had some help. . . .' Rather hesitantly Josh told the missionary about the little men who had helped them. He told him the whole story—of the Portuguese skeletons, of the great cave and of Isaiah's way of repaying their kindness. He ended with an outline of the seaman's death and their subsequent trek over the mountains.

'So you met the Bushmen and they showed you kindness,' mused the missionary, emotionally moved. 'You have been more successful than I—and I have been in Africa for nine years.'

He signalled to one of the Herero women, who brought in large slices of a juicy melon while the other woman cleared the plates from the table.

'The Bushmen are a tragic people—so very tragic. It is most unusual for them to show themselves to strangers. You must have met a remote group who have little contact with other tribes. You have been lucky.'

In spite of the guttural accent Hugo Walder had a scholar's command of the English language.

'Why are the Bushmen such a tragic people?'

The missionary wiped melon juice from the thick beard about his lips before he answered. Conversation in this remote African village was a luxury in which he was rarely able to indulge himself, and there was not a man of his acquaintance, white or black, to whom he could have expressed a sympathetic opinion about the little Bushmen. In consequence he had to think about his words.

'Why is the Bushman a tragic figure? It is because he is an anomaly in this age. He should rightly be extinct. He does not own cattle, neither does he till the land. He will not live in a village such as this one, and so he cannot be overrun and made to pay homage to an overlord. He will not understand that the land from which he and his people have fought a living for longer than history belongs to anyone. To him it is not something that can be picked up and taken, and so the land belongs to no one but itself. Unfortunately he has the same nonconformist ideas about cattle. When a Bushman is hungry he looks for food. An elephant or a cow is all the same to him. Lastly, of course, he has no powerful tribe to back his actions. Africa is no different from any other part of the world in one respect: the weak are bullied by the strong. The only difference is that in a civilised country bullying is carried on within certain accepted limits. Here there are none. Death is the only boundary. The Bushman will not conform to the will of those about him, so he is hunted and killed. The Bushman is an elusive prey with only limited power to fight back, and so the whole thing has become something of a sport. The party that found you was supposed to be a hunting party – it *was* a hunting party – but I think their quarry was the little men who helped you to cross the desert.'

Josh remembered Xhube as he had told the sign-story of the Portuguese wanderers whose bones lay in the mountain gully, and recalled the pride and sensitivity within the little golden-skinned man.

Miriam's thoughts were of the shy and beautiful smile that had belonged to the gentle Bele.

'But you are a missionary. Surely your teachings are against such things? Can't you put a stop to the killing?'

'My child, every Sunday I preach to an empty church. The Herero watched me build it with my own hands. They did not help. I treat their illnesses and their injuries. I fall to my knees and pray to a god they cannot comprehend. Things have improved since I learned their language, but they have first to accept me as a man before they will listen to what I have to say. I must teach them by example and by proving to them that their life and their hardships are mine also – that I will not desert them when things become even harder.

'I was with Tjamuene when Jonker and his Afrikaners came from the south and took the valley of the hot springs for his own, forcing the Herero to move here to Otjimkandje. That helped, but I have far to go.'

Hugo Walder stroked down his heavy black beard.

'It may seem a strange and sad thing to say, but your dead companion may have done a great service to that little tribal group. They will never again trust strangers. Because of that they may stay alive for a few more years. Who knows?

'I came here to bring the word of the Lord to a people who have walked their own path for centuries. I doubt if my mission will succeed during my lifetime. It requires much patience, and the things that are bad can only be changed slowly. Sometimes because of my years they seek my advice. Perhaps that is to be the sum of my life's work. Who can say?'

During the missionary's sincere and quiet-voiced talk Daniel's head had leaned sideways against Miriam and his eyes drooped closed. Hugo Walder saw it and immediately rose from the table.

'What am I thinking of? You must be so tired, and all I can do is talk. I am being a selfish old man because I enjoy your company so much. Come, I will show you to your huts. I think you will find them quite comfortable. Tomorrow we will discuss your plans and see what I might be able to do to help them.'

Sam Speke was given a hut adjoining the mission. Josh carried the sleeping Daniel to a larger hut on the far side of the church. After showing them in through the blanket-covered door and lighting a single yellow-flamed oil-lamp for them the gruff but kindly German missionary wished them 'Good night' and left them alone.

When he returned to his hut Hugo Walder sat down to think. After a while he crossed to the piles of ageing and tattered newspapers and, selecting one bundle, untied the string that held it together and began slowly thumbing through the pages.

The mud walls of Josh and Miriam's hut were unadorned, and above them a latticework of bowed saplings supported the thick dried-grass thatch of the roof. An upside-down lizard, red-eyed in the lamplight, was spreadeagled motionless against the thatch, waiting for an exploring fly to walk into the range of its whiplash tongue.

Two beds made up from cured animal-hides covered with colourful woven blankets were ready for them, one for Daniel and the larger one for Josh and Miriam. The lamp stood on a rough square table in the centre of the one-roomed hut, and three stools were placed around it. Hugo Walder had even managed to gather together an assortment of cooking-pots, and two large earthenware jars of water stood near the door.

After undressing Daniel and tucking him into his bed Miriam said to Josh, 'Do you realise that this is our very first home?'

Josh smiled wryly. 'That doesn't exactly make me the greatest of providers.'

'Don't say that.'

Miriam came to him quickly. 'Do you remember where I spent my childhood? In that rock cave on Bodmin Moor? This is far, far better than that. We are all three of us here because of you, Josh. Four people from *Pride of Liverpool* are alive because you insisted we should head inland instead of following the coast.'

She kissed him and he held her close, surrendering to his need for her. Miriam responded immediately, and the fears and uncertainties of the previous weeks fell away. They were alone, and for the moment there was only an all-consuming love for each other. It was a force as primitive and powerful as any that might be found in the untamed lands surrounding the mud walls of the hut in Otjimkandje.

Later that night Miriam lay awake in the crook of Josh's bare arm. Above them in the roof the lizard scratched a zig-zag path across the tight-knit thatch. The drums of the village had long since fallen silent and with them the loud voices of the Herero men returning to their huts. From the cattle-pens there was only the occasional complaint from a cow crowded by her fellows. Miriam had lain awake for a long time before she felt a slight movement from the arm about her.

'Are you awake, Josh?' she whispered.

'Yes.' His whisper was hoarser than her own as his arm

tightened about her.

'What will we do now? I mean, now that we've reached safety?'

'I don't know. Probably move on to a place where there are more Europeans. Where they might have need of an engineer. But first I must learn more of the country – who it belongs to, and how the law is administered. Whatever happens, I am not going back to prison, Miriam. I would rather die here.'

'You won't have to go prison again, Josh. Sam is the only one who knows anything about your past and he won't say anything.'

'Oh, I trust Sam. But if we made our way to a place where there was a British administrator he would ask questions. Then he would have to inform the owners of *Pride of Liverpool* of our survival, and before long news would come back that I am a convicted man.'

'Then why move on? Perhaps there are some mines in this area where you can can work.'

'I haven't heard of any – certainly none that might need a mine engineer. Not that it would be necessary for them to have engines. I had a thorough apprenticeship, and there are many other jobs I could do. Blacksmith, founder, smelter – I'll do anything.'

'It would be a completely new start, Josh. We could stay here and forget there was ever anyone or anything before. You and I and Daniel could build a whole new life together.'

'All right. I'll find out all I can about the country from Hugo Walder first thing in the morning.'

Miriam slid her arm across his chest and snuggled closer to him.

'Then I'll not worry about the future anymore. Everything is going to be all right – and we'll always be together.'

CHAPTER EIGHT

Sam Speke was as contented with his little hut as Josh and Miriam were with theirs, and by morning the strain of the arduous trek from the sea had begun to fall away from all of them. Hugo Walder visited them early, assuring himself that they had slept well and were provided with all they required.

'I had a visit from one of the chief's messengers last night,' he said. 'Tjamuene wishes to meet you this morning. You have aroused his curiosity. White men coming here from the south are rare enough. White men, a woman and a child coming from the north are unheard of!'

Tjamuene had his own tiny kraal within the village. It consisted of some thirty thatched round huts sited within a six-foot-high wall of sticks and dried grass.

The missionary had sent word ahead of him that he was bringing the newcomers, and they found the chief waiting, seated beneath a tree on a pile of cow hides, a lion skin draped about his shoulders. The chief was flanked by the warriors of his personal bodyguard – tall, powerfully built men each armed with a broad-bladed battle-assegai.

If Tjamuene's idea had been to impress his visitors, then he was successful. Josh thought it would be a brave or foolish man who would dare to attack a chief surrounded by such warriors.

'Welcome!' Tjamuene spoke English with difficulty. 'You have come far.'

'From beyond the desert and across the sea,' agreed Josh.

Mutjise spoke to his father in their own tongue, and the chief nodded, carefully appraising the newcomers.

'From the lands of the Little Father. It is far.' His face took on a calculated expression. 'You have guns, Mutjise tells me.'

'We have guns.'

'It is good. Chief Jonker of the Afrikaners would be angry if the Herero had guns. It would mean war. But you are of the Little Father's people. You will hunt for us.'

'We will need more powder,' said Sam Speke.

Again there was a conversation between father and son.

'Mutjise will fetch you whatever you need.'

'Then I am sure they will be happy to hunt for Tjamuene's people for as long as they stay in Otjimkandje,' said Hugo Walder before Josh could speak. 'But their travels are not yet over. They have far to go to reach the towns of their own people.'

This time the talk between Tjamuene and Mutjise was carried out in lengthy whispers, and the missionary took the opportunity to explain his intervention.

'Unless it is made clear to Tjamuene that you are only passing through he would regard you as being a permanent hunter for the Herero. That would not please Jonker. It might provide him with an excuse to fall upon Otjimkandje and order me from the country.'

Tjamuene spoke again, looking at Josh. 'There will always be milk in my house for you and yours.' He pointed to Daniel. 'This is your son?'

'Yes, he is my son.'

Tjamuene called over his shoulder, and a tall boy of about ten years of age came forward proudly. Tjamuene put a hand on the youngster's shoulder briefly, then motioned him forward towards Josh.

'This is my son, Kasupi. He will be as a brother and a shadow to your son. You may go now.'

It had been a good meeting. Mutjise was smiling, and there was satisfaction on the faces of the tribal elders standing behind the chief. Only Tjamuene felt an emptiness in his heart. He was chief of the Herero, but because of Chief Jonker and the Afrikaners he was unable to guarantee the safety of his visitors, or offer a guide to take them on their way. He could only give away his younger son to them.

'Tjamuene was well pleased,' said Hugo Walder as they left the chief's kraal. His relief was apparent. 'He has paid you two of the highest honours it is possible for him to bestow. Telling you there will always be milk for you in his house means you are as close to being part of his household as is possible for a stranger. And poor Kasupi has taken on an awesome responsibility. To him has been given the task of protecting Daniel —

absolutely. If danger threatens, he will be expected to give up his own life to save him. If Daniel has an accident and hurts himself, Kasupi will be whipped for not preventing it from happening.'

'You can't put responsibility like that upon a young boy!' Miriam was shocked.

'For Kasupi it is a great honour. It shows his father's trust in him.' Hugo smiled. 'It also means that you must get used to having that young man sleeping in your doorway at night and staying with you every minute of the day while you are here. He is part of your family now.'

Miriam was not at all sure it was an arrangement of which she wholeheartedly approved, but her opinion would have made little difference to Tjamuene. His gesture had been one that contained more than friendship. As Hugo Walder knew and Josh had guessed, there was a secondary motive. They had arrived as strangers from an unknown land, with unexplained intentions. Kasupi would certainly be a guide and companion for Daniel. He would also report to his father any suspicious moves the newcomers made.

'Well, now you have met Tjamuene. What would you like to do today? Are you still tired? Perhaps you would like to rest?'

'How soon can we move on?' asked Sam Speke. 'And how many days' travelling-time is it to the Cape Colony?'

The thought of what he might do with the gold he had hanging inside his shirt was beginning to weigh almost as heavily on him as the bag itself.

'Well, now.' The missionary became more serious. 'First it will be necessary to let Jonker know you are here. Then you will need his approval to pass through his territory. Once you have that no one will dare to attack you. Without it you would not get far. Then you will need an ox-wagon. When the time comes I will supply that for you, together with drivers. As for the journey itself, it will take you longer than three months.'

Josh was astounded. Until now he had believed that they were at the borders of civilisation, that towns and villages occupied by Europeans were only a few days' travelling away.

Hugo Walder interpreted his expression correctly and smiled. 'This is not like any of the places you have ever known before, my friends. This land where we stand is not wanted by any of those countries who are fighting elsewhere for colonies. The Cape was once a Dutch colony. Now it lives uneasily under the British flag and, as more and more of your countrymen arrive there, the Boers – the Dutch – move farther away to escape their jurisdiction. Even so, you will travel five hundred miles from here before you reach the first Boer farm. On the way you will pass through three mission stations. If you are lucky, you may avoid the tribal wars that are going on. If not. . . .' Hugo Walder shrugged. 'No place on this great earth is God-forsaken, but I sometimes think the Lord has yet to look upon this corner of Africa.'

The missionary saw that his words had cast a pall of deep gloom over his guests and he put a friendly great hand on Josh's shoulder.

'I am sorry – but as a missionary it is my task to light a candle to guide Him to us. Come and see the candle I have built for His glory. The church of Otjimkandje.'

Upon their arrival the previous evening the mission church had seemed large and imposing to the travel-weary party. Today they saw it was both small and incomplete. Inside there were only four long benches, and wood and crude building materials were strewn about. But at one end of the building beneath a high glassless window a silver and mother-of-pearl crucifix stood on a spotless white cloth that covered most of a wooden table, and the area around it was swept clean.

'As you can see, there is much to be done. It is very slow work, and I feel it is more important for me to learn the Herero language. That takes much of my time, but is necessary if I am to translate the hymns and prayers into Herero. Then I also have my garden to attend to. My allowance is small, and I must feed myself as much as I can.'

Hugo Walder looked about the little incomplete church with pride.

'Here I am selfishly happy, watching it grow slowly with time. However, it will have to wait a while longer. My tools are worn out, and it will be many months before more arrive from the Cape – Chief Jonker of the Afrikaners permitting.'

Josh picked up a poor-quality hand-axe from the floor. The

head of it had cracked down one side of the handle-holder.

'A blacksmith could do something with this.'

'My friend, there are so many things a blacksmith could do in Otjimkandje. Unfortunately there is not a blacksmith north of the Rehoboth Mission Station. The last one we had was an Ovambo tribesman who was put to death by Jonker. He realised the error of his ways too late and now Jonker, too, is without a blacksmith.'

Josh became thoughtful. 'Did the last blacksmith only carry out repairs, or did he also make things?'

'He did everything! To the west of here, not many miles distant, is much of the ore that makes iron and the Ovambo used it a great deal. We have other tribesmen living here who can make iron, but they lack the skill to make useful tools.'

'Well, if there is still some of the last blacksmith's equipment to hand, I think I can do something about these worn-out tools.'

After the conversation with Miriam the previous night it seemed to Josh that this was a great opportunity to exercise his skills as a blacksmith and at the same time help this man who had so little and yet was prepared to give so much to others.

'You get some of your men to produce some iron and I'll see about setting up a smithy.'

'You are a blacksmith?'

The joy on the missionary's face was touching.

'I'm an engineer. Learning to work as a smith was part of the training. I can do that while Sam does the hunting.'

'And when I'm not hunting I'll help with some of this.' Sam pointed to the unfinished church furniture. 'I'm pretty useful at carving and carpentry and the like. It will keep me out of mischief before we move on.'

Hugo Walder took a deep breath and spoke with a voice choked with emotion.

'I think the Lord must have sent you as a reproach to me for my lack of faith. My friends, your stay here is going to be a happy time for me.'

When Josh first began working on the smithy and stripped off his shirt the Herero tribesmen flocked from all over the village to look upon the vivid red scar that bisected Josh's back from shoulder to waist. When Hugo Walder asked about it Josh said only that the wound had been caused by a soldier's sabre, and the missionary asked no more questions.

By the end of two weeks Josh, assisted by Herero workmen, had almost completed the setting up of the smithy. Although no man had raised a hand to assist Hugo Walder in the building of his church, Tjamuene had taken a great interest in Josh's project. He had even handed over the crude anvil which had belonged to the murdered Ovambo blacksmith and which the Herero chief had appropriated as a piece of furniture.

It was then that Jonker's Afrikaners paid their long-awaited call.

The Afrikaners, known to the Herero as 'Aich-ai' — 'the warlike people' — rode into the village at midday, a party of about forty of them. They were shouting arrogantly, half their number brandishing muskets and most wearing at least one item of European-style clothing. The speed and recklessness of their riding kicked up a cloud of dust and scattered Herero cooking-fires.

There were no streets in Otjimkandje, only wide open spaces between the rows of huts. Jonker's men ignored these natural thoroughfares and rode direct to the mission, forcing their way between the closely packed huts and trampling over everything that lay in their path.

The manner of their arrival led Josh to think the worst and, putting aside the bellows he was shaping, he hastily loaded and primed his pistol. Tucking it into his belt, told Miriam to stay inside their hut. There was no sign of Daniel, who was off somewhere with Kasupi, and Sam Speke had gone on a hunting trip with Mutjise.

Josh returned to his embryo smithy close to the church walls and awaited the arrival of the Afrikaners. They rode straight at him, waiting until the very last minute before tugging hard on the short reins, causing their horses to rear and mill about, foam flying from abused mouths.

One of the horsemen said something to Josh in a harsh and unfamiliar language. Josh shook his head without taking his eyes from the Afrikaner's pock-marked face, and Chief Jonker's man repeated his brief statement.

'If you say it in English, I'll try to answer you,' said Josh, and this time it was the Afrikaner's turn to look blank.

At that moment the bearded German missionary came from his church, his demeanour unruffled. Armed horsemen riding up to his church could have been an everyday occurrence.

'You would appear to have a language problem,' he said, smiling at Josh. Turning to the leader of the Afrikaner horsemen, he spoke to him in the same harsh language Josh had just heard.

The conversation moved back and forth between the two men, and from the frequent nods in his direction Josh knew he was the subject of their talk.

Eventually Hugo Walder turned to Josh. 'Jonker has heard of your presence here. He would like to meet all of you.'

'The way he was putting it didn't sound much like a request to me,' commented Josh, jerking his head at the Afrikaner horseman.

'Coming from Chief Jonker even the vaguest suggestion should be interpreted as a command,' said the missionary.

'When does Chief Jonker want to see us?'

Hugo Walder put the question to Jonker's emissary.

Josh did not need a translation of the single-word answer to know that he was expected to set forth immediately.

'How long a journey is it?'

'Two days by ox-cart, a matter of hours only if we had horses.'

Josh looked at the smithy taking shape about him. 'I've another week's work to do here. Tell them we'll set off to visit their Chief Jonker then.'

Hugo Walder gave an amused smile. 'Yes, Jonker's orders bring out the worst in me also. All the same, I think we should make immediate arrangements for the journey.'

Josh pushed his way between the Afrikaner horses, slapping the rump of one of them to make it move out of his way and almost unseating its rider. Between the little church and Hugo Walder's hut was a small garden on which the missionary had put in a great many hours' work. The effort of carrying water to it was a daunting task in itself. The healthy green of the plot's well-ordered crops had been evidence of the missionary's perseverance. The arrogant Afrikaners had charged their horses through the fertile little plot and churned up mature plants and frail seedlings alike.

Josh pointed to the chaos. 'Tell Jonker's men I would have been happy to set off immediately. Unfortunately my departure will be delayed until this has been set right.'

Without another look at the horsemen Josh walked back to the smithy and resumed work on the bellows.

Hugo Walder translated Josh's words exactly as they had been spoken.

From his horse the Afrikaner looked down at Josh, his nostrils flaring angrily. Jerking his restless horse to a halt he said, in Afrikaans, 'I have carried Chief Jonker's words to you. You would do well to obey them.'

Pulling the horse's head around, he led the other horsemen away, carefully avoiding the missionary garden.

'What happens now?' Josh said to the missionary as they walked together back to his hut to deposit his pistol and tell Miriam what had been said.

The missionary smoothed his beard and smiled. 'Who knows? Perhaps the great Jonker will call personally with his invitation.'

Josh looked to see if he was serious, and the big German missionary shook his head. 'If that happened, Jonker would not come alone and we would be left in a deserted village. Tjamuene and his people would flee before him. But that must not happen, my young friend. We must prepare ourselves to pay Chief Jonker a visit.'

'What is it about him that makes him so terrifying?' asked Miriam. 'What has he done?'

'If you are asking me for a list of his misdeeds, it would save much time if I listed the few things he has *not* done.'

The missionary began pacing the confined area of the hut.

'Jonker is the younger son of a thief and murderer who fled from the Cape Colony with a band of like-minded followers. They were not really a tribe, and so for want of a name they became known as the Afrikaners – the people of Jager Afrikaner, as Jonker's father called himself. They were a strange mixed band with some white blood flowing in their veins. When the father died Jonker, as a younger son, inherited nothing. So, gathering all the worst elements of his father's people about him, he fought his way northwards, conquering the people and taking whatever he wanted. He forced Tjamuene to leave Ai-gams, in the valley of the hot springs, and now Jonker lives there and has opened up some form of trading post, exchanging stolen cattle for brandy, guns – and now horses. He calls his new capital "Winterhoek".'

'And all the other tribes pay homage to him in the hope that he will leave them alone?'

'That is so.'

While they were talking they became aware of a growing commotion outside the hut. At first Josh thought it was nothing more than excitement caused by the visit of the horsemen; but the noise was swelling and coming nearer, and now a desperate wailing accompanied the general hubbub.

The missionary was the first to the door of the hut, and as Josh and Miriam emerged into the bright sunlight the noisy crowd swarmed about them.

The missionary snapped a few questions at the noisy Herero. When he turned back to Josh he was almost as agitated as Tjamuene's people.

'What is it? What's happening?' Josh asked.

'It is Jonker's men.' Hugo Walder's face had paled beneath his beard. 'They saw Daniel over by the cattle-pens with Kasupi. They have carried both boys away with them.'

'How many miles is it to Jonker's village?' Josh intended going there on foot; he had already dismissed an ox-cart as being too slow.

'Thirty – thirty-five miles,' replied the missionary. 'But you cannot go alone!'

'He won't be alone. I'm going too.'

Miriam was busy stowing food into one of the haversacks that had stood them in such good stead on their travels from the coast.

Josh did not even start to argue with her. One look at her determined expression was sufficient to tell him it would have been a waste of time.

'What is Tjamuene doing about his own son?' he asked the missionary.

Hugo Walder spread his hands wide. 'He dare do nothing. To march on Jonker's village would mean annihilation for his tribe. Tjamuene is father to his people first – to Kasupi second.'

'Will he at least provide us with guides to show us the way to Jonker?'

'There will be no need for any Herero to come. I will take you.'

Josh paused in the act of slinging the powder-horn over his shoulder.

'There's no reason why you should involve yourself in this. You are here to preach the gospel to the Herero. If you offend Jonker, all your years of work will be undone. Just give us a guide.'

'My work will be finished here unless I am seen to do something to return Daniel. If it is seen that Chief Jonker holds me in such little regard that he can come here and interfere with those afforded my protection, then I might as well return to Germany. No, my friends, this outrage affects the lives of us all. Give me a moment or two to change my footwear and I will be ready.'

It seemed that the whole village assembled to watch their departure, the Herero warriors standing in humiliated silence. Only Tjamuene, their chief, was absent.

By taking advantage of the bright moon and sleeping for only two hours they reached Jonker's village early in the morning of the next day, taking the despotic chief completely by surprise.

The village was sited in a beautiful fertile valley, and from the wide pass in the hills above it looked very large and well laid out. There was even a train of ox-wagons trundling westwards from the village on a well-defined road.

The long forced march had brought Miriam close to the point of exhaustion, but now they had come to within a mile of the place to which her son had been taken she was stubbornly determined not to allow her tiredness to show.

'Is that Jonker's hut?' Josh pointed to a large square-built building closely surrounded on three sides by many of the now familiar round huts and with a large empty space on the fourth.

'I don't know.' Hugo Walder ran a cloth kerchief around his neckband. He had grown unused to walking long distances since moving to Otjimkandje. 'But it is the largest hut in the village, and Chief Jonker would not settle for anything less.'

Josh checked the priming in his pistol. 'It might be as well if you waited up here, Miriam.'

'I could have stayed in Otjimkandje if I'd wanted to avoid danger,' retorted Miriam. 'We'll go down there together.'

'Do you have any plan in mind?' asked the missionary as they set off down the hill to Chief Jonker's village.

'None – beyond getting Daniel and Kasupi back and returning to Otjimkandje.'

Hugo Walder could think of a great many reasons why Josh's simple and naïvely direct plan should fail – not least of them being the thousand or so armed warriors who occupied the huts they were rapidly approaching.

But luck has always reserved a special place for the brave and the foolhardy. They had arrived at a time when most of the men were beating the valley a couple of miles away to flush out a lioness who had killed a herd boy and one of his charges, and so the determined trio were actually in the open space in front of the large hut before their presence caused a stir.

Nevertheless, by the time they stood before the entrance to the hut it seemed that everyone who remained in the village was noisily rushing to surround them.

The sound brought a man from inside the hut. He was not a particularly impressive figure, being slightly built in comparison with the Herero of Tjamuene's tribe. The only distinctive thing about him was the leopard-skin cloak he wore slung over one shoulder.

'I'm looking for Chief Jonker of the Afrikaners,' Josh blurted out before the other man could speak.

'I see you have brought the Little Father with you. Does he have so short a memory that he has forgotten the chief of the Afrikaners so soon?'

The leader of the warlike Afrikaners smiled mockingly at Hugo Walder. His English was more strongly accented than the missionary's, although a recent influx of traders from the Cape Colony had given him some practice.

Slowly and deliberately Josh began to draw the heavy pistol from his belt, but the strong hand of the powerful missionary reached out quickly and took his wrist in a bone-crushing grip. Behind them the noise from the Afrikaners swelled ominously.

Chief Jonker looked deliberately at the hand gripping Josh's wrist, then raised his eyes to Josh's face.

'It is only to be expected that a man will sometimes act foolishly for love of his son.'

His quiet dignity was solidly backed up by half a dozen warriors standing a few yards away, their muskets aimed at the hearts of the three Europeans.

When Hugo Walder was sure Josh had seen the armed men he released his grip, a movement that was acknowledged by a nod from Chief Jonker.

'The child should not have been brought here. I gave no orders for it. The man responsible has been punished, and I have sent for your son.'

'We are grateful to Chief Jonker.' Hugo Walder inclined his head to the leader of the wild tribe of Afrikaners.

A tribeswoman dressed in the silks that were reserved for Jonker's favourite wives came around the corner of the hut holding Daniel by the hand. When he saw Miriam he released his hand and with a shout of 'Mamma!' ran to her, and she gathered him in her arms.

'I rode on a horse.'

That was all the whole frightening incident had been for him — an adventure, a ride on a horse.

'He is well,' said Chief Jonker and, looking at his affable smile, Josh found it difficult to believe that this was the man who was feared so much by Tjamuene and his Herero.

'But where are my manners?' Chief Jonker stood to one side of the doorway to his hut. 'You have travelled far. You must come inside to eat and rest.'

'No.' Josh spoke before the missionary could answer for him. 'We came for my son and the boy Kasupi. When we have them both we will return to Otjimkandje.'

'Is Chief Tjamuene of the Herero so afraid of the Afrikaners that he cowers in his village and sends strangers to beg for his son's return?'

'I know nothing of Tjamuene's feelings. I know only that he gave me Kasupi to serve my son. Because of that I have a responsibility for him.'

'That is so,' agreed Chief Jonker. 'He shall be returned to you now. It is fitting that Tjamuene should produce sons to be servants. Now that matter is settled you will stay. See! Your woman is tired.'

Now that Daniel had been safely returned to her, Miriam was indeed feeling the effects of the journey. Clasping Daniel tightly to her, she leaned heavily against one of the posts that supported the overhanging thatched roof of Chief Jonker's hut. But Josh had no wish to be a guest of this man he still believed to have ordered the abduction of Daniel.

'I intend to be clear of this place and back in Otjimkandje by nightfall. We'll all sleep safer there.'

For a brief moment the chief of the Afrikaners looked angry. He realised that Josh did not accept that he had not been responsible for carrying off Daniel. He turned and snapped an order in his own language at one of the musket-carrying warriors. As the man turned and hurried away Hugo Walder looked thoroughly alarmed and made a plea to the chief, also in the Afrikaner language.

Chief Jonker smiled thinly, his eyes still showing anger, but he said nothing.

The missionary turned to Miriam in a state of agitation. 'Turn away and cover the boy's eyes. Whatever you do, don't look until I tell you.'

He was too late. Miriam was able to push Daniel's face into her breast but she did not miss the gruesome trophy that the member of Chief Jonker's guard bore into their presence. She just managed to stifle the scream that rose to her lips.

His fingers locked in the short black crinkly hair, Jonker's man carried the severed head of the warrior who had ridden into Tjamuene's village and demanded that Josh leave to see his chief immediately.

The Afrikaner thrust the head at Josh, and he recoiled in horror, trying not to gag at this example of Jonker's savagery.

'Take it with you,' said the chief, satisfied with Josh's reaction. 'It will help you to remember that Chief Jonker does not lie. Neither does he deal lightly with those who do not obey his orders. You have your son. The man who took him has been punished. There is nothing between us now.'

'We will stay in your village and rest,' said Hugo Walder quickly.

'Good!' The Afrikaner chief waved the guard with the gruesome trophy away.

Had the face of the dead horseman not haunted Josh throughout the day it would have been difficult to fault Chief Jonker as a host. That he had full and absolute sovereignty over his tribe was beyond dispute. His every command, every gesture was obeyed immediately. He also possessed a natural dignity and charm that would certainly have impressed Josh and Miriam greatly had they not had tangible proof of his primitive cruelty.

The feast he put on for them after they had rested and the dancing he ordered in the space outside his hut went on until well into the night. Jonker asked many questions of his guests and seemed very impressed when he heard Josh had a knowledge of smithying and ironwork. There were many guns in his village that needed repair, and wagons, too. Would Josh not consider moving to Winterhoek where Jonker could find much more work for him? Many traders were arriving in the town with wagons damaged from the long overland haul.

Josh replied that he had no intention of operating the smithy at Otjimkandje permanently. He planned to move south to the Cape Colony as soon as possible.

'That will not be for a very long time,' said Jonker. 'There is much trouble in the land. I cannot allow you to go on until I can be sure of your safety. An attack upon you would be an attack against me. It might even bring trouble from the government at the Cape. No, you must stay. I have trouble enough.'

Josh knew from the way the Afrikaner chief spoke that his words constituted an order, not a suggestion. His talk of trouble was exaggerated. If trading wagons could get through, then so could Josh.

But Chief Jonker accepted that Josh should remain at Otjimkandje and help Hugo Walder with his mission church. He also extracted a promise from Josh that he would carry out any work that Jonker might send him from time to time and also train an Afrikaner tribesman in the art of smithying.

That night Chief Jonker and his guests parted, if not as friends, then certainly with more warmth than had been present upon their arrival in the Afrikaner village at Winterhoek.

The next morning Chief Jonker rose early to see his visitors on their way and demonstrated that there was both generosity and a bizarre sense of humour in his nature.

He loaned his visitors an ox-wagon and an escort to take them back to Otjimkandje, and gave Josh two gifts. The first was a new musket together with a quantity of lead and powder. The second gift was the horse that had belonged to the man Jonker had beheaded.

'The gun will kill from afar,' said Chief Jonker, touching the musket. 'With this you need never be short of meat.'

Reaching out, he pulled the pistol from Josh's belt. 'With a gun like this you may only shoot a chief when you stand before him. It is better to send him a message from afar with a long gun.'

On their way back to Otjimkandje the party met up with Sam Speke, Mutjise and a much enlarged hunting party of Hereros heading for Jonker's village. Not all of Tjamuene's warriors were as ready as their chief to accept an insult to the tribe.

The Hereros approached in battle formation, and Jonker's men prepared to meet an attack. Only the swift intervention of Hugo Walder prevented an incident.

Even when Mutjise and his warriors saw Daniel and Kasupi and heard of the fate of Jonker's lieutenant, they looked at the tribesmen from Winterhoek with hot-eyed suspicion. The missionary deemed it wiser to send Jonker's men back to their village with the ox-cart and walk the remainder of the way to Otjimkandje with the Hereros.

Along the way Josh jokingly asked Sam Speke whether he had intended taking on the whole of the well-armed Afrikaner tribe with his small hunting party and one musket.

'No,' replied the seaman seriously. 'But Mutjise wouldn't have thought twice about it. I don't think he's afraid of anything. Me, I'd have appealed to Chief Jonker's better nature.'

He pulled the bag of gold from inside his shirt. 'Mutjise tells me Jonker has developed an expensive taste for brandy as well as guns and is in debt to the traders. I'm sure we'd have been able to come to some arrangement.'

'You'd have parted with your gold for Daniel?' Miriam asked.

Sam Speke shrugged. 'Well . . . I'd have given him your share first, of course. But likely as not I'll waste most of mine, anyway.'

'You take care of it, Sam. One day some sensible woman will come along and snap you up. When she does you'll be able to put that money to good use.'

Sam Speke said nothing, but Miriam had touched upon a subject to which he had been giving a great deal of thought since their arrival at Otjimkandje. Among the Herero a man was not expected to run his own household, and the girl sent by Tjamuene to help with Sam's chores looked upon it as a living-in situation. She was an attractive pleasant girl, but Sam did not know how his companions would react if he told them that he seriously contemplated marrying a Herero girl.

The incident with Chief Jonker marked a turning-point in Hugo Walder's mission among the Herero. Warriors of the all-powerful Afrikaner chief had carried off a son of their own leader.

The Little Father had gone after him and returned the boy to his people. In order to achieve this he must have had the protection of a very powerful god. Such a god should not be offended.

The Herero tribe, led by their chief, flocked to the little church to learn about the missionary's god and his ways.

While Hugo Walder scattered the seeds of his religious teachings among the people, Josh brought his smithy into full operation and Sam Speke proved that not only was he a competent carpenter but was also capable of producing wood-carvings of considerable skill and imagination to decorate walls and pulpit.

While all this was happening, Miriam transformed her hut into a comfortable home, and Daniel pried into the childish mysteries of village life in company with his faithful guardian Kasupi. Miriam spent much of her day surrounded by inquisitive women. It was very difficult to order them from the hut as they pretended not to understand what she was saying. Eventually she gave up and made the best of their presence by making them teach her the Herero names for all her household items. Soon she had gained a fair command of their language.

The shipwrecked party had found their way to the village of Otjimkandje in early March of the year 1846, when the minor change in the weather introducing winter had just begun. By November, when the hot airless days of summer were upon the land, the essential work on the interior of the church was complete.

It had been a pleasant season, and somehow the urgency of moving on to seek other communities had faded. Josh's temporary smithy was kept busy from dawn to dusk with work for the Herero and the Afrikaner chief.

The small valley where the Herero village was situated was also a pleasant and healthy place. It had a permanent supply of water and ample grazing on the surrounding plains for all the cattle the tribe possessed. When cattle sickness decimated Jonker's herds during July it was far enough away to prevent the Afrikaner chief from casting envious eyes upon its prosperity.

One evening Hugo Walder invited the others to his hut for the main meal of the day. An easy relationship had developed between them, each aware of the strengths and weaknesses of the others and appreciating their worth.

The meal was over before the missionary broached a subject that had been increasingly on his mind since the completion of the church became an accomplished fact.

'This has been a most enjoyable evening,' he began. 'In fact this has been a splendid year. Because of your arrival I have seen so many of my hopes achieved. Your presence has been a great help and a constant pleasure. I realise it is a selfish pleasure. My life is here, serving God. My happiness is in His service. For you life has other things to offer. You are young.' The missionary paused uncertainly, toying with the spoon on the table in front of him. 'What I am trying to say is that I realise you have made a great sacrifice by remaining here to help me. I have always known you must go your way one day. I don't think Chief Jonker will put any obstacle in your way now. You can take my own ox-wagon and a Herero driver and I will help you in any way I can. That, coupled with my constant prayers, is the only way I know of expressing my deepest gratitude to you all.'

Now it had been said, the big bearded missionary felt relieved but very sad. He had believed for a long time that it was only a form of loyalty to him that had kept Josh and the others in Otjimkandje.

Josh and Miriam, too, were relieved that the missionary had broached the subject. It had kept them talking until very late into the night during recent weeks – but not because they wished to hasten their departure.

Josh cleared his throat noisily.

'Yes, it's something we have been thinking a lot about – at least, Miriam and I have.'

Hugo Walder nodded. 'Then I was right to speak of it. Have you decided when you would like to leave? It is becoming hotter every day. Soon travelling will be most uncomfortable – although some traders are beginning to arrive by sea at Whalefish Bay. It might be possible to arrange a sea passage to the Cape Colony for you.'

Miriam shuddered at the thought of ever again travelling by sea, but it was Josh who spoke.

'That isn't quite what we had in mind. As I said, Miriam and I have given it much thought. We've been very happy here – and are still happy, thanks to your great kindness. I'm pleased you feel we have helped you, and I believe there is much more we could do. I could extend the smithy to undertake simple foundry tasks, and when I was riding west of here some weeks ago I saw signs of a large copper-ore deposit. That could be exploited and a profitable trade built up, using Chief Jonker's sea route via Whalefish Bay. I know he would expect to be paid tribute, but that could be negotiated.'

Josh's words generated an air of excitement in the smoky lantern-lit interior of the hut, and Miriam took it up.

'I've picked up a fair knowledge of the Herero language. If I work hard, I feel sure I could master it, at least well enough to open a school.'

'I know we're taking a great many things for granted,' put in Josh. 'We came here uninvited and now we're proposing we should stay. But that's the way Miriam and I feel. I can't speak for Sam.'

'There's no need for anyone to speak for me.'

Josh's declaration had come as a great relief to Sam Speke. His relationship with the Herero girl who looked after him had grown into something very special for the lonely seaman. His love for the girl he had named Mary had grown slowly but very surely; and there were nights when he suffered torment as he lay awake holding her sleeping body close to his, dreading the day when Josh would decide to move on and he would have to make his own decision – whether to cut his ties with everyone and everything he had ever known, or leave this girl and the loyalty and love he had never before experienced.

'You've both said things I couldn't have put into words. If I was to leave here, I'd end up back at sea sooner or later – no matter how much money I had. That's no life for a free man. I can't offer you the talents Josh and Miriam have, Hugo, but I can promise you one thing. Give me a few years here and I'll make you some beautiful carvings for your church.'

Hugo Walder looked from one to the other, and even in the dim light from the smoky lamp it was possible to see the tears in his eyes.

'You *want* to stay but are not sure of the way I feel about it? My very, very good friends, if you say you will stay with me and help me in my work, I will go out to my little church tonight, fall on my knees and give heartfelt thanks because the Lord will have answered my prayers.'

Now this momentous decision had been reached Josh felt the need to tell the missionary something of the events that had brought him to Africa.

He began his story hesitantly, but Hugo Walder cut him short.

'I wish to hear nothing! God works in His own ways, and I neither question nor doubt Him. He guided you here and allowed me to judge the man you are. I am happy to have you as my helper and friend. What is more important is that together we can all do so much for the Herero – both in this life and in the greater one to come. My friends, life will begin anew for us in this great year.'

Looking at the honest old missionary, Josh thought he was right. Here in this remote African village Josh had found a freedom he would have in no other place.

Two hundred miles north-west of Otjimkandje another decision was being made. It had been a disastrous season here between the sea and the mountains of Gaua. No rain had fallen, and the few animals that normally lived here had died or moved on. Now the underground water-holes that had kept the Bushmen supplied for centuries were drying up one by one.

Xhube looked around at his people and thought their bodies were like the old wreck lying among the sand dunes, with little more than a gaunt frame remaining.

They sat about a single fire, picking listlessly at the flavourless pulp of a stringy giant desert aloe, the only food the women had found in two days.

It pained Xhube to see his people like this, the joy and laughter gone from their lives. There had not been a dance for many months. Life had become a daily fight for existence – and his people were not winning.

The little Bushman said what was in his mind.

'Tomorrow we will leave this place. We will go to meet the

rising sun and seek a home in the land beyond Gaua's mountains.'

His words meant little to the women. The land to the east promised little more than the land in any other direction. The only thing that would bring hope to them was water. But the men looked wide-eyed at their chief.

'Those are the lands of the Herero. To go there is to invite death for us and slavery for our women.'

'Death shares our fire now,' declared Xhube. 'And he will enslave our women more surely than the Herero.'

There was not the heart in the other men to argue. Only Hwexa expressed his disquiet.

'We do not know the lands beyond the mountains. We will be strangers in the land of others.'

'Are you any more familiar with the land beyond the grave, Hwexa? No, we must go to where there is food. Rain has fallen beyond the mountains. We must go there. We will travel fast and unseen to the desert beyond the Herero. Perhaps there we will find the freedom for which we are both concerned. The freedom to live as we will – and freedom from hunger.'

BOOK TWO

In the Herero village of Chief Tjamuene, Josh and Miriam enjoyed a good life for more than a decade. They had the friendship of the tribesmen and of the missionary. They built a wooden hut for themselves and made it a home, and with a well-contented pride they watched their son grow to near-manhood.

Daniel grew up learning the ways of the Herero alongside the things taught to him by Josh and Miriam. His friend Kasupi was always present to explain the customs of his people, and Daniel learned well. By the time he was sixteen he could hunt the lion with a spear and bring down a buck with a single musket-shot at a hundred paces. The child from Cornwall became a young man for whom the Herero warriors had respect. To the young Herero girls and their mothers he was the subject of much speculation. Such a hunter as Daniel would be a great asset to any family.

Meanwhile, in his little church Hugo Walder sowed the seeds of his religion with hope and honest belief, and was content to see God reaping a sparse but growing harvest.

These were the good years, and it was difficult to say when they first began to change.

The changes came as gradually as did the traders who pushed their way northwards from beyond the Orange River to Jonker's village in the valley of Winterhoek. The Afrikaner chief also established a trade route from his village to the small but safe anchorage at Whalefish Bay, one hundred and fifty miles to the west.

From the traders Jonker developed a taste for brandy, and his wives pestered him for the colourful silk dresses in which it pleased him to see them clothed.

But the traders demanded payment for the goods they lavished upon Jonker's people, and when the Afrikaner chief was not left with sufficient cattle of his own with which to pay his debts he turned upon those who had — and the Herero were his closest neighbours. Gradually, the small villages had their cattle wrested from them and, if they were foolish enough to raise their voices in complaint, the Herero lost their lives too. Soon there were but half a dozen Herero villages within a radius of one hundred miles of Winterhoek, and the only one of any size was Otjimkandje.

This was the way of things by the time Daniel was in his seventeenth year and Christmas Day in the year eighteen hundred and fifty-eight drew near.

CHAPTER ONE

Christmas in Africa did not possess the magic of the same day in Europe. Even Hugo Walder had to admit to that. The Holy Day needed snow, holly and the wide-eyed anticipation of children to give it the proper atmosphere. Somehow the pagan trimmings made it easier to imagine the birth in the manger and the Three Wise Men travelling on their journey to destiny.

In his own simple way the German missionary was a far greater man than any of the celebrated ancient trio. They had been given a star to follow – something visible to guide them on. There was no such guiding light sent to Hugo Walder. For years he laboured in total spiritual darkness – years when the tide of his faith sometimes ebbed so low that there was nothing but the ugly jetsam of doubt all about him.

Yet still he had gone on.

It was his belief that when the tribesmen saw for themselves the good that stemmed from His teachings they would turn to him for spiritual guidance. This was the basis of Hugo Walder's mission among the Herero.

He had not come to Otjimkandje to decry their customs, to demand that they conform to the strict rules he imposed upon himself. He tried hard not to interfere in their tribal way of life, although he was totally convinced the Church offered a better path for them to follow. He was equally certain he could show them that path by example. Because of these beliefs he determined not to take sides in the complicated and bloody tribal strife that sprung up in the lands around the village of Otjimkandje.

The tide had turned for Hugo Walder with the arrival of the survivors from *Pride of Liverpool*. Suddenly there was help with his physical problems: his church and his garden – and his schemes to make the material life of the Herero of Otjimkandje easier. He already had the attention of the villagers when Sam Speke provided him with an unexpected bridge between them.

The missionary had known that Mary was sharing Sam's bed;

but the fact was not blatantly thrust upon others, and Hugo Walder chose not to bring the matter into the open. Nevertheless, it came as a great joy to him when Sam Speke and Mary stood before him one day early in 1847 and said they wished Mary to be baptised and then have Hugo Walder marry them in his little mission church.

At first Hugo Walder tried to deter them.

'I am happy you wish to behave as an honourable man,' he said to the ex-sailor, 'and I know that here in this little village such a marriage would be accepted by all of us. But there is a whole world beyond Otjimkandje. Your marriage would be as binding out there as here. If you decided to move on, Mary, as your wife, would go with you. There are places not so very far from here where such a union would make you both outcasts. Mary is a good girl but all her life has been lived in Otjimkandje. She would be unhappy away from her own people.'

'I've thought of all that,' said the burly Sam Speke, fidgeting like a child before the missionary's honest searching eyes. 'I don't want to move any farther than here. I've knocked about the world a bit in my time and seen many places. There's none where I've been happier. Here I'm looked up to by Mary's people. I've never had that sort of respect before. I've been used to the lower deck, where you expect everyone to kick you. Even ashore it's only a sailor's money folks are after. When it's gone they'll kick you as hard as any ship's officer. No, I like it here. There's no reason why I should want to go anywhere else. If I have to – well, Mary has looked after me well here where I came as a stranger. I reckon I could do the same for her elsewhere.'

'In that case, Samuel Speke, I will be proud to marry you and Mary. You'll be getting a good wife, and she'll have as fine a man as any in Otjimkandje for her husband.'

There were a few formalities to be completed. Tribal custom decreed a bride must be bought, whether there was to be a Christian wedding or not. After suitable negotiation the bridal price was set at six cows and a small bench of the type Sam had made for the mission church. He also had to provide two goats for the wedding feast.

Sam Speke produced the Portuguese gold coins, Hugo Walder

carried out the trading for the livestock and the wedding went ahead.

It was the first marriage in the little mission church, which was packed to stifling overflowing for the occasion. Hugo Walder made it a very moving occasion and conducted the marriage in both English and Herero. The wedding set a precedent that other Herero couples were quick to follow.

Less than eighteen months later, in June 1848, the christening took place in the same little church of Victoria Mary Speke, newly born daughter of the mission's first marriage.

Then followed the good years for Hugo Walder – years when he saw the growth of Christianity in this remote village. The baptisms and marriages began to spread across the pages of the mission register. Soon Miriam's teachings, too, bore fruit. Some of her brighter pupils were sent to the Cape Colony and would one day return to their own tribe as teachers.

But Africa is a restless continent, ever changing and shifting its moods – a vast rumbling pot-pourri where fortunes swirl this way and that, like the sand shifting before the four winds.

So it was with Hugo Walder, his companions, Otjimkandje and the Herero. The good years did not disappear overnight, but by Christmas in the year of 1858 it seemed doubtful whether the life they had known and the community they had built about them would last for very much longer.

The cause of their uncertainty was Chief Jonker of the Afrikaners.

The years had not made the Afrikaner chief any more tolerant. He had always welcomed traders and accepted their presents. He was flattered by the deference they showed him as factual overlord of the whole territory.

The traders supplied Jonker with guns and powder and introduced him to brandy. Soon he was buying many barrels of spirits, but as Jonker's love of brandy grew and his debts to the traders mounted he no longer tried to find excuses for plundering Herero cattle. He helped himself to whatever he wanted. If the owners objected, they were killed. Jonker's warlike followers took their cue from their leader. Herero in remote villages were slaughtered and their possessions stolen by the well-armed Afrikaner warriors.

Soon it became a genocidal war, and only the strong personality of Tjamuene's missionary kept Jonker from treating Otjimkandje in the same manner as all the other Herero villages. It helped that Jonker received dues from the copper mined by Josh in the hills beyond the village. It was not a large working but it was profitable.

At the moment, however, Hugo Walder was very concerned with the situation. He voiced his thoughts at the Christmas meal he shared with Sam and Josh and their two families.

'I don't think Jonker will dare to raid us here,' said Josh. 'He's frightened that any interference with a mission station will bring trouble for him from Cape Town. Besides, Sam and I are building some ox-wagons for him. He needs them to bring his own goods up from Whalefish Bay if he's ever to break clear of the traders.'

'I wish I shared your confidence,' replied the missionary. 'Too many of Tjamuene's people are leaving and heading north with their cattle, while the ones arriving here to seek refuge have none. Very soon we will find ourselves with a feeding problem.'

'There'll be no helping them by hunting,' put in Daniel. 'Jonker's men and their guns have killed everything within two days' riding. Kasupi and I have been out twice in the last week and didn't find a single track around the usual water-holes.'

Almost as broad-shouldered as his father, Daniel possessed an air of confidence that was due to the responsibility he had assumed as hunter for the two families and Hugo Walder. It was nothing for him and Kasupi to be away from the village for a month at a time.

'We won't starve,' said Sam Speke. The ex-sailor had put on a great deal of weight since he had settled down ashore and he had the manner of a solid contented man. 'Our credit's good with the traders. If Jonker would allow them to come up as far as Otjimkandje, it would be even better.'

'It's the Herero I feel sorry for.' When Miriam had arrived at Otjimkandje she had still been a young girl, for all that she was a mother. She had matured into a beautiful woman. The bond of love and understanding between her and Josh had kept at bay the strain that aged many young women in Africa. 'They are terrified of Jonker and his men. It's a pity his last missionary gave up and left Winterhoek. He needs some sort of restraining influence.'

'For today let us try to forget Jonker,' said Hugo Walder. 'There was a full church for my service this morning. Perhaps prayers will do what the Herero cannot – keep Jonker from our village.'

But the Afrikaner chief chose that very day to pay a visit to Otjimkandje. He came with fifty mounted warriors, and their arrival threw confusion and terror into the Herero. Many of them were refugees from previous 'visits' made by Jonker and his men and they had witnessed the slaughter that followed. The screams of the women and the excited babble of the men brought the small party of Christmas celebrants out of the missionary's hut.

Chief Jonker of the Afrikaners showed his contempt for the chief of the Herero by riding past Tjamuene's small kraal without so much as a sideways glance. He did not stop until he and his party reached Hugo Walder's hut.

His first words made it clear that his business should have been with Tjamuene.

'Someone has been stealing my cattle. I have come here to look for them.'

The Afrikaner chief swayed in the saddle, and Josh realised he was dangerously drunk. He hoped the missionary also recognised the signs.

'Since when have the Herero of Otjimkandje been stealers of cattle?'

'The Herero have always been cattle thieves. Now I have come to claim back what is mine.'

All his listeners knew that Jonker had come to Otjimkandje because he needed cattle – Herero cattle – to pay his debts.

'This should be a matter between chiefs. Have you spoken to Tjamuene about this matter?'

'The chief of the Afrikaners does not talk to old women who tremble when the wind blows.'

Some of Jonker's followers laughed uproariously. Their chief had not been drinking alone.

Daniel wished his gun was closer to hand. He sensed serious trouble here. But the missionary had known Jonker for many years. He would not lose any battle of words. He looked pointedly up at the sky that was beginning to darken as the sun sank low over the skyline.

'It is unfortunate that the light is failing or I would help you seek your cattle amongst those in the cattle-pens. It would not do to make mistakes. Many of the cattle belong to the mission while others are owned by those who are friends of Chief Jonker. Besides, this is Christmas Day. We are celebrating the birth of the Son of God. But of course you will know of these celebrations. I remember your father died a Christian. Step down from your horse and join us in our celebrations – or return tomorrow and we will seek your cattle together. The great chief of the Afrikaners is always welcome in my mission.'

The missionary had turned the tables neatly. He had hinted that, if Jonker went off with any of the cattle, he might well be stealing missionary property – a matter that could have far-reaching consequences. Hugo Walder had also reminded Jonker that his father, who had himself once terrorised Namaland to the south, had turned to Christianity before his death and celebrated this day. Any trouble Jonker now caused would signify disrespect for his father's memory. It was something that not even a drunken Afrikaner chief would contemplate.

But Jonker had no intention of leaving without giving the missionary and his party some very disturbing news. It was even possible that the whole story of his 'missing' cattle had been invented and this was the real reason for his visit.

'The copper mine at Meneheke can be worked no more. There is too much water in the mine.'

Josh nodded. Meneheke was a copper mine on the other side of Winterhoek worked by a syndicate of Europeans with Jonker's blessing. Water had begun to seep into the workings years before, and they had ordered an engine from England – only to discover when it arrived that they had no one with the skill to put it together and set it to work. Josh had offered his services and done the job for them. He had told Andrews, the mine-owner, that the engine would never cope with any deep mining. The mine's closure came as no surprise to him. The Afrikaner chief's next words did.

'I have told Andrews he can work the copper at Sesebe.'

This was the small copper mine Josh had successfully developed with the help of the Herero. It was only a few miles from Otjimkandje, and Josh had used his knowledge of mining to make it an efficient and profitable undertaking. The mine had provided additional meaning to his life here. It was worthwhile and satisfying work. He was happy — and now Chief Jonker was saying he was taking it away.

'The mine is on Tjamuene's land. We've been working it for years. We made an agreement with you to work it — and you receive tribute.'

'The tribute is not enough. The Herero are lazy; they do not work hard enough. As Tjamuene's land is my land I have given it to Andrews.'

With that, Jonker jerked his horse's head around and he and his men rode away into the lowering dusk, leaving a stunned group of people behind them.

For all Hugo Walder's bluff about missionary cattle, in truth the mission and its occupants owned very few. Their livelihood depended heavily upon the modest income from the copper mine at Sesebe.

'Perhaps Jonker's bluffing.' Sam's words contained more hope than belief.

'Why should he bluff? He claims the land. He doesn't have to ask us what he can do with it — and he'll have no opposition from Tjamuene.'

Josh spoke bitterly, unaware of the figure that slipped noiselessly from the shadow of the nearby huts.

'My father is beyond the years when a man should have to fight to prove he is the chief. But he has sons. Would you have me lead my father's people to their deaths against the guns of Jonker's warriors?'

Mutjise was a man with much pride and, though he was more aware than anyone of Tjamuene's weak leadership, he would have no criticism of his father. He was wise enough to know that the day when the Herero could successfully rise against the Afrikaners was not now. They should have risen *en masse* when Jonker had led his men on their first foray into Hereroland. Now there was nowhere that could rightly be called 'Hereroland'. It was Afrikanerland.

'I'm sorry, Mutjise.' Josh liked the chief's eldest son and respected his position. It was not easy for him to lead and guide the tribe when another man was its head. 'But Jonker has given our mine at Sesebe to Andrews.'

'That is very bad.'

The Herero shared the profits with the mission and their men were paid for digging the ore.

'Perhaps Jonker would listen if I went to Winterhoek to speak to him.'

'No.'

Hugo Walder's rejection of the idea was decisive. On the last occasion Mutjise had gone to the Afrikaner chief to plead the cause of his people he had spent three days and nights tied to a wagon-wheel for his pains.

'It would serve no purpose,' Josh agreed. 'Jonker has already made the agreement with Andrews. I suspect the brandy he's been drinking today was part of the settlement. All I can do is speak to Andrews and ask him to employ Herero labour to work the mine for him. I expect he'll agree, especially as any sort of work is beneath the dignity of Jonker's men.'

Harold Andrews was only too happy to accept Josh's proposal. He was a merchant, not a mining man. He might even have been embarrassed at taking the mine away from Josh and the Herero but, as he explained to Josh, had he not agreed to mine the copper ore from Sesebe someone else would have been brought in. As a merchant Andrews had to remain on good terms with Chief Jonker. To fall out with him would be committing trading suicide.

Josh did not believe the trader. He had a shrewd suspicion that it had been Andrews who had pointed out to Jonker the money he was losing by not taking the lion's share of the profits from the Sesebe mine. But Josh kept his own counsel.

Then Harold Andrews made Josh a generous proposition. He wanted to expand the trading side of his business and explore the trading potential of the interior with his partner, a Boer trader named Jacobus Albrecht who had recently trekked overland with three wagons from the Boer territory beyond the Orange River, four hundred miles to the south. Andrews asked

Josh to manage the mine for him.

Josh accepted. The prospect of working with professional miners excited him. He told Miriam about it that evening.

'We're going to have a whole new community out here,' he said, gulping down great mouthfuls of food so he could talk more quickly. 'Andrews is going to build cabins and mess-halls and a smithy, and there'll be a wagon-shop run by Sam. We can go and live there in a new house. It will be just like a village at home.'

Miriam did not share Josh's enthusiasm.

'I thought we had found what we wanted here in Otjimkandje.'

Josh nodded vigorously, still carried along on the high tide of his enthusiasm. 'We have, but this will bring civilisation closer. There'll be new people to talk to.'

Miriam was aware that European civilisation could bring more than neighbours.

'Will there be other European women there?'

'Yes. Well . . . not at first, maybe. They will come later as the mine goes deeper and more men move in with their families.'

'Then I've a pretty shrewd idea of how the men will keep themselves entertained until then. No, thanks, Josh. We'll keep our home here. You know what miners are like when they've been paid. These men will be no different. I expect Andrews has made provision for selling liquor to his men?'

'Yes, he's going to build a place where they can buy drink.'

'Of course he is. That way he'll get a week's pay back from his men in one night.' Miriam shook her head sadly. 'We've seen it all before with Cornish miners. They'll arrive full of good intentions – to save their money and send for any kin they might have. Then the loneliness will get to them in the evenings, and they'll gather together to drink and talk about what they'll do when their families arrive – or when they return home. Before long their families will fade farther into the background and the girls in Otjimkandje begin to look more and more attractive to them.'

Miriam stood across the table from Josh, hands on hips in a stance that reminded him of his mother.

'I don't think you need me to spell out what happens then!'

Daniel had been listening in fascination. He had never before seen Miriam lecturing to his father in this way. He paused with a food-laden knife halfway up to his mouth.

'Spell it out for me, then, Ma. I don't know what happens then.'

Miriam transferred her glare to him and snapped, 'I'm pleased to hear it. That means the rumours I've been hearing about you and Kasupi and the young girls working the maize fields can't be true.'

Daniel choked on the maize-meal porridge. It was fortunate for him that Josh was too concerned with what Miriam had said about the miners to pay heed to his son.

'Yes, I'm aware of what miners are like when they have money in their pockets. I'll do what I can, but it will be little enough. I'll be paid by Andrews to run his mine, not to stop miners spending money on his liquor.'

Miriam shrugged. 'There's really nothing you can do, Josh, except to bring one or two of them here for a meal sometimes and try to encourage them to attend Hugo's church. They're grown men and will lead their own lives.'

'Of course they will – and there will be good and bad among them as there was at home, you'll see.'

'Will they need someone to hunt for them?' Daniel asked.

'Not on a regular basis. They'll buy cattle. Besides, there's little game to be found about here now. You told me so yourself.'

'There hasn't been,' agreed Daniel. 'But a tribesman from the north came in yesterday and said he'd seen signs along the Omuramba Omatako flats. I'd like to take Kasupi and check for myself.'

'How long do you expect to be away?'

'Two – maybe three weeks.'

'Are you and Kasupi taking a large party with you?'

'No, just the two of us. I'll take a horse for Kasupi and borrow Sam's old gun for him.'

'All right, but there have been reports of Bushmen up there. Keep out of their way and don't interfere with them.'

'I have no quarrel with our little brothers.'

Daniel gave his reply in the Bushmen's own click language. He had learned it from a Bushman slave kept by Tjamuene. Daniel was one of those fortunate beings to whom the learning of

140

languages came easily. In addition to the strange Bushman language he was fluent in Herero and most of the local tribal dialects as well as German, taught to him by Hugo Walder. He also had a working knowledge of the Dutch used by the Boer traders and voyageurs and favoured by Jonker's Afrikaners.

'Keep out of the way of Jonker's warriors,' warned Miriam. 'By all accounts they're spoiling for trouble.'

'Jonker and his men will be too busy seeing what they can take from the men coming to the Sesebe mine to go that far away.'

Josh had taken Daniel hunting on many occasions since he had first been able to ride a horse and he had no qualms about his ability to take care of himself. He was sixteen years of age, and in this country a boy was not allowed to remain a child for long. Daniel had been brought up in a Herero village where a boy was expected to do a man's share of the work at thirteen. At sixteen a Herero would be a warrior and most likely married. Although Kasupi had forgone his right to marriage when his father appointed him to be Daniel's personal bodyguard, being a favourite son of the tribal chief made him very attractive in the eyes of the young village girls. He took full advantage of the situation, and as Daniel was his constant companion it was inevitable that his tuition had covered more than native languages and customs. Daniel had become a man in everything but years.

CHAPTER TWO

The tribesman from the north had been correct. The game had returned to the Herero's traditional grazing-lands. With few Herero cattle remaining, they had no competition for the grasslands. The two hunters came across a black rhinoceros only thirty miles from Otjimkandje. They gave the animal a wide berth. A rhinoceros could be killed with the gun that Daniel had, but it would need to be a perfect shot. Anything less would leave two tons of angry and possibly wounded rhinoceros running wild. The animal's horn would have fetched a high price from the Herero tribal doctors, but it was not a worthwhile risk.

For Daniel, checking on game was merely an excuse to get out of the village and away from people. He loved the wide-open emptiness of the bushveldt. He especially enjoyed the country inland from the village, where the rolling landscape of coarse grass gave way to the desert, broken here and there by high rocky outcrops protruding hundreds of feet towards the sky. They were volcanic islands in a dried-up sea.

Everything about the desert fascinated Daniel. Here it was not the sand dunes of the coastal strip but a vast area, barren but for the stunted thorn-bushes and the occasional clump of sword-sharp grass defying sun and wind. This was the desert of the dry season which lasted for most of the year. But when the rains did come it changed, literally overnight. When that happened a man could be excused for thinking he had been transported in his dreams and had woken in a new land. The coarse dry grass had become green, and unseen tubers lying dormant beneath the ground pushed up stems topped with bright flowers to capture the magic of the rains.

There had been rain here in the last week and, although it had been no more than a brief rehearsal for the rainy season soon to come, it was enough to transform the whole desert.

'It is good to leave the smells of the village behind,' said Kasupi.

'And the weeping of the unmarried girls because we are away

will be good for the maize,' commented Daniel.

Kasupi's grin threatened to split his face.

'Their gratitude will be all the greater when you return me safely to them.'

Daniel snorted. 'One day Tjamuene will lose all his cattle to fathers demanding payment for the gratitude of daughters.'

Kasupi's smile disappeared. 'Better to lose his cattle that way than to the robber Jonker.'

Kasupi was as much the son of a chief as his older brother Mutjise. The domination of the Herero people by the Afrikaners was a constant source of shame to him. Kasupi was proud of being a Herero. He believed that had his people been allowed to buy guns they would have defeated the Afrikaners before they had established their dominance, but successive missionaries had frowned upon Herero trading for arms. Once Jonker arrived it was too late. No one was more aware of the importance of firearms than the Afrikaner chief. He promptly issued an order to every trader entering the country forbidding them to sell arms to the Herero. It was an order that was confirmed by the Cape government. Although their jurisdiction did not extend to this part of Africa, they warned traders against selling guns to any of the tribes in the region. It was a directive that rankled with Kasupi and the young men of his tribe because it seemed to be aimed directly at the Herero. The Afrikaners already had guns.

'We've left those troubles behind us for the moment, Kasupi. I can see something moving up ahead. Let's go and shoot our supper.'

But what Daniel had seen was not an animal. It was a tiny Bushman trotting along doggedly, eyes on the ground following a spoor that only he could see. When they were close enough to recognise him Kasupi kneed his horse forward excitedly. Animals he would kill only for food. A Bushman would provide sport.

Daniel galloped his horse alongside his friend and shouted at him.

'No, Kasupi! Don't hurt him. I want to find out what a Bushman is doing in this country.'

The keen-eared Bushman had heard them behind him and

was running for the shelter of a clump of thorn-bushes. When Daniel slid his galloping horse to a halt between the Bushman and his refuge the little hunter slung an arrow in his bow and pointed it mechanically in Daniel's direction.

'We come in peace,' Daniel said in the musical click language.

The hunter did not lower his bow, but neither did he let the arrow fly. As the two men looked at each other Daniel noticed the protruding ribs and emaciated body of the Bushman.

'Had we wished you harm you would already be dead.'

Daniel nodded to where Kasupi stood his horse twenty yards behind the Bushman, his musket aimed at the little man's back.

'We meet as friends.'

The Bushman stole a quick glance over his shoulder. Realising the hopelessness of his position, he lowered his bow, and his shoulders slumped helplessly.

'My people have no friends in this land.'

'It is long since your people were last here.'

'We live in the great emptiness where the sun rises.' He waved his arm to the east and the vastness of the northern Kalahari. 'There has been no water there for far too long. My people are dying.'

'How many of your people are with you?'

The Bushman held up nine fingers; but Kasupi had circled around to rein in alongside Daniel and, seeing the look on the Herero's face, the Bushman began instinctively to draw back the arrow in his bow.

'He's too old to make a good slave. Kill him!' the Herero said in English.

'Shut up!' Daniel glared at his companion. 'And stop behaving as though you were one of Jonker's warriors.'

The insult silenced Kasupi, and Daniel turned back to the Bushman.

'How long since you've eaten?'

'Many days. Some of my people are too weak to walk.'

'Then you'd better take me to them. Kasupi! Go and find something for our supper. When you've got it come back to here and follow our tracks. Here, you'd better take my gun and give me yours.'

He threw his modern gun to Kasupi and took Sam Speke's

old musket from him. Kasupi's pleasure at having the new weapon superseded all other feelings, and he rode away eager to test his skill with it.

The Bushman relaxed the taut string of his bow and slipped the small arrow into the tight curls of his hair, taking care not to scratch his skin with the sharp tip. When he caught sight of the musket Daniel was holding the Bushman moved to look at it more closely.

'This is yours?'

Daniel shook his head. 'No. It belongs to my father's friend.'

The Bushman looked at Daniel for some moments, his eyes showing nothing of his thoughts. Suddenly he turned away. 'Come, my people wait for me.'

He set off at a trot, and Daniel followed. The Bushman was weak and occasionally staggered, but he refused an invitation to ride on the horse with Daniel.

They travelled for about three miles before the Bushman led Daniel to a thick low clump of coarse grass. Here were the remainder of the little man's tribe. They were in desperate straits and had reached that apathetic state which comes to a Bushman when he has decided it is time to die.

The arrival of Daniel and their hunter roused them from this morbid surrender, and Daniel bullied them into getting a fire going. They had been afraid to light one before for fear they would be seen by local tribesmen. Daniel was able to assure them there were no tribes in the area at this time.

It was dark before Kasupi arrived, guided by the fire. Blood dripped from the soft nostrils of a reedbuck slung across the saddle in front of him.

The Bushmen's hunger was such that the meat of the reedbuck was barely scorched on the outside before they were cutting pieces from it and tearing the meat apart with their teeth, swallowing painfully.

Kasupi watched them with unconcealed contempt, Daniel with a strange mixture of pity and fascination. All he knew of these people were the stories he had heard from Sam Speke and his parents and the scant information gained from the slave of the Herero chief.

When the buck had been devoured and the fires were burning

low Daniel talked to the little hunters while Kasupi went some way from their camp and slept. Daniel asked them of their way of life, of their traditions and of their more recent troubles. The Bushmen in their turn questioned Daniel about the local tribes, their disposition and the hunting prospects in the land to the west. Not until the moon was on its downward journey did Daniel curl up in a scooped-out hollow in the sand and sleep.

When he awoke in the morning Kasupi was already up and scouring the ground about them. The Bushmen had gone without a track to show their direction. The Herero was angry, saying the Bushmen had made fools of them. Daniel was amused. He could well understand why the Bushmen trusted no one to know which way they had gone. But they had not left without expressing gratitude. Alongside his blanket Daniel found a miniature Bushman bow. It was a simple symbol of friendship.

From their hiding-place on a rocky outcrop the Bushmen watched Daniel and Kasupi ride away.

'You saw the stick-that-thunders?' asked the hunter who had brought Daniel to his people.

'I saw,' said the wrinkled man by his side.

'Then was I right?'

'You were right, Xhube. It was the one taken by those who came from the bitter water.'

'And this was the child. It was truly Gaua's will that we did not kill them to revenge the death of Bele.'

'It was truly Gaua's will,' agreed the aged Hwexa as he looked at their people, who would now live until they found the better hunting country Daniel had told them lay only a few miles distant.

Harold Andrews' men trekked in from the south with twenty ox-wagons and as much equipment as they had been able to carry from the played-out mine. Few of them were family men seeking to make money for their dependants. They were tough adventurers, living only for the day and taking as much from it as they were able. Josh recognised their type immediately. Theirs was the mentality adopted by generations of itinerant Cornish miners – the attitude of men with no purpose in life, no ambition but to drink their lives away in the shortest and most boisterous manner possible. Managing them was going to be tough.

The miners had been liberally supplied with Cape brandy for their journey, and because of this they arrived accompanied by a large party of Jonker's men. The chief himself was not with them. He had heard that a ship had been wrecked on the dangerous coast to the south of Whalefish Bay and had gone there to see what could be plundered.

In spite of all the drinking they had done, the miners wasted no time in setting up camp when they reached Sesebe. For the time being, the wagons would serve as bedroom and cookhouse, storeroom and mine office; but the men had brought with them the tools with which to begin the task of putting up buildings, and no sooner had they outspanned the trek oxen than they began digging out the foundations of their new mining camp.

Once work started the Afrikaners drifted away, and with their departure Herero from Otjimkandje moved in. They were immediately signed on and set to work.

By the end of a week the rough-timbered buildings were taking shape and the smithy, transferred from Otjimkandje, was in full operation. Sam Speke was working hard on wagons battered by a journey across the trackless country between the new mine and the old. In a month there were communal living-quarters, a cookhouse, office and bar surrounding the copper-rich dust of Sesebe mine.

By the time Harold Andrews arrived with his first wagon of trade goods the mine was in full operation.

'You've done well, Josh,' said the mine-owner, 'I knew I could rely on you to get things moving quickly.'

'The mine might be working well – but what about store-houses for the goods we trade, eh? And pens for cattle? Where are they? The speaker was a big blond sun-tanned man of about thirty. He spoke with a very strong Dutch accent.

'I'm sorry. You two haven't met. Josh, this is Jacobus Albrecht, my partner.'

The blond man nodded curtly at Josh.

'I repeat. Where are the cattle-pens?'

'What do we need cattle-pens for? The cattle coming in to

feed the mine will be slaughtered as they arrive.'

'Agh! I'm not interested in the mine. That's Harold's baby. I'm talking about profit – real profit. *That's* going to come from trading, and Jonker will pay for his goods with cattle. So we'll need a place to put them. Does that make sense to you, man?'

It made too much sense to Josh. He realised there was much more than copper behind Andrews' transfer of operations to Sesebe. It was closer to Jonker's Afrikaners, it was true. It was also much too close to Otjimkandje.

'Where is Jonker supposed to get his cattle from? His herds are already so small that he wouldn't dare deplete them any more by trading. The only herds of any size in these parts belong to Tjamuene's Herero.'

Jacobus Albrecht shrugged nonchalantly. 'Where he gets them is his own business. Kaffir cows are Kaffir cows. As long as they arrive in prime condition I don't ask any questions.'

'I'm sure you don't. But so far Jonker has left Otjimkandje and the mission alone. If he starts raiding their cattle to pay for your cheap brandy, you'll have no mine working here and then you'll learn where your steady profits are coming from.'

'You've lived among the Kaffirs too long. You're beginning to sound like a missionary. You just look after the mine, Retallick. Leave Harold and me to do the trading.'

'Start a war between Jonker and Tjamuene and you'll have no mine and no trading. You'd better be sure your partner understands that, Mr Andrews. At the first sign of trouble for Tjamuene I walk out of this mine and the Hereros go with me; and I guarantee that within months it will be making a bigger loss than you're able to cover by trading – that's if you are still able to trade.'

After looking contemptuously at Josh, Jacobus Albrecht gave him a tight-lipped smile and turned away. Striding off to his wagons, he shouted at the Africans working on them, using the bastard language the Boers expected all tribesmen who worked with them to understand.

'Come on. Get that load off. You – lazy Kaffir! Pakanisa lo bokisi. Pakanisa! Lift the box. Lift!'

'I shouldn't worry about Tjamuene's cattle, Josh. Most of our trading will be with the tribes farther inland. It's ivory and skins we're really after, not cattle.'

Harold Andrews spoke placatingly, but Josh knew that talk came easily to the trader.

'Have you explained the rules to Jonker? Or your partner? It seems to me Jacobus Albrecht has other ideas.'

'We've very little to trade that would interest Jonker. He's after guns and powder and, as you know, the Cape government has forbidden any trade in arms.'

'I didn't see any shortage of guns among Jonker's men when they came to Otjimkandje on Christmas Day.'

'You can't blame Albrecht or me for that, Josh. I've heard there's a Jew named Aaron who's supplying them. He's got a place down the coast from Whalefish Bay. His ships put whatever he wants ashore there. Albrecht's a hard trader but he won't go against the Cape government.'

'He must be the only Boer in Africa who won't,' retorted Josh.

The pleas of missionaries like Hugo Walder had resulted in the Cape administration banning arms shipments to the tribesmen who roamed and fought in the vast spaces of this unwanted corner of Africa, but it was a ban that was near-impossible to enforce. Even more so since numbers of resentful Boers had pushed farther northwards, refusing to accept any British-made laws. Their frontiers were still many miles away, but men like Jacobus Albrecht were their vanguard. If they thought selling arms to tribesmen would harm the Cape government more than themselves, then they would provide the guns.

Jacobus Albrecht and his people took their own laws with them wherever they went — and they would rewrite them to suit the occasion.

It was not long before the Sesebe mine was producing as much ore as they had the capacity to carry to Whalefish Bay to await the bi-monthly ship that came there. There were rumours that an ore-ship would soon arrive every month, and in the wagon-shop at the mine Sam Speke and his men worked away to provide more wagons to carry the extra ore, while other men were brought in from the Cape.

Mining the copper presented no problems for Josh. The ore was quarried rather than mined, a method that kept costs down.

But Josh was of the opinion that Sesebe, like the mine Andrews had owned, would one day simply run out of ore. He kept these thoughts to himself. While Andrews thought he needed him he would keep Jonker away from Tjamuene's cattle and Otjimkandje would survive.

But survival had to be paid for.

Hugo Walder rode over to the mine one evening to visit Josh and he was appalled by what he saw there. Although it was not yet dark, the wooden building that had been named 'The Miners' Inn' was well patronised, and ill-sung and bawdy songs rang out. Outside, a few Hereros sat on the slatted wooden steps, passing a jug of brandy around between them. Alongside the hut a number of Tjamuene's people lay in drunken sleep. Among them were two women. Shrill laughter indicated that more of the village women were inside.

'What sort of people have we allowed into this land, Josh?' asked the missionary as Josh came to the door of the mine office to meet him. 'How can I justify keeping my mission running on the proceeds of such evil living?'

'It's part of the price we must pay to keep Tjamuene's people alive,' Josh reminded the missionary. 'Having women here is a way of stopping the men from going looking for them at Otjimkandje.'

'I cannot bring myself to accept such a thing, Josh. To pay a toll to the Dévil in order that I may carry out the Lord's work is totally wrong.'

'You've come on a bad day, Hugo. The men were paid today. I'm working closely with Mutjise on the effect this is having on his people and I believe we're keeping it under control. I'm sure both the Devil and Chief Jonker would be happy if they thought that together they might drive missionaries away from this land.'

'Then I have surprising news for you, my friend. Jonker has applied to have an English-speaking missionary sent up to Winterhoek for the Afrikaner people.'

Josh was genuinely startled. 'A missionary? But why? He's had three missionaries before and driven every one of them out — but I've no need to tell you. You know more about it than anyone.'

'Ah! That is where Jonker is being very clever. I and the others were German- or Dutch-speaking. Now there is a strong British administration at the Cape—strong enough to prevent Jonker from getting as much powder and guns as he would like. He thinks if he can get a British missionary he will be in a stronger position than the Herero or any other tribe. He might even be allowed to bring in new guns and powder and shot.'

'The British will never accept that! They must know what's happening here—what Jonker is trying to do. They won't send him another missionary.'

'It isn't up to them, Josh. Besides, what church will refuse the opportunity to save a soul—especially where other churches have failed? Jonker's request has already been granted. The London Missionary Society is sending him a man from England. He may already be on his way.'

'I suppose we really ought to be pleased. He could turn out to be a restraining influence on Jonker.'

'Never! The most we can hope for is that the new missionary has the strength of purpose to stay at Winterhoek—and the ability to remain alive.'

'Jacobus Albrecht wants me to act as a guide and take him inland. He's going to try to reach Lake Ngami.' Daniel broke the news to his family at the Sunday-evening meal.

Miriam paused in the act of serving him his plate. 'Wouldn't that mean crossing the Kalahari Desert?'

'Only the northern part. Pa and I went halfway there two years ago. It's not bad country.'

'How do you feel about taking him?'

'I don't care for Albrecht one way or the other, but I'd like to see Lake Ngami. Is it all right if I go?'

Miriam had grave reservations. Daniel was an only child, and it was difficult for her to accept that a sixteen-year-old was capable of looking after himself out in the uncompromising desert of the Kalahari.

Josh had more confidence in his son's ability and he recognised the eager look in Daniel's eyes. Setting aside his dislike of the Boer, he agreed.

'It's all right with me—but don't do Albrecht any favours.

Agree on a share of his profits before you tell him you'll accept. What men will you be taking with you — Hereros?'

'No. Albrecht says he'll feel safer with Jonker's armed Afrikaners around him.'

'H'm! I'm not so sure that's a good idea. The Bechuana chief at Lake Ngami might not be pleased at having such a well-armed party riding into his territory. You'd better be sure Albrecht saves the best of his trade goods for him. Whatever you do, don't underestimate the Bechuana, Daniel. For all their apparent timidity they're fierce enough to have beaten the Zulu in battle.'

'Do you really believe Daniel will be safe travelling with Jacobus Albrecht?' The question came from the darkness beside him as Josh lay half-asleep. Miriam had asked the same question half a dozen times since he had given Daniel permission to go on the journey. Josh turned over with an exaggerated sigh and slid an arm beneath Miriam, pulling her to him.

'Should I have said he mustn't go? Made him stay here with us?'

'No, of course not.' She snuggled into Josh. 'I'm just a worrier, that's all — and you and Daniel are all I have. I know he's such a very capable boy but I sometimes think we expect him to be able to do anything a man can do. He's not a man yet.'

'Oh! And how old was I when you decided I was man enough for you?'

'Have you forgotten the mess I made of both our lives when I was a lot older than Daniel?'

Josh squeezed her comfortingly. 'I haven't forgotten one thing about you, but all that's in the past. People do some funny things when they're in love.'

'That's another thing that worries me, Josh. How is Daniel ever going to meet any nice girls when we're living way out here?'

Josh grinned in the darkness. 'One minute you're telling me our son is still a child; the next you're trying to marry him off! Perhaps you'll decide whether he's a man or a boy so I can get some sleep.'

'It's not a laughing matter, Josh Retallick. Some things are more important than sleep!'

'All right, you've convinced me. Come here.'

'That wasn't what I meant. . . .'

Although she protested, her resistance was merely a token one and she came to him readily enough. Afterwards she lay still beside Josh, listening to his heavy breathing as he slept. She thought of Daniel and of his future. Of what the future held for Josh and herself. They had found their freedom here in this ungoverned land. It was an unquestioned freedom that would not have been possible anywhere else in the world. Even if it ever became known that Josh was a convicted felon, nothing could be done about it while they remained within these undefined borders.

But Josh's freedom depended so much on others: Tjamuene and Jonker. Otjimkandje was the last remaining Herero village. The rest of the large tribe had fled hundreds of miles away to escape Jonker. How long would the unpredictable Afrikaner allow this village to remain? At the moment he needed the Herero to work the copper mine at Sesebe. He was also reluctant to offend Hugo Walder. The German missionary had powerful friends at the Cape. But Jonker was getting deeper and deeper in debt to the traders who supplied him with brandy and with silk for his wives. He was probably receiving guns and powder, too, and the Cape government's ban on their sale would have increased the price he had to pay for them. One day his need for the Herero cattle would outweigh all other considerations.

If the mission closed down, what then? Where could Josh go? The only place was the Cape Colony — and there was British justice there. Even after all these years Miriam knew that someone would remember that Josh Retallick had been sentenced to transportation for life for conspiracy to treason.

The thoughts of the past caused her to remember the families she and Josh had left behind in Cornwall. Soon after they had settled in Otjimkandje Josh had sent one letter to inform his parents they were alive and well. He had not said where he was and he knew that by the time the letter reached them it would have passed through so many hands no one would know from whence it had originated. The news would have been passed on to her mother and to their friends. But that had been twelve years ago. She wondered what they were all doing now, whether

Josh's parents and her mother were still alive.

Her memories strayed to others they had known all those years before. She wondered about Preacher Thackeray, the man she had married while she was carrying Daniel, Josh's son, inside her; the man to whom the law still bound her. It was the first time for many years that the past had returned to her thoughts in this manner. It was not a good feeling. Lying awake in the darkness, Miriam felt suddenly afraid and turned for comfort to the sleeping bulk of Josh lying beside her. For a long time she clung to him as though the darkness might spirit him away.

CHAPTER THREE

'Come on, damn you. Throw those guns inside and hitch your horses to this wagon. If we don't get out of this vlei, we won't need guns and you might as well have left them behind.'

Jacobus Albrecht tongue-lashed the reluctance of the Afrikaners to help pull the ox-wagons through a bed of wet glutinous mud.

The expedition to Lake Ngami had degenerated into near-disaster. Jacobus Albrecht had delayed it until the end of the accepted rainy season, even though these inland areas had suffered a severe drought for four years. At first this year had seemed no different. The rains had threatened, but only from a tantalising distance. Then, when the trek to the Lake was a week north-west of Winterhoek, the skies darkened and a morning wind brought the clouds scudding in across the Kalahari. With them came the rain. It came down so hard that men and horses were blinded by a near-impenetrable curtain of water. It lashed into their faces and poured inside the canvas of the wagons. The oxen, plodding forward in dogged resignation, became confused when the flickering tongue of the lightning brought deafening thunder in its wake. River-beds that had been dry and dusty for decades filled to overflowing and were impassable. The small expedition swung off course first to the east and then to the north in an effort to ford rivers and find higher ground. For two days they lost their sense of direction altogether. It seemed to them that no matter which way they turned the rain still beat into their faces. Then they floundered into the vlei, and the oxen sank to their knees in mud and the axles of the wagons were under inches of water.

Jacobus Albrecht's expedition had ten grim days of this weather. It was impossible to hunt, and tempers flared at the slightest imagined provocation. The party did not go hungry. Two of the oxen broke legs in the treacherous terrain and had to be slaughtered.

'I should have my head examined!' said Jacobus Albrecht.

'Trusting wagonloads of trade goods to a wet-nosed kid who wouldn't know a vlei from a kopje!'

Daniel had grown tired of explaining that the timing of the expedition had been the trader's choice and marshland or hill was equally indistinguishable when rain prevented a wagon-driver from seeing as far as his lead ox.

'Half my goods are ruined already from this damn rain. If we ever get as far as Lake Ngami, I'll be lucky to break even.'

'We'd stand more chance of shifting this wagon if you wasted less of your breath on the Afrikaners and put that whip away. It's not helping oxen or men to pull any harder.'

'I'll do what the hell I want,' said the big Boer, and as if to emphasise his words he cracked the tip of the long bull-hide whip viciously across the flanks of his leading pair of oxen. The sudden pain caused them to throw up their heads and their horns clashed together in panic.

Daniel did not like Jacobus Albrecht's way of handling either the animals or the Afrikaners. He used the bull-hide whip far too frequently on the oxen and had twice curled its heavy leather thong about the shoulders of an Afrikaner, accusing him of riding too close to the oxen and scaring them.

Then on the eleventh day after the start of the rains they woke to see a blue sky above them, and as the sun rose higher it spread a steamy layer of haze above the sodden ground. For the first time in days they were able to get a good fire going and have hot coffee and a filling meal.

While it was cooking, Jacobus Albrecht examined the loads on his wagons while Daniel and Kasupi rode to the top of a small rise, hoping to see a recognisable landmark. For as far as they could see the land rose and fell in gently rolling folds and with its unfamiliar cloak of green plant life and shallow low-lying lakes it presented an unfamiliar landscape.

When they returned to the camp-fire the Boer had completed his inspection. The loads had been well packed and protected, and the rain-damage was negligible. But he was still no more kindly disposed towards Daniel.

'Well, where are we?'

'I don't know,' Daniel replied honestly. 'We might have been going around in circles for days. But we won't go far wrong if we continue to head north-east.'

'What you really mean is that we're lost and you *hope* that's the right way to go?'

Daniel looked at the big man in surprise. Lake Ngami was to the north-east. Sooner or later, if they kept heading that way, they would reach a landmark that either he or Kasupi would recognise. It might not be for a couple of days, but with no shortage of water two days' travelling in this country meant nothing.

'Can you think of an alternative?'

Jacobus Albrecht made no reply, and Daniel went on, 'Get the Afrikaners to help the wagons up that far slope. The ridge is wide and flat and runs in the right direction. I'll take Kasupi with me and scout ahead.'

'Don't get lost!' was the Boer's sarcastic parting remark.

'He is not a good man,' said Kasupi when they paused on the ridge and looked back. They could hear the Boer's shouted orders and the crack of his whip. 'No Herero would treat oxen like that. They, too, have been through a bad time. He should stay and rest them for a day.'

'I'm glad you didn't suggest it,' said Daniel. 'I don't think he's too pleased with us at this moment.'

'I say nothing to him,' replied the Herero. 'He has no ears for my people.'

The two friends rode until midday when in the distance they sighted a low jagged outcrop against the skyline that neither recognised. They were probably more off course than Daniel thought, but they had plenty of time and game was plentiful.

Daniel shot a small buck and with it slung across the saddle of Kasupi's horse they set off to return to the wagons.

Daniel had never seen so many varieties of wild animal as there were all about them. They saw zebra, gnu and buck of many kinds and once saw a pride of lions running almost leisurely away from them across the wet desert.

Then they heard two shots ring out from some way ahead. They were followed by a ragged volley and then another single shot.

The two men looked at each other in alarm and without a word passing between them they kicked their heels into the horses' flanks. They heard two more shots before they gained the ridge and saw the wagons stopped in a straggling line a mile and a half away.

Jonker's Afrikaner horsemen were some distance from the wagons, milling around a number of objects lying about on the ground. Others lay singly farther away from the Afrikaners. Daniel and Kasupi slowed their horses to a canter as they headed towards the main body of riders.

When they were still to far away to establish what had been happening one of the horsemen detached himself from the group and galloped towards them. It was Jacobus Albrecht. He carried a gun and looked happy for the first time in days. Daniel and Kasupi pulled their horses to a halt as he reached them.

'I see you've been hunting too,' he said, pointing to the buck.

'But, man, we've done better than that!'

He waved his gun to where the Afrikaners were still gathered, some of them whooping loudly with glee.

'We surprised some Bushmen and killed thirteen of them. I got three for myself. Two I shot and the other one I clubbed down. I was only just in time. He damned near had an arrow fitted in his bow. It was great stuff.'

There was a shot from the scene of the slaughter, and mounting their horses the Afrikaners made their way noisily and happily back to the wagons.

The big Boer grinned. 'They've had their fun, too. There was a young Bushman girl they only wounded. She wasn't my type, but Jonker's boys enjoyed her.'

It was a quieter older Daniel who sat eating the evening meal in Otjimkandje four days later. To Miriam's repeated questioning as to why he had left the big Boer and his party to fend for themselves he would only say that he did not like the way Jacobus Albrecht ran his trading expedition.

Josh asked few questions during the meal but afterwards he announced that the elderly Tjamuene wished to speak to him about the mining camp and suggested Daniel went along with him to the chief's kraal.

They took the long way, going past the cattle-pens. Josh had recently adopted Sam Speke's habit of smoking a pipe and he stopped to light it by one of the pens.

The sudden flame caused the cattle to mill about in momentary panic, and Josh tasted dust as he drew heavily upon the pipe. He watched the cattle for some minutes until the aroma of tobacco smoke hung heavy on the night air.

'What really happened out there with Albrecht, son?'

Daniel had been expecting the question but that did not make the telling any easier. Hesitantly at first but with growing emotion Daniel told the story of the disastrous trip. Of Jacobus Albrecht's arrogance, his attitude towards Kasupi and Jonker's Afrikaners, and his uncontrolled rages when the bad weather hit them. It was a story he needed to tell someone. He was still a young man and in spite of his proven capability was dogged with a young man's uncertainty. He felt that he had somehow failed; that had he possessed a stronger personality he might have prevented Albrecht's expedition from becoming a complete débâcle – might have prevented the massacre of the Bushmen.

It was when he was talking about this last incident that his voice choked on the words and Josh understood what was really troubling his son.

'You couldn't be held accountable for the rain,' he said at length. 'And a good trek-master would have been prepared for anything that might come his way. You'll never change his attitude towards Kasupi and the others – he's a Boer. We think they're too hard with the people of this land. They think we're too soft.'

'He said I'd been living on a mission station for too long. I'd become a kaffir-boetje.'

'Would you consider it an insult if Kasupi called you "brother"?'

'No, of course I wouldn't.'

'It is something Hugo has preached for years. Don't let a man like Jacobus Albrecht change the value of the word. As for the Bushman . . . well, you know the Herero are just as bad. They'll hunt them down and kill them wherever they find them. How did you explain your feelings to Kasupi?'

'I didn't have to. Kasupi knows how I feel about them. We've met with them before. Anyway, I told Jacobus Albrecht that the Bushmen could have guided us to Lake Ngami and that killing them was not only unnecessary but stupid. Kasupi agreed with that.'

Josh nodded in the moon-filled darkness. They walked on for a while in silence until Daniel's feelings erupted once more.

'Why do they slaughter the Bushmen wherever they find them? They don't do that to animals. The Bushmen don't go looking for trouble.'

Josh knew the outburst came straight from his son's heart and he responded, gripping his shoulder sympathetically.

'I've spent many years wondering about that myself. If you ask, you'll be told it's because the Bushman is a thief, a predator. That he neither understands nor respects ownership – particularly with regard to cattle. To him any animal is something to be killed and eaten when a man is hungry. He sees little difference between a buck and a cow. Neither does he recognise tribal boundaries. He was in this country long before any other tribe arrived and he won't accept their right to exclusive use of any part of it.'

Josh paused. They were at the entrance to Tjamuene's kraal, but his thoughts were back in the past – to twelve years before and the little family group of Bushmen who had found them when they were wandering in the hot sands of the Skeleton Coast.

'Perhaps it's even more than any of the reasons I've given to you, Daniel. For the Bushman life is a continuous battle for survival. He has no wish to war with others. He doesn't covet another man's lands or possessions. He won't fight to win power over other men. He has his own rules but he does his best to live at peace with his fellow-men. Such a philosophy makes others feel uncomfortable – inferior, even. And no man can be happy if he believes himself to be inferior to a Bushman. So he goes out to prove himself against them.'

Josh tapped out his pipe on the heel of his boot and carefully ground the wad of glowing tobacco into the hard earth.

'Don't let any man change your attitude towards the Bushmen, son. You'll be unpopular for it but you can always be sure of having Sam Speke and me behind you. Without them I doubt if any of us would be alive today.'

*

Tjamuene reclined on a pile of cow hides and blankets. The years had not gone well with him. He was an old and tired man. It showed plainly in his slow movements and dull resigned eyes. The Herero of Otjimkandje still had their village and their cattle, but Tjamuene had paid for it with his pride – the pride of a hereditary Herero chief. It had been a great price to pay.

He had watched the scorn of his young men grow with the changing of the seasons. They openly declared that death was preferable to life as a vassal of Chief Jonker.

Chief Tjamuene could have told them that the Herero people could not fight their way back from the grave; that life always held a spark of hope for the future.

He could have told them but chose to keep silent. Time would tell it for him. Jonker, like Tjamuene, was growing older. He would not live for ever. The day of the Herero would dawn once again.

Room was made for Josh and Daniel and tea was served to them by one of Tjamuene's younger wives.

'My son serves you well?' Tjamuene asked of Daniel.

'He is my friend and guide,' Daniel replied in Herero, in the formal manner one was expected to use when addressing a chief. His good manners did not pass unnoticed and there were nods of approval from the elders.

'It is good. He has told me of your troubles with the trader. The man behaves like one who has no mind to think with. You must take care. Trouble sits like a vulture on the shoulder of a fool. He can cause you much sorrow.'

Daniel nodded in acknowledgement of the chief's words, and the old man turned his attention to Josh Retallick.

'How goes the work at the mine?'

'Enough copper ore is being brought out to keep Andrews happy.'

'Is it enough to keep Jonker happy?'

Josh shrugged. 'Who knows what makes the chief of the Afrikaners happy?'

Tjamuene grunted. 'Who knows, indeed? I have heard it said you do not believe the copper will always be there for the digging?'

'There is less than a year's supply of ore. I've started tunnelling to see how deep it goes. We may find more, but once we're down to a certain depth we'll need more equipment and that will push the cost up. We'd have to increase the price of the ore and become less attractive to the buyers. If other countries can produce the ore more cheaply, we'll go out of business.'

Tjamuene nodded. 'And when that happens Chief Jonker will no longer have a need for the Herero of Otjimkandje – only for our cattle.'

'He would not dare to raid Hugo Walder's mission station.'

Mutjise's laugh was devoid of mirth. 'Even the Little Father cannot tell Chief Jonker what he dare not do.'

'Then perhaps his own missionary will be able to influence him,' said Josh. 'One has been sent for and is on his way.'

'There have been missionaries at Winterhoek before,' replied the old chief. 'Now the mission church there is strewn about the ground. There was also a time when a man could ride a hundred miles in any direction from here without losing sight of Herero cattle. Now the cattle and the Herero have gone. Only we at Otjimkandje remain – but Chief Jonker is also still with us. I fear greatly for the lives of my people, but when I ask for guns to protect them I am told, "No. The White Father far away to the south says guns must not come into this land. They would be used for killing people." At first I told myself this was good. The White Father is right. There must be no guns for killing. But then Chief Jonker and his men ride through my village and each of them has a gun and a horse. Only the Herero do not have guns. Is it the wish of the White Father that only the Afrikaners should kill and only the Herero be killed?'

'Chief Tjamuene, if you wished to talk of this, you should have asked the Little Father to come here tonight. He is the one who can talk to the White Father in the Cape Colony. I only run the mine at Sesebe.'

'I know, my friend. I should not burden you with the troubles of the Herero. They are not of your doing. Forgive me. I am an old man and the things that fill my heart pour too easily from my mouth. Forgive me.'

'There is nothing to forgive. I too, feel these things. I have spoken to Andrews about Jonker's guns. He says they are not being brought in by his ships. I believe him.'

'Thank you. But let us speak of the matter for which I asked you to call on me. It concerns the women from Otjimkandje who come to Sesebe.' ·

Josh had realised this was behind Tjamuene's summons. The men at the mine were well paid, with little on which to spend their money but drink and Herero women. The women had taken to hanging about the mining camp. There they could earn more money and trinkets in one night than most of their fellow-tribeswomen acquired during a lifetime of more moral activities — and with none of the hard work that accompanied tribal life. Recently their numbers had increased, and Josh had noticed that some of the more regular visitors had more than bangles and beads as mementoes of their way of life. Sesebe would soon have its population increased by children who would belong to neither the European community of their fathers nor the tribe of their mothers.

'It is not natural that a man should be without a woman,' said the chief. 'We knew when Andrews and his men came to Sesebe that some of our women would go there. That had to be accepted. There are many of our women who have known men before. Women who have lost their men and have no families to take care of them. For these women it does not matter that they give themselves to the men at the mine. They can do as they will. But when our young girls see the gifts given to these women they say, "Come, we will go and get gifts for ourselves." This is not good. It is bad for the foolish young girls and it makes my young men angry.'

Josh nodded seriously, 'It is wrong, Tjamuene. But it is difficult for me to tell a Herero woman who has known a man from one who has not.'

'That is so,' Tjamuene accepted. 'Mutjise will go to Sesebe to send the young girls home.'

Josh saw serious trouble ahead of him if the proud Mutjise went to Sesebe and arbitrarily ordered the young Herero girls back to Otjimkandje in front of the tough miners.

'It's not fitting that the first son of a chief should carry out such a task,' he said diplomatically. 'Let Kasupi come and point out the young girls to me. I'll see that they return to Otjim-kandje.'

Kasupi was often at Sesebe with Daniel. His presence would pass unnoticed and he would be more discreet than the man who would one day be the chief of the Otjimkandje Herero.

'Good!' The old chief nodded his agreement. 'If only all the troubles of the Herero could be settled as easily.'

'They could if they didn't have a Chief Jonker behind them,' commented Josh.

As they made their way back to their own hut Josh said, 'We've got to handle this pretty carefully. If the miners realise what we're doing, it will cause a resentment that might build up to serious trouble for Tjamuene. Come to Sesebe with Kasupi tomorrow and make sure he understands the need to carry this out quietly. See how many of these girls there are, get their names and give them to me. I'll have them rounded up and sent packing. That way the miners will only be angry with me, and that's nothing too unusual.'

Jacobus Albrecht returned to Sesebe five weeks after Daniel's return. The remainder of his trading trip had been no more successful than the first few weeks. There had been an argument between the trader and the Afrikaners about the direction they should take. The trader had won and led the party straight out into the featureless wastes of the Kalahari Desert, too stubborn to acknowledge that he was wrong. Half the Afrikaners deserted him; and then the strain of pulling the laden wagons became too much for the heat-stricken oxen. They began to die.

Albrecht abandoned two of his wagons in the sands of the Kalahari before he would admit his mistake and change his direction northwards. Soon afterwards his weakened party met up with a sub-chief of the Bechuana who made exaggerated demands for gifts before allowing the trader into his territory.

Jacobus Albrecht grudgingly parted with some of his trade goods in exchange for a promise of ivory. The ivory never came, but the demands of the Bechuana grew daily more menacing. Eventually the Boar decided to cut his losses and head back to Sesebe.

The Bechuana said they could not go until they had given

him more gifts. After two days of argument Jacobus Albrecht and his small party of Afrikaners quietly packed their wagons and made a run for it.

All pretence of friendship gone, Bechuanas pursued them and in the ensuing fight three of the Afrikaners were killed. But the guns of the trader's party inflicted heavy casualties on the Bechuanas and they withdrew leaving Jacobus Albrecht to find his way back to Sesebe as best he could.

He blamed Daniel for the unsuccessful outcome of his expedition, but the Boer received little sympathy from the miners when his exhausted party eventually returned. They were of the same opinion as Josh. Jacobus Albrecht was an experienced trader and should have prepared his expedition more carefully. In the strangely perverse way of men who have to perform manual work for a living the miners were pleased that the venture of Andrews' partner had not succeeded. Far from deriding Daniel for his part in the affair they fêted him as a man who had 'put one over' on the trader!

Josh was not happy that part of their lauding Daniel took the form of treating him to drinks in the Miners' Inn. But he said nothing, and soon there were many other things to keep him busy.

CHAPTER FOUR

The Jew, Aaron, rode into Sesebe at midday on a hot January day in 1860. He was driving a large covered wagon pulled by a team of raw-boned oxen. Seated beside him on the high seat and dressed like a slim youth in cotton twill trousers and a soft flannel shirt was his daughter Hannah.

It was the hour when the day shift of miners stopped work to eat, and many of them sat drinking with the off-duty miners in the inn. They spilled out on to the wide veranda in front of the inn, feet up on the hand-rail, taking advantage of the light breeze that blew through the mining town.

The arrival of strangers in Sesebe was unusual enough. When one of them was a girl – even one aged only fifteen and wearing boy's clothing – it became a major event. The whistling and cat-calling brought miners pouring from the inn and living-quarters to add their voices of crude approval to the ribald din.

Ignoring the many invitations for Hannah to sample the doubtful pleasures of the inn, Aaron kept the scrawny oxen plodding on to where Josh stood in the doorway of the mines office, drawn outside by the noise.

Heaving on the long reins, the black-bearded Jew brought his wagon to a halt. He climbed stiffly to the ground, the movement disturbing the dust that clung to his clothes.

'You must be Joshua Retallick?'

'That's me.'

'My name is Aaron and this is my daughter Hannah.'

The dark-eyed girl on the wagon nodded unsmilingly.

Josh shook the hand the Jew proffered but did not return the other man's smile of greeting. This was the man who was rumoured to be illegally smuggling guns in for Chief Jonker's warriors. His presence here could bring nothing but trouble.

'I thought you traded only along the coast. What brings you here?'

The Jew shrugged and held his two hands out, palms upward. 'Business. What else? Things were too quiet for us there.

We tried Whalefish Bay but found folk too unfriendly. A bit too high and mighty for the likes of us. So "Hannah," I said, "I'll take you to see a copper town. Somewhere for a young girl to see a bit of life." And so here we are.'

There was a roar of approval from the miners who had deserted the inn to crowd around the wagon. They listened to the Jew and looked slyly up at the impassive girl on the high seat of the wagon.

'You let the girl come down here, Aaron,' one of them called. 'We'll show her a bit of life.'

'Come and have a drink, girl,' shouted another. 'There's no need to be shy with us.'

Josh rounded on the miners.

'If you don't get back to work, you'll be shy of a job. Your break-time is over. The rest of you return to the inn if you've nothing better to do.'

The men grumbled and were slow to move, but Josh stood firm and gradually the crowd began to break up and the miners move away. Josh's recent purge on the young Herero girls at Sesebe had convinced them that, although they might refer to him as a narrow-minded Methodist, Josh was not a man to argue with. Some of them had tried, with the result that two miners had received cracked heads and four others were on their way back to the Cape Colony to seek fresh work.

When the miners had drifted away Josh turned back to Aaron.

'Well, now you've seen your copper town and you'd be well advised to be clear of it before dark. Apart from my wife your daughter is the first white girl to set foot in Sesebe, and I won't guarantee her safety when the serious drinking starts.'

'I'm quite capable of looking after myself.' The girl on the high wagon-seat spoke for the first time. Her voice was soft but firm and she emphasised her words with the gun she pulled from beneath the seat. Josh observed that it was a gun of far more modern design than any he had seen in this part of the world. It served to confirm the rumours he had heard about the Jew's involvement in gun-smuggling.

'I'm sure you are – but so are my miners, and there are more of them.'

He turned to the girl's father. 'What's your real reason for coming to this part of the country?'

Aaron shrugged again. 'I'm a trader. I want to make money. I met Jacobus Albrecht a few weeks ago and heard of his unhappy trek inland. . . .'

'He had bad weather and his own foolishness to blame for that,' said Josh quickly.

'I never doubted it for a minute. That's why I am so sure I can do better.'

A thought came to Josh. 'Does Chief Jonker of the Afrikaners know you're here?'

The Jewish trader made a vague movement of his hands. 'I have spoken to him about such a trek. He knows how interested I am in the interior. Mind you, I haven't seen him for some months. However, that need not bother you. I've done business with Jonker many times in the past. I know how to smooth over any objections he may have.'

'Both you and your daughter seem supremely confident of your own capabilities,' said Josh. 'If you don't mind, I'd rather not have them put to the test here in Sesebe. You'd best come to Otjimkandje and stay with us there until we've sorted out your future plans.'

'Your kind offer I'm pleased to accept,' said Aaron. 'My future plans I know already. I want to trade between Whalefish Bay and the interior. To do that I'll need to establish a store and build a house here in Sesebe.'

Aaron saw Josh's astonishment. 'I won't be trading until I've built a stout wooden building with bolts and locks. You needn't worry that it will affect you. It won't be a place to sell goods to your miners, merely a staging post between the coast and the interior. There's plenty of scope for good healthy competition there, and Jacobus Albrecht says it will be all right.'

Josh wondered whether he imagined the fleeting moment of uneasiness in the young girl's eyes when Aaron mentioned the name of the Boer trader, but her father had not finished speaking.

'You'll have no need to concern yourself with Hannah or me, Mr Retallick. I promise not to upset your miners. I've looked after my little girl since she was two years old and always steered her well clear of trouble.'

'In case you haven't noticed, your "little girl" is now a very attractive young lady,' said Josh drily. 'But we can talk about that later. You get your wagon moving along that track.' He pointed the way to Otjimkandje. 'I'll send someone on ahead to warn my wife to expect company and I'll catch up with you before you reach the village.'

Miriam had put on her 'best' home-made dress to greet the new-comers. Visitors had become increasingly rare these troubled days. The occasional trader or hunter preferred the less-inhibited pleasures of the mining town to the mission station.

The Herero messenger had told Miriam one of the visitors was a white woman. 'She's young, missus, like Daniel, and dressed like a white man – but she's a woman.' His open hands rocked on his breast to emphasise the fact.

Hugo Walder stood with Miriam as the wagon rolled up to the mission. Daniel was off somewhere with Kasupi.

The young girl showed none of her earlier bravado in the presence of Miriam. She became quiet to the point of extreme shyness. Hannah had not come into contact with many other women during her lifetime.

Her father was less inhibited.

'Miriam, eh? A lovely name. Miriam the prophetess. Sister of my great forefather and namesake, Aaron. Delighted to meet you, my dear.'

Miriam smiled. The Jew was over-effusive, but there was nothing offensive in his manner. He was a man whose zest for life was continually bubbling over.

'I'm happy to have you here, Aaron – and Hannah, too. Do you have a surname?'

'My dear Miriam, if plain Aaron was good enough in Israel, why should I try to improve upon it?'

Miriam laughed. It was a lovely sound, and Josh realised that it had been a long time since he had last heard it. Life in Otjimkandje had become all too serious in recent times.

'My father's name was Moses,' she said, 'but he didn't let his pride prevent him from claiming the name of Trago also.'

The Jew spread his arms in a gesture of defeat. 'Then who is Aaron to think himself better than Moses? Copping, my dear.

Aaron Copping. It's not the name my father was given at birth, but I like it. It's easier to say.'

Hugo Walder's welcome was far cooler than Miriam's. Like Josh he had heard the rumours of Aaron's illegal traffic in guns. He had also inherited his countrymen's vague mistrust of these children of Israel who maintained their own faith and their own language even though they were a people without a country. He would allow father and daughter to remain under the protection of the Otjimkandje mission, and in time his own warm nature would encompass them, but for the moment he reserved judgement on them.

They all went into the sizeable wooden home that many years before had replaced the Retallicks' mud hut.

'You'll be staying here with us, of course,' said Miriam.

'Please! You must not put yourselves out in any way for Hannah and me,' protested Aaron. 'The wagon has been our home for a long time. We find it quite comfortable.'

'Nonsense! All the more reason why you should enjoy the advantages of a comfortable house for a while. You come with me, Hannah. I'll show you the room that will be yours while you're here. It will give you a chance to wash some of that trail dust away before we eat.'

Hannah emerged from her room wearing the same shirt and trousers as before; but the dust had been shaken from them, and her long black hair was swept back and caught behind her head, leaving it to hang in a single thick tress halfway down her back. The style brought her high cheekbones into prominence and highlighted her expressive brown eyes. She was a tall girl, standing eye to eye with Daniel when he came in fresh from another escapade with Kasupi and the girls working the fields.

Apart from an initial polite nod of greeting the young Jewish girl ignored Daniel. He did not share her indifference and was unable to take his eyes from her throughout the meal. When Miriam quietly reminded him that it was rude to stare he coloured up alarmingly.

It was with a sense of shock that Miriam realised this was the first white girl her seventeen-year-old son had seen. She had so completely accepted their isolated way of life here at Otjimkandje that it was easy to forget there were whole communities of their own people elsewhere. Whole countries of men and women, boys and girls with settled ways, different values and a code of conduct alien to all that was accepted here.

For a few seconds Miriam missed all she had once known in Cornwall.

The feeling was quickly forgotten when the Herero girl carrying in a dish of maize-meal porridge dropped it and the dish smashed into a hundred fragments on the hard dirt floor.

Hugo Walder's unease at having someone of an alien faith living in his community fought a losing battle with his generous nature. He suggested to Aaron it might be safer for Hannah if they remained in Otjimkandje instead of setting up house in Sesebe.

'Quite true,' agreed Aaron. 'Just as it would no doubt have been safer for you to remain in Germany rather than come here. No, Father Hugo. We all take our chances – you for your church, and me for my business. It's kind of you to suggest it, and I will remember that. But there's another reason why I shouldn't stay here – Chief Jonker. I have traded with him for many years. If he thought I was transferring that trade to your Herero, we would both have serious trouble on our hands. Hannah and I will move to Sesebe when our store is finished.'

The work on Aaron's combined store and home began within a few days but it was going to be a long time in the building. Its construction was more reminiscent of a fort than a trading store. Aaron justified it by saying he wanted to be sure that whenever he had to go away neither Hannah nor his goods would be in any danger inside.

While the store was being built by Herero workmen supervised by Sam Speke, Aaron decided to put the time to good use. He knew Hannah would be safe with Miriam and suggested that Josh accompany him on a trading mission to the same mysterious lake that Jacobus Albrecht had attempted to reach on his ill-fated expedition months before.

After a token show of resistance Josh agreed. Harold Andrews was in Sesebe and could look after the mine while Josh was away. Daniel wanted to go with them and was more than a little surprised and hurt when Josh refused.

'It's not that I don't want you with us,' Josh explained, seeing his son's disappointment, 'but with Sam working in Sesebe and Hugo Walder taking ship to the Cape for some meeting I want someone here I can trust to look after your mother and Hannah.'

Daniel was only partly mollified. He was never happier than when he was away from the village on a hunting or exploration trip. However, he knew his father's reasons were sound. There was no threat from the Herero, but the unpredictable Jonker was an ever-present menace.

The proposed expedition created great excitement in Otjim-kandje. Josh intended taking about forty Herero warriors with him, and there was much competition to be among those chosen. It was so unusual for the subjugated tribe to venture such a distance from their village that Mutjise himself decided to go. The Herero had neither horses nor guns, but to trek long miles with spears in their hands and a hunting song on their lips would make them feel like men again – warriors, breathing the air of the hills and plains and desert.

The send-off was all a Herero warrior could have wished. The old chief Tjamuene sat surrounded by his household to witness their departure, and the women of the village sent them on their way with the exciting ululating cry that had sent genera-tions of warriors and hunters on their journeys with hearts filled with pride.

It was quiet in Otjimkandje with so many men away. Daniel's awareness of his responsibility quickly wore off. Hannah did not help. She behaved as though he did not exist.

Daniel found her indifference both irritating and puzzling. It was totally removed from the behaviour of the Herero girls. They would giggle and nudge each other when he and Kasupi approached them. If one of them were alone, she would walk past with eyes demurely fixed upon the ground until she was alongside. Then she would raise her eyes to look slyly sideways from between long black lashes.

Hannah did none of these things. She went about whatever she happened to be doing as though he was not there, ignoring him completely. It was as though he did not exist for her. It annoyed him even more to know that she spoke freely to his mother and to the Herero women who frequented the house, and he had heard her laughter ring out when one of the young Herero men brought some produce from the mission garden to the kitchen.

After some weeks Daniel could take her diffidence no longer. Choosing a time when he knew his mother was away at Hugo Walder's house, he went into the kitchen and found Hannah alone, kneading the coarse bread the women made.

It would have been impossible for the Jewish girl not to know of his presence, but she said nothing as she pummelled the brown dough with her fists. In her own time she finished and carried the wooden board with the mixture to a corner cupboard and placed it inside. Rinsing her hands in a small bowl of water she dried them on the apron she wore, then made to walk from the room past Daniel.

He put an arm across the open doorway in front of her and she stopped abruptly. For the first time since she and her father had arrived in Otjimkandje she looked directly at him and he became acutely aware of the depth of her dark eyes.

Daniel wanted her to say something, to be the first to speak; but he found her eyes so disturbing, her look so intense, that he was thrown off balance.

'Why are you in such a hurry to leave the kitchen?'

The weakness in his own voice was apparent to him.

Hannah looked faintly surprised. 'Hurry? I'm in no hurry to leave, but I've finished what I was doing and have other things to do elsewhere. So if you will kindly remove your arm. . . .'

His arm stayed where it was. He had won. She had spoken to him.

'So you *can* speak!'

'I can speak.' Her self-assurance was so complete as to be unnerving. 'But I've been brought up to believe that speech is a gift from God. To waste it is to belittle its value and insult Him.'

Daniel was bewildered by such a deep philosophy.

'It's not wasting words to say "Good day" to me, is it?'

'Yes. You are quite capable of seeing what sort of day it is for yourself. You don't need me to tell you.'

'It isn't supposed to be a way of telling what sort of day it is.' Daniel was floundering; his confrontation with Hannah had rebounded on him and he could see no way of extricating himself.

'It's ordinary courtesy, that's all.'

'You mean it's just like the courtesy shown by yourself and that friend of yours when you talk about me in Herero when I'm standing within hearing?'

Daniel's jaw dropped. 'But you can't speak Herero. You've never been in this land before.'

The blood rushed to his face at the thought of the first conversation he and Kasupi had held about Hannah when she ventured forth from the Retallick house the day after her arrival in Otjimkandje with her father.

Secure in the knowledge that she could not know the language they had discussed her virtues and defects, and Kasupi had stated after due deliberation and discussion that Hannah would one day develop into a woman who could bring much pleasure into the life of a man like Daniel.

Daniel had scornfully replied that she had as much bosom as a hearth snake and he would as soon try to lie along the thin branch of a tree as make love to her.

There had been other remarks made in her presence since then, and his face burned at the thought of some of them.

'I have been trading north of the Orange River with my father since I could first talk,' said Hannah bitingly. 'I doubt if you could teach me any new languages. As I said earlier, words are not meant to be wasted. None of yours has been.'

To complete his utter rout at her hands Hannah's next words were in the Herero tongue.

'Words are like arrows. A man should not let them fly unless he knows where they will land.'

At that moment Miriam arrived back at the house carrying a large basket of vegetables.

'Hello, you two. It's nice to see you getting together at last. I was beginning to think you didn't like one another.'

Daniel fled from the house, and Miriam looked after him startled.

'Oh dear! Have I interrupted something?'

Hannah laughed. 'No, there's nothing to worry about. Daniel and I have just discovered that we speak the same language. We'll get along fine now.'

*

Aaron's trip towards Lake Ngami was as successful as Jacobus Albrecht's had been disastrous. He and Josh made their way steadily north-westwards without a hitch. It was a great help having Hereros with them. In former days, before Jonker had come upon the scene, some of the Hereros had led a semi-nomadic life, taking their cattle to wherever the grass grew, following the rains and searching for new grazing- and hunting-grounds. A few of their escort had been with these people. They knew the country and were able to follow the elephant tracks from water-hole to water-hole, always heading towards their goal, 'the great water'.

Only six weeks from the time they left Otjimkandje, Aaron and Josh rode off to a nearby ridge to shoot down a big bull elephant with enormous tusks. It would provide much-needed meat as well as a handsome profit. Good ivory was much sought after by the captains of trading ships.

The huge grey animal turned with flapping ears and slowly lashing trunk to meet their advance. As they moved closer it began to sway, shifting its four-ton bulk from side to side, lifting its front feet alternately, choosing its moment to charge.

Before it had arrived at a decision Josh brought it down with a single shot. The huge creature buckled at the knees and collapsed sideways, raising a huge cloud of dust as it crashed to the ground.

Not until the dust had settled did the two men see the shimmering blue line on the flat horizon.

They had reached Lake Ngami!

Recklessly galloping their horses, they confirmed their discovery and tasted the bitter waters of the lake before riding back to the wagons. They had seen enough for a decision to be reached to make a camp some miles away from the reed-beds and mud-flats of the huge inland lake. It abounded with mosquitoes and the deadly tsetse fly which could kill off all their oxen.

The lake reflected the blue of the sky as they squatted in the shade of their wagons watching the Herero warriors bringing in the meat of the bull elephant.

Josh felt a great sense of contentment and achievement inside him.

'This is the life, Aaron. It's better than being shut away in a mine office, with dust and noise all around. I sometimes wonder how I put up with it.'

'This is a great country,' agreed the bearded Jew, beaming as two huge bloody-ended tusks were stowed away inside one of his wagons. 'Have you seen the tracks about here? Some of them are better than Cape roads – and they are all made by elephants. There must be hundreds of them. A man could get rich on ivory alone in this place.'

'It might well prove less troublesome than many other items of trade,' said Josh pointedly. He had seen the Jewish trader and Mutjise in earnest conversation on a number of occasions. Their talk always broke off abruptly whenever he approached. Josh had not forgotten his earlier reservations. Aaron was a shrewd trader with a reputation for dealing in forbidden goods. Mutjise wanted the Herero to become a great nation once again. There was one commodity which might well satisfy the ambitions of both men – guns!

'With so much ivory here for the hunting what more could any man wish for?' asked the trader with exaggerated wide-eyed honesty. 'Unless it be copper, perhaps?'

'You can forget copper this far inland,' said Josh. 'It's here all right. We've passed some first-class ore in a number of places along the way. But most of it's too far from the sea. Transport problems would make it uneconomical to mine.'

'Isn't that just like the good Lord!' said Aaron, rolling his eyes towards the sky. 'He shows us the door to the promised land and then goes off with the key still in His pocket.'

Josh smiled. It was impossible not to like this black-bearded man. A keen trader he most certainly was, but he was always cheerful and even-tempered. They had been lucky and the trip had gone well this far, but Josh thought Aaron would have been the same had they met with adversity all along the way.

'It's a pity Daniel couldn't have come with us,' said Josh. 'A trip like this would have made up for the last one.'

'Ah yes! The trek with Jacobus Albrecht.'

Something about the way Aaron spoke the Boer trader's name reminded Josh of Hannah's expression when Jacobus Albrecht had been mentioned on the day of her arrival in Sesebe.

'Of course, I was forgetting you know him. I must admit it

surprised me that he agreed to your opening a trading post at Sesebe. Jacobus Albrecht doesn't impress me as a man who would invite competition into his territory.'

'No, he's used to getting his own way,' agreed Aaron, his manner more serious than usual. 'Perhaps that's way he's let me open my store.'

Josh looked at him uncomprehendingly.

'Jacobus Albrecht wants to take Hannah for his wife.'

'But she's a mere child!' Josh was shocked.

'Oh no.' Aaron Copping stroked his beard and looked directly into Josh's eyes. 'Hannah is enough of a woman to refuse to have anything to do with him.'

'What about you?' Josh sensed the Jew was being devious. 'Don't tell me you would agree?'

Aaron shrugged. 'With Hannah what I think would make little difference. She will marry whoever she decides to take for a husband.' He smiled. 'If Jacobus Albrecht believes it could be him, then who am I to bring disillusionment into his life?'

The calculating look returned to his face again. 'No, I don't think Jacobus is the man for her. For a man of my religion it would be nice to think she might choose to marry someone with a more appropriate name. A good strong Hebrew name like – Daniel?'

The dark-bearded Jew began nodding his head thoughtfully 'Yes, there's a good name. Daniel. The good book says he was a man of strong beliefs. Prepared to enter a lion's den rather than back down.' Aaron looked up at Josh and smiled again. 'But perhaps such a dramatic sign of his faith will not be necessary.'

As it happened, Daniel had found his own special lion's den in which to set foot. After his humiliating conversation with Hannah he located Kasupi and together they made a desultory foray into the maize fields. The young girls working among the tall wind-rattled plants were as giggling and willing as ever, but Daniel found he had lost his taste for women.

Leaving his companion to make uncomfortable love to the enthusiastic and overdeveloped younger daughter of a tribal elder, Daniel rode into Sesebe. His ego was immediately boosted by the welcome given to him by the miners in the Miners' Inn. Two new men had recently come up from the Cape and Daniel was introduced to them as 'the one who put it across Jacobus Albrecht'.

The story of the previous year's trek was told and retold. Incidents, real and imagined, grew as darkness covered the mining camp and brandy blurred the young man's memory and loosened his tongue.

As loud laughter and the singing of bawdy songs drowned conversation in the smoke-filled room Daniel leaned back in his chair and beamed about him. This was where a man belonged: among friends who understood him and respected his maturity; friends who looked up to him as a man who got out and did things, a man capable of making a fool of a hard-living Boer trader. They did not look down their noses at him or ignore him, did not try to humiliate him as Hannah had.

He frowned, and one of the miners leaned across the table and blinked drunkenly at him.

'Hey! What's the matter with you, man? Ain't you enjoying yourself? Come on, drink up. Your old man's away. Let's all make the most of it.'

He splashed Daniel another drink from the bottle and more brandy spilled over the edge of the glass on to the stained table-top.

It was sheer bad luck for Daniel that Chief Jonker chose this night to pay another of his unheralded visits to Otjimkandje. He, too, had been drinking cheap brandy with his men, but his drinking lacked the bonhomie of the miners.

Hugo Walder's mission and the Herero village were thorns in the flesh of the Afrikaner chief. He knew that one day he would have to do something about them. For as long as Otjimkandje remained, Jonker's authority would not be seen to be absolute in the country he had claimed for his own. It had been the land of the Herero before his coming and, while they clung to Otjimkandje, Tjamuene and his followers still had a claim to it. They had to go.

All the same, Jonker knew he could not risk an outright attack on the village lest a European be killed and bring the wrath of the Cape government down upon him. Jonker had once travelled to Cape Town in his younger days and he retained considerable respect for the organisation and might he had seen there. His control of his Afrikaner warriors was not sufficient to ensure the safety of Hugo Walder and the others. So Jonker was forced to resort to less direct tactics.

It was the night of a late-rising full moon and the shadows of Jonker and twenty or so mounted warriors cast long shadows before them as they rode from the bushveldt across the cleared space to the eastern fringe of Otjimkandje village.

As usual, they rode scornfully past Tjamuene's kraal and through the village, squeezing knee to knee between the closely spaced huts, the hoofs of their mounts scattering the dying embers of the deserted cooking-fires as they went.

Although it seemed no one had witnessed their arrival, the news that Jonker and his warriors were in Otjimkandje had reached every hut within minutes. As women and children trembled in the darkness of their homes men nervously fondled spears and wished the warriors who had gone off with Aaron were at hand. They had feared the Afrikaners for so long that no man ventured outside to see what Jonker wanted.

The Afrikaner chief rode directly to the mission area and he and his men reined to a halt outside Hugo Walder's hut.

'Little Father, I wish to speak to you.'

The Afrikaner was fully aware that the missionary was absent at the Cape, but he called loudly for the ears of those who listened and would report on the night's events to Hugo Walder when he returned.

'Little Father, I have heard bad reports that the Herero trade for guns with strangers from the sea. I wish to discuss this with you.' In a quieter aside to one of his men he said, 'Take five men and search the mission church. Turn over the benches and other things – but cause no damage. Do you understand?'

The Afrikaner nodded and, dismounting from his horse, beckoned for some of the other warriors to accompany him.

When they were gone Jonker swung down from his own horse and, flanked by two warriors, entered Hugo Walder's hut.

Not far away a figure hidden in the shadows retreated silently from the scene and hurried away to the Retallick house.

Kasupi had only to knock once. Miriam had been woken by

the Herero girl who helped in the house.

'Who is it?' she called from behind a bolted door.

'It's Kasupi. Is Daniel there?'

There was a brief pause. 'I thought he was with you.' The bolt was drawn back and the door opened to allow the Herero to slip inside.

'Where's Daniel? Why aren't you with him?'

'He will be all right.' Kaspui's heart pumped blood to his head madly. Daniel *had* to be all right. If anything had happened to him, the Herero would forfeit his own life. 'He went to Sesebe earlier. I thought he would have returned by now. Jonker is in the village.'

'I know. What's he doing?'

In the moonlight that filtered through the curtains Kasupi saw that Miriam held a pistol in her hand.

'He and his men are searching the church and the house of the Little Father. He will come here soon. Do you have a gun for me to use? If we keep the door locked, we can kill some of the Afrikaners and perhaps frighten the others away.'

'No! Do that and we give them an excuse to destroy the whole village and us with it. Go into the back room and don't show yourself. I'll deal with Jonker.'

Kasupi shook his head. He was the son of a Herero chief. He would not hide behind a woman when danger threatened. Besides, there was the question of Daniel's whereabouts. . . .

'You must stay inside here and keep the door bolted. Perhaps Jonker will not trouble you. I will go to find Daniel.'

'Wait!' Miriam clutched his arm. 'Find him and make sure he's safe – but don't bring him back here until the Afrikaners have gone.'

It was a promise Kasupi had no intention of keeping, but he nodded. Slipping from her grasp, he opened the door quietly and vanished into the night, heading for the pen where the few horses were kept.

Jonker and his men searched Hugo Walder's hut, but apart from deliberately moving some of his belongings to let him know they had been inside they disturbed very little. Hugo Walder would be furious at the invasion of his home, but he would have little of substance to complain about to the Cape authorities.

Jonker waited until his warriors rejoined him from the church before he moved off to the house of Josh Retallick.

'Mr Retallick?'

Once again Jonker made a great show of announcing his presence, although he was fully aware that Josh, too, was away from Otjimkandje.

'Yes, what do you want?' The door opened and Miriam stood in the doorway. She had decided to play the Afrikaner at his own game. If he wanted every move to be made in the open, witnessed by others, then she was quite prepared to have it that way.

'Tell Mr Retallick that Chief Jonker of the Afrikaner wishes to speak to him.'

'You know very well that Mr Retallick is away—just as I'm quite sure you know Father Walder is not in the village. If you want to speak to them, you must return some other time—in daylight, if you please.'

Chief Jonker was not used to having a woman speak to him in this manner in front of his men, not even a white woman.

'I come in peace but I am unhappy at the talk of guns being brought into the country for the Herero. I come to speak to the Little Father and see for myself that this is not so. The Little Father is not here and I am happy there are no guns in his house. I wish to be sure there are no guns for the Herero in your house.'

'The only gun in this house is the one I have here in my hand. You will take my word for that.'

The Afrikaner chief frowned. He did not want trouble at this house. On the other hand, he could not lose face in front of his men. He wished he had brought more brandy with him; the effects of his earlier drinking were beginning to wear off.

'I must be sure. We will look.'

Miriam used both thumbs to pull back one of the cocks on the double-barrelled pistol. The noise it made as it clicked into position was very loud in the night air.

The sound genuinely alarmed Jonker. He had not been prepared for events to go this far. He had merely wanted to remind the residents of Otjimkandje that he was the sovereign ruler of

Hereroland.

One of Jonker's men was not so sensitive to the diplomacy of the situation — or perhaps the effect of the brandy he had drunk was slower in wearing off. Contemptuously he kneed his horse forward to where Miriam stood outside the door and reached down to take the gun from her.

He had made the same mistake as his chief in underestimating Miriam's determination. Pointing the gun in the Afrikaner's direction, she closed her eyes and jerked the trigger.

There was a loud bang as the pistol jumped in her hand.

The ball sped harmlessly over the head of the Afrikaner warrior, but his horse was not used to having a gun fired at a distance of only six inches from its nostrils. The noise and flash terrified the animal and it reared back from the gun.

The warrior had been leaning forward and was caught off balance. The violent reaction of the horse threw him high into the air, and he landed with his arm twisted beneath him. His scream of pain was lost in the snorting of prancing horses as the frightened mount of the unseated warrior jumped among them.

Opening her eyes to the confused moonlit scene, Miriam waited for the holocaust she believed must now come down upon her.

To her amazement Jonker began to laugh. Following the example of their chief, the Afrikaner warriors joined in. A wound inflicted by a man from another tribe would have started a war. An injury caused by falling from a horse frightened by a woman was a joke. It was also Jonker's way of extricating himself from a situation he did not care for.

'Come!' he said to his men as the injured warrior was unsympathetically assisted to his feet. 'Before she fires again and dismounts us all.'

Still laughing, the Afrikaners rode away and Miriam slumped back against the doorpost. Her arm brushed against cold steel, and she looked down at the barrel of Hannah's musket which protruded through the door opening.

'Thank goodness you didn't fire that thing, too,' Miriam said weakly. 'That would have finished me off. The sound of my pistol frightened the life out of me. When that man fell to the ground and I thought I'd killed him I could have died myself.'

'Then you had both Jonker and me fooled,' replied Hannah. 'You were so cool I felt sure you must have known I was behind you with this.'

'Had I known I would have been even more frightened,' said Miriam. 'One bang like that was enough. I don't think I'll ever stop shaking!'

'I only hope Chief Jonker appreciated his luck, too,' said the Jewish girl. 'My gun was pointing at his heart — and I'm a very good shot. I wouldn't have missed. Had he not called off his men when he did the Afrikaners would be electing a new chief tomorrow and I would have been happy to die for it.'

There was such intense emotion in her voice that Miriam said, 'Hush, child! What a thing to say. Nobody's going to die tonight. And why should you hate Jonker so much? He's not a good man, but I doubt if he's any worse than many others in this world.'

'Yes, he is. Jonker is the worst man I've ever met. He can't be trusted.'

Hannah's hatred of Chief Jonker had to come out, and Miriam waited in silence in the doorway. It was dark just here and she knew from her own experiences that difficult words slipped out easier in the darkness.

'When we first came to Whalefish Bay I wasn't very old and we didn't have much money. But Father worked hard day and night doing anything to earn a living. After a couple of years he began trading and for a while things started to improve. Then he met Chief Jonker. He came to Father full of talk about how he would make him rich. He said he was the greatest chief in the country and he insisted that Father should trade with him alone and break with all the other tribes. Father agreed and from that time on everything that came in went to Jonker. It wasn't long before it became obvious that all we were getting in return were promises — and abuse. But we carried on trading with him because Father said that one day Jonker would allow us to trade farther inland and then everything would be worthwhile.'

Hannah paused and the only sound was her own heavy breathing.

'Eventually he did agree to allow traders to come inland — but he gave the concession to Jacobus Albrecht and Harold Andrews. We got nothing.'

Miriam resisted the urge to put out a hand and touch the girl. There had been nobody before to listen to her story and but for the emotive events of the night it would still have been bottled up inside her. But there was more to come.

'Jonker was still willing to trade with Father for "special" goods. But it meant moving away from Whalefish Bay and going a long way to the south – away from people to where there was nothing but sand and sea mists, where most of the trading was done at night so no one could see.'

'This trade was in guns?'

Hannah shrugged into the darkness. 'It must have been. When I asked Father he said the less I knew the better it would be for me.'

The emotion had drained away now, and Miriam did reach out and squeeze the girl's arm reassuringly.

'You've had a very hard life, Hannah, with no mother to turn to. That's over now. You're here among friends. Everything else is in the past.'

'Is it?' The bitterness returned to Hannah's voice. 'I don't suppose Jacobus Albrecht thinks so.'

'Albrecht? What's he got to do with anything?'

'He persuaded Jonker to allow us to come inland to trade.'

'He did that? Such generosity doesn't sound like the Jacobus Albrecht I've met.'

'Oh, he didn't do it out of kindness!' Her laugh was an ugly sound. 'He wants to marry me.'

'Good God! You're much too young to marry Jacobus Albrecht.'

'I was only fourteen when he first mentioned it.'

'The man must have been drunk!' Miriam's indignation crackled in the darkness.

'No. I could have excused him had he been drinking. He was quite sober. He told Father he wanted to take me for his wife. I was there when he said it. What made it even worse was that he didn't look at me during the whole time he was talking. I felt like some dog he wanted to buy.'

'Your father refused him, of course?'

'Had he done so we would still be down there among the sand dunes. Father didn't say no and he didn't say yes. He told Jacobus he would think about it if he helped us to get a trading concession from Jonker.'

'Well, we'll see about marriage to Jacobus Albrecht if it ever crops up again. If there's even the breath of a whisper about it, you come and see me, young lady. I've seen enough misery caused by wrong marriages. I'll not let it happen to you.'

She sensed the immense relief in the young girl at having someone to share the burden she had been carrying alone for so long. Miriam moved before the relief overflowed into tears.

'Now let's go inside and settle the house down for the night once more.'

The Afrikaners had gone, but there was to be little sleep for Miriam and Hannah that night. The sound of the shot she had fired had been heard in every hut in Otjimkandje; but it was not until the hoofbeats of the Akrikaners' horses had faded into the far distance that the Herero dared to leave their huts.

Cautiously at first, but in ever-increasing numbers, they made their way to the Retallick house. Soon the hut was surrounded by anxious villagers. When no one appeared from inside, the rumours began to circulate. 'The white mother Retallick has been killed.' 'No, it is the tall daughter of the Trader.' 'Both women have been taken by the Afrikaners.'

Finally Tjamuene himself arrived at the house surrounded by men of his personal bodyguard bearing bright flaming torches. 'Having first made sure Jonker has left,' commented Hannah disdainfully.

'Hush! At least he's come himself and hasn't sent one of his men,' said Miriam. 'He's an old man who would stand no chance against Jonker. Put some more tea in that pot, Hannah. We'll have to ask Tjamuene in.'

The old chief was full of genuine concern for the two women and relieved to see them both safe.

'Jonker has gone too far this time,' he said. 'I will post some of my own guards outside your house. The Afrikaner will not bother you again. You have Tjamuene's word for that.'

'Thank you, Tjamuene. That won't be necessary,' said Miriam firmly. 'He won't come again. If he did, and your men were here, there would be a fight and many men would be killed. It is better such a thing does not happen. Come, sit down and have some tea with us. It's very kind of you to be so concerned.'

While they drank the tea Tjamuene heard the full story of all that had happened. By the end of it he, too, was chuckling. The laughs came from deep in his ample belly and erupted in short uncontrollable bursts, spilling from his lips into his tea-cup.

'You are right,' he said, using a fat finger to wipe away the tears that overflowed from his bloodshot eyes. 'Jonker will not return. A chief who allows his warriors to be sent running by one woman would not dare to risk it happening for a second time. If it did, he would be their leader no longer.'

The Herero chief suddenly stopped laughing. 'But where is your son? Was he not here when Jonker came?'

'No.' Tjamuene had awakened the worry that was nagging at Miriam. 'He is in Sesebe tonight.'

The chief gave no hint of his thoughts. 'Kasupi is with him'

'Yes.'

It was not a lie, Miriam told herself. Kasupi would be with him by now.

'It is good. They are as brothers and both are sons to me.'

The old chief stood up to go. 'My eyes are pleased to see you well but my heart is heavy that as chief of the Herero I am not able to protect you while you are in my village. If we, too, had guns, perhaps Jonker's people would tremble in their huts at night. . . .' Tjamuene gave a resigned gesture. 'I will not live to see such a thing come to pass. All I can do is try to bring my people safely through each long day and night and leave my hopes for their future to those who will follow me.'

'You are the chief of the Otjimkandje Herero,' said Miriam. 'You have the love and respect of your people and your friends.'

'I am the chief of the Otjimkandje Herero,' agreed Tjamuene. 'And I have the love of my family and friends. A man can ask for little more.'

Nodding to Hannah, Tjamuene shook Miriam's hand and left the house with a quiet dignity that brought a ridiculous lump to Miriam's throat.

'We'd better get these tea things cleared away,' she said briskly to Hannah, 'otherwise we'll get no sleep at all tonight.'

But there were more visitors yet to come on this strange eventful night.

Miriam had extinguished one of the two lamps when she heard the pounding of hoofs on the hard dirt road leading into the village. For one fear-filled moment she thought it must be Jonker returning to take revenge for the humiliation she had caused him. Then she realised that the horses were coming along the road from Sesebe.

Lighting the second lamp again quickly, she unbolted the door and threw it open as the first of the foaming horses was reined to a halt outside the house.

'Daniel? Is that you? Where . . . ?'

'It's not Daniel, ma'am. It's me. Harold Andrews. Your boy's friend – the Herero – came galloping into Sesebe saying Jonker was attacking the village. I gathered up half a dozen of my men and we've come here as fast we could, thinking you was in trouble. There'll be more men following.'

'Oh dear! Yes, Jonker and his men have been here and there was some trouble, but it's over now. But Kasupi went to fetch Daniel. Where is he? Why isn't he with you? I thought he was at Sesebe?'

'He is, ma'am. He's spending the night at Sam Speke's place. If I send one of my men back along the road to stop the others, perhaps I might step inside and have you tell me what's been going on here tonight?'

'Of course. Please come in.'

Hannah had not gone to bed and she came into the kitchen when Miriam went indoors.

'You'd better make some more tea, Hannah. We'll give up any idea of sleep tonight.'

As the girl hurried away Miriam said to the trader, 'Is Daniel all right? Why didn't he come here with you?'

Harold Andrews looked sheepish. 'To tell you the truth, ma'am, he was drinking with some of my men last night. He's a big lad for his age and sometimes it's easy to forget he can't take a man's share of hard drink. He wasn't feeling too good. When I heard about it I thought it best he be taken to Sam Speke's place for the night. I didn't think it would be a good idea to bring him with us. He might easily have had an accident in the dark — especially if he was worried about you.'

'Mr Andrews.' Miriam was tight-lipped as she faced the trader. 'What you're trying to tell me is that my son got so drunk last night that he was incapable of getting himself home.'

It might have appeared to an onlooker that the hat Harold Andrews held in his hand had a red-hot brim.

'That's about the rights of it, ma'am.'

'Then don't beat about the bush. Say so. Now, you'd better get your men inside, and I'll tell you what's been going on to-night. But if I catch any of them leering at Hannah they can wait for you outside. Is that understood?'

'Yes, ma'am.'

Miriam glared at the other men through the open doorway, and when they had all nodded that they understood she led the way into the house and told her story yet again.

It was a very pale and shaken prodigal son who returned to the Retallick house the next morning. He had awakened feeling very sorry for himself, but received no sympathy from Sam Speke. The one-time seaman had hurled the news of the night's events at Otjimkandje in his face before his feet had swung to the heaving floor.

Sam described what might so easily have happened in the Herero village in such vivid detail that the thought of it had immediately combined with the stale brandy in his system to make Daniel violently sick.

Kasupi had been able to put his mind at ease when Daniel made his way to the stable to collect his horse. The Herero had spent a great part of the night riding back and forth between Otjimkandje and Sesebe. He, too, had a guilty conscience.

When he arrived at Otjimkandje, Daniel tried to apologise for his absence, but Miriam cut his words short.

'What happened here could not have been prevented by you. What does upset me is that you should undermine your father's authority by getting helplessly drunk with his men. You know very well he's concerned about the drinking in Sesebe getting out of hand. How can he do anything about it when his own son is as bad as the worst of them?' Daniel mumbled something about it not happening again. 'I'll believe that when you've proved it. But I tell you one thing. No son of mine is going to become a drunkard. If you make this a habit, I'll come to Sesebe and bring you back here myself if I have to go into that place and walk you out by the ear to do it. Just you remember that.'

Daniel's shame was heightened by the presence of Hannah. She stood in the kitchen making pastry, her back to them during the whole of Miriam's tirade.

'And don't think you're going to moon about here all day because your head feels like a bucket filled with thunder. We're out of meat. You can take that gun of yours and go and shoot something. You'll find the game in the east – in the opposite direction to Sesebe.'

'But I could be gone for days! What if Jonker comes back?'

'He won't; but, if you're so worried, you'd best be on your way, then you'll be back here quicker.'

'What sort of gun do you have?'

The question came from Hannah.

'A Spanish one – with rifling.'

'Show me.'

Only too pleased for an opportunity to escape from his mother's wrath Daniel went to his room and returned with his gun. It was a long-barrelled flintlock of excellent quality but a long-outdated model.

'That's a Kaffir gun. If you want to get back here in a hurry, you'd better take mine. Here!'

She handed him the gun she had placed in a corner of the kitchen the previous night. It was a new percussion rifle, far more reliable and accurate than a flintlock.

'Take the pouch, too. You'll find all the percussion caps, paper cartridges and moulded shot you're likely to need.'

Ignoring his stuttered thanks, Hannah turned her back on him and resumed her own task.

Daniel's dejection showed in the way he sat his horse as he rode away from Otjimkandje with Kasupi.

'You were very hard on him,' said Hannah quietly as she and Miriam stood together by the window watching him go.

'It was no more than he deserved.' Miriam's tone of voice belied her words.

'It was a good thing Daniel was in Sesebe last night,' commented Hannah. 'Had he been here it would have been him standing out there facing Jonker. His shot wouldn't have missed, either, and the Afrikaners would have killed him.'

'Don't you think I know that?' Miriam's voice broke as she added, 'I was giving my thanks to God for that as Daniel left to ride away just now.'

Turning away, she hurried into her bedroom before she could make a fool of herself in front of Hannah.

CHAPTER FIVE

Josh and Aaron were away for almost four months and returned well pleased with the results of their long trek. Although Lake Ngami had been discovered some years before, very few Europeans had yet been there.

The two men from Otjimkandje had not only reached the lake, but had also made friends with the unpredictable Bechuana chief who claimed the lake as his territory. More, they had established trading links with him. Their wagons were laden with ostrich feathers and elephant tusks. Some had been taken from animals shot by Josh, but the majority had been received from the Bechuana. Trade with Lake Ngami would take the form of a lengthy trek, but the profit at the end of it would make the journey well worthwhile.

Josh had also brought a few samples of copper ore back with him. Most of the deposits he had found had been too far inland to make working them a practical consideration, but there was one spot only two days' journey from Otjimkandje that looked promising. Josh thought that, if a road were made from it direct to Whalefish Bay, the distance would be little more than from Sesebe.

One of the Herero warriors with him said this copper deposit had been known to some of his people who had once had a village near the spot. They had fled before Jonker and no one had shown the ore to the Afrikaner. Josh said it would be as well to keep the secret with the Herero people.

Hugo Walder was still in the Cape Colony, and Miriam had suggested that nothing be said to Josh of Jonker's visit until the missionary returned. Daniel would not agree. Such an incident could not be kept secret in this land. If Josh were not told about it by the Herero, he would hear the details from the miners at Sesebe.

Daniel told his father about it himself that night when the family was having its evening meal. Aaron and Hannah were also there. Daniel made no attempt to hide the reason for his absence, and Hannah watched Josh very closely for his reaction.

Josh was angry – very angry. But whether it was directed at Jonker or at Daniel she did not know.

'Jonker knew we were all away,' Josh said finally. 'Otherwise he would never have dared to come here like that. But it was an insult directed against Hugo and Tjamuene rather than against us. I think we'll discuss it with Hugo on his return before we decide what action is necessary.'

He looked at Daniel and frowned. 'I thought I could rely on you to take care of things while I was away. It seems I was wrong.'

'Had he been here it would have been a different story,' Hannah blurted out. She repeated what she had said to Miriam the morning after the raid, adding, 'If Daniel had been here, you'd have come back to find none of us left alive.'

She stared so defiantly around the table when she had finished that Josh raised an eyebrow questioningly at Miriam and Aaron stopped his fork halfway to his mouth, looking from his daughter to Daniel with great interest. Her outburst took Daniel by surprise. Since the incident with Jonker she had been more civil to him and they had held a number of brief conversations, but no more. Aware of the interested expressions of the others his own face reddened and matched Hannah's.

'H'm! That may be so,' said Josh. 'But Daniel's had his seventeenth birthday. When I'm away he's the man in this house. I expect him to accept that responsibility.'

'It won't happen again,' mumbled Daniel.

'Of course it won't!' said Miriam, putting an end to the subject. 'Now, let's talk about Aaron's new house and store. I've been down there to help Hannah get things ready. It's far and away the finest building in these parts, and there's already been a delivery of trade goods from the Cape. Sam had them stored away for you.'

'I'll have to settle my debt with Sam,' said the Jew. 'He's a useful man to have around. Do you think he'd come to work for me, Josh?'

'He might. He's his own boss. There's more than enough work for his wagon-building in Sesebe; but, as you say, he's a good man to have around. Make him an offer he can't refuse.

He'd be especially useful if you intended trading with the Herero. He's married into the tribe, and they trust him.'

'I don't think I'll have any difficulty trading with the Herero,' said Aaron, 'but I'll ask Sam anyway.'

He pushed his plate from him and leaned back in his chair. 'That was a delightful meal, Miriam. Now, as a "thank you" for looking after my Hannah I've brought you back some specially treated sable antelope skins that the Bechuana traded from the Matabele Zulus. They are so dark and soft that if you cover your chairs with them you'll swear they are finest velvet.'

The remainder of that evening was spent talking about the things the two men had seen during their long return trip to Lake Ngami.

Aaron and Hannah left Otjimkandje for Sesebe the following day. Miriam was going to miss the tall Jewish girl. She had grown very fond of her and learned to appreciate her intelligence and quiet self-assurance. Miriam also felt sorry for Hannah. As the only white woman in Sesebe her every action would be observed and commented upon by the miners. She would need all her sound common sense to remain level-headed. Miriam's only consolation was that Hannah had promised to come and stay with her in Otjimkandje whenever Aaron went away for any lengthy period.

A week after their departure Hugo Walder returned from his long stay in Cape Town. He looked healthy and fit in spite of his advancing years. The meetings he had attended in the administrative capital of the Cape Colony had gone well for him. Owing to their patient diligence over the years, the German missionaries had gradually consolidated their precarious foothold in the country to the north of the Orange River. English missions, encouraged by the success of Robert Moffat at Kuruman, were concentrating their evangelical efforts on the southern Bechuana tribes and were poised to take advantage of Moffat's incredible but strong friendship with the bloody Matabele Zulu chief, Mzilikazi. They hoped he would help them to extend their sphere of influence to the more central regions of southern Africa. Because of this they were content to allow the German missionaries to work in the near-forgotten south-west corner of Africa.

Yet there were exceptions to these loosely defined missionary 'sees'. Jonker's request for an English missionary made one inroad into the influence of the German missions.

Hugo Walder had news of this religious incursion, and his words were to bring the whole life Miriam and Josh had built for themselves crashing down about their ears.

The two of them sat in the missionary's hut on the night of his return, listening to his news and looking at the many new things he had brought back with him.

'My society wishes me to establish new mission stations among the tribes to the north,' said Hugo. 'They are sending me two young missionaries from Germany to help. Their youth and enthusiasm will give my work new impetus. They will provide a newly sharpened edge to the time-tempered blade that is old Hugo Walder. No doubt they will also prove a great trial to me until they learn to accept the ways of the Herero.'

'It's time you had some help, Hugo.' Josh drew contentedly on his pipe. 'You've pushed yourself far too hard for too many years.'

'You need a woman to look after you,' commented Miriam, who was unpacking the missionary's clothes and inspecting them for tears or missing buttons before packing them away into the drawers and cupboards Sam Speke had made more than twelve years before.

'I still have much work to do for God if he will grant me the years,' said Hugo Walder. 'And now that Jonker has his own missionary perhaps I will be allowed to continue my work among the Herero untroubled by Afrikaner warriors.'

'His missionary is in Winterhoek? We've heard nothing about it. When did he arrive?'

'We came up from Cape Town to Whalefish Bay on the same ship,' said Hugo Walder. 'He arrived there from England only a few months ago.'

Miriam failed to notice Hugo Walder's reluctance to talk about Jonker's missionary. 'We'll have to invite him to Otjimkandje for a visit. It will be nice to hear the latest news from England. I don't suppose you know from which part of England he comes?'

'He told me he had been working in London for some years,'

replied the German missionary heavily. 'But before that he was working in the part of England from which you come – Cornwall.'

Miriam saw Hugo Walder's expression for the first time and she put a hand to her mouth. Josh froze as he lowered the pipe to the table in front of him.

'Yes, my very loved friends, I see you fear the worst – and I wish I could allay those fears.'

Hugo Walder's concern caused his German accent to thicken, but there could be no mistaking the name he was to give to them. 'Jonker's new missionary is a Wesleyan preacher named William Thackeray.'

'Oh no!' The room suddenly spun about Miriam as the words were torn from her. She reeled, and Hugo Walder caught her and sat her in a chair.

Josh's hands clenched so tightly that his nails drew blood from his palms.

Hugo Walder had just uttered a name that bridged fourteen happy years. A grim and unhappy past had caught up with them.

The foundering of *Pride of Liverpool* had set Josh free and the mission at Otjimkandje given him a new and worthwhile life. Now all that would change. The preacher's presence here had to be more than coincidence. What was more, according to the law Miriam was still William Thackeray's wife – and Daniel his lawful son.

Josh and Miriam looked at each other in utter despair.

'He asked about you,' said Hugo Walder, his misery almost as great as their own. 'I told him as little as was possible in the circumstances, but I fear he will seek you out.'

'He obviously told you about Miriam and me,' said Josh. 'I'd like to tell you our version of what happened—'

'He told me nothing,' interrupted Hugo Walder. 'And I have no need to know anything more about either of you. You have lived and worked here as my very good friends for fourteen years. What more does a man need to know?'

'But he must have told you what happened before we left England,' insisted Josh. 'How else could you know we have something to hide from Thackeray? Nobody here knows of his connection with us – not even Sam.'

'Ah. But you are wrong. You are wrong.'

The missionary sat down heavily on a tall-backed chair. 'It has always been one of my worldly weaknesses that I enjoy knowing what is going on in my beloved homeland. Every month my brother goes to the docks at Hamburg to put a package of newspapers on board a ship bound for the Cape Colony. From there they are sent here to me. But you already know this; you have seen me reading them many times, and I have given some of them to Daniel to improve his German.'

Josh and Miriam both winced at the mention of Daniel. The Wesleyan preacher's arrival would have a profound effect on his life.

Hugo Walder was speaking again. 'Not long before you were first brought to Otjimkandje I received newspapers which gave great prominence to the trial of a number of men on a charge of riot and treason in some little port in Cornwall, in England. The report said these men had fought with soldiers. There were rumours that it marked the beginning of an uprising such as the one France had experienced fifty years before. The leader of the rioting, so the newspapers said, was a young engineer named Joshua Retallick. They also reported that he was badly wounded during the battle.' The missionary spread his hands. 'Even had the name been a coincidence all doubts would have gone when I first saw you working in the smithy with your shirt off. That huge scar across your back is as distinctive as the spots on a leopard.'

'But that doesn't explain how you know about Miriam – or Preacher Thackeray. They weren't involved.'

'Oh, but they were,' corrected the missionary. 'One of the newspapers reported a disturbance at the end of the trial and observed that a woman evicted from the court was one Miriam Thackeray, wife of a local Wesleyan preacher, well known for his union activities. The reporter was surprised that he had not put in an appearance at the trial as a witness in your defence. For me the newspaper reports left many questions unanswered. For the reporter, too, I think.'

'You mean you have known about this all these years and yet said nothing?' Josh could hardly believe it was possible.

'What was there for me to say?' Hugo Walder tried to shrug

his silence away. 'Men and women leave their own countries for many reasons. I had mine; you have yours. Those who find their way to this part of the world usually have stronger reasons than most. There was a time when I was concerned for the child, but as Daniel grew it became ever more apparent that he was Josh's true son. It is not what you were before but what you have become that matters. For me you have become my very dear friends.'

'Even though the Church says I am another man's wife?' Miriam's eyes were brimming with tears she was fighting hard to hold back.

'I have forgiven the Herero far worse sins,' said Hugo Walder. 'The final judgement must be the Lord's. Even so, I do not think he will be any less compassionate than a humble man like myself.'

'Hugo, you are a truly wonderful man. . . .'

Miriam burst into tears and turned to Josh for comfort. He held her until the shuddering sobs grew still.

'We'll go home now, Hugo,' said Josh. 'We have much to discuss.'

'Of course.' The missionary put out his hand and rested it on Miriam's head. 'All seems black now, but it is not so. We cannot shut off our past as though it never happened. It always catches up with us. Much better, my friends, that we face it here rather than in the Kingdom of Heaven. If there is anything I can do, I will be here.'

As Josh led Miriam from the hut Hugo Walder called, 'And remember, the decision of an English court means nothing in Otjimkandje. Here you are a free man, and so you will remain.'

Josh was relieved that Daniel was not in the house when they arrived there. He did not feel like making his explanations to-night. Miriam was so upset that Josh insisted she went directly to bed.

When she had gone he stood in the doorway of their home for a very long time, smoking his pipe. He watched as the huge three-quarter moon rose, plump as a golden pumpkin, above the horizon, dominating the star-strewn sky. All about him lively fires danced in front of the Herero huts, and he listened to the village sounds as though hearing them for the first time:

loud voices, laughter, restless cattle sounds from the animal-pens —and the drums. They throbbed out across the warm and comfortable African evening. Later the singers would join in and a dance would begin.

It was during this time that Josh arrived at a decision. William Thackeray would not drive him away from Hereroland as he had from England. He and Miriam had made a good life here for themselves and Daniel. It was a life worth fighting for.

Josh went to Miriam and they talked until the sun took over the duties of the moon on the eastern horizon.

CHAPTER SIX

Josh rode into Winterhoek when the sun stood tall in the sky. It was hot, but he was not sure whether the perspiration that followed the course of his spine was caused by the heat or the thought of meeting William Thackeray again.

His name conjured up so many memories and images: of green moors and yellow gorse; miners and the heartbeat throb of mine-engines; family and friends. It brought back less pleasant memories, too: of heavy chafing wrist- and leg-irons, and the foul-smelling inhuman darkness of a prison hulk. Josh shivered in the heat. He would not forget that it was the man he was about to meet who had given him these last memories of England.

Winterhoek was three times the size of Otjimkandje and shut in by mountains. It was a straggling untidy village, the Afrikaner huts surrounded by the hovels of their Bergdama servants and hangers-on from other tribes. Away to one side were the more substantial huts of the traders.

Josh threaded his way through the village, his horse trampling the scattered rubbish of a lax and badly organised community. But there was plenty of activity at the church. William Thackeray had only been in Winterhoek for twenty-four hours but he had wasted no time. A whole gang of Bergdama men were busy rebuilding the walls of the mission. Beyond them were women working on the thatch of the previous missionary's hut. Bustling between the two was William Thackeray.

It came as a shock to Josh to see once again how small the missionary was. Josh had always been tall, and time and work had filled him out. It had done the opposite for William Thackeray. Always a slight man, he now looked fragile, with a frail man's slight stoop.

As Josh cleared the native huts and rode into the space before the church the missionary's face wrinkled as he shielded his eyes against the sunlight with one hand and looked up at the horseman.

'Why, Josh! What a pleasant surprise. How good to see you after all these years. My word, but you're looking well. Come into my house — or "hut" I believe I must call it. There's a terrible mess inside, but I'm sure we'll find somewhere to sit. At least we'll be out of this dreadful sun. I don't think I'll ever learn to accept the heat!'

He took out a large handkerchief and wiped his face, then ran the damp cloth around his stiff neckband to emphasise his words.

Josh ignored the preacher's elaborately friendly greeting and made no move to dismount.

'Let's not play games with one another, William. I have no fond memories of you, and you proved your regard for me many years ago by having me falsely convicted of involvement in your scheming. Why are you here?'

'I am here to serve God, Josh — as I have served Him elsewhere. This place was once a Wesleyan church and will be again. That's why I am here. As for the other things you speak of, they happened a great many years ago and bitterness has undoubtedly clouded memory. It would be futile for me to protest my innocence now. No doubt your own conscience rests easier for believing the worst of me.'

'If that remark refers to Miriam, I have no feelings of guilt about taking her from you. She was never your wife in anything but name, and you know it well. But for your interference she would have been my wife in Cornwall — as she *is* my wife here.'

'And Daniel . . . how is he?'

'My son is almost a man, as tall as his father and nearly as broad across the shoulders.'

The Bergdama workmen had stopped their labours. Few of them spoke or understood much English, but it needed no command of language to recognise the antagonism between their new missionary and the white man from the Herero village.

William Thackeray brought out his damp handkerchief again, and it pursued its limp course as before.

'Josh, I have been sent here at the request of the chief of the Afrikaners. I come to preach the gospel, not to follow a vendetta.'

200

'Are you saying your coming here is mere coincidence? That you didn't know Miriam and I were here? I don't believe that.'

'I won't lie to you. I thought to find you here. Some years ago I returned to Cornwall, seeking Miriam.' William Thackeray saw Josh's expression harden. 'My motives are irrelevant now. It is sufficient to say she was not there. Neither would anyone tell me anything, but I heard rumours. It was said that Miriam and Daniel were with you; that you were living as a family somewhere in Africa. If you were a free man, I knew you would be in no land that was under British rule. It greatly reduced the number of places where I needed to look. I was working in London, helping in a mission in the docks area. I spoke to seamen for years and heard nothing. Then I was told about two men, a woman and a child rumoured to have survived a shipwreck and living in a village inland from the Skeleton Coast. The sailor had heard the story when he was working on a ship trading between the Cape Colony and Whalefish Bay. I checked with the headquarters of all the missionaries in this area, and from Germany I was informed that an English family named Retallick had survived a shipwreck together with a sailor. They told me you were living at Otjimkandje with missionary Hugo Walder.'

'You went to all this trouble, yet expect me to believe you came here only to preach God's word? I may have been ready to believe you once, William, but not anymore. That was a lesson I learned well from you.'

William Thackeray shrugged his thin shoulders. 'I would most probably have done nothing with my information had a request not been received in London for a Wesleyan preacher to come here to this place, only a few miles distant from Otjimkandje. I felt it was an omen; that I was being given an opportunity. For what I did not know — but I came.'

'So here you are. What happens next?'

The narrow shoulders shrugged again. 'I carry out the work for which I was sent here. No doubt that will involve occasional visits to my fellow-missionaries. I hope to see you again, Josh. And I look forward to meeting Miriam and Daniel.'

Josh's horse danced as the shadow of a low gliding bird crossed the clearing in front of him. Josh fought the animal around in a tight circle to confront the preacher again.

'Many years ago I came to your house to see Miriam in an attempt to prevent your wedding. You refused to let me talk to her. You said it would serve no purpose. This time it's my turn to give you that same message – and I'll add a warning for your safety. Chief Jonker is hated by the Herero. Any of his men entering Otjimkandje unarmed would be hacked to pieces. You're Jonker's missionary, brought here by him in an attempt to gain some degree of respectability in the eyes of the Cape government. You'll be neither welcome nor safe in Otjimkandje – so stay away.'

He swung his horse's head to face towards Otjimkandje.

'Josh?'

Josh turned to look back at William Thackeray.

'I was in Cornwall for a few weeks last year. I saw your mother and father. They were well. Miriam's mother died several years ago. I thought you would both wish to know that.'

Josh inclined his head in acknowledgement of the news, then kneed his horse into a canter away from the mission at Winterhoek. He was more sure than ever that the arrival of Preacher William Thackeray meant serious trouble, if not actual disaster, to the happy little family in Otjimkandje. The newly recruited missionary was thinner than he had ever been before, but the light in his eyes showed his physical form was being fed to the furnaces of some inner force. William Thackeray remained what he had always been – a zealot. Once it had been for the cause of unionism, the unity of Cornish miners. Josh wondered what direction his crusading would take in this hot and explosive country. Jonker needed very little incentive to massacre Tjamuene's Herero. At the same time tribes of opposing interest were being driven from the south into ever-closer proximity by the northward trek of land-hungry Boers. One spark of ill-directed fervour could cause the country to erupt in bloody war.

When Josh arrived back at Otjimkandje he was not able to tell Miriam of his talk with William Thackeray because Aaron and Hannah were at the house and the Jewish trader was very distressed and extremely angry.

'When is someone going to do something about that man? He

is no more than a common thief, a scourge to honest traders. We can do nothing, and even the Cape government seems to be frightened of him.'

'Who are you talking about? What's happened?'

'Who else but that son of a renegade, Chief Jonker!'

'Well, stop prancing about the room; you're making me dizzy. Hannah, will you close that door, please. Your father's voice is loud, and there are too many ears about outside.'

Otjimkandje was no different from any other village. Not every man was loyal to Tjamuene. There were some who would be happy to repeat Aaron's words to Jonker in the hope of currying favour with the Afrikaner chief.

'So who cares who hears me? A thief is a thief, be he an Afrikaner chief or a Bushman slave.'

Hannah hurriedly closed the door of the hut, and Josh steered the Jewish trader to a chair and sat him firmly in it. 'For God's sake be sensible, Aaron. We can do without another of Jonker's visits!'

'*You* can do without another of Jonker's visits?' shouted Aaron. 'Me and my wagons, we've had one already.'

'Miriam, get some tea for all of us, then perhaps we'll get some sense from Aaron in place of this disjointed rambling.'

Aaron threw up his hands in a gesture of exaggerated resignation. 'Agh! What does it matter? What does anything matter anymore? It's no use trying to trade honestly in this country – not while Jonker is allowed to do whatever he wishes, with no man with the courage to stand against him.' He caught Josh's eye. 'All right! All right! I still talk in a riddle for you, so I tell you. I am on my way to Whalefish Bay with two wagonloads of the goods we traded from the Bechuana when I meet this – this – Afrikaner!'

Aaron made the word sound like an oath, and spluttering with indignation he went on, 'He and his men are waiting for me on the road. I cannot ride through them and so I have to stop. Without so much as a "Good day to you, Aaron", they jump on to my wagons and start to throw out all my elephant tusks and ostrich feathers. "What is all this about?" I ask Jonker. 'Is the chief of the Afrikaners so poor that he has to rob traders now in order to live?"'

Josh winced. 'You said that to Jonker?'

'I said much more. When a man sees all he's worked for being taken from him should he remain silent?'

Josh shook his head. 'No. Go on.'

'Jonker accused me of taking the trade away from his people and of bartering with the Bechuana without his permission. He said he was not taking everything, only that which was his due as paramount chief of all these lands.'

'A pity some of the other chiefs weren't around to hear him say that,' murmured Josh. 'He may have control of Hereroland, but there are bigger men moving in to crowd him. How much "tribute" did he take?'

'About three-quarters of the total,' replied Aaron bitterly. 'There wasn't enough left to cover the cost of the trip to Lake Ngami.'

'You said you had two wagonloads,' put in Miriam. 'But you returned from the lake with three. What happened to the other wagonload?'

'Ah!' Aaron managed a thin smile. 'Trusting I may be. Stupid I am not. The third wagonload is in my store in Sesebe.'

'Then you'll still make some profit,' said Josh, 'if you can get the wagon to Whalefish Bay without Jonker knowing.'

'A *little* profit I may make,' corrected the Jew, 'though it will be small enough when I've paid my debts. But with three wagons of goods I would have been clear of all my money worries. However, I don't intend to let that Afrikaner thief steal this load. I'd like to talk to Mutjise. If I take the wagon to my old trading post farther down the coast, I'll need him and some of his men to come along with me and wipe out my tracks as we go. If we set out at nightfall, we'll be out of sight of the Whalefish Bay road by sun-up.'

'What happens if Jonker discovers you've tricked him?' asked Josh.

Aaron spread his hands wide. 'Why should he ever find out? Mutjise will only bring trusted men, and no one from this house will tell him. But in case anything should go wrong I'd like to leave Hannah here with you. Is that all right?'

'Of course it is,' said Miriam, and she saw the pleasure that lit up Daniel's face. He had been silently watching the trader's daughter as the others talked. Hannah was aware of his interest but chose to pretend she had not even noticed his presence.

'I'll come with you if you feel an extra gun would help.' It was an unselfish offer from Daniel in the circumstances.

'Thank you. If I intended having an armed escort, I could ask for none better.' Aaron was not averse to praising Daniel in front of his daughter. 'But I travel in peace and trust I will avoid the paths of the Afrikaners. Now, perhaps you would send your friend to find his eldest brother. Tell him I would like to speak to him at the cattle-pens. It will not be thought unusual for a trader to talk to Mutjise about buying cattle.'

With all the bustle in the house that evening it was not until Josh and Miriam were alone in their bedroom that he was able to tell her about his meeting with William Thackeray. Miriam was upset at the news of her mother's death, although it came as no surprise to her. Her mother had been in indifferent health for some years before they had left England, and Miriam had accepted she would never see her again. Even so, there were memories of the hard years of poverty they had shared when Miriam's mother had done much to make her daughter's lot an easier one than her own.

Of more immediate concern was William Thackeray's next move. They were both quite certain there would be one. The missionary was a very devious and determined man. They would never be able to relax while he remained at Winterhoek.

Daniel was Josh's main worry.

'He will have to be told the whole truth,' he said to Miriam.

'But how can you tell him, Josh? What will you say? That his name is not really Retallick? That he was conceived out of wedlock and his mother married another man while carrying him? You can't tell him that, Josh. You can't!'

'Would you rather he heard it from William? I must tell him, Miriam, no matter how difficult it is for me.'

'But how? What will he do when he knows?'

'I'll take him on a hunting trip tomorrow. We'll stay away for a couple of days to give him time to think about it. It's not going to be easy for either of us but it must be done. You can see that?'

'Yes,' Miriam agreed finally. 'But what sort of man is it who

205

will travel thousands of miles to find us after all these years? Why is he here, Josh? What does he want?'

'If I knew that, I might be able to do something about it without Daniel ever knowing. William Thackeray is not a man to shout his intentions, but I've no doubt we will know soon enough.'

Chief Jonker had greeted his new missionary civilly enough upon his arrival a Winterhoek. He gave him women to repair his hut and men to help in the rebuilding of the mission church. He would, he said, be pleased to give William Thackeray all the help he needed to establish a church in the mountain-bordered valley.

But on the third morning no women arrived to tidy the now-completed hut and there was not a Bergdama workman to be seen.

William Thackeray waited patiently until noon before he strode off to speak to the Afrikaner chief. He found the way to the chief's door barred by an Afrikaner warrior bearing a gun.

'Chief Jonker rests,' said the guard. 'He says he will see no one.'

'Unless he also told you to shoot his missionary you'll let me through,' said William Thackeray. Scornfully brushing aside the weapon, he walked past the astonished tribesman.

He did not knock at the door. To do so would have given the guard time to recover his wits and upset the odds against the chance the missionary was taking.

The hut was in semi-darkness and smelled abominably of human perspiration, smoke and stale brandy fumes. Jonker was reclining on an untidy heap of bedding, the level of the brandy in the bottle he held already well down the bottle.

'What are you doing here? I am resting.'

The startled Jonker was belligerent but his eyes avoided meeting William Thackeray's.

'You said you would have men work on the mission church until it was completed. There are no men working today.'

'Even Bergdamas must have a day of rest.'

'Sunday is the usual day of rest. It gives the Bergdamas and your Afrikaners the opportunity to attend their church – when it's completed.'

This missionary was showing none of the deference Jonker had come to expect from those with whom he dealt. True, he had found white men to be far more casual when dealing with tribal authority, but with the exception of Hugo Walder he had always found missionaries eager to please. He changed his tactics.

'One of the white men from Otjimkandje came to see you. Why did you not tell me of this?'

'He came to see me because I knew him in England. It was nothing to do with you.'

'The Herero of the Little Father do not look kindly upon Chief Jonker of the Afrikaners. My people are greater than the Herero. They do not like this. Anyone from Otjimkandje is not my friend.'

'This man is not a friend. He came to tell me I must not visit Otjimkandje. Your Bergdamas must have told you we did not touch hands as do friends.'

'They told me. I wanted to hear it from you.'

William Thackeray took note that, although alcohol might have become an essential ingredient of life for the chief of the Afrikaners, it was not yet his master. He was still the man who had made his small tribe the most powerful in this corner of Africa. He had achieved this position by out-thinking his rivals, resorting to open warfare only when he was quite sure his small tribe could decisively beat the enemy. The Bergdama workmen had told him of the loud words between Josh Retallick and William Thackeray. He had known that by withdrawing the mission workmen Thackeray would come to him.

Chief Jonker had yet to learn that his new missionary was also a past master at the art of manipulating other men.

'Why is the white man from Otjimkandje not your friend?'

'That is between him and me. What about the men who should be working on my church?'

'They will be there when you return.'

'Good.'

William Thackeray hesitated before continuing. He had found out a great deal about Jonker while he was at the Cape. He had spoken to one of his previous missionaries and to officials of the

Cape government. There were traders there, too, who had left Winterhoek because of the Afrikaner chief. He thought he knew enough of the chief's own ambitions to be able to speak freely, but William Thackeray was unused to expressing his own ambitions to others.

'The British administration at the Cape has become very strong.'

Jonker took a noisy gurgling swig from his bottle.

'So I have heard.'

'You were wise to ask for a British missionary.'

'It is a chief's duty to be wiser than others, even though it is seen that the German missionaries have much power with other tribes.'

'I doubt if that will last for much longer.' Jonker's reticence returned once more, and William Thackeray said, 'The missionary at Otjimkandje is not a friend of the Afrikaners?'

'Without the Little Father the Herero of Otjimkandje would have gone north with their brothers long ago and their cattle would not be taking good grass from the mouths of Afrikaner cattle.'

That Afrikaner cattle had never grazed on Tjamuene's land meant nothing to Jonker. The Afrikaner tribe was stronger than the Herero, therefore it was their land.

'If the "Little Father", as you call him, were removed from Otijimkandje and the Herero left, what would happen to their village?'

Jonker tried to understand in which direction the conversation was travelling.

'I might bring in more Bergdamas to work the mine at Sesebe, or send for my brother to bring his tribe up from the south. But I cannot do this. The Little Father will not leave Otjimkandje.'

'But if he did', William Thackeray persisted, 'would you ask for another missionary from my church to take his place there?'

'Why? If every tribe has an English missionary, they, too, can speak to the Great Father in Cape Town.'

'If you can persuade other chiefs to ask for English missionaries, I will pass their requests on to the correct authority in the Cape. I will tell them they have been asked for because of your great influence over all other chiefs. I will make it clear that because of this great influence there must be no risk of offending Chief Jonker of the Afrikaners. His missionary must be chief of all other missionaries just as he is chief of all chiefs.'

Jonker put his bottle down on the floor carefully and looked at William Thackeray with new respect. He had never before met a missionary with ambitions that went much farther than persuading the village women to cover up breasts that only the missionary himself gazed at with undue interest. This man was different. He was a double-ended assegai, to be handled with care.

'The Little Father has been many years with Tjamuene's people. He would not leave them.'

'But what if I could persuade the Cape government to recall him?'

Jonker was puzzled. 'Why would they do that? Even I know the Little Father has done no wrong.'

'Leave that to me, Chief Jonker. It can be arranged, I assure you.'

The Afrikaner tried to discover more.

'All the white men would leave, too?'

'Yes, they, too, would go.'

'And the white woman? She would leave, too?'

'No. She would stay.'

The answer came too quickly, and Chief Jonker reached for his bottle again. This missionary had the weaknesses of all the white men the Afrikaner chief had ever known. He would not prove invincible. Jonker knew how to control such men.

'It will not be easy to persuade the other chiefs.'

'I did not say it would be easy. Neither should it be hurried. Until it's done you can help me by proving to your own people that you are happy to have a missionary with you again. I will expect you to be at my church every Sunday. We will speak again, Chief Jonker.'

William Thackeray smiled at the slightly bemused chief. 'I'm quite sure our association is going to be both happy and fruitful.'

Jonker nodded and as the door closed behind his missionary he leaned back on his bed thoughtfully. He had got his missionary—one who had brought with him the possibility of more influence with the Cape government than Jonker had dreamed of. Yet the Afrikaner chief was not happy. This man was seeing beyond a hill that had not yet been climbed and planning his own schemes for his own reasons. Jonker was used to having ambitious men about him, but they had always been men whose aims fell short of his own. If they went beyond a certain limit, he would have them killed. This missionary might prove more troublesome. He would have to be watched to ensure he did not gain too much authority.

If he did . . . ? Jonker sighed and poured more brandy down his throat. The missionary was still a man. He needed air to breathe and blood to keep him alive. Men of the Church had a great way with words. They wielded them as a warrior might wield a spear. But Jonker had always found the spear and the gun to be weapons of greater finality.

The Afrikaner chief smiled. He was no longer a young man but he would still be chief of the tribe when William Thackeray was no more than a vague memory for them. Yet he liked some of the things the missionary had said. If the Herero could be removed from Otjimkandje, Jonker would make quite sure their cattle did not leave with them. They would buy him much needed trade credit. Jacobus Albrecht was particularly well disposed towards trade in cattle and he was not fussy from whence they had come. It was a pity he had fallen out with the trader Aaron. The Afrikaners were hard on their weapons and at least half of their guns were no longer serviceable. But Jonker believed their differences would quickly be smoothed over. It had been necessary to show Aaron that being so friendly with the Herero did not meet with his approval. Such friendship could carry with it no profit for the Jew.

By morning Aaron's wagon and its escort of Hereros were far enough from the main trail to be safe from prying eyes. The Hereros had carried out their task well. Using blankets, they had carefully erased the tracks of men and wagon. There was nothing left for a curious Afrikaner to follow, and no one was likely to stumble across the tracks now. Aaron was taking the wagon across empty land where few men cared to go. It would take longer, and for many miles the strong shoulders of the Herero would be as necessary as oxen to heave the wagon wheels through the miles of soft sand, but it would be safe.

'How will the boat know when to expect us?' asked Mutjise as they rested among endless hot sand dunes.

'I sent word for them to meet me,' replied the bearded trader. 'I know that was before I set out for Whalefish Bay and we'll be a day or two late unless we can make it up by coming straight across country, but Captain Klopper will probably wait. He's done good business with me in the past.'

'What happens if he doesn't wait?'

Aaron's shrug successfully hid his inner feelings. 'Then we'll all have had a wasted journey and I will have to go north to Whalefish Bay and hope Chief Jonker isn't there to steal this load.'

It took fifteen gruelling days to reach their destination – fifteen days of toiling beneath a scorching sun, heaving the wagon up sand slopes so soft that the wagon wheels sank in to axle depth, then sliding down the far side, the wagons going down backwards so that men and oxen could hold them back. More than once they ended in a tangled heap at the bottom of the slope and had to right the wagon and repack the load.

But their perseverance paid off. When they topped the last rise and looked down upon the blue sea of a sheltered cove there was a small sailing vessel riding at anchor with sails furled not a hundred yards from the shore. The small crew were enjoying their unaccustomed leisure by swimming between the ship and the sandy beach.

'You and your men stay here,' Aaron said to Mutjise. 'When guns are being traded the fewer men who know where they're going the better it is for everyone. Tongues can't wag about things they don't know.'

Aaron took the wagon carefully down the slope, and some of the sailors came up to meet him and helped him get the wagon the last few yards on to the firm sand of the beach. There the captain of the small vessel was waiting.

'You've taken your time getting here, Aaron. Another day and I would have had to sail. It doesn't do to stay in a place like this for too long. There's been a naval frigate nosing along the coast, heading north. If we'd still been here when it came back, I'd as likely as not have had a longboat in to see what I was doing. There's a cargo on board that I don't want the likes of them knowing about.'

'Then you've got guns with you, Cap'n Klopper? Good guns I'm looking for, mind. None of your old useless flintlocks.'

'I've got some of each – but where's the rest of your wagons? I was told you'd been up to Lake Ngami and brought back some prime trade goods.'

A look of pain crossed Aaron's face.

'And so I did,' he growled. 'I was on my way to you, coming along the Whalefish Bay road, when Chief Jonker stopped me and stole most of it. Two wagonloads of good tusks and ostrich feathers.'

'Leaving you to bring me the rubbish he didn't want, I suppose?'

'Now, how many years have we done business, Cap'n Klopper? Have I ever tried to trade you rubbish? No, in this wagon I've got good ivory with a few pair topping two hundred and fifty pounds – and there are enough ostrich feathers to make your fortune in England. I kept this load back in my store and brought it out in the dead of night. I've travelled with it across country where no ox-wagon should have to go. That's why it's taken me so long to get here.'

'Hm!' Captain Klopper had known Aaron for enough years to recognise the truth. 'It seems to me high time someone singed the beard of this Afrikaner chief.'

'One day that might well happen, Captain. Sooner than Jonker realises. Now, get your men to help me with this canvas and we'll get down to business. How much are your guns this trip? You've brought plenty of power and shot?'

'More than one wagonload of trade goods will buy, Aaron. Guns are hard to come by. Prices are high.'

'But my credit? That's good, surely?' The wily old Jew knew better than to let Captain Klopper know just how desperately he needed credit at this time.

Captain Klopper shook his head. 'No credit this trip, Aaron. The Navy's getting too nosy – and your Afrikaner chief could meet up with you on your way back. We're neither of us a good enough risk for credit to be given on either side.'

Aaron said no more about it, and the two men got down to the ritual of hard bargaining. The Jew threw up his hands in mock disgust at the type of guns he was being offered, and Captain Klopper found imaginary cracks and splinters in the first-class ivory Aaron was trading.

Finally both men reached agreement and the deal was sealed with a clasp of hands and a bottle of good brandy.

It was almost dark when the last boatload of ivory was rowed out to the ship. Not until then did Aaron signal for Mutjise and his men to come down to the beach and help him to load the guns and powder on to the wagon. Even as the Hereros reached the beach the sails of the small ship were unfurling, and the clatter of its anchor chain tumbling into the chain locker rang out loud across the still water.

'You have many guns for us?' Mutjise and his men could not hide their excitement at the sight of the weapons.

'Enough.' Aaron was pleased with the results of his bartering.

'And you will teach us how to use them on the way back to Otjimkandje?'

'I'll teach you how to use them, but there won't be enough powder to make anyone an expert shot — not if you want to save any of it.'

'It must be saved. One day soon we will need to use it against Chief Jonker and his Afrikaners.'

'That's your business, and I don't want to know about it. Let's get the wagon loaded and over that ridge before we camp for the night. There's a British Navy ship around, and if they see our fires they might send men ashore to check on us. We can do without that kind of trouble. Let's have everyone with his shoulder to the wagons. Come on, heave! Up we go!'

Aaron cracked his long whip over the backs of the oxen, and the wagon creaked away from the sea's edge.

Later that night, the wagon safely away from the shore, Aaron sat eating with the Hereros.

'Why are you doing this for my people — getting guns for us and risking trouble with Jonker?'

Mutjise asked the question that had been with him for some days.

'Because I'm a trader. I get people what they want and take the goods I want in exchange. From you I will be getting cattle.'

'But we can only give you a few cattle at a time, so Jonker will not be suspicious. You could trade with him and he would pay you more with other things. He could even take all our cattle and give them to you now. I know he will try to do it one day.'

Aaron thought before answering. Mutjise was an intelligent man. He would know if Aaron tried to lie to him. But the trader was not certain of his own reasons for trading with the Herero. He urgently needed money or goods to pay off an outstanding debt to Jacobus Albrecht. Had he traded with Jonker it would have brought him greater – and quicker – profit. But so would the goods Jonker had stolen from him. Had Aaron been able to bring three wagons to Captain Klopper instead of only one he would have received guns for Mutjise and enough gold to pay Albrecht what he owed him.

'I have always tried to be an honest trader,' said the Jew eventually. 'I drive a hard bargain, yes. I deal in goods that are sometimes forbidden for political reasons. Yet I have never made a promise I have not kept and no man can claim he has been cheated by Aaron. Because of this I have no liking for a man who cheats and robs because he believes himself too strong to be stopped. Jonker has driven the Herero from their homes and scattered them over the land until only your father's people remain. The Herero are a persecuted tribe. The Jews, too, are a people without a land. We have much in common, you and I, Mutjise. The difference between us is that you have a chance to fight back and regain your lands. If I can help you to do that and defeat that thief Jonker, I will be happy.'

Mutjise had watched the heavily bearded Jew's face throughout the whole of his quiet speech. When it ended he nodded, satisfied.

'We will beat Jonker, and there will always be trade for you with my people. You will not lose because of your help to the Herero.'

'Good!' Aaron became the efficient trader once more. 'When I have some more trade goods sent up from Whalefish Bay your warriors must take me to Lake Ngami again. On the way back we'll take the wagons overland direct to the coast without returning to Sesebe. We'll all beat Chief Jonker in our own ways.'

CHAPTER SEVEN

Although he had been hoping to enjoy Hannah's company, Daniel was delighted when Josh suggested they went off together on a hunt.

'I'd like to leave Kasupi behind just this once,' said Josh. 'It's doubtful if Jonker will make a move while Hugo is in Otjimkandje but, if he does, Kasupi can come and find us.'

Daniel accepted this, and father and son set off early in the morning with Miriam and Hannah waving them on their way.

'I hope Josh is right and Jonker doesn't pay us another visit,' said Miriam, trying to take her mind off the real reason for the hunting trip as Daniel and Josh disappeared from view.

'I've go my rifle already in my room just in case,' said Hannah, smiling. 'How long do you think they'll be away?'

'I don't know.'

For an instant Miriam sounded so unhappy that Hannah looked at her quickly.

'Is something wrong?'

When Miriam seemed not to hear Hannah said, 'Please tell me. Is there something I can do to help?'

Miriam escaped from her thoughts. 'No, child. A fifteen-year-old in this country has enough troubles of her own without taking on others.'

Hannah's smile had a trace of sadness of her own this time. 'I'm not fifteen anymore, Mrs Retallick. I was sixteen yesterday.'

Miriam was instantly full of remorse, her own cares temporarily forgotten. 'Oh, Hannah! I'm só sorry. Why didn't you say something? I could at least have baked a special cake for you. To think your birthday passed without so much as a "happy birthday" wish from a single person.'

'I didn't mind,' Hannah lied. In fact the thought of it had lain inside her like a lead weight throughout the whole day. 'I nearly forgot it myself. Nobody here knows, and father began to forget it years ago when mother died and we came from the Cape. He had a lot of worries then.'

In a sudden unthinking statement that bared her soul Hannah

added, 'It's no fun remembering a birthday if no one else does.'

'Then we'll make certain this one doesn't pass entirely un-remembered. When Daniel and Josh return we'll have a special birthday tea. That's a promise, now.'

The mention of her two men brought back thoughts of William Thackeray, and Miriam lapsed once more into a deep silence.

'I wish you would share your unhappiness with me. Some-thing is troubling you very much. What is it?'

Hannah had spent most of her life with only her father for company. She had never learned the subtleties needed to wheedle secrets from other women. Miriam found her directness disconcerting. It was impossible to sidestep the girl's blunt questions.

'It's nothing you can help with, Hannah. Something from the past has caught up with me — something that should have re-mained forgotten for all time.'

'Is it a very bad thing?'

'Yes.'

'Does it affect Daniel?'

'Very much, and it's him I'm particularly worried about. It's a secret his father and I have had to live with for many years; but Daniel knows very little about our lives before we came to Otjimkandje.'

'It doesn't mean Daniel will go away from here, does it?'

Hannah accepted that Miriam was not going to tell her the nature of the trouble that had caught up with the Retallick family. The most she could hope for was to learn about its probable effect.

'I doubt it. Where is there for him to go?'

Miriam looked at the tall and attractive Jewish girl. 'You seem very concerned for Daniel. Don't tell me you've grown fond of him?'

'I don't know.' Hannah looked honestly at Miriam. 'I've never met anyone else of my own age before. I'm not sure how I feel about him.'

'H'm! Well, I'm glad you're here, Hannah. Daniel will need someone he can talk to when he and his father return.'

＊

After a day of hard riding Josh saw a small herd of gemsbok in the distance, recognisable by their grey bodies and long straight horns. They were moving away slowly, but the two men followed for more than thirty minutes without gaining on them. Then Daniel called to Josh and, jumping from his horse, examined a couple of distinctive paw-marks in the soft ground.

'Lion,' he said. 'I don't think we're the only ones after the gemsbok.'

'The lion is probably hungrier than we are,' said Josh. 'We'd better find a good place to camp before it gets dark and get a good fire going.'

Daniel nodded his agreement. 'And we'll tether the horses tonight.'

There were no rocks near them but plenty of thorn-bushes, and they used them to build a loose stockade about themselves and the horses, hoping it was high and wide enough to deter a hungry lion.

'This reminds me of our early days in Africa,' said Josh as they ate beside a crackling fire. 'We were never quite sure just how frightened of fire the wild animals were, but a good fire always made life seem more cheerful. You won't remember those times, Daniel; you were much too young. I'm talking about the weeks before we reached Otjimkandje. We were marooned in a strange country—exactly where we didn't know. We weren't even sure where we were hoping to get to. It was sheer luck that took us to Otjimkandje, and good luck too. We've all been happy there.'

'You've never said much about those early days, Pa. I know about the shipwreck—*Pride of Liverpool*, wasn't she?—and a little about our trek across the mountains to where Mutjise found us. But everything I know I've learned from Sam. You've never told me anything.'

Josh could not have wished for a more opportune moment to tell Daniel what needed to be said, but it was not going to come easily. His throat felt dry, and his heart was making noisy work of pumping blood around his body.

'There is a reason for that, Daniel. There are some things I hoped never to have to tell you, things I dismissed from my mind for many years and would dearly love to forget for ever.'

Daniel was puzzled; but Josh had his full attention, and now he had started the story the words came a little easier.

'One of them was that I joined *Pride of Liverpool* as a convict.' Josh looked into the fire and not at his son. 'I wasn't in chains – I wasn't even locked up – but that was only because I had a good friend in Cornwall. He got me sent out on a special ship bound for Australia because it carried some engines I was meant to assemble and work there. It was he who put you and your mother on the same boat with me.'

Josh glanced up and saw the disbelief on his son's face.

'It's true, Daniel. I was sentenced by an English court to be transported for life for being a party to treason and sedition.'

'Why?' It came out as little more than a hoarse whisper. 'What did you do?'

'I did nothing more than try to stop a crowd of foolish miners from fighting with soldiers for something they believed to be a just cause.'

'But, if you did nothing wrong, why were you sentenced to transportation?'

It was the cry of a young man who desperately wanted to believe his father.

'I was trapped by another man's ambitions, Daniel – a man who planned that I should be present when the miners started fighting with the military, not only present but in their midst. It didn't matter that I was calling on them not to be fools, to return to their houses. I was there for everyone to see. The Court of Assize said I was their leader and had organised the whole thing. There were some who believed in my innocence and a few – your mother was one – who knew I had done nothing wrong, but they could not convince the court.'

There was relief in Daniel's face. 'Well, nobody knows about it here, do they? So it doesn't matter anymore. Why have you told me after all this time?'

'Because there is more to the story, Daniel. Someone has arrived here who *does* know about it and was very much involved in what happened then.'

This was going to be the most difficult part of all and, try as he would, Josh could not keep emotion from affecting his voice.

'Your mother and I were sweethearts from the time we were

twelve years of age. During all the years I spent away from home learning to be a engineer she waited for me, knowing we would be married when I returned and was earning enough money to keep a wife. I came back to her, but then something terrible happened. Her father had too much to drink and attacked a girl. . . .'

Josh deliberately over-simplified this part of his story. Miriam's father had been a drunken bully who viciously raped a young widow in Josh's own home.

'A party of miners led by my father went after him, and he was killed. It was an accident, but the truth of that doesn't matter anymore. Your mother never believed it to be an accident – and she saw it happen. She was so upset she hardly knew what she was doing. She turned away from me to the one good friend she had, the man who had given us both our schooling – a preacher.'

Josh had to make a big effort not to mumble what had to be said next. The result was that it tumbled out louder than he had intended.

'Your mother was so upset that she married that preacher, Daniel. Even though she was carrying you – my child—at the time. It didn't take either of us long to realise what a terrible mistake we had both made. Even then we tried to behave honourably. For three years you were brought up as the preacher's own son. Then he plotted to have me falsely accused of treason, and stood back and said nothing when he could have proved my innocence.'

Josh was perspiring as though he had been working hard in the heat of the midday sun, the palms of his hands wet as he clasped and unclasped them.

'Not until then did we flout the laws of the Church and come together again on *Pride of Liverpool*, bound for Australia. A convict and his family.'

Josh drew in a deep breath. 'The shipwreck, terrible though it was, meant a new start for us, Daniel; a new life in a country where no one would know of my past – or so I thought; a chance to live as a free man and for us to become a family. It worked, Daniel. We've had fourteen good years. I've got a wife I love very much and a son I am proud of.'

The fire had burned low while Josh was talking, and he could not see Daniel's face.

'Now you know my secret, the reason why I've avoided talking about the past.'

'This man who had you sent to prison, the man'—Daniel could not bring himself to say the words—'the preacher you have been talking about. He's come here as Jonker's missionary, hasn't he? He's the man you went to see?'

'Yes.'

'What's his name?'

'Thackeray. William Thackeray.'

'So my name is really Daniel Thackeray.'

It came out as a flat statement that hit Josh and hurt more than any physical blow could have done.

'No! You're Daniel Retallick. My son.'

'Why haven't you told me about this before? Why?'

There was a fierce anguish in Daniel's voice.

'There was no need. I thought there would never be any reason why you should know.'

'But I had a right to know. Something like this shouldn't have been kept from me for ever.'

'Your mother and I believed otherwise, Daniel. I wouldn't have told you now had it not been for William Thackeray's arrival at Winterhoek. As it is I'd rather you heard it from me than from a stranger.'

Daniel made no reply, and they sat in silence for some minutes. Then Josh began to pile wood on to the low fire.

'Don't allow William Thackeray to ruin our lives again, Daniel. This will have come as a great shock to you and I'm sorry it was necessary for you to learn about it, but it doesn't alter the way I and your mother feel about the life the three of us have had together. It's been a good life. We're a happy loving family and we'd do the same again if we had to. I hope you'll be able to agree with us when you've had time to think about things.'

Daniel did not say another word that night. When Josh woke in the dark hours before daybreak the fire had been made up and he knew Daniel had lain awake all night. He wanted to say something to him but held back. It was up to Daniel to make the next move.

The silence continued into the morning, and Daniel avoided meeting Josh's eyes as they ate their breakfast. When it was finished Daniel saddled up his horse before kicking out the remains of the fire.

When he did speak it was the thick slurred speech of a man who has not slept and is tired.

'This hunting trip was just an excuse to get me out of Otjim-kandje so you could tell me about William Thackeray, wasn't it?'

'I wanted us to be alone when I told you. I knew it wasn't going to be easy for either of us.'

'Does that mean you don't want to shoot any fresh meat?' Daniel's interruption was devoid of emotion.

'We could use it. Why?'

Daniel pointed to westward of the camp. 'There's a small herd of eland over there. They'll have the sun in their eyes, and we could get one before they wake up to the fact that we're about.'

'Then what are we waiting for? Get after them.'

Josh was relieved to have something else to think about. He hurriedly stowed away the remainder of the breakfast things and saddled his horse while Daniel rode off to stalk the great humped antelope.

Even when he had cleared everything away and swung on to his horse Josh hung back to watch his son hunting, proud of his calm efficiency. Daniel loaded and primed his gun during his first cautious advance. Then he and his horse disappeared into a wide depression and came out of it at a gallop not fifty yards from the eland.

The startled antelope barely had time to kick up their heels before Daniel brought his horse to a slithering halt, the gun already to his shoulder.

He fired, and one of the six-feet-tall animals somersaulted in its tracks, sending up a cloud of pale orange dust as it thudded down in the earth.

The animal had stopped twitching by the time Josh reached it.

'That was a first-class shot,' he said. 'I can't remember ever seeing a better.'

222

Daniel nodded his head in acknowledgement of the well-earned praise, and Josh said no more.

The eland must have weighed a thousand pounds and cutting it up proved to be a major task. When it was completed and the horses fully laden the two riders turned their faces towards Otjimkandje.

Apart from a casual necessary remark they did not speak on the return journey. They arrived in the Herero village soon after dark, and an envious Kasupi helped them to carry the meat into the house.

'You've never seen a shot like the one that Daniel brought down this eland with,' said Josh when they were inside the house. 'I don't think there's another man in Hereroland who could have equalled it.'

Daniel's lack of reaction to the praise was not lost on Miriam. She looked to Josh quickly, and he nodded his head.

Miriam understood and pretended not to notice her son's silence.

'Well! With all that fresh meat we've got double cause for celebration. You'll never guess the secret Hannah kept from us. The day before yesterday was her birthday, and she never said a word about it. I've spent all day baking cakes and tarts. I'll invite Hugo Walder and we'll have a special birthday meal tonight for Hannah. It's not every day a girl is sixteen.'

'Fancy not telling us a thing like that! Happy birthday, Hannah.' Josh kissed the young Jewish girl on the cheek.

But Hannah was waiting for some response from Daniel. It never came.

'Here, I'll give you a hand with that.'

Josh went to the assistance of Kasupi, who was struggling into the house with the hindquarters of the eland.

Daniel turned away and walked out of the house, and Hannah followed him.

'Is something the matter, Daniel? Can I help?'

'No.'

He had not intended it to sound so harsh and abrupt, but that was the way it came out. He stood by his horse making unnecessary adjustments to a stirrup.

'Why are you and your mother so unhappy, Daniel? Please

let me do something to help.'

'It's nothing. Nothing at all.'

Gripping the pommel of his saddle, Daniel swung himself up on to the horse.

'Daniel! You're not going? My birthday treat—'

'I'm not hungry.'

He knew she was hurt and at that moment he hated himself for causing it, but he could not stay in the house for any celebration. Not tonight. Savagely he jerked the horse's head around and kicked his heels into its flanks.

'Daniel . . . where are you going?'

Ignoring the plaintive call from the darkness, Daniel shook out the reins and urged his already tired horse to a gallop.

He had nothing planned, but when the hoofs of his horse struck the hard-packed earth of the road he turned on it and headed for Sesebe.

'Josh, you'd better go after him before he does something silly,' said Miriam.

Josh listened to the sound of the horse's hoofs fading away into the night and shook his head. 'I'd like to go after him, but this is something he's got to work out for himself.'

He felt weary and heavy-hearted. The trip and the talk with his son had taken a lot out of him. He felt it had all been in vain. Aware of a silent figure standing in the darkness beyond Miriam he said, 'Didn't you say it was someone's birthday? Come along. Hannah. Let's enjoy your birthday meal. Perhaps Daniel will come back later.'

Daniel did not come back and the meal was a dismal affair. The three adults managed to find small presents for the girl and Hugo Walder told amusing stories of his recent trip to Cape Town, putting on his most jocular manner, but the shadow of Daniel's absence hung over the table like a pall.

A mile from Otjimkandje, Daniel slowed his horse to a walk. It had been a hard day for the animal, returning from the hunt with a double load before this final gallop. Daniel patted its neck reassuringly, and the horse dropped its head and blew through its nostrils. At Sesebe Daniel would put it into the stables and bed it down for the night.

The thought of Hannah and the manner in which he had left her standing outside the house came back to him. He had ruined her 'party' and he was not proud of his actions.

Then he thought of what his father had told him. . . .

His father? Even that was no longer a straightforward fact. The whole foundation on which his life had been built had crumbled away.

Then Daniel thought of the tension in his father's voice when he was telling him of those years back in Cornwall, and a feeling of deep remorse swept over him. It could not have been an easy thing to talk about. They must have been difficult years. And his mother? What torment must she have suffered?

For a moment Daniel thought of turning around and going back to Otjimkandje. It was then, although he did not realise it, that Daniel took an important step towards accepting the things he had been told and understanding the very difficult situation. He had managed to break through the barrier of his own self-pity.

His thoughts were disturbed by the sound of pounding hoofs coming from Otjimkandje. He pulled his horse off to one side of the road, and the rider was almost upon him before the star-light gave both horses away.

'Daniel, is that you?'

It was Kasupi.

'Yes, it's me.'

The presence of his friend brought back much of Daniel's earlier mood. It was a simple defensive reaction. He had wanted to sort out the confusion that was in his mind before having to converse with others.

'You left in a great hurry. Where are you going?'

'To Sesebe.'

'At this time of night and after a hunting trip? Why?'

'Because I feel like a drink.'

Daniel kneed his horse forward, urging it to a trot, thus making conversation difficult.

Kasupi brought his horse alongside Daniel's to avoid the dust it was kicking up. He did not attempt to speak again but he believed Daniel would probably have need of him later tonight. It would take a great deal of brandy to drown the unhappiness that fought within him.

The Miners' Inn was well patronised. Smoke from the miners' pipes rose above a dozen plank tables and swirled lazily around the ceiling like a heavy rain-cloud.

A number of men called to Daniel as he went into the inn, and he accepted an invitation to join a young miner named Simon van der Byl who sat at one of the tables farthest from the door. Van der Byl was only a year older than Daniel and had been one of the latest miners to reach Sesebe, coming overland with his father, who was also a miner.

The talk here was chiefly of mines and mining, but they all showed interest in Daniel's latest hunting trip.

'Only a day's ride away, you say,' said one of the men. 'What wouldn't I give for the taste of fresh eland meat.'

His words were echoed by a number of other miners, and Simon van der Byl said, 'There's a great opportunity for you, Daniel. Bring back fresh game meat to Sesebe and you'll be able to name your own price for it.'

The idea appealed to Daniel. 'All right. I'll bring you fresh meat. You'll have all you want the next time I come in here.'

'Ha! They'll have to send someone out to find you first.'

There was a sudden hush at the table, and Daniel swung around in his chair to face Jacobus Albrecht. The big Boer trader stood with a bottle in his hand.

'I found my way home, Mr Albrecht. As I remember it you were the one who got lost.'

Someone laughed, but the sound was hurriedly broken off and nobody else joined in.

Jacobus Albrecht flushed angrily. 'When I hire a guide I expect him to know where he's going and not leave me when the going gets tough.'

Now it was Daniel's turn to look angry.

'If you and your Afrikaners hadn't been so eager to kill Bushmen and rape their women, we wouldn't have been lost – and we would have got to Lake Ngami.'

There was a murmur of interest from the miners. Not all of them were from Boer stock and a few of the newer arrivals had some sympathy for the little men. A human life was not something to be taken lightly, in their opinion — and neither was a woman.

'Agh! Kaffir-boetje.'

With this Boer expression Jacobus dismissed Daniel from his thoughts and sat down with two other men at the next table.

Their presence sent Daniel back into his earlier mood and he drank in brooding silence.

To Kasupi, who waited outside, things did not look good. Had Daniel merely become hopelessly drunk Kasupi would have carried him to Sam Speke at Aaron's store, but with Jacobus Albrecht at the next table he feared trouble. There was nothing he could do about it. The inn was for white men only. Neither Herero nor Afrikaners were allowed inside. All Kaspui could do was make himself comfortable outside the window and prepare for a long wait.

The Boer trader was not allowing the presence of Daniel Retallick to spoil his enjoyment. He was as noisy as Daniel was silent.

The trader had been drinking for about an hour when someone at his table brought the talk around to Aaron and his store.

'It's a beautiful building, Jacobus. A man could fight off an army from in there. Why don't you build one like it?'

'What for? The Afrikaners are the only fighting kaffirs around here, and Jonker wouldn't turn on me. If he did, he'd get no brandy and starve to death.'

When the laughter died down the Boer said, 'Anyway, I'll have Aaron's store before too long. You wait and see.'

'How will you manage that, Jacobus? Buy him out, eh?'

'I won't have to pay anything. He'll give it to me. Just as he's going to give me that daughter of his, in spite of her high and mighty ways.'

Daniel's half-filled glass stopped in mid-air.

'Give you his daughter? Away with you, man! What would you do with his daughter, Jacobus? You're too bloody old, man!'

The speaker nudged the men on either side of him, and their ribald laughter made Daniel grit his teeth angrily.

'What do you think I'll do with his daughter? The same as I do with any other woman. I'll take her to bed and knock the

227

backside off her. I'll show you whether I'm too old or not. She'll never wear those denim trousers for riding again. One night with me and she'll find it too painful to sit it on a horse. I tell you, man—'

Daniel's pent-up temper exploded from him. Standing up, he turned and hurled the contents of his glass into Jacobus Albrecht's face.

'You've got a filthy tongue, Albrecht. Keep it for talking about your Afrikaner women—if they'll have you.'

Kasupi disappeared from the window. He had seen enough.

Jacobus went pale for a few seconds. As the blood rushed back to his face he took a dirty handkerchief from his pocket and carefully wiped the drink from around his eyes. Not until they were dry did he look up at Daniel.

'You've got a bit above yourself, young man. You've been around your Herero for so long you've come to think of yourself as a man. I'll have to teach you otherwise.'

Slowly and deliberately the Boer stood up and tucked the handkerchief inside his pocket.

Simon van der Byl jumped up and tried to push his way between Albrecht and Daniel. 'He didn' mean anything by his talk, Mr Albrecht. He's had too much drink like the rest of us. He'll apologise in the morning.'

'Of course he will,' called another voice. 'He's only a boy, Jacobus.'

'Boys are like Kaffirs,' said the Boer trader. 'They have to be taught to hold their tongues in the presence of their betters.'

He pushed Simon van der Byl to one side without taking his eyes from Daniel. 'You might be having second thoughts now, eh, boy? Thinking perhaps you heard wrong? Well, you didn't. I was talking about Aaron's daughter Hannah. I said I'll have her and that by the time I've finished with her she'll be as slack as a calving Afrikaner cow.'

Daniel's right fist swung in a great arc towards Jacobus Albrecht's face. It missed. So did the left that followed, and the next right swing.

The Boer trader smiled mockingly. 'Wish you'd kept your mouth shut now, boy? Is this what you're trying to do?'

His fist smashed on to Daniel's nose, and blood spattered in a wide circle on the floor about him.

'Or was it this?'

Albrecht's next punch took Daniel hard on the side of his face, knocking him to the ground, the room gyrating about him. He rose to one knee and spat out a tooth. Albrecht's face was somewhere in the haze above him and he lunged to his feet, arms flailing. He felt his fists strike home. Once, twice. Then a fist crashed into his face again, and Daniel went backwards over a table, lost in a world filled with brilliant coloured stars.

Again he rose to one knee, and this time it was one of Jacobus Albrecht's boots that sent him back to the floor again. Another kick as he lay on the ground broke two ribs – but by now Daniel was not aware of anything that was happening to him.

Sam Speke was woken by a mighty hammering on the door of the store.

'Who is it? What do you want at this time of night?'

'Come quickly. Daniel and Jacobus Albrecht are fighting. Hurry!'

Throwing the blankets from himself and his startled wife Mary, Sam Speke paused only to put on a pair of trousers. Pulling back the heavy bolts on the door, he flung it open and sprinted barefooted after Kasupi.

He arrived at the Miners' Inn just in time to see Jacobus Albrecht's second kick land in Daniel's ribs. Men went sprawling to either side as the burly ex-seaman pushed his way through them to where the Boer trader stood over the prostrate Daniel. He reached Albrecht in time to knock him off balance as he drew back his foot for another vicious kick.

The trader staggered among the watching miners, and they stopped him from falling. Recovering his balance, he saw who it was who had pushed him.

'Keep out of this, Sam. You and I have no quarrel.'

Sam Speke looked down at Daniel and saw the blood pouring from his shattered nose and trickling from the corner of his mouth. Anger rose like bile in his throat.

'What's the matter, Jacobus? Do you only fight children?'

'He started it – ask anyone. He struck out at me first.'

'There was no need to beat him the way you have. You

goaded him on to hit you first.' Simon van der Byl spoke the words, and there was a murmur of agreement from others.

For the first time Jacobus Albrecht realised he was in the midst of a hostile crowd. 'He started it,' he repeated.

Daniel groaned, and Sam Speke said to the men about him, 'Get him over to the store. I've a mind to finish what he started.'

'I've no quarrel with you, Sam,' Jacobus Albrecht repeated.

Stepping across Daniel's unconscious body, the angry Sam Speke brought a short powerful punch up on to the Boer trader's mouth. 'Now say we have no quarrel,' he said.

Jacobus Albrecht took two backward steps on his heels and wiped the back of a hand across his lips. It came away smeared with blood.

'You'll regret that,' he roared and lurched forward angrily. He walked straight into another powerful punch to the head. But his momentum carried him forward and he found himself wrapped in Sam Speke's powerful arms. It was a rib-crushing hold, and when the trader tried to shout it came out as no more than a faint breathless gasp. The more he struggled the tighter Sam Speke held him, constricting Albrecht's ribs, crushing all the strength from him.

Sam Speke had been involved in many seamen's brawls during his sea service and his name was known in the ports of the world for this one hold. He had more than once hugged a man to him until he lost consciousness.

But he had no intention of letting Jacobus Albrecht off so lightly. Daniel would always have an irregularity in his nose to remind him of his beating. Sam Speke had decided that Jacobus Albrecht would carry a similiar reminder.

At the moment the trader began to go limp in his arms Sam Speke released one arm and swung Albrecht around. He propelled him through the onlookers like a battering ram. Had the rough wooden wall been of a less stout construction Jacobus Albrecht's head would have gone straight through that too. As it was the trader's face suffered far more damage than the wall. Three times Sam Speke crashed it against the timber, then he released his hold on Albrecht.

The Boer trader dropped to the floor and rolled on to his back, his nose broken in half a dozen places.

Sam Speke looked at the men who crowded around, jostling for view of the trader's face.

'Anyone here got anything to say about what I've just done?'

'Nothing at all, Sam.'

'You did what needed doing, Sam.'

'He had no call to beat the boy the way he did.'

Sam had difficulty in hiding his contempt for them. They were unanimous in their approval of his actions and condemnation of Jacobus Albrecht but not one of them had done anything to prevent the Boer from beating Daniel.

He inclined his head towards the unconscious trader. 'When he comes round tell him if he thinks this isn't finished he knows where to find me.'

Daniel had already been taken to the store, and the crowd of miners parted respectfully as Sam Speke walked to the door and out into the clean air and soft moonlight of the African night.

CHAPTER EIGHT

The following day Sam Speke took Daniel back to Otjimkandje in one of the mine's wagons. He was having trouble breathing owing to the damage to his ribs, and the bruising on his face showed the severity of the beating he had taken.

Sam Speke's twelve-year-old daughter Victoria sat in the back of the wagon with Daniel, constantly bathing his brow with water, breaking off only to turn her head when a paroxysm of coughing took her. When this happened her shoulders hunched forward with pain, and she had to fight to draw in breath. The cough had been with her for a long time, and she was used to it now, but Sam frequently turned around to look at her with great concern.

When the wagon arrived at Otjimkandje, Josh's first reaction was to reach for his gun and go after Jacobus Albrecht. Sam Speke stopped him.

'You'd be doing yourself and Daniel no good, Josh. The thing began and ended last night. I've left Jacobus Albrecht with a face that will remind him of the fight every time he looks into a mirror. Daniel's nose will set. I doubt if Jacobus's will. Anyway, he's already gone from Sesebe – some say to Winterhoek, others to Whalefish Bay.'

'He'd better stay away a long time,' breathed Josh. 'I'm in your debt, Sam.'

'In my debt nothing! When we first got ashore from *Pride of Liverpool* we all shared each other's battles. It's been some years since then, and maybe we haven't seen so much of each other just lately, but I've got a long memory.'

'So have I, Sam, and good friends are all too rare. Come into the house for a while.'

'Later, Josh. As you can see, I brought young Victoria with me. I thought it might be better if she left Sesebe for a while. Jacobus Albrecht might do something to make life difficult there, and I'd like Hugo to have a look at her. She's not a strong girl, and I'm worried about her cough. She's had it a long time, and it's showing no sign of clearing up.'

'I'll tell Hugo,' said Josh. 'And don't worry about her while you're in Sesebe. I know she has plenty of relatives here but I'll keep an eye on her.'

Inside the house Hugo Walder finished examining Daniel. Although never qualifying as a doctor, the missionary had received medical training and had long ago accepted that he was as much of a doctor as they were likely to see for very many years in this part of the world.

He discovered Daniel's broken ribs and bound them up tightly. Gingerly he felt the bone in Daniel's nose between thumb and forefinger.

'He'll always have a bump to show for this little adventure,' he said. 'But it could have been worse. It is his ribs I am more worried about. I can't tell whether one of them might have punctured his lung. You'd better keep him in bed for a week or two, and he'll need careful looking after.'

'Hannah and I will take care of him,' said Miriam. 'But God help Jacobus Albrecht if he ever shows his face around Otjimkandje. I'll shoot him myself.'

'That was the way I felt,' said Josh. 'But it seems Sam has already settled the score for us. From his account I doubt if you'd recognise Albrecht if he did come here.'

'What started the fight?' asked the missionary.

'I don't know.' Josh was evasive.

'Yes, you do.' The assertion came from Hannah. 'It was what Jacobus Albrecht said about me. I overheard Sam Speke telling you. Daniel told Jacobus he had a foul mouth and then hit him when he repeated it.'

Josh cleared his throat noisily. Sam Speke had used seaman's language and been very explicit about what the Boer trader had said about Hannah. 'Er . . . yes, it was something like that.'

'Then the least I can do is to look after him while he's confined to his bed. Will that be all right, Mrs Retallick?'

'Why, yes, Hannah. We'll both look after him, but if you care to take charge of things it will be a great relief to me.'

Miriam would spend just as much time as Hannah fussing about her only son, but the Jewish girl's aggressive determination defied argument — and Aaron was not the only one with ideas about the future of his daughter Hannah and Daniel.

When Josh told Hugo Walder about Sam's young daughter the old missionary had her brought into the house in order that he could examine her. It was here that Hugo Walder came face to face with the inadequacy of his medical knowledge. One did not need to be a doctor to hear her breathing and know there was something seriously wrong with her chest, but the missionary could not give a diagnosis. He did not know what was wrong with her. But her condition was not one that would be as easily resolved as Daniel's.

Hannah turned out to be a devoted and efficient nurse. At night she would leave the door of her room open and, if Daniel did more than turn over in bed, she was up and in his room, satisfying herself he was all right. The fight had created a closer bond between them than Miriam would have dared hope for a few weeks earlier.

It had done something else. Although Daniel would never be able to forget the things he had learned on the hunting trip with his father, they no longer assumed such gigantic proportions in his mind. He now had a long time to think about them and accept much more than he might otherwise have done, much to the relief of Josh and Miriam.

There was another matter on Daniel's mind. Kasupi was a frequent visitor to his room and they had many whispered conversations together. After each of them Hannah was always rather less enthusiastic in her role of nurse, and after the latest meeting she tidied his bed with such scowling abandon that Daniel swore she must have broken at least another two ribs.

'You're lucky I haven't pitched you out on your head,' said Hannah. 'If you and that ne'er-do-well friend of yours want to make arrangements with village girls, then at least have the decency to wait until you're well out of my hearing.'

Daniel only grinned by way of reply. The 'arrangements' with the village girls were not of the kind Hannah imagined.

After a briefer than usual visit by Kasupi, Daniel called Hannah into his room.

'Yes, what do you want?' Hannah's hands were white with flour. 'I'm helping your mother with the cooking.'

'Come here a minute.'

'Daniel, what is it? I really am busy—'

'Come here.'

Hannah advanced into the room cautiously.

'Over here by the bed and close your eyes.'

'Why? Daniel, I've already said—'

Daniel let out an exasperated sigh. 'Will you do as you're told without arguing—just this once?'

Hannah did as she was told.

'Now, mind you keep your eyes tightly closed.'

She felt Daniel's hands go about her neck. It was so unexpected that she almost opened her eyes and only just managed to resist the urge.

Daniel was fastening something beneath her long hair at the back of her neck.

'All right, you can open your eyes now.'

Hannah opened her eyes and gave a gasp of delight. About her neck was a long necklace made up of pieces of delicately carved ivory and mother-of-pearl culminating in a beautiful polished mauve gemstone.

'Daniel, it's beautiful! But why? And where did you get it?'

'It's a late birthday present—to make up for the party I spoiled for you. I had it made specially by some of the women in the village. The stone I found in a river when I was out hunting about a year ago. Now you know all about the arrangements Kasupi and I have been making.'

Unwanted tears sprang to Hannah's eyes. 'Oh, Daniel, it's a lovely present. I've never owned anything so beautiful.'

Sitting down heavily on the bed beside him, she threw her arms about him and kissed him on the mouth.

She felt him wince and was immediately full of concern. 'I'm sorry, Daniel. Did I hurt you?'

Her eyes were very dark, the eyelashes about them very long. For perhaps the first time Daniel realised that Hannah was a very beautiful woman.

Hannah, too, realised that their relationship was undergoing a sudden dramatic change. She saw it in Daniel's eyes and responded to the emotions that rose within her. When Daniel reached out for her she came to him eagerly.

235

Holding her to him hurt Daniel's ribs, but the real pain went much deeper than that for both of them.

When Hannah returned to the kitchen to show the necklace to Miriam the older woman found the look on Hannah's face of far more interest to her. She recognised it immediately and felt a strange mixture of youth and age stir within her. She had once worn the same look for Josh, when she was even younger than Hannah. She knew the joy and the pain that were part of being in love, the fire and the water that tempered the steel of true love.

Her affectionate hug took Hannah by surprise. 'I'm very happy for you, Hannah.'

'Yes.' The tall dark Jewish girl coloured up. 'It's a birthday present.'

'I know.'

Miriam's fond smile said much more than her words. It said that she knew, as Hannah knew, that the gift was so much more than a birthday present. It explained why Daniel had tackled the Boer trader in the one-sided fight in Sesebe.

Aaron was less far-sighted about their relationship when he returned to Otjimkandje and heard about the fight. To him it spelled instant and total disaster for his business. Unknown to the others he owed Jacobus Albrecht money that was already overdue for payment. He could not tell the Boer trader of the long-term arrangement he had made with Mutjise to receive cattle as payment for the Herero's guns. It was quite certain now that the Boer would not agree to any deferment of a full settlement.

Aaron arrived just before dawn, having travelled as fast and as quietly as possible during the night hours in order to elude Jonker and reach the Herero village before Tjamuene's people awoke.

The guns and kegs of black powder were hurriedly carried into the grass-walled kraal of the chief and hidden away. Aaron did not want to know their exact hiding-place. It was safer for everyone this way.

Josh was puzzled by the unusual time of the party's arrival. In this country men did not travel at night. He said as much to

Aaron, but the Jew passed it off by saying they had hoped to arrive before dusk the previous evening but had run into trouble with the wagon. He said it had not been worthwhile to make camp when they were so close to home.

Although Aaron was tired, he slept for only a couple of hours before rising and going to Sesebe to his store. All was in order there, and Sam Speke was busy building an extension to house his wagon-building workshop.

Harold Andrews had been to speak to Sam, saying he hoped the fight with Jacobus Albrecht would not affect the business relationship between the mining company and Sam. He promised to try to smooth things over with the Boer trader.

Sam Speke promised to carry out any repairs to the wagons owned by Andrews and Albrecht, though he intended trying to build up other business. He would not trust his future to a man whom he had disfigured in such a violent manner.

To Aaron's great relief Jacobus Albrecht was not at Sesebe. But his relief was short-lived. He had hardly put the wagon into the yard behind the store and sent the Herero driver off with the oxen when a messenger arrived from Harold Andrews' office. Jacobus Albrecht was at Winterhoek and had said he wanted to see the Jewish trader as soon as he returned to Sesebe.

Aaron would have liked to put off the evil moment, but it was not his way of dealing with problems. Neither would it have helped. The Boer would know the moment he returned. Deferring the meeting would only make things worse—if such a thing were possible!

The Jewish trader rode to Winterhoek that same afternoon, and a feeling of apprehension overtook him as he topped the pass into the valley and saw Jonker's untidy village sprawled out before him. He was not sure whom he dreaded meeting more, the Afrikaner chief or the Boer trader.

Jacobus Albrecht was not in his store. The European who managed it for him said he was with the new missionary, and the news gave Aaron heart. If he could broach the subject of the money he owed the Boer in the missionary's presence, the Boer trader might be inclined to be more understanding towards Aaron's problems.

His hopes fell when he saw the state of the Boer's face. Even

237

the presence of a missionary could not make a man forget such an injury. Jacobus Albrecht would be out for revenge on everyone even remotely connected with his humiliation – and Aaron knew that Hannah had been at the root of the fight.

Another surprise to Aaron was seeing brandy standing on the table between the two men. It was true William Thackeray did not appear to be drinking very much, but most missionaries were opposed to alcohol on all but the most important occasions.

Jonker's missionary greeted Aaron warmly and motioned him to a chair, pouring him a drink and saying how pleasant it was to meet another trader.

'It's you traders we missionaries depend upon so much to bring the trappings of civilisation to our peoples. It makes a missionary's work much easier when a native can see tangible proof of our words; when he can see that by following our spiritual teachings his whole life can gain materially as well as spiritually.'

Aaron doubted the wisdom of such a sweeping statement. Standing on the table was one of the more doubtful material 'blessings' that traders had brought into the lives of the English missionary's new flock.

'I know I will need to lean heavily on Jacobus's knowledge of Jonker's people,' went on William Thackeray. 'He has traded with the chief for a great many years and knows a great deal about his ways.'

'I know a few of them myself,' said Aaron, thinking unhappily of the two wagonloads of trade good pilfered by the Afrikaner chief.

'Of course,' said William Thackeray. 'I was forgetting that you had traded with him. But most of your business is now with the Herero, is it not?'

'Trade is with whoever has something to sell or something to buy,' said Aaron. 'At the moment Jacobus is in favour with Chief Jonker. Next week it might change again.'

'Next week a lot of things might change,' said Jacobus Albrecht, scowling. He spoke as though he had a heavy cold. 'You owe me some money, Aaron. Where is it?'

The hopes Aaron had entertained of the Boer trader being more reasonable in the presence of the new missionary were dashed by his uncompromising tone of voice.

William Thackeray stood up.

'If you gentlemen are going to talk business, I'll find something else to do. . . .'

'No . . . please. . . .' Aaron still entertained a faint hope that the presence of the missionary might help him. 'It's business, yes – but honest business. Nothing that should not be heard by others.'

'He's right. Sit down, William.' The fact that the two men were on first-name terms was not lost on Aaron. 'This isn't going to take long. Either he has the money or he hasn't. If he can't pay, I've got a little proposition that might involve you professionally.'

'Jacobus, business hasn't been too good lately,' Aaron began his excuses. 'It's picking up now. Picking up well. The Herero are a good people. I'm sure they'll let me have a few cattle in advance for you. I'll pay the remainder of what I owe within three months – maybe two. How will that suit you?'

'It doesn't suit me at all,' growled Jacobus Albrecht nasally. 'The settlement is well overdue now, and I've been a very patient man. Profitable trading doesn't run on promises, Aaron. You should know that. As for business being bad – you've had a good trading trip to Lake Ngami. If you couldn't turn that into a profit, what hopes are there of my ever getting my money from you?'

'It was a good trip,' agreed Aaron. 'The profit would have been there but for Jonker. He took almost everything I had, claiming it as the tribute due to him for allowing me to trade in his lands.'

Jacobus Albrecht shrugged. 'Jonker makes the rules in his own land. Who's to say he won't do the same thing again? No, Aaron. I can't let the debt drag on any longer. You're a bad risk, man.'

'You said you had a proposition,' urged William Thackeray. 'One that might involve me.'

'I did,' agreed the Boer trader. He downed his drink and poured himself another. Then he leaned back in his chair and looked across the table at his Jewish counterpart, giving him an ugly smile. 'You can't pay your debt, Aaron, and as I see it

239

you have two alternatives. One, I take over your store, your wagons, oxen and all your property. It may sound hard to you, but if we were down south that's what would happen. You know it well.'

This was even worse than Aaron had anticipated but nothing showed on his face.

'If your second alternative is as attractive as your first, I can't wait to hear it.'

Jacobus Albrecht stopped smiling and leaned forward across the table, pushing his face closer to the bearded Jewish trader.

'It's much better, Aaron. It's one that no good businessman could possibly refuse. You know how I feel about Hannah. I've mentioned marriage before. Now I'll put it on a businesslike basis. You give her to me and I'll have William marry us right away. Then your debt to me will be wiped out. More, I'll have an agreement drawn up to say that should anything happen to me all my trading assets will come to you. Of course, I'll expect you to have a similar agreement drawn up in my favour.'

He leaned back in his chair again and, carrying his brandy to his mouth, watched Aaron.

'That sounds very generous to me,' murmured William Thackeray. 'Very generous indeed.'

Aaron looked from the Wesleyan missionary to the Boer trader, wondering what these two men could possibly have in common. Had they already discussed this 'business' proposition? Wiliam Thackeray might consider it a generous offer, but it left the most important detail out of the reckoning.

Hannah and her feelings.

'It's an interesting offer,' Aaron said cautiously. 'But I will have to discuss it with Hannah and see what she has to say about it.'

'What for?' Now the traditional Boer attitude to women came out. 'Agh! She's your daughter, man. You tell her what to do. Tell her she's got to marry me. That's all there is to it.'

'I don't do things that way,' said Aaron quietly. 'As you've just said, Hannah is my daughter, not some object in my store. I'll put your proposition to her. If she agrees to marry you, then so be it. If not. . . .' He spread his hand in a habitual gesture.

'You'd better do more than to *ask* her,' said Jacobus Albrecht angrily. 'You go home and *tell* her what to do. I'm not a patient man, Aaron. I've waited long enough for both Hannah and my money. You've got until sunset the day after tomorrow to give me my answer. If you can't persuade her by then, you'd better be out of that store of yours by the following morning. And don't take anything more than you are wearing away with you. Everything else is mine: building, stock, wagons, oxen and horses – the lot.'

Pale-faced, Aaron stood up. 'Thank you for your hospitality, Preacher Thackeray. I'll go now.'

William Thackeray shook the other man's hand and smiled enigmatically. 'It's been a pleasure meeting you, Aaron. I hope you can find a satisfactory solution to your business problems. It would give me much pleasure to conduct a wedding service for your daughter here in my little church.'

The Jewish trader nodded and walked slowly from the hut without a word to Jacobus Albrecht. Aaron felt very old, a feeling accentuated by his sense of failure. He would speak to Hannah, but he was aware of the almost intolerable burden he would be placing upon her. He would be asking her to choose between her own happiness and her father's ruin.

Hugo Walder was very worried about Victoria Speke. Sam had returned to Otjimkandje, and the missionary had examined his daughter for the second time. In the silence of the Herero hut her breathing rasped like a coarse-toothed saw.

'I'll be quite honest with you, Sam. If we were lower down towards the coast where they get the sea mists, or the north where there are the marshlands, I'd say she had lung fever; but I can't believe she would get that up here, or at Sesebe. But she has something seriously wrong with her chest.'

'What do you suggest I should do?'

Sam Speke doted on his little girl. Victoria had brought more happiness into his life than he had ever dreamed possible when he was sailing the oceans of the world.

'I just don't know, Sam,' Hugo Walder admitted. 'I have neither the skill nor the knowledge to treat her. I think you should take her to see a doctor at the Cape, but it would cost money.'

'Money isn't important. Victoria's health is all I care about. I'll go back to Sesebe now and find out when the next boat for the Cape is expected a Whalefish Bay. I'll take Mary and Victoria down there on it.'

'Good. Then I will write a letter of introduction to a very good doctor friend of mine in Cape Town. I am sure he will know what to do to help her.'

Mary, Sam's Herero wife, had been listening to her husband and the German missionary talking but had said nothing. She had already made plans of her own. She would see the man who had always treated her when she had been sick as a child – the man who was called to treat everyone in Otjimkandje, from the newest-born child to Chief Tjamuene. Victoria would receive a visit from the Herero tribal doctor. He would make her well.

Daniel awoke from a late-afternoon sleep to hear the sound of voices and someone sobbing. He knew his mother and father were spending the day at the wedding feast of the oldest son of a village elder. He had thought he and Hannah were alone in the house.

Swinging his feet to the floor, he stood up slowly. His health was much improved now and he spent much of the day out of bed. He considered his afternoon rest to be little more than a concession to Hannah, to keep her in Otjimkandje for as long as possible.

He went quietly towards Hannah's room. The door was partly open, and he had almost reached it when he heard Aaron's voice coming from inside.

'My child, it is a hard decision to make, I know, but it would be a good marriage for you. Jacobus Albrecht is a clever trader – far more successful than your old father.'

Daniel felt as though a chill wind had blown into the house.

'He's not clever. He's ruthless and dishonest. You're not.'

'You may be right, Hannah; but perhaps a man has to be all those things if he is to succeed. That doesn't alter the fact that he's asked for your hand in marriage. You know it isn't the first time. He's wanted to marry you for two years.'

'But I don't want to marry him.'

242

There was a short pause before Aaron spoke again.

'I owe Jacobus Albrecht a sum of money. It's not great, but it's more than I have or can hope to raise quickly. If it's not paid by the day after tomorrow, he'll take everything I own. The store — everything!'

'Unless I say I'll marry him?'

'He wants more than a promise, Hannah. He expects me to take you to him and go on to the new missionary at Winterhoek to be married right away.'

Hannah began to cry again. 'I don't have any choice, do I? I'm going to have to marry him or see you lose everything you've worked so hard for. I've got to marry him. . . .'

Daniel had heard enough. The thought of Hannah marrying Jacobus Albrecht after the things he had said about her in the Miners' Inn made his skin creep.

Back in his room Daniel dressed hurriedly, ignoring the throbbing pain in his chest. He had fought Jacobus Albrecht once over something that mattered far less then than it did now. He was not going to stand back and do nothing when Hannah's whole future happiness was at stake. There had to be another fight; but this time Jacobus Albrecht would not have the advantage, and the result would be decisive. Daniel picked up his gun from the corner of his room and began to load it carefully.

Had he listened at Hannah's door for a few moments longer Daniel would have heard something to change his whole course of action.

Through her tears Hannah repeated, 'I've got to marry him.'

'No. You don't *have* to marry him.'

Hannah looked up at her father and her misery hurt him more deeply than Jacobus Albrecht ever could. He took her by the shoulders and drew her to him.

'You are more important than anything else I have or have ever had.' He gave a short laugh. 'After all, what will I be giving up? A business that is in debt. Something that will never make a penny piece profit for as long as Jonker is chief of the Afrikaners. No, Hannah. You will not marry Jacobus Albrecht. No ill-mannered Boer is going to take my daughter for his wife.'

Hannah pushed herself away from him. 'But your store? You can't give that up. It's our home. What will we do?'

243

Aaron shrugged, then managed a smile. 'We'll do what I should have done years ago – move away from this uncivilised place. We'll go somewhere else, to where the standards of our fathers are accepted, where I can work for less profit but with much less risk.

'You know, I have just discovered what a relief your decision is to me. I would never have slept easy in my bed knowing that Jacobus Albrecht would take over my business if I died – and as for having him for a son-in-law . . . !'

Hannah knew he was only trying to make her feel better and she loved him for it.

'You are not fit enough to go hunting.'

Kasupi intercepted the armed Daniel as he made his way to the pens to get his horse.

'Oh, yes, I am.' Daniel ignored the throbbing of his ribs. This was the farthest he had walked since before the fight.

'Where are we going?'

'Mind your own business. I'm hunting alone.'

'No, you are not. I am coming with you, whether you like it or not.'

Kasupi made sure he would not be left behind by catching and saddling his own horse before helping Daniel to throw the saddle on his own unexercised and frisky horse.

'Do you know where Jacobus Albrecht is now?' Daniel asked the Herero.

'Probably at Sesebe. His wagons are there. Why do you ask?'

Daniel made no reply and, climbing on to his horse, set off at a trot. He had not travelled half a mile before the pain from his barely knitted ribs had him gritting his teeth to hide it from his travelling companion.

'We will go hungry if we have to make our meals from the game to be found along this road, Daniel.'

'I'm not hunting for food today.'

'Oh? You rise from a sickbed to hunt for pleasure?'

'No. I hunt for the same reason the Herero hunt the lion that has tasted human flesh – because it is necessary.'

Kasupi was puzzled, 'You seek a lion? There has not been one near Otjimkandje – or Sesebe – for many years.'

'Not a lion, Kasupi. I'm going to kill Jacobus Albrecht.'

Kasupi began a smile, thinking Daniel was joking with him. Then he looked at his friend's face and saw it was not a joke. He gasped in horror. 'You can't kill him, Daniel. It would bring big trouble to everyone — especially to you and your family.'

'Rather that than allow him to marry Hannah.'

Now Kasupi began to understand. He did not know what had prompted this sudden decision to kill the Boer, but if Hannah was at the core of it he knew he would not be able to turn Daniel from his purpose. He had known even before his friend had taken such a beating in defence of her good name that the trader's daughter would one day have a great influence over Daniel's life. He had been aware of Daniel's feelings for her before Daniel himself had known. But Kasupi could not allow Jacobus Albrecht to be killed because of Daniel's love for a girl. This thing had to be stopped before the two men met.

Once again Kasupi thought of Sam Speke.

Without another word he shook out the reins of his horse and kicked the willing animal into a gallop. Realising his friend's intention, Daniel gave chase, but his ribs would not accept the extra strain placed upon them and he was forced to slow his horse to a steadier pace.

Once again Sam Speke's intervention proved speedy and effective, and he stood in the path of Daniel as he slowed his horse to enter Sesebe.

'Out of my way, Sam. I'm here for Jacobus Albrecht. I won't need your help this time.'

'You'll be beyond all help if you go through with this stupidity.'

Daniel's face was white and drawn, and Sam could see he was in great pain. Daniel was not as strong as he had believed, and the ride from Otjimkandje had exhausted him. But he was still very determined.

'Stupid or not, Jacobus Albrecht is not going to marry Hannah.'

'At least we'll agree on that,' said the burly ex-seaman as he reached out and took a hold on the bridle of Daniel's horse. 'Now, what's all this about?'

'Aaron owes Jacobus money. Jacobus says that unless Aaron

245

agrees to let him marry Hannah he'll seize everything Aaron owns and leave him with nothing. Aaron's persuaded Hannah to agree to the marriage.'

'That doesn't sound like Aaron to me. He thinks far too much of his daughter to give her away to a man like Albrecht.'

'I heard it with my own ears, Sam. It will happen unless I kill Jacobus.'

'Will it? We'll see about that. How much does Aaron owe?'

'I don't know.'

'It doesn't matter much; there's more than one way of dealing with a man like Jacobus Albrecht – and shooting him is well down the list. You get off that horse and come inside. We've got some talking to do.'

'Don't try to trick me, Sam. I'm not going to allow Jacobus Albrecht to have Hannah.'

In spite of his bold words Daniel swayed in the saddle. There was agonising pain in his chest, and he felt sick.

'I'm on your side, Daniel,' declared Sam Speke. 'But you go after him in that condition and he'll kill you and still be alive to marry Hannah.'

He called to the Herero. 'Kasupi. Hold this horse while I help Daniel down and get him inside. Then go and watch the Miners' Inn. Let me know if Albrecht makes a move to leave. We'll have business with him shortly.'

Daniel would have fallen from the horse had Sam not been there to catch him and help him into the store. Leading him to his own room, he lowered him into a wide-armed hide chair and Daniel leaned back with a groan of relief.

Sam Speke grinned at him. 'What did I tell you? If Jacobus Albrecht was to walk in front of your gun right now, you wouldn't have the strength to pull the trigger.'

The ex-seaman was right. Daniel knew it.

'Here, get some of this down you. You've a job to do yet and you'll need some strength for it.'

Sam Speke reached down a bottle from a shelf and, pouring half a tumbler of brandy, handed it to Daniel.

It was growing dark outside, and Sam lit a lamp that stood on a table in the centre of the room, then drew the curtains together. He went to the bed in the corner of the room and reached beneath it to pull out a leather-bound trunk. It was fitted with a stout lock, and Sam produced the key on a cord from about his neck.

The heavy lid creaked as it swung open, and inside Daniel saw clothes and an accumulation of treasures the ex-seaman had acquired since arriving in Africa. Delving into the bottom of the trunk, Sam came up with a weighty leather bag that had a draw-string neck. Untying the cord, Sam tipped the bag upside down, and four smaller canvas bags dropped heavily on to the table.

Sam took one of them and balanced it in the palm of his hand for a few seconds, reliving the memories that were a part of by-gone years. Then he walked across to Daniel and dropped the bag into his lap.

'Here. I've been saving this against the time you would need it. I think that time has arrived.'

Daniel untied the cord wound about the neck of the bag and reached inside. His hand came out clutching a fistful of gold coins and there were more left inside the bag.

Daniel was surprised and not a little puzzled. 'I can't take this, Sam. Why, it's a fortune!'

Sam nodded. 'Yes, it's a fortune right enough. But you're tak-ing it because it belongs to you.' He pushed aside two of the remaining bags. 'Just as these belong to your ma and pa.'

'But they've never said anything to me about this.' Daniel was utterly bemused.

'It wouldn't surprise me if the whole thing had slipped from their minds,' said Sam, smiling. 'Money has never meant a great deal to either of them – not nearly as much as it did to poor Isaiah Dacket.'

Briefly Sam Speke told Daniel the story of the Bushmen and the two skeletons and the events leading to Isaiah Dacket's violent death.

'So there you have it,' he concluded. 'It should have been shared five ways but for Isaiah's greed. As it is there's four of us to have a part of the gold each. We earned it, Daniel. There was many a time in those mountains when I believed none of us would live to enjoy spending it.'

Daniel looked as though he was about to ask another question, and Sam Speke hurriedly interrupted him. 'Now be quick and swallow that brandy. I'm looking forward to seeing Jacobus Albrecht's face when you walk into the Miners' Inn and settle Aaron's account for him.'

Kasupi moved out from the shadows at the side of the Miners' Inn when they arrived, and Sam saw he had the gun he had taken from Daniel's saddle holster. Whether he had it to prevent Daniel from using the gun or to stop the Boer trader from leaving the inn Sam did not know.

'Albrecht is still in there. His table is in the far corner. There are two others with him.'

Daniel nodded. He had to concentrate on walking. His knees threatened to give way with every step he took. With Sam Speke at his side he pushed through the door and into the inn. It was not as busy as usual. At this hour the miners were being served their evening meal in the large cookhouse next door.

Daniel saw Jacobus Albrecht immediately. The Boer trader saw him at the same time and his expression froze. All talk in the room died down as the two stared at each other. Then Daniel began to walk across the room. The Boer stood up and pushed his chair back. He watched Daniel but addressed himself to Sam Speke.

'If you've come here to cause trouble, Sam, you'd best turn around and go back out through that door right now.' He drew back his coat to expose a new American-made Colt Navy percussion revolver tucked inside his belt. It was the first one seen in Sesebe, and its six pre-loaded cartridges made it a formidable weapon.

'Any trouble will be of your making,' said Daniel. 'We're here on business. I've come to settle Aaron's debt for him.'

Jacobus Albrecht was startled. Daniel saw it, and it gave him much satisfaction.

'If you've got business to discuss, I'll be going,' said one of the men at the table hurriedly. He stood up to go, and the third man at the table stood up with him.

'Sit down,' growled Sam. 'This is business we'd prefer to have witnesses to.'

The Boer trader flushed angrily at the insinuation of dishonesty, and his two companions sat down again.

'How much does Aaron owe you?' asked Daniel, embarrassed

because he could not keep his gaze from wandering to Jacobus Albrecht's smashed nose.

'We didn't work it out in money,' said the trader. 'I supplied him with beads, knives and trade goods.'

'I don't suppose you expected to be paid back in the same,' retorted Daniel. 'How much is owed to you—in gold?'

'About eighty guineas.'

'Eighty guineas?' Sam Speke exploded into anger. 'For eighty guineas you'd rob a man of his daughter or his livelihood?'

'I didn't beg Aaron to get into debt with me.' Jacobus Albrecht was aware of the indignant comments from the few men in the room. 'This is business. Had I borrowed from Aaron he'd have done the same to me.'

'I doubt that,' said Sam, looking at the Boer in disgust. To Daniel he said, 'You've got Portuguese Johannas there, each of them worth five guineas. You're the one who can count. Give him as many as necessary to pay Aaron's debt and let's get out of here. I feel in need of some air.'

Daniel opened the bag and counted out sixteen coins, placing them on the table in two golden piles. Pushing them across the table to the trader, he said, 'That's Aaron's debt paid in full. You can make out a receipt and leave it with Mr Andrews. I'll pick it up tomorrow.'

Drawing the string closed around the opening of the still-heavy bag. Daniel tucked it inside his shirt and, turning his back on the Boer trader, walked from the room.

He made it to the dirt road outside the inn before his legs gave way on him and he fell. Kasupi caught him before he hit the ground and the Herero and Sam Speke helped him back to the store.

The ex-seaman made light of his weakness. 'It's all right, Daniel. It doesn't matter now. What you just did to Jacobus Albrecht hurt him more than any violence.'

'Thanks to you, Sam. I'm still not sure you were telling the truth about that money and that I was meant to have a share of it.'

'I found the money, so the decision was mine to make,' replied Sam Speke. 'But unless I'm mistaken there's your father coming from Otjimkandje. You'll be able to ask him.'

There was more than one horse being galloped recklessly in the darkness on the road from the Herero village. The first horse slowed as it came into Sesebe and turned towards the Miners' Inn.

'Josh, is that you?'

The horse came to a halt, and the hoofbeats of at least two more drew nearer.

'Sam?' It was Josh.

'We're over here by the store. Daniel's with us.'

Josh mouthed something that was lost in the blowing of his horse and, jumping to the ground, he led the animal towards them.

'Daniel? What the hell are you playing at? You've had us all worried half to death.'

Sam Speke pushed open the door of the store, and in the light Josh saw that Daniel was being supported by the others. His anger immediately turned to concern for his son.

'Are you all right? What's happened?'

'He's more than all right, Josh. Come into the store and we'll talk. Who is that with you?'

The other horses were entering Sesebe.

'Aaron and Hannah. They came running to find me with some story of Daniel disappearing from the house and taking his gun with him.'

The other riders had headed for the light of the store, and now a tall slim figure leaped from one of the horses and ran towards them, seeing only Daniel.

'Daniel, are you hurt again? What have you done?'

Had Kasupi not still had a hold on Daniel, Hannah's rush would have bowled him over.

'Father and I were talking and I became very upset. Then I found you had gone and taken your gun with you. I thought you might have heard what we were saying and come here to find Jacobus Albrecht.'

'I did – and I found him.'

The night ride had brought a high colour to Hannah's cheeks. Now the blood drained away, and she turned deathly pale.

'You . . . you found him?' Her eyes were deep dark caverns in the darkness.

'Yes.'

'What . . . what happened? Is he . . . ?'

'I think we'd better go inside,' said Sam Speke. 'This is no place to hold such a conversation.'

'No!' Hannah looked terrified. 'I must know. Is Jacobus Albrecht . . . ? Is he dead?'

'He's not dead – but he's a very unhappy man,' said Sam Speke. 'Now, come inside and Daniel will tell you everything.'

The tension in Hannah and Aaron seeped away. Aaron sagged visibly. 'I don't know whether I should be pleased for Daniel or sorry for myself,' he said.

'You've got reason to be pleased for everyone except Albrecht,' said Sam Speke. 'But if you don't get inside and let me close this door we'll have all the mosquitoes in Sesebe inside your store.'

'You go in. I'll see you in a while. If Jacobus Albrecht is here, I want to see him. I have some unfinished business to attend to. Where is he?' asked Josh.

'Now, Josh . . . ,' Sam turned to him. 'Any business with Albrecht has already been settled – by Daniel and me.'

'The trader has left Sesebe,' said Kasupi quietly.

The others looked at Kasupi for an explanation.

'His horse was tethered at the back of the Miners' Inn. It has gone, and I heard it being ridden towards Winterhoek a few minutes ago.'

'There, that's settled. We'll go inside.' Sam Speke ushered them all into the store.

Daniel was helped by Kasupi and Hannah. When he was lowered into a chair the pain in his chest caused him to cough violently for a minute or two.

'Now, may we please have the story?' pleaded Aaron when Daniel had recovered his breath. 'Why should I be so pleased when a man is still alive who has threatened to take either my daughter or my business from me? I wish someone would tell me.'

'He won't be taking anything,' said Sam Speke. 'Your debt has been paid by Daniel.'

'Paid by Daniel?' The words came from Aaron, but the same question was evident on the faces of the others.

'Yes, thanks to Sam.'

Daniel told his story. When it had ended Josh said, 'That was your gold, Sam. Yours alone. You found it....'

Sam Speke held up a hand to silence him.

'I found it only because I was the one who went into the gully to check out the Bushman's story. It could as easily have been any one of us. I told you at the time the gold belonged to all of us. There can be no going back on that even after all these years. We went through a lot together during those first weeks. Daniel suffered as much as anyone else. There's a share for you and Miriam when the day comes that you have need of it.'

'Argue about the money later if you must,' said Aaron. 'Right now I want to have something made quite clear to me. Daniel — you paid Jacobus Albrecht eighty guineas to settle my debt?'

'I gave it to him so he would have no claim against you or Hannah.'

The Jewish trader did not miss the look that passed between Daniel and his daughter.

'I see! I see! Well, young man....' He leaned forward and tapped Daniel on the knee. 'You know what you did tonight?'

'I did what needed to be done, that's all.'

'Oh no! You did much more than that. You bought yourself a half-share in a trading business. "Aaron & Daniel, Traders". Or do you think it should be something more formal? "Copping & Retallick", perhaps?'

'You don't owe me anything, Aaron. It was Sam who gave me the money and the idea.'

'Sam is an honest man. There are so few of them I am always grateful to have one for a friend. But please don't say I owe nothing to you, Daniel. That would be foolish, and a fool for a partner I can do without. To you I owe everything. Rather than allow Hannah to marry that ill-mannered Boer animal I'd have given him everything else I owned — and he would have taken it from me. You fought Jacobus for what he said about Hannah and now you've settled my debt with him. Oi! Boy, you're practically family! What else can I do but make you a partner, eh? Tell me that?'

'That's very generous, Aaron,' said Josh. 'But there's no need—'

'Josh, I respect your opinion,' interrupted Aaron. 'But please let my partner speak for himself. This is not such a one-sided arrangement. He's spent his money for me, and I could use his skills for the trading trips I have planned to Lake Ngami. I'm no hunter and I can tell east and west only at sunrise and sunset. I *need* him. What do you say, Daniel? Do we have a partnership?'

He held out his hand and, hardly able to contain his delight, Daniel nodded his head and clasped the hand of the Jewish trader.

'We have a partnership, Aaron.'

'Now we have something to celebrate,' shouted Aaron. 'Sam —come and help me to carry in some brandy.'

'I'd better be getting back to Otjimkandje,' said Josh. 'Miriam will be worrying herself silly.'

'You can go in a minute. First you must have a drink. Come with Sam and me and choose your brandy. I've got three different types in the back of the store.'

Kasupi had not been Daniel's friend for many years without knowing when his absence would be appreciated. 'I'll take the horses around the back for some water,' he said.

When Daniel and Hannah were alone in the room she came to stand to one side of him, her finger tracing imaginary patterns on the arm of his chair.

'I thought I'd die when I realised you must have heard some of the things that were said back in your house—about me marrying Jacobus Albrecht.'

'It made me pretty upset,' admitted Daniel.

'When I found your gun was missing, too, I thought you'd come here to find him and kill him.'

'I would have done it, too, but for Sam.'

Daniel watched her finger on the chair. It came to rest against his bare arm.

'I wouldn't have married him, you know.'

'Wouldn't you?'

'No. I'd have killed myself rather than let him have me.' Daniel said nothing, and her hand gripped his arm. 'I mean it, Daniel.'

He looked up and saw the fierce passion of her expression.

'I believe you.'

Her lower lip trembled as she said, 'Thank you, Daniel.'

Something of her uncontrollable emotion passed to Daniel, and words would not come to him. Clumsily he pulled at her arm, and she dropped to her knees beside him. The next moment he was kissing her passionately, and she was responding violently.

Then her cheek rested against his, and he felt the dampness of tears as she said in a choked whisper, 'I love you, Daniel. I do love you so very, very much.'

He had no time to reply. The noise of laughter and footsteps came from the passageway outside the room, and Hannah just had time to retreat to the darker shadows in the far corner of the room before her father and the others returned.

CHAPTER NINE

It was a few days before Daniel was fit enough to make the return journey to Otjimkandje. Aaron and Hannah stayed in Sesebe. So, too, did Kasupi. The Herero expected Jacobus Albrecht to return and slept little until he heard that the trader was on his way to Whalefish Bay.

Aaron took advantage of Daniel's stay to plan his next trip to Lake Ngami. First he would go to Whalefish Bay himself, to buy the trade goods he would need. He would pay for them with Herero cattle driven from Otjimkandje by Tjamuene's men. It surprised Daniel that the Herero were willing to part with so many of their stock, but Aaron satisfied his curiosity by telling him it was part of a trading agreement he had negotiated long before with Mutjise. The future Herero chief realised, Aaron said, that in their isolated situation trade was important if they intended to break Jonker's stranglehold on their people.

Jacobus Albrecht would not trade with them; neither did the Herero want anything to do with the Boer. They wanted their own trader. Aaron and his new partner satisfied that need.

Aaron felt it wise at this early stage of the partnership to say nothing about the guns he had already supplied to Mutjise.

Hannah made no secret of her pleasure at having Daniel remain at Sesebe for a few more days, and her devotion to him was apparent to everyone who saw them together.

Miriam came to Sesebe the day after Daniel's ride, to satisfy herself that he was as well as Josh had said. She saw how the relationship of the two young people had suddenly blossomed and taxed Daniel with it.

'That girl thinks the world of you, Daniel.'

'Yes, I know.'

Miriam waited in vain for him to amplify his brief acknowledgement.

'Well? Is that all you've got to say about the situation? A lovely young girl like that is so fond of you she hides it from no one, and all you can say is, "Yes, I know"! What am I supposed to presume from that?'

'What do you want to presume, Ma?'

Daniel found it difficult to keep a straight face at his mother's exasperation. He knew it sprang not only from the hope that he would marry Hannah, but also from his mother's fondness for Aaron's daughter and a wish to prevent her from being hurt.

'I don't want to presume anything,' snapped Miriam. 'I just don't want you trifling with that girl's feelings, that's all.'

'Ma, I came to Sesebe to kill a man to save her from being hurt. I'd do the same thing again if it needed to be done. Does that sound as though I'm trifling with her feelings?'

Miriam looked at her son and saw he was in deadly earnest.

'Does Hannah know how you feel?'

'I haven't put it into words but I think she knows.'

'Tell her and be *sure* she does,' said Miriam. Standing up to go, she looked down at Daniel with a mixture of sadness and pride. 'It doesn't seem so long ago that you were a helpless little boy. You've grown up taking after your father, and I can't pay you a greater compliment than that, Daniel.'

Miriam hurried from the room before Daniel could say anything in reply, and a few moments later Hannah hurried into the room.

'What's happened? Have you and your mother had an argument? She just went out of the house as though she was about to burst into tears.'

'No, we haven't had an argument. In fact she's very happy. I expect it's the thought of losing her only son, that's all.'

'Losing a son? Why, Daniel, where are you going? I thought. . . .'

Her dismay was so evident that Daniel reached for her hand. 'Slow down, Hannah. I'm not going anywhere. I meant that Ma knows she'll be losing me to you before very long and a man has to make his own home when he marries.'

Realisation of what he had said dawned slowly and wonderfully for Hannah.

'You mean it, Daniel? You really do want me to marry you?'

'Yes, I want it very much. Will you marry me?'

'Will I? Oh, Daniel! What an idiotic question! Of course I will. Oh, I love you so much!'

Daniel tried without success to disentangle himself from Hannah when he heard Aaron coming along the passageway towards the room.

Over Hannah's shoulder Daniel saw the Jewish trader's eyebrows nearly disappear into his thick black hair.

'Please don't let me interrupt anything,' he said when Hannah finally backed away from Daniel. 'I just found a new gun I'd forgotten about. I thought my partner might like to try it on our first trip together.'

The gun was a new percussion musket with a long rifled barrel, but Hannah was not in the mood to admire guns.

'Father, Daniel has just said he'd like to marry me.'

Aaron's smile broke through his beard.

'Congratulations, my boy.' He pumped Daniel's hand, his eyes twinkling happily. 'You've just proved to me you're a businessman my own father would have been proud to know. First you buy half my business at a bargain price and then you offer to marry my daughter so that when I die you have the lot. What a businessman, to be sure.'

'Does that mean you'll let me marry Daniel?'

'If I say no, he'll set up a trading business in opposition and ruin me. What else can I do but say yes?'

'Oh, Father! I'm so happy, I really am.' Now it was Aaron's turn to be hugged.

A few minutes later Josh came into the store with Miriam to say they were about to leave for Otjimkandje, and Aaron broke the news to them.

'The two children think they are grown-up already,' he said. 'They have just told me they want to get married.'

Hannah looked apprehensively at Miriam. They had spent a lot of time together at Otjimkandje, and she knew how much Daniel meant to his mother.

'I've been wondering why they've been so long about it,' she said. 'I was three years younger than Hannah when I first realised I wanted to marry Daniel's father.'

The mention of the marriage of his parents jolted Daniel back into the reality of their situation. Josh noticed it, but Aaron was too happy to think of anything but another reason for a celebration.

'We can't have too many weeks like this one,' he stated as he came into the room bearing the indispensable brandy bottles. 'There will be no profits left. Isn't Sam back yet? He should be part of this celebration too.'

Sam Speke lived in Sesebe during the week, returning to Otjimkandje to spend Sunday with Mary and the ailing Victoria, but upon her arrival in the mining town Miriam had sought out the ex-seaman and told him that Victoria's cough had worsened and she thought he should discuss her condition with Hugo Walder.

Sam was very worried. Victoria weighed no more than a normal child of half her age, and her already weak body would have difficulty in coping with any additional burden.

When a wagon-driver returned from Whalefish Bay with the news that a passenger-ship bound for the Cape Colony was due at the end of the next month, only a few weeks away, Sam decided to return to Otjimkandje immediately and have Mary and the child prepare for the journey to Whalefish Bay.

A passenger-vessel was a rare visitor to the little port and would have a doctor aboard to attend to Victoria on the journey. It also meant the little girl would be away from Otjimkandje during the rainy season, a time when she seemed to suffer more than at any other time of the year.

Sam Speke's unexpected arrival in the Herero village caused much consternation among the crowd of villagers squatting about his hut. When they saw him many of the women scrambled to their feet and fled.

Thoroughly alarmed, the ex-seaman leaped from his horse and ran to the hut, fearing the worst. He flung open the door and walked into a dramatic scene that had been enacted in Herero houses for centuries when persistent sickness was present.

The cow-dung fire in the centre of the hut had been built up with the addition of the green wood of a sacred tree, and the whole room was filled with dense acrid smoke that stung Sam's eyes and momentarily took his breath away.

An old man, his face hidden behind a hideous mask, was communing with the spirits of the villagers' ancestors, urging the good spirits to chase away their evil companions who had taken over the sick body of Victoria.

The old 'holy' man was accompanied by a great many assistants and followers, their painted faces and bodies heavily greased with rancid animal fat. The smell inside the small hut was appalling.

Sam saw his daughter lying on the skin of a lion close to the fire. She appeared to be either drugged or in a deep trance. The old man in the mask knelt beside her, his bony hands first squeezing her thin body then sliding back over her skin as though drawing out some invisible matter from within. As he worked his companions and assistants sat cross-legged about the fire, keeping up a low monotonous chant that brought the hair rising on the back of the ex-seaman's neck. It sounded to him for all the world like a death chant.

'What the hell's going on in here?'

Sam Speke's anger exploded as he forced his way across the crowded hut towards his daughter. The men he touched on the way stopped chanting immediately, but the others carried on as though they were unaware of his presence.

He was intercepted before he reached Victoria by Mary, who stood red-eyed beside the fire.

'Don't stop him, my husband. He is a very holy man. He will make Victoria well again.'

'With all this smoke and stink she'll probably choke. She needs plenty of air and a real doctor, not all this witchcraft. Get out of my way, Mary.'

Pushing his wife roughly away, he forced his way to his daughter's side, knocking over the last two squatting men and towering over the old man in the mask.

'You—get out! And take all these others with you.'

He shook the shoulder of the 'holy' man roughly. The old man rocked back on his heels and looked up at Sam.

'Your daughter is very sick.'

'I don't need you and your ceremony to tell me that.'

'She is sick because you are not of our people and are bringing her up to ways that do not please our fathers.'

'She is learning the ways of both your fathers and mine. She will have two paths to choose from and when the time comes it will be her choice. She will take the path that is best for her.'

The old man closed his eyes for a long time. When he opened them again he said, 'The choice will be hers to make but she will make it not for herself but for another.' He looked up at the glowering ex-seaman. 'She will get well now.'

He got to his feet slowly and with difficulty; he had seen more seasons than any other man or woman in the village, and the coming rains were already attacking the joints of his body. He hobbled to the door of the hut and his followers filed out after him. Not one of them looked back at Sam.

When the last of them had gone Sam Speke picked up the frail form of his daughter and carried her to the door. He spoke over his shoulder to Mary, who crouched by the fire sobbing noisily.

'Mary, get a grip on yourself! Put out that fire and let's get some air in here. It's a wonder Victoria hasn't choked to death.'

Mary did as she was told, talking all the time between violent shuddering sobs. 'I did what I believed to be right for Victoria. . . . She has been getting worse. . . . You were not here to give me advice. . . . I spoke to Tjamuene, and he said this was the way.'

It was no use telling Mary that Tjamuene was an old man who no longer knew what was best for any of his people and who fell back on tradition as a substitute for wisdom. Tjamuene was the chief of the Herero. Mary had asked his advice, and it had been given. Not to accept it was unthinkable. She had followed the way of her people and done what was necessary.

'Well, it doesn't seem to have done Victoria any harm,' Sam admitted. She slept quietly and easily without the rasping breathing that had so upset him for many months.

He moved across to Mary and put an arm about her. 'You did what you thought was best. I'm sorry I was angry, but I'm worried about Victoria too. I came to tell you there's a ship to the Cape in a few weeks. We'll be on it, and let's hope the doctors there can do something for her.'

His words did not make Mary feel better. She was relieved that her husband was not angry with her, but the thought of travelling to the Cape Colony terrified her. She had never before travelled any farther than from Otjimkandje to Sesebe.

After his humiliation at the hands of Daniel, Jacobus Albrecht returned to Winterhoek to feed his anger with brandy, away from the eyes of others.

He had enjoyed a two-day drinking bout when William Thackeray paid him a visit. The missionary had completed his church, and Jonker ensured that his Sunday services were well attended. If a great many of his congregation were less than sober, it could not be helped. He was a missionary in a strange new land, among primitive people. He had to prove to Jonker that his way was the best; then he could apply pressure to bring about the changes that were necessary.

That did not mean William Thackeray would sit back and do nothing until then. Jonker's missionary had a full programme planned.

He called on Jacobus Albrecht in mid-morning when the trader had just left his bed, three days' growth of beard shading his face.

The Boer opened the door of his hut and reeled back from the glare of the sun.

'Agh, it's you! Come in, man, if you must.'

William Thackeray stepped into the room, wrinkling his nose in distaste at the wide variety of unsavoury smells that hung on the stale air inside the unventilated hut.

Jacobus Albrecht drew back the rough sacking curtains, then crossed to the table and swept a variety of dirty plates and mugs into a wooden bucket.

'I understand there is to be no wedding,' the missionary said.

'Wedding?' It took some moments for the words to sink in. 'You mean with Hannah?' He scowled. 'No, there'll be no wedding, but that's not the end of it. Nobody makes Jacobus Albrecht look a fool.'

Memory returning to him, he crossed to the bed in the corner of the room and heaved back the heap of bedclothes to reveal a naked black back.

'Hey, you! Get up. The party's over. Go home now.' He gave the exposed rump a slap that sounded like a whipcrack in the room.

A naked Afrikaner girl sat up, grumbling irritably.

'You hear me? Get up and go home, you Kaffir slut. I've got company.'

Only half-awake, and with a throbbing head, the girl swung her feet to the floor. Standing up with a groan, she tottered unsteadily towards the door.

'Hey! You—whatever your name is. Take your bloody clothes with you.'

Her 'clothes' consisted of a ragged dress and nothing else. Jacobus Albrecht screwed it into a ball and threw it at her. She caught it, staggered slightly and, tucking it beneath her arm, stepped naked from the hut into the blinding sunlight.

The Boer trader reached down a full flagon of cheap brandy from a shelf above the bed, found a nearly clean mug from beneath it and half-filled it with brandy.

'You want some of this?'

William Thackeray shook his head. Watching the trader as he swallowed the brandy and belched noisily, he wondered how a man could allow himself to sink so low and to live in such squalor when he had both the money and resources to make a good home for himself. But he allowed none of his thoughts to show. He needed this uncouth Boer to help him.

'Have you come here for anything special, or is this just a friendly visit?'

'I came here to sympathise with you,' replied the missionary. 'Any man who looked forward to marriage and is disappointed should have someone to commiserate with him.'

The Boer trader did not understand a great many of the words William Thackeray used when speaking but he was able to grasp the gist of his talk.

'A man doesn't need more than a few bottles of this when he's down,' he said, waving the flagon in front of the missionary. 'You ought to drink some of it yourself. It might take your mind off saving the souls of Jonker and his people for a while. I'm damned if I know why you bother anyway. If I was God, I'd do my best to keep a lot of them away from heaven—or wherever it is you're trying to send them.'

'Well, you and I don't agree about everything, do we, Jacobus? For instance, if someone had stopped my wedding, I'd be thinking up ways of getting back what I'd lost and not be skulking miles away drowning my sorrows.'

'I'm not skulking! You choose your words more carefully, Preacher. You'll bleed as easily as any other man. Don't forget that.'

'I came here to sympathise with you,' replied the missionary. 'Not to start up a quarrel. We're on the same side, you and I. But we'll neither of us get very far while Hugo Walder maintains such a strong influence over the Herero.'

'That's one of *your* problems,' stated the trader, pouring himself another half-mug of brandy.

'That's not true; it affects us both,' argued William Thackeray. 'Hugo Walder gains his strength from those who support him – the Retallicks, Sam Speke and Aaron. Prise them out and he'll fall. Then you'll have Aaron's trade and his daughter – if that's what you want – and Chief Jonker will be rid of the Herero.'

'How about you?' Jacobus Albrecht asked suspiciously. 'What do you get out of it?'

'I'll send to Cape Town asking for another of our missionaries to be sent here,' replied William Thackeray. 'If the Herero are still around, he can be missionary to them; if not, to whichever tribe Chief Jonker decides to settle in Otjimkandje.'

'Nothing for yourself but everything for the Church,' mocked the trader. 'Such piety doesn't sit well with you, Preacher. You're too ambitious. There's more in it than you've said. What is it?'

William Thackeray flushed but held back his anger. 'Nothing that will affect you. But we'll get nowhere until you stop supporting Hugo Walder's friends. A start would be to dismiss Josh Retallick from the Sesebe mine.'

'You don't like him, do you?' Jacobus Albrecht's bloodshot eyes watched the missionary speculatively over the rim of the mug. 'I wonder why.'

William Thackeray had regained his composure now. 'I knew him before either of us came to this country,' he admitted. 'But, then, Joshua Retallick was known to a great many people. He was so well known that if you were able to persuade some of your trading friends to deliver him to the British authorities in Cape Town their gratitude would go much farther than covering your expenses.'

The Boer trader lowered his mug. 'You mean he's a wanted man? What's he done?'

William Thackeray smiled enigmatically and shook his head. 'I'm saying nothing, Jacobus. It's better that way for the moment. But if you can get him to Cape Town and turn him over to the authorities I promise you the repercussions will be far-reaching. They might even be strong enough to have Hugo Walder recalled for harbouring him.'

The thin missionary got to his feet slowly and grimaced as though the movement had brought him pain.

'Think about what I've said, Jacobus. Our future could lie in your hands. Don't throw it away.'

A few days later Harold Andrews sent for Josh. He was apologetic to the point of embarrassment, but it did not soften the impact of his words. Josh was asked to leave the employ of Andrews and Albrecht.

'I'm sorry about it, Josh,' said the uncomfortable mine-owner. 'The mine is paying its way but it's not making a fortune. If it was up to me alone, I'd keep you on, but Jacobus is my partner and he says we've got to cut costs now there's another trading company working in direct opposition to us. He can't afford a mine-manager.'

'It's strange the opposition didn't worry Jacobus when he invited Aaron to Sesebe,' said Josh sarcastically. 'I wonder what could have brought about this sudden change of mind.'

'We both know the answer to that, Josh,' said Harold Andrews. 'But there's little I can do. I don't know how long the ore is going to last here, and mining is a much chancier business than trading. I can't risk having Jacobus pull out, taking most of the trading contacts with him.'

'You don't have to give me lengthy explanations. I've been expecting this. Now perhaps I'll have time to do some of the things I've been thinking about – going down to Whalefish Bay to see Sam and his family off, for instance.' He looked at the mine-owner, but Harold Andrews would not meet his eyes. 'I wish I could promise that things will work out as well for you, Harold. They won't. I've worked this mine for some years now; it's been my living – and would have been for a few more years – but without a good captain you'll have lost the copper seam in six months. I doubt whether you'll be able to pay the men's wages for long enough to find it again. I wish you well.'

Ignoring the mine-owner's hand, Josh turned and walked from the office.

Josh had not been merely trying to frighten Harold Andrews. At the moment the mine was taking ore from two shallow seams, each with only a short run. The time to be looking for more ore was now – and it needed an expert. The shallow seams might resume their run some distance away, possibly at an acute angle from the original seam. On the other hand, it might prove necessary to go deeper for the ore. This would be disastrous to inexperienced men. There was water in the mine already, and the rainy season was upon them. It would raise the level even higher.

The year of 1860 had been an evenful one. As it drew to a close Josh forecast that the Sesebe mine would not know another Christmas.

This did not necessarily mean the ore-ships would have to stop calling at Whalefish Bay. If a way could be found to prevent interference from Chief Jonker, Josh would persuade Aaron to join him in the purchase of wagons and equipment from the Sesebe mine when it ceased operations. They could then work the copper ore deposit he had discovered on their trip to Lake Ngami.

CHAPTER TEN

The rains did not last long that season. The last two weeks in December were very wet, but then the wind swung away to the south and the clouds disappeared overnight, leaving the year 1861 to arrive hot and sunny.

Using more of Daniel's money, Aaron had been able to have one wagonload of trade goods sent to Sesebe from Whalefish Bay. It was not much but there would be more soon. For now it would have to suffice.

Aaron had made arrangements with the Bechuana chief to meet him at a water-hole halfway between Lake Ngami and Otjimkandje and he did not intend letting him down. He and Daniel set off with their wagons during the rains, worried that the weather would slow them down. They had promised Sam Speke they would be in Whalefish Bay in time to see him and his family on to the boat.

The Bechuanas were waiting at the meeting-place with a fine load of ivory for them. This was the farthest north Daniel had been and he was very impressed with the country and its wealth of animal life. Hunting food was no problem, and he also managed to shoot a fine cheetah. One of the Hereros accompanying them cured the skin for him, and Daniel thought it would make a fine present for Hannah.

The vegetation hereabouts was also exceptional, with a wealth of new growth everywhere. The tall grass stood man-high, and there were hundreds of brilliant-hued flowers, but it was the trees that Daniel found of most interest. They were the giant baobab trees, with a circumference often equal to the length of a wagon. Their stunted leafless branches gave Daniel the impression that the Great Creator had made a mistake and stuck the trees into the earth upside down.

Certainly, the country here was not as harsh as that about Otjimkandje. Daniel became so enthusiastic that Aaron had to remind him he was seeing it during the rains. In the dry months it was almost as desolate as the lands with which Daniel was

266

more familiar — as he would see for himself on future trips to Lake Ngami.

They travelled direct from the water-hole to Whalefish Bay and when the rains ended were able to make excellent time. By keeping well to the north of Jonker's territory they encountered no unforeseen setbacks and arrived in Whalefish Bay ahead of Sam Speke and the others.

Aaron was well pleased to see the ship belonging to his friend Captain Klopper riding at anchor in the bay. It meant he would be able to get rid of his ivory immediately, thus eliminating the risk of having Jonker pay him a surprise late visit. It also meant he could be sure of obtaining a fair price for his goods.

Leaving Daniel with the wagons, Aaron went in search of the captain. Whalefish Bay had grown in recent years. It was no longer possible to locate anyone by standing on a hillock and shouting his name. There were now stores and houses, offices and inns. Aaron started with the latter and was successful at the second one he tried.

'I didn't expect to find you here, my friend,' said Aaron as the two men shook hands. 'Have you given up carrying the more rewarding items of trade and settled for the hard-won profits to be gained from general cargo?'

'For the present, yes,' replied the ship's captain. 'They are expecting some ships at the Cape bringing troops for Natal. All the English frigates are at sea, each anxious to be the first to sight them. They are buzzing up and down the coast like bees around a hive. Unless I was prepared to risk losing my ship and spending the remainder of my days in prison I had to load trade goods. So, here I am with a ship full of trinkets I'll be lucky to sell for much more than my crew's pay.'

'Then this must be your lucky day,' said the Jew. 'I've just returned from trading with the Bechuana and I've got two wagons with the best quality ivory you've ever clapped eyes on. I tell you, Cap'n Klopper, it breaks my heart to have to part with it.'

The captain warmed to Aaron's sales talk. He was well pleased at meeting the Jew. He would return to the Cape with a better cargo than he had anticipated.

'You'll be wanting more than ordinary trade goods for prime

ivory, I reckon?'

'Of course. But you and I are old friends, Cap'n Klopper. We trust each other. You'll pay for half the ivory with the goods you're carrying now. The other half will be paid for with our "special" merchandise, landed in the usual place.'

'When will you be there?'

'How long is it before the troopships are expected and the frigates return to running errands for the Cape Governor?'

'The troopships are expected any day. I should think it will be possible to make a delivery two months from today.'

'Good! Then we have a deal, Cap'n Klopper. If I am not at my cabin, bury the merchandise immediately behind the hut and sail away. With so many newcomers in Whalefish Bay it must soon burst at the seams. When it does people will spill out along the coast. It would be a great pity if inquisitive eyes saw you riding at anchor below the hut and spoiled a good business arrangement.'

'I'll be careful,' promised the ship's captain.

'Excellent! Now, if it's all the same to you, I'd like to complete the trade before dark. I would hate Jonker to ride in and rob me now we've made our deal.'

'I've got four men waiting in a boat inshore. I'll get them working on it. They're waiting to take a special passenger on board for Jacobus Albrecht.'

Aaron was rising from the table when Captain Klopper spoke the Boer trader's name. He promptly sat down again.

'Albrecht? You're doing business with him?'

'I haven't until now,' said the captain. 'He's promised to pay well and I have been told there will be more when I get the passenger to the Cape—although I must admit I don't like the sound of it.'

'Why not? It's not a long trip to the Cape given the right winds. A passenger will not inconvenience you for long.'

'Not if he's a willing passenger,' replied the captain. 'This one's not. He's to be turned over to the Cape Government when I get there.'

Aaron became increasingly interested. There was little love between Boers and British Government. Why should Albrecht be helping them?

268

'What's the name of this passenger?'

'The agreement's between Albrecht and me,' said Captain Klopper. 'I wouldn't tell him of any business you and I did.'

'I hope not,' snorted Aaron. 'For your sake as much as my own. Jacobus Albrecht is no friend of mine and he's up to no good. What's the name of the passenger?'

'Retallick.' Captain Klopper saw the old Jew's jaw drop open in amazement. 'You know him?'

Aaron nodded vigorously and his mouth snapped shut. 'Daniel Retallick is my new partner. I owed Albrecht some money and he gave me an ultimatum: either I gave him Hannah or he would take everything I owned. Daniel Retallick gave him the money to settle my debt. I owe him more than the money, Cap'n Klopper.'

Captain Klopper had been doing business with Aaron for many years and had watched Hannah grow from a tiny child to a beautiful girl. He had felt sorry for the motherless girl living in the harsh unloving world of the Skeleton Coast and when she was smaller had brought her many presents from the Cape. He had no love for any man who meant her harm. Jacobus Albrecht had just made another enemy.

'I'll do no business with any man who would try to take Hannah in that way,' he declared angrily. 'But the name of the passenger Albrecht wanted me to take was Josh Retallick, not Daniel.'

'Daniel's father? Why would the Cape Government want him? He's lived up here for almost fifteen years. Are you sure it wasn't Daniel?'

'I'm certain,' said the captain. 'Not that it makes any difference which one it was to be. I'll do none of Albrecht's dirty work for him. Bring your ivory down to the beach, Aaron. I'll get it on board and return with your trade goods, then I'll weigh anchor.'

'I'll be down at the boat in a few minutes,' said Aaron. 'And thank you for your information, Cap'n Klopper. The Retallicks have been very good to Hannah and me.'

'Then you'd better warn him quickly of what's afoot. Albrecht said he'd have him here for me tonight.'

Aaron ran all the way back to where he had left Daniel with

the wagons. He arrived so out of breath he could hardly get the story out to Daniel.

'Why should he think the Cape Government would be interested in your father?' he ended. 'He's a good man.'

Daniel had listened in tight-lipped silence. Now he said, 'You'd better ask Pa the answer to that yourself. I'll go to meet him and make sure he gets here safely. Kasupi will come with me. Will you loan him your gun?'

The Jewish trader handed the weapon to the Herero as the two friends saddled their horses. Kasupi flung an order at his fellow-tribesmen who had been escorting the wagons on the journey from Lake Ngami and half of the Hereros took their spears from the wagon, eager for a chance to do battle.

'Your father and the others should not be far along the road,' Kasupi explained. 'My warriors will follow us on foot as fast as they can. It is possible Jacobus Albrecht will use Afrikaners to help him to get your father. Our numbers will make them think twice before attacking.'

Daniel nodded acknowledgement of the sense of Kasupi's words. As he swung his horse around Aaron called to him, 'When you meet up with them let Sam, Mary and the child come on here and I'll see them settled in to await their ship. You and your father laager up with Kasupi's warriors. I'll join you with Sam's wagon as soon as Captain Klopper brings the trade goods ashore. Then we'll all return to Otjimkandje together.'

At about the time Captain Klopper was imparting his information to Aaron, William Thackeray was riding in to Otjimkandje.

He rode alone and as his horse picked its way between the huts he could not fail to make comparisons between the orderliness and general cleanliness of the Herero village and the dirt and untidiness of Winterhoek.

He made his way towards the cross on the church that rose high above the mud and straw huts about it. He found Hugo Walder inside hammering at the leg of a bench that had become loose.

The German missionary wiped the perspiration from his hand before greeting his English counterpart.

'You find me in a most unusual situation,' Hugo Walder said. 'I have not had to work with my hands for very many years — not since I began building this church myself. Not that I am complaining; it makes me feel very close to our Lord to think the humble thoughts of a carpenter. No, it is simply that Sam Speke and Josh Retallick have for many years done all the work for me. Now they are at Whalefish Bay.'

'I wish I had men like them at Winterhoek,' said William Thackeray. 'Chief Jonker's men are willing enough most of the time but they are workers in mud and cob only. I have no carpenters or metalworkers.' He was looking at a lectern made of fine scroll metalwork.

'Yes, that is quite beautiful,' agreed Hugo Walder. 'Josh made it when he set up his first forge in Otjimkandje.'

'You have a lovely little church here,' said William Thackeray wistfully. 'This is the first time I have been cool since I left England.'

'The church has thick walls and a double roof,' explained the German missionary. 'One must use every means at one's disposal to make life bearable in Africa. Otherwise this country will defeat even the most dedicated man.' Hugo Walder looked critically at Chief Jonker's missionary. 'You have been working too hard. You have lost much weight since we last met.'

'I haven't been too well,' admitted the Wesleyan Missionary. 'But I've recovered now.'

'H'm!' Hugo Walder did not commit himself to a reply. 'Come into my hut. I have cool water there. The trick is to bury it in wet sand in the shade and keep it damped down.'

'If you don't mind, I would rather stay here and feed my soul on the peace and coolness for a while,' said William Thackeray.

'Then I will bring water to you.'

'You'll find a satchel of mail on my horse,' said William Thackeray as he lowered himself gratefully to a seat on one of the wooden benches used by the Herero congregation. 'That's why I am here. A rider from Whalefish Bay brought me a satchel of letters and it wasn't until he had gone I saw a great many of them were for you.'

'I am obliged to you,' said Hugo Walder. 'Now rest while I fetch water.'

But the old missionary did not go directly to his hut. Instead he went to find Miriam.

She was alone in the house, Hannah having gone with Sam and Mary to Whalefish Bay, ostensibly to help with young Victoria. She had fooled no one. Daniel would be there, and it meant the young couple would be able to share each other's company on the ten-day return journey to Otjimkandje. Miriam did not mind; it was exactly what she might have done – and would now, given the opportunity. Even after all these years, when Josh was away Miriam missed him with all the unreasonable longings of a young girl.

Through her kitchen window Miriam saw the German missionary hurrying towards the house, and his haste was so uncharacteristic of the man that she went to the door to meet him.

He saw the concern on her face and immediately apologised.

'I'm sorry, my dear Miriam. I didn't mean to alarm you. I merely came to warn you – to tell you – that Jonker's missionary has arrived to pay me a visit. I thought you should know in case he calls on you.'

Miriam told herself that the constricted feeling in her chest was not fear. Ever since she had first heard of William Thackeray's arrival in Winterhoek she had known the day had to come when she would be forced to meet him again, to face him and talk to him, to hear him remind her of things that had remained with him as memories but which she had long since forgotten. Her life had been filled with so much since those faroff years in Cornwall. She could only hope his life had been the same; but he would hardly have come to Winterhoek had his years in England been filled with happiness and fulfilment.

'Where is he?' Miriam loosed the apron from about her waist and from habit smoothed her long hair back from her forehead.

'He's in the church. I came to fetch him water. He's hot and tired from the ride. I fear he's not a strong man – certainly not strong enough for Africa.'

'William Thackeray has never needed strength of body, Hugo. He finds others to do his work for him. He's very good at that. I'll take him water.'

'Are you sure? Is it wise?'

'I'll take it – and thank you for the warning.'

Miriam kept her water-jugs cool in a box made from sea-stone carried from the coast near Whalefish Bay. She removed one of them, took a cup from a hook on the dresser and made her way to the church. Hugo Walder watched her go, wondering whether he had been right to tell her. Jonker's missionary might have returned to Winterhoek without troubling her – but Hugo's instincts told him otherwise.

William Thackeray was sitting where Hugo Walder had left him, facing the altar, his back to the door.

Miriam was wearing soft shoes, and they made no sound on the packed-earth floor of thechurch . She paused inside the doorway, waiting for her eyes to adjust to the shadows. For some moments she looked at the back of the man with whom she had shared four years of her life. The grey of age had lightened the colour of his hair, and it was untidily long at the back of his neck. In Cornwall he had always been excessively fussy about his appearance. She could see, too, that he had lost a great deal of weight. Never a heavy man, his shoulder bones now protruded from his shirt like the shoulders of a cow with rinderpest.

William Thackeray turned around slowly, although she had not made a sound. When he looked at her Miriam knew that Hugo Walder had not exaggerated. William Thackeray was a very sick man.

'Miriam!' The missionary stood up, and there was an air of great expectancy about him. This was an important moment in his life, the fulfilment of many years of effort. Miriam knew in that moment that his coming here was no mere coincidence.

'I've brought you the water Hugo promised.'

'So he told you I was here.' William Thackeray smiled wryly. The moment of fulfilment had passed, unfulfilled, and he was aware of its passing.

'Hugo has been a good friend for a great many years.'

'You needn't have come to me here, Miriam. I had no intention of leaving Otjimkandje without paying a call upon you.'

'I'd rather we met in God's house with Him as a witness than in Josh's house with none.'

'It was in God's house we were married, Miriam. He was a witness to that, too.'

'Then He must have known what a mockery it was,' said

Miriam softly, 'with love for Josh in my heart and his son in my belly.'

William Thackeray winced as though she had struck him a physical blow.

'I didn't force you to marry me, Miriam. But what kind of talk is this? I haven't come here to open old wounds. It is not my intention to hurt you in any way.'

'You've never needed force to get your own way, William. Trickery and the ability to seize an advantage have always been your way. As for hurting me, and mine, you did that the day you landed at Whalefish Bay. We had a good life here at Otjim-kandje. Your coming has put an end to that.'

'It needn't, Miriam. I can still be a friend. You can never have too many friends in a harsh uncertain country like this.'

'You had your chance to prove friendship to Josh many years ago. He was on trial for a crime he didn't commit. Your evidence could have cleared him. Do you know, William, had you stood up in that court and told half of what you knew you would never have lost me. I never loved you – that you knew. But I once respected you, and respect kept me with you. When it went I had nothing but contempt and loathing in my heart for you. I couldn't live with that eating me away.

'Yes, this is a harsh and uncertain country, but I'll live and die here – for Josh. Here he is a free man and living a full life. That's unselfish unambitious love, William – something you'll never understand and so will never have. I don't know what you hoped to gain by coming here, but go back. Leave Josh and me and Daniel in peace. You do that and you'll take with you at least part of the respect I once had for you.' Miriam placed the water-jug down on a bench. 'Here's your water. Leave the jug when you've drunk your fill. Hugo will bring it back to me.'

She turned and walked out of the mission church without a backward glance. Miriam had feared this meeting, had lain awake for hours at night worrying about it. Now it was behind her, and had anyone asked what she had felt when she stood before the man who was still her legal husband she would have replied in one word.

Pity.

William Thackeray was no longer the man who had inspired

the miners of Cornwall and fused their enthusiasm into a single union, the preacher men would walk miles to hear, who had once drawn a crowd of three thousand and had them roaring agreement with his every word. Jonker's missionary was a man whose soul had been eaten away by bitterness and whose body was racked by ill-health. Yet, though Miriam had no love left for William Thackeray, she wished he had been able to know a happiness similiar to the one she shared with Josh.

Hugo Walder went into his church an hour later and found the Wesleyan preacher slumped on the stool where he had left him. He was so still the German missionary thought he was ill, but as he approached William Thackeray raised his head. His eyes were those of a weary and disillusioned man.

'Are you all right?' asked Hugo with some concern.

'Yes. I'm sorry if I alarmed you. It is so quiet in here I have been thinking – and praying.'

'Ah!' Hugo Walder gave William Thackeray one of his warm smiles. 'I understand.' He looked around the little church with affection. 'I know in our preaching we are wont to say that God is everywhere – and so he is, of course – yet I always feel closer to Him in here. Here is His peace, His compassion, His inspiration.' Hugo Walder struggled to find the words he wanted but concluded by saying simply, 'He is here.'

'I believe you, Father, but I have kept you from your duties for long enough. It is time I returned to Winterhoek.'

'Nonsense! The Afrikaners did without a missionary for many years; they can do without one for a few hours. I am having a meal prepared for you, and there is a bottle of good wine hidden away somewhere. Come, we will share it and you can tell me all about your church and how that scoundrel Jonker is treating you.'

Daniel and Kasupi met up with Sam Speke's party five miles outside Whalefish Bay. Hannah could hardly contain her excitement at the meeting, but one look at Daniel's face told her that romance would have to wait. There were other things on his mind. He drew Josh to one side and gave him Aaron's warning.

'Is he quite sure of this?'

'Yes. It's too dangerous for you to go on to Whalefish Bay.'

'He wouldn't dare do anything there.'

'Pa! Be sensible. Who'd stop him once he explained why he was doing it?'

Sam Speke jumped from his wagon and came over to them.

'Is something happening I should know about?'

'No,' said Josh. 'Everything is all right.'

'Everything is *not* all right,' contradicted Daniel. 'Jacobus Albrecht is planning to get Pa aboard a boat in Whalefish Bay and have him taken prisoner to Cape Town. He's already made all the arrangements with the captain.'

'It would take more than Jacobus Albrecht to put me on to a ship bound for the Cape,' declared Josh.

'I doubt he'd attempt such a thing alone,' said Sam Speke. 'Daniel's right, Josh. You can't go on to Whalefish Bay. Mary and I will go on with Victoria. You get back to Otjimkandje right away. You owe it to Miriam not to risk being taken to the Cape Colony.'

'Aaron said he'd meet you and arrange a place to stay,' said Daniel. 'We'll wait here for him. We've brought in some ivory from the Bechuana and he's loading trade goods.'

At that moment the Herero warriors rounded a bend in the road half a mile away, trotting in loose formation. Seeing the wagon they let out loud cries and breaking formation ran forward brandishing their spears above their heads.

'What the hell is this?' exclaimed Sam Speke. 'Quick, get to the wagon.'

'It's all right,' grinned Kasupi. 'They are my warriors who are coming to guard us. They will stay until the others arrive with Aaron.' He looked at Josh. 'No man will harm you until every one of my warriors lies dead.'

Kasupi did not know why Jacobus Albrecht should want to capture Josh, he did not particularly want to know. It was sufficient that Daniel's father was in danger. Besides, this made his Hereros feel like men, not skulking away from Jonker and his Afrikaners but standing in the open with sharp spears in their hands – warriors, prepared to die a warrior's death, facing an enemy. It was such a good feeling Kasupi half-hoped the Boer trader would have Afrikaners with him and dare to attack.

'It looks to me as though Daniel and Kasupi have full command of the situation, Josh,' said Sam Speke. 'You'd better take your orders from them.'

'They've done well enough.' Josh acknowledged the sense of the precautions that had been taken. 'All right, Sam. I'll say goodbye to you here. Take care of yourself and bring that beautiful daughter of yours back again fit and well.'

While Josh said goodbye to Mary and Victoria, Hannah asked Daniel what was happening. He told her only that Jacobus Albrecht was trying to put his father on a ship bound for Cape Town, against his will.

Hannah was completely baffled by the whole thing.

'Why? I mean, what does he hope to gain from doing such a thing? And why does he want to get him to the Cape?'

'It's a long story, Hannah. We've got a lot of time on the journey back to Otjimkandje ahead of us. I'll tell you all about it then. In the meantime you go on to Whalefish Bay with Victoria.'

'Let me stay with you here and you can tell me about it right away.'

'No. I want you to go to Whalefish Bay first. There could be fighting here if Jacobus Albrecht arrives with his friends.'

'If he does, you could use another gun. I'm as good a shot as any man.'

'I know you are, Hannah,' Daniel acknowledged, 'but Victoria needs you. The sight of all the buildings at Whalefish Bay will terrify her. Get her settled quickly and return with your father. You should be back here by morning.'

Hannah pouted but made no further argument, and when Daniel leaned forward from his horse and kissed her she was as happy as any girl in the whole of Africa. He had never before kissed her in front of others. It was by way of being a public declaration that she belonged to him, just one step from being married.

When the wagons creaked away and the waving from both parties ceased, Kasupi suggested they should make camp on some rising ground a short distance from the road. It would give them a good view of the surrounding countryside and make a useful defensive position should it become necessary.

Once they moved to the high ground Kasupi proved that in

spite of all the years he had spent as Daniel's guardian, when his apparently idle and self-indulgent ways had brought censure from the elders of the tribe, he was a chief's son. He gave orders to the warriors as though he were an experienced general, and they obeyed him without question.

He sent out single warriors to vantage-points about the camp, to report the approach of any unknown party, set guards in between and rode from one place to another keeping his men alert and ready. He reminded them they were Herero warriors and might be fighting an enemy at any moment.

'I think Kasupi is enjoying this,' commented Josh. 'And I must admit he seems to know what he's doing. Jonker will need to tread carefully when Mutjise takes over leadership of the Herero and Kasupi is given more responsibility.'

Daniel found it difficult to understand how Josh could act so calmly when his whole future freedom was in jeopardy. When he put his thoughts into words Josh smiled. 'It's a tribute to you and Kasupi. Jacobus Albrecht won't risk anything while I'm defended in such strength. He'll most probably abandon the whole idea when he realises we know about it. I expect he was hoping to get me away without anyone here knowing. People in Whalefish Bay might allow him to take me, but it wouldn't increase his popularity around Sesebe and Otjimkandje.'

'I can't understand why he should want to have you sent to the Cape. He has a grudge against Sam, Aaron and me, but you've done him no harm. Why make you suffer?'

'At a guess I would say William Thackeray put him up to it. He has always had the cunning to achieve his own ends by using someone else to do his work and have them believe he is doing them a favour. I've no doubt he persuaded Jacobus that he would be hurting all of you by getting me out of the way — even Hugo. It wouldn't do the mission any good if word got to the Cape that Otjimkandje had been sheltering an escaped convict for all these years. Yes, Hugo might even be recalled for something like that, and it would open the way for the Afrikaners to destroy Otjimkandje and lay claim to all of the Hereroland. Then Jonker would be the most powerful chief in this part of the world for sure. He would control all mineral rights, and the Cape Government could find themselves negotiating with him for permission to use Whalefish Bay. That would make his missionary a very influential man.

'Oh, yes, this sounds just like the William Thackeray I used to know. His planning is in this. No doubt he convinced Jacobus Albrecht that he'd stand to gain all the Herero cattle Jonker would take.' He grinned wryly at Daniel. 'I almost feel sorry for Chief Jonker. He has no idea what sort of man he has living in Winterhoek.'

'Is William Thackeray really that bad, Pa?'

Daniel's life had been spent among primitive and sometimes cruel people, but they were usually kind and generous to their own. Because of this Daniel had grown to near-manhood naïve in the ways of other men. Jacobus Albrecht had given him his first real taste of what other men were like in the world beyond the Herero. Now there was William Thackeray.

'Yes, Daniel. I'm afraid he is. He is also a very clever man. His words do more harm than the guns of others. Mind you, he can be charming at times – and that makes him even more dangerous. I still believed him to be my friend when he was planning to involve me in his schemes. This plan to get me to the Cape is just a beginning. There will be more trouble before William Thackeray is through.'

One of the Hereros called to them, and they looked up to see Kasupi galloping back to the camp.

Leaping to the ground he said, 'Jacobus Albrecht and four white men ride along the road from Whalefish Bay.'

'What shall we do?' Daniel asked, looking at his father.

'Nothing, unless he makes a move to attack us, but I doubt if he'll do that now.'

'I have told two of my warriors to watch them wherever they go,' said Kasupi. 'The others are returning here.'

It was a few minutes before the five white men could be seen by those in the camp. The Boer trader was immediately recognisable, but the others were not known to the men from Otjimkandje.

The five were almost level with the camp before the sunlight glinting on metal spear-heads gave away its position. The riders stopped for perhaps a full minute, their horses milling about in confusion. Then, maintaining a respectful distance, they circled around the waiting men before stopping for another brief conference. Four riders suddenly wheeled about and headed back towards Whalefish Bay. Seconds later Jacobus Albrecht dug his heels into his horse's belly and galloped after them.

'I think we've seen the last of them,' declared Josh. 'They didn't fancy facing Herero spears, Kasupi.'

'No.' The chief's son sounded disappointed. 'But I will keep guards out until Aaron returns with the rest of my men.'

The transfer of goods from the ship to the waiting wagons took longer than anticipated. A stiff onshore breeze blew up, and Captain Klopper called off his plans to work after dark and deferred the off-loading until first light, much to the chagrin of the impatient Hannah.

Aaron sent one of the Hereros to find Josh to tell him what was happening and he and Hannah prepared to bed down beneath their wagon as they had on many occasions before.

'This is just like the old days,' Aaron said to his daughter as he finished his meal of salt beef and leaned back against the wagon-wheel and gazed up at the stars. 'But things are constantly changing down here. Only up there do they remain the same.'

Hannah made no reply; she was too busy with her own thoughts.

'Do you love him so very much, Hannah?'

'Who?' Hannah was startled. Her father might have been reading her mind.

'Who?' Aaron repeated. 'Are there so many young men out here who have asked you to marry them that you can't remember which of them you have travelled all these miles to be with?'

Hannah began to protest she had come to Whalefish Bay to help Mary look after Victoria, but Aaron interrupted her.

'Hannah, my child, you are talking to your father! Do you think that after all these years I don't know your every look and mood, the things that make you sad and the all too few things that have happened to make you happy? You have been the whole reason for my life for many years now. Nothing is as important to me as your happiness. Are you quite sure you love Daniel?'

'Yes, I love him.'

She averted her eyes from her father's face. After all their years together with no one else the admission suddenly felt like a betrayal.

'Do you believe he feels the same way about you?'

'I think he does.'

Aaron looked at his daughter with a smile that was both warm and gentle.

'Yes, I think he does, too. It is good. Daniel is young and has much to learn but he is a good boy. He will be a son to be proud of, a strength in my old age. I am very happy for you, Hannah. It is a great relief to me to know that should anything happen to me you will have Daniel to look after you.'

'Oh father!' Hannah scrambled to his side of the fire and buried her face in his rough cloth jacket, hugging him tight. 'You've become a part of this land. You'll go on for ever.'

'Nothing is for ever, my child' — Aaron lightly patted his daughter's back — 'so be sure to empty the cup of life as it is filled for you. Love especially is too precious a gift to waste even a single drop.'

Aaron and his wagons reached Josh and the others shortly before noon the following day, having seen no sign of Jacobus Albrecht.

There was little likelihood of his trying to carry out his plan now. Before leaving, Aaron had seen Captain Klopper's ship weigh anchor and shake out her sails, nosing out into the long Atlantic rollers, leaning on the wind as it turned south.

Jacobus Albrecht's opportunity had passed.

CHAPTER ELEVEN

The ten-day journey to Otjimkandje in early February in the year 1861 was everything Hannah had hoped it would be. At night after the evening meal she would sit by the fire, leaning against Daniel, sleepy and happy. Then, later, she would lie in her bed beneath the wagon close enough to call softly to Daniel and know he would hear her. In her thoughts he lay alongside her, touching her, holding her and making love to her.

On the fourth night of the journey they outspanned the wagons close to a water-hole at the foot of one of the impressive mountain 'islands' that rose suddenly and dramatically in a dozen places along the road to Otjimkandje.

After they had eaten, the moon rose red and bloated over the horizon and Daniel announced he and Hannah intended climbing the slope to get a view of the surrounding countryside by moonlight.

'Take a gun with you,' called Aaron as they were about to leave. 'This is leopard country.'

Hannah pulled a face, but she took Daniel's rifle from the wagon and handed it to him before they set off hand in hand up the steep rocky slope.

'What it is to be young and in love,' sighed Aaron. 'The joy and the pain of it all.'

'You can't have had very much of the joy of love,' said Josh. 'It's been just you and Hannah for many years now, hasn't it?'

'Yes.'

Aaron said nothing for a long time; then, 'I have had much joy watching Hannah grow up through my own eyes and also seeing her as I think her mother might have done. She has grown into a fine young lady. Her mother would be proud of her. Now she has found a fine young man for herself and my joy is almost complete.'

'They make a handsome couple,' Josh agreed.

'Yet there will always be the sadness too,' mused the trader. 'Every time I look at Hannah I see her dear mother. I wish she might have been spared to see Hannah now.'

He took out a handkerchief and blew his nose noisily. 'It isn't only young men who feel joy and pain – though they think it is. I was not a young man when I met Sofia, Hannah's mother. She was the daughter of a good family in a small town in Russia, near the Black Sea. I was studying law. I was not good enough for her, and her family never missed an opportunity to remind me. But I wanted Sofia and she wanted me, so one day we ran away together.' Aaron gave a short laugh. 'For most young people running away is a brief adventure. They cross a border, are married – and return to face the secret admiration of their families and friends. It was not so with Sofia and me. We were married in Bucharest but did not return home. Instead we went on through Europe to the Netherlands and from there took ship to the Cape Colonies. That is where Hannah was born.'

Aaron paused and pushed a log of wood farther into the heart of the fire. 'Four years later Sofia died. I was trading by that time and doing quite well. But I could not stay in a place where every street, every friend, was a constant reminder to me of Sofia. So Hannah and I trekked northwards, always northwards, and along the way I traded with the English, the Boers, the Bechuana, Nama, Orlam, Witbooi, with Jonker – and now with Kasupi's people.'

A sleepy Kasupi grinned at him from across the fire.

'Yet through all this you brought up Hannah to be a lovely girl.'

'Some credit I will take for her schooling. Her beauty was a gift from her mother.'

'And now Daniel is going to take her from you.'

'Take? Take? Never! I *give* her to him. We are partners now, Daniel and me. Everything we share. I have had Hannah's childhood all to myself. He is given a woman. It is as it should be. Like I said, Daniel is a good boy. You and Miriam can be proud of him – just as I am. For Hannah I could not have wished a better husband. For me, I feared she might one day have chosen worse. So we are all happy.'

Daniel and Hannah climbed the slopes of the mountain until they looked down upon the fires of their camp twinkling far below them. The moon had cleared the horizon and left its red glow behind. A plump silver pumpkin, it hung in the sky sharing its magic glow with the whole world.

It showed Daniel and Hannah to a large flat rock, and without waiting to regain their breath after the climb they kissed until Hannah pushed Daniel away and lay gasping in his arms.

'Do you love me, Daniel?'

The moon had heard it all before and continued its ponderous course across the sky, sweeping the stars before it.

'I love you very much.'

Their lips met again, and Hannah clung to him as though frightened he might run away from her.

'When will we be married, Daniel?'

'I thought we could make it September. Soon after your seventeenth birthday.'

'But that's ages away! Why must we wait so long?'

'We have to build a house and get furniture and things up from the Cape.'

'Such things don't matter. Anyway, we could get them made in Sesebe.'

'Anything made there would be shoddy now that Sam is away. I want us to have the best house in the whole of southwest Africa.'

'Daniel, I don't think I can wait that long for you.' Hannah's voice was hoarse with longing. 'I lie awake at night imagining you are loving me. Daniel, I want you now.'

Hannah had not been brought up among other women. Aaron had been able to teach her many things, but an awareness of modesty was not one of them. She spoke of her feelings openly and honestly because she knew no other way.

Her words burned into Daniel and his body responded immediately. Hannah felt the contraction of his stomach muscles, the tension. Instinctively she knew the reason. She turned in towards him and the next moment they were lying side by side on the rock, their bodies straining hard against each other.

Her mouth moved beneath his as they kissed, and his hand found the gap where her shirt had pulled away from her denim trousers. Moving inside, it touched soft skin and followed the line of her slim body up to the warmth of her armpit. She squirmed in his grasp, and his hand closed about the firm breast that was more mature than that of a young girl but was not yet the breast of a woman.

Hannah moaned and her mouth kissed his cheek, his eyes and his ears. 'I love you! Oh, Daniel, I love you!'

She plucked at his rough shirt and then her hands were on his warm body, stroking and gripping, pulling him to her.

He released her breast and as she half-rolled away from him his hand slipped down from her ribs and caressed her hard flat stomach. She breathed in, and his hand pushed down farther, inside the waistband of her trousers, his fingers moving on until they discovered a new warmth that sent Hannah writhing into a new world of lover's ecstasy.

Daniel, too, was floating away into heady sensuousness until an alien sound broke in upon him, shattering all romance in an instant. He realised then that he had heard the sound a few moments before but had rejected it without thought.

This time there could be no ignoring the asthmatic cough that came from somewhere very close. Daniel hurriedly pulled his hand away from Hannah, and the top button of her trousers went spinning into the night.

'What's the matter?'

'Sh!' Daniel put his left hand over her mouth while the other hand reached behind him for the gun he had propped against the rock on which they lay. His fingers found the cold metal barrel and closed about it. As he drew the gun up to him he whispered, 'Stay perfectly still. It's a leopard, and I'm not sure where it is.'

Bringing the gun across Hannah's body he eased back the hammer with his thumb until it clicked into the cocked position. Then he waited and watched.

For long minutes the only sound was Hannah's carefully controlled breathing and a Herero warrior calling to one of his companions in the camp far below them. Perspiration ran from Daniel's forehead and into his eyes. He hastily wiped it away with the back of his hand. Moving his head, he searched the shadows on either side of the rock. A leopard was a powerful and fearless killer. The night and the shadows were its friends; it could charge silently and launch itself in a tremendous

285

twenty-foot leap before they even saw it.

The creature had all the advantages. All Daniel had was a gun with a single shot. There would be no second chance. If the leopard attacked, Daniel had to see it coming.

Hannah was fully aware of their danger. She lay absolutely still so as not to distract Daniel, all her romantic ideas forgotten.

The leopard gave away its new position by coughing once more. This time the sound came from behind Daniel. The animal was circling, choosing its moment to attack. Slowly and silently Daniel rolled away from Hannah to face into the darkness.

Suddenly he thought he saw a movement in the shadows thirty feet from them. The next moment he was certain. The leopard was making for some rocks on the slope just above them. Had they brought both their guns Daniel would have risked making a shot now. With one gun he dared not miss.

There was another flat rock twelve feet away on the slope above them. The leopard must have got their scent and did not appear to fear humans. Daniel guessed it would launch its attack from the flat rock. It was a calculated guess that Daniel hoped would prove correct. It *had* to be correct.

He moved again to give himself the best shot possible and had hardly settled into his new position when the big cat's head was silhouetted against the sky above the other flat rock.

Daniel had no time to congratulate himself on a good guess. The leopard knew exactly where his intended victims were and his attack came fast and frighteningly silent.

It took all Daniel's nerve to wait the fraction of a second until the leopard had launched itself clear of the rock and was in the air, forelegs extended towards him. Not until then did Daniel fire, aiming for the animal's heart.

The next few seconds were ones of utter confusion. The report of the gun mingled with the angry screams of the big cat and the smoke from the black powder as two hundred pounds of leopard crashed against Daniel and sent him somersaulting backwards from the rock, the sweet-sour smell of leopard in his nostrils.

He crashed to the ground with the breath knocked from him, not knowing quite what had happened. Then, to his great relief, he heard Hannah's alarmed voice calling to him.

'Daniel! Where are you? Are you all right?'

'I'm here and just a bit breathless, that's all — and you?'

'Not a scratch!'

Daniel rose to his feet and tripped over the leopard. It was lying full length on the ground between him and the rock on which they had been lying.

'Oh, Daniel, I was frightened!' Hannah trembled against him and he gave her a reassuring squeeze, aware that her fear had been for him and not for herself.

The shot had been heard in the camp at the base of the mountain and men were rushing up the slope towards them, waving blazing torches and shouting. Among their voices Daniel recognised his father and Aaron calling to them.

'Up here! We're all right. Bring the torches over here.'

One of the Hereros was the first to arrive and his long-drawn-out 'Aaah!' of admiration as he looked down at the body of the leopard would have satisfied the most vain hunter. Soon the whole party arrived at the scene to admire Daniel's kill.

'You were lucky to have hit him in this light,' commented Josh.

'There was no luck about it,' said Hannah indignantly. 'It was hunting us, and Daniel had to wait until it attacked before he could shoot.'

'It looks to me as though he almost waited too long,' said Aaron seriously. He touched the front of Hannah's shirt. In the torchlight Daniel could see two large patches of blood that must have fallen on her as the mortally wounded leopard passed over her head. It had died in mid-air from a shot that had passed clean through its heart.

Daniel and Hannah were never far from each other for the remainder of the journey but never again came as close to consummating their love — or as close to death — as they did on the slopes of 'The Mountain of the Leopard' as it was always known to the Herero tribe from that night on.

The wagons arrived at Sesebe to find a messenger from Otjimkandje awaiting them. He told Kasupi that he must go to the Herero village immediately. His father, Chief Tjamuene, was dying. Custom decreed that every one of his sons should be with him when his spirit left his body for the world beyond life.

Josh and Daniel went on to Otjimkandje with Kasupi, the Herero wagon escort travelling more slowly on the road behind them. Aaron promised that he, too, would come to Otjimkandje as soon as his wagon had been unloaded. He would not be allowed to see the old chief, but it would be known he had come to be close at the end. It was a very important gesture of respect. Failure to make the journey to Otjimkandje would be taken as an insult by Tjamuene's successor and would not easily be forgiven.

The Herero village was in a state of turmoil. Tjamuene had been their chief for almost fifty years. Most of his people had been born, lived a full life and died without knowing any other chief. The fact that for many years he had been little more than Chief Jonker's vassal made little difference to his status in the eyes of his own people. They still lived in the village where they had been born. They still owned cattle. They were the only Herero village left in the whole of this land they had once called their own. Chief Tjamuene's death would mean the end of an era. For the Herero people the future now held only uncertainty.

The general disruption of village life meant that Miriam's news of William Thackeray's visit did not disturb Josh as much as it might otherwise have done, and Miriam deliberately played the visit down. Jonker's missionary had come to see Hugo Walder. She had met him in the church and spoken to him there. That was all.

The visit had more effect upon Daniel. He bitterly resented William Thackeray's intrusion into his life. He would have liked to forget that the preacher had ever had a place in the lives of his mother and father. But that was not possible; his coming had brought too much unhappiness and uncertainty. There was the attempt to take Josh to the Cape Colony—an incident about which Daniel had been sworn to secrecy, since Josh did not want Miriam worrying about him whenever he left Otjimkandje. Daniel felt a simmering anger for William Thackeray begin to burn deep within him.

Late that evening Kasupi came to the house to say that Chief Tjamuene wished to speak to Josh and Daniel. He escorted them into the chief's kraal, pushing a way through aged head-men and the wailing women of the household.

Hugo Walder was with Chief Tjamuene, and candles burned at the head and foot of the skin bed on which he lay. Mutjise was also present, as were the most senior of the headmen.

Chief Tjamuene of the Herero did not look ill, only very, very tired. He turned his head towards Josh and Daniel as they came to him and managed to raise a weak hand for Josh to take.

'I am passing on, my friend,' he said, the words coming from his throat with little breath to give them strength.

'Your life has been good for your people, Tjamuene,' Josh replied.

'You, too, have served my people,' Tjamuene said and motioned for Mutjise to come close.

'This man is a friend of the Herero for all time,' the dying chief said to his eldest son. 'Be sure that all of our people and their sons who have yet to be born know of this.'

'It will be as though you were still chief for them,' agreed Mutjise.

The old chief closed his eyes. They were shut for so long Josh thought he slept, but as he was about to move quietly away Tjamuene spoke again.

'Bring Kasupi to me.'

The younger son stepped forward and, opening his eyes, Tjamuene looked upon him with affection and reached out for his hand.

'He has been a good friend to your son?' he asked Josh.

'Kasupi has been like a brother to my son and a good friend to my family. He is beyond praise.'

The old chief nodded weakly, well pleased.

'Now the time has come for him and my son to go their own ways,' said Josh unexpectedly and the old chief's eyes took on a sudden alertness as he looked at him.

'Kasupi is a leader, a man for warriors to follow. Mutjise will have need of such a brother. I give him back to the Herero. Even so, he will stay in my thoughts for all time.'

Kasupi tried hard not to show his pleasure at Josh's words. He had given Kasupi his freedom. Had these words not been said to Chief Tjamuene he would have been bound to serve

Daniel for the remainder of his life. Much as he loved his friend, Kasupi had many times longed for such freedom. Now he looked down at his father.

'So be it. Serve your brother well.' Chief Tjamuene released the hand of his son and his eyes closed again. This time Hugo Walder signalled for Josh and Daniel to leave the hut.

The old Herero chief's life died with the sun, and his people mourned loudly throughout the night.

The next few days were spent arranging his funeral feast and many of his best cattle were slaughtered, their carcasses beginning the slow process of cooking and their skulls being boiled clean to adorn the grave of the late Chief Tjamuene.

His funeral feast was attended by the chiefs of all the tribes within a radius of a hundred miles. Only Chief Jonker of the Afrikaners was absent. Aaron, Josh and Daniel were there with Hugo Walder, and Harold Andrews came from Sesebe to represent the mining company.

The rites lasted for two days and two nights, many of the participants staying awake for the whole forty-eight hours. Others crawled away to seek a few hours' sleep and then returned hoping their absence had not been noticed.

On the third day the ceremonies ended, and those men who had been closest to Tjamuene in life took his body from his kraal and buried him well away from the village. They were gone for a long time, for a chief's grave had to be marked by a mound of stones, and as he had been a great chief who had ruled his tribe for many years his burial mound needed to be of sufficient size to reflect this earthly status.

It was not until ten days after Chief Tjamuene's death that Otjimkandje returned to a normal routine and the Herero settled down to life under the chieftainship of Mutjise.

CHAPTER TWELVE

The mine at Sesebe ceased operations in May 1861, five months after Josh left the company. Had he stayed it might have been worked for a while longer. He would have brought in the engine from Andrews' previous copper mine to pump out water and gone deeper, but Harold Andrews made the decision to close with considerable relief. Chief Jonker was becoming more difficult with every day that passed. The Afrikaner chief had raised his levy on each wagonload of ore sent to the coast and brought the cost of the ore dangerously close to an uneconomical level.

When Andrews had protested Jonker had said that the mine was not producing enough ore because the Herero workers were lazy. His men waylaid them one Monday morning when they were on their way to Sesebe from Otjimkandje and beat them savagely in an effort to persuade them to work harder. The result had been that Mutjise ordered all the Herero workers back to their own village and no work was carried out at the mine for a whole week. Not until Harold Andrews had gone to the new Herero chief and pleaded with him had Mutjise allowed work to resume.

The Hereros went back to work; but the word was spread around that the Hereros were returning only because it had been agreed between their chief and the mine-owner, and had nothing to do with the threats of the Afrikaner chief.

Mutjise had his own reasons for making his contempt of Jonker common knowledge. The Herero's defeats at the hands of the Afrikaners had been due entirely to the weapons used in past battles. The Herero had fought with spears, the Afrikaners with guns, and the one-sided prohibition placed upon the trade in guns had helped Jonker to maintain his superiority over the Herero.

Mutjise knew the time had come for the proud Herero race led by his own warriors to shake off Jonker's sovereignty. The wagons of the trader Aaron had made more than one journey to the little hut by the sea, returning in the dark of night to

Chief Mutjise's kraal.

It became common for small bands of warriors to steal away before dawn on hunting trips far from the village. At first they returned with little to show for their hunting, but they became gradually more successful. If a man who ate the meat they brought broke his teeth on a lead musket-ball, nothing was ever said about it. If a woman found one in her cooking-pot, she was told it must have been shot by Kasupi, who owned a gun given to him by his friend Daniel.

Such a tense and unnatural state of affairs could not last for long. There was much resentment and ill-will on both sides. The Europeans could sense it and, though only Aaron knew the reason for the new confidence of the Herero, it was apparent to everyone that serious trouble lay ahead.

Hugo Walder preached the peace of the Lord at his Sunday services, but he knew as well as anybody that just as it needed two sides to make a war it would be necessary to persuade the same two opposing factors to work for peace. He was confident that Mutjise's people would never start a war, but he had no such confidence in Jonker's Afrikaners.

The German missionary decided it was time to return William Thackeray's visit.

He set off for Winterhoek early one morning in the middle of the year. Winter in this part of the world was no more than a slight relaxation of the burning heat, but the morning felt almost cool as he set off from the village that had been his home for so many years. His boyhood home in Germany in the wooded valley of the Rhine, with its rain and snow, was no longer real to him. Snow was no more than a dreamlike memory.

The missionary could not see himself ever returning to Europe. Home had become the familiar little church in the Herero village. He even spoke the Herero language more fluently than his native tongue now. He stopped his horse and looked back at the neat village, the round mud huts with their thatched roofs and thin threads of smoke rising from early fires. From the pens a thickening cloud of dust rose as the cattle became restless for food. It was a village awakening, a scene he had witnessed on hundreds of occasions.

Rising above the village, unobscured by smoke or dust and

proudly recording his modest success, was the cross of his church, Hugo Walder's achievement. He had brought Christianity to Otjimkandje and the Herero.

He enjoyed the ride to Winterhoek, his good mood lasting until he topped the ridge and looked down into the beautiful valley where Jonker had his untidy township.

There was surprisingly little life to be seen, only a few women and naked children. Most of the huts appeared to be deserted, the smoke of cooking-fires rising from only a dozen places.

Hugo Walder was puzzled; something here was not right. But he would not find the answers to his questions up here on the ridge. Flicking the reins, he urged his horse down the slope to Winterhoek.

The deserted air of the township extended to the mission church. The doors were closed and a thin layer of blown dust lay on the stone step in front of them. Neither did there seem to be anyone inside the mission hut. Curtains were drawn across the single window, and he could hear no movement inside when he listened outside the door.

The German missionary knocked twice and was about to leave when he thought he heard a faint sound from within. He tried the door and it opened beneath his hand. He pushed the door open wide, and the unhealthy smell of sickness rushed out past him to attack the clean sunlit day.

Hugo Walder strode into the hut and drew the curtains back as far as they would go. In the light that now filled the hut he saw the pale and emaciated figure of William Thackeray lying back in a rumpled and untidy bed.

'What in heaven's name are you doing lying here in this mess? How long have you been like this?'

William Thackeray could do little more than wave a weak hand towards the water-jug that stood on a nearby table.

The jug was a quarter full but the water smelled foul. Hugo Walder went outside and unhooked a water-bottle from his horse. Bringing it inside the hut, he poured the contents into a mug and took it to William Thackeray.

He lifted the Wesleyan missionary to a sitting position. His body was so thin and fragile that Hugo Walder felt obliged to handle him as gently as he would a small baby. Jonker's missionary drank the water as though it was the first he had tasted in days, choking over it and dribbling it helplessly down his chin.

'How long have you been in this condition?' Hugo Walder repeated when the other man had drunk his fill and lay back against his pillows, gasping for breath.

'I don't know. I've had a fever. It's been a long time.'

'Has none of Jonker's people been near you in that time?'

Hugo Walder was angry. The chief of even the most primitive tribe accepted a duty to care for a missionary when he came to live with them.

'Jonker has moved most of his tribe to another village about twenty miles away. He says it is unhealthy here.'

'Nonsense! This is one of the best spots anywhere in this country – though I am not saying it would not have been unhealthy for Jonker had I found him here today.'

William Thackeray winced as a pain caught him. 'I wish I had your energy, Hugo. I fear I have been a failure as a missionary. I should never have come to Africa.'

'You are a sick man. You will feel different when you are better.'

William Thackeray shook his head wearily. 'No. Chief Jonker stopped attending my church. When I asked him why he said I had brought no luck to his people. Since I came here nothing has gone right for him. Jonker lost what few cattle he owned through some cattle disease soon after the mine at Sesebe closed. Now Jonker has nothing to trade, and Jacobus Albrecht won't supply him with any more brandy until it can be paid for.'

'Where is Albrecht?'

'I don't know. I think he went with Jonker.'

William Thackeray lay back into his pillows. 'This is a judgement upon me, Hugo. I used God as an excuse to come here, to pursue personal ambition. It was not even an honourable ambition. I wished ill to a fellow-man, and now the illness has fallen upon me. It is His judgement.'

'It is your weak condition filling your mind with foolish thoughts,' said the German missionary as he pulled back the bedclothes and tidied William Thackeray's bed around his emaciated body. 'I will make you comfortable and then go and find someone in this place to bring you some food.'

'You are being very kind,' said William Thackeray. 'But it is a waste of your time. I am dying, Hugo. I know it and so do you. Leave me here to die alone. It is no less than I deserve.'

Hugo Walder had seen dying men before and knew William Thackeray had spoken the truth, but he would not leave a fellow-missionary alone to die in such miserable squalor. He finished tidying the bed.

'There! At least you have a little comfort. Now I go to find some food.'

He went to the nearest hut from which smoke was rising. An old woman sat in the shade outside the door, waving a desultory hand as the flies landed on her leathery wrinkled face in a vain search for moisture.

'I want food for Chief Jonker's missionary. What do you have?'

The eyes that were turned upon him held nothing but flat defeat.

'Who would hunt for an old woman who has no sons?'

The old crone nodded towards a hut from which a younger woman emerged, only to hurry back inside when she saw Hugo Walder. 'That is the one who should be taking food to the sick white man. Instead she sits and sulks because Jonker took her new husband from her to travel with him.'

'Thank you, mother. A blessing on your house.'

Hugo Walder went to the hut of the younger woman and called in through the open doorway. 'You in there. Come out! I want to talk to you.'

'I am busy. I have no time to talk.' There was fear in the voice.

'Come out here this instant. If I have to fetch you, I will take you straight to Chief Jonker.'

The trembling girl emerged from the hut, her naked bosom rising and falling rapidly. She was terrified of what was going to happen to her.

'Chief Jonker told you to feed and tend his missionary. Why have you not carried out his orders?'

'The missionary frightened me.' The Afrikaner girl burst into tears. 'In his sickness he threw himself about on his bed and said many strange things to me. There is a bad spirit in him.'

'He is Chief Jonker's missionary and he is very sick. You should be looking after him.'

'My man told me Chief Jonker is not pleased with him. He would be happy if his missionary was not alive when he returned.'

'Then listen to me, and hear me well. If the missionary dies because you have not fed him, I will bring such trouble upon Chief Jonker that he will kill both you and your man because of it. I am going back to the missionary now. You will bring him water and meat broth very quickly. Then you will clean his hut. When that is done I will ride back to Otjimkandje while you stay with him until my return. Is that understood?' The unhappy girl nodded. 'I hope so, for your sake. Now, hurry with that food and water. If you are slow, you will feel my anger as well as that of Chief Jonker.'

Hugo Walder returned to William Thackeray and found him lying just as he had left him. The Wesleyan missionary opened his eyes as his bearded colleague leaned over the bed.

'I thought you had returned to Otjimkandje.'

'I went only far enough to arrange for food and water to be brought to you. I will be leaving soon to arrange for a wagon to take you to my house, but someone will stay with you while I am gone.'

'No, I don't want that. I don't want to leave Winterhoek.'

The vehemence of his statement set William Thackeray to coughing so violently that Hugo Walder hurried to his side and held him tightly until he stopped. The Wesleyan missionary had a handkerchief clutched in his hand and he held it to his mouth as he coughed. When he finished he quickly tucked the handkerchief beneath his pillows, but not before Hugo Walder had seen the dark-red blood glistening upon it. William Thackeray was in an advanced state of lung disease. It was Hugo Walder's opinion that he had also contracted malaria. There could be no doubt that he was dying. It was a miracle he had managed to survive for so long.

'I can't leave you here with only an unreliable girl to look after you.'

'Hugo, please don't try to spare my feelings. You know I am going to die. I am aware of it myself. I have not been in Winterhoek for very long, but I have rebuilt the church here and done my best. Given time I would have grown to know and love it as you do your own church at Otjimkandje. It is all I have in the world that is familiar to me. Please allow me the selfish privilege of dying here and being the first man to have a Christian burial in the churchyard. Don't deny me that, Hugo.'

The German missionary could say nothing. He had heard William Thackeray's dying wish and felt obliged to respect it.

'There is one other thing you can do, Hugo. Bring Miriam here to see me before I die.'

William Thackeray looked up at the other man and anticipated his objections.

'I know she will not want to come. Plead with her for me. It is of great importance to us both. You must return with her, too, Hugo. I want you here. . . .'

The sick man's voice faded away and his eyelids drooped closed. His arm was dangling down at the side of the bed. It was frail and fleshless, no fatter than a man's two fingers. As Hugo lifted it and tucked it inside the bedclothes the Wesleyan preacher's lips moved in a faint whisper: 'Bring her here, Hugo. Please bring Miriam here.'

The frightened Afrikaner woman brought food within the hour. There was meat and maize porridge as well as broth. The German missionary took only the broth and fed it to William Thackeray himself.

Although he managed to get most of the food down, the effort left the sick man in a state of complete exhaustion. When Hugo Walder was sure he slept he ordered the woman to clean up the hut and stay there until he returned. She began to protest, but the missionary held up his hand and silenced her.

'It does not matter if I do not return for a whole week. You will stay here with him. You understand?'

The Afrikaner woman understood. She might not be a willing nurse, but she would not leave Chief Jonker's missionary.

On the return journey to Otjimkandje, Hugo Walder wondered how he might persuade Miriam to go with him to Winterhoek. It would not be easy, of that he was certain. He hoped he would find Josh at the house. It might be easier to reason with him.

But Josh was not at Otjimkandje. He had gone with Aaron to

the copper deposit he had found to the north of the Herero village. It was possible that at some time in the future it might be worked. Josh was carrying out a full survey of the extent and grade of the ore. He and Aaron would be away for some days.

Daniel was with Miriam, fretting because he would rather have been with Hannah at Sesebe. She was remaining there because Sam Speke was expected back from the Cape Colony any day now. He would be calling at Sesebe first, unaware of the events which had closed down the mine and left Aaron's store the sole occupied building in the mining village. Hannah should be perfectly safe inside the massively built store. It would defy a besieging army that was not equipped with cannon.

'Come in, Hugo,' called Miriam when he knocked on the door of the house. 'I've been expecting you. I called to see you this morning but you must have left early.'

'Yes, I went to visit William Thackeray at Winterhoek. I have just returned from there.'

'Oh!' Miriam's mouth snapped shut like a trap.

'He is a very sick man.'

'Africa doesn't agree with everyone. He should go home to England.'

'William Thackeray will never see England again.' Miriam's dark eyes met his and they widened. 'He is a dying man.'

'Then you'd best pray for him, Hugo. He'll have a lot to answer for when he meets the Lord.'

'I do not think you meant that to be as cruel as it sounded.'

'And why not? What do I owe William Thackeray but unhappiness?'

Miriam defied Hugo Walder's steady gaze for ten seconds, then she surrendered. 'No, you're quite right, Hugo. He's the one who's had nothing but unhappiness. I've had Josh and Daniel. I feel nothing but pity for him.'

'Enough pity to go and visit him?'

'Visit William Thackeray? Oh, no, Hugo! That's asking too much.'

'He wants to see you, Miriam, and I would come with you, of course. The desire to see you together with his wish to be buried next to the church at Winterhoek are probably the last requests he will ever make.'

Miriam opened her mouth to refuse again but she changed her mind.

'I'll think about it.'

Hugo Walder shook his head. 'There is no time for thinking. We must leave immediately. I will be surprised if he lives to see tomorrow's sunrise.'

Miriam searched the missionary's face for a sign that he was exaggerating the seriousness of William Thackeray's illness. She saw no deceit there.

The missionary received support from an unexpected quarter. Daniel said, 'I'd like to meet William Thackeray before he dies.'

'You? Why?' Miriam rounded on him. 'He's nothing to you. Why should you want to meet him?'

'Is it so unreasonable, Ma? I was born with his name. But there's another reason, too.'

He knew he had to choose his words carefully, so as not to hurt her.

'You're right when you say he means nothing to me. I've got you and Pa right here. Whatever my name was when I was born I'm Daniel Retallick now and it's a name I'm proud of. But I'd still like to meet William Thackeray. I'd like to know whether he spent all these years trying to find us because he hated Pa or because he loved you, and why he's come here to try to part you. I've never met that sort of man before.'

'I doubt whether you'll find any of the answers in the man who lies dying at Winterhoek, Daniel,' said Hugo Walder sadly. 'There is very little of the physical man left. But he is a dying man and he has much on his mind. It is possible he hopes for forgiveness before he leaves this world. I don't know. I only know it will make me very sad if I have to return to Winterhoek alone.'

'What about Chief Jonker?' asked Miriam. 'Will he be there?'

'Jonker has moved his people to another village. William Thackeray is dying in a near-deserted township, believing himself to be a complete failure, his whole life wasted. When I found him no other human had been near him for days.'

Although she fought hard against the feeling, Miriam could not prevent pity from welling up inside her. Although she tried hard to ignore them, there had been times when William Thackeray had been kind and considerate, especially in the days when she was a barefooted illiterate girl attending his chapel school.

'Well, what are we waiting for? If we don't hurry, we won't be there until morning. I can't ride a horse, so you'd better harness the horses to a small wagon. Oxen would take far too long to get there.'

After a flurry of activity they all set off in a wagon that sent every bump up through the spine of the three travellers; but Miriam insisted they continue as fast as was possible, and they reached the church at Winterhoek soon after the setting sun had erased the long shadow of the mission cross from the hut where the dying preacher lay.

The Afrikaner girl was sitting in the darkness inside the hut, close to the door. She had made some attempt to tidy the room, but her heart had not been in the task and she had made a poor job of it. The truth was that she had not expected Hugo Walder to return and the prospect of staying with the white missionary until he died terrified her. When Hugo Walder lit some candles and motioned for her to leave she fled gratefully.

Miriam was appalled by the lack of material comforts in the hut. There were only the bare essentials of life to be seen. Then she reminded herself that the man in the bed had been ill for a long time. It was probable the Afrikaner woman and her friends had stolen everything else. To the women it would be a matter of simple logic. The missionary was dying and would have no further use for his belongings. It was better to take them now and be sure of them.

Yet the poverty of the room did not shock Miriam nearly as much as the sight of the man lying there. His sunken eyes were closed and the skin on his face drawn so tightly across the bones of his face that it was like looking at a skull. She had seen much sickness and suffering since coming to Africa but she had never before seen anyone who looked like this – and still lived.

A spasm of pain crossed the taut face and the deep-sunken eyes flickered open. William Thackeray looked first at Hugo Walder and then at the others with no sign of recognition. At that moment Hugo Walder thought he had made a wasted journey to fetch Miriam from Otjimkandje. It looked as though the Wesleyan missionary was delirious.

Then William Thackeray's confusion cleared and he looked up at the German missionary. 'You've come back. Did you ... ?'

He turned his head on the pillow and saw Miriam. He tried to speak, but his laboured breathing overtook the words and for a full minute it was the only sound to be heard in the hut.

'Miriam! Thank you for coming.'

William Thackeray's eyes took in Daniel. 'So this is your son – the child I once held in my arms and loved as my own.' It was not possible to know whether the sudden pain that showed on his face was the result of remembering the past or had its origins in his present low physical state. 'You're every inch your father's son, Daniel. You'll grow up to be a fine Retallick.'

Miriam suddenly warmed towards this dying man. She was unable to feel anything more intimate for him than that. For the same reason she could feel no animosity towards him. This emaciated figure was no one she knew or had known. He was a dying stranger, entitled to her pity.

Yet William Thackeray had just said something that stirred memories of the preacher she had first met, the kind and considerate man she had once thought him to be. William Thackeray had just cast away any future doubts that Daniel might have felt about his parentage. Confirmed, as no one else could, that Daniel was indeed Josh's son.

'Sh! Don't try to speak. You need rest.' Miriam moved forward and fussed with his bedclothes, moved instinctively to do battle with untidiness.

'I must speak. There's so little time ... so little time.'

William Thackeray fought a battle with his breathing again. When he had won he pointed to an old chest of drawers against the far wall.

'Top drawer ... papers ... fetch them for me, Hugo.'

The German missionary moved across the room as William Thackeray ran his tongue about his dry thin lips.

Daniel filled a mug with water and carried it to the bed. He held it to the missionary's lips while Miriam lifted the sick man higher in the bed with frightening ease.

'Thank you.' William Thackeray nodded the water away, and

Daniel removed the mug from the lips of this man he had been prepared to hate but for whom he had nothing but pity.

There were a number of sheets of thick paper in the drawer, each page filled with neat handwriting that must have called for great concentration on the part of the sick missionary.

'Read it, Hugo. Aloud, please.'

Hugo Walder began to read, and from the very first line he had the full attention of Miriam and Daniel. William Thackeray leaned back on his pillows and listened with closed eyes.

What William Thackeray had written was a complete confession of his part in the Cornish riot for which Josh had been convicted. He told how he had sent a messenger to Josh in order to get him to the town where the riot was being staged. How Josh had gone there believing he would be able to prevent the disturbance. He mentioned names and meetings and implicated an officer who had been instrumental in having Josh arrested.

In short, the document went much farther than any evidence William Thackeray might have given before the Court of Assize which had found Josh guilty. There William Thackeray would have given only evidence enough to clear Josh of guilt. This document detailed his own responsibility for all that had gone on in that Cornish port – and much more beside.

When Hugo Walder finished reading the Wesleyan missionary said, without opening his eyes, 'There is a quill and ink in the same drawer, Hugo. I wish you to witness my signature.'

Without comment, the excited German missionary witnessed the document, adding the date and the information that the confession had been made by William Thackeray in the full knowledge of his imminent death.

'Does that win back a little of the respect you once had for me, Miriam?' The question came out as a feeble whisper.

'Yes, William.' Miriam swallowed the bitterness she felt. William Thackeray could have said something many years before.

'And your forgiveness?'

Miriam remained silent, and William Thackeray moved his head a fraction and opened his eyes to look at her.

'Will you at least try to forgive me?' he pleaded.

'I'll try.'

All the tension drained from William Thackeray's body.

'Then I'll leave you and your family in peace, Miriam. That's what you asked for.'

The dying missionary's eyes closed once more and his lips hardly moved as he whispered, 'We could have conquered the world, you and I, Miriam – and it would have been yours, all of it.'

William Thackeray never spoke again. He appeared to sleep, his breathing shallow but even. Then, half an hour later, Hugo Walder took William Thackeray's wrist to find a pulse and there was none.

'Poor William' was all Miriam could think of to say about him.

'What will you do with his confession?' asked the German missionary.

'What is there to be done? It comes fifteen years too late. Had he spoken when we were all in Cornwall our lives would have been very different. Now . . . ?' Miriam shrugged. 'Keep it until we return to Otjimkandje, Hugo.'

'All right, but the last well-intentioned task of a dying man should not be carried out in vain.'

Hugo Walder stepped to the door and looked out at the bright moonlight. 'You should have no difficulty in making your way back to Otjimkandje. I will stay here and bury William Thackeray in the morning.'

'We'll all stay here,' said Miriam. 'Whatever he did the past is over now. He's a man who has died in loneliness and has need of our prayers.'

'Then Daniel and I will carry him to his church now,' said the German missionary. 'He would have liked that. The rebuilding of it was the only thing William Thackeray believed he had successfully done for God. His soul will find peace there.'

CHAPTER THIRTEEN

Chief Jonker learned of the death of his missionary four days later when a boy sent from Winterhoek arrived at his new village. The messenger found him with Jacobus Albrecht, drinking brandy grudgingly given from the Boer's own fast-dwindling stock.

'Where is the body of the missionary now?' asked the Afrikaner chief.

'Buried in the ground by the stone hut with a cross,' replied the boy. 'The Little Father from Otjimkandje put him there. He was with your missionary when he died. So, too, were the white woman and her son.'

To Chief Jonker this spelled treachery. He had known his missionary wanted the white woman from Otjimkandje for himself. He also knew Jacobus Albrecht had taken part in an unsuccessful move to get her husband out of the land. Jonker believed that when this had failed William Thackeray had turned to the Little Father from Otjimkandje for help.

'The Little Father should not have gone to Winterhoek without first asking my permission,' he declared sulkily. For the fate of his missionary Jonker cared nothing. He had brought with him none of the authority of the Cape government Jonker had hoped for. Neither had his presence increased the Afrikaner chief's influence with the British administration. The missionary had been too filled with his own ambitions. He had promised Jonker that the chief's aims would be achieved as his own were fulfilled, but Jonker was prepared to take second place to no man and he was no longer of an age when he could afford to wait.

'Why not ride to Otjimkandje and tell Hugo Walder not to interfere with your Afrikaners, chief?' suggested Jacobus Albrecht.

Jonker glared at the trader. He had no wish to try to force a showdown with the German missionary. He was no match for him in a verbal battle. There was a time when he might have put up a good fight, but these days his thoughts took longer to change into words.

'When I wish to speak to the Little Father I will send for him to come to me.'

Jacobus Albrecht splashed more brandy into his mug and gave a short laugh.

'By that time he might be too high and mighty to come to you, Jonker. He might think the Herero are better than the Afrikaners. . . .' The trader saw a dangerous look appear on Jonker's face. 'I'm not saying they *are* better than your people,' he hastily added. 'I'm just saying what he might think. After all, the Herero still have plenty of cattle. Good big healthy cattle.'

The Boer trader did not have to spell out the comparison. The Afrikaners were left with a mere handful of scrawny unhealthy stock. But the Afrikaner chief would not let this man sitting across the table from him criticise the weakness of his tribe.

'Perhaps I should send you to Otjimkandje to fetch the white man, Retallick, to explain what has made them so rich,' he said. 'Or would you prefer to speak to the wagonmaker about it?'

Jonker laughed uproariously as Jacobus Albrecht's hand went instinctively to his misshapen nose.

'I'll settle my own debts,' the trader growled. 'That doesn't alter the fact that the Herero have more cattle than they know what to do with, while you don't have enough for trading.'

He divided the last of the brandy between the two mugs. 'I'm not going to be able to order any more of this until I've got something to trade with.'

'You order more brandy,' demanded the Afrikaner chief. 'I will give you cattle for trade. Get me powder, too, and new guns – good ones.'

'Now, that's getting pretty ambitious, Jonker. You know guns and powder aren't allowed in here. Oh, I can get them! But it will cost plenty of cattle.'

'There will be plenty of cattle.'

Chief Jonker drowned the last of the brandy, savouring the feel of its fire passing down his throat.

'Since the death of his father Mutjise has not been to see me to offer the friendship of the Herero people. Neither have I been asked to approve his selection as the new chief of the Otjimkandje Herero. I will have to go to him and show my displeasure. It is going to take many cattle to buy the protection of Chief Jonker of the Afrikaners once more.'

'Do you think he'll give them to you, Jonker?'

'Does a man have to ask to take what is rightfully his?'

'That's more like it, chief. Let me know when you're going for the cattle. We'll drive them straight to Whalefish Bay and ship them out. It will be too late for any argument about who owns them then!'

Josh and Aaron returned from the site of the copper deposits well pleased with their findings. Josh had carried out exhaustive tests and ascertained it was a very high-grade ore and far more extensive than the ore at Sesebe. It would make a good profit — but first he had to find a way to obtain Chief Jonker's agreement before he could work it without undue interference. The Afrikaner chief would want his share from the profit by way of 'tribute'. This was acceptable if his demands were reasonable, but Josh did not want to repeat the experience of Sesebe. He wanted to leave no loophole for Chief Jonker to bring in someone else to work the ore at a later date.

Josh and Aaron decided that for the moment they would say nothing to the Afrikaner chief of their find. Instead, they would begin work on the mine in secret, stockpiling the ore until such time as they might safely transport it to the coast.

The two men stayed in Otjimkandje only long enough to collect two wagonloads of mining-tools and gather together some of the men who had worked on Andrews' mine, before returning to their find.

Josh's reactions to William Thackeray's death-bed confession were even more confused than Miriam's had been. At first he was overjoyed, convinced he could take it to the Cape government and enjoy the ending of his forced exile. Miriam brought him sharply down to earth.

Before Josh could be a free man he would have to be granted a pardon by Queen Victoria, setting aside his conviction. It could only be accomplished in England and would take time.

Meanwhile he would be imprisoned in the Cape Colony.

There was no absolute guarantee a pardon would be granted. It it were refused, or the ship carrying it from England were lost, Josh would be condemned to spending the rest of his life in prison.

It was far too great a risk to take and Josh, bitterly disappointed, had to agree. Even after all these years the terrible memories of life on board a prison hulk were enough to cause him to break out in a cold sweat.

Ever since he had left the Assize Court in Bodmin as a convicted man Josh had dreamed of clearing his name and living his life free from fear of capture. Now he had to face the realisation that he might never achieve that end unless he was prepared to place the freedom he already had at risk.

It was a view not shared by Hugo Walder. He kept William Thackeray's confession and the day after Josh and Aaron departed for their new copper mine the missionary set off on a journey of his own to the Cape Colony, expecting to meet Sam Speke and his family along the road to Whalefish Bay.

Chief Jonker and a hundred of his armed warriors chose that very night to pay the promised visit to the new chief of the Herero. Jacobus Albrecht had been informed of his plans and had managed to find enough brandy to send the Afrikaner warriors on their way fortified with all the courage that brandy and superior weapons could bestow upon a fighting man.

Jonker wanted to surprise Mutjise and his people but there was no way an army of half-drunken men and a hundred horses could travel in complete silence. Hannah heard them pass by the shuttered and barred store in Sesebe.

It was doubtful whether Chief Jonker knew she was there, or would have cared if he had. One woman would not be able to stop a hundred armed warriors.

Hannah had other ideas. When the horsemen had passed by she unbarred the door and went to the hut at the back of the store where one of Aaron's Herero employees cowered in terror with his family. In answer to her questions he could only keep repeating that Jonker and all his warrors were on their way to destroy Otjimkandje.

'Then you must go and warn them,' said Hannah. 'You have

family there?'

The frightened man nodded. He had a father, mother and brothers in the village.

'Then get hold of yourself. Unless you want them all slaughtered in their sleep you will have to go and warn them. Take my horse and ride as fast as you can. You must get to Otjimkandje before Jonker's men. First warn the Retallicks, then Mutjise. Go quickly, now.'

Hannah physically pushed the man from the hut and made sure he mounted the horse and set off before she returned to the store.

Hannah had underestimated the Afrikaner chief. Jonker had been on many raids, and his army did not ride to do battle without outriders to guard against surprise attack. One of these flank outriders caught the terrified Herero from Sesebe and dragged him before Jonker.

'Where have you come from? Where were you going?'

The Herero's eyeballs rolled white in the darkness of his face but he said nothing.

'He was riding towards Otjimkandje,' said the man who had captured him. 'He probably came from Sesebe.'

'You did well,' said Jonker to his warrior. 'He will warn no one now. Kill him.'

The Herero's eyes rolled again and he began to speak. The words broke off in noisy gurgling as his captor pulled back his head and slit his throat with one slash of a sharp-bladed knife. The incident over, Chief Jonker resumed his advance upon Otjimkandje.

The village came awake to a frightening cacophony of noise as Jonker's men charged into the outskirts of the village not far from the mission church. The screams of the Herero women mingled with the shouts of Jonker's men and the firing of their guns.

The noise woke Daniel, and leaping from his bed he ran from the room, bumping into Miriam outside the door.

'It sounds like an attack on the village,' he said. 'It must be Jonker's men. Grab the old gun over the fireplace and get over to the church. I'll bring my own gun and some more ammunition.'

'What about the others – the villagers?'

'If they've got any sense, they'll make for the church, too. It's the only building we have any real chance of defending. Hurry now, Ma.'

Daniel grabbed all the powder and shot he could find and carried it to the church. As he had thought, many of the villagers were already there, but he saw immediately they were the women, children and old men only. None of the warriors was there.

Thinking the men of Otjimkandje must be trying to stem the Afrikaners' advance armed only with their spears, Daniel saw that Miriam had a loaded musket, then left the church. He made his way towards the shouts of the Afrikaners, the way illuminated by blazing thatch roofs deliberately fired by Jonker's men.

The attacking warriors were in no hurry to press home their attack, content to loot as they advanced. They were noisily firing their guns as they came, but there seemed to be little actual fighting taking place as so far the Afrikaners had met with no resistance.

Then, as Daniel knelt in the shadow of a hut watching the Afrikaners advancing towards him and trying to think of some way to stop them, he was joined by some of the missing Herero warriors. Others could be seen moving up into a rough line across the village, cutting off the approaching Afrikaners.

'I am happy to see you with us, Daniel.'

Kasupi spoke from the shadows beside him.

'We will remember you were ready to fight with us, but this is the night of the Otjimkandje Herero. Tonight we became warriors one more. Got to the church and take care of our women and children.'

A nearby roof erupted in a fountain of flames, and Daniel saw that every Herero warrior carried a gun and handled it as though familiar with its working.

'Go now, my friend. This is our fight. We have waited for it for too many years.'

Daniel knew better than to argue with Kasupi. The fact that the Herero were well armed and had kept it a secret meant that they were prepared for such an attack as this. He would only get in their way if he stayed.

Just before he entered the church he heard Kasupi shout an order to his men and the Herero warriors fired their first volley at Jonker's men. It was followed by another only a few seconds later.

Daniel smiled grimly and slipped inside the crowded stone church. Jonker had stuck his nose into a hornets' nest tonight. The stings would be painful indeed.

Outside in the flame-broken darkness the Herero divided into two parties, one led by Kasupi, the other by their chief Mutjise. They formed two straight lines, right across the village. One line would move forward until they were close enough to see the Afrikaner looters and open fire. Then the second line would move ahead of them while the others reloaded.

It was an orderly and thoroughly well-organised operation. Swiftly and efficiently they swept the Afrikaners from the village ahead of them, inflicting heavy casualties. Behind the musket-carrying warriors came others with assegais to despatch the Afrikaner wounded.

Jonker himself was lucky to escape with his life. Going forward on his horse after the first volley hit his men, he was caught in the second and had his horse shot from beneath him.

But there was no shortage of Afrikaner horses. By the time Jonker's men realised what was happening and turned to flee many of their number lay spilling their blood in the dusty spaces of Otjimkandje.

The Herero had won a great victory of vengeance. For the loss of three women and a baby they had killed thirty of Jonker's men and captured forty guns and eighteen horses.

What was more important was that tonight the Herero had broken Jonker's iron grip on their people. Never again would he and his tribe dare to claim sovereignty over the Herero.

It was more than two hours since Hannah had sent the messenger to Otjimkandje. His mission was urgent and he had a fast horse. He should have been there in half that time.

She wondered what would happen. Mutjise and his warriors would defend the village, of that she was sure; but it was possible that Daniel would try to get Miriam out and bring her to Sesebe before the fighting started. If all had gone well, they might arrive at any time.

When the knock came Hannah had no hesitation. Running to the door, she unbarred it and flung it open.

'Daniel . . . !'

But it was not Daniel. The man standing in the doorway was Jacobus Albrecht.

Hannah tried to slam the door shut, but the big Boer was too quick for her. He put his boot in the doorway and prevented it from closing. Hannah was terrified but she did not lose her head. She stamped hard on his toe. Jacobus Albrecht swore, then put his shoulder to the door, knocking it open and sending Hannah staggering back along the passageway.

Turning, she ran to her room. This time she reached it before the Boer and shut and bolted the door hurriedly. She turned to pick up her gun but to her dismay remembered she had left it just inside the door to the storeroom.

Hannah ran to the window above her bed. There was a glass window opening inwards with a stout shutter outside. She opened the glass window as Jacobus Albrecht lifted the latch on the door and found it bolted against him.

The Boer put his weight against the door and it gave slightly. This was not made of thick timber as was the front door. Taking a pace backwards, the Boer trader gave the door a hefty kick with the heel of his boot and the door burst open, taking the bolt staple clean out of the door-frame.

Hannah had opened the glass window but the shutter had two large bolts, both of them stiff and heavy, and she could not slide them open in time.

Standing on her bed, she turned to face Jacobus Albrecht as he came across the room at her. His smile had just begun when Hannah kicked out at his face. The Boer jerked his head to one side, but the kick landed, splitting his lower lip.

'You bitch!'

Hannah kicked again, but this time Jacobus was ready for her. He caught her foot between his two hands and twisted. Hannah overbalanced and fell backwards on to the bed. Releasing his hold on her foot, Jacobus Albrecht dropped to the bed on top of her.

'That's better. Now, you just behave and you'll enjoy it.

You're going to learn what it's like to lay with a real man instead of a young boy.'

The Boer trader smelled of brandy but he was not drunk. Hannah pummelled at his body, then tried to scratch his face, but he caught both her wrists and taking her arms above her head held both her wrists in his huge left hand while his right fumbled at her trousers, ripping and pulling as Hannah bucked and struggled beneath him.

The Boer's face came down close to hers and Hannah butted him, her forehead cracking hard against his disfigured nose. It hurt. Bringing up his right hand, Jacobus Albrecht struck her hard on the side of the jaw.

Everything went blank for Hannah. It seemed to her it could only have been for a matter of seconds, but it must have been longer than that because she regained consciousness aware of Jacobus Albrecht's body undulating on top of her, crushing her chest and making breathing difficult.

Then she felt the Boer inside her, hurting. She moaned and bit back a sob as her body began to move in time with the movements of the man above her. She wanted to stop it but could not. She hated herself and him but still her body would not stay still. The moans that escaped from her throat had nothing to do with the pain inside her. That was something she was no longer aware of.

The Boer began gasping as, head back, he drove farther into her and her moans became shouts, half-screams.

Then an animal grunt came from Jacobus Albrecht and his body shuddered to a stop. He released his grip on her wrists and her arms dropped down to his body, sliding from his back to his waist — and to his belt.

Her left hand touched metal. It was the Boer trader's American revolver, held in its holster by a short leather strap that came undone when she slid a finger beneath it.

The Boer's convulsions ended, he lay with his full weight upon her. Hannah, too, was still now, her body her own once more.

Raising himself to one elbow, the Boer looked down at her face and grinned.

'There, didn't I tell you you'd enjoy it? Where did you learn to do it like that, eh? It wasn't from the Retallick brat, that's for sure.'

Too late Jacobus Albrecht saw the expression upon Hannah's face. He grabbed down for his gun and heard the click of the hammer being thumbed back as Hannah pushed the barrel up into his stomach and pulled the trigger.

The .36 calibre bullet tore up through the Boer's stomach and blasted a hole in his heart big enough to take a pocket watch.

Hannah pushed with all her strength and the body of the big Boer rolled away from her and fell to the floor.

She sat up retching, the gun still in her hand. Jacobus Albrecht lay on his back on the floor, his mouth open, leaking blood, his eyes staring up at something he would never see.

His trousers were still undone, and looking at his exposed body Hannah remembered how her own body had responded to his. She had given herself to him.

'Oh God! What have I done? Daniel! Daniel!'

She never had to think about her next action. It was something that had to be done. Something evil inside her that had to be destroyed.

Lifting the gun slowly as though in a dream, Hannah put the cold steel barrel to her temple and pulled the trigger.

CHAPTER FOURTEEN

Sam Speke met Hugo Walder on the road and told him there was a vessel at anchor at Whalefish Bay, awaiting the arrival of a high government official from the Cape Colony who was on a brief and well-protected visit to this unclaimed territory.

In return, Hugo Walder was able to tell Sam Speke of the closing of the mine at Sesebe and of the deaths of Chief Tjamuene and William Thackeray.

It left Sam with plenty to think about as he drove the slow ox-wagon on towards Sesebe.

His trip to the Cape had been entirely successful. Even before the ship had reached the Cape, Victoria had shown signs of improvement. The doctors in the capital of the expanding colony examined the girl and declared that, although her lungs showed signs of weakness, she was now well on the road to recovery. They thought it probable that the dust of the copper workings in the dry desert soil of Sesebe had done much to irritate her lungs. If she stayed away from such conditions, there was no reason why she should not make a complete recovery.

As the wagon neared Sesebe, Sam Speke looked at the deserted buildings on the horizon. There was nothing here to irritate Victoria's lungs now. He wondered how the closure was affecting Aaron's business.

Of a sudden he felt he was nearing home and he cracked the long whip over the backs of the stolid oxen in a vain attempt to goad them to greater speed.

Sesebe was indeed a deserted town. It seemed unnatural to be arriving at midday without a sound coming from the Miners' Inn, but the door to Aaron's store stood open and Sam Speke hauled the oxen to a halt in front of it and handed Mary and Victoria down to the ground.

'Hello! Is anyone there? Aaron? Hannah?'

Nobody came to the door, and Sam Speke frowned. Anyone in the store should have heard the creaking of the ox-wagon from a quarter of a mile away. There had to be someone inside;

they would not have gone away leaving the front door open.

He walked into the store and along the passageway. Mary and Victoria behind him.

There was no one in the storeroom, and then Sam Speke saw the door to Hannah's room standing half-open. He pushed on it and his nose wrinkled at the dry acrid smell of a burnt-out lamp-wick. He had taken one pace into the room when he stopped suddenly. The light from the sunlit passageway sliced through the doorway and fell upon the wide-eyed face of Jacobus Albrecht staring up from the floor. Beyond him Hannah lay contorted in death upon the bed, a vast dark stain on the bed cover around her head.

Sam Speke slammed the door shut and turned quickly. 'Mary, get Victoria outside quickly!'

Mary Speke did not ask her husband what he had seen. The look of horror on his face was sufficient. She stopped Victoria from coming any farther and hurried her back along the passageway to the warm sunshine outside.

Sam Speke waited until his wife and daughter were out of the store before he opened the door to the room of death again.

There were candles in the room and he lit them. The disarray of Albrecht's clothing and the gun held in Hannah's stiff fingers were enough to tell Sam Speke the whole story. He prised the gun from her hand, the task made no easier by the tears that welled up and clouded his eyes.

'You poor child. You poor dear child.'

Sam Speke straightened Hannah on the bed as best he could and covered her body with a sheet he took from a cupboard in the room.

He dragged the body of Jacobus Albrecht from the room and into the passageway outside. Looking down at the flattened nose, he regretted that he had not killed the Boer trader instead of merely disfiguring him.

Going out of the house, he found Mary waiting at the wagon with Victoria. In a choked voice he told her what had happened.

Mary made no attempt to hold back her tears.

'Poor Hannah – and poor Daniel!' was all she was able to say for some time. When she regained some measure of self-control she was able to tell her husband that there was no one else in the mining village. There were signs that the hut behind the store had been occupied until very recently and that the occupants had left in a great hurry, but apart from themselves there was neither human nor animal left alive in Sesebe.

'Take the wagon out of sight beyond the end house,' said Sam Speke. 'There's something I must do before I leave.'

'Are you going to bury Hannah here?'

'No. The decision on that belongs to her father. Just take the wagon out of sight and I'll be with you in a few minutes.'

When his self-appointed task was complete, Sam Speke rejoined his wife and daughter and wheeling the oxen back on to the track he pointed them towards Otjimkandje.

Twenty minutes out of Sesebe he met up with the last person he wanted to see. Daniel was cantering his horse towards the mining 'ghost' town and he was in a happy and talkative mood.

'Sam! Mary! It's good to see you again – and Victoria! You look a different girl.' He leaned forward from the saddle and gave her a kiss. 'It's wonderful to see you looking well again.'

Before Sam Speke could interrupt his chatter he said, 'You arrived a day too late, Sam. You missed a great battle. Jonker and his Afrikaners attacked Otjimkandje last night, but somehow Mutjise had got hold of a whole lot of guns. Our Herero gave the Afrikaners the hiding of their lives. They taught them a lesson they'll never forget. I'm on my way to tell Hannah about it now. Did you see her? She'll be—'

'Daniel!' Sam Speke could not allow him to chatter on any longer. 'Listen to me.'

For the first time Daniel saw the strained expressions on the faces of the others.

'Daniel, we've just come from Sesebe. Something happened there last night, too.'

'To Hannah?'

'Yes . . . to Hannah. She's dead, Daniel.'

'Dead?' Daniel was so stunned he was unable to accept what Sam Speke had said to him. 'Dead? But . . . how, Sam? Not Jonker? I'll kill him . . . I swear I'll kill him.'

'It wasn't Jonker. Here, Daniel. Get down off that horse and we'll take a walk.'

In a daze, Daniel swung down off his horse and walked beside Sam Speke, away from the wagon. Sam told him what he had found, leaving out as many of the details as he could.

'I left Hannah lying on the bed. I didn't know what Aaron would want to be done.'

'Aaron's not in Otjimkandje. He's two days' ride away at the new copper mine with Pa.'

'Then I'll send a wagon back to bring her to Otjimkandje. We'll bury Hannah near Hugo's church.'

'Where's Albrecht's body?' Daniel asked fiercely.

'I pitched it into the copper workings. I didn't want to have anything to do with a burial for him.'

Daniel nodded his agreement, still numb with shock at the news of Hannah's death. 'You go on to Otjimkandje, Sam. Tell Ma what's happened and ask Mutjise to send a rider for Aaron, then get a wagon back to Sesebe.'

'Where will you be?'

'I'm going on to Sesebe.'

Sam Speke put a hand on his arm. 'Don't, Daniel. Nothing you do will bring her back to life. Remember her as she was, not as she is now.'

'I'll always remember her as she was, Sam. But I've got to go to her. We were to be married this year, and as Aaron's not here it's up to me to be with her until she's taken to Hugo's church.'

Sam Speke let his hand drop away. 'It doesn't make a deal of sense to me, Daniel – but I doubt if I'd feel any different if she was mine. Go and do what you need to. I'll have a wagon back as quickly as I can.'

Kasupi led forty mounted Herero warriors to Sesebe to escort his friend and the body of Hannah back to Otjimkandje. On the way they found the body of the messenger sent to warn the villagers. His body was placed on the wagon alongside Hannah.

Hannah was buried in the mission churchyard three days later. Aaron, upon his arrival, had declared he would rather she be laid to rest in a place where she was among friends than adhere to the rites of a religion he had long since given up practising.

As the coffin made by Sam Speke was lowered into the ground the Jewish trader stood a lonely figure at the graveside. In the absence of Hugo Walder, Josh said a few prayers, and the brief service was attended by Mutjise, Kasupi and many of the villagers who had been looking forward to attending the wedding feast of Daniel and Hannah later in the year.

Daniel, too, stood alone, isolated by his grief. Of all those at the graveside only Miriam knew how deeply Hannah's death had affected him. He would never speak of it to anyone, but the deep sense of loss was something that would return to haunt many lonely camp-fires.

Josh would not allow Aaron to return to Sesebe and be alone there with memories of Hannah. He insisted that the trader remain at Otjimkandje.

Later that evening Sam Speke came to the Retallick house and the talk turned to what the future now held for all of them.

Aaron was the first to state his views and he spoke in a flat voice full of despair, far removed from his usual extravert self.

'For me, I am ready to give up. Everything I did was for Hannah. Now she is gone, so what is there to work for – me?' He shrugged. 'I could open a shop in Cape Town and make a living in comfort.'

'Don't make any decision yet, Aaron,' said Josh. 'This has hit you hard, and we all grieve with you, but you're needed in this country. We need you – every one of us. If you give up now, progress will be set back thirty years.'

'Progress?' Aaron was bitter. 'You can call it progress when the tribes use my guns to raid and kill each other? When a white man attacks a girl in her own home and causes her to take her life?' His voice broke as he cried, 'My God! If that is progress, it is better we leave this country alone and take our progress back with us.'

Aaron broke down and wept, and there was nothing anyone could do to comfort him.

The long uncomfortable silence that followed was ended by Josh.

'The tribes were fighting long before we got here, Aaron. Jonker brought his first guns up to this country with him from the south to terrorise all the other tribes. What you've done is to give Mutjise's people a chance to fight back and end Jonker's reign of terror. Neither is there anything that can be done about the Jacobus Albrechts of this world. If anyone is to blame for allowing him to roam free, it's me. I should have killed him after he gave Daniel such a beating. Fortunately there are few men like him, but they are to be found wherever there are men and women.'

'I know! I know!' Aaron spoke in an emotion-choked voice. 'Tell it to me next month – or next week – and I might understand. But not today. Not today.'

'Come back to the copper mine with me for a while,' said Josh. 'Help me to build a few huts and get people working there. We'll be able to make it a full-time operation now. I doubt if Jonker will try to stop it after his defeat.'

'Do you intend staying there?' asked Sam Speke.

'For a while. We don't know how the Cape government will react to this battle between the Afrikaners and the Herero. They might decide to send troops up here and find out what it's all about. I'd rather not be here if they do come.'

Sam Speke snorted. 'There's little fear of that. Half of them in the Cape don't even know of Whalefish Bay! Otjimkandje could be on the moon for all they know – or care.'

'All the same, I think I'll go to the new mine for a while,' said Josh. 'Miriam and I have already talked it over.'

'But what about this confession made by Jonker's preacher? Hugo was very excited about it when he told me. You shouldn't have to hide anymore.'

'I wish I had as much faith in it as Hugo. Whatever William Thackeray wrote doesn't alter the fact that I'm a convicted felon. If I stay out of the way, I can be sure there'll be no trouble for me. I prefer it to be that way.'

'How about you, Daniel?' asked Miriam. Her son's withdrawn unhappiness worried her. 'You haven't said anything yet. Do you have any plans?'

'Yes. I'd like to get away from Otjimkandje.'

There were too many things around the Herero village to remind him at this time of Hannah. He wanted to forget everything about her until he could remember her as she had been and not as a corpse with the side of her head blown away. Sam

Speke had been right; Daniel should not have gone to the store.

'Do you have any idea where you want to go?' asked Josh.

Daniel looked at Hannah's father and recognised that the bearded Jew's sorrow was as deep as his own and his heart went out to him.

'That depends upon Aaron. If he decides to carry on trading, I'll move up to Lake Ngami and stay there for a while – perhaps build a permanent trading store among the Bechuana and encourage them to make use of it.'

Everyone in the room looked to the Jewish trader, who said nothing for some moments. Then he shrugged his shoulders. 'All right. For Hannah's sake I'll carry on as Daniel's partner – but only if Sam comes in with us and takes full charge of the store at Sesebe. I don't want to have to return there for a long time.'

'That will suit me fine,' said Sam Speke. 'The mining has stopped, so there's nothing to make Victoria ill again. All the stuff for wagon-making is there, and you'll be needing plenty of transport if you're going to trade between Whalefish Bay and Lake Ngami. The new mine will keep me pretty busy, too, I expect.'

'There are all of Andrews' old wagons to work on,' said Josh. 'When you were away there was no one here able to do a repair job that would last. We'll need wagons fairly soon to carry timbers to the mine to build new huts. As Miriam and I will be spending a lot of time there I'd like to build something substantial for us.'

'Doesn't this copper mine have a name?' asked Sam Speke.

'The Herero say there used to be many rhino there,' said Daniel. 'They called it "the place of the rhino", or "Ongava".'

'That's a good name for a mine,' said Josh. 'May the Ongava mine prosper in a peaceful land.'

And so the decisions were made. Hannah was dead and nothing would ever be quite the same again, but they would go on. The Ongava mine would be worked and would make money, but not in a peaceful land. The life they had all known until now was over. Otjimkandje would no longer be the hub of their very existence and the last bastion of the Herero.

The news of Jonker's first defeat travelled fast. Soon those Hereros who had fled far to the north to escape his tyrannical rule began to flock back to their homeland.

At the same time other Europeans were already beginning their exploratory treks to the unknown corners of the land that was soon to be known as South-West Africa.

CHAPTER FIFTEEN

Daniel threw himself wholeheartedly into the task of establishing a trading post at Lake Ngami. He arrived there at the end of 1861, taking with him all the store goods from Sesebe in five wagons driven by Herero wagoners.

Aaron had gone in the opposite direction. Mutjise had paid him in full for the guns he had bought, and the trader was supervising the cattle drive to Whalefish Bay.

Daniel found it a long gruelling haul to Lake Ngami and he established two smaller posts between the two main points of trade. Here he would keep small supplies of goods for local tribesmen and food for his wagoners. He did not think it was good policy to let the small local tribesmen see wagonloads of goods passing through their territory without allowing them a share of the trade. Daniel knew that if he wanted to maintain regular trade he needed friends. The harsh country and long distances involved were enemies enough.

The Bechuana chief at Lake Ngami was happy to have Daniel build a trading post at his village, but he would not allow the Herero to work there. Relations between the two tribes had recently been strained by a pair of unscrupulous Portuguese traders working southwards from Angola. They had brought with them a large party of northern Herero and camped near a Bechuana village not far away. Trading was good and the Portuguese could have seen a handsome profit by honest dealing, but that was not enough for them. At the end of the day the Herero turned on their Bechuana hosts, murdered the men and departed with all the trade goods and the Bechuana women.

'It is not that I expect your Herero to do the same,' explained the Bechuana chief. 'But the deed weighs heavily upon my people. Trouble is easier to prevent than to stop.'

Tolotebe, the Bechuana chief, spoke perfect English and was a well-educated man. His father had held a disputed chieftainship and in order to safeguard his son's life and ensure his succession had sent him as a four-year-old child many weeks' journey to the south, to the mission station at Kuruman. There he had lived with the Moffat family and learned the language and high principles of the exceptional Scots missionary.

Tolotebe had gained something more. By a strange quirk of circumstance the missionary had formed a warm and enduring friendship with one of the bloodiest and most powerful chiefs in the whole of the African continent – Mzilikazi, chief of the warlike Matabele Zulus.

Breaking away from the main Zulu nation, Mzilikazi had fought his way northwards to settle his people on the far side of the Limpopo River, close enough for his foraging warriors to have caused trouble to the Bechuana, despite the wide desert that separated them.

Thanks to Tolotebe's association with Moffat, the fighting impis of Mzilikazi's army did not sweep through his country like hungry locusts. Instead, peaceful emissaries passed between the two tribal chiefs and trade links were established.

Daniel learned of this trade one day when he saw a group of unfamiliar natives in the Bechuana village. Tall, well-built and very black they were almost naked but carried themselves with such an air of dignity that it fell hardly short of arrogance. Each of the men was armed with a spear such as Daniel had never before seen. It was not the throwing spear of the Herero or the Bechuana, but a short broad-bladed assegai designed for close combat.

When he asked one of the men working on the store who they were he was told they were men of the mighty Matabele.

That night Daniel met two of their leaders across the fire outside Tolotebe's hut. He had been invited to discuss trade with them. The men wanted to know what items would bring most profit to the Matabele and to tell Daniel what they expected to receive in return.

'It is a far journey to our lands,' said one. 'It is better that only the things that will bring much in return are carried.'

'Then I'd say you'd do well to bring ostrich feathers,' said Daniel. 'I would prefer ivory, but for the amount your men could carry over a long distance feathers would be easier.'

'We will bring both,' promised the spokesman.

'Why not let me come to you?' asked Daniel. 'Two of my

wagons can carry as much as fifty men.'

'No.' The Matabele's tone signified that this was not a matter open to discussion. 'Mzilikazi wants none of the white man's wagons to come among his people. He says they do not bring more prosperity – only more trouble.'

'Then take me to him and let him hear my words. I might be able to make him change his mind.'

'Mzilikazi's mind is his alone. Only Mzilikazi can change it.' The Matabele stood up, and his companion rose with him. 'Tolotebe will tell you of the goods we need. You will bring them here and we will have elephant tusks and ostrich feathers for you.'

'I seem to have offended them,' said Daniel as the two men walked away from the fire. 'I'm sorry. I didn't mean to.'

'Only young men are so easily offended,' smiled Tolotebe. 'Had you offended the Matabele they would not trade with you. They were merely telling you to choose your words more carefully, that was all.'

Daniel grinned in return. 'Thank you, Tolotebe. I stand corrected. But I would very much like to meet Mzilikazi. Would some of your people guide me to him?'

'No.' Tolotebe's face lost its humour. 'Mzilikazi and I are friends, but it is not wise to presume on such a friendship. There can be no help for you from the Bechuana for such a journey.'

Although it seemed he could expect no help to be forthcoming from anyone, Daniel had been impressed by the men he had seen and was determined to make the journey to the land of the Matabele.

With this aim in mind he took to hunting and exploring the land far to the east of Lake Ngami. He travelled at least a hundred miles and was shown the few water-holes known to the Bechuana hunters accompanying him. Then he pushed still farther into the burning desert that the Bechuanas called the 'land of the little people'. Bushman country.

It became increasingly apparent that, in order to reach Matabeleland, Daniel would have to go northwards, skirting Lake Ngami before swinging westwards across the desert region. It would be a dangerous expedition, especially as he would have to rely upon his own resources and scant knowledge of the Kalahari desert region.

The solution to this problem arrived in a dramatic manner in mid-1862. Daniel and his party of half a dozen Bechuanas had killed a zebra in broken bush country on the edge of the desert, and two of the hunters were skinning the animal, when another of the tribesmen came to him.

'There is a little man out there.' He extended an arm that vaguely took in the whole landscape of sand and coarse brown grass. 'He wishes to speak to you.'

'A Bushman wants to talk to me?'

'Those were his words.'

'Why didn't you bring him here to me?'

'He would not come and he says he will speak only to you.'

'All right. Cut me off a fore-quarter of the zebra to take with me. I expect he wants food.'

Daniel mounted his horse, and one of the Bechuanas slung the large joint of meat up in front of him.

'Now, where did you see this Bushman?'

The direction was as vague as before. 'You go that way. You will find him.'

Daniel moved off slowly, balancing the meat on the saddle before him.

He covered two hundred yards before a thin figure rose from the ground before him. Daniel reined in his horse and spoke in the Bushman language. 'Your message was given to me. I have come and I have brought food.'

'You have had good hunting. Xhube's people have fed from your hand before today.'

Daniel looked more closely at the Bushman. 'I remember. It was almost four years ago in Hereroland.'

'It was the land of my people long before the Herero came,' corrected the Bushman. 'And I have not come for food, though it is very welcome. I have some of your people. They are very sick.'

'My people?' Daniel was surprised. He knew of no Europeans in this part of the country.

'Three of them. They came from that way.' He pointed to the north. 'We watched them for two days. They walked first to the 'sun and then away from it. They do not know where they are.'

'Are all three of them sick?'

'Yes. One of the children and the man are very bad.'

'*One* of the children? You mean you found two children and a man wandering out here?'

'Yes.'

'Then you'd better take me to them quickly.'

The Bushman turned and trotted away, and Daniel rode slowly after him. The Bushman's camp was a mile distant, hidden in a small depression where water seeped into a sandy hole dug three feet in the ground.

The Europeans were all under one small grass shelter, and Daniel was appalled at their condition. The man's clothes were ragged and torn, and he wore no shoes. The children turned out to be two girls who could have been no more than four and six years of age. The younger had shoes, but the older girl was in as desperate a state as the man. The hair of both children was bleached to a washed-out gold colour by the sun, and their skin was burned brown.

Two of the little Bushmen took the meat from Daniel with difficulty as his horse shied away from the smell of the rancid fat with which the Bushmen had rubbed their bodies.

As Daniel hooked his reins over a low bush and kneeled on the ground beside the ragged trio the youngest girl struggled to a sitting position, ignoring Daniel's order to 'lie still'.

'I want a drink.'

Daniel's water-bottle was looped on the pommel of his saddle and he called to Xhube to fetch it for him.

He held the bottle to the girl's mouth, and she drank noisily and much too fast, choking herself. Daniel had to pummel her back to check her coughing, and then she lay on the ground exhausted. The sound had brought movement from the man, who now began to thresh about on the ground, mumbling unintelligibly. Daniel tried to quieten him and force water between his parched lips, but the man would not take it and continued to mumble incoherently about someone he called 'Isabella'.

Daniel wiped off the perspiration that soaked the delirious white man before turning to the conscious white girl again.

'Is your name Isabella?'

'No, I'm Anne. Auntie Isabella's dead. Mummy's dead.' She prodded the other little girl. 'Nell's asleep.'

Nell was so still that Daniel was afraid she might be dead. He checked her pulse and was relieved to find her still alive, though her breathing was feeble and shallow.

'Xhube?' he called to the Bushman. 'Get one of your women to cut up some of the meat into small pieces and boil it. I want to get some food inside these people. They need nourishment.'

The ribs of the sick man protruding from beneath his unhealthy skin confirmed Daniel's words.

While he waited for the meat to be prepared, Daniel sat the man up in the crook of his arm and managed to get him to swallow a couple of sips of water. Then Daniel did the same for the elder girl, though it was with a great deal more difficulty. A few minutes later a Bushman woman came along with an evil-smelling poultice which she laid on the foreheads of the man and the girl named Nell.

'That will help to take away the fever,' explained Xhube.

Daniel had heard too much of the legendary medical skills of the Bushmen to cast doubt on the statement.

When the meat had been boiled to the point of disintegration Daniel fed the three patients with some of the hot meat-juice. The younger girl insisted she was able to eat by herself, and after she had swallowed enough to satisfy a grown man Daniel took the rest away from her.

'She, too, was very sick when we found her,' said Xhube. 'But the man was carrying her and she had more strength than the others.'

He pointed to the other girl. 'This one is still very sick. She will be lucky if she ever leaves the desert.'

'Well, we won't give up yet.'

When the three wanderers had been fed Daniel rode back to the Bechuanas and sent two of them off to Lake Ngami with instructions to bring out a wagon to meet him. Until then he would move the man on a litter. The girls could be carried in the arms of the Bechuana hunters.

Daniel spent the night at the Bushman camp, feeding the man and Nell once more before night fell. He fancied that the man was not quite so feverish during the night, and little Anne slept

327

soundly now her belly was full, but there was little change in the condition of Nell.

Then, in the cool of the dawn, Daniel felt the brow of the man and knew the fever had left him. As Daniel took his hand away the sick man's eyes flickered open and he looked up at Daniel, his initial shock giving way to disbelief.

'It's all right,' Daniel reassured him. 'You're safe now. There's nothing to worry about.'

The man's eyes suddenly opened. 'The others? Where are they?'

'Don't worry about anything. Nell and Anne are right here beside you. They're both sleeping.'

'Nell? Anne?' There was puzzlement on his face for a few moments, and then all the animation drained away and he closed his eyes as though in great pain. 'Yes, Nell and Anne. We are all that are left. Just the three of us.'

'There were more? How many? Where are they now?'

The man opened his eyes again, and the pain in them made Daniel wince.

'There were eleven of us. Eleven. Three men and our families taking the word of the Lord to the natives. My wife and our baby – and the others.' He closed his eyes, but tears forced their way from the wrinkled corners of them. 'Now they're dead. All of them. Isabella, Mary – every one of them.' He opened his eyes and looked past Daniel.

'The natives didn't want us. Their chief said so. We trekked all the way to the Zambezi River to bring them the Word, and they didn't want us. They made us leave. The babies were dying, but they wouldn't listen. They made us leave.'

'Sh! Try to rest now.'

Mention of the Zambezi River had startled Daniel. It was a great river about two hundred and fifty miles to the north-west. Daniel had never before met anyone who had seen it. He tried to quieten the sick man; but he rambled on as the fever returned, and the disjointed wanderings of his mind told a terrible story of suffering and death.

'The wagon's gone, Isabella. We can't get it back. The river's too deep. . . . Cover the baby's face; the flies are here again. Clouds of them. They're trying to eat us. . . . No, Isabella, you must put the baby down. God's taken her for His own. God's taken her. He's taken Lizzie and Roger. . . . He's taking us all. He doesn't want us to be here. He doesn't want these people for his own. . . .'

His voice trailed away, and Daniel stood up, shaken. His own sorrow was as nothing when compared with what this man had suffered. He thought the sick man slept until he saw another tear trickle from between the closed eyelids and course down his face.

Daniel turned away to leave the man to his terrible delirious ramblings when, without opening his eyes, the man asked, 'What's your name?'

'Retallick. Daniel Retallick.'

'Thank you for your kindness, Daniel. I am Charles Deacon. The children are Nell and Anne Gilmore. Where are we?'

'You are in the northern Kalahari. Tomorrow we'll be setting off for Lake Ngami. I have a trading store in a Bechuana village there.'

'Bechuana?' Charles Deacon's face came alive again. 'Then I was nearly to Kuruman. I had nearly made it.'

Kuruman was Robert Moffat's mission station more than five hundred miles to the south, but Daniel did not spoil Charles Deacon's brief moment of joy at his supposed achievement.

'Get word to Kuruman. Tell them what happened. They should be told Nell and Anne are safe.'

'Do the girls have anyone there?'

'No, not now. Mother, father, brother . . . they all died at the Zambezi.'

Daniel looked across to the two sleeping orphans, then back to the haggard man who had fled with them from so much tragedy.

'You must sleep now. We'll soon have you back at Kuruman.'

'Thank you. It has been a very long nightmare.'

When Daniel next checked Charles Deacon slept as soundly as the two girls he had brought from the far Zambezi River.

Daniel decided to let the man sleep as long as he was able, and later that morning he sat and talked with the Bushman leader, Xhube.

'What would you have done with these people had I not

arrived here?' he asked.

'I knew you were coming,' he said in a matter-of-fact voice.

'You knew? How could you?'

The Bushman grinned. 'I knew,' he repeated.

It would be useless to question him further. Daniel never doubted that the little Bushman was telling the truth. He was equally sure that Xhube could not have explained it had he wanted to. He knew, that was all.

'You have come a long way to hunt when there is much game to be found near Ngami.' Xhube called the lake by the Bushman name meaning 'Bitter Water'.

Daniel smiled at the Bushman's shrewd observation.

'You are right. I seek more than animals to hunt.'

Xhube waited politely for Daniel to explain.

'I wish to know the country well so I may journey safely to the land of Mzilikazi and the Matabele.'

'You hunt with the Bechuana. They know the way. Why not ask them to take you?'

'I have. They fear Mzilikazi too much. They say he will not be pleased if they take a white man to him.'

'They do well to fear him,' said Xhube. 'But the way is not hard – for a Bushman.'

'You know the way to the land of the Matabele?'

Xhube nodded.

'Then, will you guide me? If I can get to Mzilikazi and persuade him to allow me to trade direct with him, I promise you your family will never be short of food again. I will leave small stores for you along the way.'

Xhube looked into his face to see if he spoke the truth. He was satisfied with what he saw there.

'Yes, I will guide you across our lands to where there is running water. But you must find Mzilikazi yourself. He is not a friend of my people.'

'I could not ask for more.'

Daniel was elated. After all his efforts of the last months the way was now clear for him to travel to Matabeleland. He dismissed the thought that it might prove dangerous. Reports of the ways of great chiefs were always exaggerated to legendary proportions.

'When do you wish to go?' asked Xhube.

'As soon as I have taken the man and the children to Lake Ngami and they are fit to continue their journey.'

. 'When you are ready return to this place,' said the Bushman. 'If we are not here, wait. We will come for you. But it is better that we leave before the rains begin.'

The Bushmen were relieved to see the sick white people leave. They had feared they might die in their camp. Such an event would have forced them to leave for ever one of their most important water-holes. It was part of their tradition that no one might stay in a place of death. It said much for them that they had even risked it happening and not left the sick trio to die in the hot sand of the Kalahari.

On the second morning after Daniel had left the Bushmen the older girl's fever broke and she stared wide-eyed at Daniel and his Bechuana companions. So frightened was she of the Bechuanas in particular that Daniel took her on his horse with him.

Her young sister was far less concerned and she chattered ceaselessly to everyone. The hunters from the Lake Ngami village vied with each other for the pleasure of carrying her.

Charles Deacon's condition was not so satisfactory. His fever had returned and he threw himself about with such force that Daniel was unable to feed him and had to tie him to the rough litter the Bechuanas had made for him.

By the third day Daniel was really concerned about the sick missionary. He was delirious for most of the time and his condition slowed down their progress. Daniel applied poultices of herbs given to him by the Bushman women, but they had little effect. Not until the sun was sinking over the horizon that day did the sick man become rational, but he was so weak that he could hardly swallow the water that Daniel held up to his mouth.

It was now that Daniel had to make a difficult decision. He could either stay out here in the killing heat in the hope that Charles Deacon might improve with rest after a few days, or he must move forward as fast as he could to try to reach more hospitable country in time to save the man's life.

Daniel decided to go on. The two girls influenced this decision. They were still so weak that the heat exhausted them very quickly. If either of them developed a fever again, he doubted whether they would have the strength to overcome it.

He explained his decision to Charles Deacon in the darkness. The sick missionary accepted it in the same stoic manner he had shown throughout the whole of his brief and terrible experience of Africa.

'I put my earthly body in your hands, Daniel. My spiritual being I gave to God long ago. I can't hope to understand why I have been chosen to undergo the trials of the last weeks. Perhaps if I live I may one day know it was not in vain. If I die, I shall join those I loved above all others on this earth.'

His words made it easier for Daniel when Charles Deacon joined his loved ones at dawn the following day after an all-night march. He was buried in a shallow unmarked grave of sand, the exact spot forgotten by all except the warm Kalahari wind, never knowing that the news of the appalling losses suffered by his party would be carried in the mission and church magazines of the world. The sacrifices of Charles Deacon, his family and friends inspired many others to lift their own missionary efforts to new heights.

Later that day they were met by a wagon from Lake Ngami being driven by Aaron with Josh acting as an outrider and a dozen Bechuanas providing an escort. One of them was the warrior who had jogged a hundred miles through heat and foot-burning sand to bring help.

'Some trade goods arrived at Whalefish Bay when we were both there,' said Josh, explaining their presence. 'Aaron and I decided to come up here to see how you were getting on.'

He looked at Nell, whom he had taken from Daniel's arms. 'I didn't expect you to be trading for pretty little girls. But we were told there was a man with them.'

'There was — and a very brave man,' replied Daniel. 'He lost his own family yet managed to bring these two back to safety all the way from the Zambezi River. He died at sun-up this morning.'

'It was a miracle you found them,' commented Aaron, looking out over the vast wastes of the northern Kalahari.

'I didn't find them,' explained Daniel. 'They have to thank a little Bushman for that.'

'So even the Bushmen are different here. Elsewhere they run and hide from strangers.'

'The leader of this group is rather special. I met him first about four years ago when I was out hunting with Kasupi. He and his people came originally from the coast. I gave him meat, and he has a good memory. He's an honest and intelligent little man.'

'I'm not arguing with you,' said Josh. 'You should know better than to think you have to justify your friendship with a Bushman to me. I've always thought it sad that they should be such a persecuted people.'

'I'm sorry,' said Daniel. 'I've got so used to defending myself whenever I talk about Bushmen it's become a habit. This one is going to guide me as far as Matabeleland as soon as I've seen Nell and Anne safely on their way.'

'On their way to where?' asked Aaron, looking at the two little girls, who were waiting for beds to be made up for them in the wagon. 'I think a week at Lake Ngami will build up their strength. But what shall we do with them then? Do they have any family in Africa?'

'I doubt it. Charles Deacon told me their parents and brother died with the others at the Zambezi River. But he said they were known at the Kuruman Mission.'

'What sort of a party was this, for God's sake?' Josh asked. 'They obviously knew nothing about looking after themselves. What were they doing going that far north in the first place?'

'You've already answered that,' replied Daniel. 'They were at the Zambezi River "for God's sake". They were missionaries with their families. Eleven of them set off. Nell and Anne are the only survivors.'

'Well, now Hugo is back I'll ask him to write to the Cape and call for a full enquiry into such a foolhardy trek. In the meantime these two mites can stay with your mother and me at Ongava.' Josh smiled. 'I can imagine the look on her face when I return with two little girls. That reminds me. I'm to tell you it's time you paid a visit home.'

'I will – after I've been to see Mzilikazi. But you said Hugo had returned. What happened about Thackeray's confession? Are you a free man again?'

Josh dropped his glance to the ground. He did not want Daniel to see his eyes. 'Yes, I'm a free man – just as long as I stay in this land.'

'You mean you've been refused a pardon?'

'No, not in so many words. Hugo says a pardon might take years to come through.' He grimaced helplessly. 'I think he's trying to let me down lightly. I believe he, too, realises it's hopeless.' Josh's manner suddenly became brisk. 'However, there are more important things to think about. Let's settle these children down in the wagons.'

There would be no more talk of a pardon. It had been a brief flare-up of hope, no more. Only Miriam would ever know the deep and bitter disappointment within Josh.

Once back at Lake Ngami, Daniel was kept busy with his preparations for the journey to Matabeleland. He was uncertain of his welcome there, so would not take a wagon. Instead he loaded a selection of the best trade goods on to two pack-oxen and chose a good horse for himself. When he was almost ready, Josh announced that he would travel with him as far as the Bushman meeting-place. Aaron would stay with the two children until his return. The bluff Jewish trader was finding their presence a painful mixture of stirred memories, both happy and sad. The happiness was in rediscovering the joy of having a curious and guileless child take his hand as they walked together. The sadness was remembering that Hannah had done the same thing many years before.

Josh and Daniel had a pleasant trek to the meeting-place. Trek-oxen cannot be hurried, and the slow journey together gave Josh time to learn more about his son now he was a man. He missed him, as did Miriam. Their permanent home was now at Ongava, but Miriam was not as happy there as she had been in Otjimkandje.

Yet things had changed in the Herero village too. When they had lived in fear of the Afrikaners the Herero looked to the Europeans as more than friends. They were all that stood between themselves and a powerful enemy. Now the Herero had beaten the Afrikaners and found a new pride, a proud independence. They relied upon no one but themselves.

Although nothing in their relationship had changed outwardly, Miriam felt that they—and Hugo Walder—were not welcome in Otjimkandje but were tolerated because of past links with the tribe.

Hugo agreed with her and said their presence was a reminder of the days when the Herero were a subservient people. It was not a comfortable memory for Mutjise's people to live with. The missionary hoped the attitude of the Herero would change as they became more used to their new status.

Josh doubted whether there could be such a simple solution. Mutjise was an ambitious chief who had been effective ruler of the Herero for years before his father's death and he was impatient with the old ways of his people. Now he was their official chief and had won for them a great victory in battle. Other Herero were returning to their homeland, and Mutjise wanted to be paramount chief of all the Herero. Some of the others would not be happy with his ambitions. There would be more fighting, but Josh believed Mutjise would win in the end.

The Otjimkandje chief was also fortunate in having a brilliant general in his younger brother, Kasupi. Once the Herero had been united Josh believed Mutjise would use his brother's qualities to extend his influence still farther. He would not be satisfied until he dominated all the neighbouring tribes—including Jonker's Afrikaners. It made the future uncertain for everyone in the country.

But for the moment it lay in the future, and Josh and Daniel plodded their slow way across the Kalahari.

The Bushmen were not at the meeting-place, but there was water and good hunting nearby and they passed two days pleasantly until Xhube and his people arrived.

Josh picked out the family leader immediately, although there were many more lines on the Bushman's face now.

Daniel began to introduce Josh to the Bushmen, but Xhube stopped him.

'We have met before, your father and my people. It was many, many years ago. When you were no older than my grandchild there.'

Xhube pointed to a shy pot-bellied child who peered at them

335

from behind the legs of its mother.

'It was a meeting that brought you much sorrow,' said Josh. 'I do not look back with pride on what happened then.'

For the first time Daniel realised that this was the same Bushman who had helped his parents and Sam after the shipwreck. It had happened so far from here that he had never associated the incident with these Bushmen of the Kalahari.

'There have been greater and lesser sorrows in the years since then,' said Xhube, the pain of his persecuted people in his eyes. 'The thing that happened then was not of your making. We were friends, you and I.'

'I owe you much,' said Josh with great feeling. 'Had it not been for you we might have turned back to the coast and I doubt if we would have survived to be here today.'

'The seasons have gone well with you,' declared Xhube. 'Is it the same with your woman and the other white man?' His expressive hands moulded a shape in the air that immediately told Daniel the Bushman was enquiring after Sam Speke.

'They are well. And your people?'

'There are few of us left' — Josh could see less than a third of the original number Xhube had once led — 'but we live. We have travelled far, and the good things have not always stayed with us. Now we have this land.'

Xhube indicated the semi-desert land about them. 'This is good land for us. No one else wants it. Cattle will not live here, and there are not so many animals that others wish to come here to hunt. Yet there is enough to keep us alive. We have water — and some seasons the rains come.' The little Bushman smiled. 'Who could ask for more from life?'

'Perhaps I can bring you and your people a few good years,' said Daniel. 'With regular supplies of food from my trading wagons your tribe will grow strong once more.'

'I hear what you say and am happy,' replied Xhube. 'Because it is said in friendship it is as welcome as the rain, but white men have come into our lands before and they have moved on. The tall tribes have been here, too. They fought with each other, then they also went away. One day you will go from here. Only the Bushman and the desert stay. All around us there is much change. We are told of this by Bushmen who have heard it from brothers. While there is nothing here for other people to want my family will survive. Our needs are few.'

Daniel thought it was little enough to ask from life, but what the Bushmen received would probably be even less. Men like Jacobus Albrecht were trekking steadily northwards, not passing through but looking for places to settle. They would find the scales of survival finely balanced. The Bushman needed little to keep him alive. That 'little' might be the difference between life and death to a settler – or so he would probably claim. Until the little Bushman was accepted as something more than an animal he had no chance of being allowed to live his simple life.

The men talked until well into the night. Josh and Daniel had brought food, but it was a quieter, wearier camp than the ones Josh remembered from years before. There was no dancing and no singing. For all Xhube's expressed confidence in the future Josh thought the Bushmen had lost their zest for life, had accepted the inevitability of their fate.

Daniel and the Bushmen set off soon after first light the next morning.

'Take care of my son, Xhube,' said Josh. 'You will find him a good hunter, but to his mother he is still her only child.'

'He will be as my own son,' replied the Bushman, touching hands with Josh.

Josh knew that Xhube's words meant he would lay down his own life for Daniel if necessary.

He watched them move off in single file and merge with the sun-flooded skyline. He hoped such a dramatic sacrifice would not be necessary, but the Matabele occupied lands that were far distant and remote. Mzilikazi was their absolute ruler, a chief of a type as yet unknown in this part of Africa.

CHAPTER SIXTEEN

Aaron remained at Lake Ngami to run the trading store in Daniel's absence, and Josh took the two young Gilmore girls to Miriam in Ongava.

It was a lively trip. Both girls had recovered from their long ordeal, and the curiosity of Anne in particular was insatiable. She wanted to know everything about what was going on around her and displayed a keen and searching intelligence.

Nell Gilmore was much quieter than her sister. The death of her parents had been more real for her than for the younger Anne. Both girls completely captured the heart of Josh by the end of the trip, and they were no less successful with Miriam.

'What will we do with them, Josh?' asked Miriam when the two girls had been tucked up in the room they had built for Daniel, a room that had not previously been used.

'We'll have to send word to the mission at Kuruman, telling them we have the girls here.'

'And then . . . ?'

Josh knew what Miriam wanted him to say, but he avoided committing himself for as long as possible.

'We'll have to be guided by what they say at Kuruman.'

'Josh Retallick, you are the most exasperating man I have ever known! Your own son rescues two young girls miles out in a desert, their parents dead and no one in this world to care for them. Aren't you going to suggest we keep the girls with us? And if you say "No" I'll call you a liar. You've spent weeks with them on the way from Lake Ngami, and I've seen the way you look at them. They've been delivered into our hands, and we've love enough for both of them.'

Josh grinned. 'Does it matter whether I suggest it or not? Mind you, I don't know what Kuruman will think of the idea. We haven't a lot to offer two young girls out here.'

'You mean they would have had more on the Zambezi River? With everyone dying off like flies around them?' Miriam snorted indignantly. 'No, Josh. We won't *ask* whether we can keep them here with us. We'll *tell* them.'

Josh said no more. Hugo Walder could write to the missionary, Moffat, at Kuruman and suggest it would be better for the girls to remain with them in Hereroland. He hoped Moffat would agree with the arrangement. Nothing short of armed intervention would persuade Miriam to give up the two young girls now.

They took the two girls with them to Otjimkandje and found Hugo Walder with two younger men — one of them little more that Daniel's age. They were new missionaries, sent to replace the man who had spent so many years caring for the Herero people.

'My society has recalled me to Cape Town,' Hugo Walder said, making a determined effort to hide the sadness in his voice. 'I suppose I should feel flattered that they have sent two men to continue my work, but I will miss my little church and my people.'

He introduced the newcomers as Theodore Wohlfarth and Wilhelm Doelker, both German. Neither of the two new missionaries was fluent in English. Their society, for reasons best known to itself, had taught them only Dutch and basic Herero. This lack of communication made them appear to Miriam to be more shy and consequently younger than they probably were.

'They've arrived at an opportune time to learn the hazards of missionary work,' said Josh grimly. He lifted the two girls from the wagon. 'Meet Nell and Anne Gilmore. They are the only survivors of a missionary party of eleven who set off to the Zambezi River.'

The younger of the new missionaries looked closely at the two young girls, then spoke rapidly to Hugo Walder in German. Hugo Walder replied briefly, and Wilhelm Doelker nodded his head.

Hugo Walder turned back to Josh and Miriam. 'Wilhelm says he recognises these children. They arrived in Cape Town with their parents only eight months ago and immediately went up-country to Kuruman.'

'Then they must have headed north within weeks of their arrived there,' commented Josh. 'I hope your two young men heed the warning, Hugo. This land doesn't give a second chance to those who are not fully prepared for all its moods.'

'I have told them,' replied Hugo Walder. 'For their own sakes I hope they have listened.'

Josh brought up the subject of the girls remaining with him and Miriam, and the old missionary promised to write to Moffat.

The news of Hugo Walder's departure had taken much of the pleasure of the visit away for Miriam. When she climbed down from the wagon she stood on tiptoe and kissed the big bearded missionary, much to his delight and the surprise of his young colleagues.

'Oh, Hugo, what are we going to do without you? Can't you persuade your society to allow you to stay at Otjimkandje?'

'No, that would be self-indulgent. I go wherever I can best serve God. My society believes I am needed in Cape Town. Perhaps it is right.' He nodded towards the two children. 'At least if I am there I might be able to prevent another such tragedy as they have survived. I could ensure that all missionaries understood what to expect in a strange new land.'

'There is one last favour I would like from you before you go,' said Josh quietly.

'Of course, my friend. What is it?'

'Marry Miriam and me in your church here in Otjimkandje. I thought about it soon after William Thackeray died, but it didn't matter very much then. Now you are leaving I would like us to be married here where we have found so much happiness; and it should be by you who have been our greatest friend.'

Miriam slipped her hand in Josh's and squeezed it happily.

'It could be important, Hugo,' she said. 'We want to keep Nell and Anne with us and we could hardly ask you to recommend us to Kuruman knowing we were not married.'

'That would not have stopped me,' said Hugo Walder firmly. 'You are as married as any two people I have ever known. But I am glad you wish it to be recorded in the house of God. It will give me great pleasure.'

Josh and Miriam were married the next evening in the mission church of Otjimkandje, with only Sam Speke and Mary to witness the ceremony. There was nothing unusual in it for Mary. Among her people it was often not possible for a young man to raise the bridal price at the time when passion decreed he should live with the partner of his choice. It often happened that there were one or more children of the union before it became official. Besides, she and Sam had lived together before they were married.

Many miles from Otjimkandje, life was not progressing smoothly for Daniel. The unpredictable rainy season was due, and with the long hot year drawing to a close there was little water to be found in the vast spaces of the desert country. For this reason Xhube had taken Daniel far to the north, to where there was the muddy trickle of a river. Once they had located it they turned eastward for the land of the Matabele.

Unfortunately, the drawbacks of this route soon made themselves known. He and the Bushmen now had all the water they needed—but they were plagued by great swarms of mosquitoes and tsetse flies.

Daniel soon learned to button his shirt up to the neck and fasten his sleeves at the wrist, but there was no way of protecting his face and hands.

By the second day of travelling along the river-bank Daniel's face was an ugly mass of swollen stings, his eyelids puffy and throbbing, and the backs of his hands driving him mad with their constant itching.

Then disaster struck. Both oxen died within hours of each other and, apart from a few items he gave to the Bushmen and the little that his horse could carry, the trade goods, presents for Mzilikazi, had to be abandoned.

But worse was to follow. Daniel's horse had come in for its share of tsetse stings and it began to walk stiff-legged, its head hanging low, not bothering to shake off the flies that gathered in clusters about its eyes. Daniel walked the horse behind the Bushmen, stooping frequently to allow the dejected animal to drink from the river.

Towards sunset the condition of the horse had worsened. For the last hour it had staggered along on legs as elastic as those of a drunken man.

Daniel was so distressed by his horse's sickness that when it next paused for a drink at the water's edge he paid more attention to the animal than to his surroundings. He was within ten feet of an expanse of river-grass that rose tall and green, half-in, half-out of the water. Concealed by the grass, submerged except for the tip of its snout and two yellow-and-black pebble-sized eyes, was a fifteen-foot-long crocodile, its pale soft-leather belly pressed against the mud of the river-bed.

It was this mud that helped to deaden the advance of the ugly creature. It moved slowly forward with the exaggerated stealth of a chameleon, hard reptilian eyes never off its target. The crocodile covered the last few feet in a headlong rush of surging water, expelled air from the gross body erupting noisily from between long yellow-toothed jaws.

The horse was too ill and lethargic to move back from this violent headlong attack and with a sideways twist of its jaws the crocodile grasped the foreleg of the unfortunate horse and toppled it into the river on its side.

Daniel managed to grab his gun from the saddle holster, but before he could unhook the pouch containing powder and shot, the feebly struggling horse was dragged further out into the river.

The Bushmen came running back to the scene and noisily and enthusiastically jabbed at the huge crocodile with their ineffective spears. The powerful amphibian was goaded to a near-frenzy. Its heavy tail swung to one side and bowled over one of the more daring of the Bushmen. Fortunately for the little man Daniel saw him fall and was able to drag him half-conscious from the water before the sluggish current could carry him away.

Their efforts were all in vain. The crocodile had carried the horse to deeper water now, sheer weight dragging the sick horse down to its death.

'Get back! Get back! It has a mate.'

A sharp-eyed Bushman had seen the brief flurry of disturbed water as the eyes and nostrils of another crocodile momentarily broke surface some yards downstream.

Hurriedly everyone splashed their way out of the waters of the river, and within seconds there was nothing to show for the life-and-death struggle of the horse but the disconsolate group standing on the river-bank.

Looking at the faces of his companions, Daniel saw nothing but unhappiness and defeat. The Bushmen blamed themselves for the mishap. They had undertaken to guide him safely to Matabeleland and now they had allowed him to lose his most precious possession, his horse.

Daniel waited until Xhube looked at him and he managed to produce a weak smile for the Bushman leader.

'We are fortunate. It might be one of us at the bottom of the river now.' Daniel shuddered at the thought. 'Shall we move on away from the river? I don't fancy making camp here tonight.'

When the Bushmen saw that Daniel did not appear to be unduly upset about the accident they cheered up and followed him up the incline away from the river.

They made camp near the top of a low hill. Daniel had his gun but no powder or shot. Without them he felt dejected and vulnerable.

The next morning Daniel had more than powder and shot to worry about. He woke in a burning fever with his teeth chattering together and the feeling that he was floating upwards to meet the sun.

Daniel had malaria.

The Bushmen recognised the illness immediately but stood around helplessly, unsure what to do. They had left their women behind in the Kalahari, not wishing to risk them in a strange land, and it was the women who knew the things that had to be done when a man had bad fever.

They only knew they had to bring Daniel's temperature down. Their method was primitive but effective. Carrying Daniel down the slope closer to the river they scooped a shallow grave in the sandy soil and put him in it, covering his body with a thin layer of sand until only his head was showing above ground. Then for the remainder of the day they brought water from the river to keep the sand moist and his body cool.

Daniel came out of the fever for a brief while at dusk, and Xhube fed him with fish caught from the river and baked in mud in the heart of their fire.

'I'm a trouble to you, Xhube,' gasped Daniel when he had eaten as much as he could take. 'First my horse and now me.

You'll be sorry you offered to bring me on this journey.'

'Save your strength for eating,' said the Bushman leader. 'You have eaten a fish so small it would not satisfy a bigger fish.'

'Give me the bigger fish tomorrow, Xhube. I'll be better then.'

But Daniel was not better, and fever still had a tight grip on him. Xhube was worried. He had seen his own people die from just such a fever as this and he knew white men were not as strong as Bushmen.

His companions did nothing to ease his mind. They were not happy so close to the river. They feared the crocodiles and the spirits who possessed their ungainly bodies. Such spirits were not kindly disposed towards the little men from the great desert country. Xhube's men did not want to stay. They wanted to return to the Kalahari – without Daniel.

When they put it to Xhube he refused to consider it. 'No. We have said we would take him to the land of the Matabele. I have told his father his life is my life. I will not leave him.'

'But this is not a good place for us,' argued one of his warriors. 'He will die here and we may die with him.'

'That is true,' agreed Xhube. 'And so tomorrow we will go on.'

'But the way ahead is hard. The land of the Matabele is far.'

'All these things are true,' said Xhube. 'We will have to move fast and rest only a little. The white man is very sick, so he must be carried.'

He looked at each face in turn. 'We will carry him to the land of the Matabele.'

One after another the Bushmen dropped their eyes before their chief's look and Xhube knew he had won. He was still their leader and they would do as he told them.

Xhube drove his men to the edge of exhaustion – which meant they travelled twice as far each day as any other man would have deemed possible. Their stamina was truly incredible and during the few hours' sleep Xhube allowed them they lay on the ground like dead men. Apart from this brief daily rest they stopped only when Daniel had one of his infrequent lucid periods. Then the Bushman chief would ply him with as much food and water as he could force down his throat.

It was difficult to assess whether Daniel's condition was improving. One hour he would be in a raging fever, tossing his body around, his mind assailed by delirious fantasies, the next he would sleep peacefully, undisturbed by the jogging of the improvised stretcher being carried by the uncomplaining little men.

Then came a day when it became necessary to cross the meandering river. Once more Xhube's men expressed their fears to him. On the far side of the river was Matabele country. Not their hunting-grounds only, but also their kraals and grazing-lands. They were liable to encounter groups of warriors in training and patrolling impis. The Bushmen felt they had come far enough.

Xhube understood their fears and sympathised with them, but he had made a promise to Josh and he meant to keep his word.

'We will cross the river tomorrow,' he said. 'Then we will move as Bushmen. We will not be seen by the Matabele. When we sight one of their kraals we will take him' – he pointed to Daniel – 'and leave him outside a hut before dawn. They will find him and care for him. I will have kept my word and we will return to our land.'

He looked about him at the tired faces of his men and smiled. 'Do not fear, we will all see the desert again. This I know.'

After this there could be no further argument. Xhube was a man of visions. They came to a selected few of their people. They were not to be questioned or doubted. Like the sun, the wind and the origins of the world they defied all explanation. But, like the sun, the wind and the world, they were real.

Nevertheless, the faith of the little Bushmen underwent a severe test the next morning. They awoke with the sun to find themselves inside a circle of Matabele warriors. The big black men squatted silently and menacingly, the blades of their broad stabbing assegais glinting ominously red in the light of the early sun. As the Bushmen rose from their shallow scraped sleeping-holes the Matabele stood up, their glistening well-muscled bodies towering above the little desert people.

The leader of the Matabele impi pointed his spear at Daniel, who was in the throes of one of his delirious dreams.

345

'Who is this white man? Why have you brought him here, so far from your hunting-places?'

'He is a trader on his way to see the great chief Mzilikazi. He fell sick along the way. We are hurrying to get him to the kraal of your people.'

The tall Matabele warrior frowned. He was Muvandi, one of Mzilikazi's ablest and most trusted indunas or generals. He had been returning from an expedition undertaken to punish a wayward subjugated tribe when his path had crossed the tracks of the Bushmen. Sending the main body of his men home, he had followed the tracks to this place.

Only the presence of the white man had stopped him from slaughtering the Bushmen immediately. Now he was uncertain. His standing with the Matabele chief gave him the power of life or death over any other tribe, but he would not dare to risk offending Mzilikazi by killing a man who was on his way to see him.

'Is Mzilikazi expecting the white man?'

'Why else would he ask me to bring him to your land? Since he became sick we have travelled night and day. It would not be good if he died and the great chief Mzilikazi was unhappy because of it.'

Xhube was well aware of the original intentions of the Matabele induna. The Bushman's guile was the only shield he possessed against the assegais of the most powerful warrior nation Africa knew.

'Your unhappiness will be even greater if the white man is not expected,' said Muvandi menacingly. 'Mzilikazi does not like the shadow of a white man to fall on his lands. Come, we have a full day's journey to his kraal.'

Muvandi forced the pace almost as hard as Xhube, but it was the Matabele induna who called for the brief rest periods.

They passed several small villages along the way but had not come within sight of Mzilikazi's kraal by nightfall. With the onset of darkness they were forced to slow their pace, but Muvandi kept them moving.

Not until more than half the night had gone did Xhube smell the smoke that lingered from a thousand cooking-fires. It hung on the air like the night itself, covering the land. There was no

346

escape from it. When they travelled for another half an hour before reaching the first of the quiet bee-hive huts Xhube knew this must be a kraal such as none of his people had ever seen.

Muvandi and his men threaded their way between the huts until they entered the maze that was Mzilikazi's own inner kraal. Here the induna led them to an empty hut with a hard cattle-dung floor.

'Mzilikazi sleeps' he said. 'I will speak to him in the morning. I will send for one of our healers to attend the white man. Do not try to leave. I have warriors outside.'

The Matabele healer arrived within minutes, disgruntled at being called from his sleep and insulted at having to share a hut with a party of Bushmen who rubbed themselves with animal fat and never washed. The healer wrinkled his nose at their offensive odour, but he was here at Muvandi's command and knew better than to complain. Without attempting to hide his distaste he went about the business of doctoring Daniel.

After the jostling he had received on the long journey the rest did Daniel as much good as the ministrations of the reluctant healer. By morning his fever had subsided and he slept fitfully as incantations were said over him and a variety of medicaments applied to his aching body.

Xhube, on the other hand, was becoming increasingly nervous as time went by without anything happening. He wondered whether the Matabele chief was thinking up a new and particularly unpleasant fate for the Bushmen.

It was mid-morning before a commotion outside the hut brought the little hunters to their feet. Seconds afterwards the light coming in through the doorway was abruptly blocked by the huge figure of a man. Six feet four inches tall, he must have weighed at least two hundred and sixty pounds. Entwined in his tight black hair was the warrior ring of the Matabele fighting man, and a leopard skin flung over one shoulder proclaimed his royal status. Mzilikazi had come visiting.

The Matabele healer flung himself to the ground in abasement, and Xhube and his men hurriedly followed suit to pay homage to the absolute ruler of ten thousand people, conqueror of a vast land.

The huge chief ignored the grovelling of the men in the hut.

347

Closely followed by Muvandi he stooped over Daniel, who lay on his improvised stretcher.

'This man is nothing to me,' he boomed in a deep voice. 'Let those who brought him here be put to death.'

With this brief pronouncement Mzilikazi turned to leave.

'If someone is to be punished for my presence here, then let it be me, not the Bushmen.'

Daniel's voice was weak, but it was sufficient to halt the Matabele chief. He looked back at the sick white man.

'You would die in place of these who are as nothing?'

'Willingly. I owe them my life – as they once saved the lives of my father and mother. If someone must die, it should be me.'

'Why have you come to my kraal?'

'To seek trade. I have exchanged goods with your warriors at Lake Ngami. I liked what they brought. They were pleased with my trade goods.'

'There are many men, English, Boers and Portuguese, who would like to trade with Mzilikazi. I have refused them. Why, then, should I allow you to trade here?'

The effort of talking was draining the strength from Daniel at a time when he needed to use all the persuasive powers he possessed.

'Because I am an honest man' was all he could think of to say.

Mzilikazi looked at him for a long moment, then gave a deep-throated chuckle. 'Then you are not as other traders. We will speak more of this when you are well.

'You hear me?' he spoke sternly to the grovelling healer. 'You will make him well and bring him to me.'

To Muvandi he said, 'Send someone to take the little men across the river. They may return to their desert.'

Having given life to the Bushmen and threatened death to the healer, Mzilikazi, the all-powerful, took the daylight away from the hut once more – and was gone.

348

CHAPTER SEVENTEEN

Xhube left Mzilikazi's kraal that same morning, in the company of a small impi. The Matabele warriors were not pleased at being given the task of ensuring the safe conduct of the little men through their lands. Their duty was not made easier when they met another impi returning from a foray into the land of the Manyika tribe. They were forced to endure gibes of 'goatherders', and worse. The homeward-bound impi also made elaborate moves to get up-wind of the small party. The Matabele were a scrupulously clean people and the Bushmen's habits offended the nostrils of Mzilikazi's warriors.

Daniel was sorry to have his little friends leave him. They had saved his life as surely as he had secured their freedom. But he knew he was likely to see them again. They would be waiting for him on his return journey to Lake Ngami.

Mzilikazi's healer spared no effort to safeguard his own life by nursing his charge back to health. Even so, it was eleven days before Daniel was well enough to walk from the hut by himself. He wandered slowly about the kraal, an object of curiosity to the children. Warriors and women pretended not to notice him.

The village was as well ordered as Otjimkandje but on a vastly larger scale. Daniel was further impressed when his ever-attendant healer told him this was the kraal of only one of Mzilikazi's regiments. There were others of similar size dotted over the whole of Mzilikazi's land.

A few days later Mzilikazi sent for Daniel. The Matabele chief was holding court in a huge area in the centre of the village surrounded by members of his household. His armed personal bodyguard were in close proximity, standing between the chief and his people.

Mzilikazi sat on a throne of cow hides in the shade of a wide-branched tree, his leopard skin draped carelessly across one shoulder. Out here in the sunlight Daniel could see the grey hair of the warrior chief. Mzilikazi was an old man but he was still enormous and regally impressive.

349

As Daniel was led up to the chief he saw the way the indunas and headmen called before Mzilikazi behaved. They first saluted him with a cry of 'Bayete!' which meant 'Greetings, great one,' then fell on their knees at a respectful distance to state their case.

Sometimes Mzilikazi would make a brief reply. On other occasions he would dismiss a request with a peremptory movement of his hand.

All around the square were women and children, gathered to take advantage of an opportunity to gaze upon their great and feared chief.

Mzilikazi greeted Daniel with an affable wave and motioned him to a seat beside him in the shade.

'You are better, trader?' The chief's manner was friendly and courteous.

'Thank you, yes,' Daniel replied. 'I have been well looked after.'

'Good!' Mzilikazi nodded approvingly at the healer, who backed away with a feeling of huge relief, his knees weak beneath him.

'Have you ever seen a kraal the size of this one in the lands of the Bechuana?'

'No,' replied Daniel truthfully. 'Nor in the lands of the Herero, or the Afrikaner, or the Bergdama.'

Mzilikazi's eyebrows met across the bridge of his wide nose.

'You have travelled to many places and met many people. Could none of these tribes give you elephant teeth and the things you seek?'

'Yes, but there is fighting between the tribes in Hereroland. War is not good for trade.'

The big chief chuckled. 'You are the first man who has sought the Matabele to find peace, trader. But you have been living with the Bechuana. They are at war with no one.'

'No, and I have a store there still, but I wanted to come out and find new trade.'

'Yet you bring no present of trade goods with you?'

'I brought them,' said Daniel. 'But the last of them is inside a crocodile's belly now.'

He told Mzilikazi how he had lost his oxen and then his

horse, and added, 'But when I next come to trade I'll bring a wagon with the best in my store—'

'*If* you come again,' corrected Mzilikazi. He had negotiated with white men before. They had a clever way of twisting a man's words to their own advantage. It was necessary with them to be sure that each word had the same meaning for both parties.

Daniel understood this. 'All right, *if* you agree to allow me to trade with your people, perhaps you would permit me to build a store. I will pay you rent for the land, of course.'

Mzilikazi smiled. 'The land is like the sky and the waters of the river. A man cannot take a handful and say "This is mine". It belongs to no one – and to everyone. The Matabele fought for the right to live here. Because I won that right I can say this man will stay and that man must go. That is all. So how can you pay me for land that is not mine to give? If I say you may stay, you will give me presents because you are grateful. But I have not yet decided. Sit with me now and see how Mzilikazi rules his children.'

Daniel would have liked to continue the discussion on trading, to settle the issue there and then, but he knew better than to make any attempt to force the chief's hand.

He sat in silence, listening to Mzilikazi's people bring their troubles before their chief. In the main they were minor disputes. Mzilikazi's opinion was sought over a disputed bride-price. A man's calf had strayed into another's herd and ownership was disputed. A warrior from one of the bachelor impis sought permission to marry; the request was refused, the Matabele chief considering that the man had not yet proved himself a man in battle. Until he had blooded his spear he would not be man enough for a Matabele girl beneath a marriage blanket.

Then came more serious complaints. A wife was alleged to have been unfaithful to her husband. She and the lover were brought to kneel before their chief. She kneeled with downcast eyes, but the young man was unrepentant, his eyes fixed on a point beyond Mzilikazi's left shoulder while the woman's husband gave his evidence in a tremulous voice. The husband was old and withered, and Daniel found his sympathies lying with the young adulterers.

351

Mzilikazi listened carefully to the evidence. The couple had been caught in the act of making love. There could be no doubting their guilt. Nevertheless, the chief asked them whether the husband's evidence was true. The wife began to cry, and the young man's eyes went to her before he looked at Mzilikazi's face for the first time.

'It is true.'

Mzilikazi acknowledged the young man's honesty in the briefest inclination of his head before making a quick signal to his bodyguard. Four of them moved forward, and the girl began screaming and sobbing loudly as two of the warriors pinioned her arms and dragged her away.

The young man rose to his feet and walked calmly away between the other two armed men.

'It is a pity,' said Mzilikazi. 'I have just lost a good warrior.'

Only then did Daniel realise he had witnessed the Matabele chief sentencing two of his subjects to death. They would be taken to a spot beyond the village and speared by their guards.

Yet this double execution paled into insignificance when compared with what followed.

A group of twenty-five mature and experienced warriors came from the crowd and kneeled before Mzilikazi. Their cry of 'Bayete' rang out loud and clear above the buzz of the crowd's interest.

'You have been away a long time, Nyamatakah,' said Mzilikazi to their induna. 'The news you bring back to me is good?'

'It is good,' said Nyamatakah. 'We found the village of Chiweshe and punished him for raiding his neighbours. He and all his warriors were killed, as you ordered.'

'And how many of your warriors did you lose?'

The induna held up all the fingers of one hand and one finger of the other. 'They died as men.'

Mzilikazi accepted the news with apparent satisfaction.

'Your families have been without you for too long,' he said. 'Tell them to step forward. I would see them.'

Eagerly, the wives and children stepped into the clearing, happy at the honour bestowed upon them.

'Closer!' boomed their chief. 'Come closer.'

The women and children moved forward to kneel beside

their husbands and fathers.

'And the families of those who died,' said the Matabele chief. 'Let them come forward and kneel in a place apart from the others.'

A smaller group of women and children moved forward. They did not smile.

When they were settled, Mzilikazi turned his attention back to the induna.

'You will have brought me back many cattle, Nyamatakah?'

The induna shook his head sadly. 'Chiweshe and his people were poor. He did not deserve to be a chief. His cattle were few and old. A man could lay his fingers beneath their ribs.'

Mzilikazi leaned towards him, his eyes glittering angrily. 'Then it could not have been Chiweshe's cattle you left to graze in the valley of the Umniati River with those of Chiweshe's herd-boys you allowed to live?'

Nyamatakah mouthed like a fish, but it was a full minute before words came.

'I know nothing of this.'

'Then it seems I must help your memory,' said the Matabele chief as his bodyguard moved to surround the warriors and their families.

'Take Nyamatakah's wife to the stake.'

The induna started to his feet, but the broad flat blades of the assegais held by the bodyguard beat him to his knees again.

Others from the bodyguard were dragging a young woman from among the families. They carried her screaming to a four-foot-high stake driven into the ground nearby, the top of it sharpened to a point. As Daniel watched in incredulous horror the warriors lifted the screaming woman high into the air and brought her body down upon the stake. The point quite literally cut off her scream.

As the men of the bodyguard stood back Nyamatakah's wife crouched before the assembled crowd, knees bent and arms dangling, but her body was held as erect as a Matabele warrior by the stake. She was quite dead.

Daniel's stomach contracted violently and for a second he thought his malaria-wrecked body would let him down and cause him to faint in front of the assembled Matabele people.

Mzilikazi was talking again.

'How is your memory now, Nyamatakah? Do you remember Chiweshe's cattle?'

Still the induna hesitated and the angry chief called, 'Fetch out Nyamatakah's young son.'

'No!' The erring induna leaped to his feet, but the crossed assegai-handles of the bodyguard prevented him from running forward to throw himself at the feet of the chief. 'It is true! I took Chiweshe's cattle and hid them in the valley of the Umniati River.'

'I know it is true,' said Mzilikazi. 'But I wanted to hear it from your lips. Now I will speak. The wives and children of every one of you will die on the stakes on the execution hill, and you will watch them. Then it will be your turn to die also. All your goods and cattle will be shared between the families of those who were killed in the attack on Chiweshe's village.'

There was a long despairing moan from the doomed families. It stopped when Mzilikazi held up his hand.

'Nyamatakah's impi did not lose six men by Chiweshe's hand. His men were not Matabele! They ran from battle. It became a hunt for our warriors. No, Nyamatakah, my six men died because they were loyal to me and had not agreed to steal Chiweshe's cattle. They died by the spears of their brothers.'

Mzilikazi spoke to the induna of his bodyguard. 'Before these men die remove their warrior rings. They are not Matabele fighting men. I cast them out from my tribe. Kill them and feed their bodies to the dogs.'

Only at this sentence did the condemned men show any signs of emotion, but they were quickly escorted away, one man between two warriors of the bodyguard. Their families, herded like goats, were taken to the execution hill.

Daniel turned from watching them to see that the chief's eyes were upon him.

'You are shocked, trader. You do not agree with the sentence I have just passed?'

Daniel shook his head, not trusting himself to speak until he had more control of himself.

'It's not the way of my people. Human life is valued by us.'

'Good! Then my people are safe from you and yours. You

354

will not come across the river to hunt my people as do the Boers. To kill them with guns and steal their cattle. That is not your way?'

There was a bitterness in his voice that Daniel was quick to recognise and felt able to match.

'I, too, have suffered at the hands of the Boers. I hunt only animals, not men or women.'

'Then we can trade. Build a hut here and make it ready for your trade goods. You will stay with my people until the rains have ended and it is easier to travel. My warriors will then go with you along the road to Lake Ngami.'

The thought of remaining so long as a guest of this harsh and cruel man did not appeal to Daniel, but he knew that if he wished to trade with the Matabele he had no alternative.

Mzilikazi saw his hesitation and knew the reason for it.

'You will be safe here,' he said. 'Safer than one of my warriors would be among white men. You have seen me punishing my people today. It gives me no pleasure. But many years ago I and my people were Zulus ruled by the great Shaka. I was sent on just such a raid as Nyamatakah. I, too, kept the cattle to myself, but those cattle were numbered as the stars in the sky and I had with me many warriors. We fought our way to this land where we live feared by all men. If Nyamatakah had tried to do the same with the few warriors he took with him, he would one day have met with a stronger army and been beaten. The news would have travelled far; but it would not be said, "Nyamatakah has been beaten in battle." Men would say, "Mzilikazi's warriors have been beaten in battle." Then others would try to do the same, and my people would know no peace. Think about it and you will understand my ways more clearly, trader.'

It was then that Daniel realised that Mzilikazi was more than a warrior chief. His reputation for being a great leader was justified. Even so, Daniel could not forget the cruelty he had just witnessed.

'Was it necessary for the families of these men to die with them?'

'Yes, for two reasons. Among their families were fine sons who would have grown up to be warriors – perhaps great

355

warriors. They would never forget it was Mzilikazi who killed their fathers. One day, perhaps not until my son ruled the Matabele, they would think themselves strong enough to turn on their chief.'

'And the second reason?'

'Ah! That one is not so deep, trader. It was necessary to make an example of them. My warriors are brave men. They learn to fight and to kill and are not afraid of death – for themselves. But they would not wish to bring it upon their families.' Mzilikazi rested a large hand on Daniel's shoulder. 'A people are only as strong as their laws, trader. The Matabele are a mighty people. Their laws must be strong enough to be obeyed. The first of these laws is that all men must obey their chief. The punishment for breaking that law must be greater than for any other.'

He dropped his hand and Daniel had a quick flash of intuition that the great Matabele chief who was always surrounded by advisers, indunas and headmen yet remained a lonely man.

'You are still young, trader. I do not expect you to understand everything about my people. But build your hut, stay with us a while and learn our ways. Afterwards I do not think you will be happy living among any others.'

CHAPTER EIGHTEEN

Chief Jonker saw the arrival of the rains, then he took to his bed and died within a few days. It was the end of a legend. He and his Afrikaners had been the scourge of South-West Africa for a quarter of a century, until his defeat by Mutjise.

Unlike Tjamuene, Jonker left no strong son to take his place and his passing left a vacuum that only bitter strife would fill.

For all the years of his leadership the Afrikaner tribe had occupied the best valleys and grazing-land, denying access to all other tribes. Now Jonker was dead, and even while he lay breathing his last the other tribes were closing in like jackals around a corpse to seize pieces of the land the lion of the Afrikaners had won and held.

Waiting for someone to take the initiative, the tribes and sub-tribes held their guns and spears in readiness: Herero, Nama, Topnaar, Veldshoendraer—and many more. The holocaust of war was about to descend upon the land, and for a decade progress would mark time.

Josh had seen it coming for a long time as had many others. Sam Speke brought two wagons loaded with trade goods from Whalefish Bay to Sesebe and on his own authority added another loaded with powder and shot. He spoke seriously to Kasupi about the situation and could see the unquenchable war-lust burning in the young Herero's eyes.

The one-time sailor believed that when the rains ceased and powder could be kept dry the Herero would spearhead an attack on the tribe that had terrorised the country for so long. Ignoring Mary's protests that no harm would come to them, he loaded everything from the Sesebe store on the ox-wagons and with his wife and Victoria set out for the new mine at Ongava.

Their arrival stopped all work there until Sam Speke and his Herero drivers were able to assure the miners that war had not already broken out.

'I just couldn't think what else to do, Josh,' said the burly storekeeper as they all sat down to a meal together. 'War is coming soon and it will affect every one of us. I've had no news from Aaron or Daniel for months and don't know what their thoughts are about keeping a store fully stocked in the midst of a land torn by war. I doubt if they have even heard of Jonker's death and the troubles facing us here. I thought the best thing to do was pull out and take everything to their new store at Lake Ngami.'

'It makes sense, Sam, and I'm sure they'll be able to use the stores,' Josh agreed. 'I know no more than you about things at Lake Ngami. The last news I had was a fortnight ago. An Ovambo tribesman was passing through and he said Aaron was worried about Daniel. It has been many months since he left to visit Mzilikazi and there has been no word of him. Aaron is staying at the Lake, expecting Daniel to arrive with every day that comes.'

'Daniel will come back safely. Kasupi says he can out-think and out-shoot any man who's been born of woman.'

It was Victoria who spoke. She entered the hut with a Gilmore girl clutching each of her hands and cast her opinion into the conversation.

'Did he, now?'

Miriam looked at Sam Speke's daughter with great interest. It was the first time she could remember Victoria speaking without first being asked a direct question. The fifteen-year-old had blossomed into a striking young lady since her health had been restored to her. She was far removed from the spindly underweight sickly child who had caused such concern to her father.

Victoria was one of those fortunate girls who inherit the best of both parents. She had the grace and ready smile of her mother and the honest gaze and quickness to learn of her father. Her skin colour, too, was inherited from them both. It was a beautiful golden colour, slightly paler than the skin of a Bushman.

'Since when have you been the confidante of the leader of Mutjise's army?' asked Miriam.

Victoria's smile was contagious, and Miriam found herself smiling with her.

'Since he started telling me all about Daniel. Kasupi says if Daniel would lead half the Herero warriors they could overrun

Ovambaland and Damaraland and own all the land between the Kalahari and the sea.'

'I wouldn't know about that, Victoria. But I'm worried about him now.'

Miriam turned to Josh. 'Why don't we all go to Lake Ngami with Sam?'

The idea took Josh by surprise, but after he had thought about it for a few moments he realised the suggestion made much sense. The threat of war hung over the mine as it did the rest of the country. During recent weeks nearly half of Josh's work-force had drifted away to become warriors again. Josh did not blame them. A Herero man had to look to his future in the same way as anyone else.

The warriors who followed Kasupi strutted the villages of the Herero, fierce pride lifting their heads high. A man wanted to be with them. There were more battles to be fought, great victories to be won. When the warriors returned to talk of their exploits about the camp-fires there could be only scorn for those who had remained behind. When full-scale war began there would be no men left to work Ongava.

'Why not?' Josh said to Miriam. 'At the rate my miners are leaving the mine will have to close in a few weeks anyway.'

Miriam hugged him in relief and Josh smiled above her head at Sam Speke.

'Stay with us here for a couple of days while I wind things up, Sam. Then we'll all set off together. No doubt Mutjise and Kasupi will be pleased to have our miners helping to fight their battles and will keep the other tribes away from the mine. I'll send a horseman to Whalefish Bay to pass the word that there will be no ore arriving there for a while.'

He held Miriam away from him. 'You'll need to pack all your valuables and take them with us. Leave nothing behind that can't be replaced should it be stolen.'

Later, after Josh had told his mine-workers what he intended doing, he went into the bedroom of the hut to find Miriam close to tears.

'What's the matter? What's happened?'

Miriam clung to him and rubbed her face fiercely against the front of his coarse shirt.

'Nothing. I'm just being silly, but packing everything seems so final — more final than the move from Otjimkandje. Do you think we'll ever return?'

Josh kissed the top of her head gently. 'Who knows? War can change so many things, Miriam — and war is coming.'

Miriam nodded vigorously. 'I know — and it's all so unnecessary. With Jonker dead everyone could live in peace now. Nobody needs any more land than he has at the moment.'

'Ambition doesn't end because one man dies. Jonker has left a legacy that will lure a great many men to their deaths.'

Miriam pushed herself away from Josh. 'Then I'd better get on with this packing. After hearing what Kasupi is saying about Daniel it's better we go to Lake Ngami before he returns and comes to visit us. The farther Daniel stays from Hereroland the better. I didn't bring him up to become a Herero war-chief.'

It was as though their departure from Ongava was the signal the country had been waiting for. Full-scale hostilities broke out almost immediately. Kasupi led his men on a raid to Winterhoek, which had once more become the capital of the Afrikaners. In a fierce and bloody battle the Herero wreaked a terrible revenge on the children of Jonker. When they rode back to Otjimkandje they left two-thirds of the Afrikaner fighting force and a quarter of their women and children staining the dust of Winterhoek with their life's blood.

Within a week it was the turn of Otjimkandje to be attacked by a force of Namas under a chief from the south. When this battle was over the Herero had even more cause for celebration. They not only broke up the attack and inflicted heavy casualties, but also killed the Nama chief and captured his three sons. The two eldest were promptly put to death, but the youngest, hardly more than a boy, was released after he had promised allegiance to Mutjise.

It was the time of the Herero.

Aaron extended a delighted welcome to the travellers from Hereroland, although he thought some disaster must have overcome Mutjise and his people for them all to have left Hereroland. When Josh explained their reasons for descending upon him with all their own—and Aaron's—possessions the trader agreed it was the wisest course to have taken.

'You should have brought the two new missionaries with you,' he declared. 'But they will be safe in Mutjise's village. That one will lead his people to great things, you wait and see.'

'And so he might,' said Miriam. 'But he'll find it difficult to protect the missionaries. Mary says they rode off as calm as you like, saying they felt Hugo Walder had spent too much time in Otjimkandje and neglected the remainder of Hereroland.'

'Don't they realise that if it hadn't been for Hugo there would have been no Otjimkandje—and no Hereroland?'

'They don't want to know,' said Josh. 'They are young men out to make their own names. There's little room in their hearts to give credit to another. And on the subject of young men— have you heard how Daniel is getting on in Matabeleland?'

Much of the pleasure that came from meeting old friends left Aaron's face and he was uncharacteristically lost for words.

'What is it?' Miriam immediately feared the worst. 'Has something happened to him?'

'I don't know,' Aaron replied unhappily. 'I've heard a rumour that he was taken ill whilst on his way to Matabeleland, but I can't run down the source of the rumour and I can't find out any more. I've tried.' The old trader spread his hands apologetically. 'Tolotebe won't allow any of his men to take me to Mzilikazi, and I can't find the Bushmen. I've spent days in the desert looking for them.'

'I'll go out there myself tomorrow,' said Josh. 'The Bushmen are wary of strangers but they know me.'

'I'll come with you,' said Sam Speke.

'Then be sure to return with Daniel or some news of him,' said Miriam. 'Or you'll have me out there searching with you.'

It was a busy time unloading trade goods and personal belongings and settling the seven new arrivals in an establishment that normally catered for a maximum of two men.

Fortunately, the Bechuana chief proved particularly helpful by providing two large huts for the newcomers. Aaron had already told him they came to Lake Ngami to search for Daniel. Tolotebe was unhappy about his inability to help them in this respect but he did not dare send uninvited messengers to Mzilikazi's land. They would be killed long before they reached the Matabele chief and might cause an impi to be sent against Tolotebe's people to remind him that visitors were not welcome north of the Limpopo River.

There was another reason. Tolotebe had been the first to hear the rumours from the desert country that a dying Daniel had been left with the Matabele. It did not make sense to stir up trouble looking for a man who was already dead.

Josh and Sam set off at dawn to begin their search for the elusive little Bushmen. The rains had only recently ended and the 'desert' was a canvas liberally splashed with the bright colours of flowers and the remarkably rapid-growing grasses. It made the task of the two searchers much harder. There were small catchments of water to be found all over the land, much of it caught in rock-pools buried just beneath the surface in remote places known only to the Bushmen. It might be months before Xhube had to fall back on his traditional water-holes.

Intending to be out for only three days, the two men continued their fruitless search for a full week before they were forced to acknowledge defeat. Xhube was either making the most of the opportunity to hunt new territory or he was deliberately avoiding Josh.

The two men returned to Tolotebe's village depressed by their failure — to find their efforts had been unnecessary. A party of four of Mzilikazi's warriors had arrived from Matabeleland, having cut straight across the flowering desert. They were an advance party sent on by Daniel and carried a note from him. He was well and instructed Aaron to send to Sesebe for more stores as he was following with many tusks and ostrich feathers as well as a few fine animal skins.

The atmosphere had changed dramatically. Now there was nothing to do but to relax and wait for Daniel to arrive. It was a full year since Miriam had last seen him.

While they waited news came to them that the situation in South-West Africa had deteriorated still further. They learned that the Afrikaners had carried out a raid on the harbour settlement of Whalefish Bay. Meeting with little resistance, they had helped themselves to whatever they wanted and set fire to a couple of buildings.

A few days after this they had news of a more serious incident.

The bodies of the two young Otjimkandje missionaries were found twenty miles from the Herero village. They had been hacked to death and robbed of everything they had with them and their naked and mutilated bodies left beside the track. No tribe would admit responsibility for their murder and, although Mutjise sent parties of armed men scouring the countryside, they learned nothing.

Now there was no missionary at Otjimkandje, and Hugo Walder's work of more than twenty years might never have been.

Not until late April did Daniel arrive at Lake Ngami. He had with him a large party of bearers 'recruited' by the Matabele from neighbouring tribes.

Miriam hugged her son to her, observing that he was much thinner than when he had left and had the hollow-eyed look of a man who carried malaria in his blood. The illness was something he would carry with him for ever, but Miriam would work hard to put some meat back on his ribs.

Daniel was surprised and pleased to have all his family and friends at Lake Ngami to witness the success of his trading mission to the land of the legendary Mzilikazi. He was delighted, too, that Nell and Anne were now part of the Retallick family and he gave a specially warm greeting to Victoria. He completely won her heart by treating her as a young woman and not as a child.

Daniel found it difficult to look at her in any other way. Her figure told its own story and her expressive brown eyes were as bold and guileless as Hannah's had once been.

The simile brought with it a brief moment of painful memory, but it quickly passed and Daniel was able to smile when he told Sam Speke loudly, 'You've got a beautiful young lady for a daughter, Sam. Don't go accepting any offers of marriage for her until I've put in my bid.'

Sam Speke was only half-joking when he replied, 'One day you'll be reminded of that offer, Daniel. It was made before witnesses.'

They all found much to talk about during the days ahead. There was almost a year's news to exchange, and this in a country where the arrival of an unscheduled ship five hundred miles away provided days of speculation.

Daniel told them of his illness and the loyalty of the Bushmen, and Miriam gave up a silent prayer for the little Bushman and his family. It was a ritual she had performed on many occasions in earlier years.

Josh was aware of many gaps in Daniel's story, but he said nothing until all the women had gone to bed and the men remained seated around the fire outside the store drinking brandy and smoking pipes as they breathed in the woodsmoke-scented night air.

'You've had an interesting trek, son, and been lucky with your friendships – but you've told us very little about Mzilikazi himself.'

Daniel had seen his father's look when he had not taken one of his earlier stories through to a logical conclusion. To have done so would have meant bringing in details of one of the many executions he had witnessed. Yet, although he had expected to be questioned about Mzilikazi, he was not sure he had any answers to give.

He watched the smoke that was being sucked upwards from the fire dancing with the light warm breeze from the desert.

'I suppose there are many reasons for not talking about Mzilikazi,' he said thoughtfully. 'And I didn't want to speak in front of Ma or Mary about some of the things I've seen him do. He's a cruel man, more cruel than any man I've ever known.'

Daniel told them of the execution of the men of the impi and their families and of the methods employed.

Sam Speke had been listening so intently he had allowed his pipe to go out. He sucked on it and pulled a wry face as he took in a mouthful of bitter ash. Spitting it to the ground, he said, 'The man sounds mad. What sort of people are the Matabele that they allow such a man to rule them?'

'They are a wonderful people.' Daniel leaned forward, attracting the full attention of the others with the forcefulness of his words. 'The Matabele are honest, courageous and have incredible discipline. What's more, Mzilikazi is everything a good chief ought to be. It may not seem that way to you after hearing of some of the things he does, but his ways are right for his people. His punishments appear cruel to you and me – but only the guilty are punished. If there is any doubt about the guilt of anyone brought before him, they are set free. His people would follow him anywhere, even to certain death. That's what they think of him.'

He paused and looked around at the faces of his father, Aaron and Sam chiselled into deep shadowed facets by the glow from the dying fire.

'If I haven't said very much about Mzilikazi himself, it's because I'm not certain of my own feelings for him. It appals me to see the number of executions he orders, yet I have a tremendous respect for him both as a chief and as a man.'

'Will you go back to Matabelleland?' queried Josh.

'Oh yes.' The answer came without hesitation. 'I've a large hut there for trade and there's good business to be done with the Matabele.'

Aaron's teeth glinted momentarily in the firelight. He had made a trader of this young man already.

'That's not the only reason, though,' added Daniel. 'I've promised Mzilikazi I will go back and I wouldn't break my word to him. Perhaps that's also why he's such a great chief. I would never consider breaking my word to him, and I'm just as confident he will honour his promises to me.'

'And what promises has he made?' asked Aaron.

'That I can trade freely with the Matabele tribe and that my life will be as sacred as his own while I am in any lands over which he has jurisdiction.'

'Then you've done well, Daniel.' Josh knocked the bowl of his pipe gently against a log, pitching the pellet of ash and damp tobacco into the fire. 'You've not only come to a satisfactory business arrangement, but you've also found yourself a powerful friend at the same time.'

As Daniel lay down on the floor of his hut and pulled the blanket up to his chin he knew his father was right. Josh had put into words what Daniel had found so hard to accept until now.

Mzilikazi had become his friend.

CHAPTER NINETEEN

The stories of the ferocity of the conflict in Hereroland grew with every visitor who arrived at Lake Ngami from the south-west. They came from the members of various tribes, some non-participants in the battles being fought, others refugees from the fighting. Tolotebe fed the latter and allowed them a brief time to rest but always sent them on their way again after a day or two. To harbour anyone from a warring tribe might have been construed as involvement by other combatants, and the Bechuana chief wanted no part in this war.

Each traveller told his own story, but they all agreed on one thing. The hub of the war was Otjimkandje, and Mutjise and his Herero warriors had not lost a single battle.

Communications between Whalefish Bay and the interior had ceased after the first raid on the small trading port. Even the hardy Boers, who had for years brought goods overland from their Free State, now turned their wagons around well short of Hereroland. Aaron and Daniel had good reason to thank Sam for his initiative in bringing the wagons from Sesebe. They alone continued trading and were never short of food to eat.

When there was a long lull in the fighting they intended sending the goods they had collected to Whalefish Bay, but they would need to ask for a Herero escort to take them there.

Before that happened word reached Lake Ngami that Hugo Walder had returned to Otjimkandje to investigate the deaths of the two missionaries. He sent a message to Josh that as soon as he had completed his unpleasant task he would come to Lake Ngami.

As Hugo Walder was mounted and his messenger had travelled on foot he arrived a mere twenty-four hours after his letter. He had more grey hairs and looked very tired, but he was as indomitable as ever.

'Why did you come all the way up here and make me chase halfway across Africa to find you?'

Miriam kissed his bearded cheek affectionately. 'Had we known you were coming we would never have left Otjimkandje. But why did the Cape authorities send you? Have they realised after all these years that it was only your influence that kept the peace in Hereroland?'

'In Cape Town? My dear Miriam, they know nothing about Hereroland – or Damaraland, or Namaland, or any other land if it comes to that. They think we give tea-parties every week-end for chiefs and their wives.' He snorted. 'Do you know what one of the ladies gave me as a present when she knew I was returning here?' Without waiting for a reply he said, 'Boot polish! Can you imagine that? I am ordered here to investigate the murder of two missionaries and someone thinks I should have boot polish! They live in a different world in the Cape Colony.'

Josh smiled sympathetically; it was difficult to imagine the German preacher living among such people. Hugo Walder was a natural missionary and was at home only with the tribes who lived far from civilisation. He was wasted in Cape Town.

'Have you learned anything about the deaths of Wohlfarth or Doelker?'

'No, and I doubt if I will now. It was most probably an Afrikaner raiding party – there was one in the area at the time – but we will never know for certain. They were young fools to have left Otjimkandje at such a time, but death is a high price to pay for foolishness.'

'True,' said Miriam. 'Yet there are some who would say it is foolish for an unarmed man to ride hundreds of miles in such an uncertain land just to visit old friends.'

'Ach! Then such people would be wrong,' declared Hugo Walder. 'I have something here that I would have ridden a thousand miles to deliver personally.'

The missionary had a small pouch slung over his shoulder. Undoing it tantalisingly slowly, he drew out a large envelope sealed with a large red wax seal and handed it to Josh.

The name written in bold black script on the envelope was 'Joshua Retallick, Esquire'. There was no address. Turning the envelope over, Josh saw that the seal was that of the Governor of the Cape Colony.

'What is it?'

Hugo Walder gave a sigh of mock exasperation. 'The only way to find out is to open the envelope.'

Josh took a skinning-knife from his belt and carefully slit the end of the envelope. From inside he drew out a parchment document with another seal attached to it by two red ribbons. The document dropped open, and Josh immediately saw the bold signature, 'Victoria R.'

He began to read, and those watching saw his eyes widen and his jaw drop loose.

'Josh ... ? It isn't ... ?'

Josh nodded humbly to Miriam. 'Yes. It's a royal pardon. It sets aside my conviction.'

'Oh, Josh, I'm so happy! After all these years they've accepted your innocence. You're a free man once more.'

Miriam and Josh clung to one another for a few moments and Josh accepted the congratulations of Daniel and Sam Speke. Then he looked to Hugo Walder for an explanation.

The German preacher appeared slightly embarrassed. 'It was granted a long time ago,' he said. 'But no one had thought of sending it out to the Cape Colony from England. We would not have it now if I had not asked the Governor himself to make some enquiries about it.'

'And there would be no pardon at all but for your efforts. Bless you, Hugo.'

Miriam hugged him, and Hugo Walder beamed happily.

'What can I say?' asked Josh huskily. 'After all these years I didn't think it mattered to me anymore. I was wrong. It matters more than you'll ever know, Hugo. There will no longer have to be a part of my mind closed off to everyone, a need to be careful what I tell about my past to strangers. It means more than I can put into words, Hugo.'

'Then thank me by saying a prayer for the man who made it possible,' said Hugo Walder. 'He will have had much against him when he stood before the Lord.'

'I'll say one for a wonderful friend, too,' said Miriam. 'We've been very lucky, you and I, Josh.'

Josh nodded happily, trying to resist the urge to open out the Royal Pardon and read it again.

'What will you do now?' Sam Speke posed the question.

'Do?' The full impact of the pardon suddenly hit Josh. 'I . . . I don't know. It will need thinking about.'

Josh had made quite a lot of money during his years in Africa. He and Miriam could go anywhere. Return to England even. He looked to where the two young Gilmore sisters were playing together not far away. He and Miriam could take them to England, give them a good education and a new start in life, far from the dark memories of Africa.

'I just don't know,' he repeated. 'I don't know.'

Josh and Miriam slept very little that night. Hugo Walder had opened new doors for them at the very time when events in Hereroland had squeezed them into an unfamiliar corner of Africa.

They lay side by side in the small round hut, Josh's arm about Miriam's shoulders. Above them in the thatch an upside-down lizard scratched its way in search of insects. Somewhere nearby a cricket rasped its tuneless melody, and outside the drums of the Bechuana still attacked the night.

'Would you like to return to Cornwall, Miriam?'

She turned to face him. 'It's something I've thought about many times, but before the girls came to us I could think of no reason for going. There's no one left alive there I want to see again. How about you?'

Josh thought hard about the high Cornish moor, the bushes and grass, the greenness of everything. He thought of his mother and father in their little granite-grey cottage on the slopes of the tor.

'I would like to see the family again.' They had been away for a long time, but things changed slowly in Cornwall. He would find work again as a mine-engineer if he needed to.

'They would love the girls,' Miriam said. 'But what about Daniel? Do you think he would come with us?'

'It would be unfair to expect it of him. He has his future here. He'll do well. Would you go to England without him?'

Miriam thought hard about it. Her immediate reaction was to say she would not leave their only son, but she realised it was a mother's instinct and an unreasonable one. Daniel would return to the Matabele. Even if she and Daniel stayed in Africa she might not see him for years at a time. Meanwhile, massive strides were being made in world-wide travel. Hugo had told them of the steam-driven ships he had seen in Table Bay at the Cape, ships that belched black smoke like floating engine houses and made the voyage from England in thirty-five days. Daniel and Aaron were good partners. They were well on their way to becoming wealthy men. There was no reason why Daniel should not come to visit them in Cornwall.

None of this sound logic would fill the emptiness she would know having Daniel living two continents away from her. But Miriam knew what her answer to Josh must be. It would have been easier to say had Hannah lived to exercise a cautionary influence upon Daniel. Then suddenly she thought of the young Victoria. This time it was her intuition as a woman and not as a mother that told Miriam that one day the young girl would become the biggest single influence upon Daniel's life.

'Yes, I would go to Cornwall and leave Daniel here. I think he'll be in good hands.'

Josh rose on one elbow to look down at Miriam in the dim light shining through the glassless window.

'Then we'll go? We'll go – home?'

'Yes.'

Josh and Miriam told Daniel and the others of their decision the following morning.

'Your mother would be happier if you came with us – and so would I,' said Josh. 'I can't think of any one thing that would make me happier than to have us return to Cornwall as a complete family.'

'I can't come,' said Daniel. 'I must go back to Mzilikazi. But I'll think of you often and be very happy knowing you are both safe there, far from the wars of Hereroland. It will give me less to worry about.'

'I wish I were able to say the same about you,' declared Miriam.

Daniel smiled. 'I'll be under the protection of Mzilikazi, Ma. Can you think of anyone better able to take care of me?'

'Yes, a good wife,' said Miriam firmly.

'How about you, Sam?' asked Josh. 'Will you return to England with us?'

Sam looked at Mary and Victoria before answering.

'There's nothing for me in England that I haven't already got here, Josh. It wouldn't be fair to ask Mary to start learning new English ways.'

He did not bother to add that during their visit to the Cape Colony with their sick daughter he and Mary had been ostracised by the European community because theirs was a marriage between the two differing races. He would not take Mary and Victoria back to England and risk their becoming objects of curiosity.

'I'm glad you've made that decision, Sam,' said Daniel. 'I was hoping you'd come to Matabeleland with me for a year or so – bringing Mary and Victoria with you, of course.'

Daniel saw the doubt on the burly ex-seaman's face. 'I've already discussed it with Mzilikazi. He's fascinated by the trek-wagons he's seen belonging to the Boers. I told him I would willingly give him one of mine but that you could make him a new one – made especially for him. He talked about nothing else for days. When I left he was already having a hut built for the three of you.'

'Do you think we'll be safe, Daniel? I'm not worried for myself, but what about Mary and Victoria?'

Miriam was looking at Victoria. The young girl was willing her father to agree to go with Daniel.

'You will be going at Mzilikazi's invitation, Sam. I know of no better guarantee than that. Oh, I know I spoke about Mzilikazi's harsh justice, but he's a man of his word. You'll all be better protected than you will be this side of the Kalahari.'

'Go, Sam,' this from Aaron. 'I'll stay here and look after your possessions. By the time you decide to return things might have quietened down in Hereroland and we can shift our store from Sesebe to Otjimkandje. That might suit you well enough.'

Sam Speke knew it would suit Mary very well. She was never completely at ease away from her own people. But Victoria . . .? He turned to his daughter and caught her expression as she looked at Daniel. At that moment he saw as clearly as Miriam where the interests of his daughter lay.

'All right, we'll come with you, Daniel.'

Miriam had not shifted her gaze from Victoria during all the talk. Now the young girl returned her look, and Miriam smiled. Victoria's expression was one of triumphant confidence. She knew what she wanted. She would be spending a lot of time with Daniel in the months ahead, and with her looks and determination she could afford to be confident.

'Then everything is settled,' said Hugo Walder. 'I can look forward to having delightful company on my return journey to Cape Town.'

He smiled at Miriam. 'I only wish I was more observant, then perhaps I could prepare you for the latest fashions at the Cape. I believe women set great store by such things.'

'Well, here's one who doesn't,' said Miriam, her chin going up defiantly. 'My clothes will be clean and well mended, just the way they've always been. We'll not waste good money on frills and the like because everyone else is wearing them.'

Josh smiled to himself. Miriam had changed little since she was a barefoot girl. Her attitude towards what other people thought of her dress had been the same then. Nevertheless, she would be as excited as a child at Christmas when she had the opportunity of looking around the stores at the Cape. It would give him a great deal of pleasure to buy her all the things she was claiming not to want.

'When were you thinking of leaving?' asked Hugo Walder.

'We don't have to think about that yet,' said Miriam alarmed at the thought of an early parting with Daniel. 'Let's all relax and enjoy ourselves together while we can.'

Nobody argued with her. It was pleasant to have nothing to do but fish in the bitter waters of the lake and hunt the animals that came there to drink.

But they had enjoyed only a few days of relaxation when a Bechuana herd-boy ran into the village shouting that an armed Matabele impi was advancing upon the village from the north. The Bechuana hastily gathered up their belongings and fled into the desert to the south while the Europeans gathered up their guns to prepare for the worst.

The impi soon came in view but they were marching in a relaxed manner, not advancing in the 'head and horns' formation they used for attack. As the warriors drew closer Daniel saw they were men of Mzilikazi's own formidable bodyguard, led by the induna Muvandi. These were the foremost warriors in the Matabele army, each pledged to give his life willingly for the chief. Mzilikazi would not waste such warriors on a raid. This was not a war-party.

Daniel put aside his gun and went out to meet Muvandi. Those watching saw the induna advance and salute Daniel with a raised hand. Even at a distance of three hundred yards they saw the smile of the induna.

Daniel brought Muvandi back to meet the others, the induna greeted each of them courteously and to Hugo Walder he said, 'Even in my country we have heard of "The Little Father". Mzilikazi will be pleased to know I have given you his greetings.'

'Muvandi has come to escort us back to Matabeleland,' Daniel said to Sam Speke. 'Mzilikazi heard of the troubles in Hereroland and was afraid it might affect us here. Muvandi was sent to fetch us. He would like us to leave tomorrow.'

'Tomorrow?' Miriam echoed. 'But that means this will be our last day together.'

'For a while,' Daniel said gently. 'You've been telling me yourself that England is only a month away by sea. We'll write and if I haven't come to visit you in three years' time, then you must come back here again to see me.'

'Three years!' Miriam whispered. She managed to make it sound a lifetime. 'So much can happen in that time.'

'Ma, this is supposed to be a happy time,' Daniel reminded her. 'After all the years of hardship you've both suffered Pa's name has been cleared. You can return home with your heads held high. I'm staying here because I've got a trading agreement with the most powerful chief in the whole of this part of Africa. Things could hardly be better.'

'I know.' Miriam shook her head vigorously. 'It's a mother's privilege to worry, that's all.'

Josh put an arm about her shoulders and spoke to Daniel. 'She's all right, son. Wait until we get back to Cornwall. There won't be a single household on the moor that doesn't know Daniel Retallick is trading with Mzilikazi.'

He rubbed his chin ruefully. 'Mind you, unless things have changed an awful lot since I was last there they won't have heard of Mzilikazi, and if he's got nothing to do with the price of gin or corn they won't care a lot, either.'

'It isn't necessary to go to England to find such an attitude,' said Hugo Walder. 'I'll introduce you to people in the Cape Colony who are exactly the same.'

They were up until late that evening, the men working hard to pack the wagons for the journey to Matabeleland and Miriam and the Gilmore children helping first Mary and Victoria with their packing and then drifting from wagon to wagon talking. Miriam resisted the urge to stay close enough to Daniel to reach out a hand and touch him whenever she thought of their imminent parting.

The next morning the farewells were exaggeratedly subdued, everyone deliberately playing down the occasion for their own particular reason.

Only when the final ox was inspanned did Miriam's feelings threaten to overflow in choked tears. To the young Victoria she said quietly, 'Daniel is a good man, Victoria. He'll make you a good husband one day. Take care of him.'

She was gone before Victoria could reply and she clung to Daniel for long minutes, pressing her face into his shoulder, fighting to control the emotions that threatened her self-control.

Finally it was Daniel himself who gently held her away from him.

'Take care of yourself, Ma. I'll be thinking of you and happy to know you and Pa will be back in England. Write to me through Hugo. He'll make sure I get your letters.'

He kissed her quickly and she stood away from him, hands clenched tightly at her sides.

The parting between father and son was easier. They gripped hands and looked at each other in a silence that said more than words. It was a look that spoke of love and mutual respect. They were each of them men to be reckoned with.

Both parties set off at the same time and they waved until distance and the heat of the day distorted the wagons and hid them from view in a shimmering haze as they disappeared into a new future.

They were pioneers. Each in his own way had given something new to the land they were now leaving.

To the west went those who were leaving the frontiers of Africa, the life they had known gone for ever! Josh and Miriam, returning to England to take up life again in a land they had known long before; the young Gilmore girls, memories of their terrible suffering already fading; Hugo Walder, the first white man to live among the tribes of Hereroland and teach them the faith of his order, a man who by his integrity and dedicated example had brought much honour to his calling.

To the east went those who would push the frontiers still farther into the vast unknown continent. To Daniel and Victoria the future held excitement and fulfilment. Africa was their home. They had known no other. Sam and Mary had forged a link between the old and the new with love and respect. It was a way that would be accepted by neither side for generations to come, but it was a beginning.

Watching both parties leave was Aaron, the trader. His thick long beard and chosen calling were representative of a people who had managed to keep their unique identity for two thousand years without the encouragement of a homeland. To the Herero he had given guns to bring them back from the brink of extinction. To Africa he had given his wife and daughter.

EPILOGUE

The steam clipper *Great Britain* bound from Melbourne, Australia, via Cape Town nosed into Liverpool dock on 25 May 1864. Listed among her passengers were 'Joshua Retallick, esq.' and 'wife'.

Six thousand miles away in the northern Kalahari, Pieter van der Stel and his small party of Boer trekkers were in trouble. They had been seventeen days without finding fresh water, and during the heat of the afternoon three of the oxen pulling their two wagons had dropped dead.

Pieter van der Stel was lost. The party had left the Orange Free State more than twelve months before, lured northwards by the promise of land and unlimited opportunity in the Portuguese west-coast colony of Angola.

From isolated farms and villages hundreds of Boers had been doing the same thing. Fiercely independent and resentful of the inexorable advance of British influence and control from Cape Town they moved northwards and eastwards in search of a new land, free from the laws and petty disciplines of the British.

Such was the background of Pieter van der Stel, his brother Jan and their wives and thirteen children. There had been fifteen children when they set off, but Pieter van der Stel had lost two. One, a girl of three, had fallen from the wagon-seat and been crushed by the wheel of the big canvas-topped wagon. The other, a baby born on the long trek, had simply wasted away and died because the milk of its underfed mother contained no nourishment.

They were both laid in the ground with all the formality that the prayer-book had to offer. Pieter van der Stel was a Christian man. His children had Christian burials, their bodies lain to rest in Christian coffins of rough-planed wood. A large bundle of the cheap planks dangled from the rear of each wagon, brought especially for such a grim purpose, a constant reminder of the hardships expected along the way.

376

But this was the hardest time of the whole trek. Today their situation was desperate. They had used the last drop of water, and the oxen were staggering.

Pieter van der Stel had altered course for Lake Ngami a week before and he expected to sight the water at any moment. He was blissfully unaware that the lake was still fifty miles away, and on his present course he would pass its northernmost extremity without ever sighting water.

Xhube knew it. He also knew of the Boers' desperate plight. He and his tiny family group had watched them for two days, Xhube being torn between instinctive shyness and the thought of his special relationship with Daniel.

'Today their oxen die. Tomorrow it will be their turn,' said the troubled Bushman leader.

'Death walks close beside all of us,' replied the aged Hwexa, the oldest member of Xhube's tribe. 'When he takes our hand there is no one may break his grip – not even you, Xhube.'

'I remember a time when our people lay in the sun and the skin of their bellies touched their backbones. It was a white man who saved us then.'

'He is a friend and the son of a friend. There are few such men for our people, Xhube.'

'You speak the truth. But can I look a friend in the face as a man and say I watched his people die and did nothing?'

Xhube rose to his feet, his mind made up. 'No, Hwexa. Tell the women to bring water. I will go and speak to the white men.'

Pieter van der Stel saw Xhube and his three hunters coming across the hot sand towards him. Behind the Bushman chief came Hwexa and the four women carrying water-filled eggshells and moving more slowly.

'Jannie,' the Boer called to his brother. 'Come here and bring your gun. Tell the boys to have their guns handy, too. Some Bushmen are coming. Do nothing until I tell you.'

Xhube's resolution faltered when he saw the big Boer and his brother walking out to meet him carrying their muskets in front of their bodies. Behind them, sheltered by the two wagons, he glimpsed a number of younger men, similarly armed.

377

His hunters had also seen and were unhappy.

'It will be all right,' explained Xhube. 'They must take care because they do not know us.'

His words lacked conviction. Xhube was beginning to think he might have erred in coming to the assistance of these white men, but he could have done no less.

However, there was no need to risk all his small tribe. He told his hunters to stay where they were and wait for the women.

They stopped about forty yards from the advancing Boers, and Xhube went on alone. He felt very vulnerable as he walked towards the Boers and was constantly aware of the musket-barrels which protruded from behind the two wagons.

He and the Boers met in the open desert, the Boers towering over the little Bushman.

Xhube smiled his greeting. 'You are tall and we have seen you from afar. We have water and you have none. What we have is yours. I will guide you to the bitter water and show you fresh water along the way.'

Xhube's words were accompanied by gestures, first to his people who waited patiently behind him and then to the wagons.

'What's he saying?' Jan van der Stel asked his brother.

'I don't know. I think he's asking us to give him and his people food, or something.'

'Hell, man! What does he take us for? Can't he see we're desperate for water?'

Xhube realised the Boers did not understand him and he turned, walking a few paces towards the waiting hunters and women.

'Come, bring the water.'

His soft call went unheard as a sharp-eyed boy behind one of the wagons called, 'Pa! Those Bushman women have water.'

The loud shout frightened Xhube's women and one of them turned away and began running.

'Stop! Bring the water here.' Xhube's cry was louder, more urgent.

It was too late. The tragic misunderstanding between the two parties had to run its inevitable course. Peiter van der Stel

378

hrew his gun up to his shoulder and shouted, 'Shoot the women first! We want that water.'

He fired, and one of the fleeing women crashed to the ground. She fell upon one of the two ostrich eggs she had been carrying and the water from it diluted her blood as it seeped into the hot sand of the Kalahari. The other egg fell on the soft sand, the water held in by the plug of dried grass.

Xhube ran to prevent Jan van der Stel from firing, but before he could reach him a musket-ball from one of the guns behind the wagons tore its way through his chest and bowled him over.

Muskets were crashing, and all the women were down now. The desperate Bushmen strung arrows in their tiny bows and ran at the two Boers as they reloaded their weapons with experienced swiftness.

One of the arrows found its mark in the neck of Jan van der Stel, but it was not poisoned as the Bushmen had not been prepared for hunting. The arrow was no more painful than the sting of a large bush-wasp, and the Boer shot dead the Bushman who had fired it at him.

The massacre was over in less than two minutes, and the two Boer women and the children were soon gathering up the precious water-filled eggs.

'Pa! This one's still alive.'

One of the van der Stel boys leaned over Xhube. Pieter van der Stel strode to where the Bushman lay on his back, blood bubbling from the hole in his chest and dribbling from the side of his mouth.

The Boer raised his gun to bring the butt down and finish the dying man. He found himself looking into the unwavering eyes of the Bushman and unexpectedly lowered the gun.

'Agh! Leave him. He's as good as dead already.' Pieter van der Stel ushered his family back to the wagons where he and his brother doled out the water sparingly to humans and oxen.

No trace was ever found of the van der Stel trekkers. The two families, their oxen and wagons found their last resting-place in the Kalahari desert of Xhube's people, the exact spot known only to the wind, the sand and the silent elusive Bushman from whom the desert keeps no secrets.

Xhube lived long enough to crawl to a rock and claw himself to a sitting position with his back to it. He watched the Boers leave and the sun overtake them, and when he died his shadow stretched as far as that of the tallest man who had ever walked the land.

HISTORICAL BACKGROUND

This book has as its setting the South West Africa of the 1840s and 1850s and whilst the majority of events and characters are ficitious, the tribes and the lands they occupied were, and are, very real.

The first man to make his home there was the Bushman. He had no need to make tribal boundaries, the whole of the land was his. There *were* no other tribes. For thousands of years he wandered at will and it was this very freedom that was to prove his downfall. When other tribes invaded he was unable to adapt to their ways. Their cattle grazed the land therefore he hunted them as he had always hunted grazing animals. Their crops grew from the land therefore they must be his also. When the newcomers sought him out to kill him the Bushman had no tribal structure to call upon for help. He was an individual and the numbers of the strangers defeated him. The Bushman, a natural victim, lost his place and became a diminutive enigma.

The Herero tribesman had his boundaries, but they were wide. He himself said, 'Wherever Herero cattle have grazed, there is Hereroland.' By the early years of the 19th century he was firmly established in an area of 100,000 square miles, from Rehoboth to Grootfontein, and from Gobabis to the sea. His was the power of numbers and he possessed the arrogance of a ruling race. His cattle raised dust to the sky from horizon to horizon. The sun shone to warm *his* back, the rains fell to water *his* stock.

But then, in 1823, the tribesmen of Jonker Afrikaner invaded the land. One of the Orlam tribes, the Afrikaners had moved northwards from the Cape over a period of many years, settling for a while on the Orange River, ruled by their chief, Jager Afrikaner. When Jager died he left his younger sons without an inheritance. One of them gathered together all the wildest elements of his late father's tribe and led them northwards to carve out a territory of his own. That son was Jonker. Armed with guns, his followers fell upon the Hereros, stripping them of everything they owned. He built himself an empire about the hills of modern-day Windhoek and stamped his name indelibly upon the history of his adopted land.

There were many tribes, many chiefs, but only Jonker rose above the fiction I was able to weave about the others. For as long as he lived, he ruled absolutely. When he died at Okahandja in 1861 it was the end of an important chapter in history. The strength went from his Afrikaner tribe and Jonker's empire fell apart. If I have bent his image in order to tell my story — I apologise to his memory.

But my story is set in a harsh, scorched and uncertain land, and in the difficult days of the mid-19th century. Jonker lived there. So too did the Herero and the Bushman. Their lives have been documented by the historian. They, together with the characters of my story, truly reaped a Harvest of the Sun.

E.V.T.